William Painter, Joseph Jacobs

The palace of pleasure

Elizabethan versions of Italian and French novels from Boccaccio, Bandello,

Cinthio, Straparola, Queen Magaret of Navarre and others - Vol.III

William Painter, Joseph Jacobs

The palace of pleasure
Elizabethan versions of Italian and French novels from Boccaccio, Bandello, Cinthio, Straparola, Queen Magaret of Navarre and others - Vol.III

ISBN/EAN: 9783742855763

Manufactured in Europe, USA, Canada, Australia, Japa

Cover: Foto ©Andreas Hilbeck / pixelio.de

Manufactured and distributed by brebook publishing software
(www.brebook.com)

William Painter, Joseph Jacobs

The palace of pleasure

THE
Palace of Pleasure

ELIZABETHAN VERSIONS OF ITALIAN AND FRENCH NOVELS
FROM BOCCACCIO, BANDELLO, CINTHIO, STRAPAROLA,
QUEEN MARGARET OF NAVARRE,
AND OTHERS

DONE INTO ENGLISH

BY WILLIAM PAINTER

NOW AGAIN EDITED FOR THE FOURTH TIME

BY JOSEPH JACOBS

VOL. III.

LONDON: PUBLISHED BY DAVID NUTT IN THE STRAND
MDCCCXC

TABLE OF CONTENTS.

VOLUME III.

TOME II.—*Continued.*

The second Tome

of the Palace of Pleasure,

contayning store of goodlye histories,

Tragical matters, and other Mo-
rall argumentes, very re-
quisite for delight
and profyte.

Chosen and selected out of

diuers good and commen-
dable Authors:

and now once agayn corrected and
encreased

By William Painter, Clerke of the
Ordinance and Armarie.

Imprinted at London, in

Fleat strete, by Thomas
Marshe.

THE TWENTY-THIRD NOUELL.

The infortunate mariage of a Gentleman, called Antonio Bologna, wyth the Ducheſſe of Malfi, and the pitifull death of them both.

THE great Honor and authority men haue in thys World, and the greater their eſtimation is, the more ſenſible and notorious are the faultes by theim committed, and the greater is their ſlaunder. In lyke manner more difficult it is for that man to tolerate and ſuſtayne Fortune, which al the dayes of his life hath lyued at his eaſe, if by chaunce he fall into any great neceſſity than for hym whych neuer felt but woe, miſhap, and aduerſity. Dyoniſius the Tyraunt of Scicilia, felt greater payne when hee was expelled his Kyngdome, than Milo did, beinge baniſhed from Rome: for ſo mutch as the one was a Soueraygne Lorde, the ſonne of a Kynge, a Iuſticiary on Earth, and the other but a ſimple Citizen of a Citty, wherein the People had Lawes, and the Lawes of Magiſtrates were had in reuerence. So lykewyſe the fall of a high and lofty Tree, maketh greater noyſe, than that whych is low and little. Hygh Towers, and ſtately Palaces of Prynces bee ſeene further of, than the poore Cabans, and homely Sheepeheardes Sheepecotes: the Walles of lofty Cittyes more a looſe doe Salute the Viewers of the ſame, than the ſimple Caues, which the Poore doe digge belowe the Mountayne Rockes. Wherefore it behooueth the Noble, and ſutch as haue charge of Common wealth, to lyue an honeſt Lyfe, and beare their port vpright, that none haue cauſe to diſcourſe vppon their wicked deedes and naughty life. And aboue all modeſty ought to be kept by Women, whom as their race, Noble birth, auɗhority and name, maketh them more famous, euen fo their vertue, honefty, chaftity, and continencie more prayfe worthy. And behoueful it is, that like as they wiſhe to be honoured aboue all other, ſo their life do make them worthy of that honour, without difgracing their name by deed or worde, or blemiſhing that brightneſſe which may commend the fame. I greatly feare that all the Princely faɗes, the exploytes and conqueſts done by the Babylonian Queene Semyramis, neuer was recommended wyth futch prayfe, as hir vice had ſhame in records by thofe which left remembrance of auncient aɗs. Thus I fay, becaufe a woman being as it were the Image of fweetneffe, curtefie and ſhamefaſtneſſe, ſo foone as ſhe ſteppeth out of the right traɗ, and abandoneth the fweete fmel of hir duety and modefty, befides the denigration of hir honour, thruſteth her felfe into infinite Troubles, caufeth ruine of futch whych ſhould bee honoured and prayfed, if Womens Allurementes folicited theym not to Folly. I wyll not heere Indeuour my felfe to feeke for examples of Samfon, Salomon or other, which fuffred themfelues fondly to be abufed by Women : and who by meane of them be tumbled into great faults, and haue incurred greater perils: contentinge my felfe to recyte a ryght pitifull Hiftory done almoft in our tyme, when the French vnder leadinge of that notable Capitayne Gafton de Foix, vanquiſhed the force of Spayne and Naples at the Iourney of Rauenna in the time of the French Kynge called Lewes the twelfth, who married the Lady Mary, Daughter to Kynge Henry the feuenth, and Sifter to the Viɗorious Prynce of worthy memory kynge Henry the eyght, Wyfe (after the death of the fayd Lewes) to the puiſſaunt Gentleman Charles, late Duke of Suffolke. In the very tyme then lyued a Gentleman of Naples called Antonio Bologna, who hauing bin mafter of Houfehold to Fredericke of Aràgon, fomtime king of Naples, after the French had expelled thofe of Aragon out of that Citty, the fayde Bologna retyred into Fraunce, and thereby recouered the goods, which hee poffeffed in his countrey. The Gentleman befides that he was valiant of his perfone, a good man of Warre, and wel efteemed amongs the beft, had a paffing numbre of good graces, which made him to be loued and cheriſhed of euery

wight: and for riding and managing of greate horfe, he had not
his fellow in Italy: he could alfo play exceedynge well and trim
vpon the Lute, whofe fayning voyce fo wel agreed therevnto, that
the mofte melancholike perfons would forget their heauineffe,
vpon hearing of his heauenly noyfe: and befides thefe qualyties,
he was of perfonage comely, and of good proportion. To be fhort:
nature hauing trauayled and difpoyled hir Treafure Houfe for in-
riching of him, he had by Arte gotten that, which made him moft
happy and worthy of prayfe, which was, the knowledge of good
letters, wherein he was fo well trayned, as by talke and difpute thereof, he made thofe to blufh that were of that ftate and
profeffion. Antonio Bologna hauing left Fredericke of Aragon
in Fraunce, who expulfed out of Naples was retired to king Lewes,
went home to his houfe to lyue at reft and to auoyd trouble, forgetting the delicates of Courtes and houfes of great men, to bee
the only hufband of his owne reueneue. But what? it is impoffible to efchue that which the heauens haue determined vpon vs:
or to fhunne the vnhappe which feemeth to follow vs, as it were
naturally proceeding from our mother's Wombe: in futch wyfe as
many times, he which feemeth the wifeft man, guided by miffortune, hafteth himfelf with ftouping head to fall headlonge into bys
death and ruine. Euen fo it chaunced to this Neapolitane Gentleman: for in the very fame place where he attained his aduauncement, he receiued alfo his diminution and decay, and by that
houfe which preferred hym to what he had, he was depryued,
both of his eftate and life: the difcourfe whereof you fhall vnderftande. I haue tolde you already, that this Gentleman was
Mayfter of the kinge of Naples houfehold, and beyng a gentle
perfon, a good Courtier, wel trained vp, and wyfe for gouernment
of himfelf in the Courte and in the feruice of Princes, the
Ducheffe of Malfi thought to intreate him that he would ferue
hir, in that office which he ferued the King. This Ducheffe was
of the houfe of Aragon, and fifter to the Cardinall of Aragon,
which then was a rych and puiffant perfonage. Being refolued,
and perfuaded, that Bologna was deuoutly affected to the houfe
of Aragon, as one brought vp there from a Chylde: fhee fent for
him home to his Houfe, and vpon hys repaire vfed vnto him thefe,

or like Woordes: "Mayfter Bologna, fith your ill fortune, nay
rather the vnhap of our whole Houfe is futch, as your good Lord
and Mayfter hath forgon his ftate and dignity, and that you therwithall haue loft a good Maifter, without other recompence but
the prayfe which euery man giueth you for your good feruice, I
haue thought good to intreat you to doe me the honor, as to take
charge of the gouernment of my Houfe, and to vfe the fame, as
you did that of the King your maifter. I know well that the
office is to vnworthy for your calling; notwithftanding you be
not ignorant what I am, and how neare to him in bloud, to whom
you haue bene a Seruaunte fo faythfull and Louing; and albeit
that I am no Queene, endued with greateft reuenue, yet with that
little portyon I haue, I beare a Pryncely heart: and futch as you
by experience do knowe what I haue done, and dayly do to thofe
which depart my feruice, recompenfing them according to theyr
paine and trauaile: magnificence is obferued as well in the Courts
of poore Princes, as in the ftately Palaces of great Kings and
monarches. I do remember that I haue read of a certain noble
gentleman, a Perfian borne, called Ariobarzanes, who vfed great
examples of curtefie and ftoutneffe towards King Artaxerxes,
wherewith the king wondred at his magnificence, and confeffed
himfelf to be vanquifhed: you fhal take aduife of this requeft,
and in the meane time do think you will not refufe the fame,
afwell for that my demaund is iuft, as alfo being affured, that
our Houfe and race is fo well imprinted in your heart, as it is impoffible that the memory thereof can be defaced." The gentleman hearynge that curteous demaund of the Ducheffe, knowing
himfelfe how deeply bound he was to the name of Aragon, and
led by fome vnknowen prouocation to his great il luck, anfwered
hir in this wife: "I would to God, Madame, that with fo good
reafon and equity I were able to make denyall of your commaundment, as iuftly you maye require the fame: wherfore for the
bounden duety which I owe to the name and memorie of the
houfe of Aragon, I make promife that I fhall not only fuftaine
the trauell, but alfo the daunger of my Lyfe, dayly to be offred for
your feruice: but I feele in mynde I know not what, which commaundeth me to withdraw my felfe to lyue alone at home within

my lyttle houſe, and to be content with that I haue, forgoing
the ſumptuous charge of Prynces houſes, which Lyfe would be wel
liked of my ſelf, were it not for the feare that you Madame ſhould
be diſcontented with my refuſall, and that you ſhould conceiue,
that I diſdained yqur offred charge, or contempne your Court for
reſpeᴄt of the great Office I bare in the Courte of the Kyng, my
Lord and Mayſter: for I cannot receiue more honour, than to ſerue
hir, which is the paragon of that ſtock and royal race.　Therfore
at all aduentures I am reſolued to obey your will, and humbly to
ſatiſſy the duety of the charge wherein it pleaſeth you to imploy
me, more to pleaſure you for auoiding of diſpleaſure, then for
deſire I haue to lyue an honorable lyfe in the greateſt Princes
houſe of the world, ſith I am diſcharged from him in whoſe name
reſteth my comfort and only ſtay, thinking to haue liued a ſolitarye
life, and to paſſe my yeres in reſt, except it were in the pore
abilitye of my ſeruice to that houſe, wherunto I am bound continually to be a faithfull ſeruaunt.　Thus Madame, you ſee me
to be the readieſt man of the world, to fulfil the requeſt, and
accompliſhe ſutch other ſeruice wherein it ſhall pleaſe you to
imploy me." The Ducheſſe thanked him very heartily, and gaue
him charge of all hir houſholde traine, commaunding ech perſon
to do him ſutch reuerence as to hir ſelf, and to obey him as
the chief of al hir family.　This Lady was a widow, but a paſſing
faire Gentlewoman, fine and very yong, hauing a yong ſonne
vnder hir guard and keping, left by the deceaſed Duke hir huſband,
togither with the Duchy, the inheritaunce of hir child.　Now conſider hir perſonage being ſutch, her eaſy life and delycate bringing vp, and hir daily view of the youthly trade and manner of
Courtiers lyfe, whether ſhe felt hir ſelf pryckt wyth any deſire,
which burned hir heart the more inceſſantly, as the flames were
hidden and couert: from the outward ſhew whereof ſhee ſtayed hir
ſelf ſo well as ſhee coulde.　But ſhee followinge beſte aduice, rather
eſteemed the proofe of Maryage, than to burne wyth ſo lyttle
fire, or to incurre the exchange of louers, as many vnſhamefaſte
ſtrumpets do, which be rather giuen ouer, than ſatiſſied with pleaſure of loue.　And to ſay the truthe, they be not guided by wiſe-
dom's lore, which ſuffer a maiden ripe for mariage to be long

vnwedded, or yong wife long to liue in widowe's ftate, what affurance fo euer they make of their chafte and ftayed lyfe. For bookes
be to full of futch enterpryfes, and houfes ftored with examples of
futch ftolne and fecrete practifes, as there neede no further proofe
for affurance of our caufe, the daily experience maketh plaine and
manifeft. And a great folly it is to build the fantafies of chaftitye
amid the follies of worldly pleafures. I will not goe about to
make thofe matters impoffible, ne yet will iudge at large, but that
there be fom maydens and Wyues, which wifelye can conteine
themfelues amongs the troupe of amorous futers. But what? the
experience is very hard, and the proofe no leffe daungerous, and
perchaunce in a moment the mind of fome peruerted, which all
their lyuyinge dayes haue clofed theyr Eares from the Sute of thofe
that haue made offer of louyng feruice. And hereof we neede not
run to forrayne Hyftories, ne yet to feeke records that be auncient,
fith wee may fee the daily effects of the lyke, practifed in Noble
houfes, and Courtes of Kyngs and Prynces. That this is true,
example of this fayre Ducheffe, who was moued wyth that defyre
which pricketh others that be of Flefh and Bone. Thys Lady waxed
very weary of lying alone, and gryeued hir Hearte to be wythoute
a match, fpecially in the Nyght, when the fecrete filence and darkeneffe of the fame prefented beefore the eyes of hir mind, the
Image of the pleafure which fhe felt in the lyfe tyme of hir deceafed
Lord and Hufband, whereof now feelyng hir felfe defpoyled, fhe
felt a contynuall Combat, and durft not attempt that which fhe
defyred moft, but efchued the thyng wherof hir Mind lyked beft.
"Alas (fayd fhee) is it poffyble after the tafte of the Value of
honeft obedyence whych the Wyfe oweth vnto hir Hufband, that I
fhould defyre to fuffer the Heat whych burneth and altereth the
martyred mynds of thofe that fubdue themfelues to loue? Can
futch attempt pierce the heart of me to become amorous by forgetting and ftraying from the limmetts of honeft life? But what
defire is this? I haue a certayne vnacquaynted luft, and yet very
well know not what it is that moueth me, and to whom I fhall vow
the fpoyle thereof. I am truely more fond and foolyfhe than euer
Narciffus was, for there is neyther fhadow nor voyce, vpon which
I can well ftay my fight, nor yet fimple Imagination of any worldly

man, whereuppon I can arreſt the conceypt of my vnſtayed heart, and the defires which prouoke my mynde. Pygmalion loued once a Marble Piller, and I haue but one defire, the colour whereof is more pale than death. There is nothyng which can geue the ſame ſo mutch as one ſpot of vermilion rud. If I doe diſcouer theſe appetites to any wight, perhaps they will mock me for my labor, and for all the beauty and Noble byrth that is in me, they will make no confcience to deeme me for their ieſting ſtock, and to folace themſelues with reherſall of my fond conceits. But ſith there is no enemy in the field, and that but ſimple ſuſpicion doth aſſayle me, why breake I not the ſame, and deface the entier remem-braunce of the lightneſſe of my brayne? It appertayneth vnto mee to ſhewe my ſelfe, as iſſued from the Noble houſe of Aragon : to me it doeth belonge to take heede how I erre or degenerate from the royall bloud whereof I came." In this ſort that fayre Wydow and young Princeſſe fantaſied in the night vppon the diſcourſe of hir appetites. But when the day was come, ſeeing the great multitude of the Neapolitan Lords and Gentlemen that marched vp and downe the Citty, eyinge and beholdinge their beſt beloued, or vſing talke of loue with them whoſe ſeruaunts they were, all that which ſhe thought vpon in the night, vaniſhed ſo ſone as the flame of burned Straw, or the Pouder of Cannon ſhot, and purpoſed for any reſpect to liue no longer in that ſort, but promiſed the conqueſt of ſome frend that was luſty and diſcreete. But the difficulty reſted in that ſhe knew not vpon whom to fixe hir loue, fearing to bee ſlaundered, and alſo that the light diſpoſition and maner of moſt part of youth were to be ſuſpected, in ſutch wiſe as giuing ouer al them which vauted vpon their Gennets, Turkey Palfreis, and other Courſers alonge the City of Naples, ſhee purpoſed to take repaſt of other Veniſon, than of that fond and wanton troupe. So hir miſhap began already to ſpin the threede which choked the Ayre and Breath of hir vnhappy life. Yee haue heard before that Mayſter Bologna was one of the wiſeſt and moſt perfect Gentlemen that the land of Naples that tyme brought forth, and for his Beauty, Proportion, Galantneſſe, Valiaunce, and good grace, without com-pariſon. His fauour was ſo ſweete and pleaſant, as they which kept him company, had ſomwhat to do to abſtayne their affection.

Who then could blame thys fayre Princeffe, if (preffed wyth defire
of match, to remoue the ticklifh inftigations of her wanton flefh, and
hauing in hir prefence a man fo wife) fhee did fet hir minde on
hym, or fantafy to mary him? Would not that party for calming
of his thirft and hunger, being fet at a table before fundry forts of
delicate viands, eafe his hunger? Me thinke the perfon doth greatly
forget himfelfe, which hauing handfaft vpon occafion, fuffreth the
fame to vanifh and fly away, fith it is wel known that fhe being
bald behinde, hath no place to feafe vpon when defire moueth vs
to lay hold vpon hir. Which was the caufe that the Ducheffe
became extremely in loue with the mayfter of hir houfe. In futch
wyfe as before al men, fhe fpared not to prayfe the great perfections of him whom fhe defired to be altogether hirs. And fo fhe
was inamored, that it was as poffible to fee the night to be voide
of darkneffe, as the Ducheffe without the prefence of hir Bologna,
or els by talke of words to fet forth his prayfe, the continuall
remembrance of who (for that fhee loued him as hirfelfe) was hir
onely minde's repaft. The Gentleman that was full wyfe, and had
at other times felt the great force of the paffion which proceedeth
from extreeme loue, immediatly did mark the countenaunce of
the Ducheffe, and perceyued the fame fo neere, as vnfaynedly hee
knew that very ardently the Lady was in loue with him: and albeit
he fawe the inequality and difference betweene them both, fhe
being forted out of the royall bloud, and himfelf of meaner calling,
yet knowing loue to haue no refpect to ftate or dignity, determined
to folow his fortune, and to ferue hir which fo louingly fhewed hir
felfe to him. Then fodaynely reprouing his fonde conceit, he fayd
vnto himfelf: "What folly is that I enterprife, to the preiudice
and peril of mine honor and life? Ought the wifedome of a Gentleman to ftray and wandre through the affaults of an appetite rifing
of fenfuality, and that reafon gieue place to that which doeth
participate with brute beafts depriued of all reafon by fubduinge
the minde to the affections of the body? No, no, a vertuous man
ought to let fhine in him felfe the force of the generofity of his
minde. This is not to liue according to the fpirite, when pleafure
fhall make vs forget our duty and fauegard of our Confcience.
The reputation of a wife Gentleman refteth not only to be valiant,

and fkilfull in feates of armes, or in feruice of the Noble: but needefull it is for him by difcreation to make himfelfe prayfe worthy, and by vanquifhinge of himfelfe to open the gate to fame, whereby he may euerlaftingly make himfelfe glorious to all posterity. Loue pricketh and prouoketh the fpirite to do well, I do confeffe, but that affection ought to be addreffed to fome vertuous end, tending to mariage, for otherwife that vnfpotted Image fhall be foyled wyth the villany of Beaftly pleafure. Alas," fayd he, "how eafie it is to difpute, when the thyng is abfent, which can both force and violently affayle the Bulwarks of moft conftant hearts. I full well doe fee the troth, and doe feele the thing that is good, and knowe what behoueth mee to follow: but when I view the percles beauty of my Lady, hir graces, wifedome, behauiour and curtefie, when I fee hir to caft fo louinge an eye vpon me, that fhe vfeth fo great familiarity, that fhe forgetteth the greatneffe of hir houfe to abafe hirfelfe for my refpect: how is it poffible that I fhould be fo foolifh to difpife a duety fo rare and precious, and to fet light by that which the Nobleft would purfue wyth all reuerence and deuoyre? Shall I be fo voyde of wifdome to fuffer the yonge Princeffe to fee hirfelfe contempned of mee, thereby to conuert hir loue to teares, by fetting hir mynde upon an other, that fhall feek mine ouerthrow? Who knoweth not the fury of a woman: fpecially the Noble dame, by feeing hirfelfe defpifed? No, no, fhe loueth me, and I will be hir feruaunt, and vfe the fortune proffred. Shal I be the firft fimple Gentleman that hath married or loued a Princeffe? Is it not more honourable for mee to fettle my mind vpon a place fo high, than vppon fome fimple wench by whom I fhall neyther attayne profit, or aduancement? Baldouine of Flaunders, did not he a Noble enterprife when he carried away Iudith the daughter of the French kynge, as fhe was paffing vpon the Seas into England, to be married to the kynge of that Countrey? I am neither Pirat nor Aduenturer, for the Lady loueth me. What wrong doe I then to any perfon by rendringe loue agayne? Is not fhe at liberty? To whom ought fhee to make accoumpt of hir deedes and doinges, but to God alone and to hir owne Confcience? I wyll loue hir, and cary lyke affection for the loue which I know and fee that fhe beareth vnto me, beinge affured that the fame is directed to good ende, and that a Woman fo wyfe as fhe is, will not hazard the bleamifh of hir honor." Thus Bologna framed the plot for intertaynment of the Ducheffe (albeit hir loue already was fully bent vpon him) and fortified hym felfe agaynft all perillous myfhap and chaunce that might fucceede, as ordinarily you fee that Louers conceyue all things for their aduauntage, and fantafie dreames agreeable to their moft defire, refemblinge the Mad and Bedlem perfons which haue before their eyes, the figured Fanfies whych caufe the conceipt of their fury, and ftay themfelues vpon the vifion of that which moft troubleth their offended Brayne. On the other fide, the Ducheffe was in no leffe care of hir Louer, the will of whom was hid and fecret, whych more did vexe and torment hir, than the fire of loue that burned hir feruently. She could not tell what way to hold, to do him vnderftand hir heart and affection. She feared to difcouer the fame vnto hym, doubtinge eyther that fome fond and rigorous aunfwere, or the reueylinge of hir mynde to hym, whofe prefence pleafed hir more than all of the men of the World. " Alas," fayd fhee, " am I happed into fo ftraunge mifery, that with mine owne mouth I muft make requeft to him, which with all humility ought to offer mee hys feruice? Shall a Lady of futch bloud as I am, be conftrayned to fue, where all other be required by importunate inftance of their Suters? Ah loue, loue, what fo euer he was that clothed thee wyth futch puiffaunce, I dare fay he was the cruell ennimy of man's freedom. It is impoffible that thou hadft thy being in heauen, fith the clemency and curteous influence of the fame, inuefteth man with better benefits, than to fuffer hir nourfe children to be intreated with futch rigor. He lieth which fayth that Venus is thy mother, for the fwetenes and good grace that refteth in that pitifull Goddeffe, who taketh no pleafure to fee louers perced with fo egre trauayles as that which afflicteth my heart. It was fome fierce cogitation of Saturne, that brought thee forth, and fent thee into the worlde to breake the eafe of them which liue at reft without any paffion or griefe. Pardon me Loue, if I blafpheme thy maiefty, for the ftreffe and endleffe grief wherein I am plunged, maketh me thus to roue at large, and the doubts, which I conceyue, do take away the health and foundneffe

of my mynde, the little experience in thy fchole caufeth this
amaze in me, to be folicited with defire that counterfayeth the
duty, honor, and reputation of my ftate: the party whom I loue,
is a Gentleman, vertuous, valiant, fage, and of good grace. In
this there is no caufe to blame Loue of blindneffe, for all the
inequality of our houfes, apparant vpon the firft fight and fhew of
the fame. But from whence Iffue Monarchs, Prynces and great
Lords, but from the naturall and common Maffe of Earth, whereof
other men do come? what maketh thefe differences betwene thofe
that loue ech other, if not the fottifh opinion which we conceiue
of greatneffe, and preheminence: as though naturall affections
bee like to that ordayned by the fantafie of men in their lawes
extreme. And what greater right haue Princes to ioyne wyth a
fimple Gentlewoman, than the Princeffe to mary a Gentleman, and
futch as Anthonio Bologna is, in whom Heauen and Nature haue
forgotten nothinge to make him equall with them which march
amongs the greateft. I thinke we be the dayly flaues of the fond
and cruell fantafie of thofe Tyraunts, which fay they haue puiffance
ouer vs: and that ftraininge our will to their tiranny, we be ftill
bound to the chaine like the Galley flaue. No, no, Bologna fhall
be my Hufband, for of a freend I purpofe to make my loyall and
lawful Hufband, meaning therby not to offend God and men
together, and pretend to liue without offence of confcience, wherby
my foule fhal not be hindred for any thyng I do, by marying him
whom I fo ftraungely loue. I am fure not to be deceyued in
loue. He loueth me fo mutch or more as I do him, but he dareth
not difclofe the fame, fearing to be refufed and caft of with
fhame. Thus 2 vnited wils, and 2 hearts tied togethers with
equal knot cannot chofe but bryng forth fruites worthy of futch
fociety. Let men fay what they lift, I will doe none otherwyfe
than my heade and mynd haue already framed. Semblably I
neede not make accompt to any perfone for my fact, my body, and
reputation beynge in full liberty and freedome. The bond of
mariage made, fhall couer the faulte whych men woulde fynde,
and leauyng myne eftate, I fhall do no wrong but to the greatneffe
of my houfe, which maketh me amongs men right honorable. But
thefe honors be nothyng worth, where the Mynd is voyd of conten-

tation, and wher the hearte pryckte forwarde by defire leaueth the
Bodye and Mynde reftleffe wythout quiet." Thus the Ducheffe
founded hir enterpryfe, determining to mary hir houfhold Mayfter,
feeking for occafion and time, meete for difclofing of the fame,
and albeit that a certaine naturall fhamefaftneffe, which of cuftome
accompanieth Ladies, did clofe hir mouth, and made hir to deferre
(for a certain time) the effect of hir refolued minde: yet in
the ende vanquifhed with loue and impacience, fhe was forced to
breake of filence, and to affure hir felf in him, reiecting feare
conceiued of fhame, to make hir waye to pleafure, which fhe
lufted more than mariage, the fame feruyng hir, but for a Mafke
and couerture to hide hir follies and fhameleffe lufts, for which fhe
did the penaunce that hir folly deferued. For no colorable dede
or deceytful trompery can ferue the excufe of any notable wyckedneffe. She then throughly perfuaded in her intent, dreamyng
and thinking of nought elfe, but vpon the imbracement of hir
Bologna, ended and determined hir conceits and pretended follies:
and vpon a time fent for him vp into hir chamber, as commonly
fhe did for the affaires and matters of hir houfe, and taking him a
fide vnto a window, hauing profpect into a garden, fhe knew not
how to begin hir talk : (for the heart being feafed, the mind troubled, and the witts out of courfe, the tongue fayled to do his office,) in futch wife, as of long time fhe was vnable to fpeake one
onely woord. He furprifed with like affection, was more aftonied
by feeing the alteration of his Ladie. So the two Louers ftoode
ftill like Images beholding one another, without any mouing
at all, vntill the Lady the hardieft of them bothe, as feelinge the
moft vehement and greateft gryef, tooke Bologna by the hand,
and diffembling what fhe thought, vfed this or futch language:
" If any other befides your felfe (Gentleman) fhould vnderftand the
fecret which now I purpofe to dyfclofe, I doubt what fpeeach
were neceffary to colour, what I fhall fpeake: but being affured
of your difcretion and wifdom, and with what perfection nature
hath indued you, and Arte, hauing accomplifhed that in you, which
nature did begin to worke, as one bred and brought vp in the
royal court of the feconde Alphonfe, of Ferdinando, and Frederick
of Aragon my coufins, I wil make no doubt at all to manifeft to

you the hidden fecretes of my heart, being well perfuaded that
when you fhall both heare and fauor my reafons, and taft the light
which I bring forth for me, eafily you may iudge that mine aduice
cannot be other than iuft and reafonable. But if your conceits
fhall ftraye from that whych I determine, I fhal be forced to
thinke and faye that they which efteeme you wife and fage, and
to be a man of good and ready wytte, be marueloufly deceiued.
Notwithftanding my heart foretelleth that it is impoffible for
mayfter Bologna, to wandre fo farre from equitie, but that by and
by he wil enter the lyftes and dyfcerne the White from Blacke, and
the Wronge fro that whych is Iuft and Ryghte: for fo mutch as
hitherto I neuer faw thinge done by you, which Prepofterated or
peruerted the good iudgement that all the world efteemeth to
fhine in you, the fame well manifefted and declared by your
tongue, the right iudge of the Mynde, you knowe and fee how I
am a Wydow through the Death of that Noble Gentleman of good
remembrance, the Duke my Lord and hufbande: you be not ignoraunt alfo, that I haue lyued and gouerned my felf in futch wife
in my Widow ftate, as there is no man fo hard and feuere of iudgement, that can blafon reproch of mee in that whych appertayneth
to the honeftye and reputation of futch a Lady as I am, bearyng
my port fo righte, as my confcience yeldeth no remorfe, fuppo-
finge that no Man hathe wherewith to byte and accufe me. Touchyng the order of the goods of the Duke my Sonne, I have vfed
them with diligence and difcretion, as befides the Dettes, whych I
haue dyfcharged fithens the death of my Lord: I haue purchafed a
goodly Manor in Calabria, and haue annexed the fame to the
Dukedome of his heire: and at this day doe not owe one peny to
any creditor that lent money to the Duke, which he toke vp to fur-
nifh the charges in the warres, which he fuftayned in the feruice of
the Kinges our foueraine Lords in the late warres for the Kyngdome
of Naples. I haue as I fuppofe by this meanes ftopped the flaunderous mouth and giuen caufe vnto my fonne, during his life to
accompt himfelf bound vnto his mother: now hauing till thys
time liued for other, and made my felfe fubiect more than nature
could beare, I am entended to chaunge both my lyfe and condition. I haue tyll thys time run, trauayled, and remoued to the

Caſtels andLordeſhips of theDukedome,to Naples and other places, being in mind to tary as I am a widow.   But what new affayres and new councel hath poſſeſt my mynd?   I haue trauayled and payned my ſelf inoughe: I haue to long abidden a widowe's lyfe: I am determined therefore to prouyde a Huſbande, who by louing me, ſhall honor and cheryſh me according to the loue which I ſhall beare hym, and my deſert.   For to loue a man without mariage, God defend my hearte ſhould euer think, and ſhal rather dye a hundred thouſand deathes, than a deſire ſo wicked ſhould ſoyle my conſcience, knowyng well that a woman which ſetteth hir honor to ſale, is leſſe than nothing, and deſerueth not the common ayre ſhould breathe vpon hir, for all the reuerence that men do beare vnto them.   I accuſe no perſon, albeit that many noble women haue their forheds marked, with the blame of diſhoneſt lyfe, and being honored of ſome, bee neuertheleſſe the common Fable of the Worlde.   To the intente then that ſutch myſhappe happen not to me, and perceyuyng my ſelfe vnable ſtyll thus to lyue, beyng younge as I am, and (God bee thanked) neyther deformed nor yet paynted, I had rather bee the louyng Wyfe of a ſymple feere, than the Concubyne of a kynge or greate Prynce. And what? is the myghty Monarche able to waſhe away the faulte of hys Wyfe whych hath abandoned him contrary to the duety and honeſty whych the vndefyled bed requyreth? no leſſe then Prynceſſes that whilom treſpaſſed with thoſe whych were of baſer ſtuffe than themſelues.   Meſſalina with hir imperiall robe could not ſo wel couer hir faults, but that the Hiſtorians, do defame hir with the name and title of a common woman. Fauſtina the Wyfe of the ſage Monarch Marcus Aurelius, gayned lyke reporte by rendringe hir ſelfe to others pleaſure, byſides hir lawfull Spouſe.   To mary my ſelfe to one that is myne equall, it is impoſſible, for ſo mutch as there is no Lorde in all this Countrey meete for my degree, but is to olde of age, the reſt being dead in theſe later Warres.   To mary a huſband that yet is but a childe, is folly extreeme, for the inconueniences which daily chaunce thereby, and the euil intreaty that Ladies do receyue when they come to age, when their nature waxeth cold, by reaſon whereof, imbracements be not ſo fauourable, and their huſbandes glutted

with ordinary meate, vſe to run in exchange: wherefore I am reſolued without reſpite or delay, to chooſe ſome well qualified and
renoumed Gentleman, that hath more vertue than richeſſe, that is
of better Fame and brute, then of wealth and reuenue, to the entent
I may make him my Lord, Eſpouſe, and Huſbande. For I cannot imploy my loue vpon treaſure, which may bee taken away
from him, in whom richeſſe of the minde doth fayle, and ſhall bee
better content to ſee an honeſt Gentleman with little liuing, to be
prayſed and commended of ech Degree for his good Deedes, than
a rich Carle curſſed and deteſted of all the World. Thus mutch I
ſay, and it is the ſumme of all my ſecretes, wherein I pray your
councel and aduice. I know that ſome wil be offended with my
choiſe, and the Lords my Brothers, ſpecially the Cardinall will
thincke it ſtraunge, and receyue the ſame with ill Digeſture, that
mutch a do ſhall I haue to bee agreed with them and to remoue the
griefe they ſhall conceyue againſt mee for this myne attempt:
wherefore I would the ſame ſhould ſecretly be kept, until without
peril and daunger eyther of my ſelf or him, whome I pretende to
marry, I may publiſh and manyfeſt, not my loue but the mariage
which I hope in God ſhall ſoone bee conſummate and accompliſhed wyth one, whome I doe loue better than my ſelf, and who as I
ful well do know, doeth loue me better than his owne propre lyfe."
Mayſter Bologna, which tyll then hearkned to the oration of the
Ducheſſe without mouing, feeling himſelfe touched ſo neare, and
hearinge that his Lady had made hir approche for mariage, ſtode
ſtill aſtonnied, hys tongue not able to frame one word, onely ſan-
taſied a thouſand chimeraes in the Ayre, and formed like number
of imaginations in his minde, not able to coniecture what hee was,
to whom the ducheſſe had vowed hir loue, and the poſſeſſion of
hir beauty. He could not thinke that this ioy was prepared for
hymſelfe, for that his Lady ſpake no word of him, and he leſſe durſt
open his mouth, and yet was wel aſſured that ſhe loued him beyond
meaſure. Notwithſtanding knowing the fickleneſſe and vnſtable
heart of women, he ſayd vnto himſelfe that ſhe would change hir
mynde, for ſeeing him to be ſo great a Coward, as not to offer his
ſeruice to a Lady by whom hee ſaw himſelfe ſo many times both
wantonly looked vppon, aud intertayned wyth ſome ſecreſie more

than familiar. The Ducheffe which was a fine and fubtile dame,
feeinge hir friend rapt with the paffion, and ftanding ftill vn-
mooueable through feare, pale and amazed, as if hee had bene accufed and condempned to dy, knew by that Countenaunce and
aftonifhment of Bologna, that fhe was perfectly beloued of him :
and fo meaning not to fuffer him any longer to contynue in that
amaze, ne yet to further feare hym, wyth diffembled and fayned
mariage of any other but wyth hym, fhe tooke hym by the hand,
and beholdinge him with a wanton and luring eye, (in futch fort
as the curious Philofophers themfelues would awake, if futch a
Lampe and Torche did burne wythin theyr ftudies,) fhe fayde thus
vnto hym : "Seignor Anthonio, I pray you be of good cheere,
and torment not your felfe for any thing that I haue fayd : I know
well, and of long time haue perceyued what good and faythful
lone you beare mee, and with what affection you haue ferued me,
fithens you firft came into my company. Thinke me not to bee
fo ignorant, but that I know ful wel by outward fignes, what fecret thoughts be hid in the inner heart : and that coniectures many
times do geue me true and certayne knowledge of concealed things :
and am not fo foolifh to thinke you to be fo vndifcrete but that
you haue marked my Countenaunce and maner, and thereby haue
knowen that I haue bene more affectioned to you, than to any
other : for that caufe (fayde fhee, ftrayninge hym by the hand
very louingly, and wyth cheerefull colour in hir face) I fware vnto
you, and doe promife that if you thinke meete, it fhalbe none
other but your felf whom I wil haue, and defire to take to hufband
and lawful fpoufe, beynge affured fo much of you, as the loue
which fo longe time hath ben hidden and couered in our hartes,
fhall appeare by fo euident proofe, as onely death fhal end and
vndo the fame." The Gentleman hearing futch fodain talke, and
the affurance of that which he moft wifhed for, albeit he faw the
daunger extreme wherunto he launched himfelf by efpoufing this
great Ladie, and the ennimies he fhould get by entring futch aliaunce : notwythftandynge building vpon vaine hope, and thinking at length that the choler of the Aragon brother would paffe
away if they vnderftoode the maryage, determined to purfue the
purpofe, and not to refufe that greate preferment, being fo pro-

digally offred : for which caufe hee anfwered his Lady in this manner: "If it were in my power madame, to bryng to paffe that,
which I defire for your feruice by acknowledging the benefits and
fauors which you depart vnto me, as my mind prefenteth thanks
for the fame, I would think my felf the happyeft Gentleman that
lyueth, and you the befte ferued Prynceffe of the world. For one
beter beloued (I dare prefume to fay, and fo long as I liue wil
affirme) is not to be found. If tyll thys time I delayed to open
that which now I difcouer vnto you, I befeeche you madame to
impute it to the greatneffe of your eftate, and to the duty of my
calling and office in your houfe, being not feemelye for a feruaunte
to talk of futch fecrets with his Lady and Miftreffe. And truely
the payne which I haue indured to hold my peace, and to hyde
my grief, hath ben more noyfom to me than one hundred thoufand
like forrowes together, although it had bene lawfull to haue reuealed them to fome trufty friend: I doe not denye madame, but
of long time you did perceiue my follie and prefumption, by ad-
dreffing my minde fo high, as to the Aragon bloud, and to futch a
princeffe as you be. And who can beguile the Eye of a louer,
fpecially of hir, whofe Paragon for good minde, wifedome and gentleneffe is not? And I confeffe to you befides, that I haue moft
euidentlye perceiued how a certain loue hath lodged in your gracious hearte, wherwith you bare me greater affection, than you dyd
to anye other within the compaffe of your family. But what?
great Ladyes heartes be fraught with fecretes and conceites of other
effects than the Minds of Symple Women, which caufed me to
hope for none other guerdon of my loyal and faithful affection, than
Deathe, and the fame very fhort, and fith that little hope accompanyed wyth great, nay, rather extreme paffion, is not able to giue
fufficient force, both to fuffer and to ftablifh my heart with conftancye. Nowe for fo mutch as of your motion, grace, curtefie
and liberality the fame is offred, and that it pleafeth you to accept
me for yours, I humblye befeche you to difpofe of me not as hufband, but of one whych is, and fhalbe your Seruaunt for euer, and
futch as is more ready to obey, than you to commaund. It refteth
now Madame, to confyder how, and in what wife our affayres are
to be directed, that thynges being in affurance, you may fo liue

without perill and bruite of flaunderous tongues, as your good fame
and honeft report may continue without fpot or blemifh." Beholde the firft Acte of this Tragedy, and the prouifion of the fare
which afterwardes fent them bothe to their graue, who immediatly
gaue their mutual faith: and the houre was affigned the next
day, that the faire Princeffe fhould be in hir chamber alone, attended vpon with one onely Gentlewoman which had ben brought vp
with her from the cradle, and was made priuy to the heauy mariage
of thofe two louers which was confummate in hir prefence.
And for the prefent time they paffed the fame in words: for
ratification whereof they went to bed togither: but the pain in
the end was greater than the pleafure, and had ben better for
them bothe, yea and alfo for the third, that they had fhewed themfelues fo wyfe in the deede, as difcrete in keeping filence of that
which was don: for albeit theyr mariage was fecrete, and therby
politikely gouerned themfelues in their ftelthes and robberyes of
Loue, and that Bologna more ofte helde the ftate of the Stewarde
of the Houfe by Daye, than of Lorde of the fame, and by Nyghte
fupplyed that Place, yet in the ende, the thynge was perceyued
whych they defyred to bee clofely kepte. And as it is impoffyble to tyll and culture a fertyle Grounde, but that the fame
mufte yelde fome Fruycte, euen fo the Ducheffe after many
pleafures (being ripe and plentifull) became with childe, which at
the firfte aftonned the maried couple: neuertheleffe the fame fo
well was prouided for, as the firft Childbed was kept fecret, and
none did know thereof: the Childe was nourced in the Towne, and
the father defired to haue him named Frederick, for remembraunce
of the parents of hys Wyfe. Nowe fortune whych lieth in dayly
wayte and ambufhment, and lyketh not that men fhould longe
Loyter in Pleafure, and Paffetime, being enuious of futch profperity, cramped fo the Legges of our two Louers, as they muft
needes chaunge their Game, and learne fome other practife: for fo
mutch as the Ducheffe beinge great with Childe agayne, and deliuered of a Girle, the bufineffe of the fame was not fo fecretly
done, but that it was difcouered. And it fufficed not that the
brute was noyfed through Naples, but that the found flew further
of: As eche man doth know that Rumor hath many mouthes, who

wyth the multitude of hys Tongues, and Trumps, Proclaymeth in
diuers and fundry places, the things which chaunce in al the
Regions of the Earth: euen fo that bablinge foole, caried the
newes of that fecond Childbed to the eares of the Cardinall of
Aragon the Ducheffe brother, being then at Rome. Think what
Ioy, and Pleafure the Aragon brothers had, by hearinge the report of their Sifter's fact: I dare prefume to fay, that albeit they
were extremely wroth wyth this happened Slaunder, and wyth
that difhoneft fame which the Ducheffe had gotten throughout
Italy, yet farre greater was their forrow and griefe for that they
did not know what hee was, that fo curteoufly was allied to their
houfe, and in their loue had increafed their Ligneage: and therefore fwelling wyth defpite, and rapt with fury to fee themfelues
fo defamed by one of their Bloude, they purpofed by all meanes
whatfoeuer it coft them, to know the lucky Louer that had fo wel
tilled the Ducheffe their Sifter's field. Thus defirous to remoue
that fhame from before their eyes, and to bee reuenged of a wrong
fo notable, they fent Efpials round about, and fcouts to Naples, to
view and fpy the behauiour and talke of the Ducheffe, to fettle
fome certayne Iudgement of him, which ftealingly was become
their Brother in lawe. The Ducheffe Courte beinge in thys
trouble, fhe dyd contynually perceiue in hir houfe, hir brothers
men to marke hir countenance, and to note thofe that came thither
to vifite hir, and to whom fhe vfed greateft familiaritie, bicaufe it is
impoffible but that the fire, although it be raked vnder the afhes,
muft giue fome heat: and albeit the two Louers vfed eche others
company, without fhewing any Sygne of their affection, yet they
purpofed to chaung theyr eftate for a tyme, by yelding truce to
their pleafures: yea, and although Bologna was a wife and prouident perfonage, fearing to be furprifed vpon the facte, or that
the Gentlewoman of the chamber corrupted with money, or forced
by.feare, fhould pronounce any matter to his hinderance or dis-
aduantage, determined to abfent himfelf from Naples, yet not fo
fodainly but that he made the Ducheffe his faithfull Lady and companion priuy of his intent: and as they were fecretly in their
chamber together, he vfed thefe or futch like words: "Madame,
albeit the right good intent and vnftained confcience, is free from

faulte, yet the iudgement of men hath further relation to the exterior apparance, than to vertue's force and innocency it felf, as
ignoraunt of the fecrets of the thought: and fo in things that be
well done, wee muft of neceffity fall into the fentence of thofe,
whom beaftly affection rauifheth more, than ruled reafon. You
fee the folempne watch and guarde whych the Seruaunts of the
Lordes your Brothers do within your houfe, and the fufpition
which they haue conceiued by reafon of your fecond Childbed,
and by what meanes they labor truely to know how your affayres
procede, and things do paffe. I feare not death where your
feruice may be aduaunced, but yf herein the Maiden of your
Chamber be not fecrete, if fhe bee corrupted, and if fhe keepe
not clofe that which fhee ought to doe, it is not ignoraunt to you
that it is the loffe of my lyfe, and fhall dye fufpected to bee a
Whoremonger and varlot, euen I, (I fay) fhal incurre that Peryll,
whych am your true and Lawfull Hufband. Thys feparation
chaunceth not by iuftyce or defert, fith the caufe is to ryghteous for
vs: but rather your brethren will procure my death, when I fhall
thinke the fame in greateft affurance. If I had to do but wyth
one or two, I would not chaunge the place, ne march one ftep
from Naples, but be affured, that a great band, and the fame well
armed will fet vppon me: I pray you, madame, fuffer me to retire
for a time, for I am affured that when I am abfent, they will neuer
foile their hands or imbrue their fweardes in your Bloud. If I
doubted any thing at all of Peryll touchyng your owne perfon, I
had rather a hundred hundred tymes die in your Company, than
lyue to fee you no more: but out of doubt I am, that if our affaires
were difcouered, and they knew you to be begotten with Chyld by
me, your fafety would be prouided for wher I fhould fuftain the
penaunce of the fact, committed without fault or finne: and therfore I am determined to goe from Naples, to order mine affaires,
and to caufe my Reuenue to be brought to the place of mine
abode, and from thence to Ancona, vntyl it pleafeth God to
mitigate the rage of your brethren, and recouer their good wills
for confent to our mariage. But I meane not to do or conclude
any thing without your aduife, and if thys intente doe not like
you, gyue me Councell Madame, what I were befte to doe, that

both in Lyfe and Death you may knowe your faythfull feruaunt
and louing Hufband is ready to obey and pleafe you." This good
Lady hearing hir hufband's difcourfe, vncertayne what to do,
wept bitterly, as well for grief to lofe his prefence, as for that fhe
felt her felf with child the third time: the fighes and teares, the
fobbes and heauy lookes, which fhe threwe forth vppon hir forrowful hufband, gaue fufficient witneffe of hir payne and Gryef: and
if none had hard hir, I thynke her playntes would haue well expreffed hir inwarde fmarte of mynde. But like a wife Ladye feing
the alleaged reafons of hir hufbande, licenfed him although agaynfte
hir minde, not wythout vtterance of thefe fewe Words, before hee
went out of hir Chamber: "Deare hufbande, if I were fo well
affured of the affe∂yon of my Brethren, as I am of my mayde's
fidelity, I would entreat you not to leaue me alone: fpecially in
the cafe I am, beynge wyth Chylde: but knowyng that to be iuft
and true whych you haue fayde, I am content to force my wyll
for a certayne tyme, that hereafter we may lyue at reft together,
ioyning our felues in the companye of our Chyldren and Famylye,
voyde of thofe troubles, whych greate Courts ordinarily beare
within the compaffe of their Palaces. Of one thing I muft intreat you, that fo often as you can by trufty meffenger, you fend
me word and intelligence of your health and ftate, bicaufe the
fame fhall bring vnto me greater pleafure and contentation, than
the welfare of mine owne: and bicaufe alfo, vpon futch occurrentes as fhall chaunce, I may prouyde for myne owne affaires,
the furety of my felf, and of our Children." In faying fo, fhe
embraced him very amoroufly, and he kiffed hir with fo greate
forrow and grief of heart, as the foule was ready out of his Body
to take hir flight, forowful beyond meafure fo to leaue hir whome
he loued, for the great curtefies and honor which hee had receiued
at hir hands. In the end, fearing that the Aragon efpials woulde
come and difcrie them in thofe priuities, Bologna tooke his leaue,
and bad his Lady and fpoufe Farewell. And this was the fecond
Acte of this Tragicall Hiftorie, to fee a fugitife hufband fecretly
to mary, efpecially hir, vpon whome hee ought not fo mutch as
to loke but with feare and reuerence. Behold here (O ye folifh
louers) a Glaffe of your lightneffe, and yee Women, the courfe of

your fond behauyor.   It behoueth not the wife fodainly to execute
their firft motions and defyres of their heart for fo mutch as they
may be affured that pleafure is purfued fo neare with a repentaunce fo fharp to be fuffred, and hard to be digefted, as their
voluptuoufneffe fhall vtterly difcontent them.   True it is, that
mariages be don in heauen and performed in earth, but that faying may not be applied to fooles, which gouerne them felues by
carnall defires, whofe fcope is but pleafure, and the reward many
times equall to their follie.   Shall I be of opinion that a houfhold
feruaunt oughte to follicite, nay rather fuborne the Daughter of
his Lorde without punyfhment, or that a vyle and abieᶜt perfon
dare to mount vpon a Prynces Bed?   No, no, pollicye requyreth
order in all, and eche wight ought to bee matched according to
theyr qualytye, wythout makynge a Paftyme of it to couer theyr
Follyes, and knowe not of what Force Loue and Defteny be, except
the fame be refyfted.   A goodly thinge it is to Loue, but where
reafon loofeth Place, Loue is wythoute his effeᶜte, and the fequele
rage and Madneffe: leaue we to difcourfe of thofe which beleue
that they be conftrayned to folowe the Force of theyr Mynde, and
may eafilye fubdue themfelues to the Lawes of Vertue and Honefty,
lyke one that thrufteth hys Heade into a Sack, and thynkes he can
not get out: futch people do pleafe themfelues in theyr loffe, and
thinke all well that is noyfome to their Health, daily folowyng
theyr owne delyghtes.   Come wee againe then to fir Bologna, who
after he had left hys Wyfe in hir Caftell, went to Naples, and hauing
feffed a rent vpon hir lands, and leuyed a good fumme of Money,
he repayred to Ancona a city of the patrimonye of the Romane
church, whither hee caryed the two Chyldren, which he had of
the Ducheffe, caufyng them to be brought vp with fuche Dyligence
and care, as it is to be thought a Father well affeᶜtyoned to hys
Wyfe would doe, and who delyghted to fee a Braunch of the Tree,
that to hym was the beft beloued Fruyᶜt of the World.   There he
hyred a houfe for hys trayne, and for thofe that wayted vppon hys
Wyfe, who in the meane tyme was in great care, and could not
tell of what Woode to make hir arrowes, perceyuing that hir Belly
began to fwell, and grow to the tyme of hir deliuery, feeing that
from Day to Day, hir Brothers feruaunts were at hir back, voide

of Counfel and aduife, if one euenyng fhe had not fpoken to the
Gentlewoman of her chamber, touchyng the doubts and peryl
wherein fhe was, not knowing how fhe might be deliuered from
the fame. That maiden was gentle and of a good mind and
ftomake, and loued hir miftreffe very derely, and feeing hir fo
amazed and tormenting hir felf to death, mindyng to fray hir no
further, ne to reproue hir of hir fault which could not be amended,
but rather to prouyde for the daunger wherunto fhe had hedlong
caft hir felfe, gaue hir this aduyfe: " How now, Madame " (fayd
fhee,) " is that wyfdom whych from your Chyldhode hath ben fo
famyliar in you, diflodged from your breft in time when it ought
chiefly to reft for incountryng of thofe mifhaps that are comming
vpon vs ? think you to auoid the dangers, by thus tormentyng
your felf, except you fet your hands to the work therby to gyue
the repulfe to aduerfe fortune ? I haue heard you many tymes
fpeake of the Conftancye and Force of Mynde, whych ought to
fhine in the deedes of Princeffes, more clerely than amongs thofe
dames of bafer houfe, and whych ought to make them appeare
like the funne and the little ftarres: and yet I fee you nowe
aftonned, as though you had neuer forfeene, that aduerfity chaunceth fo wel to catch the great within his clouches, as the bafe and
fimple fort. It is but now that you haue called to remembraunce
that which might infue your mariage with fir Bologna ? Did hys
onely prefence affure you againft the waits of fortune, and was it
the thought of paines, feares and frights, which now turmoileth
your dolorous mind ? Ought you thus to vexe your felfe, when
nede it is to thinke how to faue both your honor, and the fruicte
wythin your intrailes ? If your forrow be fo great ouer fir Bologna,
and if you feare your childbed wil be defcried, why feeke you
not meanes to attempt fome voyage, for couering of the fact, to
beguile the eyes of them whych fo diligently do watch you ?
Doth your hearte faile you in that matter ? whereof do you dreame ?
why fweat and freat you before you make me anfwer ? " " Ah
fweete hearte," (anfwered the Ducheffe,) " if thou felteft the payne
which I do fuffer, thy tongue would not be fo mutch at wyll, as
thou fheweft it now to bee for reproofe of my fmall Conftancie.
I do forrow fpecially for the caufes which thou alleageft, and

aboue all, for that I know well, that if my Brethren had neuer fo
litle intelligence of my beynge with Chyld, I were vndone and my
Lyfe at an end, and peraduenture poore Wench, thou fhouldeſt
beare the penaunce for my finne. But what way can I take,
that ſtil theſe Candels may not giue light, and I voided of the
Trayne whych ought to wayghte vpon my Brethren? I thinke if
I fhould defcend into Hell, they would know, whither any fhadowe
there were in loue with me. Now geſſe if I fhould trauayle the
Realme, or retire to any other place, whither they would let me
liue in peace? Nothing leſſe, for fufpe they would, that the
caufe of my departure proceeded of defyre to liue at liberty, to
dallye wyth hym, whom they Iudge to be other than my lawfull
hufbande: and it may fo be, that as they bee Wicked and fufpicious, fo will they doubte of my beynge wyth Chylde and thereby
fhall I bee farre more infortunate by trauaylyng, than here in
miferie amidde myne anguifhe: and you the refte that be keepers
of my Councell, fall into greater Daunger, vppon whome no doubte
they will bee reuenged: and flefhe themfelues for your vnhappy
waiting and attendance vpon vs." "Madame," fayd the bolde
Maiden, "be not afraide, and followe mine aduife, for I hope that
it fhall be the meanes both to fee your fpoufe, and to rid thofe
troublefome verlets out of your houfe, and in like maner fafely to
deliuer you into good affuraunce." "Say your mind," quod the
Ladye, "for it may bee, that I wyll gouerne my felf according to
the fame." "Mine aduife is then," fayd the Gentlewoman, "to
let your houfhold vnderftand, that you made a Vowe to vifite the
Holy Temple of our Lady of Loretto, (a Famous Pilgrimage in Italy)
and that you commaund your Trayn to make themfelues ready to
wayt vpon you for accomplyfhment of your deuotion, and from
thence you fhall take your Iourney to foiourne at Ancona, whither
before you goe hence, you fhall fend your Moueables and Plate,
wyth futch Moneye as you thynke neceffarye for furnyfhing of
your Charges: and afterwards God will performe the reſt, and
through his holy mercy will guyde and direct al your affaires." The
Ducheſſe hearing the mayden fpeake her good aduife and amazed
of her fodayne inuention, could not forbear to imbrace and kyſſe
hir, bleſſing the houre wherein fhe was borne, and that euer fhe

chaunced into hir Companye, to whome afterwards fhee fayd:
"My Wenche, I had well determined to gyue ouer myne eftate
and Noble porte, ioyfully to lyue a fimple Gentlewoman with my
deare and welbeloued Hufband, but I could not deuyfe how I
fhould conuenyently departe thys countrey without fufpition of
fome folly: and fith that thou haft fo well inftructed mee for
brynging that fame to paffe, I promyfe thee that fo diligentlye
thy counfel fhal be performed, as I fee the fame to be right good
and neceffary: for rather had I fee my hufband, beynge alone
without title of Ducheffe or great Lady, than to liue without him
beautified with the graces and Names of Honor and preheminence."
This deuifed plot was no foner grounded, but fhe gaue order for
execution of the fame, and brought it to paffe with futch dexterity as the Ladye in leffe than VIII. Dayes had conueyed and
fente the moft part of hir Moueables, and fpecially the chyefeft
and befte to Ancona, taking in the meane time hir way towards
Loretto after fhe had bruted hir folempne vow made for that Pilgrimage. It was not fufficient for this folyfh Woman to take a
Hufband more to glut hir libidinous appetite, than for other
occafion, except fhee added to hir finne another excreable im-
pietie, making holy places and dueties of deuotion, to be as it
were the fhadowes of hir folly. But let vs confider the force of
Louers rage, which fo foone as it hath feafed vpon the minds of
men, we fee how maruellous be the effects thereof, and with what
ftraint and puiffaunce that madneffe fubdueth the wife and
ftrongeft worldlings: who woulde thinke that a great Lady befides
the abandoning hir eftate, hir goodes and Chyld, would haue mif-
pryfed hir honor and reputation, to follow like a vagabond, a pore
and fimple Gentleman, and him befides that was the houfehold
feruaunt of hir Courte? and yet you fee this great and mighty
Ducheffe trot and run after the Male, like a female Wolfe or Lioneffe
(when they goe to fault,) and forget the Noble bloud of Aragon
whereof fhe was defcended, to couple hir felf almoft with the
fimpleft perfon of all the trimmeft Gentlemen of Naples. But
turne we not the example of follies to be a matter of confequence:
for if one or two become bankrupt of theyr honor, it followeth
not, good Ladyes, that theyr fact fhould ferue for a matche to your

deferts, and mutch leffe a patron for you to folow. Thefe Hyftories be not wryten to trayne and trap you to purfue the thoufand
thoufand flippery fleightes of Loue's gallantife, but rather carefully to warne you to behold the femblable faultes, and to ferue
for a drugge to dyfcharge the Poyfon which gnaweth and fretteth
the integrytie and foundneffe of the foule. The wyfe and fkilfull
Apothecary or compofitor of drugges, dreffeth Vipers flefh to purge
the patyent from hote corrupted bloud which conceyueth and engendreth Leprofie within hys Body. In lyke manner, the fonde
loue and wycked rybauldry of Semiramis, Pafiphae, Meffalina,
Fauftina, and Romilda is fhewed in wryt, that euery of you maye
feare to be numbred and recorded amongs futch common and difhonourable women. You Princes and great Lords read the follies
of Paris, the adulteries of Hercules, the dainty and effeminate life
of Sardanapalus, the tiranny of Phalaris, Bufiris, or Dyonifius of
Sicile, and fee the hiftory of Tiberius, Nero, Caligula, Domitian,
and Heliogabalus, and fpare not to recompte them amongs our
wanton youthes which foile themfelues villaines more filthily than
the fwine do in the durt: al this intendeth it an inftruction for
your youth to follow the infection and whoredome of thofe
Monfters? Better it were all thofe bokes were drenched in bottom-
leffe depth of feas, than Chriftian life by their meanes fhould be
corrupted: but the example of the wicked is induced for to efchue
and auoid them, as the life of the good and honeft is remembred
to frame and addreffe our behauior in this world to be praife
worthy and commended: otherwyfe the holineffe of facred writ
fhould ferue for an argument to the vnthrifty and luxurious to
confirm and approue their beaftly and licencious wickedneffe.
Come we againe then to our purpofe: the good Pilgrime of
Loretto went forth hir voyage to atchieue hir deuotions, by vifiting
the Saint for whofe Reliques fhe was departed the country of the
Duke hir Sonne: when fhe had done hir fuffrages at Loretto, hir
people thought hir voiage to be at an end, and that fhe would haue
returned again into hir Countrey: but fhe faid vnto them, that
forfomutch as fhe was fo neare Ancona, being but xv. myles of,
fhe would not retyre but fhe had feen that auncient and goodlye
city, which diuers Hyftories do greatly recommend, as wel for the

antiquitie, as for the pleasant seat therof. Al were of hir aduise, and went forward to see the antiquities of Ancona, and she to renue the pleasures whych she had before begon with hir Bologna, who was aduertised of all hir determination, restyng now like a God, possessed with the Iewels and rychesse of the Duchesse, and had taken a fayre palace in the great Streat of the City, by the gate wherof the traine of hys Lady must passe. The Harbinger of the Duchesse posted before to take vp lodging for the train, but Bologna offred vnto hym hys Palace for the Ladye. So Bologna whych was already welbeloued in Ancona, and newely entred Amytye and greate Aquayntaunce wyth the Gentlemen of the Cytye, wyth a goodlye troupe of them, wente forthe to meete hys Wyfe, to whom he presented his house, and besought hir that shee and hir trayne would vouchsafe to lodge there. She receiued the same very thankfully, and withdrew hir selfe vnto his house, who conducted hir thither, not as a husband, but like him that was hir humble and affectionate seruaunte. But what needeth greate dyscourse of Woordes? The duchesse knowing that it was impossible but eche man must be priuy to hir facte, and know what secretes hath passed betweene hir and hir Husband, to the ende that no other opynyon of hir Childebed should be conceyued, but that whych was good and Honest, and done synce the accomplyshment of the Maryage, the morrow after hir arryuall to Ancona, assembled all her Trayne in the Hall, of purpose no longer to keepe cloase that sir Bologna was hir Husbande, and that alreadye shee had had two Chyldren by him, and agayne was great with childe, with a third. And when they were come togither after dynner, in that presence of hir husbande, shee vsed vnto them these woordes: "Gentlemen, and al ye my trusty and louyng seruaunts, hyghe tyme it is to manyfest to euery of you, the thing which hath ben done before the Face, and in the presence of hym who knoweth the most obscure and hydden secrets of our thoughts. And needefull it is not to keepe silente that which is neyther euyll done ne hurtfull to any person: If things myght be kept secrete and styl remaine vnknowen, except they were declared by the doers of them, yet would not I commit the wrong in concealyng that, which to dyscouer vnto you doth greatly delite me, and deliuereth my mind from exceeding grief, in futch wife as if the flames of my defire could break out with futch violence, as the fire hath taken heate within my mind, ye fhould fee the fmoke mount vp with greater fmoulder than that which the mount Gibel doeth vomit forth at certayne feafons of the yeare. And to the intent I may not keepe you long in this fufpect, this fecret fire wythin my Heart, and that which I fhal caufe to flame in open ayre, is a certain opinion which I conceiue for a mariage by me made certain yeares paft, at what time I chofe and wedded a hufband to my fantafie and liking, defirous no longer to liue in Widow ftate, being vnwilling to do the thing that fhould preiudice and hurt my confcience. The fame is done, and yet in one thing I haue offended, which is by long keepyng fecrete the performed mariage: for the wycked brute difpearfed through the realme by reafon of my childbed, one yeare pafte, hath difpleafed fome: howbeit my confcience receiueth comforte, for that the fame is free from fault or blot. Now fhall ye know therefore what he is, whom I acknowledg for my Lord and fpoufe, and who it is that lawfully hath me efpoufed in the prefence of this Gentlewoman here prefent, which is the witneffe of our Nuptials and accorde of mariage. This gentleman alfo Antonio Bologna, is he to whom I haue fworn and giuen my faith, and hee againe to mee hath ingaged his. He it is whom I accompt for my fpoufe and hufband, (and with whome henceforth) I meane to reft and contynue. In confideration whereof, if there be any heere amongs you all, that fhal miflike of my choyfe, and is willing to wayt vppon my fonne the Duke, I meane not to let them of their intent, prayinge them faithfully to ferue him, and to be careful of his perfon, and to be vnto him fo honeft and loyall, as they haue bene to me fo longe as I was their miftreffe. But if any of you defire ftil to make your abode wyth me, to be partakers of my Wealth and woe, I will fo entertayne them as they fhall haue good caufe to be contented, if not let them departe hence to Malfi, and the fteward fhal prouide for them according to their degre: for touching my felf I do mind no more to be termed an infamous Ducheffe: rather would I be honored wyth the Tytle of a fymple Gentlewoman, or wyth that eftate whych fhee can haue that hath an honeft hufband, and wyth whom fhe holdeth

faithfull and loyall company, than reuerenced with the glory of a
Pryncesse, subiect to the despite of slaunderous tongues. Ye know"
(said she to Bologna) "what hath passed betwene vs, and God is
the witnesse of the integrity of my Conscyence, wherfore I pray
you bryng forth our Chyldren, that eche Man may beholde the
Fruytes raysed of our allyance." Hauynge spoken those Woordes,
and the Chyldren broughte forthe into the Hall, all the companye
stoode styll so astonned wyth that newe successe and tale, as
though hornes sodainly had started forth their heads, and rested
vnmoueable and amazed, like the great marble piller of Rome
called Pasquile, for so mutch as they neuer thought, ne coniectured
that Bologna was the successor of the duke of Malfi in his mariage
bed. This was the preparatiue of the catastrophe and bloudy end
of this tragedie. For of all the Duchesse seruaunts, there was not
one that was willing to continue wyth theyr auncient mistresse,
who with the faithfull maiden of hir chamber remained at Ancona,
enioying the ioyful embracements of hir Husbande, in all sutch
Pleasure and Delyghts as they doe, whych hauyng lyued in fear, be
set at liberty, and out of al suspition, plunged in a sea of ioy, and
fleting in the quiet calme of al passetime, where Bologna had none
other care, but how to please his best beloued, and she studied
nothing else but how to loue and obey him, as the wyfe ought to
doe hir husband. But thys fayre Weather lasted not long, for as
the ioyes of men do not long endure but wast in lyttle time, so
bee the delights of louers lesse firme and stedefast and passe away
almost in one moment of an houre. Now the seruaunts of the
Duchesse which wer retired, and durst tary no longer with hir,
fearing the fury of the cardinal of Aragon brother to the Lady, the
verye Day they departed from Ancona, deuised amongs themselues
that one of them should ride in post to Rome, to aduertise the
cardinal of the ladye's maryage, to the intente that the Aragon
brethren myght conceiue no cause to seke reuenge of theyr dis-
loyalty. That determination spedily was accomplished, one posting
towardes Rome, and the rest galloping to the countrey Castles of
the duke. These newes reported to the Cardinal and his brother,
it may be coniectured how gryeuously they toke the same, and
that they were not able to digest them wyth modestye, the yongest

of the brethren, yalped forth a Thoufand Curffes and defpytes, agaynfte the fymple fexe of womankind. "Ha," faid the Prince (tranfported with choler, and driuen into deadly furie) "what law is able to punifh or reftrayne the folyfh indifcretion of a Woman, that yeldeth hir felf to hir own defires? What fhame is able to brydle and withdrawe a Woman from hir mind and madneffe? Or with what fear is it poffible to fnaffle them from execution of theyr filthineffe? Ther is no beaft be he neuer fo wilde, but man fometime may tame, and bring to his lure and order. The force and diligence of Man is able to Make mylde the ftronge and Proude, and to ouertake the fwyfteft Beafte and Foule, or otherwyfe to attayne the hygheft and deepeft things of the world: but this incarnate diuelifh beafte the Woman, no force can fubdue hir, no fwiftneffe can approch hir mobylity, no good mind is able to pre-uent hir fleightes and deceites, they feem to be procreated and borne againfte all order of Nature, and to liue withoute Lawe, whych gouerneth al other things indued with fome reafon and vnderftanding. But howe great abhomination is this, that a Gentlewoman of futch a houfe as ours is, hath forgotten hir eftate, and the greatneffe of hir deceafed hufband, with the hope of the toward youthe of the Duke hir fonne and our Nephew. Ah, falfe and vile bytch, I fweare by the Almighty God and by his bleffed wounds, that if I can catch thee, and that wicked knaue thy chofen mate, I wil pype ye both futch a wofull galiard, as in your imbrace-ments ye neuer felt like ioy and mirthe. I wil make ye daunce futch a bloudy bargenet, as your whorifh heate for euer fhall be cooled. What abufe haue they committed vnder title of mariage, whych was fo fecretly don, as their children do witneffe their lecher-ous loue, but theyr promife of faith was made in open aire, and ferueth for a cloke and vifarde of their mofte filthy whoredom. And what if mariage was concluded, be we of fo little refpect, as the carion beaft could not vouchfafe to aduertife vs of hir entent? Or is Bologna a man worthy to be allied or mingled with the roial bloud of Aragon and Caftille? No, no, be he neuer fo good a gentleman, his race agreeth not with kingly ftate. But I make to God a vow, that neuer wyll I take one found and reftful flepe, vntill I haue difpatched that infamous fact from our bloud, and

that the caitif whoremonger be vfed according to his defert." The
cardinal alfo was out of quiet, grinding his teeth togither, chattering forth of his Spanifh mofel Jack an Apes Pater-nofter, promis-
ing no better vfage to their Bologna than hys yonger brother did.
And the better to intrap them both (without further fturre for that
time) they fent to the Lord Gifmondo Gonfago the Cardinal of
Mantua, than Legate for pope Iulius the fecond at Ancona, at
whofe hands they enioyed futch friendfhip, as Bologna and all his
family were commaunded fpedily to auoid the city. But for al
that the Legat was able to do, of long time he could not preuail,
Bologna had fo greate intelligence wythin Ancona. Neuerthel
whiles hee differred his departure, he caufed the moft part of his
trayne, his Children and goods to be conueyed to Siena, an auncient
Citty of Thofcane, which for the ftate and liberties, had long time
bin at warres with the Florentines, in futch wyfe as the very fame
day that newes came to Bologna that hee fhould depart the Citty
within xv. daies, hee was ready, and mounted on horfeback to
take hys flight to Siena, whych brake for forrow the hearts of the
Aragon brethren, feeinge that they were deceiued, and fruftrate of
their intent, bicaufe they purpofed by the way to apprehend
Bologna, and to cut him in peeces. But what? The tyme of his
hard lucke was not yet expired, and fo the marche from Ancona,
ferued not for the Theatre of thofe two infortunate louers ouerthrow, who certaine moneths liued in peace in Thofcane. The
Cardinall night nor day did fleepe, and his brother ftill did wayt
to performe hys othe of reuenge. And feeinge their ennimy out
of feare, they difpatched a poft to Alfonfo Caftruccio, the cardinall
of Siena, to entreat the lord Borgliefe, cheyfe of the Seigniory
there, that their Syfter, and Bologna fhould be banifhed the
Countrey, and limits of that Citty, which wyth fmall fuite was
brought to paffe. Thefe two infortunate, Hufband and Wyfe,
were chafid from all places, and fo vnlucky as whilom Achaftus
was when he was accurfed, or Oedipus, after his father's death, and
inceftious mariage wyth his mother, vncertayne to what Sainct to
vow themfelues, and to what place to take their flight. In the
ende they determined to goe to Venice, but firft to Ramagna,
there to imbarke themfelues for to retyre in faulfty to the citty

enuironned wyth the Sea Adriaticum, the richeſt in Europa.
But the poore ſoules made their reconinge there wythout their
hoaſte, faylinge halfe the price of their banket. For being vppon
the territory of Forly, one of the trayne a farre of, did ſee a troupe
of horſemen galloping towardes their company, which by their
countenaunce ſhewed no ſigne of peace or amity at all, which
made them conſider that it was ſome ambuſh of theyr Enimyes.
The Neapolitan gentleman ſeeing the onſet bendinge vppon
them, began to feare death, not for that hee cared at al for his
miſhap, and ruine, but his heart began to cleaue for heauineſſe
to ſee his Wyfe and little Children ready to be murdered, and
ſerue for the paſſetime of the Aragon Brethren's eyes, for whoſe
ſakes he knew himſelfe already predeſtinate to dy, and that for
deſpite of him, and to accelerate his death by the ouerthrow of hys
Wyfe and Children, he was aſſured that they would diſpatch them
all before his face and preſence. But what is there to be done,
where counſell and meanes to eſcape do fayle? Full of teares
therefore, aſtoniſhment and feare, he expected death ſo cruell as
man could deuiſe, and was already determined to ſuffer the ſame
with good courage, for any thing that the Ducheſſe could ſay vnto
him. He might well haue ſaued himſelf and his eldeſt ſonne by
flight, being both wel mounted vpon two good Turkey horſſes,
whiche ran ſo faſt, as the quarrel out of a Croſbow. But he loued
to mutch his wife and children, and woulde kepe them company
both in lyfe and death. In th'ende the good Lady ſayd vnto him :
" Sir, for all the ioyes and pleaſures which you can do me, for
God's ſake ſaue your ſelfe and the litle infant next you, who can
well indure the galloping of the horſe. For ſure I am, that you
being out of our company, we ſhall not neede to feare any hurt :
but if you do tary, you wil be the cauſe of the ruine and ouerthrow of vs all, and we ſhal receiue thereby no profit or aduauntage : take this purſe therefore, and ſaue yourſelf, attending better fortune in time to come." The poore Gentleman Bologna
knowing that his wife had pronounced reaſon, and fearing that it
was impoſſible from that time forth that ſhe or hir Traine could
eſcape their hands, taking leaue of hir, and kiſſing his chyldren not
forgetting the money which ſhe offred vnto him, willed his ſer-

uants to faue themfelues by futch meanes as they thought beft.
So gieuing fpurs vnto his horfe, he began to fly amayne, and his
eldeft fonne feeing his father gone, began to followe in like forte:
and fo for that time they two were faued by breaking of the in‑
tended ill luck lyke to light vpon them. And where he thought
to refcue himfelfe at Venice, he turned another way, and by great
Iourneys arriued at Millan. In the meane time the horfemen were
approched neere the Ducheffe, who feeing that Bologna had faued
himfelfe, very courteoufly began to fpeake vnto the lady, were it
that the Aragon brethren had geuen theym that charge, or feared
that the Lady would trouble them with hir importunate Cries, and
Lamentations. One therefore amongs the Troupe fayde thus vnto
hir: "Madam, we be commaunded by the Lordes your brethren, to
conduct you home vnto your houfe, that you may receiue agayne
the Gouernment of the Duchy, and the order of the Duke your
fonne, and do maruell very mutch at your folly, for giuing your
felfe thus to wander the Countrey after a man of fo fmal reputa‑
tion as Bologna is, who when he had glutted his lufting lecher‑
rous minde with the comelines of your noble Perfonage, wil des‑
poyle you of your goods and honour, and then take his Legs into
fom ftraung countrey." The fimple Lady, albeit greeuous it was
vnto hir to heare futch fpeech of hir hufband, yet helde hir peace
and diffembled what fhe thought, glad and wel contented with
the curtefy done vnto hir, fearinge before that they came to kyll
hir and thought hirfelfe already difcharged, hopinge vppon their
courteous Dealinges, that fhee, and hir Chyldren from that tyme
forth fhould lyue in good affuraunce. But fhe was greatly de‑
ceyued, and knew within fhorte fpace after, the good will that hir
Brethren bare hir: for fo foone as thefe Gallants had conducted
hir into the kyngdome of Naples, to one of the Caftels of hir
fonne, fhe was committed to pryfon wyth hir chyldren, and fhe
alfo that was the fecretary of hir infortunate mariage. Til this
time Fortune was contented to proceede with indifferent quiet
againft thofe Louers, but henceforth yee fhall heare the Iffue of
theyr little profperous loue, and how pleafure hauing blinded them,
neuer forfooke them vntil it had giuen them the ouerthrow. It
booteth not heere to recite any Fables or Hyftories, contenting my

felf that Ladies do reade wythout to many weping teares, the pitifull end of that myferable princeffe, who feeing hir felfe a Prifoner
in the company of hir litle chyldren and welbeloued Mayden,
paciently liued in hope to fee hir Brethren appayfed, comforting
hir felfe for the efcape of hir hufband out of the hands of his
mortal foes. But hir affurance was changed into an horrible feare
and hir hope to no expectation of furety, when certayne dayes
after hir imprifonment, hir gaoler came in, and fayde vnto hir:
"Madame, I do aduife you henceforth to confider and examine
your Confcience, for fo mutch as I fuppofe that euen thys very
day your Lyfe fhall be taken from you." I leaue for you to thinke
what horrour, and traunce affayled the feeble heart of this poore
Lady, and wyth what eares fhe receyued that cruell meffage, but
hir cryes, and moanes together with hir fighes and lamentations
declared with what chere fhe receyued the aduertifement. "Alas"
(fayd fhe) "is it poffible that my brethren fhould fo far forget
themfelues, as for a fact nothing preiudicial vnto them, cruelly to
put to death their innocent Sifter, and to imbrue the memory of
their fact, in the bloud of one which neuer did offend them?
Muft I againft al right and equity be put to death before the
Iudge or Maieftrate haue made triall of my lyfe, and knowne the
righteoufneffe of my caufe? Ah God, moft rightfull and bounti-
full father, beholde the mallice of my Brethren, and the Tyrannous
cruelty of thofe which wrongfully doe feeke my bloud. Is it a
finne to marry? Is it a fault to fly, and auoide the finne of
Whoredome? What Lawes be thefe, where marriage bed, and
ioyned matrimony is purfued wyth lyke feuerity, that Murder,
Theft, and Aduoutry are? And what Chriftianity in a Cardinall,
to fhed the bloud which hee ought to defend? What profeffion is thys, to affayle the innocent by the hygh way fide, and
to reue them of lyfe in place to punifh Theeues and Murderers?
O Lord God thou art iuft, and doft al things in equity, I fee wel
that I haue trefpaffed againft thy maiefty in fome more notoryous
crime than in marriage: I moft humbly therefore befeech thee to
haue compaffion on mee, and to pardon myne offences, accepting
the confeffion, and repentaunce of mee thine humble feruaunt for
fatiffaction of my finnes, which it pleafed thee to wafhe away in

the precious bloud of thy fonne our Sauiour, that being fo puri-
fied, I may appeare at the holy banket in thy glorious kingdome."
When fhee had thus finifhed hir prayer, two or three of the minis-
ters which had taken hir befides Forly, came in, and faid vnto hir:
"Now Madame make ready your felfe to goe to God, for beholde
your houre is come." "Prayfed be that God" (fayd fhe) "for
the wealth and woe that it pleafeth hym to fend vs. But I befeech
you my friendes to haue pitty vppon thefe lyttle Babes and innocent creatures: let them not feele the fmarte whych I am affured
my Brethren beare agaynfte their Poore vnhappy Father." "Well
well, madame," fayd they, "we wil conuey them to futch place
as they fhal not want." "I alfo recommend vnto you" (quod fhe)
"this pore imprifoned mayden, and entreate hir well, in confideration of hir good feruice done to the infortunate Ducheffe of Malfi."
As fhe had ended thofe words, the two Ruffians did put a coarde
about her neck, and ftrangled hir. The mayden feeing the piti-
ous Tragedy commenfed vpon hir mayftreffe, cried out a maine,
curfing the cruell malice of thofe tormenters, and befought God
to be witneffe of the fame, and crying out vpon his diuine Maies-
ty, fhe humbly praied vnto him to bend hys iudgement agaynft
them which caufeleffe (being no Magiftrates,) had killed fo innocent creatures. "Reafon it is" (fayd one of the Tyrants) "that thou
be partaker of thy mayftreffe innocency, fith thou haft bene fo
faythfull a Minifter, and meffenger of hir flefhly follies." And
fodaynly caught hir by the hayre of the head, and in fteade of a
Carcanet placed a roape about her necke. "How nowe" (quoth
fhee,) "is this the promifed fayth you made vnto my lady?" But
thofe words flew into the Ayre wyth hir Soule, in company of the
myferable Ducheffe. And now hearken the moft forowfull fcene
of all the Tragedy. The little Chyldren which had feene all this
furious game executed vpon their mother and hir mayde, as nature prouoked them, or as fome prefage of their myfhap might
leade them thereunto, kneeled vpon their knees before thofe Tyrants, and embracinge their Legges, wayled in futch wyfe, as I
thinke that any other, except a pitileffe heart fpoyled of all humanity, would haue had compaffion. And impoffible it was for
them, to vnfolde the embracementes of thofe innocent creatures,

whych feemed to foreiudge their death by Sauage lookes and Countenaunce of thofe Royfters: whereby I think that needes it muft
be confeffed, that nature hath in hir felfe, and in vs imprinted
fome figne of diuination, and fpecially at the Houre and tyme of
death, fo as the very beaftes doe feele fome forewarninges, although
they fee neyther Sworde, nor Staffe, and indeuoure to auoyde the
cruell Paffage of a thynge fo Fearefull, as the feparation of two
thynges fo neerely vnyted, euen the Body, and Soule, which for
the motiou that chaunceth at the very inftant, fheweth how na-
rure is conftrained in that monftrous diuifion, and more than horrible ouerthrow.   But who can appeafe a heart determined to
worke mifchief, and hath fworne the death of another forced thereunto by fome fpecial commaundment?   The Aragon brethren
ment hereby nothing elfe, but to roote out the whole name and
race of Bologna.   And therfore the two minifters of iniquity did
like murder and flaughter vpon thofe two tender babes, as they
had done before vpon their mother not without fome motion of
horror, for an act fo deteftable.   Behold here how far the cruelty
of man extendeth, when it coueteth nothing elfe but vengeance,
and marke what exceffyue choler the mind of them produceth,
whych fuffer themfelues to be forced and ouerwhelmed with fury.
Leaue we apart the cruelty of Euchrates, the Sonne of the kinge
of Bactria, and of Phraates the Sonne of the Perfian Prynce, of
Timon of Athenes, and of an infinit number of thofe which were
rulers and gouernors of the Empyre of Rome: and let vs match
with thefe Aragon brethren, one Vitoldus Duke of Lituania, the
cruelty of whom, conftrained his own fubiects to hang themfelues
for feare leafte they fhould fall into his furious and bloudy hands.
We may confeffe alfo thefe brutall brethren to be more butcherly
than euer Otho Erle of Monferrato, and prince of Vrbin was, who
caufed a yeoman of his chamber to be wrapped in a fheete pou-
dred with fulpher and brimftone, and afterwards kindled with a
Candle, was fcalded and confumed to death, bicaufe he waked not
at an hour by him appointed: let vs not excufe them alfo from
fome affinity with Manfredus the fonne of Henry the fecond emperor, who fmoldered hys own father, being an old man, between
two Couerlets.   Thefe former furies might haue fome excufe to

couer their cruelty, but thefe had no other color but a certain beaftly madneffe which moued them to kil thofe litle Children their nephews, who by no means could preiudice or anoy
the Duke of Malfi or his title, in the fucceffion of his Duchie,
the mother hauing withdrawen hir goods, and had her dowrie affigned hir: but a wicked hart wrapt in malice muft nedes bring
forth femblable workes. In the time of thefe murders the infortunate Louer kept himfelf at Millan with his fonne Frederick, and
vowed himfelf to the Lord Siluio Sauello, who that tyme befieged
the Caftell of Millan, in the behalf of Maximilian Sforcia, which in
the end he conquered and recouered by compofition wyth the
French within. But that charge being atchieued, the general
Sauello marched from thence to Cremona with hys Campe, whyther Bologna durft not folow, but repayred to the Marquize of
Britone, in whych tyme the Aragon brethren fo wroughte as hys
goods were confifcate at Naples, and he dryuen to hys fhiftes to
vfe the Golden Duckates which the Ducheffe gaue him to relieue
himfelfe at Millan, whofe Death althoughe it were aduertifed by
many, yet hee could not be perfuaded to beleue the fame, for that
diuers which went about to betray him, and feared he fhoulde flie
from Millan, kept his beake vnder the water, (as the Prouerb is,)
and affured him both of the Lyfe and welfare of his Spoufe, and
that fhortly his Brethren in law would be reconciled becaufe many
Noble men fauored hym well, and defired his returne home to hys
countrey. Fed and filled with that vaine hope, he remayned more
than a yeare at Millan, frequentyng good company, who was well
entertayned of the rycheft marchaunts and beft Gentlemen of the
Cytye: and aboue all other, he had famyliar acceffe to the houfe
of the Ladye Hippolita Bentiuoglia, where vppon a Daye after
Dynner, takyng hys lute in hand, whereon he could exceedyngly
well play, he began to fing a fonnet, whych he had compofed vppon the difcourfe of hys myffortune, the tenor whereof infueth.

The Song of Antonio Bologna, the hufband of the Ducheffe of Malfi.
If loue, the death, or tract of tyme, haue meafured my diftreffe,
Or if my beatinge forrowes may my languor well expreffe:
Then loue come foone to vifit me, which moft my heart defires,

And fo my dolor findes fome eafe, through flames of fanfies fires.

The time runnes out his rollinge courfe, for to prolong myne eafe,

To th' end I fhall enioy my loue, and heart himfelfe appeafe,

A cruell darte brings happy death, my foule then reft fhall find :

And fleepinge body vnder Toumbe, fhall dreame time out of

     mynde,

And yet the Loue, the Time, nor Death, lookes not how I decreace :

Nor geueth eare to any thinge, of this my wofull peace.

Full farre I am from my good hap, or halfe the ioye I craue,

Whereby I chaung my ftate wyth teares, and draw full neere

     my graue.

The courteous Gods that giues me lyfe, now mooues the Planets all :

For to arreft my groning ghoft, and hence my fprite to call.

Yet from them ftill I am fepard, by thinges vnequall heere,

Not ment the Gods may be vniuft, that breedes my chaunging

     cheere.

For they prouide by their forefight, that none fhall doe me harme:

But fhe whofe blafing beauty bright, hath brought me in a

     charme.

My miftreffe hath the powre alone, to rid me from this woe :

Whofe thrall I am, for whom I die, to whom my fprite fhall goe.

Away my foule, goe from the griefs, that thee oppreffeth ftill,

And let thy dolor witneffe beare, how mutch I want my will.

For fince that loue and death himfelfe, delights in guiltleffe bloud,

Let time tranfport my troubled fprite, where deftny feemeth

     good.

This fong ended, the poor Gentleman could not forbeare from pouring forth his luke warme Tears, which abundantly ran downe his heauy Face, and his pantinge Sighes truly difcouered the alteration of his mynde, whych mooued ech wight of that affembly to pitty his mournful State : and one fpecially of no acquaintance, and yet knew the deuifes that the Aragon Brethren had trayned and contriued againft hym : that vnacquaynted gentleman his name was Delio, one very well learned, and of trim inuention, who very excellently hath endited in the Italian vulgar tongue. This Delio knowing the Gentleman to be hufband to the deceafed

Ducheffe of Malfi, came vnto him, and taking him afide, faid: "Sir, albeit I haue no great acquaintance with you, this being the firft time that euer I faw you, to my remembrance, fo it is, that vertue bath futch force, and maketh gentle myndes fo amorous of their like, as when they doe beholde ech other, they feele them-felues coupled as it were in a bande of mindes, that impoffible it is to diuide the fame: now knowinge what you be, and the good and commendable qualities in you, I coumpt it my duty to reueale that which may chaunce to breede you damage. Know you then, that I of late was in company with a Noble man of Naples, whych is in this Citty, banded with a certaine company of horfemen, who tolde mee that he had a fpeciall charge to kill you, and therefore prayed me (as it feemed) to require you not to come in his fight, to the intent he might not be conftrayned to doe that which fhould offend his Confcience, and grieue the fame all the dayes of his life: moreouer I haue worfe Tidinges to tell you: the Ducheffe your Wyfe deade by violent hand in prifon, and the moft part of them that were in hir company: befides this affure your felfe, that if you doe not take heede to that which this Neapolitane Capitnyne hath differred, other wyll doe and execute the fame. This mutch I haue thought good to tell you, bicaufe it would very mutch grieue me, that a Gentleman fo excellent as you be, fhould be murdered in that myferable wyfe, and I fhould deeme my felfe vnworthy of lyfe, if knowing thefe practifes I fhould diffemble the fame." Whereunto Bologna aunfwered: "Syr Delio, I am greatly bound vnto you, and geue you hearty thankes for the good will you beare me. But in the confpiracy of the brethren of Aragon, and of the death of my lady, you be deceyued, and fome haue giuen you wrong intelligence: for within thefe two dayes I receyued letters from Naples, wherein I am aduertifed, that the right honorable and reuerend Cardinal and his Brother be almoft ap-peafed, and that my goods fhall bee rendred agayne, and my dear Wyfe reftored." "Ah fyr," fayde Delio, "how you be beguiled and Fedde wyth Follyes, and nourifhed with fleigbts of Court: affure your felfe that they which write thefe trifles, make futch fhamefull fale of your lyfe, as the Butcher doth of his flefh in the Shambles, and fo wickedly betray you, as impoffible it is to inuent

a treafon more deteftable : but bethinke you well thereof." When
he had fayd fo, he tooke hys leaue, and ioyned hymfelfe in company of fine and pregnaunt Wyttes, there affembled together. In
the meane tyme, the cruell Spirite of the Aragon Brethren were
not yet appeafed with the former murders, but needes muft finifh
the laft act of Bologna hys Tragedy by loffe of hys Lyfe, to keepe
hys Wyfe and Chyldren company, fo well in an other Worlde as
he was vnited with them in Loue in this frayle and tranfitory
paffage. The Neapolitan gentleman before fpoken of by Delio,
whych had taken this enterprife to fatiffie the barbarous Cardinall
to berieue his Countreyman of lyfe,'hauinge chaunged his mynde,
and differring from day to day to forte the fame to effect, it
chaunced that a Lombarde of larger Confcience than the other, in-
ueigled with Couetoufneffe, and hired for ready Money, practifed
the death of the Ducheffe poore hufband : this bloudy beafte was
called Daniel de Bozola that had charge of a certayne bande of
footemen in Millan. Thys newe Iudas and peftilent manqueller,
who wythin certayne dayes after knowinge that Bologna oftentymes Repayred to heare Seruice at the Church and conuent of S.
Fraunces, fecretly conueyed himfelf in ambufh, hard befides the
church of S. Iames, (being accompanied wyth a certayne troupe
of Souldiers) to affayle infortunate Bologna, who was fooner flayne
than hee was able to thinke vpon defence, and whofe mifhap was
futch, as hee whych kylled hym had good leyfure to faue himfelfe by reafon of the little purfuite made after hym. Beholde
heere the Noble fact of a Cardinall, and what fauer it hath of
Chriftian purity, to commit a flaughter for a fact done many
yeares paft vpon a poore Gentleman which neuer thought him
hurt. Is thys the fweete obferuation of the Apoftles, of whom
they vaunt themfelues to be the Succeffours and followers ? And
yet we cannot finde nor reade, that the Apoftles, or thofe that
ftept in their trade of lyfe, hyred Ruffians, and Murderers to cut
the Throates of them which did them hurt. But what ? it was in
the tyme of Iulius the fecond, who was more martiall than Chris-
tian, and loued better to fhed bloud than giue bleffing to the
people. Sutch ende had the infortunate mariage of him, whych
ought to haue contented himfelfe wyth that degree and honor that

he had acquired by the deedes and glory of his vertues, fo mutch
by ech wight recommended : we ought neuer to climb higher than
our force permitteth, ne yet furmount the bounds of duty, and
leffe fuffer our felues to be haled fondly forth with defire of brutal
fenfuality. Which finne is of futch nature, that he neuer giueth
ouer the party whom he mayftereth, vntil he hath brought him to
the fhame of fome Notable Folly. You fee the miferable difcourfe
of a Princeffe loue, that was not very wyfe, and of a Gentleman
that had forgotten his eftate, which ought to ferue for a lookinge
Glaffe to them which bee ouer hardy in makinge Enterprifes, and
doe not meafure their Ability wyth the greatneffe of their Attemptes :
where they ought to mayntayne themfelues in reputation, and
beare the title of well aduifed : forefeeing their ruine to be
example for all pofterity, as may bee feene by the death of Bologna, and by all them which fprang of him, and of his infortunate
Spoufe his Lady and Maiftreffe. But we haue difcourfed
inough hereof, fith diuerfity of other hyftories do call vs
to bring the fame in place, which were not mutch
more happy than the bloudy end of thofe,
whofe Hyftory ye haue already heard.

THE TWENTY-FOURTH NOUELL.

The difordered Lyfe of the Counteffe of Celant, and how fhee (caufinge the County of Mafino to be murdered,) was beheaded at Millan.

Not wythout good caufe of long tyme haue the wyfe, and dif-crete, Prudently gouerned their Children, and taken great heede ouer their Daughters, and thofe alfo whom they haue chofen to bee their Wyues, not in vfing them lyke Bondwomen, and Slaues, to beereiue them of all Liberty, but rather to auoyde the murmur, and fecrete flaunderous Speach of the common people, and occafions offred for infeftion, and marrying of Youth, fpecially circumfpeft of the affaultes bent agaynft Maydens, being yet in the firfte flames of fire, kindled by nature in the hearts, yea of thofe that be the wyfeft, and beft brought vp. Some doe deeme it very ftraunge, that folempne Guard bee obferued ouer thofe which ought to lyue at lyberty, and doe confider how lyberty and the bridle of Lycence let flip vnto Youth, they breede vnto the fame moft ftrong and tedious Bondage, that better it had bene for youth to haue beene chaynced, and clofed in obfcure Pryfon, than marked wyth thofe blottes of infamy, which Sutch Lycence and Lyberty doe conduce. If England doe not by experience fee Maydens of Noble Houfes Infamed through to mutch vnbrideled, and frank maner of Lyfe, and their Parents defolate for futch villanyes, and the name of their houfes become Fabulous and Ridiculous to the people: furely that manner of Efpiall and watch ouer Children, may be noted in Nations not very farre conuening from vs, where men be Ielous of the very Fantafie of them, whom they think to be indued with great vertues, and of thofe that dare with their very Lookes geue attaynt, to behold their Daughters : but where examples be euident, where all the World is affured of that which they fee by daily experience, that the fruifts of the difordered, breake out into light, it behooueth no more to attend the daunge-rous cuftomes of Countreyes, to condefcend to the fottifh Opi-nions of thofe, whych fay that youth to narrowly looked vnto, is trayned vp in futch grofeneffe, and blockifhneffe of fpyrite, as impoffible it is afterwardes the fame fhoulde do any thinge prayfe worthy. The Romayne maydens whilom were Cloyftered within their Fathers Pallaces, ftill at their Mothers Elbowes, and notwith-ftanding were fo wel brought vp, that thofe of beft ciuility and fineft trained vp in our age, fhall not be the feconde to one of the leaft perfect in the Citty. But who can learne ciuility and vertue in thefe our dayes? our Daughters noufled in companies, whofe mouthes run ouer with Whorifh and filthy talke, wyth behauiour full of Ribauldry, and many fraughted wyth facts leffe honeft than Speach is able to expreffe. I doe not pretend heereby to depriue that fexe of honeft and feemely talke, and company, and lefte of exercife amonges the Noble Gentlemen of our Englyfhe Soyle, ne yet of the Liberty receyued from our Aunceftours, only (me thyncke) that requifite it were to contemplate the manners and inclination of wils, and refrayne thofe that be prone to wantonneffe, and by lyke meanes to reioyce the mindes of them that be bent to heauineffe, deuided from curtefie and Ciuility, by attendinge of whych choyfe, and confidering of that difference, impoffible it is but vertue muft fhyne more bright in Noble houfes than homelyneffe in Cabanes of Pefauntes, and Countrey Carles: who oftentymes better obferue the Difcipline of our Predeceffours in education of their Chyldren, than they which prefume to prayfe themfelues for good fkil in vfe and gouernment of that age, more troublefome and payneful to rule, than any other wythin the compaffe of man's lyfe. Therefore the good and wife Emperour Marcus Aurelius would not haue his Daughters to be trayned vp in Courts. "For (quod he) what profit fhall the Nurfe receyue by learning hir may-den honefty and vertue, when our workes intice them to daliaunce and vice, apprehending the folly of thofe that bee amorous?" I make this difcourfe, not that I am fo rigorous a Iudge for our maydens of England, but that I wifh them fo reformed, as to fee and be feene fhould be forbidden, as affured that vertue in what place fo euer fhe be, cannot but open things that fhall fauor of hir excellency. And now to talke of an Italian Dame, who fo long as hir firft hufband (knowing hir inclination) kept hir fubiect, liued in reputation of a modeft and fober wyfe. Nothing was feene in hir that could defame hir renoume. But fo foone as the fhadow of that free captiuity was made free by the death of hir hufband, God knoweth what pageant fhe played, and how fhee foyled both hir owne reputation, and the honour of hir fecond Mate, as yee fhall vnderftande if with pacience yee vouchfafe to reade the difcourfe of thys prefent Hyftory. Cafal, (as it is not vnknowen) is a Citty of Piedmont, and fubiect to the Marquize of Montferrato, where dwelled one that was very rich, although of bafe birth, named Giachomo Scappardone, who being growne wealthy, more by wicked art, and vfury, to mutch manifeft, than by his owne diligence, toke to Wife a yong Greeke mayden, which the Marchiones of Montferrato mother of Marquize Guglielmo, had brought home wyth hir from the voyage that fhee made into Grætia wyth hir hufbande, when the Turkes ouerran the countrey of Macedonia, and feafed vpon the Citty of Modena which is in Morea.   Of that mayden Scapperdone had a Daughter indifferent fayre, and of behauiour liuely and pleafaunt, called Bianca Maria. The Father dyed wythin a while after hir birth, as one that was of good yeares, and had bin greatly turmoyled in getting of riches, whofe value amounted about one Hundred Thoufand Crownes. Bianca Maria arriued to the age of fixteene, or feuenteene yeares, was required of many, afwell for hir Beauty, Gentlenes, and good grace, as for her goods, and riches.   In the ende fhe was maried to the Vicecount Hermes, the Sonne of one of the chiefeft Houfes in Millan, who incontinently after the mariage, conueyed hir home to hys houfe, leauing his Greeke mother to gouerne the vfuries gotten by hir dead hufband.   The Gentleman which amongs two greene, knew one that was ripe, hauing for a certayne tyme well knowen, and learned the maners of hys Wyfe, faw that it behooued hym rather to deale wyth the Bit and brydle than the fpur, for that fhe was wanton, full of defire, and coueted nothing fo mutch as fond and difordered liberty, and therefore without cruell dealing, difquiet, or trouble, hee vfed by little and little to keepe hir in, and cherifhed hir more than his nature willingly would fuffer, of purpofe to holde hir wythin the boundes of duty.   And although the Millan Dames haue almoft like lyberties that ours haue, yet the Lord Hermes kept hir wythin Dores, and fuffred hir to frequent none other houfe and company, but the Lady Hippolita Sforcia, who

vppon a day demaunded of him wherefore hee kept in his wyfe fo
fhort, and perfuaded hym to geue her fomewhat more the Brydle,
bicaufe diuers already murmured of this order, as to ftrayte and
Frowarde, efteeming hym eyther to be to mutch fond ouer hir, or
elfe to Jealous. "Madame," fayde the Millanoife, "they whych at
pleafure fo fpeake of me, know not yet the nature of my Wyfe,
who I had rather fhould be fomewhat reftrayned, than run at
Rouers to hir difhonour, and my fhame. I remember wel madame
the proper faying of Paulus Emilius that notable Romane: who
being demauned wherefore he had put away his Wyfe being a
Gentlewoman fo fayre and beautifull. 'O,' quod he and lifted
vp his leg whereupon was a new payre of Bufkins) 'yee fee this
fayre Bufkin, meete and feemely for this Leg to outward apparance
not greeuous or noyfome, but in what place it hurteth me, or
where it wringeth yee doe neyther fee nor yet feele. So I, madame,
do feele in what place my Hoafe doeth hurt and wring my Legge.
I know madame what it is to graunt to fo wanton a dame as my
Wyfe is, hir will, and how farre I ought to flip the rayne: iealous
I am not vpon the fayth I beare vnto God, but I feare what may
chaunce vnto me. And by my trouth, madame, I geeue her
Lycence to repayre to you both Day and Nyght, at whatfoeuer
hour you pleafe, being affured of the vertuous company that
haunteth your houfe: otherwyfe my Pallace fhall fuffyce hir pleafure for the common ioy of vs both, and therefore I wifh no more
talk hereof, leaft too importunate fuites do offend my nature, and
make me thinke that to be true whych of good will I am loth to
fufpect, contenting my felfe with hir Chaftity, for feare leaft to
mutch liberty do corrupt hir." Thefe words were not fpoken
wythout caufe, for the wyfe hufband faw wel that futch beafts,
albeit rudely they ought not to be vfed, yet ftifly to be holden
fhort, and not fuffred too mutch to wander at will. And verily
his prophecy was to true for refpect of that which followed: who
had not bene maried full vi. yeares, but the Vicecount Hermes
departed thys World, whereof fhe was very fory bycaufe fhe loued
him derely, hauing as yet not tafted the licorous baites of futch
liberty, as afterwards fhe drank in gluttonous draughts, when after
hir hufband's obfequies, fhe retired to Montferrato, and then to

Cafal to hir Father's houfe, hir mother being alfo dead, and fhe
a lone woman to ioy at pleafure the fruiét of hir defires, bendinge
hir only ftudy to gay and trimme Apparell, and imployed the
mornings with the vermilion rud to colour hir cheekes by greater
curiofity than the moft fhameleffe Curtifan of Rome, fixing hir
eyes vppon ech man, gyring, and laughing with open mouth, and
pleafantly difpofed to talk and reafon with euery Gentleman that
paffed by the ftreate. This was the way to attayne the glorious
feaft of hir triumphant filthines, who wan the prife aboue the moft
famous women whych in hir tyme made profeffion of thofe armes,
wherewith Venus once difpoyled Mars, and toke from him the
ftrongeft and beft fteeled armure of all his furniture. Thinck not
fayre maydes, that talk and clattering with youth is of fmall
regarde. For a Citty is halfe won when they within demaunde for
parle, as loth to indure the Canon fhot. So when the eare of yong
Wyfe or mayde is pliant to lafciuious talk, and deliteth in wanton
words, albeit hir chaftity receyue no damage, yet occafion of fpeach
is miniftred to the people, and perchaunce wyth futch difaduan-
tage, as neuer after hir good name is recouered. Wherefore needefull it is, not only to auoyde the effeét of euill, but alfo the leaft
fufpition : for good fame is requifite for the Woman, as honeft lyfe.
The great Captain Iulius Cæfar, (which firft of al reduced the
common wealth of Rome in fourme of monarchie) beinge once
demaunded wherefore hee hadde refufed hys Wyfe before it was
proued that fhe had offended with Clodius, the night of the facri-
fices done to the Goddeffe Bona, anfwered fo wyfely as truely,
that the houfe of Cæfar ought not onely to be voyde of whordome
but of fufpition therof. Behold therfore what I haue fayd, and
yet doe fay againe, that ye oughte to take greate heede to youre
felues, and to laugh in tyme, not reclinyng your eares to vncomely
talke, but rather to follow the nature of the Serpent, that ftoppeth
his eare with his tayle, to auoide the charms and forceries of the
Enchaunter. Now this Bianca Maria was fued vnto, and purfued
of many at Cafall that defired hir to Wyfe, and amonges the reft
two did profer themfelues, which were the Lord Gifmondo Gonzaga, the neere kinfman of the Duke of Mantua, and the Counte
of Celant, a great Baron of Sauoy, whofe landes lie in the vale of

Agofta. A great paftyme it was to thys fyne Gentlewoman to feede hir felf wyth the Orations of thofe two Lordes and a ioye it was to hir, to vfe her owne difcourfe and aunfwers expreffinge with right good grace fundry amorous countenances, intermingling therwithall fighes, fobbes, and alteration of cheere, that full well it might haue bene fayde, of loue trickes that fhee was the only dame and miftreffe. The Marchyoneffe of Montferrato defirous to gratify the Lord of Mantua his fonne in law, endeuored to induce this wanton Lady to take for fpoufe Gifmondo Gonzaga, and the fute fo well proceeded, as almoft the mariage had bene concluded if the Sauoy Earle had not come betwixte, and fhewed forth his Nobleneffe of minde, when he vnderftode how things did paffe, and that another was ready to beare away the pryfe, and recouer his miftreffe. For that caufe he came to vifit the Lady, who intertayned him wel, as of cuftom fhe did al other. And for that he would not employe hys tyme in vayne, when he founde hir alone and at conuenyent leyfure, began to preache vnto hir in thys wyfe with futch countenaunce, as fhe perceyued the Counte to be far in loue with hir.

The Oration of the Counte of Celant to his Ladye.

" I am in doubt Madame, of whome chiefly I ought to make complaynt, whether of you, or of my felfe, or rather of fortune which guideth and bryngeth us together. I fee wel that you receiue fome wrong, and that my caufe is not very iuft, you taking no regarde vnto my paffion which is outragious, and leffe hearkeninge vnto my requeft that fo many times I haue giuen you to vnderftand onely grounded vpon the Honeft loue I beare you. But I am befides this more to be accufed for fuffering an other to marche fo far ouer my game and foyle, as I haue almoft loft the tracte of the pray after which I moft defire, and fpecially doe condemne my Fortune, for that I am in daunger to lofe the thyng which I deferue, and you in peryll to paffe into that place where your captiuity fhalbe worfe than the flaues by the Portugales condemned to the mines of India. Doeth it not fuffife you that the Lord Hermes clofed you vp the fpace of v. or vi. yeares in his Chamber, but wil you nedes attempt the reft of your youthly daies amid the Mantuanes, whofe fufpicious heads are ful of hammers working in the

VOL. III.   D

fame? Better it were madame, that we approchynge neerer the
gallante guife of Fraunce, fhould live after the lyberty of that Countrey, than bee captiue to an Italian houfe, whych wyll reftrain you
with like bondage, as at other tymes you haue felt the experience.
Moreover ye fee what opinion is like to be conceiued of you,
when it fhalbe bruted that for the Marquize feare, you haue maried
the Mantuan Lord. And I know well that you like not to be
efteemed as a pupil, your nature cannot abyde compulfion, you
be free from hir authority, it were no reafon you fhould be conftrained. And not to ftay in framing of orations, or ftand vpon
difcourfe of Words, I humbly befeche you to behold the conftant
loue I beare you, and being a Gentleman fo Wealthy as I am, none
other caufe induceth me to make this fute, but your good grace
and bryngynge vp, whych force me to loue you aboue any other
Gentlewoman that liueth. And althoughe I myghte alleage other
reafons to proue my faying, yet referre I my felf to the experience and bounty of youre mynd, and to the equity of your Iudgement. If my paffion were not vehement, and my torment without
comparifon, I would wifh my fained griefs to be laughed to fcorne,
and my diffembled payne rewarded with flouts. But my loue
being fincere and pure, my trauail continuall, and my griefs
endleffe, for pity fake I befeche you madame to confider my
faithfull deferts with your duetiful curtefie, and then fhall you
fee how mutch I ought to be preferred before them, which vnder
the fhadow of other mens puiffance, do feke to purchafe power to
commaund you : where I do faithfully bynd and tye my word and
deede continually to loue and ferue you, wyth promyfe al the dayes
of my Lyfe to accomplifh your commaundements. Beholde if it
pleafe you what I am, and with what affection I make mine humble
playnt, regard the Meffanger, loue it is himfelf that holdeth me
within your fnares, and maketh mee captyue to your beauty and
gallant graces, which haue no piere. But if you refufe my fute,
and caufe me breath my words into the aire, you fhalbe accufed of
cruelty, ye fhall fee the entier defaict of a gentleman which loueth
you better than loue himfelfe is able to yelde flame and fire to
force any wight to loue mortal creature. But, verily, I beleue the
heauens haue departed in me futch aboundance, to the intent in

louyng you with vehemence fo greate, you may alfo thinke that
it is I which ought to be the Friend and fpoufe of that gentle and
curteous Lady Bianca Maria, which alone may cal her felf the
miftreffe of my Heart." The Ladye whych before was mocked and
flouted wyth the Counte his demaunds, bearing thys lafte difcourfe,
and remembring his firft mariage, and the natural iealofie of
Italyans, half wonne, without making other countenance, anfwered
the Counte in thys manner: "Syr counte, albeyt that I am obedy-
ente to the wyll and commaundemente of madame the Marchyoneffe,
and am loth to dyfpleafe hir, yet wil I not fo farre gage my
lybertye, but ftill referue one poynt to faye what reafteth in my
thoughte. And what fhoulde lette me to chofe futch one, to
whome I fhalbe both his life and death? And whereof beinge
once poffed, it is impoffyble to be rid and acquited? I affure
you, if I feared not the fpeach and fufpition of malycious mindes,
and the venime of flaunderous Tongues, neuer hufband fhould
bryng me more to bondage. And if I thought that he whom I
pretend to chofe, would be fo cruel to me, as others whom I know,
I would prefently refufe mariage for euer. I thanke you neuertheleffe, both of your aduertifements giuen me, and of the honor
you doe me, your felf defiryng to accomplifh that honor by maryage to be celebrated betweene vs. For the fidelity of which your
talke, and the little diffimulation I fee to be in you, I promife
you that there is no gentleman in this countrey to whom I giue
more puiffance ouer me, than to you, if I chaunce to mary, and
thereof make you fo good affurance, as if it were already done."
The Counte feeing fo good an entry would not fuffer the tyme to
flip, but beating the Bufhes vntill the praye was ready to fpryng,
replyed: "And fith you know (madame) what thing is profitable,
and what is hurtfull, and that the benefite of lyberty is fo mutch
recommended, why doe you not performe the thinge that may
redounde to your honor? Affure mee then of your word, and
promife me the faith and loyaltie of maryage, then let me alone to
deale wyth the reft, for I hope to attayn the effect without
offenfe and difpleafure of any." And feeing hir to remaine in a
mufe without fpeaking word, he toke hir by the hand and kiffing
the fame a million of tymes, added thefe Words: "How now,

madame, be you appalled for fo pleafaunt an affault, wherin
your aduerfary confeffeth himfelfe to be vanquifhed? Courage,
madame, I fay courage, and beholde him heere which humbly praieth
you to receiue him for your lawfull hufband, and who fweareth vnto
you all futch amitye and reuerence that hufband oweth to hys loyall
fpoufe." "Ah, fyr Counte," fayd fhe, "and what wyll the Marquize fay, vnto whom I haue wholly referred my felf for mariage?
fhal not fhe haue iuft occafion to frowne vppon mee, and frowardly
to vfe me for little refpect I beare vnto hir? God be my witneffe
if I would not that Gonzaga had neuer come into this countrey:
for although I loue him not, yet I haue almoft made him a
promyfe, which I can not kepe." "And fith there is nothing don,"
(faid the Sauoy Lord) "what nede you to torment your felfe? wyl
the Marquize wrecke hir tyrannie ouer the will of hir fubiectes,
and force Ladyes of hir Lande to marie againfte their lufte? I
thinke that fo wyfe a princeffe, and fo well nurtured, will not fo
far forget hir felf, as to ftraine that which God hath left at lyberty
to euerye wight: promife me onely maryage and leaue me to deale
wyth the reft: other thynges fhalbe wel prouided for." Bianca
Maria vanquifhed with that importunity, and fearing againe to fal
into feruytude, hoping that the Counte would mainteine futch
liberty as he had affured, agreed vnto hym and plyghted vnto him
her faithe, and for the tyme vfed mutuall promifes by wordes refpec-
tiuely one to another: and the better to confirme the fact, and to
let the knotte from breakyng, they bedded themfelues togethers.
The Counte very ioyfull for that encountre, yelded futch good
beginning by his countenance, and by Famyliar and continuall
haunte with Bianca Maria, as fhortly after the matter was knowen
and came to the Marqueffe eares, that the Daughter of Scappardone had maryed the Counte of Celant. The good lady albeit that
fhee was wroth beyond meafure, and willingly would haue ben
reuenged vpon the bride, yet hauing refpect to the Counte, which
was a noble man of great authority, fwallowed down that pille
wythout chewing, and prayed the Lord Gonzaga not to be offended,
who feing the light behauiour of the Ladie, laughed at the matter,
and prayfed God for that the thing was fo wel broken off: and he
did forefee already what iffue that Comedye would haue, beynge

very famylyar for certayne Dayes in the Houfe of Bianca Maria.
Thys maryage then was publyfhed, and the folempnity of the
Nuptyals were done very pryncely, accordyng to the Nobylity of
hym whych had maryed hir: but the augurie and prefage was
heauy, and the melancholike face of the feafon (which was obfcured and darkened about the time they fhould go to church)
declared that the mirth and ioy fhould not long continue in the
houfe of the counte, according to the common faying: *He that
loketh not before he leapeth, may chaunce to ftumble before he
fleepeth.* For the lord of Celant being retird home to his valeys
of the Sauoy mountains, began to loke about his bufineffe, and
perceiued that his wife furpaffed al others in light behauiour and
vnbrideled defires, whereuppon hee refolued to take order and ftop
hir paffage before fhe had won the field, and that frankly fhe
fhould goe feke hir ventures where fhee lift, if fhe would not be
ruled by his aduife. The foolifh Counteffe feeing that hir hufband
well efpied hir fond and foolyfh behauior, and that wifely he went
about to remedy the fame, was no whit aftonied, or regarded his
aduife, but rather by forging complaints did caft him in the
teeth fometymes with hir riches that fhe brought him, fometime
with thofe whom fhe had refufed for his fake, and with whom
farre of fhe liued lyke a fauage creature amid the mountaine
deferts and baren dales of Sauoy, and tolde him that by no meanes
fhe minded to be clofed and fhut vp like a tameleffe beaft.
The Counte which was wyfe, and would not breake the Ele
vppon his knee, prouidently admonifhed hir in what wife a Ladye
ought to efteeme hir honor, and how the lighteft faults of Noble
forts appeare mortal finnes before the world: and that it was not
fufficient for a Gentlewoman to haue hir body chaft, if hir fpeach
were not according, and the minde correfpondent to that outward
femblance, and the conferuation agreable to the fecret conceiptes
of Mynd: "And I fhall be ful fory fwete Wife" (fayd the Counte)
"to giue you caufe of difcontent: for wher you fhalbe vexed and
molefted, I fhall receiue no ioy or pleafure, you being [fuch one
as ought to be the fecond my felf, determining] by God's grace
to keepe my promife, and vfe you like a wyfe, if fo be you
regard me with duety femblable: for reafon will not that the

head obey the members, if they fhew not themfelues to be futch as depend vpon the health and life of it. The hufband being the Wyue's chiefe, ought to be obeyd in that which reafon forbiddeth: and fhee referring hir felfe to the pleafure of hir head, forceth him to whom fhe is adioyned, to do and affay all trauayle and payne for hir fake. Of one thinge I muft needes accufe you, which is, that for trifles you frame complaynt: for the mynde occupied in folly, lufteth for nothinge more than vayne things, and thofe that be of little profite, fpecially where the pleafure of the Bodye is onely confidered: where if it follow reafon, it diffembleth his griefes with wordes of wyfedome, and in knowing mutch, fayneth notwithftanding a fubtile and honeft ignoraunce: but I may bee mutch deceyued herein, by thinking that a Woman fraught with fickle Opinions may recline her eares to what fo euer thing, except to that whych deliteth hir mynde, and pleafeth the defires framed wyth in hir foolyfhe fantafie. Let not thys fpeach be ftraunge vnto you, for your woordes vttered without difcretion, make me vfe thys language: finally (good madame) you fhall fhew your felfe a Wyfe and louing wyfe, if by takinge heede to my requefts, you faythfully follow the advife thereof." The Counteffe whych was fo fine and malicious as the Earle was good and wyfe, diffembling her griefe, and coueringe the venome hidden in hir mynde, began fo well to play the hypocrite before hir hufbande, and to counterfayte the fimple Dame, as albeit he was right politike, yet he was within hir Snare intrapt, who flattered him wyth fo fayre Wordes, as fhe won him to goe to Cafal, to vifite the lands of hir Inheritaunce. We fee whereunto the intent of this falfe Woman tended, and what checkmate fhe ment to geue both to hir hufband, and hir honour: whereby we know that when a woman is difpofed to giue hir felfe to wickedneffe, hir mynde is voyd of no malyce or inuention to fort to ende any daunger or perill offered vnto hir. The factes of one Medea (if credite may be gieuen to Poets) and of Phædra, the Woman of Thefeus, wel declare with what beaftly zeale they began and finifhed their attempts: the eagles flight is not fo high, as the Foolyfhe defires, and Conceiptes of a Woman that trufteth in hir owne opinion, and treadeth out of the tract of duety, and way of Wyfedome. Pardon

me, good Ladies, if I fpeake fo largely, and yet think not that I
mean to difplay any other but futch, as forget the degree wherin
their Aunceftours haue placed them, and whych digreffe from the
true path of thofe that haue immortalized the memory of themfelues, of their hufbands, and of the houfes alfo whereof they
came. I am very lothe to take vppon mee the office of a flaun-
derer, and no leffe do mean to flatter thofe, whom I fee to their
great fhame, offende openly in the fight of the worlde: but why
fhould I dyffemble that which I know your felues would not conceyle, yf in confcyence yee were requyred? It were extreame
follye to decke and clothe vice wyth the holy garment of Vertue,
and to call that Curtefie and Ciuylity, whych is manyfeft whoredom
and Trechery: let vs terme ech thyng by his due Name, and not
deface that whych of it felfe is faire and pure: let vs not alfo ftaine
the renoume of thofe, whom their own Vertue do recommende.
This gentle Counteffe beeing at Cafal, making mutch of hir hufbande, and kiffing him with the kiffe of treafon, and of him
being vnfainedly beloued and cherifhed, not able to forget his
fermons, and mutch leffe hir own filthy lyfe, feeyng that with hir
Counte it was impoffyble for hir to liue and glut her lecherous
luft, determined to runne away and feeke hir aduenture: for the
brynging to paffe wherof fhe had already taken order for money,
the intereft wherof growing to hir daily profite at Millan: and
hauynge leuied a good fumme of Ducates in hande, vntyll hir
other rents were ready, fhe fled away in the night in companye of
certayne of hir men which were priuie to her doeings. Hir retire
was to Pauie, a City fubiecte to the ftate and Duchy of Millan,
where fhe hired a pryncely pallace, and apparelled the fame according to hir eftate and Trayne of hir hufband, and as her owne
reuenue was able to beare. I leaue for you to thinke what buzzings
entred the Counte's head, by the fodayne flight of his wife, who
would haue fent and gone him felfe after to feke hir out, and
bryng hir home againe, had he not well confidered and wayed his
owne profite and aduantage, who knowing that hir abfence would
rid out of his head a fardell of fufpitions which he before conceiued, was in the ende refolued to lette hir alone, and fuffer hir
remaine in what place fo euer fhe was retired, and whence hee

neuer minded to cal hir home agayne. " I were a very foole,"
(faid he) " to keepe in my Houfe fo pernicious and fearfull an
enimy, as that arrant whore is, who one day before I beware will
caufe fome of hir ruffians to cut my throte, befides the Vyolatyon
of hir holye Maryage Bed : God defende that futch a Strumpet by
hir prefence fhould any longer profane the houfe of the Lord of
Celant, who is well rewarded and punifhed for the exceffiue loue
whych he bare hir : let hir goe whether fhee lift, and lyue a God's
name at hir eafe, I do content my felf in knowing what Women be
able to do, wythout further attempt of fortune or other proofe of
hir wycked Lyfe." He added further, that the honor of fo Noble a
perfonage as he was, depended not upon a woman's mifchief : and
affure your felfe the whole race of woman kind was not fpared by
the Counte, againft whom he then inueyed more through rage than
reafon, he confidered not the honeft fort of women, which deface
the vyllany of thofe that giue themfelues ouer to theyr own lufts,
wythout regarde of modefty and fhame, which oughte to be
Famylyar, as it were by a certain Naturall inclynatyon in all degrees
of Women and Maydens. But come we again to Bianca Maria,
holding now hir Courte and open houfe at Pauie, wher fhe got fo
holy a fame, as miftreffe Lais of Corinth did, whofe trumprie was
neuer more common in Afia than that of this fayre dame, almoft
in euery corner of Italy, and whofe conuerfation was futch as hir
frank liberty and famyliar demeanor to ech wyghte, well witneffed
hir horryble Lyfe. True it was that her reputatyon ther was very
fmal, and fhe hired not hir felfe, ne yet toke pains by fetting hir
body to fale, but for fome refonable gayne and earneft pain : howbeit fhe (of whom fomtimes the famous Greke orator would not
buy repentaunce for fo high a pryce) was more exceffiue in Sale
of hir Merchaundyfe, but not more wanton : for fhe no fooner
efpyed a comely Gentleman that was youthly, and well made, but
would prefently fhew him fo good countenance, as he had ben a
very foole, that knewe not what prouender this Colt did neigh :
whofe fhameleffe Gefture Maffalina the Romane princeffe dyd
neuer furmount, except it were in that fhee vifited and haunted
common houfes : and this dame vfed hir difports wythin hir owne,
the other alfo receiued indyfferently Carters, Galleye flaues, and

Porters: and thys halfe Greeke did hir paftyme wyth Noble Men that were braue and luftye: but in one thing fhee well refembled hir, whych was, that Meffalina was foner wearye with trauayle, than fhe fatiffied with pleafure and the filthy vfe of hir body, like vnto a fink that receyueth al filth, wythout difgorgyng any throwne into the fame: this was the chafte lyfe which that good Lady led, after fhe had taken flight from hir hufband. Marke now whether the Milanois that was hir firft hufbande, were a groffe headed perfon or a foole, and whither hee were not learned and fkilful in the fcience of Phifiognomy, and time for him to make ready the rods to make hir know hir duety, therwith to correct hir wanton youth, and to cut of the lufty twigs and proud fciences that foked the moifture and hart of the ftock and braunches. It chaunced whiles fhe liued at Pauie, in this good and honorable port, the Counte of Maffino called Ardizzino Valperga came to the Emperour's feruice, and therby made hys abode at Pauie with one of his brothers: the Counte being a goodly Gentleman young and gallant in apparel, giuen to many good quallities had but one onely fault, which was a mayme in one of his legges, by reafon of a certain aduenture and blow receiued in the warres, although the fame toke away no part of his comelineffe and fyne behauyor. The Counte I fay, remaining certayne days at Pauie beheld the beauty and fingularity of the Counteffe of Celant, and ftayed with futch deuotion to view and gaze vpon hir, as manye times he romed vp and down the ftreate wherein fhe dwelt to find meanes to fpeak vnto hir. His firft talke was but a *Bon iour:* and fimple falutation, futch as gentlemen commonly vfe in company of Ladies, and at the firfte brunte Valperga coulde fettle none other iudgement vpon that Goddeffe, but that fhe was a wife and honeft dame, and yet futch one as needed not the Emperor's camp to force the place, which as he thought was not fo well flanked and rampired but that a good man of Armes myght eafily winne, and the breache fo liuely and fautable, as any fouldier might paffe the fame: he became fo famyliar with the Lady, and talked with hir fo fecretly, as vpon a day being with hir alone, hee courted in this wife: "Were not I of all men mofte blame worthy, and of greateft folly to be reproued, fo long time to be acquainted with a Lady

fo faire and curteous as you be, and not to offre my feruice life
and goodes to be difpofed where you pleafed? I fpeake not thys,
Madame, for any euil and finifter iudgement that I conceyue of
you, for that I prayfe and efteeme you aboue any Gentlewoman
that euer I knew til this day, but rather for that I am fo wonderfully attached with your good graces, as wrong I fhould doe
vnto your honor and my loyal feruice towards you, if I continued
dumbe, and did conceyle that whych inceffantly would confume
my heart with infynyte numbre of ardent defyres, and waft myne
intrailes for the extreame and burning loue I beare you. I do require you to put no credite in me, if I refufe what it fhall pleafe
you to commaund me: wherfore Madame, I humbly befech you
to accepte me for your owne, and to fauor me as futch one, whych
with all fidelity hopeth to paffe hys time in your company."
The Counteffe although fhe knew ful wel that the fire was not fo
liuely kindled in the ftomacke of the Counte as hee wente aboute
to make hir beleue, and that his wordes were to eloquent, and countenance to ioyfull for fo earneft a louer as hee femed to be, at thys
firft incountry: yet for that he was a valiant Gentleman, yong, lufty,
and ftrongly made, minded to retaine him, and for a tyme to ftaye
hir ftomacke by appeafying hir gluttonous appetite in matters of
loue, with a morfell fo dainty, as was thys Mynion and luftye
young Lorde: and when the Courage of hym began to coole, another fhoulde enter the liftes. And therefore fhe aunfwered hym
in thys wife: "Although I (knowying the vfe and manners of men,
and with what Baits they Hoke for Ladies, if they take not heede,
hauing proued their malice and little loue,) determined neuer to
loue other than mine affection, ne yet to fauoure Man excepte it
bee by fhewyng fome Familiar manner to heare theyr talke, and
for paftime to hearken the braue requefts of thofe which fay they
burne for loue, in the mids of fome delyghtfome brooke. And
albeit I think you no better than other bee, ne more fayhfully,
more affectyonate, or otherwyfe moued than the reft, yet I am
contente for refpecte of youre honoure, fomewhat to beeleue
you and to accepte you for myne owne, fith your dyfcretyon is
futch (I trufte) as fo Noble a Gentleman as you bee, wyll hym
felfe declare in thofe Affayres, and when I fee the effecte of my

hope fucceede, I cannot be fo vnkynde, but wyth all honefty fhall affaye to fatiffy that your loue." The Countee feeing hir alone, and receyuing the Ladie's language for his aduantage, and that hir countenance by alteration of hir minde did ad a certayne beauty to hir face, and perceyuing a defire in hir that he fhould not vfe delay, or be to fqueimifh, fhe demaunding naught elfe but execucion, tooke the prefent offred time, forgetting all ceremonies, and reuerence, he embraced hir and kiffed hir a Hundred Thoufande tymes. And albeit fhee made a certayne fimple and prouoking refiftance, yet the louer notinge them to be but preparatiues for the fport of loue, he ftrayed from the bounds of honefty, and threw her vppon a fielde Bed wythin the Chambre, where hee folaced hymfelfe wyth hys long defired fuite. And finding hir worthy to be beloued, and fhe him a curteous gentleman, confulted together for continuaunce of their amity, in futch wife as the Lorde Ardizzino fpake no more but by the mouth of Bianca Maria, and dyd nothynge but what fhe commaunded, being fo bewrapped wyth the heauy Mantell of hir Beaftly Loue, as hee ftill abode nyght and day in the houfe of his beloued: whereby the brute was noyfed throughout the Citty, and the fonges of their Loue more common in ech Citizen's mouth, than Stanze or Sonnettes of Petrarch, Played and Fayned vpon the Gittrone, Lute, or Lyra, more fine and witty than thofe vnfauery Ballets that be tuned and chaunted in the mouthes of the common fort. Beholde an Earle well ferued, and dreffed by enioying fo falfe a Woman, which had already falfified the fayth betrouthed to hir hufband, who was more honeft, milde, and vertuous than fhe deferued. Beholde alfo, yee Noble Gentlemen, the fimplicity of this good Earle, how it was deceyued by a falfe and filthy ftrumpet, whofe ftincking lyfe and common vfe of body woulde haue withdrawen ech fimple creature from mixture of their owne wyth futch a Carrion. A leffon to learne al youth to refrayne the Whoorifhe lookes of lighte conditioned Dames, a number (the more to be pittied) fhewinge foorth themfelues to the Portfale of euery Cheapener, that lift demaunde the pryce, the grozenes whereof before confidered, were worthy to be defied and loathed. This Ladye feeinge her Louer noufled in hir luft, dandled him with a thoufand trumperyes, and made

hym holde the Mule, while other enioyed the fecrete fporte which
earſt hee vſed hymſelf. This acquayntance was ſo dangerous to
the Counte, as ſhe hir ſelfe was ſhameleſſe to the Counte of Celant:
for the one bare the armes of Cornwall, and became a ſeconde
Aƈeon, and the other wickedly led his lyfe, and loſt the chiefeſt
of that hee loked for by the ſeruice of great Princes, throughe the
treaſon of an arrante common queane. Whiles this Loue contynued in al Pleaſure and lyke contentation of either parts: fortune
that was ready to mounte the ſtage, and ſhew in ſight that her
mobylytye was no more ſtable than a woman's wyll: for vnder
ſutch habite and ſexe Painters and Poets deſcribe hir) made Ardizzino ſufpeƈe what deſire ſhe had of chaunge: and within a while
after, ſawe himſelfe ſo farre miſliked of his Lady, as though he had
neuer bene acquainted. The cauſe of which recoile was, for that
the Counteſſe was not contented with one kind of fare, whoſe Eyes
were more greedy than hir ſtomake able to digeſt, and aboue al
deſired chaunge, not ſeking meanes to finde him that was worthy
to be beloued and intertayned of ſo great a Lady, as ſhe eſteemed
hir ſelfe to be, and as ſutch of their owne opinion thinke themſelues, who counterfaiƈe more grauitie and reputation than they
doe, whome Nature and vertue for theyr maieſty and holynes
of lyfe make Noble and praiſe worthy. That deſire deceiued hir
nothing at all, for a certaine time after that Ardizzino poſſeſſed
the forte of this fayre Counteſſe, there came to Pauia, one Roberto
Sanſeuerino earle of Gaiazzo, a yong and valiaunte gentleman,
whoſe Countreye lyeth on this ſide the Mountaines, and was verye
famylyar with the Earle of Maſſino. This vnfaythful Alcina and
cruel Medea had no ſoner caſt hir Eye vppon Signor di Gaiazzo,
but was pierced with loue in ſutch wife, as if forthwith ſhee had
not attayned hir deſyres, ſhe would haue run mad, bycauſe that
Gentleman bare a certayne ſtatelye repreſentatyon in hys Face,
and promyſed ſutch dexteritie in hys deedes, as ſodaynly ſhe
thought him to be the man that was able to ſtaunch hir filthy
thurſt. And therfore ſo gently as ſhe could, gave ouer hir Ardizzino, with whom ſhe vtterly refuſed to ſpeake, and ſhunned hys
company when ſhe ſaw him, and by ſhutting the gates agaynſt
him: the Noble man was notable to forbeare from throwing forth

fome words of choler, wherby fhe tooke occafion both to expell him, and alfo to beare hym futch difpleafure, as then fhe confpired his death, as afterwards you fhall perceyue. This greate hatred was the caufe that fhe fell in loue as you haue harde wyth the Counte of Gaiazzo, who fhewed vnto him all figne of Amitye, and feeing that hee made no greate fute vnto hir, fhe wrote vnto him in this manner.

The Letter of Bianca Marie, to the Counte of Gaiazzo.

SIR, I doubt not by knowing the ftate of my degree, but that ye blufh to fee the violence of my mynd, which paffing the limites of modefty, that ought to guard futch a Lady as I am, forceth me (vncertayn of the caufe) to doe you vnderftand the gryef that doeth torment me, which is of futch conftraynt, as if of curtefie ye do not vouchfafe to come vnto me, you fhall commyt two faults, the one leauing the thing worthy for you to loue and regard, and which deferueth not to be caft of, the other in caufing the Death of hir, that for Loue of you, is bereft of reft: wherby loue hath uery little in me to feafe vpon, either of heart or liberty. The eafe of which gryef proceedeth from your only grace, which is able to vanquyfhe hir, whofe victorious hap hath conquered all other, and who attending your refolut aunfwer, fhal reft vnder the mercifull refuge of hope, whych deceiuing hir, fhal fe by that very meanes the wretched end of hir that is al your owne.

Bianca Maria Counteffe of Celant.

The yong Lorde mutch maruelled at this meffage, were it for that already hee was in loue with hir, and that for loue of his friend Ardizzino, durft not be known therof, or for that he feared fhe wold be ftraught of wits, if fhe were defpifed, he determined to goe vnto hir, and yet ftayed thinking it not to be the part of a faythfull companyon to deceiue his Friend: but in the end pleafure furmounting reafon, and the beauty ioyned wyth the good grace of the Lady hauing blinded him, and bewitched his wits fo wel as Ardizzino, he toke his way towards hir houfe, who waited for him wyth good deuotion, whither being arriued, he failed not to vfe like fpech that Valperga did, either of them (after certain reuerences and other fewe words) minding and defyringe one kinde of intertayne-

ment. This practize dured certayn months, and the Counteſſe was
ſo farre rapt with her new louer, as ſhe only employed hir ſelf to
pleaſe him, and he ſhewed himſelf ſo affected as therby ſhe thought
to rule and gouerne him in all things: wherof ſhe was afterwards
deceiued as you ſhall vnderſtand the maner. Ardizzino ſeing
himſelf wholly abandoned the preſence and loue of his Lady,
knowing that ſhe railed vpon him in al places where ſhe came,
departed Pauia halfe out of his wittes for Anger, and ſo ſtrayed
from comely ordyr by reaſon of his rage, as hee diſplayed the
Counteſſe thre times more liuely in hir colours, than ſhe could be
paynted, and reproued hir wyth the termes of the vileſt and moſte
common ſtrumpet that euer ran at rouers, or ſhot at random.
Bianca Maria vnderſtode hereof, and was aduertiſed of the vile
report that Ardizzino ſpread of hir, throughout Lombardie, which
chaffed hir in ſutch wyſe as ſhe fared like the Bedlem fury, ceaſing night nor day to playne the vnkindnes and folly of hir reiected
louer: ſomtimes ſaying, that ſhe had iuſt cauſe ſo to do, then
flattering hir ſelfe, alledged, that men were made of purpoſe to
ſuffer ſutch follyes as were wroughte by hir, and where they
termed themſelues to bee Women's Seruauntes, they ought at theyr
Myſtreſſe Handes to endure what pleaſed them. In the end, not
able any longer to reſtrayne hir choler, ne vanquiſh the appetite
of reuenge, purpoſed at all aduenture to prouide for the death
of her auncient Enimy, and that by meanes of him whom ſhe had
now tangled in her Nettes. See the vnſhamefaſtneſſe of this mas-
tife bitche, and the rage of that Female Tiger, howe ſhee goeth
about to arme one friend againſt an other, and was not content
onely to abuſe the Counte Gaiazzo, but deuiſed how to make him
the manqueller. And as one night they were in the middeſt of
their embracements, ſhe began pitifully to weepe and ſigh, in ſutch
wiſe as a man would haue thought (by the vexation of hir hearte)
that the ſoule and body would haue parted. The younge Lorde
louingly enquired the cauſe of hir heauineſſe: and ſayd vnto hir,
that if any had done hir diſpleaſure, hee would reuenge hir cauſe
to hir contentment. She hearing him ſay ſo, (then in ſtudie vpon
the deuice of hir Enimie's death) ſpake to the Counte in this manner: "You know ſir, that the thing whych moſte tormenteth the

Gentle heart and minde that can abide no wronge, is defamation
of honoure and infamous reporte. Thus mutch I fay for that the
Lord of Maffino, (who to fay the trouth, was fauoured of me in like
forte as you be now) hath not been afhamed to publifhe open
flaunders agaynft me, as thoughe I were the arranteft Whore that
euer had giuen her felf ouer to the Galley flaues alongs the fhore
of Scicile. If he had vaunted the fauour which I haue done him
but to certayne of his privat Friendes, I had incurred no flaunder
at all, mutch leffe any lyttle fufpition, but hearyng the common
reportes, the wrongfull Woordes and wycked brutes that he hath
rayfed on me: I befeech you fyr, to do me reafon that he may
feele his offence and the fmart for his committed fault againft hir
that is al yours." The Lord Sanfeuerino hearyng this difcourfe,
promifed hir to do hys beft, and to teache Valperga to talke
more foberly of hir, whom he was not worthy for to ferue, but in
thought. Notwithftandyng, he fayde more than he ment to do,
for he knew Ardizzino to be fo honeft, fage and curteous a
perfonage, as hee would neyther doe nor fay any thing without
good caufe, and that Ardizzino had iufter quarell agaynft him,
by takyng that from hym whych hee loued (althoughe it was
after his difcontinuance from that place, and vpon the onely
requeft of hir.) Thus he concluded in mind ftyl to remayne the
fryend of Ardizzino, and yet to fpend his time with the Counteffe,
which he did the fpace of certayn months without quarelling with
Valperga, that was retired to Pauie, with whom he was conuer-
fant, and liued familiarly, and moft commonly vfed one table and
bed togither. Bianca Maria feeing that the Lord of Gaiazzo cared
not mutch for hir, but onely for his pleafure, determined to vfe
like practife againft him, as fhe did to hir former louer, and to
banifh him from hir Houfe. So that when he came to fee hir, either
fhe was ficke, or hir affaires were sutch, as fhe could not kepe hym
company: or elfe hir gate was fhut vpon him. In the end (playing
double or quit) fhe prayed the fayd Lord to fhewe hir futch pleafure and friendfhip, as to come no more vnto hir, bicaufe fhe was
in termes to goe home to hir hufband the Counte of Celant, who
had fent for hir, and feared leaft his feruaunts fhoulde finde her
houfe ful of futers, alleaging that fhe had liued long inoughe in

that moſt ſinful life, the ligheſt faultes whereof were to heynous
for dames of hir port and calling, concluding that ſo long as ſhe
lyued ſhe would beare him good affection for the Honeſt Company
and conuerſation had betwene them, and for hys curteſie towards
hir. The yong Earle, were it that he gaue creadit vnto hir tale or
not, made as though he did beleue the ſame, and without longer
dyſcourſe, forbare approche vnto hir houſe, and droue out of his
heade al the Amorous affection which he caried to the Piedmont
Circes. And to the ende he might haue no cauſe to thinke vpon
hir, or that his preſence ſhould make hym ſlaue againe to hir that
firſt purſued him, he retired in good time to Millan : by which
retire hee auoided that miſhap, wherwith at length this Peſtilent
women would haue cut him ouer the ſhinnes, euen when his mind
was leaſt theron. Such was the malice and miſchief of hir heart,
who ceaſing to play the whore, applied hir whole paſtime to
murder. Gaiazzo being departed from Pauie, thys Venus once
agayne aſſayed the embracements of hir Ardizzino, and knew not
wel how to recouer hym agayne, bycauſe ſhe feared that the other
had diſcouered the Enterpryſe of his Murder. But what dare not
ſhee attempte whoſe mynde is ſlaue to ſinne ? The firſt aſſayes
be harde, and the minde doubtfull, and conſcience gnaweth vpon
the worme of repentaunce, but the ſame once nouſled in vice, and
rooted in the heart, it is more pleaſaunte, and gladſome for the
wicked to execute, than vertue is familiar to thoſe that follow hir :
So that ſhame ſeparate from before the eyes of youth, riper age
nourſed in impudency, their ſight is ſo daſeled, as they can ſee
nothing that eyther ſhame or feare can make them bluſh, which
was the cauſe that this Lady, continuinge ſtill in hir miſchiefe, ſo
mutch practiſed the freendes of hym whom ſhe deſired to kill,
and made ſutch fit excuſe by hir Ambaſſades, as hee was content
to ſpeake to hir, and to here hir Iuſtifications, whych were eaſy
inough to doe, the Iudge being not very guilty. Shee promiſed
and ſwore that if the fault were proued not to be in him, neuer
man ſhould ſee Bianca Maria, (ſo long as ſhe lyued) to be other
than a friend and ſlaue to the Lord Ardizzino, wholly ſubmitting
hirſelfe vnto his will and pleaſure. See how peace was capitulated
betweene the two reconciled Louers, and what were the articles of

the fame, the Lorde of Maffino entringe Poffeffion agayne of the fort that was reuolted, and was long tyme in the power of another. But when he was seazed agayne, the Lady faw full wel, that hir recouered friend was not fo hard to pleafe, as the other was, and that wyth him fhe liued at greater liberty. Continuing then their amorous Daunce, and Ardizzino hauing no more care but to reioyce himfelfe, nor hys Lady, but to cherifhe and make mutch of hir friend, beholde eftfoones the defire of Bloud and wyll of murder, newly reuiued in that new Megera, who incited (I knowe not with what rage,) fanfied to haue him flayne, whych refufed to kill hym, whom at this prefent fhee loued as hirfelfe. And he that had inquired the caufe thereof, I thyncke none other reafon coulde be rendred, but that a brayneleffe heade and reafonleffe minde, doe thincke moft notable murders, and myfchiefe be eafie to be brought to paffe, who fo ftrangely proceeded in difordred Luftes, which in fine caufed their myferable fhame, and ruine, wyth the death of hirfelfe and hym, whom fhe had ftirred to the fact, boldeninge him by perfuafion, to make him beleue Vyce to bee Vertue, and Glorioufly commended hym in hys follies, whych you fhall heare by readinge at lengthe the difcourfe of thys Hyftory. Bianca Maria, feeing hirfelfe in full poffeffion of hir Ardizzino, purpofed to make hym chiefe executioner of the murder, by hir intended, vpon Gaiazzo, for the doing whereof one night holdinge hym betwene hir armes, after fhee had long time dalyed with hym, like a cunninge Maiftreffe of hir Art, in the ende weauinge and trayning hir treafon at large, fhe fayd thus vnto him : "Syr, of long time I haue bene defirous to require a good turne at your hands, but fearing to trouble you, and thereupon to be denied, I thought not to be importunate : and albeit the matter toucheth you, yet did I rather holde my peace then to here refufall of a thinge, which your felfe ought to profer, the fame concerning you." "Madame," fayd hir Louer, "you know the matter neede to be haynous and of great importaunce, that I fhould deny you, fpecially if it concerne the bleamifh of your honor. But you fay the fame doth touch mee fomewhat neerely, and therefore if ability be in me, fpare not to vtter it, and I wyll affay your fatiffaction to the vttermoft of my power." "Syr," fayd fhe, "is the Counte of Gaiazzo one of your very frends?" "I thinke" (aunſwered Valperga) "that he is one of the ſureſt freends I haue, and in reſpeƈt of whoſe frendſhip, I will hazarde my ſelfe for him no leſſe than for my Brother, being certaine that if I have neede of him, he will not fayle to do the like for me. But wherefore doe you aſke me that queſtion?" "I will then tel you," ſayd the Traytreſſe (kiſſing him ſo ſweetely as euer he felt the like of any Woman,) "for ſomutch as you be ſo deceyued of your opinion in him who is wicked in diſſembling of that, which maliciouſly lieth hidden in hys heart. And briefly to ſay the effeƈt: aſſure your ſelfe hee is the greateſt and moſt mortall Ennimy that you haue in the Worlde. And to the intent that you do not think this to be ſome forged Tale, of light inuention, or that I heard the report of ſome not worthy of credit, I will ſay nothinge but that whych hymſelfe did tell me, when in your abſence he vſed my company. He ſware vnto me, without declaration of the cauſe, that hee coulde neuer bee mery, nor hys mynde in reſt, before hee ſaw you cut in pieces, and ſhortly woulde giue you ſutch aſſaulte, as al the dayes of our lyfe, you ſhoulde neuer haue luſt or mynde on Ladies loue. And albeit then, I was in choler agaynſt you, and that you had miniſtred ſome cauſe, and reaſon of hatred, yet our firſt loue had taken ſutch force in my hart, and I beſought him not to do that enterpriſe ſo long as I was in place where you did remayne, becauſe I cannot abide (wythout preſent death) to ſee your finger ake, mutch leſſe your lyfe berieued from you. Vnto which my ſute his Eare was deafe, ſwearing ſtill and proteſting that either he would be ſlayne himſelfe, or elſe diſpatch the Countee Ardizzino. I durſt not" (quod ſhe) "ne wel could as then aduertiſe you thereof, for the ſmal acceſſe that my ſeruants had vnto your lodging, but now I pray you to take good heede by preuenting his diuelifhe purpoſe: For better it were for you to take his lyfe, than he to kill and murder you, or otherwyſe work you miſchiefe, and you ſhal be eſteemed the wiſer man, and he pronounced a traytor to ſeeke the death of him, that bare him ſutch good will. Doe then accordinge to myne aduice, and before he begin, doe you kill hym, by the which you ſhall ſaue your ſelfe, and doe the part of a valyaunt knight, biſides, the ſatiſſying of the mynde of hir that

aboue al pleafures of the World doth chiefly defire the fame. Experience now will let me proue whether you loue me or not, and what
you will do for hir that loueth you fo dearly, who openeth this confpired murder, afwell for your fafety, as for lengthening of the lyfe
of hir, which wythout yours cannot endure: graunt this my fute
(O friend moſt deare) and fuffer me not in forrowfull plight to
be defpoyled of thy prefence: and wilt thou fuffer that I ſhoulde
dy, and that yonder Proude, Trayterous, and vnfaythfull varlet
ſhould liue to laugh mee to fcorne?" If the Lady had not added
thofe laſt words to hir foolifh fermon, perchaunce fhe might haue
prouoked Ardizzino to folow hir Counfell: but feeing hir fo ob-
ſtinately continue hir requeſt, and to profecute the fame with futch
violence, concluding vpon hir owne quarrel, his confcience throb-
bed, and his minde meafured the malice of that Woman, with the
honeſty of him, againſt whom that tale was told, who knew his frend
to be fo found and truſty, as willingly he would not do the thinge
that ſhould offend him, and therefore would geue no credit to
falfe report without good, and apparant proofe: for which caufe
hee was perfuaded that it was a malicious tale deuifed by fome
that went about to fowe debate betweene thofe two friendly earles.
Notwithſtanding, vpon further paufe, and not to make hir chafe,
or force hir into rage, he promifed the execution of hir curfed wil,
thanking hir for hir aduertifement, and that he would prouide for
hys defence and furety: and to the intent that ſhee might thyncke
he went about to performe his promife, he tooke his leaue of
hir to goe to Millan, which hee did, not to follow the abhominable will of that rauenous Maſtife, but to reueale the matter to his
companion, and direct the fame as it deferued. Being arriued at
Millan, the chiefe Citty of Lombardy, he imparted to Gaiazzo
from poynct to poynct the difcourfe of the Counteſſe, and the
peticion ſhee made vnto hym, vppon the conclufion of hir Tale:
"O God" (fayd the lord Sanfeuerino,) "who can beware the traps
of Whoores, if by thy grace our hands be not forbidden, and our
hearts and thoughts guided by thy goodnes? Is it poſſible that
the Earth can breede a Monſter more pernicious than this moſt
Peſtilent Beaſt? Thys is truely the grift of hir Father's vfury, and
the ſtench of all hir Predeceſſours villanyes: it is impoſſible of a

Kyte or Cormerant to make a good Sparhauk, or Tercle gentle.
This carion no doubt is the Daughter of a Vilayne, fprong of the
bafeft race amongs the common people, whofe mother was more
fine than chafte, more fubtile than fober: this minion hath forfaken hir hufband, to erect bloudy Skaffoldes of murder amid the
Nobles of Italy: and were it not for the difhonour which I fhould
get to foyle my hands in the bloude of a Beaft fo corrupt, I
woulde teare hir with my Teeth in a hundreth Thoufand peeces:
how many times hath fhe entreated mee before: in how many
fundry fortes with ioyned handes hath fhe befought mee to kill
the Lorde Ardizzino? Ah, my Companion, and right well beloued
Freende, can you thincke mee to bee fo Trayterous, and Cowarde a
Knaue, as that I dare not tell to them to whome I beare difpleafure
what mallice lurketh in my heart?" "By the fayth of a Gentleman," (fayd Ardizzino,) "I would be fory my mynd fhould feaze
on futch Folly, but I am come to reueale thys vnto you, that the
Song might found no more wythin myne eares. It behoueth vs
then, fith God hath kept vs hytherto, to avoyde the ayre of that
infection, that our braynes be not putrified, and from henceforth
to fly thofe Bloudfuckers, the Schollers of Venus: and truely great
difhonour would redound to vs, to kill one an other for the onely
paftime and fottifh fanfie of that mynion: I haue repented me an
hundred times when fhe firft mooued mee of the deuice to kill
you, that I did not geeue a hundred Poignaladoes wyth my
Dagger, to ftop the way by that example for all other to attempt
futch Butcheries: for I am well affured that the mallyce whych
fhee beareth you, proceedeth but of the delay you made for fatis-
faction of hir murderous defire, whereof I thancke you, and yelde
my felfe in all caufes to imploy my lyfe, and that I haue, to do
you feruice." "Leaue we of that talk" (fayd Gaiazzo) "for I
haue done but my duety, and that which ech Noble heart ought to
euery wight, doing wrong to none, but prone to help, and doe
good to all: whych is the true marke and Badge of Nobility.
Touching that malignant Strumpet, hir owne lyfe fhall reuenge
the wrongs which fhe hath gone about to venge on vs. In meane
while let vs reioyce, and thincke the goods, and richeffe fhee hath
gotten of vs, wil not caufe hir Bagges mutch to Strout and Swel.

To be fhort, fhe hath nothing whereby fhe may greatly laugh vs to fcorne, except our good entertainment of hir night and day do prouoke hir: let other coyne the pence henceforth to fill her Coafers, for of vs (fo farre as I fee) fhe is deceyued." Thus the two Lordes paffed forth their tyme, and in all Companies where they came, they fpent their Talke, and Communication of the disordered lyfe of the Counteffe of Celant. The whole Citty alfo rang of the fleights and meanes fhe vfed to trappe the Noblemen, and of her pollicies to be rid of them when her thirft was ftanched, or diet grew lothefome for want of chaunge. And that whych greued hir moft, an Italyan Epigram blafed forth hir prowes to hir great difhonour, whereof the Copy I cannot get, and fome fay that Ardizzino was the author: for it was compofed, when he was difpoffeffed of pacience: and if fhee coulde haue wreked hir will on the knights, I beleeue in hir rage fhe would haue made an Anathomy of their Bones. Of whych hir two enimies, Ardizzino was the greateft, agaynft whom hir difpleafure was the more, for that he was the firft with whom fhe entred fkirmifh. Nothing was more frequent in Pauy, than villanous Iefts, and Playes vppon the filthy Behauiour of the Counteffe, which made hir afhamed to goe out of hir Gates. In the ende fhee purpofed to chaunge the Ayre and place, hoping by that alteration to ftay the Infamous Brute, and Slaunder: fo fhe came to Millan, where firft fhe was inuefted wyth ftate of honour, in honeft Fame of Chafte lyfe fo longe as Vicount Hermes liued, and then was not purfued to ftaunch the thirft of thofe that did ordinarily draw at hir Foun-tayne. About the tyme that fhe departed from Pauy, Dom Pietro de Cardone a Scicilian, the Baftard Brother of the Counte of Colifano, whofe Lieuetenaunt he was, and their father flayn at the Battayle of Bicocca wyth a band of horfemen arriued at Milan. This Scicilian was about the age of one or two and twenty yeres, fomwhat black of face, but well made and fterne of countenance: whiles the Counteffe foiorned at Milan, this gentleman fell in loue with hir, and fearched all meanes he coulde to make hir hys friende, and to enioy hir: who perceyuing him to be young, and a Nouice in Skirmifhes of Loue, lyke a Pigeon of the firft coate, determined

to lure him, and to ferue hir turne in that which fhee purpofed to
doe on thofe agaynft whom fhee was outragioufly offended. Now
the better to entice thys younge Lorde vnto her Fantafye, and to
catch hym wyth hir bayte, when hee paffed through the Streate, and
faluted hir, and when he Syghed after the manner of the Spaniard,
rominge before hys Lady, fhee fhewed him an indifferent mery Countenaunce, and fodaynely reftrayned that Cheere, to make hym tafte
the pleafure mingled with the foure of one defire, which he could not
tel how to accomplifh: and the more faynt was his hardines for that
he was neuer practifed in the daliance and feruice of Lady of noble
houfe or calling, who thinck_ing that the Gentlewoman was one of
the Principall of Millan, he was ftraungely vexed, and tormented for
hir loue, in futch wyfe as in the night he could not reft for fanta-
fing, and thynking vpon hir, and in the Day paffed up and downe
before the Doore of her lodging. One eueninge for his difport hee
went forth to walke in company of another Gentleman, which well
could play vppon the Lute, and defired him to gieue awake vnto hys
Lady, that then for iealoufie was harkeninge at hir window, both
of the founde of the Inftrument, and the Ditty of hir amorous
Knight, where the Gentleman fong thys Sonet.

The death with trenchant dart, doth brede in breft futch il,
As I cannot forget the fmart, that thereby rifeth ftil.
Yet neertheleffe I am, the ill it felfe in deede,
That death with daily dolours deepe, within my breaft doth breede.

I am my Miftreffe thrall, and yet I doe not kno,
If fhe beare me good will at all, or if fhe loue or no.
My wound is made fo large, with bitter wo in breft,
That ftill my heart prepares a place to lodge a carefull gueft.

O dame that hath my lyfe and death at thy defire.
Come eafe my mind, wher fancies flames doth burne like Ethna
          fire,
For wanting thee my life is death and doleful cheere,
And finding fauor in thy fight, my dayes are happy heere.

Then he began to figh fo terribly, as if already fhe had geuen fentence, and difinitiue Iudgement of his farewell, and difputed with his fellow in futch fort, and wyth Opinion fo affured of hys contempt, as if he had bene in loue with fome one of the Infants of Spayne: for which caufe he began very pitifully to fing thefe verfes.

That God that made my foule, and knows what I haue felt,
Who caufeth fighes and forows oft, the fely foule to fwelt,
Doth fee my torments now, and what I fuffer ftill,
And vnderftands I taft mo griefs, than I can fhew by fkill.

Hee doth confent I wot, to my ill hap and woe,
And hath accorded with the dame that is my pleafaunt foe,
To make my boyling breft abound in bitter bliffe,
And fo bereue me of my reft, when heart his hope fhall miffe.

O what are not the fongs, and fighs that louers haue,
When night and day with fweete defires, they draw vnto their
     graue,
Their grief by frendfhip growes, where ruth nor pity raynes,
And fo like fnow againft the Sun, they melt away with pains.

My dayes muft finifh fo, my deftny hath it fet,
And as the candle out I goe, before hir grace I get.
Before my fute be heard, my feruice throughly knowne,
I fhalbe layd in Toumbe ful low, fo colde as Marble ftone.

To thee fayre Dame I cry, that makes my fenfes arre,
And planteft peace within my breft and then makes fodain war:
Yet at thy pleafure ftill, thou muft my fowre make fweete,
In graunting me the fauour due, for faythfull Louers meete.

Which fauor geue me now, and to thy Noble mynde,
I doe remayne a Galley flaue, as thou by proofe fhall finde.
And fo thou fhalt releafe my heart from cruell bandes,
And haue his fredome at thy wil that yelds into thy handes.

So rendring all to thee, the gods may ioyne vs both
Within one lawe and league of loue, through force of conftant
    troth.
Then fhalt thou miftreffe be, of lyfe, of Limme and all,
My goods, my golde, and honour, loe! fhall fo be at thy call.

Thys gentle order of loue greatly pleafed the Lady, and therefore
opened hir gate to let the Scicilian lorde, who feeing hymfelfe
fauoured (beyond all hope) of his Lady, and cheerefully intertayned, and welcommed with great curtefie ftoode fo ftill afton-
nied, as if hee had beene fallen from the Cloudes: but fhe which
coulde teache hym good manner, to make hym the minifter of hir
myfchiefe, takynge hym by the hande, made hym fit downe vpon
a greene Bed befydes hir, and feeing that he was not yet imbolde-
ned, for all hee was a Souldiour, fhee fhewed hir felfe more hardy
than hee, and firfte affayled hym wyth talke, fayinge: " Syr, I
praye you thinke it not ftraunge, if at thys houre of the nyght,
I am bolde to caufe you enter my houfe, beinge of no great acquayntaunce wyth you, but by hearinge your curteous falutations: and wee of thys Countrey bee fomewhat more at liberty
than they in thofe partes from whence you come: befides it lyketh
mee well (as I am able) to honour ftraunge gentlemen, and to
retayne theym with right good willinge heart, fith it pleafeth
theym to honour mee wyth repayre vnto my houfe: fo fhall you
be welcome ftyll when you pleafe to knocke at my Gate, whych
at all tymes I wyll to be opened for you, wyth no leffe good wyll
than if yee were my naturall Brother, the fame wyth all the thinges
therein, it may pleafe you to difpofe as if they were your own."
Dom Pietro of Cardonne well fatiffied, and contented wyth thys
vnlooked for kyndneffe, thanked her very Curteoufly, humbly praying hir befides to dayne it in good parte, if he were fo bolde to
make requefte of loue, and that it was the onelye thynge which
hee aboue all other defyred mofte, fo that if fhee would receiue
him for hir friende and Seruaunt, fhee fhoulde vnderftande him to
be a Gentleman, which lightly woulde promife nothing excepte
the accomplifhment did followe: fhe that fawe a greater onfet
than fhe loked for, anfwered hym fmilyng with a very good grace:

"Sir, I haue knowne very many that haue vouched ſlipperie pro-
myſes, and proffered lordly ſeruices vnto Ladies, the effect wherof
if I myght once ſee, I would not thinke that they coulde vaniſhe ſo
ſoone, and conſume like ſmoake." "Madame" (ſayde the Scicilian) "yf I fayle in any thing which you commaunde mee, I praye
to God neuer to receiue any fauor or grace of thoſe Curteſies
whych I craue." "If then" (quod ſhee) "you wyl promiſe to
employ your ſelfe aboute a buſineſſe that I haue to do when I
make requeſt, I wyll alſo to accept you for a friende, and graunt
ſutch ſecrecie as a faithful louer can deſyre of his Lady." Dom
Pietro which would have offred hym ſelfe in Sacrifice for hir, not
knowyng hir demaunde, tooke an othe, and promyſed hir ſo
lyghtly as madly afterwardes he did put the ſame in proofe. Beholde the preparatiues of the obſequies of their firſt loue, and the
guages of a bloudie Bed: the one was prodigall of hir honoure,
the other the tormente of his reputation, and neglected the duety
and honor of his ſtate, which the houſe wherof he came, commaunded hym to kepe. Thus all the nyght he remained with
Bianca Maria, who made him ſo wel to like hir good entertaynment and imbracementes, as he neuer was out of her Company.
And the warie Circes fayned her ſelf ſo fare in loue wyth hym,
and vſed ſo many toyes and gametricks of her filthy ſcience,
as he not onelye eſteemed hym ſelfe the happieſt Gentleman of
Scicilia, but the moſt fortunate wight of all the Worlde, and by
bibbing of hir Wyne was ſo ſtraungely charmed with the Pleaſures of his fayre Myſtreſſe, as for hir ſake he would haue taken
vpon him the whole ouerthrowe of Milan, ſo well as Bloſe of
Cumes to ſette the Cittye of Rome on fire, if Tyberius Gracchus
the ſedicious, woulde haue giuen it him in charge. Sutch is the
manner of wilde and fooliſh youth, whych ſuffreth it ſelfe to be
caried beyonde the boundes of reaſon. The ſame in time paſt
did ouerthrow many Realmes, and cauſed the chaunge of diuers
Monarchies: and truely vnſeemely it is for a man to be ſubdued
to the will of a common ſtrumpet. And as it is vncomly to ſubmit him ſelfe to ſutch one, ſo not requiſite to an honeſt and vertuous Dame, his maried Wyfe. Which vnmanly deedes, be occa-
ſions that diuers Fooliſhe Women commit ſutch filthy factes, with

their infpekable trumperies begiling the fimple man, and perchance through to mutch lofing the Bridle raynes to the lawfull
Wyfe, the poore man is ftrangely deceyued by fome adulterous
varlet, whych at the Wyue's commaundment, when fhe feeth
oportunity, wil not fhrinke to hazarde the honour of them both,
in futch wife as they ferue for an example vppon a common Scaffold to a whole generation and Pofterity. I wyll not feeke farre
of for examples, being fatiffied with the folly of the Baftard Cardonne, to pleafe the cruelty and malice of that infernall fury the
Counteffe, who hauinge lulled, flattered, and bewitched with hir
louetricks (and peraduenture with fome charmed drinke) her new
Pigeon, feeinge it time to folicite his promife, to be reuenged of
thofe, whych thought no more of hir confpiracies and trayterous
deuifes, and alfo when the time was come for punifhinge of hir
whoredome, and chaftifing of the breach of fayth made to hir hufbande, and of hir intended murders, and fome of them put in execution, fhe I fay, defirous to fee the ende of that, which in thought
fhe had contryued, vppon a day tooke Dom Pietro afide, and
fecretly begaŋ this Oration: "I take God to witnes (fir) that
the requeft which I pretend prefently to make, proceedeth of defire rather that the Worlde may know how iuftly I feeke meanes
to mayntayne myne honour, than for defire of reuenge, knowinge
very well, that there is nothing fo precious, and deere vnto a woman, as the preferuation of that ineftimable Iewell, fpecially in a
Lady of that honourable degre whych I mayntayne amonge the
beft. And to the intent I feeme not tedious with prolixity of
words, or vfe other than direct circumftances before him that hath
offred iuft reuenge for the wrongs I haue receyued: knowe you
fir, that for a certain tyme I continued at Pauie, kepynge a houfe
and Trayne fo honeft, as the beft Lords were contented wyth
myne ordinarye: It chaunced that two honeft Gentlemen of Noble
Houfe haunted my Palace in lyke fort, and with the fame intertainment whych as you fee, I doe receiue ech Gentleman, who
beyng well intreated and honoured of me, in the ende forgat themfelues fo farre, as without refpect of my ftate and callinge, wythout regard of the race and family wherof they come, haue attempted the flaunder of my good name, and vtter fubuerfion of my

renoume: and fufficient it was not for them thus to deale with mee
poore Gentlewoman, without defert (excepte it were for admyt-
tyng them to haue acceffe vnto my houfe) but alfo to continue
their Blafphemies, to myne extreame reproach and fhame: and
howe true the fame is, they that know me can well declare, by
reafon whereof, the vulgar people prone and ready to wycked reportes, haue conceiued futch opynion of me, as for that they fee me
braue and fine in Apparell, and fpecyally throughe the flaunderous fpeache of thofe gallantes, do deeme and repute me for a
common Whoore, wherof I craue none other wytneffe than your
felfe and my confcience. And I fweare vnto you, that fith I
came to Milan, it is you alone that hath vanquifhed, and made the
Triumphe of my Chaftytye: and yf you were abfent from this
Citye, I affure you on my fayth that I would not tarry heere xxiiii.
houres. Thefe infamous ruffians I fay, thefe perfecuters and ter-
magantes of my good name, haue chafed mee out of all good
Cityes, and made me to be abhorred of ech honeft company, that
weary I am of my lyfe, and lothe to lyue any longer except fpedye
redreffe bee had for reuengement of thys wronge: wherefore except I finde fome Noble Champion and Valyaunte Perfonage to
requyte thefe Vyllains for their fpitefull Speach blafed on me in
euerye Corner of Towne and Countreye, and to paye them theyr
rewarde and hire that I may lyue at Lybertye and quyet, Sor-
rowe wyll eyther confume mee or myne owne handes fhall has-
ten fpedye Death." And in fpeakyng thofe Woordes, fhee beganne to weepe with futch abundance of teares ftreaming downe
hir Cheekes and Necke of Alabafter hewe, as the Scicilian whych
almoft had none other God but the Counteffe, fayd vnto hir:
"And what is he, that dare moleft and flaunder hir that hath in
hir puiffaunce fo many Souldiers and men of Warre? I make a
vow to God, that if I know the names of thofe two arrant vil-
laynes, the which haue fo defamed my Myftreffe name, the whole
worlde fhall not faue their liues, whofe carrion Bodies I will hew
into fo many gobbets, as they haue members vpon the fame:
wherefore Madame" (fayd he, imbracing her) "I pray you to grieue
your felfe no more, commit your wronges to me, only tell me the
names of thofe Gallaunts, and afterwards you fhall vnderftande

what difference I make of woorde and deede, and if I doe not
trimme and dreſſe theym ſo finely, as hereafter they ſhall haue
no neede of Barber, neuer truſt me any more." Shee, as reuiued
from death to lyfe, kyſſed and embraced him a thouſand tymes,
thankinge hym for his good will, and offering him all that ſhe
had. In the ende ſhe tolde him that hir enimies were the counties
of Maſſino and Gaiazzo, which but by theyr deaths alone were
not able to amend and repayre hir honour. "Care not you" (ſayde
hee) "for before that the Sunne ſhall ſpreade his Beames twice
24 houres vpon the earth, you ſhall heare newes, and know
what I am able to do for the chaſtiſement of thoſe deuils." As he
promiſed, bee fayled not to do : for wythin a whyle after as Ardizzino was goinge to ſupper into the Citty, he was eſpyed by hym,
that had in company attendaunt vppon hym fyue and twenty men
of Armes, which waited for Ardizzino, in a Lane on the left hand
of the Streate called Merauegli, leading towards the church of
Sainct Iames, through which the Countee muſt needes paſſe.
Who as he was going very pleaſantly diſpoſed with his brother,
and 5 or 6 of his men, was immediately aſſayled on euery
ſide, and not knowinge what it ment, would haue fled, but the
Wayes, and Paſſages were ſtopped rounde aboute : to defende himſelfe it auayled not hauing but their ſingle Swords, and amid the
troupe of ſutch a bande that were throughly armed, which in a
moment had murdred, and cut in peeces all that company. And
although it was late, yet the Countie Ardizzino many times named
Dom Pietro, which cauſed hym to be taken, and impriſoned by the
Duke of Bourbon, that was fled out of Fraunce, and then was Lieutenaunt for the Emperour Charles the fifth in Milan. Whoſoeuer was
aſtonned and amazed with that Impriſonment, it is to bee thoughte
that the Scicilan was not greatly at his eaſe and quiet, who
needed no torments to force him confeſſe the faſt, for of his owne
accorde voluntarily he dyſcloſed the ſame, but he ſayde he was
prouoked thervnto by the perſuaſion of Bianca Maria telling the
whole diſcourſe as you haue heard before. ' She had already
intelligence of this chaunce, and might haue fled and ſaued hir
ſelfe before the faſt (by the confeſſion of Dom Pietro) had ben
diſcouered, and attended in ſome ſecrete place till that ſtormie

time had bene calmed and appeafed. But God which is a right-full iudge woulde not fuffer hir wickedneffe ftretch any further, fith fhe hauing found out futch a nimble and wilful executioner, the Countee of Gaiazzo could not long haue remained aliue, who then in good time and happy houre was abfent out of the City. So foone as Dom Pietro had accufed the Counteffe, the Lord of Bourbon fente her to pryfon, and being examined, confeffed the whole matter, truftinge that hir infinite numbre of Crownes woulde haue corrupted the Duke, or thofe that reprefented his perfon. But hir Crownes and Lyfe paffed all one way. For the day after hir imprifonment fhee was condempned to lofe hir heade: and in the meane time Dom Pietro was faued, by the diligence and fuite of the Captaynes, and was employed in other Warres, to whom the Duke gaue him, for that he was lothe to lofe fo notable a Souldiour, the very right hand of his Brother the Countee of Colifano. The Counteffe hauing fentence pronounced vppon hir, but trufting for pardon, would not prepare hir felfe to dy, ne yet by any meanes craue forgiuenes of hir faults at the hands of God, vntil fhe was conueyed out of the Caftell, and ledde to the common place of execution, where a Scaffolde was prepared for hir to play the laft Acte of thys Tragedy. Then the miferable Lady began to know hirfelfe, and to confeffe hir faults before the people, denoutly praying God, not to haue regard to hir demerites, ne yet to deter-mine his wrath agaynft hir, or enter with hir in iudgement, for fo mutch as if the fame were decreed accordinge to hir iniquity, no faluation was to be looked for. She befought the people to pray for hir, and the countee of Gaiazzo that was abfent, to pardon hir malice, and treafon which fhe had deuifed agaynft him. Thus miferably and repentantly dyed the Counteffe, which in hir lyfe refufed not to imbrace and follow any wickednes, no mifchiefe fhee accompted euill done, fo the fame were imployed for hir plea-fure and paftime. A goodly example truely for the youth of our prefent time, fith the moft part indifferently do launch into the gulfe of difordred lyfe, fuffring themfelues to bee plunged in the puddles of their owne vayne conceiptes, without confideration of the mifchieues that may enfue. If the Lord of Cardonne had not bene beloued of his generall, into what calamity had he fallen for

yeldinge himfelfe a pray to that bloudy Woman who had more
regarde to the light, and wilfull fanfie of hir, whom he serued like
a flaue, than to his duety and eftimation? And truely all futch be
voyde of their right wits, which thincke themfelues beloued of a
Whoore. For their amity endureth no longer than they fucke
from their purffes and bodies any profit or pleafure. And becaufe
almoft euery day femblable examples be feene, I will leaue of this
difcourfe, to take me to a matter, not farre more pleafaunt than
this, although founded vpon better grounde, and ftablifhed upon
loue, the firft onfet of lawfull mariage, the fucceffe whereof
chaunced to murderous ende, and yet the fame intended by neyther
of the beloued: as you fhall be iudge by the continuance of
reading of the hiftory enfuing. Beare with me good Ladyes (for
of you alone I craue this pardon) for introducing the Whoorifh
lyfe of the Counteffe, and hir bloudy enterprife : bicaufe I know
right wel, that recitall of murders, and bloudy facts wearieth the
mindes of thofe that loue to lyue at reft, and wifh for fayre weather
after the troublefome ftormes of raging Seas, no leffe than the
Pilote and wife Mariner, hauing long time endured and cut the
perillous ftraicts of the Ocean Sea. And albeit the corruption of
our nature be fo great, as follies delighte vs more than erneft
matters fraught wyth reafon and wifedome, yet I thinke not that
our mindes be fo peruerted and diuided from trouth, but fometimes
wee care and feeke to fpeake more grauely than the countrey
Hynde, or more foberly than they, whofe lyues do beare the marke
of infamy, and be to euery wight notorious for the onely name of
their vocation. Suffifeth vs that an Hyftory, be it neuer fo full
of fporte and pleafure, do bring with it inftruction of our lyfe, and
amendement of our maners. And wee ought not to be fo curious
or fcrupulous, to reiect merry and pleafant deuifes that be voide
of harmeful talke, or wythout futch glee as may hynder the education of Youth procliue, and ready to choofe that is corrupt, and
naught. The very bookes of holy fcriptures doe defcribe vnto vs
perfons that bee vicious, and fo deteftable as nothing more, whofe
factes vnto the fimple may feeme vnfeemely, vpon the leaft recitall
of the fame. And fhall wee therefore reiect the readinge, and
efchue thofe holy bookes? God forbid, but with diligence to

beware, that we do not refemble thofe that be remembred there for example, forfomutch as fpeedely after finne, enfueth grieuous, and as fodayne punifhment. For which caufe I haue felected thefe Hiftoryes, of purpofe to aduertife Youth, how they that follow the way of damnable iniquity, fayle not fhortly after their great offences, and execution of their outragious vices, to feele the iuft and mighty hand of God, who guerdoneth the good for their good works and deedes, and rewardeth the euil for their wickednes and mifchiefe. Now turne we then to the Hyftory of two, the rareft Louers that euer were, the performaunce, and finifhinge whereof, had it bene fo profperous as the beginning, they had ioyed ioyfully the Fruicts of their intent, and two noble houfes of one City reconciled to perpetuall frendfhip.

THE TWENTY-FIFTH NOUELL.

*The goodly Hyſtory of the true, and conſtant Loue between Rhomeo
and Ivlietta, the one of whom died of Poyſon, and the other of
ſorrow, and heuineſſe : wherein be compryſed many aduentures of
Loue, and other deuiſes touchinge the ſame.*

I AM ſure that they which meaſure the Greatneſſe of Goddes
workes accordinge to the capacity of their Rude, and ſimple vnder-
ſtandinge, wyll not lightly adhibite credite vnto thys Hiſtory, ſo
wel for the variety of ſtraunge Accidents which be therein de-
ſcribed, as for the nouelty of ſo rare, and perfeᴄ̄t amity. But they
that haue read Plinie, Valerius Maximus, Plutarche, and diuers
other Writers, do finde, that in olde time a great number of Men
and Women haue died, ſome of exceſſiue ioy, ſome of ouermutch
ſorrow, and ſome of other paſſions: and amongs the ſame, Loue
is not the leaſt, whych when it ſeazeth vppon any kynde and
gentle ſubieᴄ̄t, and findeth no reſiſtaunce to ſerue for a rampart to
ſtay the violence of his courſe, by little and little vndermineth,
melteth and conſumeth the vertues of naturall powers in ſutch
wyſe as the ſpyrite yealdinge to the burden, abandoneth the place
of lyfe: which is verified by the pitifull, and infortunate death of
two Louers that ſurrendered their laſt Breath in one Toumbe at
Verona a Citty of Italy, wherein repoſe yet to thys day (with
great maruell) the Bones, and remnauntes of their late louing
bodies: an hyſtory no leſſe wonderfull than true. If then perticular
affeᴄ̄tion which of good right euery man ought to beare to the
place where he was borne, doe not deceyue thoſe that trauayle, I
thincke they will confeſſe wyth me, that few Citties in Italy, can
ſurpaſſe the ſayd City of Verona, aſwell for the Nauigable riuer
called Adiſſa, which paſſeth almoſt through the midſt of the ſame,
and thereby a great trafique into Almayne, as alſo for the proſpeᴄ̄t
towards the Fertile Mountaynes, and pleaſant valeys whych do
enuiron the ſame, with a great number of very clere and lyuely
fountaynes, that ſerue for the eaſe and commodity of the place.
Omittinge (bifides many other ſingularities) foure Bridges, and an

infinite number of other honourable Antiquities dayly apparaunt
vnto thofe, that be to curious to viewe and looke vpon them.
Which places I haue fomewhat touched, bicaufe thys moſt true
Hiſtory which I purpoſe hereafter to recite, dependeth thereupon,
the memory whereof to thys day is ſo wel known at Verona, as
vnneths their blubbred Eyes be yet dry, that ſaw and beheld that
lamentable fight.   When the Senior Efcala was Lord of Verona,
there were two families in the Citty, of farre greater fame than the
reſt, aſwell for riches as Nobility: the one called the Monteſches,
and the other the Capellets: but lyke as moſt commonly there is
diſcorde amongs theym which be of ſemblable degree in honour,
euen ſo there hapned a certayne enmity betweene them: and for
ſo mutch as the beginning thereof was vnlawfull, and of ill foundation, ſo lykewyſe in proceſſe of time it kindled to ſutch flame, as
by diuers and ſundry deuyſes praᵭtiſed on both ſides, many loſt
their lyues.   The Lord Bartholmew of Efcala, (of whom we haue
already ſpoken) being Lord of Verona, and ſeeing ſutch diſorder in
his common weale, aſſayed diuers and ſundry waies to reconcile
thofe two houſes, but all in vayne: for their hatred had taken
ſutch roote, as the fame could not be moderated by any wyſe
counſell or good aduice: betweene whom no other thing could be
accorded, but geuing ouer Armour, and Weapon for the time, attending ſome other ſeaſon more conuenient, and wyth better leyſure
to appeaſe the reſt.   In the time that theſe thinges were adoing,
one of the family of Monteſches called Rhomeo, of the age of 20
or 21. yeares, the comlieſt and beſt conditioned Gentleman that
was amonges the Veronian youth, fell in loue with a yong Gentlewoman of Verona, and in few dayes was attached with hir Beauty,
and good behauiour, as he abandoned all other affaires and buſines,
to ſerue and honour hir: and after many Letters, Ambaſſades,
and preſents, he determined in the ende to ſpeake vnto hir, and
to diſcloſe hys paſſions, which he did without any other praᵭtiſe.
But ſhe which was vertuouſly brought vp, knew how to make him
ſo good anſwer to cut of his amorous affe᭰tions, as he had no luſt
after that time to returne any more, and ſhewed hir ſelf ſo auſtere,
and ſharpe of Speach, as ſhe vouchſafed not with one looke to
behold him.   But how mutch the young Gentleman ſaw hir whiſt,

and filent, the more he was inflamed: and after he had continued
certayne months in that feruice wythout remedy of his griefe, he
determined in the ende to depart Verona, for proofe if by chaunge of
the place he might alter his affection, faying to himfelfe: "What
do I meane to loue one that is fo vnkinde, and thus doth difdayn
me: I am all hir owne, and yet fhe flieth from me: I can no longer
liue, except hir prefence I doe enioy: and fhe hath no contented
mynde, but when fhe is furtheft from me: I will then from henceforth
Eftraunge my felfe from hir, for it may fo come to paffe by not beholding hir, that thys fire in me which taketh increafe and nourifhment by hir fayre Eyes, by little and little may dy and quench." But
minding to put in proofe what he thought, at one inftant hee was
reduced to the contrary, who not knowing whereupon to refolue,
paffed dayes and nights in marueilous Playnts, and Lamentations: for Loue vexed him fo neare, and had fo well fixed the Gentlewoman's Beauty within the Bowels of his heart, and mynde,
as not able to refift, hee faynted with the charge, and confumed by
little and little as the Snow agaynft the Sunne: whereof hys
parenttes, and kinred did maruayle greatly, bewaylinge hys
miffortune, but aboue all other one of hys Companyons of riper
Age, and Counfell than hee, began fharpely to rebuke him: for the
loue that he bare him was fo great as hee felt hys Martirdome, and
was pertaker of hys paffion: which caufed him by ofte viewyng
his friend's difquietneffe in amorous panges, to fay thus vnto him:
"Rhomeo, I maruell mutch that thou fpendeft the beft time of
thine age, in purfute of a thing, from which thou feeft thy felf
defpifed and banifhed, wythout refpecte either to thy prodigall
difpenfe, to thine honor, to thy teares, or to thy myferable lyfe,
which be able to moue the moft conftant to pity: wherefore I
pray thee for the Loue of our auncient amity, and for thyne health
fake, that thou wilt learn to be thine owne man, and not to alyenat
thy lyberty to any fo ingrate as fhe is: for fo farre as I coniecture by things that are paffed betwene you, either fhe is in loue
wyth fome other, or elfe determineth neuer to loue any. Thou
arte yong, rich in goods and fortune, and more excellent in beauty
than any Gentleman in thys Cyty: thou art well learned, and the
onely fonne of the houfe wherof thou commeft: what gryef would

it bee to thy poore olde Father and other thy parentes, to fee the
fo drowned in this dongeon of Vyce, fpecially at that age wherein
thou oughteft rather to put them in fome Hope of thy Vertue?
begyn then from henceforth to acknowledge thyne error, wherein
thou haft hitherto lyued, doe away that amorous vaile or couerture
whych blyndeth thyne Eyes and letteth thee to folow the ryghte
path, wherein thine aunceftors haue walked: or elfe if thou do
feele thy felf fo fubiect to thyne owne wyll, yelde thy hearte to
fome other place, and chofe fome Miftreffe accordyng to thy
worthyneffe, and henceforth doe not fow thy Paynes in a Soyle fo
barrayne whereof thou reapeft no Fruyete: the tyme approcheth
when al the Dames of the Cyty fhal affemble, where thou mayft
behold futch one as fhall make thee forget thy former gryefs."
Thys younge Gentleman attentyuely hearyng all the perfuad-
yng reafons of hys fryend, began fomewhat to moderate that heate
and to acknowledge all the exhortatyons which hee had made
to be directed to good purpofe: and then determined to put
them in proofe, and to be prefent indifferently at al the
feafts and affemblies of the City, without bearing affection more
to one Woman than to an other: and continued in thys manner of
Lyfe, II. or III. monthes, thinking by that meanes to quench the
fparks of auncient flames. It chaunced then within few dayes
after, about the feaft of Chryftmaffe, when feafts and bankets
moft commonly be vfed, and mafkes accordinge to the cuftome
frequented, that Anthonie Capellet being the Chief of that Familye,
and one of the principall Lords of the City too, made a banket, and
for the better Solempnization thereof, inuited all the Noble men
and dames, to which Feaft reforted the moft part of the youth
of Verona. The family of the Capellets (as we haue declared in
the beginninge of thys Hyftory) was at variance with the Montes-
ches, which was the caufe that none of that family repaired to
that Banket, but onelye the yong Gentleman Rhomeo, who came
in a mafke after fupper with certaine other yong Gentlemen: and
after they had remained a certayne fpace with their vifards on,
at length they did put of the fame, and Rhomeo very fhamefaft,
withdrew himfelf into a Corner of the Hall: but by reafon of the
light of the Torches which burned very bright, he was by and by

knowen and loked vpon of the whole Company, but fpecially of
the Ladies, for befides his Natiue Beauty wherewyth Nature had
adorned him, they maruelled at his audacity how hee durft prefume
to enter fo fecretly into the Houfe of that Famyllye which had litle
caufe to do him any good.   Notwithftanding, the Capellets dis-
fembling their mallice, either for the honor of the company, or
elfe for refpeçt of his Age, did not mifufe him eyther in Worde
or Deede : by meanes whereof wyth free liberty he behelde and
viewed the Ladies at hys Pleafure, which hee dyd fo well, and wyth
grace fo good, as there was none but did very well lyke the
prefence of his perfon : and after he had particularly giuen
Iudgement vppon the excellency of each one, according to his
affeçtion, hee fawe one Gentlewoman amonges the refte of fur-
paffinge Beautye who (althoughe hee had neuer feene hir tofore)
pleafed him aboue the reft, and attributed vnto bir in heart the
Chyefeft place for all perfeçtion in Beautye : and feaftyng hir in-
ceffantlye with piteous lookes, the Loue whych hee bare to his firft
Gentlewoman, was ouercomen with this newe fire, that toke futch
norifhment and vigor in his hart, as he was not able neuer to quench
the fame but by Death onely : as you may vnderftande by one of
the ftrangeft difcourfes, that euer any mortal man deuifed.   The
yong Rhomeo then felying himfelfe thus toffed wyth thys newe
Tempeft, could not tell what countenaunce to vfe, but was fo furprifed and chaunged with thefe laft flames, as he had almoft forgotten himfelfe, in futch wife as he had not audacity to enquyre
what fhe was, and wholly bente himfelf to feede hys Eyes with
hir fighte, wherewyth he moyftened the fweete amorous venome,
which dyd fo empoyfon him, as hee ended hys Dayes with a kinde
of moft cruell death.   The Gentlewoman that dydde put Rhomeo
to futch payne was called Iulietta, and was the Daughter of Capellet, the mayfter of the houfe wher that affembly was, who as
hir Eyes did rolle and wander too and fro, by chaunce efpied
Rhomeo, which vnto hir feemed to be the goodlieft perfonage
that euer fhee fawe : and Loue (which lay in wayte neuer vntill
that time,) affayling the tender heart of that yong Gentlewoman,
touched hir fo at the quicke, as for any refiftance fhe coulde make,
was not able to defende his forces, and then began to fet at naught

the royalties of the feaſt, and felt no pleaſure in hir heart, but
when ſhe had a glimpſe by throwing or receiuing ſome ſight or
looke of Rhomeo. And after they had contented eche others
troubled heart with millions of amorous lookes which oftentimes
interchangeably encountred and met together, the burning Beames
gaue ſufficient teſtimony of loue's priuy onſettes. Loue hauing
made the heartes breache of thoſe two louers, as they two ſought
meanes to ſpeake together, Fortune offered them a very meete and
apt occaſion. A certayne Lord of that troupe and companye tooke
Iulietta by the Hande to Daunce, wherein ſhee behaued hir ſelfe
ſo well, and wyth ſo excellent grace, as ſhee wanne that Daye
the priſe of Honour from all the Damoſels of Verona. Rhomeo
hauynge foreſeene the place wherevnto ſhee mynded to retire,
approched the ſame, and ſo dyſcretelye vſed the matter, as hee
founde the meanes at hir returne to ſit beſide hir: Iulietta when
the daunce was finiſhed, returned to the very place where ſhe was
ſet before, and was placed betwene Rhomeo and an other gentleman called Mercutio, which was a courtlyke Gentleman, very well
be loued of all men, and by reaſon of his pleaſaunt and curteous
behauior was in euery company wel intertayned. Mercutio that
was of audacity among Maydens, as a Lyon is among Lambes, ſeazed
incontynently vpon the hande of Iulietta, whoſe hands wontedly
were ſo cold both in Wynter and Sommer as the Mountayne yce,
although the fire's heat did warm the ſame. Rhomeo whych ſat
vppon the left ſide of Iulietta, ſeynge that Mercutio held hir by
the right hand, toke hir by the other that he myght not be deceiued
of his purpoſe, and ſtrayning the ſame a little, he felt himſelf ſo
preſt wyth that newe fauor, as he remayned mute, not able to
aunſwer: but ſhe perceyuyng by his chaunge of color, that the
fault proceded of the vehemence of loue, deſyryng to ſpeake vnto
hym, turned hir ſelfe towards hym, and wyth tremblyng voyce
ioyned with virginal ſhamefaſtneſſe, intermedled with a certayn
baſhfulneſſe, ſayd to hym: "Bleſſed be the houre of your neare
approche:" but myndyng to procede in further talke, loue had ſo
cloſed vp hir mouth, as ſhe was not able to end hir Tale. Wherunto the yong Gentleman all rauiſhed with ioy and contentation,
ſighing, aſked hir what was the cauſe of that ryght fortunate

bleffing: Iulietta, fomwhat more emboldened with pytyful loke
and fmyling countenance, faid vnto him: "Syr, do not maruell yf I
do bleffe your comminge hither, bicaufe fir Mercutio a good tyme
wyth frofty hand hath wholly frofen mine, and you of your curtefy
haue warmed the fame agayne." Wherunto immediatly Rhomeo
replyed: "Madame, if the heauens haue ben fo fauorable to
employe me to do you fome agreeable feruice, being repaired hither
by chance amongs other Gentlemen, I efteeme the fame well
beftowed, crauying no greater benefite for fatiffaction of all my
contentations receiued in this World, than to ferue obey and honor
you fo long as my lyfe doth laft, as experience fhall yeld more
ample proofe when it fhall pleafe you to geue further affaye:
moreouer, if you haue receiued any Heat by touche of my Hand,
you may be well affured that thofe flames be dead in refpect of
the lyuely Sparkes and violent fire which forteth from you fayre
Eyes, which fire hath fo fiercely inflamed all the moft fenfible parts
of my body, as if I be not fuccored by the fauoure of your good
graces, I do attend the time to be confumed to duft." Scarfe had
he made an ende of thofe laft words but the daunce of the Torche
was at an end: whereby Iulietta, which wholly burnt in loue,
ftraightly clafpyng her Hand with hys, had no leyfure to make
other aunfwer, but foftly thus to fay: "My deare frend, I know
not what other affured wytneffe you defire of loue, but that I let
you vnderftand that you be no more your own, than I am yours,
beying ready and dyfpofed to obey you fo farre as honour fhal
permyt, befeechying you for the prefent tyme to content your
felfe wyth thys aunfwere, vntyll fome other feafon meeter to Com-
mvnicate more fecretly of our affaires." Rhomeo feeing himfelfe
preffed to part of the Company, and for that hee knew not by
what meanes he myght fee hir agayne that was hys Life and Death,
demaunded of one of his friends what fhee was, who made aunfwer
that fhe was the Daughter of Capellet, the Lord of the houfe, and
Mayfter of that daye's feaft (who wroth beyonde meafure that
Fortune had fent him to fo daungerous a place, thought it impoffible to bring to end his enterprife begon.) Iulietta couetous on
the other fide, to know what yong Gentleman he was which had fo
curteoufly intertayned hir that Nyght, and of whome fhee felt

the new wound in hir heart, called an olde Gentlewoman of honor
which had nurfed hir and brought her vp, vnto whom fhe fayd
leaning vpon hir fhoulder: "Mother, what two young Gentlemen
be they which firft goe forth with the two Torches before them."
Vnto whome the old Gentlewoman told the name of the houfes
wherof they came. Then fhe afked hir againe, what young gentleman that was which holdeth the vifarde in his hand, wyth the
damafke cloke about him. "It is" (quod fhe) "Romeo Mon-
tefche, the fonne of youre Father's capytall Enimye and deadly foe
to all your kinne." But the Mayden at the onely Name of Mon-
tefche was altogyther amazed, defpayrynge for euer to attayne to
hufband hir great affectyoned fryend Rhomeo, for the auncyent
hatreds betweene thofe two Families. Neuertheleffe fhe knewe fo
well how to diffemble hir grief and difcontented Minde, as the olde
Gentlewoman perceiued nothing, who then began to perfuade hir
to retire into hir Chamber: whom fhe obeyed, and being in bed,
thinking to take hir wonted reft, a great tempeft of diuers thoughtes
began to enuiron and trouble hir Mynde, in futch wyfe as fhee
was not able to clofe hir Eyes, but turninge heere and there, fantafied diuers things in hir thought, fometimes purpofed to cut of the
whole attempte of that amorous practife, fometimes to continue
the fame. Thus was the poor pucell vexed with two contraries,
the one comforted hir to purfue hir intent, the other propofed the
immynente Perill wherevnto vndyfcretly fhe headlong threwe hir
felf: and after fhe had wandred of long time in this amorous Labe-
rinth, fhe knew not whereuppon to refolue, but wept inceffantly,
and accufed hir felfe, faying: "Ah, Caitife and myferable Creature,
from whence do rife thefe vnaccuftomed Trauayles which I feele
in Mynde, prouokynge mee to loofe my refte: but infortunate
wretch, what doe I know if that yong Gentleman doe loue mee
as hee fayeth. It may be vnder the vaile of fugred woordes he
goeth about to fteale away mine honore, to be reuenged of my
Parentes whych haue offended his, and by that meanes to my
euerlaftinge reproche to make me the fable of the Verona people."
Afterwardes fodainly as fhe condempned that which fhe fufpected
in the beginning, fayd: "Is it poffible that vnder futch beautye
and rare comelyneffe, dyfloyaltye and treafon may haue theyr

Syedge and Lodgynge? If it bee true that the Face is the faythfull
Meſſanger of the Mynde's Conceypte, I may bee aſſured that hee
doeth loue mee: for I marked ſo many chaunged Colours in his
Face in time of his talke with me, and ſawe hym ſo tranſported
and beſides himſelfe, as I cannot wyſhe any other more certayne
Iucke of Loue, wherein I wyll perſyſt immutable to the laſte gaſpe
of Lyfe, to the intente I may haue hym to bee my huſband: for
it maye ſo come to paſſe, as this newe aliaunce ſhall engender a
perpetuall peace and Amity betweene hys Houſe and mine." Ar-
reſtinge then vppon this determynation ſtyll, as ſhe ſaw Rhomeo
paſſinge before hir Father's Gate, ſhe ſhewed hir ſelfe with merry
countenance, and followed him ſo with loke of Eye, vntill ſhe had
loſt his ſight. And continuing this manner of Lyfe for certaine
Dayes, Rhomeo not able to content himſelf with lookes, daily did
behold and marke the ſituation of the houſe, and one day amongs
others hee eſpied Iulietta at hir Chamber Window, bounding vpon
a narrow Lane, ryght ouer againſt which Chamber he had a Gardein
which was the cauſe that Rhomeo fearing diſcouery of their loue,
began the day time to paſſe no more before the Gate, but ſo ſoone
as the Night with his browne Mantell had couered the Earth, hee
walked alone vp and downe that little ſtreat: and after he had
bene there many times, miſſing the chiefeſt cauſe of his comming,
Iulietta impacient of hir euill, one night repaired to hir window,
and perceiued throughe the bryghtneſſe of the Moone hir friend
Rhomeo vnder hir window, no leſſe attended for, than hee hymſelfe was waighting. Then ſhe ſecretly with Teares in hir Eyes,
and wyth voyce interrupted by ſighes, ſayd: "Signior Rhomeo,
me thinke that you hazarde your perſon to mutch, and commyt the
ſame into great Daunger at thys time of the Nyght, to protrude
your ſelf to the Mercy of them which meane you little good. Who
yf they had taken would haue cut you in pieces, and mine honor
(which I eſteme dearer than my lyfe,) hindred and ſuſpected for
euer." "Madame" aunſwered Rhomeo, "my Lyfe is in the Hand
of God, who only can diſpoſe the ſame: howbeyt yf any Man had
ſoughte menes to beryeue mee of my Lyfe, I ſhould (in the preſence of you) haue made him knowen what mine ability had ben
to defend the ſame. Notwythſtandyng Lyfe is not ſo deare, and

of futch eftimation wyth me, but that I coulde vouchfafe to facry-
fice the fame for your fake : and althoughe my myfhappe had bene
fo greate, as to bee dyfpatched in that Place, yet had I no caufe
to be forrye therefore, excepte it had bene by lofynge the meanes,
and way how to make you vnderftande the good wyll and duety
which I beare you, defyrynge not to conferue the fame for anye
commodytye that I hope to haue thereby, nor for anye other
refpecte, but onelye to Loue, Serue, and Honor you, fo long as
breath fhal remaine in me." So foone as he had made an end of
his talke, loue and pity began to feaze vpon the heart of Iulietta,
and leaning hir head vpon hir hand, hauing hir face all befprent
wyth teares, fhe faid vnto Rhomeo : "Syr Rhomeo, I pray you
not to renue that grief agayne : for the onely Memory of futch
inconuenyence, maketh me to counterpoyfe betwene death and
Lyfe, my heart being fo vnited with yours, as you cannot receyue
the leaft Iniury in this world, wherein I fhall not be fo great a
Partaker as your felf : befeechyng you for conclufion, that if you
defire your owne health and mine, to declare vnto me in fewe
Wordes what youre determynation is to attaine : for if you couet any
other fecrete thing at my Handes, more than myne Honoure can
well allowe, you are marueloufly deceiued : but if your defire be
godly, and that the frendfhip which you proteft to beare mee, be
founded vppon Vertue, and to bee concluded by Maryage, receiuing me for your wyfe and lawfull Spoufe, you fhall haue futch
part in me, as whereof without any regard to the obedience and
reuerence that I owe to my Parentes, or to the auncient Enimity of
oure Famylyes, I wyll make you the onely Lord and Mayfter [ouer
me], and of all the thyngys that I poffeffe, being preft and ready
in all poyntes to folow your commaundement : but if your intent
be otherwyfe, and thinke to reape the Fruycte of my Virginity, vnder
pretenfe of wanton Amity, you be greatly deceiued, and doe pray
you to auoide and fuffer me from henceforth to lyue and reft amongs
myne equals." Rhomeo whych looked for none other thyng, holding vp his Handes to the Heauens, wyth incredible ioy and contentation, aunfwered : "Madame, for fo mutch as it hath pleafed
you to doe me that honour to accepte me for futch a one, I accorde
and confent to your requeft, and doe offer vnto you the beft part

of my heart, which fhall remayn with you for guage and fure tes-
timony of my faying, vntill futch tyme as God fhall giue me leaue
to make you the entier owner and poffeffor of the fame. And to
the intent I may begyn myn enterpryfe, to morrow I will to the
Frier Laurence for counfell in the fame, who befides that he is my
ghoftly father is accuftomed to giue me inftruction in al my other
fecret affaires, and fayle not (if you pleafe) to meete me agayne in
this place at this very hour, to the intent I may giue you to vnderftand the deuice betwene him and me." Which fhe lyked very
well, and ended their talke for that time. Rhomeo receyuing none
other fauour at hir hands for that night, but only Wordes. Thys
Fryer Laurence, of whom hereafter wee fhall make more ample mention, was an auncient Doctor of Diuinity, of the order of the Fryers
Minors, who befides the happy profeffion which he had made in
ftudy of holy writ, was very fkilful in Philofophy, and a great
fearcher of nature's Secrets, and exceeding famous in Magike
knowledge, and other hidden and fecret fciences, which nothing
diminifhed his reputation, bicaufe hee did not abufe the fame.
And this Frier through his vertue and piety, had fo well won
the citizens hearts of Verona, as he was almoft the Confeffor
to them all, and of all men generally reuerenced and beloued:
and many tymes for his great prudence was called by the lords of
the Citty, to the hearing of their weighty caufes. And amonges
other he was greatly fauored by the Lorde of Efcale, that
tyme the principall gouernor of Verona, and of all the Family of
Montefches, and of the Capellets, and of many other. The young
Rhomeo (as we haue already declared) from his tender age, bare a
certayne particuler amity to Frier Laurence, and departed to him
his fecrets, by meanes whereof fo foone as he was gone from Iulietta, went ftrayght to the Fryers Francifcians, where from poinct
to poinct he difcourfed the fucceffe of his loue to that good father,
and the conclufion of mariage betwene him and Iulietta, adding
vpon the ende of talke, that hee woulde rather choofe fhamefull
death, than to fayle hir of his promife. To whom the good Frier
after he had debated diuers matters, and propofed al the inconueniences of that fecret mariage, exhorted hym to more mature deliberation of the fame: notwithftandinge, all the alleged perfua-

fions were not able to reuoke his promyfe. Wherefore the Frier
vanquifhed with his ftubborneffe, and alfo forecafting in his mynde
that the mariage might be fome meanes of reconciliation of thofe
two houfes, in th'end agreed to his requeft, intreating him, that he
myght haue one dayes refpit for leyfure to excogitate what was beft
to be done. But if Rhomeo for his part was carefull to prouide for his
affayres, Iulietta lykewife did her indeuour. For feeing that fhee
had none about her to whom fhe might difcouer her paffions, fhee
deuifed to impart the whole to hir Nurfe which lay in her Chamber,
appoynéted to wayte vppon hir, to whom fhe committed the
intier fecrets of the loue betwene Rhomeo and hir. And although
the olde Woman in the beginninge refifted Iulietta hir intent, yet
in the ende fhe knew fo wel how to perfuade and win hir, that fhe
promifed in all that fhe was able to do, to be at hir commaundement. And then fhe fent hir with all diligence to fpeake to
Rhomeo, and to know of him by what meanes they might be
maried, and that he would do hir to vnderftand the determination
betwene Fryer Laurence and him. Whom Rhomeo aunfwered, how
the firft day wherein he had informed Fryer Laurence of the matter,
the fayde Fryer deferred aunfwere vntil the next, which was the very
fame, and that it was not paft one houre fithens he returned with
finall refolution, and that Frier Laurence and he had deuifed, that
fhe the Saterday following, fhould craue leaue of hir mother to go
to confeffion, and to repayre to the Church of Saynét Francis,
where in a certayne Chappell fecretly they fhould be maried, praying hir in any wyfe not to fayle to be there. Which thinge fhe
brought to paffe with futch difcretion, as hir mother agreed to hir
requeft: and accompanied onely wyth hir gouerneffe, and a young
mayden, fhe repayred thither at the determined day and tyme.
And fo foone as fhe was entred the Church, fhe called for the good
Doétor Fryer Laurence, vnto whom anfwere was made that he was
in the fhriuing Chappell, and forthwith aduertifement was gieuen
him of hir comming. So foone as Fryer Laurence was certified of
Iulietta, hee went into the body of the Church, and willed the olde
Woman and yong mayden to go heare feruice, and that when hee
had heard the confeffion of Iulietta, he would fend for them
agayn. Iulietta beinge entred a little Cell wyth Frier Laurence,

he fhut faft the dore as he was wont to do, where Rhomeo and he
had bin together fhut faft in, the fpace of one whole hour before.
Then Frier Laurence after that he had fhriued them, fayd to Iulietta:
"Daughter, as Rhomeo here prefent hath certified me, you be
agreed, and contented to take him to hufband, and he likewife you
for his Efpoufe and Wyfe. Do you now ftill perfift and continue
in that mynde?" The Louers aunfwered that they defired none
other thing. The Fryer feeing theyr conformed and agreeable
willes, after he had difcourfed fomewhat vppon the commendation
of mariage dignity, pronounced the vfuall woordes of the Church,
and fhe hauing receyued the Ring from Rhomeo, they rofe vp
before the Fryer, who fayd vnto them: "If you haue any other
thing to conferre together, do the fame wyth fpeede: for I purpofe that Rhomeo fhall goe from hence fo fecretly as he can."
Rhomeo fory to goe from Iulietta fayde fecretly vnto hir,
that fhee fhould fend vnto hym after diner the old Woman,
and that he would caufe to be made a corded Ladder the fame
euening, thereby to climbe vp to her Chamber window, where at
more leifure they would deuife of their affaires. Things determined betwene them, either of them retyred to their houfe with
incredible contentation, attendinge the happy houre for confummation of their mariage. When Rhomeo was come home to his
houfe, he declared wholly what had paffed betwen him and Iulietta,
vnto a Seruaunt of his called Pietro, whofe fidelity he had fo greatly
tryed, as he durft haue trufted him with hys life, and commaunded
hym wyth expedition to prouide a Ladder of Cordes wyth 2 ftrong
Hookes of Iron faftned to both endes, which he eafily did, becaufe
they were mutch vfed in Italy. Iulietta did not forget in the
Euening about fiue of the Clocke, to fend the olde Woman to
Rhomeo, who hauing prepared all things neceffary, caufed the
Ladder to be deliuered vnto her, and prayed hir to require Iulietta
the fame euening not to fayle to bee at the accuftomed place. But
if this Iorney feemed long to thefe two paffioned Louers, let other
Iudge, that haue at other tymes affayed the lyke: for euery minute
of an houre feemed to them a Thoufande yeares, fo that if they had
power to commaund the Heauens (as Iofua did the Sunne) the
Earth had incontinently bene fhadowed wyth darkeft Cloudes. The

apoynƈted houre come, Rhomeo put on the moſt ſumptuous
apparell hee had, and conduƈted by good fortune neere to the
place where his heart tooke lyfe, was ſo fully determined of hys
purpoſe, as eaſily hee clymed vp the Garden wall. Beinge arriued
hard to the wyndow, he perceyued Iulietta, who had already ſo well
faſtned the Ladder to draw him vp, as without any daunger at all,
he entred hir chambre, which was ſo clere as the day, by reaſon of
the Tapers of virgin Wax, which Iulietta had cauſed to be lighted,
that ſhe might the better beholde hir Rhomeo. Iulietta for hir
part, was but in hir night kerchief: who ſo ſoon as ſhe perceyued
him colled him about the Neck, and after ſhee had kiſſed and re-
kiſſed hym a million of times, began to imbrace hym betwene hir
armes, hauing no power to ſpeake vnto him, but by Sighes onely,
holding hir mouth cloſe againſt his, and being in this traunce
beheld him with pitifull eye, which made him to liue and die
together. And afterwards ſomewhat come to hir ſelfe, ſhe ſayd
with ſighes deeply fetched from the bottom of hir heart: "Ah
Rhomeo, the exampler of al vertue and gentlenes, moſt hartely
welcome to this place, wherein for your lacke, and abſence, and
for feare of your perſon, I haue guſhed forth ſo many Teares as the
ſpring is almoſt dry: but now that I hold you betwen my armes,
let death and fortune doe what they liſt. For I count my ſelfe
more than ſatiſſied of all my ſorrowes paſt, by the fauour alone of
your preſence." Whom Rhomeo with weeping eye, giuing ouer
ſilence aunſwered: "Madame, for ſomutch as I neuer receyued ſo
mutch of fortune's grace, as to make you feele by liuely experience
what power you had ouer me, and the torment euery minute of the
day ſuſtained for your occaſion, I do aſſure you the leaſt grief
that vexeth me for your abſence, is a thouſand times more paynefull than death, which long time or this had cut of the threede of
my lyfe, if the hope of this happy Iourney had not bene, which
paying mee now the iuſt Tribute of my weepings paſt, maketh me
better content, and more glad, than if the whole Worlde were at
my commaundement, beſeeching you (without further memory of
auncient griefe) to take aduice in tyme to come how we may content our paſſionate hearts, and to ſort our affayres with ſutch
Wyſedome and diſcretion, as our enimies without aduantage may

let vs continue the remnant of our dayes in reſt and quiet." And
as Iulietta was about to make anſwere, the Olde woman came in
the meane time, and ſayd vnto them : " He that waſteth time in
talke, recouereth the ſame to late. But for ſo mutch as eyther of
you hath endured ſutch mutuall paynes, behold (quoth ſhee) a
campe which I haue made ready : " (ſhewing them the Fielde bed
which ſhee had prepared and furniſhed,) whereunto they eaſily
agreed, and being then betwene the Sheets in priuy bed, after they
had gladded and cheriſhed themſelues with al kinde of delicate
embracements which loue was able to deuiſe, Rhomeo vnlooſing
the holy lines of virginity, tooke poſſeſſion of the place, which
was not yet beſieged with ſutch ioy and contentation as they can
iudge which haue aſſayed like delites. Their marriage thus conſummate, Rhomeo perceyuing the morning make to haſty approch,
tooke his leaue, making promiſe that he would not fayle wythin a
day or two to reſort agayne to the place by lyke meanes, and
ſemblable time, vntil Fortune had prouided ſure occaſion vnfear-
fully to manyfeſt their marriage to the whole Worlde. And thus
a month or twayne, they continued their ioyful mindes to their
incredible ſatiſſaction, vntil lady Fortune enuious of their proſperity,
turned hir Wheele to tumble them into ſuch a bottomleſſe pit, as
they payed hir vſury for their pleaſures paſt, by a certaine moſt
cruell and pitifull death, as you ſhal vnderſtand hereafter by the
diſcourſe that followeth. Now as we haue before declared, the
Capellets and the Monteſches were not ſo well reconciled by the
Lord of Verona, but that there reſted in them ſutch ſparks of
auncient diſpleaſures, as either partes waited but for ſome light
occaſion to draw togethers, which they did in the Eaſter holy
dayes, (as bloudy men commonly be moſt willingly diſpoſed after
a good time to commit ſome nefarious deede) beſides the Gate of
Bourſarie leading to the olde caſtel of Verona, a troupe of Capellets rencountred with certayne of the Monteſches, and without
other woordes began to ſet vpon them. And the Capellets had
for Chiefe of their glorious enterpriſe one called Thibault, coſin
Germayne to Iulietta, a yong man ſtrongly made, and of good
experience of armes, who exhorted his Companions with ſtout
Stomakes to repreſſe the boldnes of the Monteſches, that ther

might from that time forth no memory of them be left at all.
The rumoure of this fray was difperffed throughout al the corners
of Verona, that fuccour might come from all partes of the Citty
to depart the fame. Whereof Rhomeo aduertized, who walked
alonges the Citty with certayne of his Companions, hafted him
fpeadily to the place where the flaughter of his Parents and alies
were committed: and after he had well aduifed and beholden
many wounded and hurt on both fides, he fayd to hys Companions:
"My frends let vs part them, for they be fo flefht one vpon an
other, as will all be hewed to pieces before the game be done."
And faying fo, he thruft himfelfe amids the troupe, and did no
more but part the blowes on eyther fide, crying vpon them aloud:
"My freends, no more, it is time henceforth that our quarel ceafe.
For befides the prouocation of God's iuft wrath, our two families
be flaunderous to the whole World, and are the caufe that this
common wealth doth grow vnto diforder." But they were fo egre
and furious one agaynft the other, as they gaue no audience to
Rhomeo his councel, and bent theymfelues too kyll, dyfmember
and teare eche other in pieces. And the fyght was fo cruell and
outragious betweene them as they which looked on, were amafed
to fee theym endure thofe blowes, for the grounde was all couered
with armes, legges, thighes, and bloude, wherein no figne of coward-
nes appeared, and mayntayned their feyghte fo longe, that none
was able to iudge who hadde the better, vntill that Thibault Coufin
to Iulietta inflamed with ire and rage, turned towardes Rhomeo
thinkinge with a pricke to runne him through. But he was fo
wel armed and defended with a priuye coat whiche he wore
ordinarily for the doubt he had of the Capellets, as the pricke
rebounded: vnto whom Rhomeo made anfweare: "Thibault thou
maieft know by the pacience which I haue had vntill this prefent
tyme, that I came not hether to fyght with thee or thyne, but to
feeke peace and attonemente betweene vs, and if thou thinkeft
that for defaulte of courage I haue fayled myne endeuor, thou
doeft great wrouge to my reputacion. And impute thys my
fuffrance to fome other perticular refpecte, rather than to wante
of ftomacke. Wherfore abufe mee not but be content with this
greate effufion of Bloude and murders already committed. And

prouoke mee not I befeeche thee to paffe the boundes of my good
will and mynde." "Ah Traitor," fayd Thibaulte, "thou thinkefte
to faue thy felfe by the plotte of thy pleafaunt tounge, but fee that
thou defende thy felfe, els prefently I will make thee feele that thy
tounge fhal not gard thy corps, nor yet be the Buckler to defende
the fame from prefent death." And faying fo, he gaue him a blow
with fuch furye, as hadde not other warded the fame hee had cutte
of his heade from his fhoulders, and the one was no readyer to
lende, but the other incontinentlye was able to paye agayne, for
hee being not onelye wroth with the blowe that hee had receiued,
but offended with the iniury which the other had don, began to
purfue his ennemy with fuche courage and viuacity, as at the third
blowe with his fwerd hee caufed him to fall backewarde ftarke
deade vppon the grounde with a pricke vehementlye thrufte into
his throte, whiche hee followed till hys Sworde appeared throughe
the hynder parte of the fame, by reafon wherof the conflicte ceaffed.
For befides that Thibault was the chiefe of his companye he was
alfo borne of one of the Nobleft houfes within the Cittye, which
caufed the Poteftate to affemble his Souldiers with diligence for
the apprehenfion and imprifonment of Rhomeo, who feyeng yl
fortune at hande, in fecrete wife conuayed him felfe to Fryer
Laurence at the Friers Francifcanes. And the Fryer vnderftandinge
of his facte, kepte him in a certayne fecrete place of his couente
vntil fortune did otherwyfe prouyde for his fafe goinge abroade.
The bruite fpred throughout the citty, of this chaunce don vpon
the Lorde Thibault, the Capellets in mourning weedes caufed the
deade bodye to be caryed before the fygnory of Verona, fo well to
moue them to pytty, as to demaunde iuftice for the murder: before
whom came alfo the Montefches, declaryng the innocencye of
Rhomeo, and the wilfull affault of the other. The councell affembled and witneffes heard on both partes a ftraight commaundemente was geuen by the Lorde of the Cittye to geeue ouer theire
weapons, and touchinge the offence of Rhomeo, becaufe he hadde
killed the other in his owne defence, he was banifhed Verona for
euer. This common miffortune publifhed throughout the Citty,
was generally forowed and lamented. Som complayneth the death
of the Lorde Thibault, fo well for his dexteritye in armes as for the

hope of his great good feruice in time to come, if hee hadde not
bene preuented by futch cruell Death. Other bewailed (fpecially
the Ladies and Gentlewomen) the ouerthrow of yong Rhomeo, who
befides his beauty and good grace wherwith he was enriched, had
a certayne naturall allurement, by vertue whereof he drew vnto
him the hearts of eche man, like as the ftony Adamante doth the
cancred iron, in futch wife as the whole nation and people of Verona lamented his mifchaunce : but aboue all infortunate Iulietta,
who aduertifed both of the death of hir cofin Thibault, and of the
banifhment of hir hufband, made the Ayre found with infinite
number of mornefull playnts and miferable lamentations. Then
feeling hirfelfe to mutch outraged with extreeme paffion, fhe went
into hir chamber, and ouercome with forrowe threwe hir felfe
vpon hir bed, where fhe began to reinforce hir dolor after fo
ftraunge fafhion, as the moft conftant would haue bene moued to
pitty. Then like one out of hir wits, fhe gazed heere and there,
and by fortune beholding the Window whereat Rhomeo was wont
to enter into hir chamber, cried out : " Oh vnhappy Windowe, oh
entry moft vnlucky, wherein were wouen the bitter toyle of my
former mifhaps, if by thy meanes I haue receyued at other tymes
fome light pleafure or tranfitory contentation, thou now makeft me
pay a tribute fo rigorous and paynefull, as my tender body not able
any longer to fupport the fame, fhall henceforth open the Gate to
that lyfe where the ghoft difcharged from this mortal burden, fhal
feeke in fome place els more affured reft. Ah Rhomeo, Rhomeo,
when acquayntaunce firft began betweene vs, and reclined myne
eares vnto thy fuborned promiffes, confirmed with fo many othes,
I would neuer haue beleeued that in place of our continued amyty,
and in appeafing of the hatred of our houfes, thou wouldeft haue
fought occafion to breake the fame by an acte fo fhamefull, whereby
thy fame fhall be fpotted for euer, and I miferable wretch defolate
of Spoufe and Companion. But if thou haddeft beene fo gready
after the Cappelletts bloud, wherefore didft thou fpare the deare
bloud of mine owne heart when fo many tymes, and in futch
fecret place the fame was at the mercy of thy cruell handes? The
victory which thou fhouldeft haue gotten ouer me, had it not bene
glorious inough for thine ambitious minde, but for more trium-

phant folempnity to bee crowned wyth the bloude of my deareſt kinſman? Now get thee hence therefore into ſome other place to deceiue ſome other, ſo vnhappy as my ſelfe. Neuer come agayne in place where I am, for no excuſe ſhall heereafter take holde to aſſwage mine offended minde: in the meane tyme I ſhall lament the reſt of my heauy lyfe, with ſutch ſtore of teares, as my body dried vp from all humidity, ſhall ſhortly ſearch reliefe in Earth." And hauing made an ende of thoſe hir wordes, hir heart was ſo grieuouſly ſtrayned, as ſhee coulde neyther weepe nor ſpeake, and ſtoode ſo immoueable, as if ſhe had bene in a traunce.   Then being ſomewhat come agayne vnto hirſelfe, with feeble voyce ſhee ſayd: "Ah, murderous tongue of other men's honor, how dareſt thou ſo infamouſly to ſpeake of him whom his very enimies doe commend and prayſe? How preſumeſt thou to impute the blame vpon Rhomeo, whoſe vnguiltines and innocent deede euery man alloweth? Where from henceforth ſhall be hys refuge, ſith ſhe which ought to bee the onely Bulwarke, and aſſured rampire of his diſtreſſe, doth purſue and defame him? Receyue, receyue then Rhomeo the ſatiſfaction of mine ingratitude by the ſacrifice which I ſhal make of my proper lyfe, and ſo the faulte which I haue committed agaynſte thy loyaltye, ſhall bee made open to the Worlde, thou being reuenged and my ſelfe puniſhed." And thinking to vſe ſome further talke, all the powers of hir body fayled hir wyth ſignes of preſent death. But the good olde Woman whych could not imagine the cauſe of Iulietta hir longe abſence, doubted very mutch that ſhe ſuffred ſome paſſion, and ſought hir vp and downe in euery place wythin hir Father's Pallace, vntill at length ſhee founde hir lyinge a long vpon hir Bed, all the outwarde parts of hir body ſo colde as Marble. But the goode Old woman which thought hir to bee deade, began to cry like one out of hir Wittes, ſaying: "Ah deare Daughter, and Nourſechylde, howe mutch doeth thy death now grieue mee at the very heart?" And as ſhe was feeling all the partes of hir body, ſhee perceyued ſome ſparke of Lyfe to bee yet within the ſame, whych cauſed hir to call hir many tymes by her name, til at length ſhe brought her oute of her founde, then ſayde vnto her: "Why Iulietta, myne owne deare darelyng, what meane you by this tormoylinge of your ſelfe? I

cannot tel from whence this youre behauiour and that immoderate heauines doe proceede, but wel I wot that within this houre
I thought to haue accompanied you to the graue." "Alas good
mother" (aunfwered woful Iulietta) "do you not moft euidently
perceiue and fee what iuft caufe I haue too forrow and complayne,
loofyng at one inftante two perfons of the world which wer vnto
mee moft deare?" "Methinke," aunfweared the good woman,
"that it is not feemely for a gentlewoman of your degree to fall
into fuch extremetye: for in tyme of tribulation wyfedome fhould
moft preuaile. And if the lord Thibault be deade do you thinke
to get him agayn by teares? What is he that doth not accufe his
ouermutch prefumption: woulde you that Rhomeo hadd done that
wronge to him, and hys houfe, to fuffer himfelfe outraged and
affayled by one to whom in manhoode and proweffe he is not
inferioure? Sufficeth you that Rhomeo is alyue, and his affayres
in futche eftate whoe in tyme may be called home agayne from
banifhmente, for he is a greate lorde, and as you know well allied
and fauored of all men, wherefore arme your felfe from henceforth
with pacyence: for albeit that Fortune doth eftraunge him from
you for a tyme, yet fure I am, that hereafter fhee will reftore him
vnto you agayne wyth greater ioye and Contentatyon than before.
And to the Ende that wee bee better affured in what ftate he is,
yf you wyll promyfe me to gyue ouer your heauyneffe, I wyll to
Daye knowe of Fryer Laurence whether he is gone." To which requeft Iulietta agreed, and then the good woman repayred to S.
Frauncis, wher fhee founde Fryer Laurence who tolde her that the
fame nyghte Rhomeo would not fayle at hys accuftomed houre
to vifite Iulietta, and there to do hir to vnderftande what he
purpofed to doe in tyme to come. This iorney then fared like the
voiages of mariners, who after they haue ben toft by greate and
troublous tempeft feeyng fome Sunne beame pearce the heauens
to lyghten the lande, affure themfelues agayne, and thinkinge to
haue auoyded fhipwracke, and fodaynlye the feas begynne to
fwell, the waues do roare with futch vehemence and noyfe, as if
they were fallen agayne into greater danger than before. The affigned hour come, Rhomeo fayled not accordinge to hys promife
to bee in his Garden, where he founde his furniture preft to mount

the Chamber of Iulietta, who with difplayed armes, began fo
ftrayghtly to imbrace hym, as it feemed that the foule would haue
abandoned hir body. And they two more than a large quarter of
an hour were in futch agony, as they were not able to pronounce
one word, and wetting ech others Face faft clofed together, the
teares trickeled downe in futch abundance as they feemed to be
throughly bathed therein, which Rhomeo perceyuing, thinking to
ftay thofe immoderate teares, fayd vnto hir: " Myne owne deareft
freend Iulietta, I am not now determined to recite the particulars
of the ftraung happes of frayle and inconftaunte Fortune, who in a
moment hoifteth a man vp to the hygheft degree of hir wheele,
and by and by, in leffe fpace than in the twynckeling of an eye,
fhe throweth hym downe agayne fo lowe, as more mifery is prepared for him in one day, than fauour in one hundred yeares: whych
I now proue, and haue experience in my felfe, which haue bene
nourifhed delicately amonges my frends, and maynteyned in futch
profperous ftate, as you doe little know, (hoping for the full per-
feftion of my felicity) by meanes of our mariage to haue recon-
cifed our Parents, and frends, and to conduft the refidue of my
lyfe, according to the fcope and lot determined by Almighty God:
and neuertheleffe all myne enterprifes be put backe, and my pur-
pofes tourned cleane contrary, in futch wife as from henceforth I
muft wander lyke a vagabonde through diuers Prouinces, and
fequeftrate my felfe from my Frends, wythout affured place of
myne abode, whych I defire to let you weete, to the intent you
may be exhorted in tyme to come, paciently to beare fo well
myne abfence, as that whych it fhal pleafe God to appoint." But
Iulietta, al affrighted wyth teares and mortal agonies, would not
fuffer hym to paffe any further, but interruptinge his purpofe,
fayd vnto hym: " Rhomeo, how canft thou be fo harde hearted
and voyde of all pity, to leaue mee heere lone, befieged with fo
manye deadlye myferies? There is neyther houre nor Minute,
wherein death doth not appeare a thoufand tymes before mee, and
yet my miffehappe is futch, as I can not dye, and therefore doe
manyfeftlye perceyue, that the fame death preferueth my lyfe,
of purpofe to delight in my gryefes, and tryumphe ouer my euyls.
And thou lyke the mynifter and tyrante of hir cruelty, doeft make

no confcience (for ought that I can fee) hauing atchieued the
Summe of thy defyres and pleafures on me, to abandon and forfake me: whereby I well perceyue, that all the lawes of Amity
are deade and vtterly extinguyfhed, forfomutch as he in whom
I had greateft hope and confidence, and for whofe fake I am become an enimy to my felf, doth difdayne and contemne me. No,
no Rhomeo, thou muft fully refolue thy felfe vppon one of thefe
II. points, either to fee me incontinently throwen down headlong from this high Window after thee: or elfe to fuffer me to
accompany thee into that Countrey or Place whither Fortune fhall
guide thee: for my heart is fo mutch tranfformed into thine, that
fo foone as I fhall vnderftande of thy departure, prefently my lyfe
will depart this wofull body: the continuance whereof I doe not
defire for any other purpofe, but only to delight my felfe in thy
prefence, to bee pertaker of thy miffortunes: and therefore if euer
there lodged any pity in the heart of gentleman, I befeeche the
Rhomeo with al humility, that it may now finde place in thee, and
that thou wilt vouchfafe to receyue me for thy feruaunt, and the
faithful companion of thy mifhaps: and if thou thinke that thou canft
not conueniently receyue me in the eftate and habite of a Wyfe, who
fhall let me to chaunge myne apparell? Shall I be the firft that haue
vfed like fhiftes to efcape the tyranny of parentes? Dofte thou doubt
that my feruice will not bee fo good vnto thee as that of Petre thy
feruaunte? Wyll my loyaltye and fidelity be leffe than his? My
beauty which at other tymes thou haft fo greatly commended, it is
not efteemed of thee? my teares, my loue, and the aunciente pleafures
and delights that you haue taken in mee fhal they be in obliuyon?"
Rhomeo feing hir in thefe alterations, fearing that worffe inconue-
nience would chaunce, tooke hir agayne betweene hys armes, and
kiffing her amoroufly, fayd: Iulietta, the onely miftreffe of
my heart, I pray thee in the Name of God, and for the feruent
Loue whych thou beareft vnto me, to doe away thofe vayne cogitations, excepte thou meane to feeke and hazard the deftruction of
vs both: for if thou perfeuer in this purpofe, there is no remedye
but wee mufte both perifh: for fo foone as thyne abfence fhalbe
knowen, thy Father will make futch earneft purfute after vs, that
we cannot choofe but be difcried and taken, and in the ende cruelly

punifhed, I as a theefe and ftealer of thee, and thou as a dyfobe-
dyent Daughter to thy Father: and fo in ftead of pleafaunt and
quiet Lyfe, our Dayes fhalbe abridged by moft fhamefull Death.
But if thou wylt recline thy felf to reafon, (the ryght rule of
humane Lyfe,) and for the tyme abandon our mutuall delyghts, I
will take futch order in the time of my banifhment, as within three
or foure Months wythoute any delay, I fhalbe reuoked home agayne:
but if it fall out otherwyfe (as I truft not,) howfoeuer it happen,
I wyll come agayne vnto thee, and with the helpe of my Fryendes
wyll fetch the from Verona by ftrong Hand, not in Counterfeit
Apparell as a ftraunger, but lyke my fpoufe and perpetuall companion: in the meane tyme quyet your felfe, and be fure that
nothing elfe but death fhall deuide and put vs a funder." The
reafons of Rhomeo fo mutch preuailed with Iulietta, as fhee made
hym thys aunfwere: "My deare fryend, I wyll doe nothing contrary to your wyll and pleafure: and to what place fo euer you
repayre, my hearte fhall bee your owne, in like forte as you haue
giuen yours to be mine: in the meane while I pray you not to
faile oftentimes to aduertife me by Frier Laurence, in what ftate
your affaires be, and fpecially of the place of your abode." Thus
thefe two pore louers paffed the Night togither, vntil the day
began to appeare which did dyuyde them, to their extreame
forrow and gryef. Rhomeo hauinge taken leaue of Iulietta, went
to S. Fraunces, and after he hadde aduertyfed Frier Laurence of
his affaires, departed from Verona in the habit of a Marchaunt
ftraunger, and vfed futch expedytyon, as without hurt he arriued at
Mantuona, (accompanied onely wyth Petre his Seruaunt, whome
hee haftily fente backe agayne to Verona, to ferue his Father)
where he tooke a houfe: and lyuying in honorable companye,
affayed certayne Monthes to put away the gryefe whych fo tormented him. But duryng the tyme of his abfence, miferable
Iulietta could not fo cloke hir forrow, but that through the euyll
colour of hir face, hir inwarde paffion was difcryed: by reafon
whereof hir Mother, who heard hir oftentimes fighing, and inces-
fantly complayning, coulde not forbeare to fay vnto hir:
"Daughter, if you continue long after thys fort, you wyll haften
the Death of your good Father and me, who loue you fo dearely as

our owne lyues: wherefore henceforth moderate your heauineſſe, and endeuor your ſelf to be mery: think no more vpon the Death of your coſin Thibault, whome (ſith it pleaſed God to cal away) do you thinke to reuoke wyth Teares, and ſo withſtande his Almightye will?" But the pore Gentlewoman not able to dyſſemble hir griefe, ſayd vnto hir: "Madame, long time it is ſithens the laſt Teares for Thibault were poured forth, and I beleue that the fountayne is ſo well ſoked and dried vp, as no more will ſpryng in that place." The mother which could not tell to what effect thoſe Woords were ſpoken held hir peace, for feare ſhe ſhould trouble hir Daughter: and certayne Dayes after ſeeing hir to continue in heauineſſe and continuall griefs, aſſaied by al meanes poſſible to know, aſwell of hir, as of other the houſholde Seruauntes, the occaſion of their ſorrow, but al in vayne: wherwith the pore mother vexed beyonde meaſure, purpoſed to let the Lord Antonio hir Husband to vnderſtand the caſe of hir Daughter: and vppon a day ſeeing him at conuenient leiſure, ſhe ſayd vnto him: "My Lord, if you haue marked the countenaunce of our daughter, and hir kinde of behauior ſithens the Death of the Lord Thibault hir Coſyn, you ſhall perceiue ſo ſtraunge mutation in hir, as it will make you to maruell, for ſhe is not onely contented to forgoe meate, drinke and ſlepe, but ſhe ſpendeth hir tyme in nothinge elſe then in Weeping and Lamentatyon, delighting to kepe hir ſelf ſolytarye wythin hir Chamber, where ſhe tormenteth hir ſelf ſo outragiouſly as yf wee take not heede, hir Lyfe is to be doubted, and not able to knowe the Oryginall of hir Payne, the more difficulte ſhall be the remedye: for albeit that I haue ſought meanes by all extremity, yet cannot I learne the cauſe of hir ſickneſſe: and where I thought in the beginning, that it proceded vpon the Death of hir Coſin, now I doe manifeſtly perceiue the contrary, ſpecially when ſhe hir ſelf did aſſure me that ſhe had already wept and ſhed the laſt teares for him that ſhe was mynded to doe: and vncertayne whereuppon to reſolue, I do thinke verily that ſhe mourneth for ſome deſpite, to ſee the moſt part of theyr companions maried, and ſhe yet vnprouyded, perſuading with hir ſelfe (it may be) that wee hir Parents do not care for hir: wherefore deare Huſband, I heartely beſeech you for our reſt and hir quiet, that hereafter ye be carefull

to prouyde for hir fome maryage worthy of our ftate." Whereunto the Lord Antonio, willingly agreed, faying vnto hir: "Wyfe,
I haue many times thought vppon that whereof you fpeake, notwythftandyng fith as yet fhee is not attayned to the age of xviii.
yeares, I thought to prouide a hufband at leyfure: neuertheleffe
things beinge come to thefe Termes, and knowing the Virgins
chaftity is a dangerous Treafure, I wyll be mindfull of the fame
to your contentation, and fhe matched in futch wyfe, as fhe fhall
thynke the tyme hitherto well delayed.   In the meane while
marke dylygently whyther fhe bee in loue wyth any, to the end
that we haue not fo greate regarde to goodes, or the Nobylity of
the houfe wherein we meane to beftow hir, as to the Lyfe and
Health of our Daughter who is to me fo deare as I had rather die
a Begger without Landes or goods, than to beftow hir vpon one
which fhall vfe and intreat hir il."   Certayne dayes after that the
Lorde Antonio had bruted the maryage of his daughter, many
Gentlemen were futers, fo wel for the excellency of hir Beauty, as for
hir great Rycheffe and reuenue.   But aboue all others the alyaunce
of a young Earle named Paris, the Counte of Lodronne, lyked the
Lord Antonio: vnto whom lyberally he gaue his confent, and
told his Wyfe the party vppon whom he dyd mean to beftow his
Daughter.   The mother very ioyful that they had found fo honeft
a Gentleman for theyr Daughter, caufed hir fecretly to be called
before hir, doyng hir to vnderftande what things had paffed
betwen hir father and the Counte Paris, difcourfing vnto hir the
beauty and good grace of the yong Counte, the vertues for which
he was commended of al men, ioyning therevnto for conclufion the
great richeffe and fauor which he had in the goods of fortune, by
means whereof fhe and hir Fryends fhould liue in eternal honor:
but Iulietta which had rather to haue ben torne in pieces than to
agree to that maryage, anfwered hir mother with a more than accuftomed ftoutneffe: "Madame, I mutch maruel, and therewithal
am aftonned that you being a Ladye difcrete and honorable, wil
be fo liberal ouer your Daughter as to commit hir to the pleafure
and wil of an other, before you do know how hir mind is bent:
you may do as it pleafeth you, but of one thing I do wel affure
you, that if you bring it to paffe, it fhal be againft my wil: and

touching the regard and eſtimation of Counte Paris, I ſhal firſt loſe
my Lyfe before he ſhal haue power to touch any part of my body:
which being done, it is you that ſhal be counted the murderer, by
deliueryng me into the handes of him, whome I neyther can, wil,
or know whiche way to loue: wherefore I praye you to ſuffer me
henceforth thus to lyue, wythout taking any further care of me,
for ſo mutche as my cruell fortune hath otherwyſe diſpoſed of
me." The dolorous Mother which knewe not what Iudgement to
fixe vpon hir daughter's aunſwere, lyke a woman confuſed and
beſides hir ſelfe went to ſeeke the Lord Antonio, vnto whom without conceyling any part of hir Daughter's aunſwer, ſhe dyd him
vnderſtand the whole. The good olde man offended beyond
meaſure, commaunded her incontinently by Force to be brought
before him, if of hir own good will ſhe would not come: ſo ſoone
as ſhe came before hir Father, hir eyes full of teares, fel down at
his fete, which ſhe bathed with the luke warme drops that dis-
tilled from hir Eyes in great abundance, and thynkyng to open
hir mouth to crye him mercy, the ſobbes and ſighes many tymes
ſtopt hir ſpeach, that ſhee remained dumbe not able to frame a
Woorde. But the olde man nothing moued with his Daughter's
Teares, ſayd vnto hir in great rage: "Come hither thou vnkynd
and dyſobedient Daughter, haſt thou forgotten how many tymes
thou haſt hearde ſpoken at the Table, of the puiſſance and autho-
ryty our auncyente Romane Fathers had ouer their chyldren?
vnto whom it was not onelye lawfull to ſell, guage, and otherwyſe diſpoſe them (in theyr neceſſity) at their pleaſure, but alſo
which is more, they had abſolute power ouer their Death and Lyfe?
With what yrons, with what torments, with what racks would
thoſe good Fathers chaſten and correct thee if they were a liue
againe, to ſee that ingratitude, miſbehauior and diſobedience which
thou vſeſt towards thy Father, who with many prayers and requeſtes hath prouided one of the greateſt Lords of this prouince to
be thy huſband, a Gentleman of beſt renoume, and indued wyth
all kynde of Vertues, of whom thou and I be vnworthy, both for
the notable maſſe of goods and ſubſtance wherewith he is enriched,
as alſo for the Honoure and generoſitie of the houſe whereof hee
is diſcended, and yet thou playeſt the parte of an obſtinate and

rebellyous Chyld agaynft thy Father's will. I take the omnipo-
tency of that Almightye God to witneffe, which hath vouchfafed
to bryng the forth into this world, that if vpon Tuefday nexte
thou faileft to prepare thy felfe to be at my Caftell of Villafranco,
where the Counte Paris purpofeth to meete vs, and there giue thy
confent to that whych thy Mother and I haue agreed vppon, I will
not onely depriue thee of my worldly goodes, but alfo will make
the efpoufe and marie a pryfon fo ftraight and fharpe, as a thoufande times thou fhalt curfe the Day and tyme wherein thou waft
borne : wherfore from henceforth take aduifement what thou doeft,
for excepte the promife be kept which I haue made to the counte
Paris, I will make the feele how greate the iuft choler of an
offended Father is againft a Chylde vnkynde." And without ftay-
ing for other anfwer of his Daughter, the olde man departed the
Chamber, and lefte hir vppon hir knees. Iulietta knowing the
fury of hir Father, fearing to incurre his indignation, or to prouoke
his further wrath, retired for the day into hir Chamber, and contriued that whole Nyght more in weeping then flepyng. And the
next Morning fayning to goe heare feruice, fhe went forth with
the woman of hir Chamber to the Fryers, where fhe caufed father
Laurence to be called vnto hir, and prayed him to heare hir confeffion : and when fhe was vpon hir knees before hym, fhee began
hir Confeffion wyth Teares, tellinge him the greate mifchyefe that
was prepared for hir, by the maryage accorded betweene hir Father
and the Counte Paris: and for conclufion fayd vnto him : " Sir,
for fo mutch as you know that I cannot by God's law bee maried
twice, and that I haue but one God, one hufband and one faith,
I am determined when I am from hence, with thefe two hands
which you fee ioyned before you, this Day to ende my forowful
lyfe, that my foule may beare wytneffe in the Heauens, and my
bloude vppon the Earth of my faith and loyalty preferued."
Then hauyng ended hir talke, fhee looked about hir, and feemed
by hir wylde countenaunce, as though fhe had deuifed fome
finifter purpofe: wherefore Frier Laurence, aftonned beyonde
meafure, fearyng leaft fhe would haue executed that which fhe
was determyned, fayd vnto hir: "Miftreffe Iulietta, I pray you
in the name of God by little and little to moderate youre con-

ceiued griefe, and to content your felf whilft you bee heere, vntill
I haue prouided what is beft for you to doe, for before you part
from hence, I will giue you futch confolation and remedy for
your afflictions, as you fhall remaine fatyffied and contented."
And refolued vppon thys good minde, he fpeedily wente out
of the Churche vnto his chamber, where he began to confider of
many things, his confcience beyng moued to hinder the marriage
betwene the Counte Paris and hir, knowing by his meanes fhe had
efpoufed an other, and callynge to remembraunce what a daungerous enterprife he had begonne by committyng hymfelf to the
mercy of a fymple damofell, and that if fhee fayled to bee wyfe
and fecrete, all theyr doyngs fhould be difcried, he defamed, and
Rhomeo hir fpoufe punifhed. Hee then after he had well debated
vpon infinite numbre of deuifes, was in the end ouercome with
pity, and determined rather to hazarde his honour, than to fuffer
the Adultery of the Counte Paris with Iulietta: and being determined herevpon, opened his clofet, and takynge a vyall in his
Hande, retourned agayne to Iulietta, whom he found lyke one
that was in a Traunce, wayghtinge for newes, eyther of Lyfe or
Death: of whome the good olde Father demaunded vpon what
Day hir maryage was appoynted. "The firfte daye of that ap-
poyntment (quod fhee) is vppon Wednefdaye, whych is the Daye
ordeyned for my Confente of Maryage accorded betweene my
father and Counte Paris, but the Nuptiall folemnitye is not before
the x. day of September." "Wel then" (quod the religious
father) "be of good cheere daughter, for our Lord God hathe
opened a way vnto me both to deliuer you and Rhomeo from the
prepared thraldom. I haue knowne your hufband from his cradle,
and hee hath daily committed vnto me the greateft fecretes of hys
Confcience, and I haue fo dearely loued him agayne, as if hee had
ben mine owne fonne: wherefore my heart can not abide that
anye man fhould do him wrong in that fpecially wherein my
Counfell may ftande him in ftede. And forfomutch as you are his
wyfe, I ought lykewyfe to loue you, and feke meanes to delyuer
you from the martyrdome and Anguifh wherewyth I fee your
heart befieged: vnderftande then (good Daughter) of a fecrete
which I purpofe to manifeft vnto you, and take heede aboue all

thinges that you declare it to no liuing creature, for therein confifteth your life and Death. Ye be not ignorant by the common report of the Cityzens of this City, and by the fame publifhed of me,
that I haue trauailed throughe all the Prouinces of the habytable
Earthe, wherby duryng the continuall tyme of xx. yeres, I haue
foughte no reft for my wearied body, but rather haue many times
protruded the fame to the mercy of brute beafts in the Wyldernefle,
and many times alfo to the mercilefle Waues of the Seas, and to
the pity of common Pirates together with a thoufand other Daungers and fhipwracks vppon Sea and Land. So it is good Daughter
that all my wandring Voyages haue not bene altogethers vnpro-
fitable. For befides the incredible contentation receiued ordinarily in mind, I haue gathered fome particular fruyct, whereof by
the grace of God you fhall fhortly feele fome experience. I haue
proued the fecrete properties of Stones, of Plants, Metals, and other
thinges hydden within the Bowels of the Earth, wherewith I am
able to helpe my felfe againfte the common Lawe of Men, when
neceffity doth ferue: fpecyally in thynges wherein I know mine
eternal God to be leaft offended. For as thou knoweft I beynge
approched as it were, euen to the Brymme of my Graue, and that
the Tyme draweth neare for yeldynge of myne Accompte before the
Audytor of all Audytors, I oughte therefore to haue fome deepe
knowledge and apprehenfion of God's iudgement more than I
had when the heat of inconfidered youth did boyle within my lufty
body. Know you therefore good daughter, that with thofe graces,
and fauours which the heauens prodigally haue beftowed vpon me, I haue learned and proued of long time the compofition of a certayne Paafte, which I make of diuers foporiferous
fimples, which beaten afterwards to Pouder, and dronke wyth a
quantyty of Water, within a quarter of an houre after, bringeth the
receiuer into futch a fleepe, and burieth fo deepely the fenfes
and other fprites of life, that the cunningeft Phifitian will iudge
the party dead: and befides that it hath a more marueillous effect,
for the perfon which vfeth the fame feeleth no kinde of griefe,
and according to the quantity of the dough, the pacient remayneth
in a fweete fleepe, but when the operation is wrought and done,
hee returneth into his firft eftate. Now then Iulietta receiue myne

inſtruction, put of all Feminine affection by taking vppon you a
manly ſtomacke for by the only courage of your minde conſiſteth
the hap or miſhap of your affayres. Beholde here I geue you a
Vyale which you ſhall keepe as your owne propre heart, and the
night before your mariage, or in the morninge before day, you
ſhall fil the ſame vp with water, and drink ſo mutch as is contayned
therein.   And then you ſhall feele a certayne kynde of pleaſaunt
ſleepe, which incrochinge by litle and litle all the partes of your
body, wil conſtrayne them in ſutch wyſe, as vnmoueable they ſhal
remayne : and by not doing their accuſtomed dueties, ſhall looſe
their naturall feelinges, and you abide in ſutch extaſie the ſpace
of 40 houres at the leaſt, without any beating of poulſe or other
perceptible motion, which ſhall ſo aſtonne them that come to ſee
you, as they will iudge you to be deade, and according to the cuſtome of our Citty, you ſhal be caried to the Churchyarde hard by
our Church, where you ſhall be intoumbed in the common monument
of the Capellets your aunceſtors, and in the meane tyme we will
ſend word to lord Rhomeo by a ſpeciall meſſanger of the effect
of our deuice, who now abideth at Mantua.   And the night following I am ſure he will not fayle to be heere, then he and I
together will open the graue, and lift vp your body, and after the
operation of the Pouder is paſt, hee ſhall conuey you ſecretly to
Mantua, vnknowen to all your Parents and frends. Afterwards
(it may be) Tyme, the mother of Truth, ſhall cauſe concord betwene the offended City of Verona, and Rhomeo.   At which time
your common cauſe may be made open to the general contenta-
cion of all your frends." The words of the good father ended, new
ioy ſurpriſed the heart of Iulietta, who was ſo attentiue to his
talke as ſhe forgat no one poynct of hir leſſon. Then ſhe ſayd
vnto him : "Father, doubt not at all that my heart ſhall fayle in
performaunce of your commaundement : for were it the ſtrongeſt
Poyſon, or moſt peſtiferous Venome, rather would I thruſt it into
my body, than to conſent to fall in the hands of him, whom I
vtterly miſlike : with a right ſtrong reaſon then may I fortifie my
ſelfe, and offer my body to any kinde of mortall daunger to approch
and draw neare to him, vpon whom wholly dependeth my Life and
all the ſolace I haue in this World."   "Go your wayes then my

daughter" (quod the Frier) " the mighty hand of God keepe you, and
hys furpaffing power defende you, and confirme that will and good
mynde of yours, for the accomplifhment of this worke." Iulietta
departed from frier Laurence, and returned home to hir father's
Pallace about 11. of the clock, where fhe found hir mother at the
Gate attending for hir: And in good deuotion demaunded if fhee
continued ftill in hir former follies? But Iulietta with more gladfome cheere than fhe was wont to vfe, not fuffering hir mother to
afke agayne, fayd vnto hir: " Madame I come from S. Frauncis
Church, where I haue taried longer peraduenture than my duety
requireth: how be it not without fruict and great reft to my
afflicted confcience, by reafon of the godly perfuafions of our
ghoftly Father Frier Laurence, vnto whom I haue made a large
declaration of my life. And chiefly haue communicated vnto him
in confeffion, that which hath paft betwene my Lord my father
and you, vpon the mariage of Countee Paris and me. But the good
man hath reconciled me by his holy words, and commendable
exhortations, that where I had minde neuer to mary, now I am
well difpofed to obey your pleafure and commaundement. Wherfore, madame, I befeech you to recouer the fauor and good wyl of
my father, afke pardon in my behalfe, and fay vnto him (if it pleafe
you) that by obeying his Fatherly requeft, I am ready to meete
the Countee Paris at Villafranco, and there in your prefence to
accept him for my Lorde and hufband: In affuraunce whereof, by
your pacience, I meane to repayre into my Clofet, to make choife
of my moft pretious Iewels, that I being richly adorned, and
decked, may appeare before him more agreeable to his mynde,
and pleafure. The good mother rapt with exceeding great ioy,
was not able to aunfwere a word, but rather made fpeede to feeke
out hir hufband the Lord Antonio, vnto whom fhe reported the
good will of hir daughter, and how by meanes of Frier Laurence
hir minde was chaunged. Whereof the good olde man maruellous
ioyfull, prayfed God in heart, faying: " Wife this is not the firfte
good turne which we haue receiued of that holy man, vnto whom
euery Cittizen of this Common wealth is dearely bounde. I would
to God that I had redeemed 20 of his yeares with the third
parte of my goods, fo grieuous is to me his extreme old age.'

The felfe fame houre the Lord Antonio went to feeke the Countee
Paris, whom hee thought to perfwade to goe to Villafranco. But
the countee told him agayne, that the charge would be to great,
and that better it were to referue that coft to the mariage day,
for the better celebration of the fame. Notwithftanding if it were
his pleafure, he would himfelfe goe vifite Iulietta: and fo they
went together. The Mother aduertifed of his comming, caufed hir
daughter to make hir felfe ready, and to fpare no coftly Iewels
for adorning of hir beauty agaynft the Countee's comming, which
fhe beftowed fo well for garnifhing of hir Perfonage, that before
the Countee parted from the houfe, fhee had fo ftolne away his
heart, as he liued not from that time forth, but vpon meditation of
hir beauty, and flacked no time for acceleration of the mariage day,
ceafing not to be importunate vpon father and mother for th'ende
and confummation thereof. And thus with ioy inough paffed forth
this day and many others vntil the day before the mariage, againft
which time the mother of Iulietta did fo well prouide, that there
wanted nothing to fet forth the magnificence and nobility of their
houfe. Villafranco whereof we haue made mention, was a place
of pleafure, where the Lord 'Antonio was wont many tymes to recreate himfelfe a mile or two from Verona, there the dynner was
prepared, for fo mutch as the ordinary folemnity of neceffity mufte
be done at Verona. Iulietta perceyuing hir time to approache
dyffembled the matter fo well as fhee coulde: and when tyme
forced hir to retire to hir Chamber, hir Woman would have waited
vppon hir, and haue lyen in hir Chambre, as hir cuftome was: but
Iulietta fayd vnto hir: "Good and faithfull mother, you know that
to morrow is my maryage Day, and for that I would fpend the moft
parte of the Nyght in prayer, I pray you for this time to let me
alone, and to morrow in the Mornyng about vi. of the clocke come
to me agayne to helpe make mee readie." The good olde woman
willing to follow hir minde, fuffred hir alone, and doubted
nothyng of that which fhe did meane to do. Iulietta beinge
within hir Chambre hauing an eawer ful of Water ftanding vppon
the Table filled the viole which the Frier gaue her: and after fhe
had made the mixture, fhe fet it by hir bed fide, and went to Bed.
And being layde, new thoughtes began to affaile hir, with a con-

ceipt of grieuous Death, which brought hir into futch cafe as fhe
could not tell what to doe, but playning inceffantly fayd: "Am
not I the moft vnhappy and defperat creature, that euer was
borne of Woman? For mee there is nothyng left in this wretched
worlde but mifhap, mifery, and mortall woe, my diftreffe hath
brought me to futch extremity, as to faue mine honor and confcience, I am forced to deuoure the drynke whereof I know not the
vertue: but what know I (fayd fhe) whether the Operatyon of thys
Pouder will be to foone or to late, or not correfpondent to the due
tyme, and that my fault being difcouered, I fhall remayne a Fable
to the People? What know I moreouer, if the Serpents and other
venomous and crauling Wormes, whych commonly frequent the
Graues and pittes of the Earth wyll hurt me, thynkyng that I am
deade. But howe fhall I indure the ftynche of fo many carions
and Bones of myne aunceftors whych reft in the Graue, yf by fortune I do awake before Rhomeo and Fryer Laurence doe come
to help mee?" And as fhee was thus plunged in the deepe contem-
platyon of thynges, fhe thought that fhe faw a certayn vifion or
fanfie of hir Coufin Thibault, in the very fame fort as fhee fawe
him wounded and imbrued wyth Bloud, and mufing how that fhe
muft be buried quick amongs fo many dead Carcafes and deadly
naked bones, hir tender and delycate body began to fhake and
tremble, and hir yelowe lockes to ftare for feare, in futch wyfe as
fryghtned with terroure, a cold fweate beganne to pierce hir heart
and bedewe the refte of al hir membres, in futch wife as fhe
thought that an hundred thoufand Deathes did ftande about hir,
haling hir on euery fide, and plucking hir in pieces, and feelyng
that hir forces diminyfhed by lyttle and lyttle, fearing that through
to great debilyty fhe was not able to do hir enterpryfe, like a furious and infenfate Woman, with out further care, gulped vp the
Water wythin the Voyal, then croffing hir armes vpon hir ftomacke,
fhe loft at that inftante all the powers of hir Body, reftyng in a
Traunce. And when the morning lyght began to thruft his head
out of his Oryent, hir Chaumber Woman which had lockte hir in
with the Key, did open the doore, and thynkyng to awake hir,
called hir many tymes, and fayd vnto hir: "Miftreffe, you fleepe
to long, the Counte Paris will come to raife you." The poore olde

Woman fpake vnto the wall, and fange a fong vnto the deafe. For
if all the horrible and tempeftuous foundes of the world had bene
cannoned forth out of the greateft bombardes and founded through
hir delycate Eares, hir fpyrites of Lyfe were fo faft bounde and ftopt,
as fhe by no meanes coulde awake, wherewith the pore olde Woman
amazed, began to fhake hir by the armes and Handes, whych fhe
found fo colde as marble ftone. Then puttyng Hande vnto hir
Mouthe, fodainely perceyued that fhe was dead, for fhee perceyued
no breath in hir. Wherefore lyke a Woman out of hir Wyttes,
fhee ranne to tell hir mother, who fo madde as a Tigre, berefte of
hir Faunes hied hir felfe into hir Daughter's Chaumber, and in
that pitiful ftate beholdynge hir Daughter, thinkyng hir to be deade,
cried out: "Ah cruell Death, which haft ended all my ioye and
Blyffe, vfe the laft fcourge of thy wrathfull ire agaynft me, leaft by
fufferyng mee to liue the reft of my woefull Dayes, my Torment doe
increafe." Then fhe began to fetch futch ftrayning fighes, as hir
heart did feeme to cleaue in pieces. And as hir cries began to encreafe, behold the Father, the County Paris, and a great troupe of
Gentlemen and Ladies, which were come to honour the feafte, hearing no fooner tell of that which chaunced, were ftroke into futch
forrowfull dumpes as he which had beheld their Faces would eafily
haue iudged that the fame had ben a day of ire and pity, fpecially
the Lord Antonio, whofe heart was frapped with futch furpaffing
woe, as neither teare nor word could iffue forth, and knowing not
what to doe, ftraight way fent to feeke the moft expert Phifitians
of the towne, who after they had inquired of the life paft of Iulietta, deemed by common reporte, that melancoly was the caufe of
that fodayne death, and then their forows began to renue a frefh.
And if euer day was Lamentable, Piteous, Vnhappy, and Fatall,
truly it was that wherein Iulietta hir death was publifhed in Verona:
for fhee was fo bewayled of great and fmall, that by the common
playnts, the Common wealth feemed to be in daunger, and not
without caufe: for befides hir naturall beauty (accompanied with
many vertues wherewith nature had enriched hir) fhe was elfe
fo humble, wife, and debonaire, as for that humility and curtefie
fhe had ftollen away the hearts of euery wight, and there was
none but did lament hir Miffortune. And whileft thefe thinges

were in this lamented ftate, Frier Laurence with diligence dis-
patched a Frier of his Couent, named Frier Anfelme, whom he
trufted as himfelfe, and deliuered him a Letter written with hys
owne hande, commaunding him expreffely not to giue the fame
to any other but to Rhomeo, wherein was conteyned the chaunce
which had paffed betwene him and Iulietta, fpecially the vertue
of the Pouder, and commaunded him the nexte enfuinge Nighte
to fpeede himfelfe to Verona, for that the operation of the
Pouder that time would take ende, and that he fhould cary wyth
him back agayne to Mantua his beloued Iulietta, in diffembled
apparell, vntill Fortune had otherwife prouided for them. The
frier made futch haft as (too late) hee arriued at Mantua, within a
while after. And bicaufe the maner of Italy is, that the Frier
trauayling abroade ought to take a companion of his couent to
doe his affaires wythin the City, the Fryer went into his couent,
and for that he was within, it was not lawfull for him to come oute
againe that Day, bicaufe that certain dayes before, one relygious
of that couent as it was fayd, dyd dye of the plague : wherefore
the Magiftrates appoynted for the health and vifitation of the
fick, commaunded the Warden of the Houfe that no Friers fhould
wander abrode the city, or talke with any Citizen, vntil they were
licenfed by the officers in that behalfe appoynted, which was the
caufe of the great mifhap which you fhal heare hereafter. The
Friar being in this perplexitye, not able to goe forth, and not knowyng what was contayned in the Letter, deferred hys Jorney for that
Day. Whilft things were in thys plyght, preparation was made
at Verona, to doe the obfequies of Iulietta. There is a cuftome
alfo (which is common in Italy,) to laye all the beft of one lignage
and Familye in one Tombe, wherevppon Iulietta was intoumbed,
in the ordinary Graue of the Capellettes, in a Churcheyarde, hard
by the Churche of the Fryers, where alfo the Lord Thibault was
interred, whofe Obfequies honorably done, euery man returned :
whereunto Pietro, the feruaunt of Rhomeo, gaue hys affyftance :
for as we haue before declared, hys mayfter fente hym backe
agayne from Mantua to Verona, to do his father feruice, and to
aduertife him of that which fhould chaunce in his abfence there :
who feeyng the Body of Iulietta, inclofed in Toumbe, thinkyng

with the refte that fhee had bene dead in deede, incontinently tooke
pofte horfe, and with dylygence rode to Mantua, where he founde
his Mayfter in his wonted houfe, to whom he fayde, wyth hys
Eyes full of Teares: " Syr, there is chaunced vnto you fo ftraunge
a matter as if fo be you do not arme your felfe with Conftancye, I
am afrayed that I fhall be the cruell minyfter of your Death : be
it known vnto you fir, that yefterday morning my miftreffe Iulietta left hir Lyfe in thys Worlde to feeke reft in an other : and
wyth thefe Eyes I faw her buryed in the Churchyarde of S. Frauncis." At the founde of whych heauye meffage, Rhomeo begann
woefullye to Lamente, as though hys fpyrites gryeued wyth the
Tormente of his Paffion at that inftant would haue abandoned his
Bodye. But ftronge Loue which woulde not permytte him to
faynt vntyl the extremity, framed a thoughte in hys fantefie, that
if it were poffyble for him to dye befides hir his Death fhould be
more gloryous, and fhee (as he thought) better contented : by reafon whereof, after he had wafhed his face for feare to difcouer
his forrowe, hee wente out of his Chamber, and commaunded hys
man to tarry behynd him, that he myght walke through out all
the Corners of the Citye, to finde propre remedye (if it were poffyble) for hys gryefe. And amonges others, beholdynge an Apotica-
rye's fhop of lyttle furnyture and leffe ftore of Boxes and other
thinges requifite for that fcyence, thought that the verye pouerty
of the mayfter Apothecarye would make hym wyllingle yeld to that
which he pretended to demaunde : and after he had taken hym
afide, fecretly fayde vnto him : " Syr, if you be the Mayfter of the
Houfe, as I thynk you be, beholde here Fifty Ducates, whych I
gyue you to the intent you delyuer me fome ftrong and vyolente
Poyfon that within a quarter of an houre is able to procure Death
vnto hym that fhall vfe it." The couetous Apothecarye entyfed by
gayne, agreed to his requeft, and faynying to gyue hym fome
other medycine before the People's Face, he fpeedily made ready a
ftrong and cruell Poyfon, afterwardes he fayd vnto him foftly :
" Syr, I guye you more than is needefull, for the one halfe is able
to deftroy the ftrongeft manne of the world : " who after he hadde
receyued the poyfon, retourned home, where he commaunded his
man to departe with diligence to Verona, and that he fhould make

prouifion of candels, a tynder Boxe, and other Inftrumentes meete
for the opening of the graue of Iulietta, and that aboue all things
hee fhoulde not fayle to attende his commynge befides the
Churchyarde of S. Frauncis, and vppon Payne of Life to keepe hys
intente in filence. Which Pietro obeied in order as hys maifter
had requyred, and made therin futch expedityon, as he arriued in
good time to Verona, taking order for al things that wer commaunded him. Rhomeo in the meane while being folycyted
wyth mortall thoughtes caufed incke and paper to be broughte
vnto hym, and in few words put in wryting all the difcourfe of his
loue, the mariage of him and Iulietta, the meane obferued for confummation of the fame, the helpe that he had of Frier Laurence,
the buying of his Poyfon, and laft of all his death. Afterwardes
hauing finifhed his heauy tragedy, hee clofed the letters, and
fealed the fame with his feale, and directed the Superfcription
thereof to hys Father: and puttyng the letters into his purffe, he
mounted on horfebacke, and vfed futch dylygence, as he arriued
vppon darke Nyght at the Citye of Verona, before the gates were
fhut, where he founde his feruaunte tarying for him with a Lan-
terne and inftrumentes as is before fayd, meete for the opening of
the graue, vnto whome hee faid: "Pietro, helpe mee to open this
Tombe, and fo foone as it is open I commaunde thee vppon payne
of thy life, not to come neere mee, nor to ftay me from the thing
I purpofe to doe. Beholde, there is a letter which thou fhalt prefent to morrow in the mornyng to my Father at his vpryfing,
which peraduenture fhall pleafe him better than thou thinkeft."
Pietro, not able to imagine what was his maifter's intent, ftode
fomewhat aloofe to beholde his maifter's geftes and Countenance.
And when they had opened the Vaulte, Rhomeo defcended downe
two fteppes, holdyng the candel in his hand and began to behold
wyth pityfull Eye, the body of hir, which was the organ of his
Eyes, and kyft it tenderly, holdyng it harde betwen his armes,
and not able to fatiffie him felfe with hir fight, put hys fearefull
handes vppon the colde ftomacke of Iulietta. And after he had
touched hir in many places, and not able to feele anye certayne
Iudgemente of Lyfe, he drewe the Poyfon out of hys boxe, and
fwallowyng downe a great quantytye of the fame, cryed out:

"O Iulietta, of whome the Worlde was vnworthye, what Death
is it poffyble my Hearte coulde choofe oute more agreeable than
that whych yt fuffereth harde by thee? what Graue more Gloryous,
than to bee buried in thy Toumbe? what more woorthy or excellent Epytaphe can bee vowed for Memorye, than the mutuall
and pytyfull Sacryfice of our lyues?" And thinkinge to renue
his forrowe, his hearte began to frette through the vyolence of
the Poyfon, whiche by lyttle and lyttle affailed the fame, and
lookyng about hym, efpied the Bodye of the Lorde Thibault,
lying nexte vnto Iulietta, whych as yet was not al together putrified, and fpeakyng to the bodye as though it hadde bene alyue,
fayde: "In what place fo euer thou arte (O Coufyn Thibault) I
moft heartely do crye the mercye for the offence whych I haue
done by depryuing of thy Lyfe: and yf thy Ghoft doe wyfhe and
crye out for Vengeaunce vppon mee, what greater or more cruell
fatyffaction canfte thou defyre to haue, or henceforth hope for,
than to fee him whych murdered thee, to bee empoyfoned with
his owne handes, and buryed by thy fide?" Then endynge hys
talke, felyng by lyttle and lyttle that his lyfe began to fayle,
falling proftrate vppon his knees, wyth feeble voyce hee foftely
fayd: "O my Lord God, which to redeeme me dideft difcend
from the bofom of thy Father, and tookeft humane flefhe in the
Wombe of the Vyrgine, I acknowledge and confeffe, that this
body of myne is nothing elfe but Earth and Duft." Then feazed
vppon wyth defperate forrow, he fell downe vppon the Body of
Iulietta with futch vehemence, as the heart faint and attenuated
with too great torments, not able to beare fo hard a vyolence,
was abandoned of all his fenfe and Naturall powers, in futch
forte as the fiege of hys foule fayled him at that inftant, and his
members ftretched forthe, remayned ftiffe and colde. Fryer
Laurence whych knew the certayne tyme of the pouder's operation, maruelled that he had no anfwere of the Letter which he
fent to Rhomeo by his fellowe Fryer Anfelme, departed from S.
Frauncis and with Inftruments for the purpofe, determined to open
the Graue to let in aire to Iulietta, whych was ready to wake: and
approchyng the place, hee efpied a lyght within, which made him
afraide vntyll that Pietro whych was hard by, had certyfied hym

that Rhomeo was with in, and had not ceafed there to Lamente
and Complayne the fpace of halfe an Houre : and when they two
were entred the Graue and finding Rhomeo without Lyfe, made
futch forrowe as they can well conceyue whych Loue their deare
Fryende wyth lyke perfection. And as they were making theyr
complaints, Iulietta rifing out of hir traunce, and beholding light
within the Toumbe, vncertayne wheather it were a dreame or
fantafie that appeared before his eyes, comming agayne to hir
felfe, knew Frier Laurence, vnto whom fhe faid : "Father, I pray
thee in the name of God to perfourme thy promife, for I am
almoft deade." And then frier Laurence concealing nothing from
hir, (bycaufe he feared to be taken through his too long abode in
that place) faythfully rehearfed vnto hir, how he had fent frier
Anfelme to Rhomeo at Mantua, from whom as yet hee had receiued no aunfwere. Notwithftanding he found Rhomeo dead in
the graue, whofe body he poynćted vnto, lyinge hard by hir,
praying hir fith it was fo, paciently to beare that fodayne misfortune, and that if it pleafed hir, he would conuey hir into fome
monaftery of women where fhe might in time moderate hir forrow,
and giue reft vnto hir minde. Iulietta had no fooner caft eye
vppon the deade corps of Rhomeo, but began to breake the fountayne pipes of gufhing teares, which ran forth in futch aboundance, as not able to fupport the furor of hir griefe, fhe breathed
without ceafing vpon his mouth, and then throwen hir felfe vppon
his body, and embracing it very hard, feemed that by force of
fighes and fobs, fhe would haue reuiued, and brought him againe
to life, and after fhe had kiffed and rekiffed hym a million of
times, fhe cried out : "Ah the fweete refte of my cares, and the
onely port of all my pleafures and paftimes, hadft thou fo fure a
hearte to choofe thy Churchyarde in this place betwene the armes
of thy perfeċt Louer, and to ende the courfe of thy life for my
fake in the floure of thy Youth when lyfe to thee fhould have bene
moft deare and deleċtable ? how had this tender body power to
refift the furious Coumbat of death, very death it felfe here prefent ?
how coulde thy tender and delicate youth willingly permit that
thou fhouldeft approch into this filthy and infeċted place, where
from henceforth thou fhalt be the pafture of Worms vnworthy of

thee? Alas, alas, by what meanes fhall I now renue my playnts, which time and long pacience ought to haue buried and clearely quenched? Ah I, miferable and Caitife wretch, thinking to finde remedy for my griefs, haue fharpned the Knife that hath gieuen me this cruell blow, whereof I receiue the caufe of mortall wound. Ah, happy and fortunate graue which fhalt ferue in world to come for witneffe of the moft perfect aliaunce that euer was betwene two moft infortunate louers, receyue now the laft fobbing fighes, and intertayment of the moft cruell of all the cruell fubiects of ire and death." And as fhe thought to continue hir complaynts, Pietro aduertifed Frier Laurence that he heard a noyfe befides the citadell, wherewyth being afrayd, they fpeadily departed, fearing to be taken: and then Iulietta feeing hir felfe alone, and in full Liberty, tooke agayne Rhomeo betweene hir armes, kiffing him with futch affection, as fhe feemed to be more attaynted with loue than death, and drawing out the Dagger which Rhomeo ware by his fide, fhe pricked hir felfe with many blowes againft the heart, fayinge with feeble and pitiful voice: "Ah death the end of forrow, and beginning of felicity, thou art moft hartely welcome: feare not at this time to fharpen thy dart: giue no longer delay of life, for feare that my fprite trauayle not to finde Rhomeo's ghoft amongs futch number of carion corpfes: and thou my deare Lord and loyall hufband Rhomeo, if there reft in thee any knowledge, receyue hir whom thou haft fo faythfully loued, the onely caufe of thy violent death, which frankely offreth vp hir foule that none but thou fhalt ioy the loue whereof thou haft made fo lawfull conqueft, and that our foules paffing from this light, may eternally liue together in the place of euerlafting ioy." And when fhe had ended thofe wordes fhee yelded vp hir ghoft. While thefe thinges thus were done, the garde and watch of the Citty by chaunce paffed by, and feeing light within the graue, fufpected ftraight that there were fome Necromancers which had opened the Toumbe to abufe the deade bodies for ayde of their arte: and defirous to knowe what it ment, went downe into the vaut, where they found Rhomeo and Iulietta, with their armes imbracing ech other's neck, as though there had bene fome token of lyfe. And after they had well viewed them at leyfure, they perceyued in what cafe they were:

and then all amazed they fought for the theeues which (as they thought) had done the murther, and in the ende founde the good father Fryer Laurence, and Pietro the feruaunte of deade Rhomeo (whych had hid themfelues under a ftall) whom they caryed to Pryfon, and aduertyfed the Lord of Efcala, and the magiftrates of Verona of that horrible murder, which by and by was publifhed throughoute the City. Then flocked together al the Citizens, women and children leauyng their houfes, to loke vppon that pityful fighte, and to the Ende that in prefence of the whole Cytie, the murder fhould be knowne, the Magiftrates ordayned that the two deade Bodies fhould he erected vppon a ftage to the view and fight of the whole World, in futch forte and manner as they were found withyn the Graue, and that Pietro and frier Laurence fhould publikely bee examyned, that afterwardes there myght be no murmure or other pretended caufe of ignoraunce. And thys good olde Frier beyinge vppon the Scaffold, hauinge a whyte Bearde all wet and bathed with Teares, the Iudges commaunded him to declare vnto them who were the Authors of that Murder, fith at vntimely houre hee was apprehended with certayne Irons befides the Graue. Fryer Laurence, a rounde and franke Man of talke, nothyng moued with that accufation, anfwered them with ftoute and bolde voyce : " My maifters, there is none of you all (if you haue refpect vnto my forepaffed Life, and to my aged Yeres, and therewithall haue confideration of this heauy fpectacle, where- unto vnhappy fortune hathe prefently brought me) but doeth greatly maruell of fo fodaine mutation and change vnlooked for fo mutch as thefe three fcore and Ten or twelue Yeares fithens I came into this Worlde, and began to proue the vanities thereof, I was neuer fufpected, touched, or found guilty of any crime which was able to make me blufhe, or hide my face, although (before God) I doe confeffe my felf to be the greateft and moft abhomi- nable finner of al the redeemed flocke of Chrift. So it is notwyth- ftanding, that fith I am preft and ready to render mine accompte, and that Death, the Graue and wormes do dailye fummon this wretched corps of myne to appeare before the Iuftyce feate of God, ftill wayghtyng and attending to be carried to my hoped graue, this is the houre I fay, as you likewife may thinke wherein I am

fallen to the greateft damage and preiudice of my Lyfe and honeft
porte, and that which hath ingendred thys fynyfter opynyon of mee,
may peraduenture bee thefe greate Teares which in abundaunce
tryckle downe my Face as though the holy fcriptures do not witneffe, that Jefus Chrift moued with humayne pitty, and compaffion, did weepe, and poure forth teares, and that many times teares
be the faythfull meffengers of a man's innocency. Or elfe the moft
likely euidence, and prefumption, is the fufpeċted hour, which (as
the magiftrate doth fay) doth make mee culpable of the murder,
as though all houres were not indifferently made equall by God
their Creator, who in his owne perfon declareth vnto vs that there
be twelue houres in the Day, fhewing thereby that there is no
exception of houres nor of minutes, but that one may doe eyther
good or ill at all times indifferently, as the party is guided or forfaken by the fprite of God : touching the Irons which were founde
about me, needefull it is not now to let you vnderftand for what
vfe Iron was firft made, and that of it felfe it is not able to increafe
in man eyther good or euill, if not by the mifchieuous minde of
hym which doth abufe it. Thus mutch I haue thought good to
tell you, to the intent that neyther teares nor Iron, ne yet fufpeċted houre, are able to make me guilty of the murder, or make
me otherwyfe than I am, but only the witneffe of mine owne
confcience, which alone if I were guilty fhould be the accufer,
the witneffe, and the hangman, whych, by reafon of mine age
and the reputation I haue had amonges you, and the little time
that I haue to liue in this World fhoulde more torment me within,
than all the mortall paynes that could be deuifed : but (thankes
be to myne eternall God) I feele no worme that gnaweth, nor
any remorfe that pricketh me touching that faċt, for which I
fee you all troubled and amazed : and to fet your harts at reft,
and to remoue the doubts which hereafter may torment your
confciences, I fweare vnto you by all the heauenly parts wherein
I hope to be, that forthwith I will difclofe from firft to laft the
entire difcourfe of this pitifull tragedy, whych peraduenture fhall
driue you into no leffe wondre and amaze, than thofe two poore
paffionate Louers were ftrong and pacient, to expone themfelues to
the mercy of death, for the feruent and indiffoluble loue betwene

then." Then the Fatherly Frier began to repeate the beginning
of the loue betwene Iulietta, and Rhomeo, which by certayne
fpace of time confirmed, was profecuted by wordes at the firft,
then by mutual promife of mariage, vnknown to the world. And
as within few dayes after, the two Louers feelinge themfelues
fharpned and incited with ftronger onfet, repaired vnto him vnder
colour of confeffion, protefting by othe that they were both
maried, and that if he woulde not folempnize that mariage in
the face of the Church, they fhould be conftrayned to offend God
to liue in difordred luft: in confideration whereof, and fpecially
feeing their alliaunce to be good, and comfortable in dignity,
richeffe and Nobility on both fides, hoping by that meanes perchaunce to reconcile the Montefches, and Capellets, and that
by doing futch an acceptable worke to God, he gaue them the
Churches bleffing in a certayne Chappel of the friers church whereof
the night following they did confummate the mariage fruicts in
the Pallace of the Capellets. For teftimony of which copulation,
the woman of Iuliettae's Chamber was able to depofe: Adding
moreouer, the murder of Thibault, which was Coufin to Iulietta :
by reafon whereof the banifhment of Rhomeo did followe, and
howe in the abfence of the fayd Rhomeo, the mariage being kept
fecret betwene them, a new Matrimony was intreated wyth the
Countee Paris, which mifliked by Iulietta, fhe fell proftrate at his
feete in a Chappell of S. Frauncis church, with full determination
to haue killed hirfelf with hir owne hands, if he gaue hir not
councell how fhe fhould auoyde the mariage agreed betwene hir
father and the Countee Paris. For conclufion, he fayd, that
although he was refolued by reafon of his age, and neareneffe
of death to abhorre all fecrete Sciences, wherein in his younger
yeares he had delight, notwithftanding, preffed with importunity,
and moued with pitty, fearing leaft Iulietta fhould do fome
cruelty agaynft hirfelfe, he ftrayned his confcience, and chofe
rather with fome little fault to grieue his minde, than to fuffer
the young gentlewoman to deftroy hir body, and hazarde the
daunger of hir foule : and therefore he opened fome part of his
auncient cunning, and gaue her a certayne Pouder to make hir
fleepe, by meanes whereof fhe was thought to be deade. Then he

tolde them how he had fent Frier Anfelme to cary letters to Rhomeo
of their enterprife, whereof hitherto he had no aunfwere. Then
briefly he concluded how he found Rhomeo dead within the graue,
who as it is moft likely did impoyfon himfelfe, or was otherwife
fmothered or fuffocated with forow by findinge Iulietta in that
ftate, thinking fhee had bene dead. Then he tolde them how
Iulietta did kill hirfelfe with the Dagger of Rhomeo to beare him
company after his death, and how it was impoffible for them to
faue hir for the noyfe of the watch which forced theym to flee
from thence. And for more ample approbation of his faying, he
humbly befought the Lord of Verona and the Magiftrats to fend
to Mantua for Frier Anfelme to know the caufe of his flack returne, that the content of the letter fent to Rhomeo might be
feene: to examine the Woman of the Chamber of Iulietta, and
Pietro the feruaunt of Rhomeo, who not attending for further requeft, fayd vnto them: "My Lordes, when Rhomeo entred the
graue, he gaue me this Pacquet, written as I fuppofe with his owne
hand, who gaue me expreffe commaundement to deliuer it to his
father." The pacquet opened, they found the whole effe
ftory, fpecially the Apothecarie's name, which fold him the Poyfon,
the price, and the caufe wherefore he vfed it, and all appeared to
be fo cleare and euident, as there refted nothing for further verifi-
cation of the fame, but their prefence at the doing of the particulers thereof, for the whole was fo well declared in order, as they
were out of doubt that the fame was true: and then the Lord
Bartholomew of Efcala, after he had debated with the Magiftrates
of thefe euents, decreed that the Woman of Iulietta hir chamber
fhould bee banifhed, becaufe fhee did conceale that priuy mariage
from the Father of Rhomeo, which if it had beene knowne in
tyme, had bred to the whole Citty an vniuerfall benefit. Pietro
becaufe he obeyed hys mayfter's commaundement, and kept clofe
hys lawfull fecrets, according to the well conditioned nature of a
trufty feruaunt, was fet at liberty. The Poticary taken, rackt, and
founde guilty, was hanged. The good olde man Frier Laurence, as
well for refpe
common wealth of Verona, as alfo for his vertuous life (for the
which hee was fpecially recommended) was let goe in peace, with-

out any note of Infamy. Notwithſtanding by reaſon of his age,
he voluntarily gaue ouer the World, and cloſed himſelfe in an
Hermitage, two miles from Verona, where he liued 5 or 6 yeares,
and ſpent hys tyme in continuall prayer, vntil he was called out of
this tranſitory worlde, into the blifful ſtate of euerlaſting ioy.
And for the compaſſion of ſo ſtraunge an infortune, the Montes-
ches, and Capellets poured forth ſutch abundaunce of teares, as
with the fame they did euacuate their auncient grudge and choler,
whereby they were then reconciled : and they which coulde not
bee brought to attonement by any wiſedome or humayne councell,
were in the ende vanquiſhed and made frends by pity : and to im-
mortalizate the memory of ſo intier and perfeɛt amity, the Lord of
Verona ordayned, that the two bodies of thoſe miraculous Louers
ſhould be faſt intoumbed in the graue where they ended their lyues,
in which place was ereɛted a high marble Piller, honoured
with an infinite number of excellent Epytaphes, which
to this day be apparaunt, with ſutch noble memory,
as amongs all the rare excellencies, wherewith
that City is furniſhed, there is none more
Famous than the Monument of Rhomeo
and Iulietta.

THE TWENTY-SIXTH NOUELL.

Two gentlemen of Venice were honourably deceiued of their Wyues, whofe notable practifes, and fecret conference for atchieuinge their defire, occafioned diuers accidentes, and ingendred double benefit : wherein alfo is recited an eloquent oration, made by one of them, pronounced before the Duke and ftate of that Cittye : with other chaunces and actes concerninge the fame.

HEERE haue I thought good to fummon 2 Gentlewomen of Venice to appeare in Place, and to mount on Stage amongs other Italian Dames to fhew caufe of their bolde incountrey agaynft the Folly of their two Hufbands, that vncharitably without refpect of neyghbourhoode, went about to affayle the honefty of eyther's wyfe, and weening they had enioyed others felicity, by the womens prudence, forefight and ware gouernment, were both deceiued, and yet attayned the chiefeft benefit that mariage ftate doth looke for : fo that if fearch bee made amonges antiquities, it is to be doubted wheather greater chaftity, and better pollicy could be founde for accomplifhment of an intended purpofe. Many deedes haue ben done by women for fauegard of their Hufbandes lyues, as that of the Minyæ, a fort of Women whofe hufbandes were imprifoned at Lacedæmon, and for treafon condemned, who to faue their liues, entred into prifon the night before they fhould dy, and by exchange of apparell, deliuered them, and remayned there to fuffer for them. Of Hipficratea alfo the Queene and Wyfe of Mithridates king of Pontus, who fpared not hir Noble beauty and golden lockes to manure hir felfe in the vfe of armes, to keepe hir hufband company in perils and daungers : and being ouercome by Pompeius, and flying away, neuer left him vnaccompanied, ne forfooke futch trauayle as he himfelfe fuftayned. The like alfo of Æmilia, Turia, Sulpitia, Portia, and other Romane Dames. But that futch haue preuented their hufband's folly, feldome we reade, fauing of Queene Marie, the Wife of Don Pietro king of Arragon, who marking the infolency of hir hufband, and fory for his difordred life, honeft iealoufie opening hir continent

eyes, forced hir to feeke meanes to remoue his wanton acts, or at
leaftwife by pollicy and wife forefight to make him hufbande and
culture his own foy'le, that for want of feafonable tillage was barren
and voyde of fruicte. Wherefore confulting with the Lord chamberlayne, who of cuftome brought whom the king liked beft, was
in place of his woman beftowed in his Bed, and of her that night
begat the yong Prynce Giacomo, that afterwardes proued a
valiaunte, and wife king. Thefe paffing good pollicies of women
many times abolifh the frantik lecherous fits of hufbands gieuen
to fuperfluous lufts, when firft by their chaft behauiour and
womanly patience they contayne that which they be loth to fee or
heare of, and then demaunding counfell of fobriety and wifedome,
excogitate fleights to fhun folly, and expell difcurtefie, by hufbande's carelef̄e vfe. Sutch practifes, and deuifes, thefe two
Gentlewomen whom I now bringe forth, difclofe in this difcourfe
enfuing. In the Citty of Venice, (which for riches and fayre
Women excelleth all other within the region of Italy) in the time
that Francefco Fofcari, a very wyfe Prynce, did gouerne the ftate,
there were two young Gentlemen, the one called Girolamo Bembo,
and the other Anfelmo Barbadico, betwene whom as many times
chaunceth amongs other, grew futch great hatred and cruel hofti-
lity, as ech of them by fecret and all poffible meanes deuifed to
doe other fhame and difpleafure, which kindled to futch outrage,
as it was thought impoffible to be pacified. It chaunced that at
one tyme both of them did mary two noble young Gentlewomen,
excellent and fayre, both brought vp vnder one Nurfe, and loued
ech other lyke two Sifters, and as though they had been both borne
of one body. The Wyfe of Anfelmo, called Ifotta, was the
Daughter of Meffer Marco Gradenigo, a man of great eftimation
in that Citty, one of the procuratours of San Marco, whereof there
were not fo great number in thofe dayes as there bee now, becaufe
the Wyfeft men, and beft Approued of Lyfe were chofen to that great
and Noble dignity, none allotted thereunto by Bribes or Ambition.
The Wyfe of Girolamo Bembo was called Lucia, the Daughter of
Meffer Gian Francefco Valerio Caualiere, a Gentleman very well
learned, and many times fent by the State, Ambaffador into diuers
Countreys, and after he had bene Orator wyth the Pope, for his

wifedome in the execution of the fame was in great eftimation
wyth the whole Citty. The two Gentlewomen after they were
maried, and heard of the hatred betwene their Hufbandes, were
very forrowfull and penfiue, becaufe they thought the Freendfhyp
and Loue betwene them twayne, continued from their tender
yeares, could not bee, but with greate difficulty kept, or elfe
altogither diffolued and broken. Notwithftanding beyng difcrete
and wyfe, for auoyding occafion of eche Hufbande's offence, determined to ceafe their accuftomed conuerfation and louinge Familiarity, and not to frequent others company, but at Places and
Tymes conuenient. To whom Fortune was fo fauourable, as not
onely theyr Houfes were neere together but alfo adioyninge, in the
Backfides whereof theyr Gardeyns alfo Confined, feperated onely
wyth a lyttle Hedge, that euery day they myght fee one another,
and many tymes talke together: moreouer the Seruauntes, and
People of eyther houfes were freendly, and familiar, whych didde
greately content the two Louynge Gentlewomen, bicaufe they alfo
in the abfence of theyr Hufbandes, myghte at pleafure in their
Gardens difport themfelues. And continuing this order the fpace
of three yeares neyther of them within that terme were with chylde.
In which fpace Anfelmo many times viewing and cafting his eyes
vpon Madonna Lucia, fell earneftly in loue with hir, and was not
that day well at eafe, wherein he had not beholden hir excellent
beauty. She that was of Spirite, and Wit fubtle, marked the
lookes and maner of Anfelmo, who neyther for loue, ne other caufe
did render like lookes on him, but to fee to what ende his louing cheere and Countenaunce would tend. Notwithftanding fhe
feemed rather defirous to behold him, than elfwhere to imploye
hir lookes. On the other fide the good behauiour, the wife order
and pleafaunt beauty of Madonna Ifotta was fo excellent and
plaufible in the fight of mayfter Girolamo, as no Louer in the World
was better pleafed with his beloued than he with hir: who not
able to liue wythout the fweete fight of Ifotta (that was a crafty
and wily Wench) was by hir quickly perceiued. She being right
honeft and wife, and louing hir hufband very dearely, did beare
that countenaunce to Girolamo, that fhe generally did to any of
the Citty, or to other ftraunger that fhe neuer faw before. But hir

husband more and more inflamed, hauing loft the liberty of himfelfe, wounded and pierced with the amorous arowes of Loue, coulde
not conuert his minde to any other but to miftreffe Lucia. Thefe
two women wonted to heare feruice euery day ordinarily at the
church of Sanfantino, bicaufe they lay long a bed in the mornings,
and commonly feruice in that church was fayd fomewhat late:
their pewes alfo fomwhat diftant one from an other. Whether
their 2 amorous hufbands continually vfed to follow them a
loofe of, and to place themfelues where eyther of them might beft
view his beloued: by which cuftome they feemed to the common
people to be iealous ouer their Wyues. But they profecuted the
matter in futch wyfe, as eyther of them without fhipping, fought
to fend other into Cornouale. It came to paffe then, that thefe
2 beloued gentlewomen one knowing nothing of another's intent,
determined to confider better of this loue, becaufe the great good
will long time borne, fhould not be interrupted. Vppon a certayne
day when their hufbands were abrode, reforting together to talk at
their Garden hedge according to theyr wonted manner, they began
to be pleafaunte and merry: and after louynge falutations, Mis-
treffe Lucia fpake thefe Woordes vnto hir Companyon: "Ifotta my
deare beloued fifter, I haue a tale to tell you of your hufband, that
perchaunce will feeme ftraunger than anye newes that euer you
heard." "And I" (anfwered miftreffe Ifotta) "I have a ftory to
tel you that wil make you no leffe to wonder than I at that which
you haue to fay, and it may be will put you into fome choler and
chafe." "What is that?" quod the one and other. In the ende
eyther of them told what practizes and loue their hufbands went
about. Whereat although they were in great rage for theyr hufbandes follye, yet for the time they laughed out the matter, and
thought that they were fufficient (as in very deede they were, a thing
not to be doubted) and able to fatiffie their hufbands hunger and
therewithall began to blame them and to fay that they deferued
to learn to play of the Cornets, if they had no greater feare of
God, and care of honefty than their hufbands had. Then after
mutch talke of this matter, concluded that they fhould do wel to
expect what their hufbands would demaund. Hauing taken order
as they thought meete, they agreed dailye to efpye what fhoulde

chaunce, and purpofed firft with fweete and pleafaunte lookes to
bayte and lure eche other feere, to put them in hope therby that
they fhould fatiffie their defires, which done for that tyme they
departed.   And when at the Church at Sanfantino or other place in
Venice, they chanced to meete their louers, they fhewed vnto them
chearful and mery Countenaunce : whych the Louers well notyng,
were the gladdeft Men of the Worlde : and feeing that it was impoffible in Speache to vtter their Myndes, they purpofed by Letters to
fignify the fame.   And hauing found Purciuants to goe betwene
parties (whereof this City was wont to be ful) either of them wrote
an Amorous Letter, to his beloued, the content whereof was, that
they were verye defyrous fecretly to talke with them, thereby to
expreffe the burnynge affectyons that inwardly they bare them,
whych without declaration and vtterance by Mouthe in theyr
owne prefence, woulde breede them Torments more bytter than
Deathe.   And wythin fewe Dayes after (no greate dyfference of
Tyme betweene,) they wrote their Letters.   But Girolamo Bembo
hauing a pregnant Wit, who coulde well Endite both in profe, and
Rime, wrote an excellent fonnet in the prayfe of his Darling in
Italian Meeter, and wyth hys Letter fent the fame vnto hir, the
effect whereof doth follow.

> A liuely face and pearcing beauty bright
> Hath linkt in loue my fely fences all :
> A comely porte, a goodly fhaped wight
> Hath made me flide that neuer thought to fall :
> Hir eyes, hir grace, hir deedes and maners milde,
>   So ftraines my heart that loue hath Wit begilde.
>
> But not one dart of Cupide did me wounde,
> A hundred fhaftes lights all on me at ones :
> As though dame kind fome new deuife had founde,
> To teare my flefh, and crafh a two my bones :
> And yet I feele futch ioy in thefe my woes
>   That as I die my fprite to pleafure goes.
>
> Thefe new found fits futch change in me doe breede,
> I hate the day and draw to darkneffe, lo !

Yet by the Lampe of beauty doe I feede
In dimmeft dayes and darkeft nights alfo,
Thus altring State and changing Diet ftill,
I feele and know the force of Venus will.

The beft I finde, is that I doe confeffe,
I loue you Dame whofe beauty doth excell :
But yet a toy doth breede me fome diftreffe,
For that I dread you will not loue me well,
Than loue yee wot fhall reft in me alone :
And flefhly breft, fhall beare a heart of ftone.

O goddeffe mine, yet heare my voyce of ruthe,
And pitie him that heart prefents to thee :
And if thou want a witneffe for my truth
Let fighes and teares my iudge and record be,
Vnto the ende a day may come in haft,
To make me thinke I fpend no time in wafte.

For nought preuayles in loue to ferue and fue
If full effect ioyne not with words at neede,
What is defire or any fanfies newe
More than the winde ? that fpreades abroade in deede,
My words and works, fhall both in one agree,
To pleafure hir, whofe Seruaunt would I bee.

The fubtill Dames receiuing thofe amorous letters and fong,
difdanfully at the firft feemed to take them at the bringers hands,
as they had determined, yet afterwardes they fhewed better countenaunce. Thefe letters were toffed from one to an other, whereat
they made great paftime, and thought that the fame would come
to very good fucceffe, eyther of theym keepinge ftyll their Hufbande's Letter, and agreed without iniury done one to an other
trimly to deceyue their hufbands. The maner how you fhall
perceyue anone. They deuifed to fend word to their Louers, that
they were ready at al times to fatiffie their futes, if the fame might
be fecretly done, and fafely might make repayre vnto their houfes,
when their Hufbands were abfent, which in any wife they fayde,

muſt be done in the night, for feare leaſt in the day tyme they were
diſcried. Agayne theſe prouident and ſubtill Women had taken
order wyth their Maydes, whom they made priuy to their practyſe
that through their Gardens they ſhould enter into other's houſe,
and bee ſhut in their Chambers without Lyght, there to tary for
their Huſbands, and by any meanes not to bee ſeene or knowne.
This order preſcribed and giuen, Miſtreſſe Lucia firſt did hir louer
to vnderſtand, that the night infuing at foure of the Clock at
the Poſterne dore, which ſhould be left open, he ſhould come into
hir houſe, where hir mayde ſhould be ready to bring him vp to hir
Chaumbre, becauſe hir huſband Maiſter Girolamo woulde that
Night imbarke himſelfe to goe to Padua. The like Miſtreſſe Iſot-
ta did to Maiſter Girolamo, appointing him at fiue of the clock,
whych ſhe ſayd was a very conuenient time, bicauſe mayſter Anſelmo that night would ſup and lye with certayne of his Fryends
at Murano, a place beſides Venice. Vpon theſe newes, the 2
Louers thought them ſelues the moſt valiaunt and fortunate of the
World, no Enterpriſe now there was but ſeemed eaſie for them to
bring to paſſe, yea if it were to expell the Saracens out of Hieruſalem, or to depriue the great Turke of his Kingdome of Conſtantinople. Their ioy was ſutch, as they coulde not tell where they
were, thinking euery houre a whole day till night. At length the
tyme was come ſo long deſired, and the Huſbandes accordingly
gaue diligent attendaunce, and let their Wyues to vnderſtande,
(or at leaſt wyſe beleeued they had) that they could not come home
that night for matters of great importaunce. The Women that
were very wiſe, ſeeing their ſhip ſayle wyth ſo proſperous wynde,
fayned themſelues to credite all that they offered. Theſe young
men tooke eyther of them his Gondola (or as we tearm it theyr
Barge) to diſport themſelues, and hauing ſupped abroade, rowed
in the Canali, which is the Water that paſſeth through diuers
Streates of the Citty, expecting their appoyncted houre. The
Women ready at three of the Clocke, repayred into their Gardens, and after they had Talked, and Laughed together a pretty
whyle, went one into an other's houſe, and were by the maydes
brought vp to the Chaumbers. There eyther of them the Candle
being light, began diligently to view the order and ſituation of the

Place, and by little and little marked the chiefeft things they looked for, committing the fame to memory. Afterwards they put out
the Candle, and both in trembling maner expected the comming of
their Hufbandes. And iuft at four of the Clocke the Mayden of
Madonna Lucia ftoode at the dore to wayte for the comminge of
Maifter Anfelmo, who within a while after came, and gladly was
let in by the mayde, and by hir conducted vp to hir Bed fide. The
place there, was fo dark as Hel, and impoffible for him to know
his Wyfe. The two Wyues were fo like of bigneffe and Speach
as by darke wythout great difficulty they could be known: when
Anfelmo had put of his clothes, he was of his Wyfe amoroufly
intertayned, thinking the Wyfe of Girolamo had receyued him betwene hir armes, who aboue a Thoufande times kiffed hir very
fweetely, and fhe for hir parte fweetely rendred agayne to hym fo
many: what followed it were Folly to defcribe. Girolamo lykewife at 5 of the clocke appeared, and was by the mayde conueied
vp to the Chamber, where he lay with his own Wife, to their great
contentations. Now thefe 2 hufbands thinking they had ben imbraced by their beloued Ladies, to feeme braue, and valiaunt men
of Warre, made greater proofe of their Manhoode, than they were
wont to do. At what time their Wyues (as it pleafed God to manifeft by their deliuery) were begotten with child of 2 fayre Sons,
and they the beft contented Women of the World. This practife
continued betwene them many times, fewe weekes paffing but in
this fort they lay together. Neyther of them for all this perceiued
themfelues to be deluded, or conceyued any fufpition of colluflon for
that the chamber was ftill without light, and in the day the Women commonly fayled not to be together. The time was not longe
but their Bellies began to fwell, whereat their Hufbandes were
exceeding ioyfull, beleeuing verily that eyther of them had fixed
Hornes vpon the other's head. Howbeit the poore men for all their
falfe Beliefe had beftowed theyr Laboure vppon their owne Soyle,
watred onely with the courfe of their proper Fountayne. Thefe
two Iolly Wenches feeyng themfelues by thys amorous practize to be with Childe, beganne to deuife howe they might
break of the fame, douting leaft fome flaunder and ill talke
fhould rife: and thereby the hatred and malice betwene theyr hus-

bandes increafe to greater fury.   And as they were aboute thys
deuife, an occafion chaunced vtterly to diffolue theyr accuftomed
meetynges, but not in that forte as they woulde haue had it.   For
the Women determined as merily they had begon fo iocundlye to
ende: but Fortune the guide of Humane Lyfe, difpofeth all enterpryfes after hir owne pleafure, who lyke a puiffant Lady caryeth
with hir the fucceffe of eche attempte.   The beginning fhe offereth
freely to him that lift, the Ende fhe calleth for, as a ranfome or
trybute payable vnto hir.   In the fame ftreate, or as they call it
Rio, and Canale, not farre from theyr Houfes, there dwelled a young
Woman very fayre and comely, not fully twenty yeares of age,
which then was a Widow, and a lyttle before the wife of M. Nic-
colo Delphino, and the Daughter of M. Giuoanni Moro, called
Gifmonda: fhe befides hir Father's Dowrye (which was more than
a Thoufand Pound) had left hir by hir Hufband, a great Porcyon
of Money, Iewels, Plate, and houfhold Furnitures.   Wyth hir
fell in Loue Aloifio Fofcari, the Nephewe of the Duke, who making
greate fute to haue hir to Wyfe, confumed the time in beholding his Ladye, and at length had brought the matter to fo good
paffe, as one Nighte fhe was contented, at one of the Wyndowes of
hir Houfe directly ouer agaynfte a little lane, to heare him fpeake.
Aloifio maruellous glad of thofe defired Newes, at the appoynted
Nyght, about fyue or fixe of the Clocke, with a Ladder made of
Roapes (bicaufe the Window was very high) went thyther alone.
Beyng at the place and making a figne concluded vppon betweene
them, attended when the gentlewoman fhould throw down hir cord
to draw vp the Ladder accordingly as was appointed, which not
longe after was done.   Gifmonda when fhee had receiued the ende
of the Ladder, tied it faft to the iawme of the wyndow, and gaue a
token to hir Louer to mount. He by force of loue being very venturous, liuely and luftely fcaled the Wyndow: and when he was vppon the Top of the fame, defirous to cafte himfelfe in, to embrace
his Lady, and fhee not readye to receiue him, or elfe vppon other occafion, he fel downe backewarde, thinking as he fell to haue
faued himfelfe twice or thryce by catchyng holde vppon the Ladder,
but it would not be.   Notwithftanding, as God would haue it, the
poife of his Body fell not vppon the pauement of the ftreate fully,

but was ftayed by fome lets in the fall, whych had it not bene fo, no doubt he had bene flayne out of hande, but yet his bones were fore brufed and his heade deepely wounded. The infortunate Louer feeing himfelfe fore hurt wyth that pityfull fall, albeyt hee thought that hee had receiued his Death's Wounde, and impoffyble to liue any longer, yet the loue that he bare to the Widow, did fo far furmount hys payne and the gryefe of hys Body fore crufhed and broken, that fo well as he could, hee rofe vp, and with his hands ftayed the Bloud that ranne from hys Heade, to the intente yt myghte not rayfe fome flaunder vppon the Widow whom hee loued fo wel: and went alonges the ftreate towarde the houfes of Girolamo and Anfelmo aforefaid. Being come thither wyth greate difficulty not able to goe anye further for verye payne and gryefe, hee faynted and fell downe as deade, where the Bloude iffued in futch aboun-daunce, as the Grounde therewyth was greatly imbrued, and euery one that faw him thought him to be voide of Lyfe. Miftreffe Gifmonda exceeding forrowful for this mifchaunce, doubted that he had broken his Necke, but when fhe faw hym depart, fhe com-forted him fo well as fhe could, and drewe vp the Ladder into hir Chamber. Sutch Chaunces happen to earneft Louers, who when they think they haue fcaled the top of theyr Felicity, fodaynly tomble downe into the Pit of extreme defpayre, that better it had ben for them leyfurely to expect the grace of their Ladyes at con-uenient place and houre, than hardily without prouidence to aduen-ture lyke defperat fouldiers to clym the top of the vamure, without meafurying the height of the Wals, or viewynge the fubftaunce of theyr Ladders, do receyue in the ende cruell repulfe, and fal down headlonge either by prefent Death or mortall Wounde, to receyue euerlaftyng reproche and fhame. But turne we agayne now to this difgraced Louer, who lay gafping betwene Lyfe and Death. And as he was in this forrowful ftate, one of the Captaynes, a Noble man appointed to fee orders obferued in the Nighte, wyth hys bande (which they call Zaffi) came thither: and finding hym lying vpon the ground, knew that it was Aloifio Fofcari, and caufing him to be taken vp from the place wher he lay, (thinking he had ben dead) commanded that he fhould be conueyed into the Church adioyn-ing whych immediately was done. And when he had wel confi-

dered the place where hee was founde, hee doubted that eyther
Girolamo Bembo or Anfelmo Barbadico, before whofe Dores hee
thought the murder committed, had kylled him, which afterwards
he beleued to be true, bycaufe he heard a certayne noyfe of mennes
Feete at one of their Doores: wherefore he deuided his company,
placyng fome on the one fide of their houfes, and fome on the other,
befieging the fame fo well as he coulde. And as Fortune woulde
he founde by Neglygence of the mayds, the dores of the ii. houfes
open. It chaunced alfo that Nyght that the two Louers one in
other's Houfe were gone to lye with their Ladyes, who hearynge
the hurly burly, and fturre made in the houfe by the Sergeants,
fodaynely the Women lept out of their Beds, and bearyng their
apparell vppon theyr fhoulders, went home to their houfes throughe
their Gardeins vnfeene of any, and in fearefull wyfe did attende
what fhould be the End of the fame. Girolamo, and Anfelmo not
knowing what rumor and noife that was, although they made haft
in the Darke to cloth themfelues, were by the Offycers without
any field fought, apprehended in ech other's Chamber, and remained Pryfoners at theyr mercy: whereat the Captayne and hys
Band did greatly maruell, knowyng the Hatred betweene them.
But when Torches and Lyghts were brought, and the two Gentlemen caried out of Doores, the wonder was the greater for that
they perceyued them almofte Naked, and pryfoners taken in eche
other's Houfe. And befydes thys admiratyon, futch murmur and
flaunder was bruted, as the quality of euerye Vulgar Heade
coulde fecretlye deuyfe or Imagyne, but fpecyally of the innocente Women, who howe faultleffe they were, euery Man by what
is fayde before maye conceyue, and yet the cancred Stomackes
of that Troupe bare futch Malyce agaynfte them, as they iarred
and brawled agaynft them lyke curryfhe Curres at ftraunge
Dogges whom they neuer fawe before. The Gentlemen immediately were caried to pryfon, ignorant vppon what occafion:
afterwards vnderftandinge that they were committed for the murder of Aloifio Fofcari, and impryfoned like theeues, albeit they
knew themfelues guiltleffe of murder or Theft, yet their gryef and
forrowe was very greate, beynge certayne that all Venice fhould
vnderftande howe they betweene whome had ben mortall hatred,

were nowe become copartners of that whych none but the true
poffeffours ought to enioy : and althoughe they coulde not abyde
to fpeake together, lyke thofe that deadly dyd hate one another,
yet both theyr myndes were fyxed vppon one thought.   In the
ende, conceyuing Fury and defpite agaynfte theyr Wyues, the place
being fo darke that no Lyght or Sunne coulde pierce into the
fame, whereby wythout fhame or difdayne one of them began
to fpeake to another, and with terrible Othes they gaue theyr
fayth to difclofe the troth in what fort eyther of them was taken
in other's Chamber, and frankely told the way and ineane howe
eche of them enioyed hys Pleafure of other's Wyfe : whereupon the
whole matter (according to their knowledge) was altogether by
little and little manifeft and knowne.   Then they accompted theyr
Wiues to be the moft arrant ftrumpets within the whole City, by
difprayfing of whom theyr olde rancor was forgotten, and they
agreed together like two Fryends, who thought that for fhame
they fhould neuer be able to looke Men in the face, ne yet to fhew
themfelues openlye within the Citye, for forrow whereof they
deemed Death the greateft good turne and beft Benefit that could
chance vnto them.   To be fhort, feeing no meanes or occafion to
comfort and relieue theyr penfyue and heauy ftates, they fell into
extreeme defpayre, who afhamed to lyue any longer, deuifed way
to rid them felues of Lyfe, concludyng to make themfelues guilty
of the murder of Aloifo Fofcari : and after mutch talke betweene
them of that cruell determination, ftyll approuing the fame
to be theyr beft refuge, they expected nothyng elfe, but when
they fhould be examined before the Magiftrates.   Fofcari as is
before declared was carryed into the Churche for Deade, and
the Pryeft ftraightly charged wyth the keepynge of hym, who
caufed hym to be conueyed into the myddes of the Church,
fetting II. Torches a Light, the one at his heade, and the other
at his feete, and when the Company was gone, he determined to
goe to bed the remnant of the Nyght to take his reft : but before
he went, feeing the Torches were but fhort, and could not laft pafte
two or three houres, he lighted two other, and fet them in the others
place, for that it fhould feeme to his frends, if any chaunced to
come what care and worfhip he beftowed vpon him.   The Prieft

ready to depart, perceiued the Body fomewhat to moue, with that looking vppon his Face, efpyed his eyes a little to begin to open. Wherewithall fomewhat afraide, he crying out, ran awaye: notwithftanding his Courage began to come to him again, and laying his hand vpon his breaft, perceiued his heart to beate, and then twas out of doubt that he was not dead, although by reafon of loffe of his bloud he thought little life to remaine in him: wherefore he with one of his fellow priefts which was a bed, and the Clerck of the Parifh, caried maifter Fofcari fo tenderly as they could into the Priefts Chamber, which adioined next the Church. Then he fente for a furgeon that dwelt hard by, and required him diligently to fearch the Wounde, who fo well as he could purged the fame from the corrupt Bloud, and perceiuvng it not to be mortall, fo dreffed it wyth Oyles and other precious ointments, as Aloifio came agayn to hymfelfe: and when he had anoynted that recouered body wyth certayne Precious and comfortable Oyles, he fuffred him to take his reft: the Prieft alfo went to bed and flepte till it was Daye, who fo foone as he was vp, went to feeke the Captayne to tel him that Maifter Aloifio was recouered. The Captaine at that tyme was gone to the pallace at San. Marco, to giue the Duke aduertifement of thys Chaunce, after whom the Prieft went and was let in to the Duke's Chamber: to whom he declared what he had done to Aloifio. The Duke very glad to heare tell of his Nephewe's lyfe, although then very penfiue for the newes broughte vnto him by the Captayne, intreated one of the Signor de notte, to take with him two of the beft furgions, and to call him that had already dreffed his Nephew, to goe to vifite the wounded Gentleman, that hee might be certified of the truth of that Chaunce. All which together repaired to the Pryefte's Chaumber, where fyndinge hym not a fleepe, and the Wounde fayre inoughe to heale, dyd therevnto what their cunning thoughte meete: and then they began to inquire of hym, that was not yet full recouered to perfecte fpeache, howe that chaunce happened, telling hym that he might frankelye confeffe vnto them the trouthe. The more dilygent they were in this demaunde, bicaufe the Surgeon that dreffed him fyrft, alleaged, that the Wounde was not made with Sworde, but receiued by fome greate fall or blowe with Mace or

Clubbe, or rather feemed to come of fome high fall from a
Wyndowe, by reafon his Head was fo gryevoufly brufed. Aloifio
hearynge the Surgeons fodayne demaunde, prefentlye aunfwered,
that he fell downe from a Wyndowe, and named alfo the Houfe.
And he had no fooner fpoken thofe Woordes, but he was very
angry wyth him felfe and forrye: and wherewithall his difmayde
Spyrites began to reuyue in futch wyfe, as fodainlye he choyfe
rather to dye than to fpeake any thynge to the dyfhonoure of
myftreffe Gifmonda. Then the Signior di notte, afked hym what
he dyd there aboute that Tyme of the Nyght, and wherfore hee dyd
clymb vp to the Wyndowe, beynge fo hyghe: whych hee coulde not
keepe fecrete, confyderyng the Authorytye of the Magyftrate that
demaunded the queftyon, albeyt hee thoughte that yf his Tongue
hadde runne at large, and commytted a Faulte by rafhe fpeakynge,
hys Bodye fhould therefore fuffer the fmart: wherefore before hee
woulde in any wyfe gyue occafion to flaunder hir, whome hee
loued better than hys owne Lyfe, determined to hazarde hys Lyfe
and Honoure, to the mercye of Iuftice, and fayde: "I declared
euen nowe, whych I cannot denye, that I fell downe from the
wyndowe of Myftreffe Gifmonda Mora. The caufe thereof
(beeynge now at ftate, wherein I knowe not whether I fhall Lyue
or Dye) I will truelye dyfclofe: Myftreffe Gifmonda beynge a
Wydowe and a younge Woman, wythoute anye Man in hir Houfe,
bycaufe by reporte fhee is very rych of Iewels and Money, I purpofed to robbe and dyfpoyle: wherefore I deuyfed a ladder to
clymbe vp to hir Wyndowe, with Mynde full bent to kill all thofe
that fhould refifte me: but my mifhappe was futch as the Ladder
being not well faftened fell downe, and I my felfe therwithall, and
thinking to recouer home to my lodging with my corded Ladder,
my Spirites beganne to fayle, and tombled downe I wotte not
where." The Signor de notte, whofe name was Domenico Mari-
perto hearing him fay fo, maruelled greatly, and was very forie,
that all they in the Chamber, which were a great number, (as at
futch chaunces commonly be) dyd heare thofe Woordes: and
bicaufe they were fpoken fo openly, he was forced to faye vnto
hym: "Aloifio, it doth not a little grieue me that thou haft committed futch follye, but for fo mutch as forrowe now will not

ferue to remedye the Trefpaffe, I mufte needes fhew my felfe both faithfull to my countrey, and alfo carefull of niine honor, withoute refpect of perfons: wherefore thou fhalte remaine here in futch fafe cuftody as I fhal appoint, and when thou art better amended, thou muft according to defert be referred to the Gaole." Leauing him there vnder fure keeping, he went to the counfell of the Dieci, (which magiftrates in that City be of greateft authority) and finding the Lords in Counfell, he opened the whole matter vnto them: the prefidentes of the Counfell which had hearde a great numbre of complaynts of many Theftes don in the Nyght wythin the Citye, tooke order that one of the Captaynes that were appoynted to the dilygente Watche and keepyng of Aloifio, remayning in the Pryefte's Houfe, fhould caufe him to be examined, and with tormentes forced to tell the truth, for that they did verely beleeue that hee had committed many Robberies befides, or at the leaft was priuy and acceffarie to the fame, and knew where the Theues were become. Afterwardes the fayd Counfell did fitte vppon the matter of Girolamo Bembo and Anfelmo Barbadico, found at myde Night naked in eche other's Chambre, and commytted to Pryfon as is before remembred: and bicaufe they had many matters befides of greater importaunce, to confult vppon, amongs which the warres betwene them and Philippo Maria Vifconte, Duke of Milane, the aforefayde caufes were deferred tyll an other tyme, notwythftandyng in the meane while they were examyned. The Duke himfelfe that tyme being in Counfell, fpake moft feuerely againft his Nephew: neuertheleffe he did hardly beleeue that his Nephew being very rich, and indued with great honefty, would abafe himfelfe to a vice fo vile and abhominable as theft is, whereuppon he began to confider of many thinges, and in the ende talked with hys Nephew fecretly alone, and by that meanes learned the trouth of the whole matter. In like maner Anfelmo and Girolamo were Examined by Commiffioners appoyncted by the ftate, what one of them did in an other's chamber, at that houre of the night, who confeffed that many tymes they had feene Aloifio Fofcari, to paffe vp and down before their houfes at times inconuenient, and that night by chaunce one of them not knowing of another, efpied Aloifio, thinking that he lingered about their

houſes to abuſe one of their Wyues, for which cauſe they went
out, and with their Weapons ſodenly killed him : which confeſſion
they openly declared accordingly, as whereupon before they were
agreed. Afterwardes with further circumſtaunce being examined
vpon the Article of being one in another's Chaumber, it appeared
that their firſt tale was vtterly vntrue : of all which contradictions
the Duke was aduertiſed, and was driuen into extreeme admiration, for that the truth of thoſe diſorders coulde not be to the full
vnderſtanded and knowne. Whereuppon the Dieci, and the
aſſiſtauntes were agayne aſſembled in councell accordinge to the
maner, at what time after all things throughly were debated and
ended, the Duke being a very graue man, of excellent Witte, aduaunced to the Dukedome by the conſent of the whole State, as
euery of theym were about to riſe vp, hee ſayde vnto them : " My
Lordes, there reſteth one thinge yet to be moued, which peraduenture hitherto hath not bene thought vpon : there are before vs
two complaynts, the effect whereof in my iudgement is not
throughly conceyed in the Opinions of diuers. Anſelmo Barbadico, and Girolamo Bembo, betwene whom there hath bene euer
continuall hatred, left vnto them as a man may ſay euen by Fathers
Inheritance both of them in eyther of their Chaumbers, were apprehended in a manner naked by our Sergeaunts, and without Torments, or for feare to bee racked vpon the onely interrogatories of
oure miniſters, they haue voluntarily confeſſed that before their
houſes they killed Aloiſio our Nephew : and albeit that our ſayde
Nephew yet liueth, and was not ſtriken by them or any other as
ſhould appeare, yet they confeſſe themſelues guilty of murder.
What ſhall be ſayd then to the matter, doth it not ſeeme doubtfull ?
Our Nephew again hath declared, that in going about to rob the
houſe of Miſtreſſe Giſmonda Mora, whom he ment to haue ſlayne,
he fel downe to the Ground from the top of a window, wherefore
by reaſon ſo many robberies haue bene diſcouered within the
Citty, it may be preſumed that hee was the theefe and malefactor,
who ought to be put to the torments, that the truth may be knowne,
and being found guilty, to feele the ſeuere puniſhment that he
hath deſerued. Moreouer when he was found lying vpon the
ground, he had neither Ladder nor Weapon, whereupon may bee

thought that the fact was otherwife done, than hitherto is confeffed. And becaufe amongs morall vertues, temperance is the
chiefeft and worthy of greateft commendation, and that iuftice
not righteoufly executed, is iniuftice and wronge, it is meete and
conuenient for vs in thefe ftraunge accidents, rather to vfe temperaunce than the rigor of iuftice : and that it may appeare that I
do not fpeake thefe words without good grounde, marke what I
fhall faye vnto you. Thefe two moft mortall enimies doe confeffe
that which is impoffible to be true, for that our Nephew (as is
before declared) is a liue, and his wounde was not made by Sworde,
as hee himfelfe hath confeffed. Now who can tell or fay the contrary, but that fhame for being taken in their feuerall Chambers,
and the difhonefty of both their Wyues, hath caufed them to
defpife life, and to defire death? we fhall finde if the matter be
diligently inquired and fearched, that it will fall out otherwife
than is already fuppofed by common opinion. For the contrariety
of examinations, vnlikelihoode of circumftances, and the impoffibility of the caufe, rendreth the matter doubtfull : wherefore it is
very needeful diligently to examine thefe attempts, and thereof
to vfe more aduifed confideration. On the other fide, our Nephew
accufeth himfelfe to be a theefe and which is more, that hee ment
to kill Miftreffe Mora when hee brake into hir houfe. Vnder
this Graffe, my Lords, as I fuppofe, fome other Serpent lieth hiden,
that is not yet thought of. The Gentleman yee know before this
time was neuer defamed of futch outrage, ne fufpected of the
leaft offence that may be obiected : befides that, all yee doe know,
(thanks therefore be geuen to almighty God) that he is a man of
great richeffe, and poffeffions, and hath no neede to rob : for
what neceffity fhould driue him to rob a widowe, that hath of his
owne liberally to beftow vpon the fuccour of Widowes? Were
there none els of fubftance in the Citty for him to geue attempt
but to a Wyddowe, a comfortleffe creature, contented with quiet
lyfe to lyue amonges hir family within the boundes of hir owne
houfe? What if hir richeffe, Iewels and plate be great, hath not
Aloifio of his owne to redouble the fame? but truly this Robbery
was done after fome other manner than hee hath confeffed : to
vs then my Lords it appertayneth, if it fo ftande with your plea-

fures, to make further inquiry of the fame, promifinge vnto you
vppon our Fayth, that wee fhall imploy our whole diligence in the
true examination of thys matter, and hope to bring the fame to
futch good ende, as none fhall haue caufe to blame vs, the finall
fentence whereof fhall bee referued to youre iudgement." Thys
graue requeft and wife talke of the Duke pleafed greatly the Lordes
of the Counfayle, who referred not onely the examination, but alfo
the finall fentence vnto hym. Whereuppon the wyfe Prynce
beinge fully enformed of the chaunce happened to his Nephewe,
attended onely to make fearch, if he could vnderftand the occafion why Bembo and Barbadico fo foolifhly had accufed themfelues of that which they neuer did. And fo after mutch counfayle, and great tyme contriued in their feueral examinations, his
Nephew then was well recouered, and able to goe abroade, being
fet at liberty. The Duke then hauinge beftowed hys trauayle
with the other two prifoners, communicated to the Lords of the
aforefayd councel called Dieci the whole trouth of the matter.
Then he caufed with great difcretion, proclamation to be made
throughout Venice, that Anfelmo and Girolamo fhold be beheded
betwene the two Pyllers, and Aloifio hanged, whereby he thought
to know what fute the women would make, eyther with or againft
their Hufbandes, and what euidence miftreffe Gifmonda woulde
geue againft Aloifio. The brute hereof difperfed, diuers talke
thereuppon was rayfed, and no communication of any thing els in
open ftreats, and priuate houfes, but of the putting to death of
thofe men. And bicaufe all three were of honorable houfes, their
kinfmen, and Friendes made fute by all poffible meanes for theyr
pardon. But their Confeffions publifhed, the rumor was made
worfe, (as it dayly chaunceth in like cafes) than the matter was in
deede, and the fame was noyfed how Fofcari had confeffed fo many
theftes done by him at diuers tymes, as none of his freends or Kin
durft fpeake for him. Miftreffe Gifmonda which bitterly lamented
the mifchaunce of hir Louer, after fhe vnderftoode the confeffion
hee had made, and euidently knew that becaufe hee woulde not
bleamifh hir honour, he had rather willingly forgo his owne, and
therewithall his lyfe, felt hir felfe fo oppreffed with feruent loue,
as fhee was ready prefently to furrender hir ghoft. Wherefore

fhee fent him woorde that he fhould comfort himfelfe, becaufe
fhee was determined to manifeft the very trouth of the matter, and
hoped vppon hir declaration of true euidence, fentence fhoulde bee
reuoked, for teftimony whereof, fhee had his louinge letters yet to
fhewe, written to hir with his owne handes, and would bring forth
in the iudgement place, the corded ladder, which fhe had kept ftil
in her chamber. Aloifio hearinge thefe louing newes, and of the
euidence which his Lady woulde giue for his defence, was the
gladdeft man of the worlde, and caufed infinite thankes to be
rendred vnto hir, wyth promife that if hee might bee rid and difcharged out of prifon, he woulde take hir for his louing fpoufe and
wyfe. Whereof the gentlewoman conceyued finguler folace, louing
hir deere freende with more entier affection than hir owne foule.
Miftreffe Lucia, and miftreffe Ifotta, hearing the difpercled voyce
of the death of their hufbands, and vnderftanding the cafe of mis-
treffe Gifmonda by an other woman, layd their heads together
likwife to deuife meanes for fauing their hufbandes liues: and
entring into their Barge, or Gondola, wente to feeke miftreffe Gifmonda and when they had debated vppon the trouthe of thefe
euents, concluded with one affent to prouide for the fafegarde and
deliuerye of theyr hufbandes, wherein they fhewed themfelues
both wife and honeft. For what ftate is more honorable and of
greater Comforte than the marryed Lyfe, if in deede they that haue
yoaked themfelues therein be conformable to thofe Delightes, and
contentation which the fame conduceth? Wealth and Riches
maketh the true vnyted couple to reioyce in the Benefits of Fortune,
graunted by the fender of the fame, either of them prouiding for
difpofing thereof, againft the decripite time of olde age, and for
the beftowing of the fame vppon the Fruicte accrued of theyr
Bodies. Pouerty in any wife dothe not offend them, both of them
glad to laboure and trauaile like one Body, to fuftaine theyr poore
and neady Lyfe, eyther of them Comfortably doth Minyfter comforte in the cruell tyme of Aduerfity, rendring humble thankes to
God for hys fharp Rodde and Punyfhment enflicted vppon them
for their manyfolde finnes commytted againfte hys maieftye,
trauailinge by night and Daye by fweatinge Browes to get browne
Breade, and drynke ful thin to ceafe the Cryes and pytifull crau-

inges of their tender Babes, wrapt in Cradle and inſtant on their
mother to fill their hungry mouthes. Aduerſe fortune maketh
not one to forſake the other. The louing Wyfe ceaſeth not by
paynfull ſute to trot and go by Night and day in heate and colde
to relieue the miſerye of hir huſband. He likewiſe ſpareth not
his payne to get and gayne the liuyng of them both. He abrode
and at home according to his called ſtate, ſhe at home to ſaue the
Lucre of that Labor, and to doe ſutch neceſſary trauayle incident to
the married kinde. He carefull for to get, ſhe heedeful for to ſaue,
he by trafique and Arte, ſhee by diligence and houſholde toile. O
the happy ſtate of married folke : O ſurpaſſing delights of mariage bed : which maketh theſe 11. poore Gentlewomen, that by
honorable pollicy ſaued the honor of themſelues and honeſty of
theyr huſbandes, to make humble ſute for their preſeruation, who
were like to be berieued of their greateſt comforts. But come we
again to declare the laſt act of this Comical diſcourſe. Theſe maried
Women, after this chaunce befell, vpon their huſbandes impryſonment, began to be abhorred of their Friendes and Parentes, for that
they were ſuſpected to be diſhoneſte, by reaſon whereof dolefully
lamenting their Misfortune, notwithſtandynge their owne conſcience
voyde of faulte, dyd byd them to be of good cheere and comfort.
And when the daye of execution came, they dyd theyr Friends and
Parents to vnderſtand that their conceiued opinyon was vntrue,
and prayed them to forbeare their diſdain and malice, till the truth
ſhould be throughly manifeſted, aſſuring them that in the End their
owne innocencie and the guiltleſſe cryme of their Huſbands ſhould
openly be reuealed to the Worlde. In the meane time they made
requeſt vnto their Friendes, that one of the Lordes called Auogadori
might be admitted to vnderſtande their caſe, the reſt to be referred to themſelues, wherein they had no neede either of Proctor
or Aduocate. This requeſt ſeemed verye ſtraunge to their friends,
deeming their caſe to be ſhameful and abhominable : neuertheles
diligently they accomplyſhed their requeſt and vnderſtandyng that
the Counſell of the Dieci had commytted the matter wholy to the
Duke, they made a ſupplicatyon vnto hym in the name of the three
Gentlewomen, wherein they craued nothing elſe but theyr matter
might be hearde. The Duke perceiuying hys aduiſe like to take

effect, affigned them a Day, commaundinge them at that tyme
before hym and the Lords of the Councell and all the College of the
eftate to appeare. The Day being come, all the Lordes affembled,
defirous to fee to what iffue this matter would grow. On the
morning the three Gentlewomen honeftly accompanied with other
Dames, went to the Palace, and goynge along the ftreate of San
Marco the people began to vtter many raylyng words againft them:
fome cried out (as we fee by vnftable order the vulgare people in
like cafes vfe to do) and doinge a certain curtify by way of difdain
and mockery : "Behold the honest women, that without fending
their hufbands out of Venice, haue placed them in the Caftell of
Cornetto, and yet the arrante Whoores bee not afhamed to fhewe
them felues abrode, as thoughe they hadde done a thynge that
were Honefte and prayfe worthye." Other fhot forth theyr Boltes,
and wyth theyr Prouerbes proceedyng from their malicious Mouthes
thwited the pore Women at their pleafure. Other alfo feeyng
Myftreffe Gifmonda in their Company, thought that fhe went to
declame againft maifter Aloifio Fofcari, and none of them all
hapned on the trouth. Arryued at the pallace, afcending the
marble ftaires or fteps of the fame, they were brought into the
great hal, wher the Duke appointed the matter to be heard. Thither
repaired the friends and thofe of neareft kin to the three Gentlewomen, and before the matter did begin, the Duke caufed alfo the
thre prifoners to be brought thither. Thither alfo came many
other Gentlemen, with great defire to fee the end of thofe euents.
Silence being made the Duke turning his face to the women, fayd
vnto them : "Ye Gentlewomen haue made requefte by fupplyca-
tyon to graunt you publike audyence accordyng to Iuftice, for that
you do alleage that Law and order doth fo require, and that euery
wel ordred common wealth condemneth no fubiecte withoute due
anfwere by order of lawe. Beholde therefore, that we defirous to
do Iuftice, bee ready in Place to heare what ye can fay." The
two hufbands were very angrie and wrathfull againft their
wiues, and the more their ftomackes did fret with choler and difdayne, by how mutch they faw their impudente and fhameleffe
wiues wyth futch audacity to appeare before the maiefty of a
counfel fo honourable and dreadfull, as though they had ben the

moft honefte and chaft Women of the World. The two honefte
wiues perceyued the anger and difpleafure of their hufbands, and
for all that were not afrayde ne yet difmayde, but fmyling to themfelues and fomewhat mouing their heads in decente wyfe feemed
vnto them as though they had mocked them. Anfelmo more
angry and impacient then Girolamo, brake out into futch furie,
as had it not ben for the maiefty of the place, and the Companye of
People to haue ftayed him, woulde haue kylled them : and feyng he
was not able to hurt them, he began to vtter the vyleft Woords,
that he poffibly could deuife agaynft them. Miftreffe Ifotta
hearing hir hufband fo fpytefully to fpit forth his poyfon in the
prefence of that honourable affemblye, conceiued courage, and
crauinge licence of the Duke to fpeake, with merrye countenance
and good vttrance began thus to fay her mind: "Moft excellent Prince, and yee right honourable Lordes, I doe perceyue
how my deare hufbande vncomely and very difhoneftly doth
vfe himfelfe agaynft me in this noble company, thincking alfo
that mayfter Girolamo Bembo is affected with like rage and
minde agaynft this Gentlewoman myftreffe Lucia hys wyfe, although more temperate in words, he do not expreffe the fame.
Agaynft whom if no reply be made, it may feeme that he doth well
and hath fpoken a truth, and that we by filence do condemne our
felues to be thofe moft wicked women whom hee alleageth vs to be.
Wherefore by your gratious pardon and licence (moft honourable)
in the behalfe of miftreffe Lucia and my felfe, for our defence
I purpofe to declare the effect of my mynde, although my purpofe
be cleane altered from that I had thought to fay, being now iuftly
prouoked by the vnkinde behauiour of him whom I loue better
than my felfe, and whofe difloyalty, had hee beene filent and not fo
rafhly runne to the ouerthrow of me and my good name, coulde I
haue concealed, and onely touched that which had concerned the
Purgation and fauegard of them both, which was the onely intent
and meaning of vs, by making our humble fupplication to your
Maiefties. Neuertheleffe, fo farre as my feeble force fhall ftretch,
I will affay to do both the one and the other, although it be not
appropriate to our kinde in publike place to declayme, nor yet to
open futch bold attempts, but that neceffity of matter and opor-

tunity of time, and place dothe bolden vs to enter into these termes, whereof we craue a thoufand pardons for our vnkindely dealings, and render double thanks to your honours, for admitting vs to fpeake. Be it knowne therefore vnto you, that our husbands agaynft duety of loue, lawes of mariage, and againft all reafon, do make their heauy complaynts, which by and by I will make playne and euident. I am right well affured, that their extreme rage and bitter hearts forrow do proceede of 2 occafions: The one, of the murder whereof they haue falfely accufed theymfelues: the other of iealoufie, which grieuoufly doth gnawe their hearts, thinking vs to be vile, and abhominable Women, becaufe they were furprifed in ech other's Chaumber. Concerning the murder, if they haue foyled their handes therein, it appertayneth vnto you my Lords to render their defert. But how can the fame be layd to our charge, for fomutch as they (if it were done by them) committed the fame without our knowledge, our help and counfel? And truly I fee no caufe why any of vs ought to be burdened with the outrage, and mutch leffe caufe haue they to laye the fame to our charge: for meete it is that he that doth any vnlawful act, or is acceffary to the fame, fhould fuffer the due penalty and feuere chaftifement accordingly as the facred lawes do prefcribe, to be an example for other to abftayne from wicked facts. But hereof what neede I to difpute, wherein the blind may fee to bee none offence, becaufe (thankes bee to GOD) Mayfter Aloifio liueth, which declareth the fonde Confeffion of our vngentil husbandes to bee contrary to trouth? And if fo be our hufbands in deede had done futch an abhominable enterprife, reafon and duety had moued vs to forrowe and lament them, becaufe they be borne of noble bloud, and be gentlemen of this noble Citty, which like a pure virgin inuiolably doth conferue hir lawes and cuftomes. Great caufe I fay, had we to lament them, if lyke homicides, and murderers they had fpotted their bloud with futch fowle bleamifh thereby deferuing death, to leaue vs yong Women Widowes in wofull plight. Nowe it behoueth me to fpeake of the Iealoufie they haue conceyued of vs, for that they were in ech other's Chamber, which truly is the doubtfull knot and fcruple that forceth all their difdaine and griefe. This I knowe well is the Nayle that

pierceth their heart: other caufe of offence they haue not: who
like men not well aduifed, without examination of vs and our de-
meanour, bee fallen into defpayre, and like men defperate, haue
wrongfully accufed themfelues: but becaufe I may not confume
words in vayne, to ftay you by my long difcourfe from matters of
greater importaunce, I humbly befeech you (right excellent prince)
to commaunde them to tell what thing it is, which fo bitterly doth
torment them." Then the Duke caufed one of the noble men affis-
taunt there, to demaund of them the queftion: Who aunfwered
that the chiefeft occafion was, bicaufe they knew their Wyues to
be Harlots, whom they fuppofed to be very honeft: and forfomutch as they knew them to be futch, they conceyued forrow and
griefe, which with futch extremity did gripe them at the heart, as
not able to fuftayne that great Infamy, afhamed to be fene of men,
were induced through defire of death to confeffe that they neuer
did. Miftreffe Ifotta hearing them fay fo, began to fpeak agayne,
turning hir felfe vnto them: "Were you offended then at a thynge
which yee thought inconuenient and not meete to be done? Wee
then haue greateft caufe to complayne. Why then fweete Hufband
went you to the Chaumber of miftreffe Lucia at that time of the
night? What had you to do there? What thing thought you to
finde there more than was in your own houfe? And you Mayfter
Girolamo, what conftrayned you to forfake your Wyue's Bed to
come to my Hufband's, where no man euer had, or at this prefent
hath to do but himfelfe? Were not the Sheetes of the one fo
white, fo fine, neate, and fweete as the other? I am (moft noble
Prince) fory to declare my Hufbande's folly, and afhamed that hee
fhould forfake my Bed to go to an other, that did accompt myfelfe
fo well worthy to entertayne hym in myne owne, as the beft Wyfe
in Venice, and now through his abufe, I abftayne to fhewe my
felfe amonges the Beautifull, and noble Dames of this Citty.
The lyke mifliking of hirfelfe is in miftreffe Lucia, who (as you
fee) may be numbred amongs the fayreft. Eyther of you ought to
haue bene contented with your Wyues, and not (as wickedly
you haue done) to forfake them, to feeke for better breade than is
made of Wheate, or for purer Golde than whereof the Angell is
made: O worthy deede of yours, that haue the Face to leaue your

owne Wyues, that be comely, fayre, and honeft, to feeke after
ftraunge Carrion. O beaftly order of Men that cannot conteyne
their luft within the boundes of their owne Houfe, but muft goe
hunt after other Women as Beaftes do after the nexte of their
kinde that they chaunce vppon. What vile affection poffeffed your
hearts to luft after others Wyfe? You make complaynte of vs,
but wee with you haue right good caufe to be offended, you
ought to bee grieued with your owne diforder, and not with others
offence, and thys your affliction patiently to beare, bycaufe you
went about to beguile one an other's Loue, lyke them that be
weary, and Glutted with their owne fare, feekinge after other
daynties more delicate if they were to be founde. But prayfed
be GOD and our prouident difcretion, if any hurt or fhame hath
chaunced, the fame doth light on you. Moreouer I know no
caufe why men fhould haue more liberty to doe euill than we
Women haue: albeit through the weaknes and cowardife of our
Sexe, yee men will doe what ye lift. But ye be now no Lords, nor
we Seruaunts, and hufbands we do you call, bicaufe the holy
Lawes of Matrimony (which was the firft Sacrament giuen by
GOD to Men after the creation of the Worlde) doe require equall
fayth, and fo well is the hufband bound to the Wyfe as fhe vnto
him. Go to then and make your complaynt: the next Affe or
Beaft ye meete take hir to be your Wyfe. Why do yee not know
that the balance of iuftice is equall, and wayeth downe no more
of one fide than of other ? But let vs nowe leaue of to reafon of
this matter, and come to that for which we be come hither. Two
things (moft ryghteous Prynce) haue moued vs to come before
your maiefty, and all this honourable affembly, which had they
not bene, we would haue bene afhamed to fhewe our Faces, and
leffe prefumed to fpeake or once to open our Lippes in this Noble
audience, which is a place only meete for them that be moft
Expert, and eloquent Orators, and not for vs, to whom the Needle,
and Diftaffe be more requifite. The firft caufe that forced vs to
come forth of our owne houfe, was to let you underftand that our
Hufbands be no murderers, as is fuppofed, neyther of this Gentleman prefent maifter Aloifio, ne yet of any man els: and thereof
we haue fufficient and worthy teftimony. But herein we neede

not to trauaile mutch, or to vfe many wordes: for neyther maifter
Alofio is flayne, ne any other murdred that is known or manifeft
hitherto.   One thyng refteth, which is that Madonna Lucia and
I do humbly befeech youre excellente Maieftye, that youre grace
and the authoritye of the right honourable Lords here prefent, will
vouchfafe to reconcile vs to our hufbands, that we may obtayne
pardon and fauor at their handes, bicaufe we haue fo manifeftly
made their acts to appeare, and for that we be the offence, and
they the Offendours, and yet by their owne occafions, we haue
committed the Error (if it may be fo termed.)   And now to come
to the conclufion, I doe remember, fithens I was a Chylde, that I
haue heard the Gentlewoman my mother faye (whofe foule God
pardon) many times vnto me, and other my fifters, and to mis-
treffe Lucia, that was brought vp with vs, being by hir inftructed
in diuers good and vertuous Leffons, that all the honor a woman
can doe vnto hir hufband, whereby fhe beautifieth him and his
whole race and family, confifteth in hir honeft, chaft, and vertuous lyfe, without which, fhe oughte rather to die than liue.
And that a Gentleman's Wyfe when fhe hath giuen hir body to the
vfe of an other man, is the common marke for euery man to point
at in the ftreate where fhe goeth, hir hufband therby incurring
reproche and fhame, whych no doubt is the greateft iniury and
fcorne that an honeft Gentleman can receiue, and the mofte fhamefull reproche that can deface his houfe.   Which Leffon we fo well
remembryng, defirous not to fuffer the careleffe and vnbrideled
appetites of our hufbandes to be vnrained, and runne at large to
fome difhoneft Ende, by a faithfull and commendable pollicy, did
prouide for the mifchyefe that myghte enfue.   I neede not heere
rehearfe the enimytye and debate that manye yeares did raigne
betweene our hufbandes Fathers, bicaufe it is knowne to the
whole City.   Wee too therefore here prefente, the Wiues of thofe
noble Gentlemen, brought vp together from oure Cradle, perceiuing
the malyce betwene our hufhandes, made a vertue of Neceffity,
deemynge it better for vs to lofe our fweete and auncient conuerfation, than to mynifter caufe of difquietneffe.   But the neareneffe
of our houfes would not that naturall hatred fhoulde defraude
and take away olde ingrafted amity.   Wherefore many times

when our Hufbands were gone forth, we met together, and talked
in our Gardens, betwene whych there is but a flender hedge befet
with Primme and Rofes, which commoditye in their abfence we
did difcretly vfe. And as fometimes for pleafure we walked with
oure hufbandes there, ye (fhee turninge vnto them) did caft your
eyes vpon ech other's wyfe, and were ftrayghte way in loue, or elfe
perchance you fained your felues to bee, whych efpied by vs,
many times betwene our felues did deuife vppon the fame, and
red your amorous letters, and fonnet fent vnto vs. For which
difloyalty and treafon toward vs your Wyues, we fought no difhonour to youre perfons, wee were content to fuffer you to bee
abufed with your fond loue, we blabbed it not abroade to our
Goffips, as many leude and fantafticall women bee wont to doe,
thereby to rayfe flaunder to our hufbands, and to fturre vp ill
reporte vpon them, whofe infirmities it becommeth vs to conceale
and hide. We deuifed meanes by fome other way to let you
underftand your fault, and did caft vpon you many times right
louinge lookes. Which although it were agaynfte our owne
defire, yet the caufe, and full conclufion of the fame, was to
practife, if it were poffible, to make you frendes: But confideringe
that this loue, and allurementes of eyther parts, could not tend to
other end, as wee coniectured, but to increafe difpleafure, and to
put the fwords into your handes, we therefore confulted, and
vniformely in one minde agreed for the appeafinge, and fatiffaction of all partes, at futch nightes as ye fayned to go into diuers
places about earneft affayres as yee alleaged, Miftreffe Lucia
with the help of Caffandra my mayde, through the Gardeine came
into my chamber, and I by meanes of Iane hir maide by like way
repayred vnto hirs. And yee poore men guided by our maydes
were brought vnto your chambers where ye lay with your owne
Wyues, and fo by tilth of others land in ftraunge foyle (as yee
beleeued) yee loft no labour. And bicaufe your embracements
then, were like to thofe atchieued by amorous Gentlemen, vfinge
vs with more earneft defire than you were wont to do, both wee
were begotten with childe: which ought to be very gladfome,
and gratefull vnto you, if yee were fo fayne to haue children as
yee fhewed your felues to bee. If then none other offence doth
grieue you, if remorfe of Confcience for other caufe doeth not

offend you, if none other forrowe doeth difpleafe you : gieue ouer
your griefe. Remit your difpleafure. Be glad, and ioyfull. Thanke
vs for our pollicy and pleafaunt difport that wee made you.
If hitherto yee haue ben enimies, henceforth be frends, put of that
auncient mallice fo long continued, mitigate your hatefull moode,
and liue yee from henceforth like friendly Gentlemen, yelde vp your
rancor into the lap of your Countrey, that fhee may put him in
exile for euer, who like a pitifull, and louing mother woulde
gladly fee all hir children of one accorde and minde.   Which if
yee doe, (ye fhall do fingulare pleafure to your friendes), ye
fhall doe great difcomfort to your foes, yee fhall do fingular
good to the commonwealth, yee fhall doe greateft benefit to your
felues, ye fhall make vs humble Wyues, yee fhall encreafe
your pofterity, yee fhall be prayfed of all men, and finally
fhall depart the beft contented that euer the World brought
forth.   And now becaufe yee fhall not thinke that wee haue
picked out thys Tale at our fingers ends, thereby to feeke your
fauegard and our owne Fame, and prayfe, beholde the letters
which you fent vs, beholde you owne handes fubfcribed to the
fame, beholde your feales affigned thereunto, which fhall render
true teftimony of that which vnfaynedly we haue affirmed."
Then both deliuered their letters, which viewed and feene, were
well knowne to be their owne hufbandes handes, and the fame fo
well approued hir tale, as their hufbands were the gladdeft
men of the world and the Duke and Seignory maruayloufly fatisfied and contented.   In fo mutch as the whole affembly with
one voyce, cried out for their hufbands deliueraunce.   And fo
with the confent of the Duke and the whole feignory they were
clearely difcharged.   The Parents, Cofins, and Friends of the
husbands and wyues were wonderfully amazed to heere this long
hyftory, and greatly prayfed the maner of their deliuery, accoumpt-
ing the women to be very wife, and miftreffe Ifotta to be an
eloquent gentlewoman, for that fhee had fo well defended the
caufe of their hufbands and of themfelues.   Anfelmo and Girolamo
openly in the prefence of all the people embraced, and kiffed
their Wyues with great reioyfing.   And then the hufbands fhaked
one an other by the hands, betwene whom began a Brotherly
accorde, and from that time forth liued in perfect amity, and

Friendſhip, exchaunging the wanton loue that eyther of them
bare to other's wyfe into Brotherly Friendſhip, to the great delight
of the whole Citty.   When the multitude aſſembled, to heare this
matter throughly was ſatiſſied, the Duke with cheerefull Countenaunce lookinge toward Giſmonda, ſayde thus vnto hir: "And
you fayre Gentlewoman, what haue you to ſay: Bee bolde to vtter
your minde, and wee wil gladly heare you." Miſtreſſe Giſmonda
baſhfull to ſpeake, began wonderfully to bluſh, into whoſe cheekes
entred an orient rud, intermixed with an alabaſter white, which
made her countenaunce more amiable than it was wont to be.
After ſhe had ſtode ſtill a while with hir eyes declined towards
the ground, in comly wiſe lifting them vp againe with ſhamefaſt
audacity ſhe began thus to ſpeake: "If I moſt Noble Prince, in
open audience ſhould attempt to diſcourſe of Loue, whereof I
neuer had experience, or knew what thing it was, I ſhould be
doubtfull what to ſay thereof, and peraduenture durſt not open
my mouth at al.   But hearing my father (of worthy memory)
many times to tel that your maieſty in the time of your youth diſdained not to open your heart to receiue the amorous flames of
loue, and being aſſured that there is none but that doth loue little
or mutch, I do not doubt but for the words which I ſhal ſpeake,
to obtaine both pity and pardon.   To come then to the matter:
God I thanke him of his goodneſſe, hath not permitted me to bee
one of thoſe women, that like hipocrites do mumble their Pater-
noſter to ſainčts: appearing outwardly to be devout and holy
and in Fruič doe bring forth Deuils, and al kinds of vices, ſpecially
ingratitude, which is a vice that doth ſuck and dry vp the foun-
tain of godly Piety.   Life is deare to mee (as naturally it is to all)
next which I eſteeme myne honor, which is to be preferred before
life, bicauſe without honor life is of no regard.   And where man
and woman do liue in ſhame notorious to the world, the ſame
may be termed a liuing death rather than a life.   But the loue
that I beare to mine onely beloued Aloiſio here preſent, I do
eſteeme aboue al the Iewels and treaſures of the world, whoſe
perſonage I do regard more than mine owne Lyfe.   The reaſon
that moueth me thereto is very great, for before that I loued him
or euer ment to fixe my mind that way, he dearely regarded me,
continually deuiſing which way he might win and obtain my

loue, fparing no trauel by Night and Day to feeke the fame. For
which tender affection fhould I fhew myfelf vnkind and froward?
God forbid. And to be playn with your honors, he is more deare
and acceptable vnto me, than the balles of mine own eyes, being
the chiefeft things that appertain to the furniture of the body of
man, without which no earthly thing can be gladfome and ioyful
to the fenfe, and feelinge. Laft of all his amorous, and affectionate
demonftration of his loue towards me, by declaringe himfelfe to
be carefull of mine honor, rather more willinge to beftow his
owne, than to fuffer the fame to be touched with the leaft fufpicion of difhonefty, I can not choofe, but fo faythfully imbrace,
as I am ready to guage my life for his fake, rather than his finger
fhoulde ake for offence. And where hath there bene euer found
futch liberality in any louer? What is he that hath bene euer fo
prodigall, to employ his life (the moft fpeciall pledge in this
worlde,) rather than hee would fuffer his beloued to incurre dif-
honoure? Many hyftoryes haue I red, and Chronicles of our time,
and yet I haue found few or none comparable vnto thys Gentleman, the like of whom be fo rare and feldome as white Crowes,
or Swannes of colour blacke. O finguler liberality, never hearde
of before. O fact that can neuer be fufficiently prayfed. O true
loue moft vnfayned. Maifter Aloifio rather than he would haue
my fame any one iote to be impayred, or to fuffer any fhadow of
fufpition to bleamifh the fame, frankly hath confeffed himfelfe to
be a theefe, and murdrer, regardinge mee and mine honor more
than himfelfe, and life. And albeit that he might a thoufand
wayes haue faued himfelfe without the imprifonment and aduerfity which he hath fuftayned : neuertheleffe after he had fayd,
beinge then paft remembrance through the fall, that he fell downe
from my window, and perceyued how mutch that confeffion would
preiudice and hurt my good name, and hurt the known honefty
of the fame, of his good wyll did chofe to dye rather than to fpeake
any words that might breede yll opinion of mee, or the leaft
thinge of the worlde that might ingender infamy and flaunder.
And therefore not able to revoke the words hee had fpoken of the
fall, nor by any meanes coulde coloure the fame, hee thought to
faue the good name of another by his owne hurt. If he then thus
redily and liberally hath protruded his life into manifeft daunger

for my benefit and faueguard, preferring mine honour aboue the
care of himfelfe, fhall not I abandon all that I haue, yea and
therewithall hazard mine honor for his faluation? But what?
Shall I difdayne bountifully to imploy my felfe and all the
endeuor of my Frendes for his deliuery? No, no (my Lords) if
I had a thoufand liues, and fo many honors at my commaundement, I woulde giue them al for his releyfe and comfort, yea
if it were poffible for me to recouer a frefh x.c.m. lyues, I
woulde fo frankly beftow them all, as euer I defired to liue, that
I might enioy mine owne Aloifio. But I am forry, and euer
fhal be forry, for that it is not lawful for me to do more for him,
than that which my power and poffibility is able. For if he
fhould die, truely my life could not endure: if he were depriued
of life, what pleafure fhould I haue to liue in this world after him:
whereby (mofte honorable and righteous iudge,) I beleeue before
the honeft, not to loofe any one iote of myne honor, bicaufe I
being (as you may fee) a younge Woman and a Widow defirous
to marry againe, it is lawful for me to loue and to bee beloued, for
none other intent (whereof God is the onely iudge) but to attaine
a hufbande according to my degre. But if I fhould lofe my
reputation and honor, why fhould not I aduenture the fame for
hym, that hath not fpared hys own for me? Now to come to the
effect of the matter, I do fay wyth al dutifull reuerence, that it
is an accufation altogither falfe and vntrue, that euer mayfter
Aloifio came to my houfe as a Theefe againft my wil. For what
neede he to be a thefe, or what nede had he of my goodes, that is
a Lorde and owner of twenty times fo mutch as I haue? Alas
good Gentleman, I dare depofe and guage my lyfe, that he neuer
thoughte mutch leffe dyd any robbery or thing vnlawful, wherewith iuftly he may be charged, but he repayred to my houfe
with my confent, as a louing and affectionate Louer, the circum-
ftance whereof, if it be duly marked, muft aduouch the fame to
be of trouth infallible. For if I had not giuen him licence to
come, how was it poffible for him to conuey his ladder fo high,
that was made but of Ropes, and to faften the fame to the iaume
of the window, if none within did helpe hym? Againe, howe could
the Window of the Chaumber be open at that time of the night,
which is ftill kept fhut, if it had not bene by my confent? But

I with the helpe of my mayde threwe downe to him a little Rope,
whereunto he tyed his Ladder and drewe the fame vp, and making
it fo faft, as it could not vndo, gaue a figne for him to Mounte.
But as both our ill Fortune would haue it, before I could catch
any hold of him, to mine ineftimable griefe and hart's forrow he
fell downe to the ground.   Wherefore (my Lords) I befeech your
honours to reuoke the confeffion wherein he hath made hymfelfe
to be a theefe.   And you maifter Aloifio declare the trouth as it
was, fith I am not afhamed in this honourable affemble to tel the
fame.   Beholde the letters (my Lordes) which fo many tymes he
wrote vnto me, wherein hee made fuite to come to my fpeache,
and continually in the fame doth call me Wyfe.   Beholde the
Ladder, which till nowe, did ftill remayne in my chaumber.   Beholde
my maide, whych in all mine affayres, is as it were myne owne
hande and helper."   Aloifio being hereupon demaunded by the
Lordes of the articles, which fhe in hir tale had recited, confeffed
them al to be true: who alfo at the fame inftant was difcharged.
The Duke greatly commended them both, hir for hir ftoute
audacity, in defence of an innocent Gentleman, and him for his
honour, and modefty, by feeking to preferue the Fame and good
reporte of a vertuoufe Gentlewoman.   Whych done, the Counfell
difaffembled and brake up.   And the friendes of both the parties
accompanied them home to the houfe of miftreffe Gifmonda,
where to the great reioyce, and pleafure of all men, they were
folemnely maried in fumptuous and honourable wife, and Aloifio
with hys Wyfe lyued in great profperity long time after.   Miftreffe
Lucia, and miftreffe Ifotta, at the expyred tyme were deliuered
of two goodly fonnes, in whom the Fathers tooke great Ioy, and
delight.   Who wyth their Wyues after that tyme liued very
quietly, and well, one louing an other like naturall Brethren, many
times fporting among themfelues difcretely at the deceipts of their
Wyues.   The wifedome of the Duke alfo was wonderfully extolled
and commended of all men, the fame whereof was increafed
and bruted throughout the Region of Italy.   And not without caufe.   For by hys prudence and aduife, the Dominion of the
State, and Common wealth was amplified and dilated.   And yet
in th'ende being old and impotent, they vnkindly depofed him
from his Dukedom.

THE TWENTY-SEVENTH NOUELL.

The Lorde of Virle, by the commaundement of a fayre younge Wydow called Zilia, for hys promife made, the better to attaine hir loue, was contented to remayne dumbe the fpace of three yeares, and by what meanes he was reuenged, and obtayned hys fuite.

THEY that haue fpent their youth in humayne follies, and haue followed the Vanities of loue, not addicted to the contemplation of high fecrets, nor haue made entry here on Earth, to inlarge and amplyfy the boundes of their honor and Eftimation. Thofe Worldlings (I fay) and embracers of tranfitory pleafures, fhall witneffe with me, and confirme, this olde and auncient Theme and propofition to be true which is: that the Beauty, and comely grace of a Woman, is the very true and naturall adamant (for the attractiue power, and agreeable quality there inclofed,) to draw vnto it the hearts, and affections of men: which hath made man beleue, that the fame onely effence, was fent downe from aboue to ferue both for ioy and torment together. For the amplyfyinge of which propofition, I will not bring forth, the immoderate loue of Paris by forfaking his owne Natiue country of Troy, to vifite fayre Helena in Greece, nor yet tell how Hercules gaue ouer his mace to handle the Diftaffe, vpon the commaundement of Omphale, nor yet how Sampfon and Salomon were fotted in the flaueries of Dalida and other concubines. But my difcourfe here folowing fhall ring out a loud Peale, of a meane Gentlewoman, of Piedmount, that fhewed no fauor or Curtefy at all to her fuppliant, a Gentleman not inferior to Paris for his actiuity and proweffe: which for her feruice and atchyeues of her loue, refufed not to bee dombe the fpace of many yeares, and to giue ouer the beft porcion of his fences wherewith the Almighty, made Man differente from brute and fauage Beaftes. If this thing declare not fufficiently the force and power of that attractiue and drawing power in woman, no other example is worthy to be preferred. Thofe aforefayd and many other haue voluntarily yoaked themfelues in the chains of loue's obedience, rendreth the maffe of

their mirye corps to the flauery thereof, but that any haue
franckely tyed vp their Tongue, the chiefeft Inftrument of the
bodies furniture: in honorable affembly or where dexterity of
feruice fhoulde make him glorious, the like of that fubiection
was neuer feene or founde. And yet our fathers dayes did fee
this miracle wrought by a Woman, vpon a Gentleman very wife,
and well trained vp in all good exercyfe. This example, and
what this Malapert Dame did gaine, by the penance of this louing
knight, fhal in this difcourfe be manifeftly pronounced. The
City of Thurin (as is well knowne to them that haue trauelled
Piedmont) is the ornament and bulwark of al the Countrey, fo
well for the natural fite of the place, as for the artificial and indus-
trious worke of man's hande, which hath inftaured and furnifhed
with great magnificence, that which nature had indifferently
enryched, for the rudeneffe and litle knowledg of the time paft.
Now befides this ftately and ftrong city, there ftandeth a litle
towne named Montcall, a place no leffe ftrong, and of good
defence, than wel planted in a faire and rich foyle. In this Towne
there dwelt a Gentlewoman a widow called Zilia, beautiful amongs
the moft excellent fayre Gentlewomen of the countrey, which
country (befides other happy and heauenly influences) feemeth to
be fpecially fauored, for hauing the moft faireft and curteous
Gentlewomen, aboue any other within the compaffe of Europa.
Notwithftanding this faire Silia, degenerating from the nature of
hir climate was fo haggard and cruel, as it might haue ben thought,
fhe had ben rather nourifhed and brought vp amid the moft
defert mountaines of Sauoy, than in the pleafant and rich Cham-
pian Countreye, watred and moyftened with Eridanus, the father
of Riuers, at this Day called the Pau, the largeneffe whereof doth
make men to maruel, and the fertility allureth ech man to be defirous to inhabit vpon the fame. This fayre rebellious Widow,
albeit, that fhe was not aboue xxiv. or xxv. yeres of age, yet
protefted neuer more to be fubiect to man, by mariage, or otherwife, thinking her felfe wel able to liue in fingle life: a Minde
truly very holy and commendable, if the pricks of the flefh do
obey the firft motions and adhortations of the fpirit, but where
youth, pleafure, and multitude of futers do addreffe their endeuour

againſt that chaſtity (which is lightly enterpryſed) the Apoſtels counſel oughte to be followed, who willeth yong widows to marry in Chriſt, to auoid the temptations of the fleſh, and to flye offenſiue ſlaunder and diſhonour before men. This miſtreſſe Zilia (hir huſband being dead) only bent hir ſelfe to enrich hir houſe, and to amplify the poſſeſſion of a little infant which ſhe had by hir late departed Huſband. After whoſe death ſhe became ſo couetous, as hauing remoued, and almoſt cut of quite the wonted port ſhe vſed in hir huſband's dayes, imployed hir maids in houſhold affaires, thinking nothing to be wel don that paſſed not through hir owne Handes. A thinge truely more prayſe worthy, than to ſee a ſorte of effeminate, fine and daynty fyngred Dames, that thinke their honor diminiſhed yf they holde but their Noſe ouer theyr Houſholde Matters, where theyr Hande and Dylygence were more requiſite, for ſo mutch as the myſtreſſe of a Houſe is not placed the Cheyfe to heare onely the reaſons of them that Labor, but thereunto to put hir hands, for hir preſente eye ſeemeth to giue a certyn perfection to the worke that the Seruauntes doe by hir commaundement. Which cauſed the Hyſtoryans in tymes paſt, to deſcribe vnto the Poſterity a Gentlewoman called Lucretia, not babbling amongs young girles, or running to feaſtes and Maigames, or Maſking in the night, withoute any regard of the honor and dygnitye of hir race and houſe, but in hir Chaumber Sowing, Spinning and Carding, amids the Troup of hir Mayden Seruaunts : wherein our miſtreſſe Zilia paſſed the moſte part of hir time, ſpending no minute of the day, without ſome honeſt exerciſe, for that ſhe the rather did for that ſhe liked not to be ſeene at Feaſts, or Bankets, or to be gadding vp and downe the ſtreetes, wandring to Gardeyns or places of pleaſure, although to ſutch places youth ſometimes may haue their honeſt repayre to refreſh their wearied bodies with vertuous recreation, and thereby reioyce the heauineſſe of their mynde. But this Gentlewoman was ſo ſeuere in following the rigorous, and conſtrayned maners of our auncients, as impoſſible it was, to ſee hir abroade : except it were when ſhe went to the Church to heare deuine ſeruice. This Gentlewoman ſeemed to haue ſtudied the diuinity of the Ægyptians which paynt Venus holding a key before hir mouth, and ſetting

hir Fote vpon a Tortus, fignifying vnto us thereby the duety of a
chafte Woman, whofe tongue ought to bee locked, that fhee
fpeak not but in tyme and place, and her feete not ftraying or
wandering, but to keepe hir felfe within the limits of hir owne
houfe, except it be to ferue God, and fometimes to render bounden
duety to them which brought them into light.   Moreouer Zilia
was fo religious (I will not fay fuperftitious) and rigorous to
obferue cuftomes, as fhe made it very fqueimifh and ftraung to
kiffe a Gentleman that met hir, a ciuility which of long time hath
bene obferued, and yet remayneth in the greateft parte of the
Worlde, that Gentlewomen do welcome ftraungers and Guefts into
their houfes with an honeft and chafte kiffe.   Notwithftandinge
the inftitution and profeffion of this Wyddow had wiped away
this poynéte of hir youth: whether it were for that fhe efteemed
hirfelfe fo fayre as all men were vnworthy to touch the vtter partes
of fo rare and pretious a veffell, or that hir great, and inimitable
chaftity made hir fo ftraunge, to refufe that which hir duety and
honour woulde haue permitted hir to graunt.   There chaunced
about this time that a Gentleman of the Countrey, called Sir Philiberto of Virle, efteemed to be one of the moft valiaunt gentlemen
in thofe parts, repayred vpon an holy day to Montcall, (whofe
houfe was not very farre of the Towne) and being at diuine feruice,
in place of occupying his Sence and Mynde in heauenly things,
and attending the holy words of a Preacher, which that day
declared the worde of God vnto the people, hee gaue himfelfe to
contemplate the excellent beauty of Zilia, who had put of for a
while hir mourninge vayle, that fhe might the better beholde the
good father that preached, and receyue a little ayre, becaufe the
day was extreme hot.   The Gentleman at the firft blufhe, when
hee fawe that fweete temptation before his eyes, thought himfelfe
rapt aboue the thirde heauen, and not able to withdraw his looke,
he fed himfelfe with the Venome which by little, and little, fo
feafed vpon the foundeft parts of hys mynde, as afterwards being
rooted in heart, he was in daunger ftill to remayne there for a
Guage, wythout any hope of eafe or comforte, as more amply this
followinge difcourfe, fhall giue you to vnderftande.   Thus all the
morning hee behelde the Gentlewoman, who made no more

accoumpt of theym, that wyth great admiration did behold hir, than they themſelues did of their life, by committing the ſame to the handes of a Woman ſo cruell. This Gentleman being come home to his lodging enquired what fayre Wyddow that was, of what calling, and behauiour, but hee heard tell of more truely than he would of good will haue known or deſired to haue ben in hir, whom he did preſently choſe to be the only miſtreſſe of his moſt ſecret thoughts. Now vnderſtandynge well the ſtubburne Nature, and vnciuile Manner of that Wyddowe, hee coulde not tell what parte to take, nor to what Sainƈt to vow his Deuotion, to make ſuite vnto hir hee thought it tyme loſt, to bee hir Seruaunt, it was not in his power, hauing already inguaged his Lyberty into the handes of that beauty, whych once holding captiue the hearte of men, will not infraunchiſe them ſo ſoone as Thought and Wyll deſire. Wherefore baytinge hymſelf with hope, and tickled wyth loue, he determined whatſoeuer chaunced, to loue hir, and to aſſay if by long ſeruice he could leniſie that harde hearte, and make tender that vnpliaunt wyll, to haue pitty vppon the payne which ſhee ſaw him to endure, and to recompence hys labourſome Trauayles, which hee thought were vertuouſly imployed for gayn-ing of hir good grace. And vpon this ſettled deliberation, he retired agayne to Virle (ſo was his houſe named) where diſpoſinge hys thinges in order, he retorned agayne to Montcall to make his long reſiaunce there, to put in readines his furniture, and to welde his artillary with ſutch induſtry, as in the ende he might make a reaſonable breach to force and take the place : for ſur-priſing whereof, hee hazarded great daungers, the rather that himſelfe might firſt be taken. And where his aſſaults and pollicies could not preuayle, hee minded to content his Fancy wyth the pleaſure and paſtyme that hee was to receyue in the contem-plation of a thing ſo fayre, and of an image ſo excellent. The memory of whom rather increaſed his paine than yelded comfort, did rather miniſter corroſiue poyſon, than giue remedy of eaſe, a cauſe of more cruell and ſodayne death, than of prolonged lyfe. Philiberto then being become a citizen of Montcal, vſed to fre-quent the Church more than hee was wont to doe, or his deuotion ſerued hym, and that bycauſe he was not able elſewhere to enioy

the prefence of hys Saynƈt, but in places and Temples of Deuotion :
which no doubt was a very holy and worthy Difpofition, but yet
not meete or requifite to obferue futch holy places for thofe
intentes, which ought not to bee prophaned in things fo fonde
and foolifhe, and Aƈtes fo contrary to the Inftitution, and mynde
of thofe, whych in tymes paft were the firfte Founders and Erec-
toures of Temples.   Seignior Philiberto then mooued wyth that
Religious Superftition, made no Confcience at al to fpeake vnto hir
wythin the Church.   And true it is, when fhe went out of the
fame, he (mooued wyth a certayne familiar curtefie, naturall to
eche Gentleman of good bringing vp) many tymes conduƈted hir
home to hir houfe, not able for all that (what fo euer hee fayd) to
win the thing that was able to ingender any little folace, which
greeued him very much : for the cruell woman fained as though
fhe vnderftoode nothing of that he fayde, and turnyng the Wayne
agaynft the Oxen, by contrary talke fhee began to tell hym a tale
of a Tubbe, of matters of hir Houfeholde, whereunto hee gaue fo
good heede, as fhee did to the hearing of his complaynts.   Thus
thefe two, of diuers Affeƈtions, and mooued wyth contrary
thoughtes, fpake one to another, without apt aunfwere to eyther's
talke.   Whereby the Gentleman conceyued an affured argument
of hys Ruine, who voyde of all hope, and meanes, praƈtifed with
certayne Dames of the Citty, that had familiar acceffe vnto hyr
houfe, and vfed frequent conuerfation wyth hys rebellious Lady
Zilia.   To one of them, then hee determined to communicate hys
fecrets, and to doe hir to vnderftand in deede the only caufe that
made him to foiorne at Montcall, and the griefe which he fuffered,
for that he was not able to difcouer his torment vnto hir, that had
giuen him the wounde.   Thys Gentleman therefore, repayred to
one of his neyghbours, a Woman of good corage, which at other
tymes had experimented what meates they feede on that fit at
Venus Table, and what bitterneffe is intermingled amid thofe
drinckes that Cupido quaffeth vnto hys Gueftes.   Vnto whom
(hauing before coniured hir to keepe clofe that whych hee woulde
declare) he difcouered the fecrets of hys mynde, expreffinge hys
loue wythout naming hys Lady before he heard the aunfwere of
hys Neyghbour, who vnderftanding almoft to what purpofe the

affections of the Pacient were directed, sayd vnto hym: "Sir, needful it is not to vse longe orations, the loue that I beare you for the honeft qualities whych hytherto I haue knowne to be in you, fhall make me to keepe filent, that whereof as yet I do not know the matter, and the affuraunce you haue, not to bee abufed by mee, conftrayneth me to warrant you, that I wyll not fpare to do you all the pleafure and honeft feruice I can." "Ah mif- treffe," (aunfwered fir Philiberto) "fo long as I lyue, I will not fayle to acknowledge the Liberality of your endeuour by offeringe your felfe paciently to heare, and fecretly, to keepe the Words I fpeake accordingly as they deferue: and that (whych is more than I require) you doe affure me that I fhall finde futch one of you as wil not fpare to gieue your ayde. Alas, I refemble the good and wyfe Captayne, who to take a forte doeth not only ayde him- felfe with the forwardneffe, and valiaunce of his Souldiers, but to fpare them, and to auoyde flaughter for makinge of way, planteth his cannon, and battereth the Walle of the fort, which hee would affaile, to the intent that both the Souldier, and the ordinaunce may perfourme and fuffife the perfection of the plat, which hee hath framed and deuifed within his pollitike heade. I haue already encouraged my fouldiers, and haue loft the better part truely in the fkirmifh which hath deliuered vnto mee my fweete cruell Ennimy. Now I am driuen to make ready the fire, which refteth in the kindled match of your conceiptes, to batter the fort hitherto inexpugnable, for any affault that I can make." "I vnderftand not" (fayd fhe fmilyng) "thefe labyrynths of your complaynts, except you fpeake more playn. I neuer haunted the Warres, ne knewe what thynge it is to handle weapons, improper and not feemely for myne eftate and kynde." "The Warre" (quod he) whereof I fpeake, is fo naturall and common, as I doubt not, but you haue fometymes affayed, with what fleightes and camis- ados men vfe to furpryfe their enimies, howe they plant their ambufhes, and what meanes both the affaylant and defendant ought to vfe." "So far as I fee" (fayd fhee) "there refteth nothing for vs, but the affurance of the field, fith wee bee ready to enter in combat: and doe thinke that the fort fhall not bee harde to winne, by reafon of the Walles, dikes, rampers, bulwarks,

platformes, counterforts, curtines, vamewres and engins which
you haue prepared, befides a numbre of falfe brayes and flanks,
placed in good order, and the whole defended from the thundringe
Cannons and Bombardes, which do amaze the wandring enemy
in the field. But I pray you leauing thefe warlike Tumults, to
fpeak more boldly without thefe extrauagantes and digreffions,
for I take pitye to fee you thus troubled: ready to exceede the
boundes of your modefty and wonted wyfedome." "Do not
maruell at all miftreffe" (quod he) "fith accordynge to new
occurrentes and alterations, the purpofe, talke, and counfel ordinarily do change I am become the feruaunt of one which maketh
me altogither lyke vnto thofe that bee madde, and bound in
Chaines, not able to fpeake or fay any thing, but what the fpyrites
that be in them, do force them to vtter. For neither will I
thynke, or fpeake any thing, but that which the Enchaunter Loue
doth commaunde and fuffer to expreffe, who fo rygoroufly doth
vexe my hearte, as in place wher bouldeneffe is moft requyfite,
hee depriueth me of force, and leaueth mee without any Countenance. And being alone, God knoweth how frankly I doe wander
in the place, where myne enemy may commaunde, and with what
hardineffe I do inuade hir prouince. Alas, is it not pity then
to fee thefe diuerfities in one felfe matter, and vpon one very
thing? Truely I would endure wyllingly all thefe trauailes, if I wyft
in the end, my feruice woulde be accepted, and hoped that my
Martirdome fhoulde fynde releefe: but liuing in this vncertainty,
I muft needes noryfh the hunger and folace of the vnhappy, which
are wifhes and vaine hopes, trufting that fome God wyll gayne me
a faythful friend that will affaye to rid me from the hell, into the
which I am throwne, or elfe to fhorten thys Miferable lyfe, whych
is a hundred tymes more paynfull than Death." In fayinge fo, he
began to fighe fo ftraungely as a man would haue thought that
two Smithes fledges working at the forge, had gyuen two blowes
at his ftomake, fo vehement was the inclofed winde within his
heart, that made him to fetche forth thofe terrible fighes, the
Eyes not forgetting to yeld forth a Riuer of Teares, which gufhynge
forthe at the centre of hys Hearte, mounted into his Braynes, at
lengthe to make iffue through the Spoute, proper to the Chanell

of futch a Fountayne. Which the Gentlewoman feyng, moued with compaffion, coulde not contain alfo from Weepyng, and therewythall fayde vnto him : "Although mine eftate and reputation, which to this day I have kept vnfpotted, defend the vfe of my good wyl in al things that may defame mine honor, yet fir, feing the extremity which you fuffer to be vnfained, I wil fomwhat ftretch my confcience, and affay to fuccor you with fo good heart, as frankely you truft me with the fecrets of your thought. It refteth then now for me to know what fhe is, to whome your deuocions be inclined whofe heart and mind I wil fo relief with the tafte of your good wil, as I dare giue warrant, her appetit fhal accept your profred feruice, and truly that woman may count her felf happy that fhal intertain the offer of a gentleman that is fo honeft and curteous, who meaneth with al fidelity to aduance and honor, not onely the fuperficial ornament of hir beauty, but the inward vertues of hir conftant mind. And truly the earth feldom yeldeth thofe frutes in the harts of men in thefe our barren days, they being ouer growen with the fhrubbes of difloialty the fame choke vp the plantes of true Fidelity, the fedes whereof are fowen and replanted in the foyle of womens hartes, who not able to depart and vfe the force and effects thereof will put vpon them conditions that bee cruell, to punifh the Foolyfh indifcreation of tryfling Louers, who difguifed with the vizard of fained friendfhip, and paynted with coloured Amity, languifhing in fighes and forrowes, goe aboute to affay to deceiue the flexible Nature of them that prodigally employ theyr honor into the hands of futch cruel, inconftante and foolyfh futers." "Ah Miftreffe" anfwered the Gentleman : "howe may I bee able to recompence that onely benefite which you promyfe me now? But be fure that you fee heere a Souldier and Gentleman prefente which fhall no leffe bee prodigall of hys Lyfe to doe you feruyce, than you bee lyberall of your reputation, to eafe his Paines. Now fith it pleafeth you to fhew futch fauour to offer me your helpe and fupport in that which payneth me, I require no more at your hands, but to beare a letter which I fhall wryte to myftreffe Zilia, with whome I am fo farre in loue, as if I do receiue no folace of my griefe, I know not howe I fhall auoyde the cuttyng of the Threede, whych the

ſpynning ſyſters haue twiſted to prolonge my lyfe, that henceforth can receiue no ſuccor if by your meanes I do not atchieue
the thing that holdeth me in bondage." The Gentlewoman was
very ſorrowful, when ſhe vnderſtoode that Seignior Philiberto had
bent his Loue vpon ſutch one, as would not conſente to that
requeſte, and mutch leſſe would render reſt vnto hys myſeryes,
and therefore enforced hir ſelfe to moue that Foolyſhe Fantaſye
out of his head. But he beyng already reſolued in thys myſhappe,
and the ſame perceyued by her in the ende ſhe ſayde : " To the
intente ſir that you may not thynke that I doe meane to excuſe
the Satyſſaƈtyon of my promyſe, make youre Letters, and of my
Fayth I wil delyuer them. And albeyt I knowe verye well what
bee the Honoures and Glorye of that Pylgryme, yet I wyll render
to you agayne the true aunſwere of hir ſpeache whereby you maye
conſider the gayne you are lyke to make, by purſuing a Woman
(although faire) of ſo ſmall deſert." The Gentleman fayled not
to gyue her heartye Thankes, prayinge bir to tarry vntyll hee had
written his letters : whereunto ſhe moſt willingly obeyed. He
then in his chaumber, began to fantaſie a hundred hundred matters to write vnto his Miſtreſſe, and after he had fixed theym in
minde tooke Incke and Paper writing as followeth.

The Letters of Seignior Philiberto of Virle, to Miſtreſſe Zelia of
Montcall.

" The paſſion extreeme which I endure, (Madame) through the
feruent loue I beare you, is ſutch, as beſides that I am aſſured
of the little affeƈtion that reſteth in you towards me agayne, in
reſpeƈt of that incredible ſeruitude which my deſire is ready to
employ, I haue no power to commaunde my force, ne yet to rid
my ſelfe from my vowed deuotion and will to your incomparable
beauty, although euen from the beginning I felt the pricks of the
mortall ſhot which now torments my mynde. Alas, I do not know
vnder what influence I am borne, nor what Fate doth guide my
yeares, ſith I doe perceyue that heauen, and loue, and hir whom
alone I honor, doe confirme themſelues with one aſſent to ſeeke
myne ouerthrow. Alas, I thinke that all the powers aboue con-
ſpired together, to make me be the faythfull man, and perpetuall

feruaunt of you my miftreffe deare, to whom alone, I yelde my
heart afflicted as it is, and the ioy of hidden thoughts nourfed in
my minde, by the contemplation and remembraunce of your
excellent and perfect graces, whereof, if I be not fauored, I waight
for death, from whych euen now I fly: not for feare of that
whych fhe can doe, or of the vgly fhape which I conceyue to be
in hir, but rather to confirme my life, this Body for inftrument to
exercife the myndes conceypts for doinge your Commaundements,
which Body I greatly feare fhall proue the vnworthy cruelty,
both of your gentle nouriture, and of thofe graces which Dame
Nature moft aboundantly hath powred in you. Be fure Madame
that you fhall fhortlye fee the Ende of him, which attendeth yet
to beare fo mutch as in him doeth lye, the vehement loue into an
other world, which maketh me to pray you to haue pity on him,
who (attending the reft and final fentence of his Death or Lyfe)
doth humbly kiffe your white and delicate handes, befeeching
God to giue to you like ioy as his is, who defireth to be,

> Wholy yours or not to be at all
> > PHILIBERTO OF VIRLE.

The Letter written, clofed and fealed, he deliuered to his neighbour, who promyfed hym agayne to bryng him anfwere at Night.
Thus this Meffenger went hir way, leauing this pore languifhyng
Gentlemen hoping againft hope, and fayning by and by fome ioy
and pleafure, wherein he bained himfelf with great contented
minde.   Then fodaynly he called againe vnto remembraunce, the
cruelty and inciuility of Zilia, which fhewed before his eyes fo
many kindes of Death, as tymes he thought vpon the fame, thinking that he faw the choler wherewith his little curteous miftreffe
furioufly did intertaine the meffenger, who findinge Zilia comming forth of a garden adioining to her houfe, and hauing faluted
her, and receiued like curteous falutation would haue framed hir
talke, by honeft excufe in the vnfemely charge and meffage: to hir
vnto whom fhe was fent, and for fome eafe to the pore gentleman
which approched nearer death than life. But Zilia break of hir
talke faying: " I maruell mutch Gentle neighbor to fee you heere
at this time of the day, knowing your honeft cuftome is to let
paffe no minute of the tyme, except it be emploied in fome vertu-

ous exercife." "Miftreffe" anfwered the meffanger, "I thank
you for the good opinion you haue of me, and doe pray you to
continue the fame. For I do affure you that nothinge vayne or
of lyttle effeĉt hath made me flacke my bufineffe at this time,
which me think I do not forflow, when I inforce my felfe to take
pitye and mercy vpon the afflicted and the fubftaunce thereof I
woulde difclofe, if I feared not to offend you, and break the loue
which of long tyme betweene vs two hath ben frequented." "I
know not" (faid Zilia) "whereunto your words do tend, althoughe
my Hearte doth throbbe, and minde doth moue to make mee
thinke your purpofed talke to bee of none other effeĉte, than to
fay a thing which may redound to the preiudice of myne honour.
Wherefore I pray you do not difclofe what fhall be contrary, (be
it neuer fo little) to the duety of Dames of our Degree." "Mys-
treffe" fayd the Neighboure, "I fuppofe that the lyttle Lykeli-
hoode touchyng in you the thinge for the helpe whereof I come,
hath made you feele fome paffion, contrary to the greefe of him
that indures fo mutch for your fake. Vnto whome without feare
of your dyfpleafure, I gaue my Faithe in Pledge to beare this
Letter." In faying fo, fhe drewe the fame out of hir Bofome, and
prefentyng it to cruell Silia, fhee fayde: "I befeeche you to
thynke that I am not ignoraunt of the evyll wherewyth the Lorde
of Virle is affeĉted, who wrote thefe letters. I promyfed him the
duety of a Meffanger towards you: and fo conftrayned by promyfe I could doe no leffe, than to delyuer you that which hee
doeth fende, with Seruyce futch as fhall endure for euer, or yf it
fhall pleafe you to accept him for futch a one as hee defireth to
be. For my parte I onelye praye you to reade the Contentes, and
accordynglye to gyue mee Aunfwere: for my Fayth is no further
bounde, but truftelye to report to hym the thinge whereuppon
you fhall bee refolued." Zilia which was not wonte to receyue
very ofte futch Ambaffades, at the firfte was in mind to breake the
Letters, and to retourne the Meffanger wythout aunfwere to hir
fhame. But in the Ende takyng Heart, and chaunging hir
affeĉtyon, fhe red the Letters not without fhewing fome very great
alteration outwardely, which declared the meanynge of hir thought
that diuerfly did ftryue wythin hir mynde: for fodaynly fhee

chaunged her Coloure twyce or thryce, nowe waxing pale lyke the increasynge Moone Eclypsed by the Sunne, when shee feeleth a certayne darkenynge of hir borowed Lyghte, then the Vermylyon and coloured Taynte came into hir Face agayne, wyth no lesse hewe than the blomed Rose newelye budded forthe, whych Encreased halfe so mutch agayne, the excellencye of that wherewyth Nature had indued hir. And then she paused a whyle. Notwythstandynge, after that shee had red, and red agayne hir Louer's letter, not able to dissemble hir foolishe anger which vexed hir heart, shee sayde vnto the mistresse messanger: "I would not haue thought that you, being a woman of good fame would (by abusinge your duety,) haue bene the ambassador of a thing so vncomely for your Estate, and the house where of you come, and towards me which neuer was sutch one (ne yet pretend to be.) And trust me it is the loue I beare you, which shall for this tyme make me dissemble what I thincke, reseruinge in silence, that whych (had it come from an other) I would haue publifhed to the great dishonour of hir that maketh so little accoumpt of my chaftity. Let it suffice therefore in tyme to come for you to thinke and beleue, that I am chafte and honeft: and to aduertife the Lord of Virle to proceede no further in his fute: for rather will I dy, than agree to the leaft poynct of that which hee defires of mee. And that he may knowe the fame, be well affured that hee shall take his leaue of that priuate talke which fometimes I vfed with him to my great dishonor, as far as I can fee. Get you home therefore, and if you loue your credit fo mutch, as you fee me curious of my chaftity, I befeech you vfe no further talke of hym, whom I hate fo mutch, as his folly is exceffiue, for I do little efteeme the amorous Toyes and fayned paffions, whereunto futch louinge fooles doe fuffer themfelues to be caried headlong." The meffenger afhamed to heare hir felfe thus pinched to the quicke, aunfwered hir very quietly without mouing of hir pacience: "I pray to God (miftreffe) that he may recouer the different difeafe al moft incurable in eyther of you twayne, the fame being fo vehement, as altered into a phrenefie, maketh you in this wyfe, incapable of reafon." Finifhing thefe wordes fhe tooke hir leaue of Zilia, and arriued to the Louer's houfe, fhe founde him

lying vpon his bed, rather dead than a liue: who feeing his
neyghbor returned backe agayne, with Face fo fadde, not tarying
for the aunfwere which fhe was about to make, he began to fay:
"Ah infortunate Gentleman, thou payeft wel the vfury of thy
pleafures paft when thou diddeft lyue at lyberty, free from thofe
trauayles which now do put thee to death, without fuffering thee
to dy. Oh happy, and more than happy had I ben, if inconftant
Fortune had not deuifed this treafon, wherein I am furprifed and
caught, and yet no raunfome can redeeme from prifon, but the
moft miferable death that euer poore louer fuffred. Ah Miftreffe,
I knowe well that Zilia efteemeth not my Letters, ne yet regardeth
my loue, I confeffe that I haue done you wrong by thus abufing
your honeft amity, for the folace of my payne. Ah fickle loue,
what foole is hee which doth commit hymfelfe to the rage and
fury of the Waues of thy foming and tempeftuous Seas? Alas I
am entred in, with great, and gladfome cheere, through the glifter-
ing fhew before myne eyes of the faynt fhining Sunne beames,
whereunto as foone as I made fayle, the fame denied me light of
purpofe to thruft me forth into a thoufand winds, tempefts, and
raging ftormes of Rayne. By meanes whereof I fee no meane at
all to hope for end of my mifhaps: and mutche leffe the fhipwracke
that fodainely may rid me from this daunger more intollerable,
than if I were ouerwhelmed wythin the bottomleffe depth of the
mayne Occan. Ah deceyuer and wily Souldiour, why haft thou
made me enterprife the voyage farre of from thy folitudes and
Wilderneffe, to geue me ouer in the middeft of my neceffity? Is
this thy maner towards them which franckly followe thy traēt,
and pleafauntly fubdue themfelues to thy trayterous follies? At
leaft wyfe if I fawe fome hope of health I would indure without
complaynt thereof: yea, and it were a more daungerous tempeft.
But O good God, what is he of whom I fpeake? Of whom do I
attend for folace and releefe? Of him truely which is borne for
the ouerthrow of men. Of whom hope I for health? Of the moft
noyfom poyfon that euer was mingled with the fubtileft druggs
that euer were. Whom fhall I take to be my Patron? He which
is in ambufh traiteroufly to catch me, that he may martir me
worffe than he hath done before. Ah cruell Dame, that meafureft

fo euill, the good will of him that neuer purpofed to trefpaffe the leaft of thy commaundements. Ah, that thy beauty fhould finde a Subiect fo ftubborne in thee, to torment them that loue and honor thee. O maigre and vnkinde recompence, to expell good feruaunts that be affectionate to a feruice fo iuft and honeft. Ah Bafilifke, coloured ouer with pleafure and fwetneffe, how hath thy fight difperfed his poyfon throughout mine heart? At leaft wife if I had fome drugge to repell thy force, I fhould liue at eafe, and that without this fute and trouble. But I feele and proue that this fentence is more than true:

> No phyficke hearbes the griefe of loue can cure,
> Ne yet no drugge that payne can well affure.

Alas, the feare cloath will not ferue, to tent the wound the time fhall be but loft, to launch the fore, and to falue the fame it breeds myne ouerthrow. To be fhort, any dreffing can not auayle, except the hand of hir alone which gaue the wounde. I woulde to God fhee fawe the bottome of my heart, and viewed the Clofet of my mynde, that fhee might iudge of my firme fayth and know the wrong fhe doth me by hir rigor and froward will. But O vnhappy man, I feele that fhe is fo refolued in obftinate mynde, as hir reft feemeth only to depend vpon my payne, hir eafe vpon my griefe, and hir ioy vpon my fadneffe." And faying fo, began ftraungly to weepe, and fighing betwene, lamented, in fo mutch as, the miftreffe meffaunger not able to abide the griefe and paynefull trauayle wherein fhee faw the poore gentleman wrapped, went home to hir houfe: notwithftanding fhe told afterward the whole fucceffe of his loue to a Gentleman, the friend of Philiberto. Now this Gentleman was a companion in armes to the Lorde of Virle, and a very familyar Freend of his, that went about by all meanes to put away thofe foolifhe, and Franticke conceypts out of his fanfie, but hee profited as mutch by his endeuour, as the paffionate gayned by his heauines: who determining to dye, yelded fo mutch to care and grief, as he fell into a greeuous ficknes, which both hindred him from fleepe, and alfo his Appetite to eate and drinke, geuing himfelfe to mufe vppon his follies, and fanfied dreames, without hearing or admitting any man to fpeake

vnto hym. And if perchaunce hee hearkened to the perfuafions
of his frends, he ceaffed not his complaynt, bewayling the cruelty
of one, whom he named not. The Phifitians round about were
fought for, and they coulde geue no iudgement of his malady
(neyther for all the Signes they faw, or any infpection of his Vrine,
or touching of his pulfe) but fayd that it was melancholie humor
diftilling from the Brayne, that caufed the alteration of his fenfe:
howbeit their Arte and knowledge were void of fkil to evacuate
the groffe Bloud that was congeled of his difeafe. And therefore
difpayryng of his health, with hands full of Money, they gaue him
ouer. Which his friend and Companion perceiuing, maruellous
forry for his affliction he ceafed not to practife all that he could
by Letters, gifts, promifes and complaynts to procure Zilia to
vifite her pacient. For hee was affured that her onely prefence
was able to recouer him. But the cruell woman excufed hir felf
that fhe was a Widow and that it fhoulde bee vnfeemely for one
of hir degree (of intente) to vifite a Gentleman, whofe Parentage
and Alliance fhe knew not. The foliciter of the Lord of Virle his
health, feeing how lyttle hys prayers auailed to his implacable
gryefe could not tell to what Sainct he might vow himfelf for
Counfell, in the ende refolued to follicite hir again that hadde
done the firft Meffage, that fhe myght eftfons deuife fome meanes
to bryng them to fpeake togither. And fynding hir for hys purpofe, thus he fayed vnto hir: "Myftreffe I maruell mutch that
you make fo little accompt of the pore lorde of Virle who lyeth
in his Bedde attending for Death. Alas, if euer pitty had place in
Woman's heart, I befeech you to gyue your ayde to help him, the
meane of whofe recouery, is not ignoraunt vnto you." "God is
my witneffe" (quod fhe) "what trauaile my heart is willing to
vndertake to helpe that Gentleman, but in things impoffible, it is
not in man to determine, or reft affured iudgement. I wil go
vnto him and comfort hym fo well as I can, that peraduenture
my Promyfes may eafe fome part of his payne: and afterward we
wil at leyfure better confider, what is beft for vs to do." Here-
vppon they wente together to fee the Pacient, that beganne to
looke more chearefull than he dyd before: who feeing the Gentlewoman, faid vnto hir: "Ah miftres, I would to God I had neuer

proued your fidelity, then had I not felt the paffing cruell Heart of hir, that efteemeth more hir honour to practife rigour and tyranny than with gentleneffe to maintaine the Lyfe of a pore feeble knight." "Sir," (faid fhe,) "be of good cheare, doe not thus torment your felfe: for I truft to gyue you remedy betwene thys and to morrowe, and wyll doe myne endeuor to caufe you to fpeake with hir, vppon whome wrongfully perchaunce you doe complayne, and who dare not come vnto you, leaft ill fpeakers conceiue occafion of fufpicion, who wil make the report more flaunderous, then remedie for the caufe of your difeafe." "Ah" (fayd the pacient) "howe ioyefull and pleafaunt is your talke? I fee wel that you defire my health, and for that purpofe would haue me drinke thofe liquors, which fuperficiallay appeare to bee fweete, which afterwardes may make my lyfe a hundred tymes more faint and feeble than now it is." "Be you there," fayed fhe? "And I fweare vnto you by my faith not to faile to keepe my promyfe, to caufe you fpeake alone with miftreffe Zilia." "Alas, miftreffe" fayd the louer, "I afke no more at your handes, that I may heare with myne own eares the laft fentence of hope or defiance." "Well put your truft in me," fayd fhe, "and take no thought but for your health. For I am affured ere it be longe, to caufe hir to come vnto you, and then you fhall fee whether, my diligence fhall aunfwere the effect of myne attempt." "Me thinke already" (quod he) "that fickneffe is not able to ftay me from going to hir that is the caufe, fith her onely remembraunce hath no leffe force in mee, than the clearneffe of the Sun beames to euaporate the thickneffe of the morning miftes." With that the Gentlewoman tooke her leaue of hym, and went home attendynge oportunity to fpeake to Zilia, whome two or three Dayes after fhe mette at Church, and they two beyng alone togither in a Chapell, fhe fayd vnto hir with fayned Teares, forced from her Eyes, and fending forth a Cloude of fighes, thefe woordes: "Madame, I nothing doubt at al, but the laft Letters which I brought you, made you conceiue fome il opinion of me, which I do gueffe by the frownyng countenance that euer fithens you haue borne me. But when you fhall knowe the hurte which it hath done, I thinke you wyll not be fo harde, and voyde of pitye,

but with pacyence hearken that whych I fhall faye, and therewythall bee moued to pitye the ftate of a pore Gentleman, who
by your meanes is in the pangs of death." Zilia, which til then
neuer regarded the payne and ficknetfe of the pacient, began to
forrow, with futch paffion, as not to graunt him further fauor
than he had already receiued, but to finde fome means to eafe him
of hys gryefe, and then to gyue hym ouer for euer. And therefore fhe fayd vnto hir neyghbor: "My good frend, I thought
that all thefe futes had beene forgotten, vntill the other day a
certen Gentleman praied me to go fee the Lord of Virle, who told
me as you do now, that he was in great daunger. And now
vnderftanding by you that he waxeth worffe, and worffe, I will
be ruled, being well affured of your honefty and vertue, and that
you will not aduife me to any thing that fhall be hurtfull to myne
honour. And when you haue done what you can, you fhal winne
of me fo mutch as nothinge, and geeue no eafe to him at all that
wrongfully playneth of my cruelty. For I purpofe not to do any
priuate fact with him, but that which fhall be meete for an honeft
Gentlewoman, and futch as a faythfull tutor of hir chaftity, may
graunt to an honeft and vertuous Gentleman." "His defire is
none other" (fayd the gentlewoman) "for he craueth but your
prefence, to let you wit by word, that he is ready to do the thing
you fhall commaund him." "Alas" fayde Zilia, "it is impoffible
for me to go to hym without fufpition, which the common people
will lightly conceiue of futch light and familiar Behauiour. And
rather would I dy than aduenture mine honor hitherto conferued
wyth great feuerity and diligence. And yet fith you fay, that he
is in extremes of death, for your fake, I wil not ftick to heare him
fpeake." "I thanke you" (fayd the Meffanger) "for the
good wil you beare me and for the help you promife vnto the
poore paffionate Gentleman, whom thefe newes wil bring on foote
againe, and who al the dayes of his life wil do you honor for that
good turne." "Sith it is fo (fayd Zilia) to morrow at noone
let him come vnto my houfe, wherein a low chamber, he fhall
haue leyfure to fay to mee his mind. But I purpofe by God's
help, to fuffer him no further than that which I haue already
graunted." "As it fhall pleafe you" (fayd hir neighbour) "for

I craue no more of you but that only fauour, which as a Meſſanger of good Newes, I go to ſhew hym, recommending my ſelfe in
the meane tyme to your commaunde." And then ſhe went vnto
the pacient, whom ſhe found walkinge vp and downe the Chaumber, indifferent luſty of his perſon, and of colour meetely freſhe
for the tyme hee left his Bed." Now when ſir Philiberto ſaw the
Meſſanger, hee ſayde vnto hir: "And how now myſtreſſe, what
Newes? Is Zilia ſo ſtubborne as ſhee was wont to be?" "You
may ſee hir" (ſayd ſhe) "if to morrowe at Noone you haue the
heart to aduenture to goe vnto hir houſe." "Is it poſſible" (ſayd
hee imbracing hir) "that you haue procured my delyueraunce
from the miſery, wherewith I haue ſo long tyme beene affeƈted?
Ah truſty and aſſured frende, all the dayes of my lyfe I wil
remember that pleaſure, and benefite, and by acknowledging
of the ſame, ſhall be ready to render like, when you pleaſe
to commaunde, or els let me be counted the moſt vncurteous
Gentleman that euer made profeſſion of loue: I will go by God's
help to ſee miſtreſſe Zilia, with intent to endure all vexation,
wherewith Dame Fortune ſhall affliƈt me, proteſting to vex my
ſelfe no more, although I ſee my wiſhed hap otherwiſe to ende
than my deſert requireth. But yet agaynſt Fortune to contend,
is to warre agaynſt my ſelfe, whereof the Viƈtory can be but
daungerous." Thus he paſſed all the day, which ſeemed to laſt
a thouſand years to hym, that thought to receyue ſome good intertaynment of hys Lady, in whoſe Bonds hee was catched before he
thought that Woman's malice could ſo farre exceede, or diſplay
hir venomous Sting. And truly that man is voyde of Senſe, whych
ſuffreth hym ſelfe ſo fondly to bee charmed, ſith the pearill of
others before time abuſed, ought to ſerue hym for exaumple.
Women be vnto mankinde a greate confuſion, and vnwares for
want of hys due foreſight, it doth ſuffer it ſelfe to bee bounde and
taken captiue by the very thing which hath no being to worke
effeƈt, but by free will. Which Inchauntment of woman's beauty,
being to men a pleaſaunt diſpleaſure, I thinke to bee decked with
that drawinge vertue, and allurement, for chaſtiſing of their
ſinnes who once fed and bayted with their fading fauour and
poyſoned ſweetneſſe, forget their owne perfeƈtion, and nouſled in

their foolifhe Fanfies, they feeke Felicity, and foueraygne delight,
in the matter wherein doth lie the fumme of their vnhaps. Sem-
blaly the vertuous and fhamefafte dames, haue not the eyes of
their minde fo blindfolde, but that they fee whereunto thofe
francke feruices, thofe difloyal Faythes and Vyces coloured and
ftuffed with exterior vertue, doe tende: Who doubt not alfo but
futch louers do imitate the Scorpion, whofe Venome lieth in his
Tayle, the ende of which is loue beinge the ruine of good Renoume,
and the Decay of former vertues. For which caufe the heauens,
the Frende of their fexe, haue giuen them a prouidence, which
thofe Gentle, vnfauoured louers terme to be rigor, thereby to proue
the deferts of Suters, afwell for their great contentation and prayfe,
as for the reft of them that do them feruice. Howbeit this iuft
and modeft prouidence, that cruel Gentlewoman practifed not
in hir louer, the Lord of Virle, who was fo humble a feruaunt of
his vnkinde miftreffe, as his obedience redounded to his great
mifhap, and folly, as manifeftly may appeare by that whych
followeth. Sir Philiberto then thinking to haue gayned mutch
by hauing made promife, liberally to fpeake to his Lady, went
vnto hir at the appoyncted hour, fo well contented truely of that
grace, as all the vnkindneffe paft was quite forgot. Now being
come to the Lodging of Miftreffe Zilia, he found hir in the deuifed
place with one of hir maydes attending vpon hir. When fhe
faw him, after a little cold entertaynment, fhe began to fay vnto
him with fayned ioy, that neuer mooued hir heart, thefe woordes:
"Now fir, I fee that your late fickneffe was not fo ftraunge as
I was geeuen to vnderftand, for the good ftate wherein I fee you
prefently to be, which from henceforth fhall make mee beleue,
that the paffions of Men endure fo long as the caufe of their
affections continue within their fanfies, mutch like vnto looking
Glaffes, which albeit they make the equality or exceffe of things
reprefented to appeare, yet when the thing feene doth paffe, and
vanifhe away, the formes alfo do voyde out of remembraunce,
refembling the wynde that lightly whorleth to and fro through
the plane of fome deepe valley." "Ah madame" aunfwered he,
"how eafie a matter it is for the griefeleffe perfon to counterfayt
both ioy and diffimulation in one very thing, which not onely

may forget the conceipt that mooueth his affections, but the obiect muft continually remayne in him, as paynted, and grauen in his minde. Which truely as you fay is a looking Glaffe, not futch one for all that, as the counterfayted apparaunce of reprefented formes hath like vigor in it, that the firft and true idees and fhapes can fo foone vanifh without leauing moft perfect impreffion of futch formes within the minde of him, that liueth vpon their onely remembraunce. In this mirror then (which by reafon of the hidden force I may well fay to bee ardent and burning) haue I looked fo well as I can, thereby to form the fuftentation of my good hap. But the imagined Shape not able to fupport futch perfection, hath made the reft of the body to fayle (weakned through the mindes paffions) in futch wife as if the hope to recouer this better parte halfe loft, had not cured both, the whole decay of the one had followed, by thinking to giue fome accomplifhment in the other. And if you fee me Madame, attayne to fome good ftate, impute the fame I befeech you, to the good will and fauor which I receiue by feeing you in a priuate place, wherein I conceyue greater ioy than euer I did, to fay vnto you the thing which you would not beleeue, by woords at other times proceeding from my mouth, ne yet by aduertifement fignified in my written letters. Notwithftanding I think that my Martirdome is known to bee futch as euery man may perceyue that the Summe of my defire is onely to ferue and obey you, for fo mutch as I can receyue no greater comforte, than to be commaunded to make repayre to you, to let you know that I am whole (although giuen ouer by Phifitians) when you vouchfafe to employ me in your feruice, and thinke my felfe rayfed vp agayne from one hundred thoufand deathes at once, when it fhall pleafe you to haue pitty vpon the griefe and paffion, that I endure. Alas, what caufeth my mifhap, that the heauenly beauty of yours fhould make proofe of a cruelty fo great? Haue you decreed Madame thus to torment mee poore Gentleman that am ready to facrifice myfelfe in your feruice, when you fhall impart fome fauour of your good grace? Do you thinke that my paffions be diffembled? Alacke, alacke, the teares which I haue fhed, the loffe of luft to eate and drinke, the weary paffed nights, the longe contriued fleepeleffe tyme the reftleffe turmoyle of my confumed corps may wel affure that my loyall heart is of better merite than you efteeme." Then feeing hir to fixe hir eyes vpon the ground, and thinkinge that hee had already wonne hir, he reinforced his humble Speache, and Sighing at fits betwene, not fparinge the Teares, whych trickled downe alongs hys Face, he profecuted his Tale as followeth : "Ah fayre amongs the fayreft, woulde you blot that furpaffing Beauty with a cruelty fo furious, as to caufe the death of him which loueth you better than himfelfe? Ah my withered eyes, which hitherto haue bene ferued with two liuely fprings to expreffe the hidden griefs within the heart, if your vnhap be futch that the only Miftreffe of your contemplations, and caufe of your driery teares, doe force the Humor to encreafe, which hitherto in futch wife hath emptied my Brayne, as there is no more in mee to moiften your drouth, I am content to endure al extremity, vntill my heart fhal feele the laft Pangue, that depriueth yee of nourifhment, and me of mine affected Ioy." The Gentlewoman, whether fhee was weary of that Oration, or rather doubted that in the end hir chaftity would receue fome affault through the difmeafured paffion which fhe faw to continue in him, anfwered with rigorous words: "You haue talked, and written inough, you haue indifferently well folicited hir, whych is throughly refolued in former minde, to keepe hir honor in that worthy reputation of degree, wherein fhe mayne-tayneth the fame amongs the beft. I haue hitherto fuffered you to abufe my patience, and haue fhewed that familiarity which they deferue not that go about leudly to affayle the chaftity of thofe Women that patiently gieue them eare, for the opinion they haue conceiued of the fhadowing vertues of like foolifhe Suters. I now doe fee that all your woordes doe tend to beguile mee, and to depriue mee of that you cannot giue mee: Which fhall bee a warning for me henceforth, more wifely to looke about my bufi-neffe, and more warely to fhunne the Charmes of futch as you bee, to the ende that I by bending mine open eares, be not fur-prifed, and ouercome wyth your enchaunted Speaches. I pray you then for conclufion, that I heare no more hereof, neyther from you, nor yet from the Ambaffadour that commeth from you. For I neyther will, ne yet pretend to depart to you any

other fauour than that which I haue enlarged for your comfort:
but rather doe proteſt, that ſo longe as you abide in this Countrey,
I will neyther goe forth in ſtreate, nor ſuffer any Gentleman to
haue acceſſe into this place except he be my neare Kinſman.
Thus for your importunat ſute, I will chaſtiſe my light conſent,
for harkeninge vnto you in thoſe requeſts, which duty and Woman-
hoode ought not to ſuffre.   And if you do proceede in theſe your
follies, I will ſeeke redreſſe according to your deſert, which till
now I haue deferred, thinking that time would haue put out the
ardent heate of your raſh, and wanton youth."   The infortunate
Lord of Virle, hearing this ſharpe ſentence, remayned long time
without ſpeach, ſo aſtonned as if he had bene falne from the
Clouds.   In the ende for al his deſpayre he replyed to Zilia with
Countenaunce indifferent merry: "Sith it is ſo madame, that you
take from mee all hope to be your perpetuall Seruaunt, and that
without other comfort or contentation I muſt nedes depart your
preſence, neuer (perchaunce) hereafter to ſpeake vnto you againe,
be not yet ſo ſqueimiſh of your beauty, and ſo cruell towards your
languiſhing louer, as to deny him a kiſſe for pledge of his laſt
farewell.   I demaund nothing here in ſecret, but that honeſtly
you may openly performe.   It is al that I doe craue at your handes
in recompence of the trauayles, paynes, and afflictions ſuffred for
your ſake."   The malitious dame full of rancor, and ſpitefull rage
ſayd vnto him: "I ſhall ſee by and by ſir, if the loue which you
vaunt to beare mee, be ſo vehement as you ſeeme to make it."
"Ah Madame" (ſayd the vnaduiſed Louer) "commaunde only, and
you ſhal ſee with what deuotion I will performe your will, were
it that it ſhould coſt me the price of my proper life."   "You ſhall
haue" (quod ſhe) "the kiſſe which you require of me if you will
make promiſe, and ſweare by the fayth of a Gentleman, to do the
thinge that I ſhall commaund, without fraude, couin or other
delay."   "Madame" (ſayd the ouer wilful louer) "I take God
to witneſſe that of the thing which you ſhall commaunde I will
not leaue one iote vndone, but it ſhall bee executed to the vtter-
moſt of your requeſt and will."   She hearing him ſweare with ſo
good affection, ſayd vnto him ſmiling: "Now then vpon your
oth which I beleue, and being aſſured of your Vertue and Noble

nature, I will alfo performe and keepe my promife." And faying
fo, fhee Embraced and kiffed him very louingly. The poore
Gentleman not knowing how dearely hee had bought that dif-
fauorable curtefie, and bitter fweetenefle, helde hir a while betwene
his armes, doubling kiffe vppon kiffe, with futch Pleafure, as his
foule thought to fly vp to the heauens being infpired with that
impoyfoned Baulme which hee fucked in the fweete and fugred
breath of his cruel miftreffe: who vndoing hir felfe out of his
armes, fayde vnto him: "Sith that I haue made the firft difclo-
fure both of the promife and of the effect, it behooueth that you
performe the reft, for the full accomplyfhment of the fame."
"Come on hardily" (fayeth hee) "and God knoweth how fpedily
you fhal be obeyed." "I wil then" (quod fhee) "and commaund
you vpon your promyfed faith that from this prefent time, vntyl
the fpace of three yeres be expyred, you fpeake to no lyuing
perfon for any thing that fhall happen vnto you, nor yet expreffe
by tonge, by found of word or fpeache what thing you wante or
els defyre, whych requefte if you do breake, I will neuer trufte
liuing man for youre fake, but wil publyfhe your fame to bee
villanous, and your perfon periured, and a promyfe breaker." I
leaue for you to think whether this vnhappy louer were amazed
or not, to heare a Commaundment fo vniuft, and therewithall
the difficulty for the performance. Notwithftanding he was fo
ftoute of hearte, and fo religious an obferuer of his Othe as euen
at that very inftant he began to do the part which fhe had commaunded, playing at Mumchaunce, and vfing other fignes, for
doing of his duetye, accordynge to hir demaund. Thus after his
ryghte humble reuerence made vnto hir, he went home, where
faining that hee had loft his fpeach by meanes of a Catarre or
reume which diftilled from his brayne, he determined to forfake
his Countrey vntill his tyme of penance was rune out. Wherfore
fetting ftaye in hys affayres, and prouydyng for his trayne, he
made him ready to depart. Notwithftanding, he wrot a Letter vnto
Zilia, before he toke hys iovrney into Fraunce, that in olde tyme
hadde ben the Solace and refuge of the miferable, as wel for the
pleafantnes and temperature of the ayre, the great wealth and
the aboundance of al thynges, as for the curtefye, gentlenes and

familyarity of the people: wherein that region may compare with any other nation vpon the earth. Now the Letter of Philiberto, fell into the hands of lady Zilia, by meanes of hys Page inſtructed for that purpoſe: who aduertiſed hir of the departure of his may-ſter, and of the deſpaire wherein hee was. Whereof ſhee was ſomewhat ſory, and offended: But yet puttinge on hir Aunciente ſeuerytye, tooke the Letters, and breakinge the Seale, found that which followeth.

THE very euill that cauſeth mine anoy
The matter is that breedes to me my ioy,
Which doth my wofull heart full ſore diſpleaſe,
And yet my hap and hard yll lucke doth eaſe.
I hope one day when I am franke and free,
To make thee do the thing that pleaſeth mee,
Whereby gayne I ſhall, ſome pleaſaunt gladneſſe,
To ſupply mine vndeſerued ſadneſſe,
The like whereof no mortall Dame can giue
To louing man that heere on earth doth lyue.
This great good turne which I on thee pretende,
Of my Conceites the full deſired ende,
Proceedes from thee (O cruell myſtreſſe myne)
Whoſe froward heart hath made mee to reſigne
The full effect of all my liberty,
(To pleaſe and eaſe thy fonde fickle fanſy)
My vſe of ſpeache in ſilence to remayne:
To euery wight a double helliſhe payne.
Whoſe fayth hadſt thou not wickedly abuſde
No ſtreſſe of payne for thee had bene refuſde,
Who was to thee a truſty ſeruaunt ſure,
And for thy ſake all daungers would endure.
For which thou haſt defaced thy good name,
And thereunto procurde eternall ſhame.
¶ That roaring tempeſt huge which thou haſt made me felt,
The raging ſtormes whereof, well neere my heart hath ſwelt
By painefull pangs: whoſe waltering waues by troubled Skies,
And thouſand blaſts of winde that in thoſe Seas do ryſe

Do promife fhipwracke fure of that thy fayling **Barke**,
When after weather cleare doth rife fome Tempeft darke.
For eyther I or thou which art of Tyger's kinde,
In that great raging gulfe fome daunger fure fhalt finde,
Of that thy nature rude the deft'nies en'mies bee,
And thy great ouerthrow full well they do forefee.
The heauens vnto my eftate no doubt great friendfhip fhoe,
And do feeke wayes to ende, and finifh all my woe.
This penaunce which I beare by yelding to thy heft
Great ftore of ioyes fhall heape, and bring my mynde to reft.
And when I am at eafe amids my pleafaunt happes,
Then fhall I fee thee fall, and fnarld in Fortune's trappes.
Then fhall I fee thee ban and curffe the wicked time,
Wherin thou madeft me gulp fuch draught of poyfoned wine.
Of which thy mortall cup, I am the offerd wight,
A vowed facrifice to that thy cruell fpight.
Wherefore my hoping heart doth hope to fee the day,
That thou for filence now to me fhalt be the pray.
¶ O Bleffed God moft iuft, whofe worthy laude and prayfe
With vttered fpeach in Skies a loft I dare not once to rayfe,
And may not well pronounce and fpeak what fuffrance I fuftain,
Ne yet what death I do indure, whiles I in lyfe remayne,
Take vengeance on that traytreffe rude, afflict hir corps with woe
Thy holy arme redreffe hir fault, that fhe no more do foe:
My reafon hath not fo farre ftrayed but I may hope and truft
To fee hir for hir wickednes, be whipt with plague moft iuft.
In the meane while great heauines my fence and foule doth bite,
And fhaking feuer vex my corps for griefe of hir defpite.
My mynde now fet at liberty from thee (O cruell Dame)
Doth giue defiaunce to thy wrath, and to thy curfed name,
Proclayming mortal warre on thee vntill my tongue vntide,
Shall ioy to fpeak to Zilia faft weping by my fide.
The heauens forbid that caufleffe wrong abroad fhold make his
        vaunt,
Or that an vndeferued death forgetfull tombe fhould haunt:
But that in written booke and verfe their names fhold euer liue
And eke their wicked deedes fhold dy, and vertues ftil reuiue.

So ſhall the pride and glory both, of hir be puniſht right,
By length of yeares, and traƈt of time. And I by vertues might,
Full recompence thereby ſhal haue and ſtand ſtill in good Fame,
And ſhe like caitif wretch ſhall liue, to hir long laſting ſhame.
Whoſe fond regard of beautie's grace, contemned hath the force
Of my true loue full fixt in hir: hir heart voide of remorſe,
Eſteemed it ſelfe right fooliſhly and me abuſed ſtill,
Vſurping my good honeſt fayth and credite at hir will.
Whoſe loyall faith doth reſt in ſoule, and therein ſtil ſhal bide,
Vntill in filthy ſtincking graue the earth my corps ſhall hide.
Then ſhal that ſoule fraught with that faith, to heuens make his
      repaire
And reſt among the heuenly rout, bedeƈt with ſacred aire.
And thou for thy great cruelty, as God aboue doth know,
With ruful voice ſhalt wepe and wayle for thy gret ouerthrow,
And when thou woldſt fayn purge thy ſelf for that thy wretched dede
No kindnes ſhal to the be done, extreme ſhal be thy mede:
And where my tongue doth want his wil, thy miſchiefe to diſplay,
My hand and penne ſupplies the place, and ſhall do ſo alway.
For ſo thou haſt conſtraynd the ſame by force of thy beheſt:
In ſilence ſtill my tongue to keepe, t'accompliſhe thy requeſt.
Adieu, farewell my tormenter, thy frend that is full mute,
Doth bid thee farewell once agayne, and ſo hee ends his ſute.

    He that liueth only to be reuenged of thy cruelty,

                    PHILIBERTO OF VIRLE.

    Zilia lyke a diſdaynefull Dame, made but a Ieſt at theeſe Letters
and Complayntes of the infortunate Louer, ſaying that ſhe was
very well content with his Seruice: and that when he ſhould
perfourme the tyme of his probation, ſhee ſhoulde ſee if he were
worthy to bee admitted into the Felowſhip of theym which had
made ſufficient proofe of the Order, and Rule of Loue. In the
meane tyme Philiberto rode by great Iourneys (as we haue ſayde
before) towardes the goodly, and pleaſaunte countrey of Fraunce,
wherein Charles the Seuenth that tyme did raygne, who miraculouſly (But gieue the Frencheman leaue to flatter, and ſpeake well
of hys owne Countrey, accordinge to the flatteringe, and vaunt-
inge Nature of that Nation) chaſed the Engliſhemen out of hys

Landes, and Auncient Patrimony in the yeare of our Lord 1451.
This Kynge had hys Campe then Warrefaringe in Gafcoine, whofe
Lucke was fo Fortunate as hee expelled hys Ennymies, and left no
Place for theym to Fortyfy there, whych Incouraged the Kynge to
followe that good Occafion, and by Profecutinge hys Victoryous
Fortune, to Profligate out of Normandie, and to difpatch himfelfe
of that Ennemy, into whofe Handes, and feruitude the Countrey
of Guyene was ryghtly delyuered, and Victoryoufly wonne, and
gotten by the Englifhmen. The kynge then beeinge in hys Campe
in Normandie, the Piedmount Gentleman the Lorde of Virle aforefayde, Repayred thereunto to Serue hym in hys Perfon, where hee
was well knowne of fome Captaynes whych had feene hym at other
tymes, and in place where worthy Gentlemen are wonte to Fre-
quente, and in the Duke of Sauoyes Courte, whych the Frenche-
men dyd very mutch Haunte, becaufe the Earle of Piedmont
that then was Duke of Sauoy had Marryed Iolanta, the feconde
daughter of Charles the Seuenth. Theefe Gentlemen of Fraunce
were very mutch fory for the Myffortune of the Lord of Virle, and
knowinge hym to be one of the Braueft, and Luftyeft Men of
Armes that was in his tyme within the Country of Piedmont,
prefented him before the King, commending vnto hys grace the
vertue, gentleneffe, and valiaunce of the man of Warre : who after
hee had done his reuerence accordinge to hys duety, whych hee
knew ful wel to doe, declared vnto him by fignes that he was
come for none other intent, but in thofe Warres to ferue hys
Maieftye : whom the King heard and thankefully receyued affuryng himfelf and promifing very mutch of the dumbe Gentleman for refpect of his perfonage which was comely and wel pro-
portioned, and therefore reprefented fome Force and greate
Dexterity : and that whych made the king the better to fantafie
the Gentleman, was the reporte of fo many worthy men which
extolled euen to the heauens the proweffe of the Piedmont knight.
Whereof he gaue affured teftimony in the affault which the king
made to deliuer Roane, the Chyefe Citye and defence of all Normandie, in the year of our Lord 1451. where Philiberto behaued
himfelf fo valiantly as he was the firft that mounted upon the
Wals, and by his Dexterity and inuincyble force, made way to the

fouldiers in the breche, whereby a little while after they entred
and facked the Enemies, dryuing them out of the Citye, and
wherein not long before, that is to fay 1430. the duke of Somerfet
caufed Ioane the Pucelle to be burnt. The king aduertifed of the
Seruice of the Dumbe Gentleman, to recompence him according
to his defert, and bycaufe hee knewe hym to bee of a good houfe,
he made him a Gentleman of his Chambre, and gaue him a good
penfion, promyfing him moreouer to continue hys liberality, when
he fhould fee him profecute in time to come, the towardneffe of
feruice which he had fo haply begon. The dumbe Gentleman
thanking the King very humbly, both for the prefent pryncely
reward, and for promife in time to come, lifted vp his hand to
heauen as taking God to witneffe of the faith, which inuiolable
he promyfed to keepe vnto his Prynce: which he did fo earneftly,
as hardely he had promyfed, as well appeared in a Skirmifhe
betweene the Frrench, and their auncient Enimies the Englyfh-
Men, on whofe fide was the valiaunt and hardy Captayne the Lord
Talbot, who hath eternized his memory in the victories obtained
vpon that People, which fometimes made Europa and Afia to
tremble, and appalled the monftruous and Warlike Countrey of
Affrica. In this conflycte the Piedmont Knighte combated with
the Lorde Talbot, agaynfte whome he had fo happy fucceffe, as
vpon the fhock and incountre he ouerthrewe both man and Horfe,
which caufed the difcomfiture of the Englifhe Men: who after
they had horfed agayne their Captain fled amaine, leauing the
field befpred with dead Bodyes and bludfhed of their Companions.
This victory recouered futch corage and boldnes to the French, as
from that tyme forth the Englifhmen began with their places
and forts to lofe alfo theyr hartes to defend themfelues. The
king excedingly wel contented wyth the proweffe and valiance
of the dumbe Gentleman, gaue him for feruice paft the Charge of
v. c. men of armes, and indued him with fome poffeffions, attending
better fortune to make him vnderftand howe mutch the vertue of
valiance ought to be rewarded and cheryfhed by Prynces that be
aided in their Neceffity with the Dylygence of futch a vertuous and
noble Gentleman. In lyke manner when a Prynce hath fomething
good in himfelf, he can do no leffe but loue and fauor that which

refembleth himfelf by Pryncely Conditions, fith the Vertue in
what foeuer place it taketh roote, can not chofe but produce good
fruiéte, the vfe whereof far furmounts them all which approche the
place, where thefe firft feedes of Nobility were throwen.   Certaine
dayes after the kinge defirous to reioyce his Knights and Captaines
that were in his trayne, and defirous to extinguifh quite the woefull time which fo long fpace held Fraunce in fearefull filence,
caufed a triumph of Turney to bee proclaimed within the City of
Roane, wherein the Lord of Virle was deemed and efteemed one
of the beft, whych further did increafe in him the good wyl of the
kyng, in futch wyfe as he determined to procure his health, and
to make him haue his fpeache againe.   For he was verye forry
that a Gentleman fo valiant was not able to expreffe his minde,
which if it might be had in counfel it would ferve the ftate of a
commonwealth, fo wel as the force and valor of his body had til
then ferued for defence and recovery of his country.   And for
that purpofe he made Proclamation by found of Trumpet throughout the prouinces as wel within his own kingdome, as the regions
adioyning vpon the fame, that who fo euer could heale that dumb
Gentleman, fhoulde haue ten thoufand Frankes for recompence.   A
Man myght then haue feene thoufands of Phyfitians affemble in
fielde, not to fkirmifh with the Englyfh men, but to combat for
reward in recouery of the pacient's fpeache, who begon to make
futch Warre againft thofe ten thoufand Frankes, as the kyng was
afrayde that the cure of that difeafe could take no effeét : and for
that caufe ordained furthermore, that whofoeuer would take in
hand to heale the dumbe, and did not keepe promyfe within a
certaine prefixed time, fhould pay the fayd fumme, or for default
thereof fhould pledge his head in gage.   A Man myght then haue
feene thofe Phificke Mayfters, afwell beyonde the Mountaynes, as
in Fraunce it felfe, retire home againe, bleeding at the Nofe,
curfing with great impiety their Patrones, Galen, Hypocrates, and
Auicen, and blamed with more than reprochful Woordes, the Arte
wherewith they fifhed for honor and richeffe.   This brute was
fpred fo far, and babblyng Fame had already by mouth of her
Trump publyfhed the fame throughout the moft part of the Prouinces, Townes, and Cities neare and farre off to Fraunce, in futch

wyſe as a Man wouldc haue thought that thc two young men (which once in the tyme of the Macedonian Warres brought Tydings to Varinius that the king of Macedon was taken by the Conſul Paulus Emilius) had ben vagarant and wandering abrode to carry Newes of the king's ediɛte for the healing of the Lord of Virle. Which cauſed that not only the brute of the Proclamation, but alſo the Credyte and reputatyon wherein the ſayd Lord was with the French king arriued euen at Montcal and paſſed from mouth to mouth, til at length Zilia the principal cauſe thereof vnderſtode the newes, which reioyced hir very mutch, ſeing the firme Amitie of the dumbe Lord, and the ſyncere faith of hym in a promiſe vnworthy to be kept, for ſo mutch as where Fraude and feare doe rule in Heartes of Men, relygyon of promiſe, ſpecially the Place of.the gyuen Fayth, ſurrendreth hys force and reuolteth, and is no more bound but to that which by good wyll he woulde obſerue. Nowe thoughte ſhee, thoughte? nay rather ſhee aſſured hir ſelfe, that the Gentleman for all hys wrytten Letter was ſtil ſo ſurpryſed wyth hir Loue, and kindled wyth her fire in ſo ample wyſe, as when hee was at Montcall: and therefore determyned to goe to Paris, not for deſire ſhee had to ſee hir pacient and penetenciarie, but rather for couetiſe of the ten thouſand Francks, wherof already ſhee thought hir ſelf aſſured, making good accompt that the dumbe Gentleman when hee ſhould ſee himſelf diſcharged of his promiſe, for gratifying of hir, would make no ſtay to ſpeak to the intent ſhe myght beare away both the prayſe and Money, whereof all others had failed tyll that tyme. Thus you ſee that ſhe, whome honeſt Amitye and long ſervice could lytle induce to compaſſion and deſire to giue ſome eaſe vnto hir moſte earneſt louer, yelded hir ſelfe to couetous gaine and greadineſſe for to encreaſe hir Rycheſſe. O curſed hunger of Money, how long wilt thou thus blinde the reaſon and Sprytes of men? Ah perillous gulfe, how many haſt thou ouerwhelmed within thy bottomleſſe Throte, whoſe glory, had it not bene for thee, had ſurpaſſed the Clouds, and bene equall with the bryghtneſſe of the Sunne, where now they bee obſcured wyth the thickneſſe of thy fogges and Palpable darkneſſe. Alas, the fruiɛts whych thou bryngeſt forth for all thine outewarde apparance, conduce no felycity to them

that bee thy poſſeſſors, for the dropſey that is hydden in their
Mynde, whych maketh them ſo mutch the more drye, as they
drynke ofte in that thirſty Fountaine, is cauſe of their alteration:
and moſte miſerable is that inſaciable deſire the Couetous haue to
glut their appetite, whych can receiue no contentment. Thys
onely Couetouſneſſe ſometimes procured the Death of the great and
rych Romane Craſſus who through GOD's punyſhment fell into
the Handes of the Perſians, for violating and ſacking the Temple
of God that was in Ieruſalem. Sextimuleus burnyng with Avarice
and greedyneſſe of money, dyd once cut of the head of hys Patron
and defender Caius Gracchus the Tribune of the People, incyted
by the Tirant, which tormenteth the hearts of the couetous. I wil
not ſpeake of a good number of other Examples of people of all
kyndes, and divers nations, to come again to Zilia. Who forgetting hir virtue, the firſt ornament and ſhining quality of hir honeſt
behauiour, feared not the wearines and trauaile of way, to commit
her ſelfe to that danger of loſſe of honor, and to yeld to the mercy
of one, vnto whom ſhe had don ſo great iniury, as hir conſcyence
(if ſhee hadde not loſt hir ryghte ſence) oughte to haue made hir
thinke that hee was not without deſire to reuenge the wrong
vniuſtly don vnto him, and ſpecially being in place where ſhe
was not known, and he greatly honoured and eſteemed, for whoſe
loue that Proclamation and ſearch of Phyſicke was made and
ordained. Zilia then hauing put in order hir affaires at home
departed from Montcall, and paſſyng the Mounts, arrived at Paris,
in that time when greateſt deſpayre was of the dumbe Knight's
recouery. Beynge arryued, wythin fewe Dayes after ſhe inquyred
for them that had the charge to entertayne ſutch as came, for the
cure of the pacient. "For (ſayd ſhe) if ther be any in the world,
by whom the knigt may recouer his health, I hope in God that I
am ſhe that ſhal haue the prayſe." Heereof the Commiſſaries deputed hereunto, were aduertyſed, who cauſed the fayre Phyſitian
to come before them, and aſked her if it were ſhe, that would take
vppon hir to cure this dumbe Gentleman. To whom ſhee aun-
ſweared. "My mayſters it hath pleaſed God to reueale vnto me a
certayne ſecrete very proper and meete for the healyng of hys
Malady, wherewithal if the pacyent wyll, I hope to make hym

ſpeake ſo well, as he dyd theſe two yeares paſt and more." "I ſuppoſe, ſayd one of the Commiſſaries, that you be not ignoraunte of
the Circumſtances of the Kynges Proclamation." "I knowe ful
wel" (quod ſhe) "the Effecte therefore, and therefore doe ſay vnto
you, that I wyll looſe my life yf I doe not accomplyſh that which
I doe promyſe ſo that I may haue Lycence, to tarry wyth hym
alone, bycauſe it is of no leſſe importaunce than hys Health." "It
is no maruell," ſayde the Commiſſary, "conſideryng your Beauty,
which is ſufficient to frame a Newe Tongue in the moſte dumbe
Perſon that is vnder the Heauens. And therefore doe your Endeuor, aſſuring you that you ſhall doe a great pleaſure vnto the
King, and beſides the prayſe you ſhall gette the good wyll of the
dumbe Gentleman, which is the moſt excellent man of the World
and therefore ſo well recompenſed as you ſhall haue good cauſe
to be contented wyth the kynges Lyberalitye. But (to the intente
you be not deceyued) the meanynge of the Edicte is, that within
fiftene dayes after you begin the cure, you muſte make hym whole,
or elſe to ſatiſfie the Paynes ordayned in the ſame." Whereunto ſhe ſubmitted hir ſelfe, blinded by Auarice and preſumption,
thinking that ſhe had like power nowe ouer the Lord of Virle, as
when ſhe gaue him that ſharpe and cruel penance. Theſe Conditions promyſed, the Commiſſaries went to aduertiſe the Knight,
how a gentlewoman of Piedmont was of purpoſe come into Fraunce
to helpe him: whereof he was maruelouſly aſtonned. Now he
would neuer haue thoughte that Zilia had borne hym ſo great
good wil, as by abaſing the pryde of hir Corage, would haue come
ſo farre to eaſe the griefe of him, whome by ſutch greate torments
ſhe had ſo wonderfully perſecuted. He thought againe that it
was the Gentlewoman his Neighboure, whych ſometymes had done
hir endeuor to helpe him, and that nowe ſhe had prouoked Zilia to
abſolue him of his faith, and requite him of hys promiſe. Muſing
vpon the diuerſitie of theſe things, and not knowing wherevpon
to ſettle hys iudgment, the deputies commaunded that the Woman
Phyſitian ſhould be admitted to ſpeake with the patient. Which
was done and brought in place, the Commiſſaries preſently withdrew themſelues. The Lord of Virle ſeeinge hys Ennemye come
before him, whom ſometimes hee loued very dearely, iudged by

and by the caufe wherefore fhe came, that onely Auaryce and
greedy defire of gaine had rather procured hir to paffe the moun-
tayns trauaile, than due and honeft Amitye, wherewith fhe was
double bound through his perfeuerance and humble feruice, with
whofe fight hee was fo appalled, as he fared like a fhadowe and
Image of a deade man.   Wherefore callyng to mynd the rigour
of his lady, hir inciuility and fonde Commaundement, fo longe
time to forbidde hys Speach, the Loue which once hee bare hir,
with vehement defire to obey hir, fodainly was fo cooled and
qualyfyed, that loue was turned into hatred, and will to ferue hir,
into an appetite of reuenge : whereupon he determined to vfe that
prefente Fortune, and to playe his parte wyth hir, vpon whom hee
had fo foolyfhly doted, and to pay hir with that Money wherewyth
fhe made him feele the Fruiĉts of vnfpcakable crueltye, to giue
example to fonde and prefumptuous dames, how they abufe
Gentlemen of futch Degree whereof the Knyghte was, and that by
hauing regarde to the merite of futch perfonages, they be not fo
prodigall of themfelues, as to fet their honour in fale for vyle reward and filthy mucke : whych was fo conftantly conferued and
defended by this Gentlewoman, agaynft the affaultes of the good
grace, beauty, valour, and gentleneffe, of that vertuous and honeft
futer.   And notwithftanding, in thefe dayes wee fee fome to
refifte the amity of thofe that loue, for an opynyon of a certayne
vertue, which they thinke to bc hydden within the corps of excellent beauty, who afterwards do fet themfelues to fale to hym that
giueth moft, and offreth greateft reward.   Sutch do not deferue
to be placed in rank of chaft Gentlewomen, of whome they haue
no fmacke at al, but amongs the throng of ftrumpets kynde, that
haue fome fparke and outward fhew of loue : for fhe which loueth
money and hunteth after gayne, wyl make no bones, by treafon's
trap to betray that vnhappy man, which fhall yelde himfelfe to
hir : hir loue tending to vnfenfible things, and futch in dede, as
make the wifeft forte to falfifie their fayth, and fel the ryghte and
Equity of their Iudgment.   The Lorde of Virle, feeing Zilia then
in his company, and almoft at his commaundement, fayned as
though hee knew hir not, by reafon of his fmall regard and leffe
intertaynment fhewed vnto hir at hir firft comming.   Which

greatly made the poore Gentlewoman to mufe.   Neuerthelefſe
fhe making a vertue of neceſſity, and feeing hir felfe to bee in
that place, from whence fhee could not depart, without the loſſe
of hir honor and Lyfe, purpofed to proue Fortune, and to com-
mitte hir felfe vnto his mercy, for all the mobilytie whych the
auncients attribute vnto Fortune.   Wherefore fhutting faſt the
doore, fhee went vnto the Knight, to whom fhe fpake thefe
words : " And what is the matter (fir knight) that now you make
fo little accompte of your owne Zilia, who in times paſt you fayd,
had great power and Authorytye ouer you ?   what is the caufe that
moueth you hereunto ?   haue you fo foone forgotten hir ?   Beholde
me better, and you fhal fee hir before you that is able to acquyte
you of youre promyfe, and therefore prayeth you to pardon hir
committed faultes done in tymes paſt by abufing fo cruelly the
honeſt and firme loue which you bare hir.   I am fhe, which
through follye and temeritie did ſtoppe your mouth, and tyed vp
your Tongue.   Giue me leaue, I befeeche you, to open the fame
agayne, and to breake the Lyne, whych letteth the liberty of your
Speache."   She feeying that the dumbe Gentleman would make no
aunfwere at all, but mumme, and fhewed by fignes, that he was
not able to vndoe his Tongue, weepyng began to kyſſe hym, imbrace hym and make mutch of hym, in futch wyfe, as he whych
once ſtudyed to make Eloquent Orations before hys Ladye, to
induce hir to pity, forgat then thofe Ceremonyes, and fpared his
talke, to fhewe hymfelfe to be futch one as fhee had made at hir
Commaundement, mufed and deuyfed altogether vpon the execu-
tyon of that, which fometyme hee hadde fo paynefully purfued,
both by Woords and contynuall Seruyce, and coulde profite nothing.   Thus waked agayne by hir, whych once had Mortyfyed
hys Mynde, aſſayed to renue in hir that, whych long tyme before
feemed to be a fleepe.   She more for feare of loſſe of Lyfe, and
the pryce of the rewarde, than for any true or earneſt loue fuffred
hym to receyue that of hir, whych the long Suter defireth to obtaine
of his miſtreſſe.   They liued in this ioy and Pleafure the fpace of
fiftene Dayes ordained for the aſſigned Terme of his Cure, wherein
the poore Gentlewoman was not able to conuert hir offended
Fryende to fpeake, although fhe humbly prayed him to fhewe fo

mutch favour as at leaſt ſhe might goe free, from either loſſe :
telling hym howe lyttle regard ſhee hadde to hir honour, to come
ſo farre to doe him pleaſure, and to diſcharge him of his promiſe.
Mutch other gay and lowlye talke ſhee hadde. But the knyghte
nothing moued with what ſhe ſayde determined to brynge hir in
ſutch feare, as he had bene vexed with heauineſſe, which came
to paſſe at the expryred tyme. For the Commiſſaries ſeeing that
their pacyent ſpake not at all, ſummoned the Gentlewoman to pay
the Penaltye pronounced in the Edict, or elſe to looſe hyr lyfe.
Alas, howe bytter ſeemed thys drynke to thys poore gentlewoman
who not able to diſſemble the gryef that preſt on euery ſyde, beganne to ſaye : "Ah, I Wretched and Caytyfe Woman, by thinking to deceiue an other, haue ſharpened the Sworde to finiſh myne
owne lyfe. Was it not enough for me to vſe ſutch crueltye towardes this myne Enemye, which moſt cruelly in double wyſe
taketh Reuenge, but I muſt come to bee thus tangled in his Snares,
and in the Handes of him, who inioying the Spoyles of myne
Honour, will with my Lyfe, depryue me of my Fame, by making
mee a Common Fable, to all Poſterity in tyme to come ?   O what
hap had I, that I was not rather deuoured by ſome Furious and
cruell beaſt, when I paſſed the mountaines, or elſe that I brake
not my Necke, downe ſome ſteepe and headlong hil, of thoſe high
and hideous mountains, rather than to bee ſet heare in ſtage, a
Pageant to the whole Citye to gaze vppon, for enterpryſing a thing
ſo vayne, done of purpoſe by him, whome I haue offended. Ah,
Signior Philiberto, what Euill rewardeſt thou for pleaſures receiued, and fauors felt in hir whom thou didſt loue ſo much, as
to make hir dye ſutch ſhameful, and dreadfull death. But O
GOD, I know that it is for worthy guerdon of my folyſh and
wycked Lyfe. Ah diſloyaltye and fickle truſt, is it poſſible that
thou be harbored in the hearte of hym which hadde the Brute to
bee the moſt Loyall and Curteous Gentleman of hys Countrey ?
Alas, I ſee well nowe that I muſt die through myne onelye ſimplicity, and that I muſte ſacrifice mine Honoure to the rygour of
hym, which with two aduauntages, taketh ouer cruell reuenge of
the lyttle wrong, wherewith my chaſtity touched him before."
As ſhe thus had finiſhed hir complainte, one came in to carrye

hir to Pryſon, whether willinglye ſhee wente for that ſhe was
already reſolued in deſire, to lyue no longer in that miſerie.   The
Gentleman contented wyth that payne, and not able for to dis-
ſemble the gryefe, which hee conceyued for the paſſion whych
hee ſawe hys Welbeloued to endure, the enioyinge of whome
renued the heate of the flames forepaſt, repayred to the Kyng,
vnto whome to the great pleaſure of the Standers by, and exceding
reioyce of hys Maieſtye (to heare hym ſpeake) he told the whole
diſcourſe of the Loue betweene hym and cruell Zilia, the cauſe of
the loſſe of his ſpeach, and the ſomme of hys reuenge." By the
fayth of a Gentleman (ſayed the king) but here is ſo ſtraunge an
hyſtorye as euer I heard : and verely your fayth and loyaltye is no
leſſe to be praiſed and commended than the cruelty and couetous-
nes of the Woman worthy of reproch and blame, which truly
deſerueth ſome greeuous and notable iuſtice, if ſo be ſhe were
not able to render ſome apparant cauſe for the couerture and
hiding of hir folly."   "Alas ſir," (ſayd the Gentleman) " pleaſeth
your maieſty to deliuer hir (although ſhe be worthy of puniſhment) and diſcharge the reſt that be in priſon for not recouery of
my ſpeach, ſith my onely help did reſt, eyther at hir Commaundemente whych had bounde me to that wrong, or elſe in the expired
time, for whych I had pleadged my fayth." To which requeſt,
the Kinge very willingly agreed, greatly prayſing the Wiſedome,
Curteſie, and aboue all the fidelity of the Lord of Virle, who
cauſing his penitenciary to be ſet at liberty, kept hir company
certayne dayes, as well to Feaſte, and banket hir, in thoſe Landes
and Poſſeſſions which the kinges maieſty had liberally beſtowed
vpon him, as to ſaciate his Appetite with ſome fruictes whereof he
had ſauoured his taſte when he was voluntaryly Dumbe.   Zilia
founde that fauour ſo pleaſaunt, as in maner ſhee counted hir
impriſonment happy, and hir trauell reſt, by reaſon that diſtreſſe
made hir then feele more liuely the force and pleaſure of Liberty,
which ſhee had not founde to bee ſo delicate, had ſhe not receyued the experience and payne thereof.   Marke heere how Fortune
dealeth with them which truſtinge in their force, deſpiſe (in reſpect of that which they doe themſelues) the little portion that
they iudge to bee in others.   If the Vayneglory, and arrogante

Prefumption of a Chaftity Impregnable had not deceiued this Gentlewoman, if the facred hunger of gold had not blinded hir, it could not haue bene knowne, wherein hir incontinency confifted, not in the Mynion delights, and alluring Toyes of a paffionate Louer, but in the couetous defire of filling hir Purfe, and Hypocriticall glory of praife among men. And notwithftanding yee fee hir gaine to ferue hir turne nothing at all but to the perpetuall reproch of hir name, and the flaunder futch as ill fpeakers and enimies of womankinde, do burden the Sexe withall. But the fault of one Woman, which by hir owne prefumption deceyued hir felfe, ought not to obfcure the glory of fo many vertuous, Fayre, and Honeft dames, who by their Chaftity, Liberality, and Curtefy, be able to deface the blot of Folly, Couetoufnes and cruelty of this Gentlewoman heere, and of all other that do refemble hir. Who taking leaue of hir Louer, went home agayne to Piedmount, not without an ordinary griefe of heart, which ferued hir for a fpur to hir Confcience, and continually forced hir to thinke, that the force of man is leffe than nothing, where God worketh not by his grace, which fayling in vs, oure worckes can fauor but of the ftench and corruption of our nature, wherein it tumbleth and toffeth lyke the Sow that walloweth in the puddle of filth and dirt. And becaufe yee fhall not thincke in generall termes of Woman's chaftity, and difcretion, that I am not able to vouche fome particular example of later years, I meane to tell you of one, that is not onely to bee prayfed for hir Chaftity in the abfence of hir hufband, but alfo of hir Courage and Pollicy in chaftifinge the vaunting natures of two Hungarian Lords that made their braggs they would win hir to their Willes, and not only hir, but all other, whatfoeuer they were of Woman-kynde.

THE TWENTY-EIGHTH NOUELL.

*Two Barons of Hvngarie aſſuring themſelues to obtayne their ſute
to a fayre Lady of Boeme, receyued of hir a ſtraung and mar-
uelous repulſe, to their great ſhame and Infamy, curſinge the tyme
that euer they aduentured an Enterpriſe ſo fooliſh.*

PENELOPE, the woful Wife of abſent Vliſſes, in hir tedious longing
for the home retourne of that hir aduenturous knight, aſſayled
wyth Carefull heart amid the troupe of amorous Suters, and within
the Bowels of hir royall Pallace, deſerued no greater fame for hir
valiaunt encountries and ſtoute defence of the inuincible, and
Adamant fort of hir chaſtity than this Boeme Lady doth by reſiſt-
ing two mighty Barrons, that canoned the Walles, and well mured
rampart of hir pudicity. For being threatned in his Princes
Court, whether al the well trayned crew of eche ſcience and profeſſion, dyd make repayre, beyng menaced by Venus' band, which
not onely ſummoned hir fort and gaue hir a camiſado by thick
Al' Armes, but alſo forced the place by fierce aſſault, ſhe lyke a
couragious and politike captayne, gaue thoſe braue and luſty
Souldiers, a fowle repulſe, and in end taking them captiues, vrged
them for their victuals to fall to woman's toyle, more ſhamefull
than ſhameleſſe Sardanapalus amid hys amorous troupe. I neede
not amplifie by length of preamble, the fame of this Boeme Lady,
nor yet briefly recompt the Triumph of hir Victory : vayne it were
alſo by glorious hymnes to chaunte the wiſedome of hir beleuing
maake, who not careleſſe of hir Lyfe, employed hys care to ſerue
hys Prynce, and by ſeruice atchieued the cauſe that draue him to
a ſouldier's ſtate. But yet for truſtleſſe faith in the pryme conference of his future porte, hee conſulted wyth a Pollaco, for a
compounded drugge, to eaſe his ſuſpect mind, whych medicine ſo
eaſed his maladie, as it not onely preſerued hym from the infected
humour, but alſo made hir happy for euer. Sutch fall the euents
of valiaunt mindes, though many tymes mother iealoſie that cancred Wytch ſteppeth in hir foote to anoy the well diſpoſed heart.
For had he ioyned to his valyaunce credite of his louynge wife,

without the blynde aduyſe of ſutch as profeſſe that blacke and
lying ſcyence, double glorye hee had gayned : once for endeuor-
yng by ſeruice to ſeeke honour : the ſeconde, for abſolute truſte
in hir, that neuer ment to beguyle him, as by hir firſte aunſwere
to his firſt motion appeareth.   But what is to be obiected againſt
the Barons ?   Let them anſwere for their fault, in this diſcourſe
enſuing : whych ſo leſſoneth all Noble Myndes, as warely they
ought to beware how they aduenture upon the honour of Ladies,
who bee not altogither of one ſelfe and yelding trampe, but wel
forged and ſteeled in the ſhamefaſt ſhoppe of Loyaltie, which
armure defendeth them againſt the fond ſkirmiſhes and vnconſi-
dred conflicts of Venus' wanton band.   The maieſties alſo of the
king and Queene, are to be aduaunced aboue the ſtarres for their
wiſe diſſuaſion of thoſe Noblemen from their hot and hedleſſe
enterpryſe, and then their Iuſtice for due execution of their forfait,
the particularity of whych diſcourſe in this wyſe doth begynne.
Mathie Coruine, ſometime king of Hungarie, aboute the yeare of
oure Lorde 1458, was a valiaunt man of Warre, and of goodly
perſonage.   Hee was the firſt that was Famous, or feared of the
Turks, of any Prynce that gouerned that kingdome.   And amongs
other his vertues, ſo well in Armes and Letters, as in Lyberallyty
and Curteſie he excelled al the Prynces that raygned in his time.
He had to Wyfe Queene Beatrice of Arragon, the Daughter of olde
Ferdinando kyng of Naples, and ſiſter to the mother of Alphonſus,
Duke of Ferrara, who in learnyng, good conditions, and all other
vertues generally diſperſed in hir, was a ſurpaſſing princeſſe, and
ſhewed hirſelf not onely a curteous and Liberall Gentlewoman to
king Mathie hir huſband, but to all other, that for vertue ſeemed
worthy of honour and reward : in ſutch wiſe as to the Court
of theſe two noble Princes, repayred the moſt notable Men of al
Nations that were giuen to any kind of good exerciſe, and euery
of them according to theyr deſert and degree welcomed and
entertained.   It chaunced in this time, that a knight of Boeme
the vaſall of Kinge Mathie, for that he was likewyſe kyng of that
countrey, born of a noble houſe, very valiant and wel exerciſed in
armes, fell in loue with a paſſing faire Gentlewoman of like nobility,
and reputed to be the faireſt of al the country, and had a brother

that was but a pore Gentleman, not lucky to the goods of fortune. This Boemian knight was alſo not very rich, hauing onely a Caſtle, wyth certain reuenues thervnto, which was ſcarce able to yeld vnto him any great maintenance of liuing. Fallyng in loue then with this faire Gentlewoman, he demaunded hir in mariage of hir brother, and with hir had but a very little dowrie. And this knight not wel forſeeing his poore eſtate, brought his wyfe home to his houſe, and there, at more leiſure conſidering the ſame, began to fele his lacke and penury, and how hardly and ſcant his reuenues were able to maintein his port. He was a very honeſt and gentle perſon, and one that delighted not by any meanes to burden and fine his tenants, contenting himſelf with that reuenue which his anceſters left him, the ſame amounting to no great yerely rent. When this gentleman perceiued that he ſtode in neede of extraordinary relyefe, after many and diuers conſyderations with himſelf, he purpoſed to folow the Court, and to ſerue king Mathie his ſouerain lord and maſter, there by his diligence and experience, to ſeke meanes for ability to ſuſtaine his wife and himſelf. But ſo great and feruent was the loue that he bare vnto his Lady, as he thought it impoſſible for him to liue one houre without hir, and yet iudged it not beſt to haue hir with him to the court, for auoidinge of further Charges incydente to Courtyng Ladyes, whoſe Delight and Pleaſure reſteth in the toyes and trycks of the ſame, that cannot be wel auoyded in poore Gentlemen, without theyr Names in the Mercer's or Draper's Iornals, a heauy thyng for them to confyder if for their diſport they lyke to walke the ſtretes. The daily thynkyng thereupon, brought the poore Gentleman to great ſorrow and heauineſſe. The Lady that was young, wiſe and diſcrete, marking the maner of hir huſband, feared that he had ſome miſliking of hir. Wherefore vpon a day ſhe thus ſayd vnto hym: "Dere huſband, willingly would I deſire a good turne at your hand, if I wiſt I ſhould not diſpleaſe you." "Demaund what you will," (ſaid the knighte) "if I can, I ſhall gladly performe it, bicauſe I do eſteeme your ſatiſfaction, as I do mine owne lyfe." Then the Lady very ſobrely praied him, that he would open vnto hir the cauſe of that diſcontentment, which hee ſhewed outwardly to haue, for that his mynd and behauiour ſeemed to bee

contrary to ordinary Cuftome, and contriued **Daye and Nyghte** in
fighes, auoydinge the Company of them that were wont fpecially
to delyght him. The Knight hearing his Ladyes requeft, panfed a
whyle, and then fayd vnto hir: "My wel beloued Wyfe, for fo
mutch as you defyre to vnderftand my thoughte and mynde, and
whereof it commeth that I am fad and penfife, I wyll tell you:
all the Heauineffe wherewith you fee me to be affected, doth
tend to this end. Fayne would I deuyfe that you and I may in
honour lyue together, accordyng to our calling. For in refpect of
our Parentage, our Liuelode is very flender, the occafion whereof
were our Parents, who morgaged theyr Lands, and confumed a
great part of their goods that our Aunceftors lefte them. I dayly
thynking hereupon, and conceiuyng in my head dyuers Imaginations, can deuife no meanes but one, that in my fanfie feemeth
beft, which is, that I go to the Court of our foueraine lord Mathie
who at this prefent is inferring Warres vpon the Turk, at whofe
hands I do not miftruft to receyue good intertainment, beynge a
moft Lyberal Prynce, and one that efteemeth al futch as be valiant
and active. And I for my parte wyll fo gouerne my felfe (by
God's grace) that by deferte I wyll procure futch lyuing and
fauour as hereafter we may lyue in oure Olde Dayes a quyet Lyfe
to oure great ftay and comforte: For althoughe Fortune hitherto
hath not fauored that ftate of Parentage, whereof we be, I doubt
not wyth Noble Courage to win that in defpyte of Fortune's Teeth,
which obftinately hitherto fhe hath denyed. And the more affured
am I of thys determination, bycaufe at other tymes, I haue ferued
vnder the Vaiuoda in Tranfiluania, agaynft the Turke, where
many tymes I haue bene requyred to ferue alfo in the Courte, by
that honourable Gentleman, the Counte of Cilia. But when I dyd
confider the beloued Company of you (deare Wyfe) the fweteft
Companyon that euer Wyght poffeffed, I thought it vnpoffible
for me to forbeare your prefence, whych yf I fhould doe, I were
worthy to fuftayne that difhonour, which a great number of careleffe Gentlemen doe, who following their pryuate gayne and Wyll,
abandon theyr young and fayre Wyues, neglectinge the fyre which
Nature hath inftilled to the delycate bodies of futch tender Creatures. Fearing therewythall, that fo foone as I fhoulde depart

the lufty yong Barons and Gentlemen of the Countrey would purfue the gaine of that loue, the pryce whereof I do efteeme aboue
the crowne of the greateft Emperour in all the World, and woulde
not forgoe for all the Riches and Precious Iewels in the fertyle
Soyle of Arabie, who no doubte would swarme togyther in greater
heapes then euer dyd the wowers of Penelope, within the famous
graunge of Ithaca, the houfe of Wandering Vliffes. Whych purfute if they dyd attayne, I fhoulde for euer hereafter be afhamed
to fhewe my face before thofe that be of valour and regard. And
this is the whole effeꞓt of the fcruple (fweete wyfe) that hyndreth
me, to feeke for our better eftate and fortune." When he had
fpoken thefe words, he held his peace. The Gentlewoman which
was wyfe and ftout, perceyuing the great loue that her hufband
bare hir, when hee had ftayed himfelfe from talke, with good and
merry Countenance anfwered hym in thys wyfe: "Sir Vlrico,"
(which was the name of the Gentleman) "I in lyke manner as you
haue done, haue deuyfed and thoughte vpon the Nobilitye and
Byrth of our Aunceftors, from whofe ftate and port (and that
wythout oure fault and cryme) we be far wyde and deuyded. Notwythftanding I determined to fet a good face vpon the matter,
and to make fo mutch of our paynted fheath as I could. In deede
I confeffe my felfe to be a Woman, and you Men doe fay that
Womens heartes be faynt and feeble: but to bee playne wyth you,
the contrary is in me, my hearte is fo ftoute and ambitious as
peraduenture not meete and confonant to power and ability,
although we Women will finde no lacke if our Hartes haue pith and
ftrength inough to beare it out. And faine woulde I fupport the
ftate wherein my mother maintayned me. Howe be it for mine
owne part (to God I yeld the thanks) I can fo moderate and ftay
my little great heart, that contented and fatiffied I can be, with
that which your abilitye can beare, and pleafure commaund. But
to come to the point, I fay that debating with my felfe of our
ftate as you full wifely do, I do verily think that you being a yong
Gentleman, lufty and valiaunt, no better remedy or deuyfe can be
found than for you to afpyre and feeke the Kyng's fauor and feruice. And it muft needes ryfe and redounde to your gaine and
preferment, for that I heare you fay the King's Maieftye doth

already knowe you. Wherefore I do suppose that hys grace (a
skilfull Gentleman to way and esteeme the vertue and valor of ech
man) cannot chose but reward and recompence the well doer to
his singular contentation and comfort. Of this myne Opinion I
durst not before thys time vtter Word or signe for feare of your
displeasure. But nowe sith your selfe hath opened the way and
meanes, I haue presumed to discouer the same, do what shal seeme
best vnto your good pleasure. And I for my parte, although that
I am a woman (accordingly as I saied euen now) that by Nature
am desirous of honor, and to shew my selfe abrode more rich and
sumptuous than other, yet in respect of our fortune, I shal be contented so long as I lyue to continue with you in this our Castell,
where by the grace of God I will not fayle to serue, loue and obey
you, and to keepe your House in that moderate sorte, as the reuenues shall be able to maintayne the same. And no doubt but that
poore liuing we haue orderly vsed, shal be sufficient to finde vs
two, and fiue or sixe seruaunts with a couple of horsse, and so to
lyue a quyet and merry Lyfe. If God doe send vs any Children, tyl
they come to lawfull age, we will with our poore liuing bryng
them vp so well as wee can and then to prefer them to some Noble
mens seruices, with whome by God's grace they may acquire
honoure and lyuing, to keepe them in their aged dayes. And I
doe trust that wee two shall vse sutch mutuall loue and reioyce,
that so long as our Lyfe doth last in wealth and woe, our contented
mindes shall rest satiffied. But I waying the stoutnesse of your
minde, doe know that you esteeme more an Ounce of honor, than
all the Golde that is in the world. For as your birth is Noble, so
is your heart and stomacke. And therefore many tymes seeing
your great heauinesse, and manyfolde muses and studies, I haue
wondred with my selfe whereof they should proceede, and amongs
other my conceipts, I thought that either my behauior and order
of dealyng, or my personage did not lyke you: or else that your
wonted gentle minde and disposition had ben altered and trans-
formed into some other Nature: many times also I was contente
to thynke that the cause of your disquiet mynde, dyd ryse vppon
the disuse of Armes, wherein you were wonte dailye to accustome
youre selfe amonges the Troupes of the honourable, a company in

dede moſt worthy of your preſence. Reuoluing many times theſe
and ſutch lyke cogitations, I haue ſought meanes by ſutch alure-
mentes as I could deuyſe, to eaſe and mitigate your troubled
minde, and to wythdraw the great vnquiet and care wherewith I
ſawe you to be affeçted. Bycauſe I do eſteeme you aboue all the
Worlde deemyng your onely gryefe to be my double Payne, your
aking Fynger, a feruent Feuer fit, and the leaſt Woe you can ſus-
tayne moſte bytter Death to me, that loueth you more dearelye
than my ſelfe. And for that I doe perceyue you are determyned
to ſerue our Noble King, the ſorrowe which without doubte wyll
aſſayle mee by reaſon of your abſence, I wyll ſweeten and lenifie
wyth Contentatyon, to ſee your Commendable deſyre appeaſed and
quiet. And the pleaſaunt Memory of your valyaunt façts beguyle
my penſiſe thoughts, hopyng our nexte meetyng ſhall bee more
ioyfull than thys our dyſiunçtyon and departure heauy. And where
you doubt of the Confluence and repayre of the dyſhoneſte whych
ſhall attempt the wynnyng and ſubduing of myne heart and vn-
ſpotted bodye, hytherto inuyolably kepte from the touch of any
perſon, caſt from you that ſeare, expel from your minde that fonde
conceipt: for death ſhall ſooner cloſe theſe mortall Eyes, than my
Chaſtitye ſhall bee defyled. For pledge whereof I haue none other
thyng to gyue but my true and ſymple fayth, whych if you dare
truſt it ſhal hereafter appeare ſo firme and inuiolable as no ſparke
of ſuſpition ſhal enter your careful minde, which I may wel terme
to be carefull, bicauſe ſome care before hand doth riſe of my
behauior in your abſence. The tryall wherefore ſhall yelde ſure
euidence and teſtimony, by paſſing my careful life which I may
with better cauſe ſo terme in your abſence, that God knoweth
wil be right penſiſe and carefull vnto mee, who ioyeth in nothinge
elſe but in your welfare. Neuertheleſſe all meanes and wayes
ſhall bee agreeable vnto my minde for your aſſurance, and ſhall
breede in me a wonderful contentation, which luſteth after
nothing but your ſatiſſaçtion. And if you liſt to cloſe me vp in
one of the Caſtell towers til your return, right glad I am there to
continue an Ankreſſe life: ſo that the ſame may eaſe your deſired
mind." The knight with great delyght gaue ear to the aunſwere
of his Wife, and when ſhe had ended hir talke, he began to reply

vnto hir: "My welbeloued, I doe lyke wel and greatly commended the ftoutneffe of your heart, it pleafeth me greatly to fee
the fame agreeable vnto mine.   You haue lightned the fame
from ineftimable woe by vnderftanding your conceiued purpofe
and determination to gard and preferue your honor, praying you
therein to perfeuere, ftill remembring that when a Woman hath
loft hir honor, fhee hath forgone the chiefeft Iewel fhe hath in
this Life, and deferueth no longer to be called woman.   And
touching my talke propofed vnto you although it be of great
importaunce, yet I meane not to depart fo foone.   But if it do
come to effeɛt I affure thee Wife, I will leaue thee Lady and
miftreffe of all that I haue.   In the meane time I will confider
better of my bufineffe, and confult with my fryendes and kins-
men, and then determine what is beft to be done.   Til when let
vs lyue and fpend our tyme fo merely as we can."   To bee fhorte
there was nothing that fo mutch molefted the knight, as the doubt
he had of his wife, for that fhe was a very fine and faire yong
Gentlewoman: And therefore he ftil deuifed and imagined what
affurance he myght finde of hir behauior in his abfence.   And
refting in this imagination, not long after it cam to paffe that the
knight being in company of diuers Gentleman, and talking of
fundry matters, a tale was tolde what chaunced to a gentleman of
the Countrey whych had obtained the fauoure and good wyll of a
Woman, by meanes of an olde man called Pollacco, which had the
name to be a famous enchaunter and Phyfitian, dwelling at Cutiano
a Citie of Boeme, where plenty of filuer mines and other metals is.
The knight whofe Caftle was not far from Cutiano, had occafion to
repaire vnto that Citye, and according to his defire found out this
Pollacco, which was a very old man, and talking with him of
diuers things, perceiued him to be of great fkil.   In eud he entreated him, that for fo mutch as he had don pleafure to many
for apprehenfion of their loue, he wold alfo inftruɛt him, how he
might be affured that hys wife did keepe hir felf honeft all the
time of his abfence, and that by certaine fignes hee might have
fure knowledge whether fhe brake hir faith, by fending his honefty
into Cornwall.   Sutch vaine truft this knight repofed in the lying
Science of Sorcery, whych although to many other is found deceit-

ful, yet to him ſerued for ſure euidence of his wiue's fidelity. This
Pollacco which was a very cunning enchaunter as you haue heard
ſayd vnto him : " Sir you demaund a very ſtraunge matter, ſutch
as wherwyth neuer hithcrto I haue bene acquainted, ne yet
ſearched the depthe of thoſe hydden ſecrets, a thyng not commonly ſued for, ne yet practized by me. For who is able to
make aſſurance of a woman's chaſtity, or tel by ſignes except he
were at the deede doing, that ſhe had don amiſſe ? Or who can
gaine by proĉtors wryt, to ſummon or ſue at ſpiritual Courte,
peremptorily to affirme by neucr ſo good euydence or teſtimony,
that a woman hath hazarded hir honeſty, except he ſweare Rem
to be in Re, which the greateſt Ciuilian that ever Padua bred
neuer ſawe by proceſſe duely tried ? Shall I then warrante you
the honeſty of ſuch ſlippery Catell, prone and ready to luſt, eaſy
to be vanquiſhed by the ſuites of earneſt purſuers ? But blame-
worthy ſurely I am, thus generally to ſpeake : for ſome I know,
although not many, for whoſe poore honeſties I dare aduenture
mine owne. And yet that number how ſmall ſo euer it be, is
worthy all due Reuerence and Honoure. Notwythſtandyng (bycauſe you ſeeme to bee an Honeſte Gentleman) of that Knowledge
which I haue, I will not bee greatelye ſqueimyſhe, a certayne
ſecrete experiment in deede I haue, wherewith perchaunce I may
ſatiſſy your demaund. And this is it : I can by mine Arte in
ſmal time, by certaine compoſitions, frame a Woman's Image, which
you continually in a lyttle Boxe may carry about you, and ſo
ofte as you liſt behold the ſame. If the wife doe not breake hir
maryage faith, you ſhall ſtill ſee the ſame ſo fayre and wel coloured
as it was at the firſt making, and ſeeme as though it newly came
from the painter's ſhop, but if perchaunce ſhe meane to abuſe hir
honeſty the ſame wil waxe pale, and in deede committing
that filthy Faĉt, ſodainly the colour will bee blacke, as arayed
with Cole or other filth, and the ſmel thereof wyl not be very
pleaſaunt, but at al times when ſhe is attempted or purſued,
the colour will be ſo yealow as Gold." This maruellous ſecrete
deuyſe greatly pleaſed the Knyght verely beleuing the ſame to be
true, ſpecially mutch moued and aſſured by the fame bruted
abrode of his ſcience, whereof the Cytyzens of Cutiano, tolde very

ftraunge and incredyble things. When the pryce was paied for
this precious Iewel, hee receiued the Image, and ioyfully returned
home to his Caftell, where tarryinge certain dayes, he determined
to repayre to the Court of the glorious king Mathie, making his
wife priuy of hys intent. Afterwards when he had difpofed his
houfehold matters in order, he committed the gouernment therof
to his Wife, and hauinge prepared all Neceffaries for his voyage,
to the great forrow and grief of his beloued, he departed and
arryued at Alba Regale, where that time the king lay with Beat-
trix his Wife, of whom hee was ioyfully receiued and entertayned.
He had not long continued in the Court, but he had obtained and
won the fauor and good wyll of all men. The king which knew
him full well very honorably placed him in his Courte, and by him
accomplifhed diuers and many waighty affairs, which very wifely
and truftely he brought to paffe according to the king's mind and
pleafure. Afterwards he was made Colonell of a certain number
of footmen fent by the king againft the Turks to defende a holde
which the enimies of God began to affaile vnder the conduct of
Muftapha Bafca, which conduct he fo wel directed and therin
ftoutly behaued himfelf, as he chafed al the infidels oute of thofe
coafts, winning therby the name of a moft valiaunt foldier and pru-
dent Captaine, whereby he merueyloufly gayned the fauor and grace
of the king, who (ouer and befides his dayly intertaynment) gaue
vnto him a Caftle, and the Reuenue in fee farme for euer. Sutch
rewards deferue all valiaunt men, which for the honour of theyr
Prince and countrey do willingly imploy their feruice, worthy no
doubt of great regard and chearifhinge, vpon their home returne,
becaufe they hate idlenes to win Glory, deuifinge rather to fpende
whole dayes in fielde, than houres in Courte, which this worthy
knight deferued, who not able to fuftayne his poore Eftate, by
politick wifdome and proweffe of armes endeuored to ferue his
Lord and countrey, wherein furely hee made a very good choyfe
Then he deuoutly prayfed God, for that he put into his minde
futch a noble enterprife, trufting dayly to atchieue greater Fame
and Glory : but the greater was his ioy and contentation, bicaufe
the Image of hys Wyfe inclofed wythin a Boxe, whych ftill hee
caried about him in hys purffe, continued frefhe of coloure with-

out alteration. It was noyſed in the Court how thys valiaunt
Knight Vlrico, had in Boeme the fayreſt and goodlieſt Lady to his
Wife that liued eyther in Boeme, or Hungary. It chaunced as a
certaine company of young Gentlemen in the Courte were together
(amongs whom was this Knight) that a Hungarian Baron ſayd vnto
him : "How is it poſſible, ſyr Vlrico, being a yeare and a halfe
ſince you departed out of Boeme, that you haue no minde to returne to ſee your Wife, who, as the common fame reporteth, is
one of the goodlieſt Women of all the Countrey : truely it ſeemeth
to me, that you care not for hir, which were great pitty if hir
beauty be correſpondent to hir Fame." "Syr," (quod Vlrico)
"what hir beauty is I referre vnto the World, but how ſo euer you
eſteeme me to care of hir, you ſhall vnderſtand that I doe loue
hir, and wil do ſo duringe my lyfe. And the cauſe why I haue
not viſited hir of long time, is no little proofe of the great aſſurance I haue of her vertue and honeſt lyfe. The argument of hir
vertue I proue, for that ſhe is contented that I ſhould ſerue my
Lord and king, and ſufficient it is for me to giue hir intelligence
of my ſtate and welfare, whych many tymes by Letters at opportunity I fayle not to do : The proofe of my Fayth is euydent by
reaſon of my bounden duety to our Soueraigne Lord of whom I haue
receyued ſo great, and ample Benefites, and the Warrefare which I
vſe in his grace's ſeruice vpon the Frontiers of his Realme agaynſt
the enimies of Chriſte, whereunto I bear more good will than I
doe to Wedlocke Loue, preferring duety to Prince before mariage :
albeit my Wiue's fayth, and conſtancy is ſutch, as freely I may
ſpend my lyfe without care of hir deuoyr, being aſſured that
beſides hir Beauty ſhee is wiſe, vertuous and honeſt, and loueth
me aboue al worldly things, tendring me ſo dearely as ſhe doth the
Balles of hir owne eyes." "You haue ſtoutly ſayd," (anſwered the
Baron) "in defence of your Wiue's chaſtity, whereof ſhe can
make vnto hir ſelfe no great warrantice, becauſe a woman ſome
tymes will bee in minde not to be mooued at the requeſts, and
gifts offred by the greateſt Prince of the World who afterwards
within a day vpon the onely ſight, and view of ſome luſty youth,
at one ſimple worde vttered with a few Teares, and ſhorter ſuite,
yeldeth to his requeſt. And what is ſhe then that can conceyue

futch affuraunce in hir felfe? What is hee that knoweth the fecretes
of hcartes which be impenetrable? Surely none as I fuppofe,
except God him felfe. A Woman of hir owne nature is mooueable and plyant, and is the mofte ambitious creature of the Worlde.
And (by God) no Woman doe I know but that fhe lufteth and
defireth to be beloued, required, fued vnto, honored aud cherifhed?
And oftentimes it commeth to paffe that the moft crafty Dames
which thincke with fayned Lookes to feede their diuers Louers, be
the firft that thruft their heads into the amorous Nets, and lyke
little Birdes in hard diftreffe of weather be caught in Louer's Lime-
twigges. Whereby, fir Vlrico, I do not fee that your Wyfe (aboue
all other Women compact of flefh and bone) hath futch priuiledge
from God, but that fhe may be foone entifed and corrupted."
" Well fir," (fayd the Boeme Knight) " I am perfuaded of that
which I haue fpoken, and verely doe beleue the effect of my beliefe moft true. Euery man knoweth his owne affayres, and the
Foole knoweth better what hee hath, than hys neighbors, do, be
they neuer fo wife. Beleue you what you thincke for good. I
meane not to difgreffe from that which I conceyue. And fuffer
me (I pray you) to beleue what I lift, fith beliefe cannot hurt me,
nor yet your difcredite can hinder my beliefe, being free for ech
man in femblable chaunces to thinke, and belieue what his mynde
lufteth and liketh." There were many other Lordes and Gentlemen
of the court prefent at there talke, and as we commonly fee (at
futch like meetinges) euery man vttereth his minde : whereupon
fundry opinions were produced touching that queftion. And
becaufe diuers men be of diuers natures, and many prefuminge
vpon the pregnancy of their wife heads there rofe fome ftur about
that talke, each man obftinate in hys alledged reafon, more froward peraduenture than reafon, more rightly required: the communication grew fo hot and talke brake forth fo loude, as the fame
was reported to the Queene. The good Lady fory to heare tell
of futch ftrife within hir Court, abhorring naturally all controuerfie
and contention, fent for the parties, and required theym from
poynct to poynct to make recitall of the beginning, and circum-
ftaunce of their reafons, and arguments. And when fhe vnderftoode the effect of al their talke, fhe fayd, that euery man at his

owne pleaſure might beleeue what he liſt, affirming it to be pre-
ſumptuous and extreme folly, to iudge all women to be of one dis-
poſition, in like ſort as it were a great errour to ſay that all men bee
of one quality and condicion: the contrary by dayly experience
manifeſtly appearing. For both in men and women, there is ſo
great difference and variety of natures, as there bee heades, and
wits. And how it is commonly ſeene that two Brothers, and
Siſters, borne at one Byrth, bee yet of contrary Natures and
Complexions, of Manners, and Conditions ſo diuers, as the thinge
which ſhall pleaſe the one, is altogeather diſpleaſaunt to the other.
Wherevppon the Queene concluded, that the Boeme knight had
good reaſon to continue that good and honeſt credit of his Wyfe,
as hauing proued hir fidelity of long time, wherein ſhe ſhewed
hirſelf to be very wiſe and diſcret. Now becauſe (as many times
we ſee) the natures and appetites of diuers men be inſaciable, and
one man ſometimes more fooliſh hardy than another, euen ſo (to
ſay the troth) were thoſe two Hungarian Barons, who ſeeming
wiſe in their owne conceiptes, one of them ſayd to the Queene in
this manner: "Madame, your grace doth wel maintaine the ſexe
of womankinde, becauſe you be a Woman. For by nature it is
gieuen to that kinde, ſtoutly to ſtand in defence of themſelues, becauſe their imbecillity, and weakenes otherwiſe would bewray
them: and although good reaſons might be alledged to open the
cauſes of their debility, and why they be not able to attayne the
hault excellency of man, yet for this tyme I doe not meane to be
tedious vnto your grace, leaſt the little heart of Woman ſhould ryſe
and diſplay that conceit which is wrapt within that little Moulde.
But to retourne to this chaſte Lady, through whom our talke
began, if we might craue licence of your Maieſty, and ſaulfe Con-
duꜫ of thys Gentleman to knowe hir dwelling place, and haue
leaue to ſpeake to hir, we doubt not but to breake with our
batteriuge talke the Adamant Walles of hir Chaſtity that is ſo
famous, and cary away that Spoile which viꜫoriouſly we ſhall
atchieue." "I know not," aunſwered the Boeme Knight, "what yee
can, or will doe, but ſure I am, that hitherto I am not deceyued."
Many things were ſpoken there, and ſundry opinions of eyther
partes alledged, in ende the two Hungarian Barons perſuaded

them felues, and made their vaunts that they were able to climbe
the Skyes, and both would attempt and alfo bring to paffe any
enterprife were it neuer fo great, affirming their former offer by
othe, and offering to Guage all the Landes, and goods they had,
that within the fpace of 5 moneths they woulde eyther of them
obtayne the Gentlewoman's good will to do what they lift, fo that
the knight were bound, neyther to returne home, ne yet to aduertife hir of their determination.   The Queene, and all the ftanders
by, laughed heartely at this their offer, mocking and iefting at
their foolifh, and youthly conceites.   Whych the Barons perceiuing, fayde: "You thinke Madame that we fpeake triflingly, and
be not able to accomplifh this our propofed enterprife, but Madame,
may it pleafe you to gieue vs leaue, wee meane by earneft
attempt to gieue proofe thereof."   And as they were thus in reafon-
inge and debating the matter, the kinge (bearinge tell of this large
offer made by the Barons) came into the place where the queene
was, at fuch time as fhe was about to diffuade them from the
frantik deuife.   Before whom he being entred the chamber, the
two Barons fell downe vpon their Knees, and humbly befought his
Grace, that the compact made betwene fir Vlrico and them might
proceede, difclofing vnto him in few wordes the effect of all their
talke, which franckly was graunted by the king.   But the Barons
added a Prouifio, that when they had won their Wager, the Knight
by no meanes fhoulde hurt his Wyfe, and from that tyme forth
fhould gieue ouer hys falfe Opinion, that women were not naturally gieuen to the futes and requefts of amorous perfons.   The
Boeme Knight, who was affured of hys Wyue's great Honefty, and
Loyall fayth, beleeued fo true as the Gofpell, the proportion and
quality of the Image, who in all the tyme that hee was farre of,
neuer perceyued the fame to bee eyther Pale or Black, but at
that tyme lookinge vpon the Image, hee perceiued a certayne
Yealow colour to rife, as hee thought his Wyfe was by fome loue
purfued, but yet fodeynly it returned agayne to his naturall hewe,
which boldned him to fay thefe words to the Hungarian Barons :
"Yee be a couple of pleafaunt, and vnbeleeuing Gentlemen, and
haue conceyued fo fantafticall opinion, as euer men of your
calling did : but fith you proceede in your obftinate folly, and

wil needes guage all the Lands, and goods you haue, that you bee able to vanquiſhe my Wyue's Honeſt, and Chaſte heart, I am contented, for the finguler credite which I repofe in bir, to ioyne with you, and will pledge the poore lyuinge I haue for proofe of mine Opinion, and ſhall accompliſhe al other your requeſtes made here, before the maieſties of the Kinge and Queene. And therefore may it pleaſe your highneſſe, ſith this fond deuice can not be beaten out of their heads, to gieue Licence vnto thofe Noblemen, the Lords Vladiſlao and Alberto, (ſo were they called) to put in proofe the mery conceipt of their diſpoſed mindes (whereof they do ſo greatly bragge) and I by your good grace and fauoure, am content to agree to their demaundes: and wee, anſwered the Hungarians, do once agayne affirme the ſame which wee haue ſpoken." The king willing to haue them gyue ouer that ſtrife, was intreated to the contrary by the Barons: whereupon the kinge perceyuinge their Follies, cauſed a decree of the bargayne to be put in writing, eyther Parties interchaungeably ſubſcribing the ſame. Which done, they tooke their leaues. Afterwards, the two Hungarians began to put their enterpriſe in order and agreed betweene themſelues, Alberto to bee the firſte that ſhould aduenture vppon the Lady. And that within ſixe Weekes after vpon his returne, the lord Vladiſlao ſhould proceede. Theſe things concluded, and all Furnitures for their ſeuerall Iorneys diſpoſed, the lord Alberto departed in good order, with two ſeruaunts directly trauayling to the caſtle of the Boeme Knight, where being arriued, hee lighted at an Inne of the towne adioyning to the Caſtle, and demaunding of the hoſte, the Conditions of the lady, hee vnderſtoode that ſhee was a very fayre Woman, and that hir honeſty, and loue towards hir huſbande farre excelled hir beauty. Which wordes nothing diſmayede the Amorous Baron, but when hee had pulled of his Bootes, and richely arayed hymſelfe, he repayred to the Caſtle, and knockinge at the Gates, gaue the Lady to vnderſtand that he was come to ſee hir. She which was a curteous Gentlewoman, cauſed him to be brought in, and gently gaue him honourable intertaynment. The Baron greatly muſed vppon the beauty, and goodlineſſe of the Lady, ſingularly commending hir honeſt order and Behauiour. And beinge ſet down, the young

Gentleman fayd vnto hir: "Madame, mooued with the fame of
your furpaffing Beauty, which now I fee to bee more excellent
than Fame with hir fwifteft Wyngs is able to cary: I am come
from the Court to view and fee if that were true, or whether lyinge
Brutes had fcattered their Vulgar talke in vayne: but finding the
fame farre more fine and pure than erft I did expect, I craue
Lycence of your Ladyfhip, to conceyue none offence of this my
boulde, and rude attempt." And herewithall hee began to ioyne
many trifling and vayne words, whych dalyinge Suters by heate
of Lufty bloude bee wont to fhoote forth, to declare theym felues
not to be Speachleffe, or Tongue tied. Which the Lady well
efpying fpeedily imagined into what Porte hys rotten Barke would
arriue: wherefore in the ende when fhee fawe his Shippe at Roade,
began to enter in prety louinge talke, by little, and little to
incourage his fond attempt. The Baron thinkinge hee had caught
the Ele by the Tayle, not well practifed in Cicero his fchoole,
ceafed not fondly to contriue the time, by making hir beleeue, that
he was farre in loue. The Lady weary (God wote) of his fonde
behauiour, and amorous reafons, and yet not to feeme fcornfull,
made him good countenaunce, in futch wyfe as the Hungarian
two or three dayes did nothing elfe but proceede in vayne Purfute,
Shee perceyuing him to bee but a Hauke of the firft Coate, deuyfed
to recompence hys Follies with futch entertaynement, as during
his life, he fhoulde keepe the fame in good remembraunce. Wherefore not long after, fayning as though his great wifedome, vttered
by eloquent Talke, had fubdued hir, fhee fayd thus vnto him:
"My Lord, the reafons you produce, and your pleafaunt gefture
in my houfe, haue fo inchaunted mee, that impoffible it is, but
I muft needes agree vnto your wyll: for where I neuer thought
during lyfe, to ftayne the purity of mariage Bed, and determined
continually to preferue my felfe inuiolably for my Hufbande:
your noble grace, and curteous behauiour, haue (I fay) fo bewitched mee, that ready I am to bee at your commaundement,
humbly befeeching your honour to beware, that knowledge hereof
may not come vnto myne Hufband's eares, who is fo fierce and
cruell, and loueth me fo dearely, as no doubt he will without
further triall eyther him felfe kill me, or otherwife procure my

death: and to the intent none of my houfe may fufpect our
doings, I fhall defire you to morrow in the morninge about nyne
of the Clock, which is the accuftomed time of your repayre
hither, to come vnto my Caftle, wherein when you be entred,
fpeedily to mount vp to the Chaumber of the higheft Tower, ouer
the doore whereof, yee fhall finde the armes of my Hufband,
entayled in Marble: and when you be entred in, to fhut the Doore
faft after you, and in the meane time I will wayte and prouyde,
that none fhall moleft and trouble vs, and then we fhall beftowe
our felues for accomplifhement of that which your loue defireth."
Nowe in very deede this Chaumber was a very ftrong Pryfon
ordayned in auncient time by the Progenitours of that Territory,
to Impryfon, and punifhe the Vaffals, and Tenants of the fame, for
offences, and Crimes committed. The Baron hearynge this Lyberall
offer of the Ladye, thinking that he had obteined the fumme of al
his ioy, fo glad as if he had conquered a whole kingdome, the
beft contented man aliue, thanking the Lady for hir curteous
anfwere, departed and retourned to his Inne. God knoweth vppon
howe merry a Pinne the hearte of this young Baron was fette,
and after he had liberally banketted his hofte and hofteffe, pleafantly difpofing himfelfe to myrth and recreation, he wente to
bed, where ioy fo lightned his merry head, as no flepe at all could
clofe his eyes, futch be the fauage pangs of thofe that afpyre to
like delyghts as the beft reclaimer of the wildeft hauk could neuer
take more payne or deuife mo fhiftes to Man the fame for the better
atchieuing of hir pray than dyd this braue Baron for brynging
hys Enterprife to effect. The nexte day early in the morning hee
rofe, dreffing himfelfe with the fweete Perfumes, and puttinge on
hys fineft fuite of Apparell, at the appoincted houre hee went to
the Caftell, and fo fecretly as he could, accordinge to the Ladies
inftruction, hee conueyed himfelfe vp into the Chaumber which
hee founde open, and when he was entred, hee fhut the fame, the
maner of the Doore was futch, as none within coulde open it without a Key, and befides the ftrong Locke, it hadde both barre and
Bolt on the outfide, wyth futch faiteninge as the Deuill himfelfe
being locked within, could not breake forth. The Lady whych
wayted hard by for his comming, fo foone as fhe perceyued that

the Doore was ſhut, ſtept vnto the ſame, and both double Locked
the Doore, and alſo without ſhe barred, and faſt Bolted the ſame,
caryng the Key away with hir. This Chamber was in the hygheſt
Tower of the Houſe (as is before ſayd) wherein was placed a Bedde
wyth good Furniture, the Wyndow whereof was ſo high, that none
coulde looke out wythout a Ladder. The other partes thereof were
in good, and conuenient order, apt and meete for an honeſt Pryſon. When the Lorde Alberto was within, hee ſat downe, wayting
(as the Iewes do for Meſſias) when the Lady according to hir
appoynctment ſhoulde come. And as he was in this expectation
building caſtles in the Ayre, and deuiſing a thouſand Chimeras in
his braine, behold he heard one to open a little wicket that was in
the doore of that Chamber, which was as ſtraight, as ſcarcely able
to receiue a loafe of bread, or cruſe of Wyne, vſed to be ſent to the
pryſoners. He thinkyng that it had ben the Lady, roſe vp, and
hearde the noyſe of a lyttle girle, who looking in at the hole, thus
ſayd vnto him : "My Lord Alberto, the Lady Barbara my miſtreſſe
(for that was hir name) hath ſent me thus to ſay vnto you : 'That
for as much as you be come into this place, by countenaunce of
Loue, to diſpoyle hir of hir honour, ſhee hath impryſoned you like
a theefe, accordinge to your deſerte, and purpoſeth to make you
ſuffer penance, equall to the meaſure of your offence. Wherefore ſo long as you ſhal remain in thys place, ſhe mindeth to force
you to gaine your bread and drinke with the arte of ſpinning, as
poore Women doe for gayne of theyr lyuinge, meanynge thereby to
coole the heate of your luſty youth, and to make you taſt the ſorrow
of ſauce meete for them to aſſay, that go about to robbe Ladyes of
theyr honour: ſhe bad me lykewiſe to tell you, that the more
yarne you ſpin, the greater ſhall be the abundance and delycacie of
your fare, the greater payne you take to earne your foode, the
more lyberall ſhe will be in dyſtrybutyng of the ſame, otherwiſe
(ſhe ſayeth) that you ſhall faſte wyth Breade and Water.' Which
determinate ſentence ſhe hath decreed not to be infringed and
broken for any kinde of ſute or intreaty that you be able to make."
When the maiden had ſpoken theſe Wordes, ſhe ſhut the lyttle
dore, and returned to hir Ladye, the Baron which thought that he
had ben commen to a mariage, did eate nothing al the mornyng

before, bycaufe he thought to be enterteyned with better and dain-
tier ftore of viandes, who nowe at thofe newes fared like one out of
his wittes and ftoode ftill fo amazed, as though his leggs would
haue fayled him, and in one moment his Spyrites began to vanyfh
and hys force and breath forfoke hym, and fel downe vpon the
Chamber flore, in futch wife as hee that had beheld hym would
haue thought him rather dead than liuyng. In this ftate he was
a great tyme, and afterwardes fomewhat commynge to himfelfe,
he could not tel whether hee dreamed, or elfe that the Words were
true, which the maiden had fayde vnto hym : In the end feeing,
and beynge verely affured, that he was in a Pryfon fo fure as
Bird in Cage, through difdayne and rage was like to dye or elfe to
lofe his wits, faring with himfelfe of long time lyke a madde Man,
and not knowing what to do, paffed the reft of the Day in walking
vppe and downe the Chaumber, rauing, ftamping, ftaring, Curs-
ynge and vfing Words of greateft Villanie, lamenting and bewail-
inge the time and day, that fo like a beaft and Brutyfh man, he
gave the attempt to difpoyle the honefty of an other man's
Wyfe. Then came to his mind the loffe of all his Lands and Goods,
which by the king's authority were put in comprimife, then the
fhame, the fcorne, and rebuke whych hee fhould receiue at other
mens handes, beyonde meafure vexed him : and reporte bruted
in the Courte (for that it was impoffible but the whole Worlde
fhould knowe it) fo gryeued hym, as his heart feemed to be ftrained
with two fharp and bityng Nailes : the Paynes whereof, forced
hym to loofe hys wyttes and vnderftandynge. In the myddes of
whych Pangs furioufly vauntyng vp and downe the Chaumber, hee
efpied by chaunce in a Corner, a Dyftaffe furnyfhed with good
ftore of flaxe, and a fpyndle hangyng thereuppon : and ouercome
wyth Choler and rage, hee was aboute to fpoyle and break the
fame in pieces : but remembryng what a harde Weapon Neceffitye
is, hee ftayed his wyfedome, and albeyt he hadde rather to haue
contryued hys leyfure in Noble and Gentlemanlyke paftyme, yet
rather than he would be idle he thought to referue that Inftrument to auoyde the tedious lacke of honeft and Familiar Company.
When fupper time was come, the mayden retourned agayne, who
opening the Portall dore, faluted the Baron, and fayde : "My

Lord, my miſtreſſe hath ſent mee to vyſite your good Lordſhyp, and to receiue at youre good Handes the effecte of your laboure, who hopeth that you haue ſponne ſome ſubſtanciall ſtore of threede for earning of your Supper, whych beynge done, ſhall be readily brought vnto you." The Baron full of Rage, Furie, and felonious moode, if before he were fallen into choler, now by proteſtation of theſe words, ſeemed to tranſgreſſe the bounds of reaſon, and began to raile at the poore wench, ſcolding and chiding hir like a ſtrumpet of the ſtews, faring as though he would haue beaten hir, or don hir ſome other miſchiefe: but his moode was ſtayed from doyng any hurt. The poore Wench leſſoned by her miſtreſſe, in laughing wiſe ſayd vnto him: "Why (my Lord) do you chaſe and rage againſte mee? Me thinks, you do me wrong to vſe ſutch reprochful words, which am but a ſeruaunt, and bounde to the commaundement of my miſtreſſe: Why ſir, do you not know that a purſiuaunt or meſſanger ſuffreth no paine or blame? The greateſt Kyng or Emperour of the Worlde, receiuing defiaunce from a meaner Prynce, neuer vſeth his ambaſſador with ſcolding Wordes, ne yet by villany or rebuke abuſeth his perſon. Is it wiſdome then for you, being a preſent pryſoner, at the mercy of your kepers, in thys diſhonorable ſorte to reuile me with diſordred talke? But ſir, leaue of your rages, and quiet your ſelfe for this preſent tyme, for my miſtreſſe maruelleth much why you durſt come (for al your Noble ſtate) to giue attemptes to violate hir good name, which meſſage ſhee requyred me to tell you, ouer and beſides a deſire ſhee hath to know whether by the Scyence of Spynning, you haue gained your meat for you ſeeme to kicke againſt the wynd, and beat Water in a morter, if you think from hence to goe before you haue earned a recompenſe for the meat which ſhal be giuen you. Wherefore it is your lot paciently to ſuffer the penance of your fond attempt, which I pray you gently to ſuſtaine, and think no ſcorn thereof hardely, for deſperate men and hard aduentures muſt needes ſuffer the daungers thereunto belonging. This is the determinate ſentence of my miſtreſſe mynd, who fourdeth you no better fare than Bread and Water, if you can not ſhewe ſome prety Spyndle full of yarne for ſigne of your good wyll at this preſent pynch of your diſtreſſe." The

Mayden feeying that hee was not dyfpofed to fhewe fome part of
wyllyng mind to gaine his lyuing by that prefixed fcyence fhut the
portall Doore, and went her way. The unhappy Baron (arryued
thether in very yll tyme) that Nyght had Neyther Breade nor
Broth, and therefore he fared accordynge to the Prouerbe : He that
goeth to bed fupperleffe, lyeth in his Bed reftleffe, for during the
whole night, no fleepe could faften hys Eyes. Now as this Baron
was clofed in pryfon fafte, fo the Ladye tooke order, that fecretly
wyth great cheare hys Seruauntes fhould be interteyned, and his
Horffe wyth fweete haye and good prouender well mainteined, all
his furnitures, fumpture horfe and caryages conueyed within the
Caftle, where wanted nothyng for the ftate of futch a perfonage
but onely Lyberty, makyng the hoft of the Inne beleue (wher the
Lord harbored before) that he was returned into Hungarie. But
now turne we to the Boeme knight, who knowynge that one of the
two Hungarian Competitors, were departed the Court and ridden
into Boeme, dyd ftill behold the quality of the inchaunted Image,
wherein by the fpace of thre or foure Dayes, in whych time, the
Baron made his greateft fute to his Ladie : he marked a certaine
alteration of Coloure in the fame, but afterwards returned to his
Natiue forme : and feeing no greater tranfformation, he was wel
affured, that the Hungarian Baron was repulfed, and imployed his
Labor in vaine. Whereof the Boeme knight was excedingly pleafed
and contented, bycaufe he was well affured, that his Wyfe had
kept hir felfe ryghte pure and honeft. Notwithftandyng hys
Mynde was not wel fettled, ne yet hys heart at reft, doubting that
the lord Vladiflao, which as yet was not departed the courte,
would obtayne the thing, and acquite the faulte, which his Companion had committed. The impryfoned Baron which all this
tyme had neither eaten nor dronken, nor in the night could fleepe,
in the mornyng, after he had confidred his mifaduenture, and well
perceyued no remedy for him to goe forth, except hee obeyed the
Ladie's heft, made of Neceffity a Vertue, and applyed himfelfe to
learne to Spynne by force, which freedome and honour could neuer
haue made him to do. Whereuppon he toke the diftaffe and
beganne to Spynne. And albeyt that hee neuer Sponne in al hys
Lyfe before, yet inftructed by Neceffity, fo well as he could, he

drewe out his Threede, now fmall and then greate, and manye
times of the meaneft fort, but verye often broade, yl fauored, yll
clofed, and worfe twifted, all oute of fourme and fafhyon, that
fundry tymes very heartely he laughed to himfelfe, to fee bis
cunning, but would haue made a cunning Woman fpinner burft
into Ten Thoufand laughters, if fhe had ben there. Thus all the
morning he fpent in fpynning, and when dynner came, his accuftomed meffenger, the mayden, repayred vnto him againe, and
opening the wyndow demaunded of the Baron how his worke went
foreward, and whether he were difpofed to manifeft the caufe of
hys comming into Boeme? Hee well beaten in the fchoole of
fhame, vttered vnto the Maide the whole compact and bargayne
made betweene him and his Companion, and the Boeme knyghte
hir mayfter, and afterwards fhewed vnto hir his Spyndle ful of
threde. The young Wenche fmylyng at hys Woorke, fayd : "By
Sainct Marie this is well done, you are worthy of victual for your
hire : for now I well perceiue that Hunger forceth the Woulf oute
of hir Denne. I conne you thanck, that like a Lord you can fo
puiffantly gayne your lyuing. Wherefore proceeding in that
which you haue begonne, I doubt not but fhortely you will proue
futche a workeman, as my miftreffe fhall not neede to put oute
hir flax to fpinne (to hir great charge and cofte) for making of
hir fmockes, but that the fame may wel be don within hir own
houfe, yea althoughe the fame doe ferue but for Kitchen Cloathes,
for dreffer bordes, or cleanynge of hir Veffell before they bee ferued
forth. And as your good deferts doe merite thankes for this your
arte, now well begonne, euen fo your new told tale of comming
hyther, requyreth no leffe, for that you haue dyfclofed the trouth."
When fhe had fpoken thefe Woords, fhe reached hym fome ftore
of meates for hys dynner, and bade hym fare well. When fhee
was returned vnto hir Lady, fhee fhewed vnto hir the Spyndle full
of threde, and told hir therewythall the whole ftory of the compact betwene the knight Vlrico, and the two Hungarian barons.
Whereof the Lady fore aftonned, for the fnares layd to entrappe
hir, was notwithftanding wel contented, for that fhee had fo well
forfeene the fame : but moft of all reioyfed, that hir hufband had
fo good opinion of hir honeft lyfe. And before fhe would aduer-

tife hym of thofe euents, fhe purpofed to attend the commyng of
the lord Vladiflao to whome fhe ment to do like penance for his
carelelfe bargayne and difhoneft opinion, accordyngly as he
deferued, maruelling very mutch that both the Barons, were fo
rafh and prefumptuous, daungeroufly (not knowing what kind of
Woman fhe was) to put their Landes and goodes in hazard. But
confidering the Nature of diuers brainfick men, which pafle not
how carelefly they aduenture their gained goods, and inherited
Lands, fo they may atchieue the pray, after which they vainely
hunt, for the preiudice and hurt of other, fhe made no accompt
of thefe attemptes, fith honeft Matrones force not vppon the futes,
or vayne confumed time of lyght brained Cockfcombs, that care
not what fond coft or ill imployed houres they wafte to anoy the
good renoume and honeft brutes of Women. But not to difcourfe
from point to point the particulers of this intended iorney, this
poore deceiued Baron in fhort time proued a very good Spinner, by
exercife whereof, he felt futch folace, as not onely the fame was
a comfortable fporte for his captiue time, but alfo for want of
better recreation, it feemed fo ioyfull, as if he had bene pluming
and feding his Hawke, or doing other fports belongyng to the
honourable ftate of a Lord. Which his wel attriued labour, the
Maiden recompenfed with abundance of good and delycate meates.
And although the Lady was many times requyred to vifite the
Baron, yet fhe would neuer to that requeft confent. In whych
tyme the knyght Vlrico ceafed not continually to viewe and re-
uewe the ftate of his Image, which appeared ftyll to bee of one
well coloured forte, and although thys vfe of hys was diuers times
marked and feene of many, yet being earneftly demaunded the
caufe thereof hee would neuer difclofe the fame. Many coniectures thereof were made, but none could attayne the trouthe.
And who would haue thought that a knight fo wyfe and prudente
had worne within his purffe any inchaunted thyng? And albeyt
the Kyng and Queene had intelligence of thys frequent practyfe of
the knight, yet they thought not mete for the priuate and fecrete
Myftery, to demaund the caufe. One moneth and a halfe was
paffed now that the Lorde Alberto was departed the Court, and
become a Caftle knyghte and cunning Spynfter: which made the

Lord Vladiflao to mufe, for that the promife made betweene them was broken, and hearde neyther by Letter or meffenger what fucceffe he had receiued. After diuers thoughts imagyned in his mynde, he conceyued that his companion had happily enioyed the ende of his defired ioy, and had gathered the wyfhed fruicts of the Lady, and drowned in the mayne Sea of his owne pleafures, was ouerwhelmed in the bottome of Obliuion: wherefore he determined to fet forward on his iourney to giue onfet of his defired fortune: who without long delay for execution of his purpofe, prepared all neceffaries for that voyage, and mounted on horfebacke with two of his men, he iourneyed towards Boeme, and within a few daies after arryued at the Caftle of the fayre and moft honeft Lady. And when hee was entred the Inne where the Lord Alberto was firft lodged, he dilygently enquyred of him, and heard tell that he was returned into Hungarie many dayes before, whereof mutch maruelling, could not tel what to fay or think. In the end purpofing to put in profe the caufe wherefore he was departed out of Hungarie, after dilygent fearche of the maners of the Lady, he vnderftoode by general voyce, that fhe was without comparifon the honefteft, wifeft, gentleft, and come- lyeft Lady within the whole Countrey of Boeme. Incontinently the Lady was aduertifed of the arriual of this Baron, and knowing his meffage, fhe determyned to paye him alfo wyth that Money whych fhe had already coyned for the other. The next Day the Baron went vnto the Caftle, and knocking at the Gate, fent in woord how that he was come from the Court of king Mathie, to vifite and falute the Lady of that Caftle: and as fhe did entertayne the firft Baron in curteous guife, and with louing Countenaunce, euen fo fhe dyd the fecond, who thought thereby that he had attayned by that pleafaunt entertaynment, the game which he hunted. And difcourfing vppon dyuers matters, the lady fhewed hir felfe a pleafaunt and Familyar Gentlewoman, whych made the Baron to thynk that in fhort tyme he fhould wyn the pryce for which he came. Notwithftanding, at the fyrfte brunt he would not by any meanes defcend to any particularity of his pur- pofe, but hys Words ran general, which were, that hearynge tell of the fame of hir Beauty, good grace and comelineffe, by hauing

occafion to repayre into Boeme to doe certayne his affaires, he
thought it labor wel fpent to ride fome portion of his iourney,
though it were befides the way, to dygreffe to do reuerence vnto
hir, whom fame aduaunced aboue the Skyes: and thus paffing his
firft vifitation he returned againe to his lodging. The lady when
the Baron was gone from hir Caftle, was rapt into a rage, greatlye
offended that thofe two Hungarian Lordes fo prefumptuoufly had
bended themfelues lyke common Theeues to wander and roue the
Countreys, not onely to robbe and fpoyle hir of hir honour, but
alfo to bryng hir in difpleafure of hir hufband, and thereby into
the Daunger and Peryll of Death. By reafon of which rage (not
without caufe conceived) fhe caufed an other Chamber to be
made ready, next Wall to the other Baron that was become futch
a notable Spynfter, and vpon the nexte returne of the Lord
Vladiflao, fhe receiued him with no leffe good entertainement
than before, and when Nyght came, caufed him to be lodged
in hir owne houfe in the Chamber prepared as before, where
he flept not very foundly all that Night, through the continuall remembraunce of hys Ladies beauty. Next morning he
perceiued himfelf to be locked faft in a Pryfon. And when he
had made him readye, thinking to defcend to bid the Lady good
Morrow, feeking meanes to vnlock the Doore, and perceiuing
that he could not, he ftoode ftyll in a dumpe. And as hee was
thus ftandyng, maruelling the caufe of his fhuttyng in fo faft,
the maiden repaired to the hole of the dore, giuing his honor an
vnaccuftomed falutation, which was that hir miftreffe commaunded hir to giue him to vnderftand, that if hee had any luft
or appetyte to his breakfaft, or if he minded from thenceforth to
eafe his hunger or conteine Lyfe, that he fhould giue him felfe
to learne to reele yarne. And for that purpofe fhe willed him to
looke in futch a corner of the Chamber, and he fhould find certaine fpindles of thred, and an inftrument to winde his yarn vpon.
"Wherefore" (quod fhe) "apply your felf thereunto, and loofe no
time." He that had that tyme beholden the Baron in the Face,
would haue thought that hee had feene rather a Marble ftone,
than the figure of a man. But conuerting his could conceyued
moode, into mad anger, he fell into ten times more difpleafure

with himfelfe, than is before defcribed by the other Baron.   But
feeinge that his mad behauiour, and beaftly vfage was beftowed
in vayne, the next day he began to Reele.   The Lady afterwardes
when fhee had intelligence of the good, and gaynefull Spinning
of the Lord Alberto, and the wel difpofed, and towardly Reeling
of the Lord Vladiflao, greatly reioyced for makinge of futch two
Notable Workemen, whofe workemanfhip exceeded the labours of
them that had been Apprentyzes to the Occupation feuen Yeares
togeather.   Sutch bee the apt and ready Wyts of the Souldiers of
Loue: wherein I would wifhe all Cupides Dearlings to be noufled
and applied in their youthly time: then no doubt their paffions
woulde appeafe, and rages affuage, and would giue ouer bolde attempts, for which they haue no thancke of the chafte and honeft.
And to thys goodly fight the Lady brought the Seruaunts of thefe
noblemen, willing them to marke and beholde the diligence of
their Mayfters, and to imitate the induftry of their gallant exercife, who neuer attayned meate before by labour they had gayned
the fame.   Which done, fhee made them take their Horfe, and
Furnitures of their Lords, and to depart: otherwife if by violence
they refifted, fhe would caufe their choller to be caulmed with
futch like feruice as they faw their Lordes doe before their Eyes.
The Seruaunts feeing no remedy, but muft needes depart, tooke
their leaue.   Afterwards fhe fent one of hir Seruaunts in poaft to
the Courte, to aduertife hir hufband of all that which chaunced.
The Boeme knight receyuing thefe good newes, declared the
fame vnto the King and Queene, and recited the whole ftory of
the two Hungarian Barons, accordingly as the tenor of his Wyues
letters did purport.   The Princes ftoode ftill in great admiration,
and highly commended the wifedome of the Lady, efteeming hir
for a very fage and politicke woman.   Afterwards the knight
Vlrico humbly befought the king for execution of his decree and
performaunce of the Bargayne.   Whereupon the king affembled
his counfell, and required euery of them to faye their minde.
Vpon the deliberation whereof, the Lord Chauncellor of the Kingdome, with two Counfellers, were fent to the Caftle of the Boeme
knight, to enquire, and learne the proceffe and doinges of the two
Lordes, who diligently accomplifhed the kinge's commaundement.

And hauinge examined the Lady and hir mayden with other of
the houfe, and the barons alfo, whom a little before the arriuall
of thefe Commiffioners, the Lady had caufed to be put together,
that by Spinning and Reeling they might comfort one another.
When the Lord Chauncellor had framed and digefted in order the
whole difcourfe of this hiftory, returned to the Court where the
king and Queene, with the Pieres and Noblemen of his kingdome,
caufed the acts of the fame to be diuulged and bruted abroade,
and after mutch talk, and difcourfe of the performaunce of this
compact, pro, and contra, the Queene taking the Ladie's part, and
fauoring the knight, the kinge gaue fentence that fir Vlrico
fhould wholly poffeffe the landes and goods of the two Barons
to him, and to his Heyres for euer, and that the Barons fhould be
banifhed the kingdomes of Hungary and Boeme, neuer to returne
vpon payne of death.   This fentence was put in execution, and
the vnfortunat Barons exiled, which fpecially to thofe that were
of their confanguinity and bloud, feemed to feuere, and rigorous.
Neuertheleffe the couenaunt being moft playne and euident to
moft men, the fame feemed to bee pronounced with greate
Iuftice and equity, for example in time to come, to leffon rafh
wits how they iudge and deeme fo indifferently of Womens beha-
viours, amongs whom no doubt there bee both good and bad as
there bee of men.   Afterwards the 2 princes fent for the Lady to
the Court, who there was courteoufly intertayned, and for this hir
wife and polliticke fact had in great admiration. The Queene then
appoynted hir to be one of hir women of honor, and efteemed hir
very deerely.   The knight alfo daily grew to great promotion well
beloued and fauored of the king, who with his lady long time
liued in greate ioy and felicity, not forgetting the cunning
Pollacco, that made him the image and likenes of his
wife : whofe frendfhip and labor he rewarded with
money, and other Benefits very
liberally.

THE TWENTY-NINTH NOUELL.

Dom Diego a Gentleman of Spayne fell in loue with fayre Gineura, and fhe with him: their loue by meanes of one that enuied Dom Diego his happy choyfe, was by default of light credit on hir part interrupted. He conftant of mynde, fell into defpayre, and aban-doninge all his frends and liuing, repayred to the Pyrene Moun-taynes, where he led a fauage lyfe for certayne moneths, and after-wardes knowne by one of hys freendes, was (by marueylous Circum-ftaunce) reconciled to hys froward miftreffe, and maryed.

Mens mifchaunces occurring on the brunts of dyuers Tragicall for-tunes, albeit vpon their firft tafte of bitterneffe, they fauor of a certayne kinde of lothfome relifh, yet vnder the Rynde of that vnfaueroufe Sap, doth lurke a fweeter honnye, than fweeteneffe it felfe, for the fruit that the Pofterity may gather, and learne by others hurts, how they may loathe, and fhun the like. But bicaufe all thinges haue their feafons, and euery thynge is not conuenient for all Times, and Places, I purpofe now to fhew a notable example of a vayne and fuperftitious Louer, that abandoned his liuing and friendes, to become a Sauage Defert man. Which Hiftory refembleth in a maner a Tragical Comedy, comprehending the very fame matter and Argument, wherewyth the greateft part of the fottifhe forte Arme themfelues to couer and defend their Follies. It is red and feene to often by common cuftome, and therefore needeleffe heere to difplay what rage doth gouerne, and headlong hale fonde and licentious youth (conducted by the pangue of loue, if the fame be not moderated by reafon, and cooled with facred Leffons) euen from the cradle to more murture and riper age. For the Tiranny of Loue amonges all the deadly Foes that vexe and afflict our mindes, glorieth of his force, vaunting hym-felfe able to chaunge the proper nature of things, be they neuer fo founde and perfect: who to make them like his luftes, trans-formeth himfelfe into a fubftaunce qualified diuerfly, the better to intrap futch as be giuen to his vanities. But hauing auouched fo many examples before, I am content for this prefent to tell the

difcourfe of two perfons, chaunced not long fithens in Catheloigne.
Of a Gentleman that for his conftancy declared two extremities
in himfelfe of loue and folly. And of a Gentlewoman fo fickle
and inconftant, as loue and they which wayted on him, be disordered, for the truftleffe grounde whereupon futch foundation of
feruice is layed, which yee fhall eafely conceiue by well viewing
the difference of thefe twayne: whom I meane to fummon to the
lifts, by the blaft of this founding trump. And thus the fame
beginneth. Not long after that the victorious and Noble Prynce,
younge Ferdinandus, the Sonne of Alphonfus Kynge of Aragon was
deade, Lewes the Twelfth, that tyme being Frenche king, vpon,
the Marches of Catheloigne, betwene Barcelona, and the Mountaynes, there was a good Lady then a Wyddow, which had bene the
Wyfe of an excellant and Noble knight of the Countrey, by whom
fhe hadde left one only Daughter, which was fo carefully brought
vp by the mother as nothinge was to deare or hard to bee brought
to paffe for hir defire, thinking that a creature fo Noble and perfect, could not be trayned vp to delicately. Now befides hir
incomparable furniture of beauty, this Gentlewoman was adorned
with Hayre fo fayre, curle, and Yealow, as the new fined golde was
not matchable to the fhining locks of this tender Infant, who
therefore was commonly called Gineura la Blonde. Halfe adaye's
iorney from the houfe of this Wyddow, lay the lands of another
Lady a Wydow alfo, that was very rich, and fo wel allied as any in
all the Land. This Lady had a Sonne, whom fhe caufed to be trayned
vp fo well in Armes and good letters, as in other honeft Exercifes
proper and mete for a Gentleman and great Lorde, for which
refpect fhee had fent him to Barcelona the chyefe Citty of all the
Countrey of Catheloigne. Senior Dom Diego, (for fo was the
Sonne of that Wydow called) profited fo well in all thynges, that
when hee was 18 yeares of age, there was no Gentleman of his
degree, that did excell him, ne yet was able to approche vnto his
Perfections and commendable Behauiour. A thing that did fo
well content the good Lady his mother as fhe could not tell what
countenaunce to keepe to couer hir ioy. A vice very common to
fond and foolifh mothers, who flatter themfelues with a fhadowed
hope of the future goodneffe of their children, which many times

doth more hurt to that wanton and wilfull age, than profit or
aduauncement. The perfuafion alfo of futch towardneffe, full oft
doth blinde the Spirites of Youth, as the Faults which follow the
fame bee farre more vile than before they were: whereby the
firft Table (made in his firft coloures) of that imagined vertue, can
take no force or perfection, and fo by incurring fundry mifhaps
the Parent and Chylde commonly efcape not without equall blame.
To come agayne therefore to our difcourfe : It chaunced in that
tyme that (the Catholike Kyng deceafed) Phillippe of Auftrich
which Succeeded him as Heyre, paffing through Fraunce came into
Spayne to bee Inuefted, and take Poffeffion of all hys Seigniories,
and Kyngdomes : which knowen to the Cittyzens of Barcelona,
they determined to receiue hym with futch Pompe, Magnificence,
and Honor, as duely appertaineth to the greatnes and maiefty of
fo great a Prince, as is the fonne of the Romane Emperour.   And
amonges other thinges they prepared a Triumphe at the Tilt, where
none was fuffred to enter the lifts, but yong Gentlemen, futch as
neuer yet had followed armes.   Amongs whom Don Diego as the
Nobleft perfon was chofen chiefe of one part.   The Archduke then
come to Barcelona after the receyued honors and Ceremonies,
accuftomed for futch entertaynment, to gratifie his Subiects, and
to fee the brauery of the yong Spanifh Nobility in armes, would
place himfelfe vpon the fcaffolde to iudge the courfes and valiaunce of the runners.   In that magnifique and Princely conflict,
all mens eyes were bent vpon Dom Diego, who courfe by courfe
made hys aduerfaries to feele the force of his armes, his manhoode,
and dexterity, on horfebacke, and caufed them to mufe vpon his
toward valiance in time to come, whofe noble Ghefts then acquired
the victory of the Campe on his fide.   Which mooued King
Phillip to fay, that in all his life he neuer faw triumph better
handled, and that the fame feemed rather a battell of ftrong and
hardy men, than an exercife of yong Gentlemen neuer wonted
to fupport the deedes of armes, and trauayle of warfare.   For
which caufe calling Dom Diego before him he fayd : "God
graunt (yong Gentleman) that your ende agree with your good
beginnings and hardy fhock of proofe done this day.   In memory
whereof I will this night that ye do your watch, for I meane to

morrow (by God's affiftance) to dub you Knight." The yong
Gentleman blufhing for fhame, vpon his knees kiffed the Prince's
hands, thanking him moft humbly of the honor and fauor which
it pleafed his maiefty to do to him, vowing and promifing to do
fo wel in time to come, as no man fhould be deceyued of their
conceyued opinion, nor the king fruftrate of his feruice, which was
one of his moft obedient Vaffals and fubiects. So the next day
he was made knight, and receyued the coller of the order at the
hands of king Phillip, who after the departure of his prince which
tooke his iorney into Caftille, retired to his owne landes and houfe
more to fee his mother, whom long time before he had not feene,
than for defire of pleafure that be in fieldes, which notwithftanding he exercifed fo wel as in end he perceyued refiaunce in townes
and Cities, to be˜an imprifonment in refpect of that he felt in
Countrey. As the Poets whilome fayned Loue to fhoote his Arrowes
amid the Woods, Forrefts, fertile Fields, Sea coafts, Shores of
great Ryuers, and Fountayne brinkes, and alfo vppon the tops of
Huge, and hygh Mountaynes at the purfute of the fundry forted
Nymphes, and fieldifh Dimigods, deeming the fame to bee a
meane of liberty to follow Loue's tract without fufpition, voyde of
company and lothfome cries of Cities, where Iealoufie, Enuy, falfe
report, and ill Opinion of all things, haue pitched their Camp, and
rayfed their Tents. And contrariwife franckly and wythout diffimulation in the fieldes, the Freende difcouering his paffion to his
Miftreffe, they enioy the pleafure of hunting, the naturall muficke of
Byrds and fometimes in pleafaunt Herbers compaffed with the murmur of fome running Brookes, they communicate their Thoughts,
beautifie the accorde and vnity of Louers, and make the place famous for the firft witneffe of their amorous acquaintaunce. In like
manner thrice, and foure times bleft be they there, who leeuing
the vnquiet toyle that ordinarily doth chaunce to them that abyde
in Cities, doe render duety of their ftudies to the Mufes wherevnto
they be moft Addicted. Now Dom Diego at his owne houfe
loued and cherifhed of his mother, reuerenced and obeyed of hys
Subiects after he had imployed fome time at his ftudy, had none
other ordinary pleafure but in roufing the Deere, hunting the
wylde Bore, run the Hare, fometimes to fly at the Hearon, or fearfnl

Partrich alongs the fields, Forefts, Ponds, and fteepe Mountaynes.
It came to paffe one day, as he Hunted the wylde Mountayne
Goate, which he had diflodged vpon the Hill top, he efpied an
olde Hart that his Dogges had found, who fo ioyfull as was
poffible of that good lucke, followed the courfe of that fwift, and
fearefull beaft. But (futch was his Fortune) the Dogges loft the
foote of that pray, and he his men : for being horffed of purpofe,
vpon a fayre Iennet, could not be followed, and in ende loofinge
the fight of the Deere, was fo farre feuered from company, as
he was vtterly ignoraunt which way to take. And that which
grieued him mofte was his Horfe out of Breath fcarce able to goe
a falfe Gallop. For which caufe he put his horne to his mouth,
and blew fo loude as he could : but his men were fo farre of, as
they could not here him. The young Gentleman being in this
diftreffe, could not tell what to doe, but to returne backe, wherein
he was more deceyued than before, for thinkinge to take the way
home to hys Caftle, wandred ftill further of from the fame. And
trotting thus a long tyme, he fpied a Caftle Situated vppon a little
Hill, whereby he knew himfelfe far from his owne houfe. Neuertheleffe hearing a certayne noyfe of Hunters, thinking they had
bene his People, reforted to the fame, who in deede were the Seruaunts of the Mother of Gineura with the golden Locks, which in
company of their Miftreffe had hunted the Hare. Dom Diego,
when he drue neere to the cry of the Hounds, faw right well that
hee was deceyued. At what tyme Night approched, and the
Shadowes darkening the Earth, by reafon of the Sunnes departure,
began to Cloth the Heauens with a Browne and mifty Mantell.
When the Mother of Gineura faw the knight which Rode a foft
pace, for that his Horffe was tired, and could trauayle no longer,
and knowing by his outward apperance that he was fome great
Lord, and ridden out of his way, fent one of hir men to knowe
what he was, who returned agayne with futch aunfwere as fhee
defired. The Lady ioyfull to entertayne a Gentleman fo excellent
and famous, one of hir next neighbors, went forwarde to bid
hym welcome, which fhe did with fo great curtefy as the
Knight fayd vnto hir : "Madame, I thinke that fortune hath done
me this fauour, by fetting me out of the way, to proue your

curtefie and gentle entertaynment, and to receyue this ioy by
vifiting your houfe, whereof I truft in time to come to be fo perfect a frend, as my predeceffors heretofore haue bene." "Sir,"
fayd the Lady, "if happineffe may be attributed to them, that
moft doe gayne, I thincke my felfe better fauored than you, for
that it is my chaunce to lodge and entertayne him, that is the
worthieft perfon and beft beloued in all Catheloigne." The Gentleman blufhing at that prayfe, fayd nothing els, but that affection
forced men fo to fpeake of his vertues, notwithftandinge futch as
hee was, he vowed from thenceforth his feruice to hir and all hir
Houfhold. Gineura defirous not to bee flacke in curtefie, fayd
that he fhould not fo do, except fhe were partaker of fome part
of that, which the knight fo liberally had offered to the whole
Family of hir Mother. The Gentleman which till that time tooke
no heede to the deuine Beauty of the Gentlewoman, beholding hir
at his pleafure, was fo aftoonned, as hee could not tell what to
aunfwere, his eyes were fo fixed vpon hir, fpendinge his lookes
in contemplation of that frefhe hew, ftayned with a red Vermilion,
vppon the Alabafter and fayre colour of hir cleare and beautifull
face. And for the imbelifhing of that naturall perfection, the
attire vppon hir head was fo couenable and proper, as it feemed
the fame day fhee had Looked for the comming of him, that afterwardes indured fo mutch for hir fake. For hir head was Adorned
with a Garlande of Floures, interlaced wyth hir Golden, and Ena-
miled hayre, which gorgeoufly couered fome part of hir Shoulders,
difparcled, and hanging down fome tyme ouer hir paffing fayre
Foreheade, fomewhyles vpon hir ruddy Cheekes, as the Sweete,
and Pleafaunt windy Breath dyd mooue them to, and fro : Yee
fhould haue feene hir wauering and crifped treffes difpofed with
fo good grace, and comelyneffe, as a man would haue thought
that Loue and the three Graces coulde not tell els where to harbor
themfelues, but in that riche and delectable place of pleafure, in
gorgeous wife laced and imbraudred. Vpon hir Eares did hang
two Sumptuous and Riche orientall Pearles, which to the artificiall
order of hir hayre added a certen fplendent brightnes. And he
that had beholden the fhining and large Forehead of that Nimph
which Gallantly was befet with a Diamonde of ineftimable price

and value, chafed with a treffe of Golde made in form of little
Starres, would haue thought that he had feene a Rancke of the
twinckeling Planettes, fixed in the Firmament in the hotteft time
of Sommer, when that fayre feafon difcouereth the order of his
glittering Cloudes. In lyke maner the fparkeling eyes of the fayre
Gentlewoman, adorned with a ftately vaulte with two Archers,
equally by euen fpaces diftinct, and deuided, ftayned with the
Ebene Indian tree, did fo well fet forth their Brightneffe, as the
eyes of them that ftayed their lookes at Noone daye's directly
vpon the Sunne, could no more be dazeled and offended, than
thofe were that did contemplate thofe two flaminge Starres, which
were in force able throughly to pierce euen the Bottome of the
inward partes. The Nofe well fourmed, iuftly placed in the
Amiable valley of the Vyfage, by equall conformity Diftinguifhed
the two Cheekes, ftayned wyth a pure Carnation, refemblinge two
lyttle Apples that were arryued to the due time of their maturity
and ripeneffe. And then hir Coralline mouth, through which
breathing, iffued out a breath more foote and fauorous than Am-
bre, Mufke, or other Aromaticall Parfume, that euer the fweete
Soyle of Arabie brought forth. She fometime vnclofing the doore
of hir Lips, difcouered two rancke of Pearles, fo finely blanched,
as the pureft Orient would blufhe, if it were compared with the
Beauty of thys incomparable whiteneffe. But hee that will take
vppon hym to fpeake of all hir infpeakable Beauty, may make his
vaunte that he hath feene all the greateft perfections that euer
dame Nature wrought. Now to come a little lower, on this frefhe
Diana appeared a Neck, that furmounted the Blaunch colour of
Mylke, were it neuer fo excellent white, and hir Stomacke fomewhat mounting by the two Pomels, and firme Teates of hir Breafts
feparated in equal diftaunce, was couered wyth a vayle, fo lofe,
and fine, as thofe two little prety Mountaynes might eafily be
Difcried, to moue, and remooue, according to the affection that
rofe in the centre of that modeft, and fober Pucelle's mynde: who
ouer, and befides all thys, had futch a pleafaunt Countenaunce,
and ioyefull cheere, as hir Beauty more than wonderfull, rendred
hir not fo woorthy to be ferued, and loued, as hir natural goodneffe, and difpofed curtefie appearing in hir Face, and hir excel-

lent entertaynement and comely Grace to all indifferently. This
was not to imitate the maner of the moſt parte of our fayre Ladies,
and Gentlewomen, who (mooued wyth what Opinion I know not)
be ſo diſdaynefull, as almoſt theyr name cauſeth diſcontentment,
and breedeth in them great imperfeɛtion. And who by thinking
to appeare more braue, and fine, by to mutch ſqueymiſhe dealing,
doe offuſcate and darken with folly their exterior Beauty, blotting,
and defacing that which beauty maketh amiable, and worthy of
honor. I leaue you now to conſider wheather Dom Deigo had
occaſion to Forgo his Speach, and to bee bereft of Senſe, being
liuely aſſayled with one ſo well armed as Gineura was with hir
Graces and Honeſty : who no leſſe abaſhed with the Port, Countenaunce, ſweete talk, and ſtately Behauiour of the knight, which
ſhe vewed to be in him by ſtealing lookes, felt a motion (not
wonted or accuſtomed) in hir tender heart, that made hir to chaunge
color, and by like occaſion ſpeachleſſe: an ordinary cuſtome in
them that be ſurpriſed with the malady of loue to loſe the vſe of
ſpeach where the ſame is moſt needefull to gieue the intier charge
in the heart, which not able to ſupport and beare the burden of
ſo many paſſions, departeth ſome portion to the eyes, as to
the faythful meſſengers of the mynde's ſecret conceipts, which
tormented beyond meaſure, and burninge with affeɛtion, cauſeth
ſometimes the Humor to guſhe out in that parte that diſcouered
the firſt aſſault, and bred the cauſe of that Feuer, which frighted
the hearts of thoſe two yong perſons, not knowing well what the
ſame might be. When they were come to the Caſtle, and dis-
mounted from their Horſſes, many Welcomes and Gratulations
were made to the knight, which yelded more wood to the fire, and
liuely touched the yong Gentleman, who was ſo outraged with
loue, as almoſt he had no minde of himſelfe, and rapt by litle, and
little, was ſo intoxicated with an Amorous paſſion, as all other
thoughtes were lothſome, and Ioye diſpleaſaunt in reſpeɛt of the
fauourable Martirdome which hee ſuffered by thinking of his fayre
and gentle Gineura. Thus the knight which in the morning dis-
poſed him ſelfe to purſue the Hart, was in heart ſo attached, as
at euening he was become a Seruaunt, yea and ſutch a Slaue, as
that voluntary ſeruitude wholly diſpoſſeſſed him from his former

Freedome. Thefe be the fruictes alfo of Folly, inuegling the lookes
of men, that launch themfelues with eyes fhut into the Gulfe of
defpayre which in ende doth caufe the ruin and ouerthrow of
him, that yeldeth thereunto.   Loue proceedeth neuer but of
opinion: fo likewife the ill order of thofe that bee afflicted with
that Paffion, ryfeth not elswhere, but by the fond perfuafion
which they conceiyue, to bee Blamed, Defpifed, and deceyued of
the thing beloued: where if they meafured that paffion according to his valor, they would make no more accoumpt of that
which doth torment them, than they do of their health, honor,
and life, which loue for their great feruice and labor deludeth
them, and recompenfeth another with that for which the foolifh
Louer imployeth thys trauel, which at length doth hafte defpaire,
and ende more than defperate, when an other enioy that, for
which hee hath fo longe time beate the Bufhes.   During the
time that fupper was preparyng, the Lady fente hir men to feeke
the huntefmen of Dom Diego, to gyue them knowledge where
he was become, and thereof to certify his mother, who when fhe
heard tell that her fonne was lodged there, was very glad beyng
a ryght good fryend and very familiar Neighbor with the Lady, the
hoftelfe of Dom Diego.   The Gentleman at fupper after he had
tafted the feruent heate that broyled in his Minde, coulde eate
little meate, beinge fatiffied with the feeding diete of his Amorous
eyes, which without any maner of Iealoufie, diftributed their
nourifhment to the heart, who fat very foberly, priuily throwing
his fecretly Prickes, with louely, and wanton lookes, vppon the
heart of the fayre Lady, which for hir part fpared not to render
vfury of rolling regardes, whereof he was fo fparing, as almoft he
durft not lift vp his eyes for dazeling of them.   After Supper, the
knight bidding the mother and Daughter good night, went to Bed,
where in fteede of fleepe, he fell to fighinge and imageninge a
thoufande diuers deuifes, fantafiyng like number of follies, futch
as they doe whofe Braynes be fraught loue.   "Alas," (fayde hee)
"what meaneth it, that alwayes I haue lyued in fo great liberty,
and nowe doe feele my felf attached with futch bondage as I cannot expreffe whofe effects neuertheleffe be faftned in me?   Haue
I hunted to be taken?   Came I from my houfe in liberty, to be

fhut vp in Pryfon, and do not know wheather I fhall be receyued,
or being receyued haue intertaynment, according to defert? Ah
Gineura, I would to God, that thy Beauty did pricke mee no worffe,
than the tree whereof thou takeft thy name, is fharp in touching, and
bitter to them that tafte it. Truely I efteeme my comming hither
happy (for all the Paffion that I indure) fith the purchafe of a
griefe fo lucky doth qualify the ioy, that made me to wander thus
ouer frankly. Ah Fayre amonges the Fayreft, truely the fearefull
Beaft which with the bloudy Hare Houndes was torne in pieces, is
not more Martired, than my heart deuided in Opinions vppon thyne
Affeƈtion. And what doe I know if thou loueft an other more
worthy to bee Fauoured of thee than thy poore Dom Diego. But
it is impoffible that any can approche the fincerity that I feele in
my heart, determining rather to indure death, than to ferue other
but fayre and golden Gineura : therefore my loyalty receyuing no
comparifon, cannot bee matched in man fufficient (for refpeƈt of
the fame) to be called feruaunt of thine excellency. Now come
what fhal, by meanes of this, I am affured that fo long as Dom
Diego liueth, his heart fhal receyue none other impreffion or
defire, but that which inciteth him to loue, ferue, and honor the
faireft creature at thys day within the compaffe of Spayne." Refolued hereupon, fweating, laboring, and trauelling upon the
framing of his loue, he founde nothing more expedient than to
tel hir his paffion, and let hir vnderftand the good wil that he
had to do hir feruice, and to pray hir to accept hym for futch, as
from that time forth would execute nothing but under the title
of hir good name. On th'otherfide Gineura could not clofe hir
eyes, and knew not the caufe almoft that fo impeched hir of
fleepe, wherefore now toffing on th'one fide, and then turning to
the other, in hir rich and goodly Bed, fantafied no fewer deuifes
than paffionated Dom Diego did. In th'end fhe concluded, that if
the knight fhewed hir any euident figne, or opened by word of
mouth any Speach of loue and feruice, fhe would not refufe to do
the like to him. Thus paffed the night in thoughts, fighes, and
wifhes betwene thefe 2 apprentifes of the thing, whereof they
that be learners, fhal foone attayne the experience, and they that
follow the occupation throughly, in fhort time be their crafts

maifters. The next day the knight would depart fo foone as he
was vp: but the good widow, imbracing the perfonage and good
order of the knight in hir heart, more than any other that fhe
had feene of long time, intreated him fo earneftly to tarry as he
which loued better to obey hir requeft then to depart, although
fayned the contrary, in the end appeared to be vanquifhed vpon
the great importunity of the Lady. Al that morning the Mother
and the Daughter paffed the time with Dom Deigo in great talke
of common matters. But he was then more aftonned and inamored
than the night before, in futch wife as many times he aunfwered
fo vnaptly to their demaunds, as it was eafily perceiued that his
minde was mutch difquieted with fome thing, that only did
poffeffe the force and vehemence of the fame: notwithftanding
the Lady imputed that to the fhamefaftneffe of the Gentleman,
and to his fimplicity, which had not greatly frequented the company of Ladies. When dinner time was come, they were ferued
with futch great fare and fundry delicates accordingly as with hir
hart fhe wyfhed to intertain the young Lord, to the intent from
that time forth, he might more willinglye make repaire to hir
houfe. After dinner he rendred thanks to his hofteffe for his
good cheare and intertainment that he had receiued, affuring hir,
that all the dayes of his Life he would imploy himfelfe to recompence hir curtefy, and with all duety and indeuor to acknowledge that fauor. And hauing taken his leaue of the mother, he
went to the Damofell, to hir I fay, that had fo fore wounded his
hearte who already was fo deeply grauen in his mind, as the
marke remained there for euer, taking leaue of hir, kiffed hir
handes, and thinking verily to expreffe that whereuppon hee
imagined all the Nyghte, his Tongue and Wits were fo tyed and
rapt, as the Gentlewoman perfectly perceiued this alteration,
whereat fhe was no whit difcontented and therefore all blufhyng,
fayde vnto him: "I pray to God fir, to eafe and comfort your
gryefe, as you leaue vs defirous and glad, long to enioy your company." "Truely Gentlewoman," (aunfwered the Knyght) "I
think my felfe more than happy, to heare that wyfh proceede
from futch a one as you be, and fpecially for the defire whych
you fay you haue of my prefence, whych fhall be euer readye

to doe that whych it fhall pleafe you to commaunde." The
Gentlewoman bafhfull for that offer, thanked hym verye heartilye
praying him wyth fweete and fmilinge Countenance, not to forget the waye to come to vifite them, beyng wel affured, that hir
mother would be very glad thereof. "And for mine owne part,"
(quod fhe) "I fhall thinke my felf happy to be partaker of the
pleafure and great amity that is betwene our two houfes." After
great reuerence and leaue taken between them, Dom Diego returned home, where he tolde his mother of the good interteyn-
ment made him, and of the great honefty of the Lady hys hofteffe:
"Wherfore madam," (quod he to hys Mother) "I am defyrous
(if it be your pleafure) to let them know how much their bounti-
full hofpitality hath tied me to them, and what defire I haue to
recompence the fame. I am therefore wyllyng to bydde them
hyther, and to make them fo good cheare, as wyth all theyr
Hearte they made me when I was wyth them." The Lady whych
was the affured fryende of the Mother of Gineura, lyked well the
aduyfe of hir fonne, and tolde him that they fhould bee welcome,
for the aunciente amity of long time betwene them, who was
wont many times to vifit one an other. Dom Diego vpon his
mother's words, fent to intreat the Lady and fayr Gineura, that it
woulde pleafe them to do him the honour to come into his houfe:
to which requeft fhe fo willingly yelded, as he was defirous to
bid them. At the appointed day Dom Diego fought al meanes
poffible honourably to receyue them: In meates whereof there
was no want, in Inftruments of all fortes, Mummeries, Morefcoes,
and a thoufand other paftymes, whereby he declared his good
bringing vp, the gentleneffe of his Spyryte, and the defire that he
had to appeare futch one as he was, before hir, which had already
the full poffeffion of his liberty. And bicaufe he would not faile
to accomplyfhe the perfection of his intent, hee inuyted all the
Gentlemen and Gentlewomen that were his neighbours. I will not
here defcribe the mofte part of the prouifion for that feaft, nor
the diuerfity of Meates, or the delycate kyndes of Wines. It fhall
fuffife mee to tell that after dynner they daunced, where the
knight tooke his miftreffe by the hand who was fo glad to fee hir

felfe fo aduanced, as he was content to be fo neare hir, that was
the fweete torment and vnfpeakable paffion of his mynd, whych
hee began to difcouer vnto hir in this wyfe: "Miftreffe Gineura
I have ben alwayes of this Minde, that Mufike hath a certeine
fecrete hydden vertue (which wel can not be expreffed) to reuiue
the thoughts and cogitations of man, be he neuer fo mornfull and
penfiue, forcing him to vtter fome outward reioyfe: I fpeake it
by my felf, for that I liue in extreme anguifh and payne, that al
the ioy of the World feemeth vnto mee difpleafaunt, care, and dif-
quyetneffe: and neuertheleffe my paffion, agreeing with the
plaintife voice of the Inftrument, doth reioyce and conceiue comforte, as well to heare infenfible thinges conformable to my defires
as alfo to fee my felf fo neere vnto hir, that hath the falue to
eafe my payne, to difcharge my difeafe, and to depryue my Mynd
from all gryefs. In like maner reafon it is, that fhe hir felfe do
remedy my difeafe, of whom I receiued the prycke, and which
is the firft foundation of all mine euil." "I can not tell" (fayd
the Gentlewoman) what difeafe it is you fpeak of, for I fhoulde
bee very vnkinde to gieue him occafion of griefe, that doth make
vs this great cheere." "Ah Lady myne," (fayd the knight,
fetching a figh from the bottome of his heart,) "the intertayne-
ment that I receyue by the continuall contemplation of your
diuine Beauties, and the vnfpeakeable brightneffe of thofe two
Beames, which twinkle in your Face, bee they that happily doe
vex me, and make me drink this Cup of bitterneffe, wherein notwithftanding I finde futch fweeteneffe as al the Heauenly Drincke
called Ambrofia, fayned by the Poets, is but Gall in refpect of that
which I tafte in mynde, feeling my deuotion fo bent to do you feruice, as onely Death fhall vnty the knot wherewith voluntarily I
Knyt my felfe to be your Seruaunt for euer, and if it fo pleafe vou,
your Faythfull, and Loyall Freende, and Hufbande." The yonge
Damofell not wonted for to heare futch Songs, did chaunge hir
coloure at leaft three or foure times, and neuertheleffe fayned a
little angre of that which did content hir moft: and yet not fo
fharpe, but that the Gentleman perceyued well enough, that fhee
was touched at the quicke, and alfo that he was accepted into hir

good Grace and Fauoure. And therefore hee continued ſtyll hys talke, all that time after dinner, vntill the Mayden made hym thys aunſwere: "Sir, I will nowe confeſſe that griefe may couer alter-ation of affeċtions proceeding of Loue. For although I had deter-mined to diſſemble that which I thinke, yet there is a thinge in my Mynde (which I can not name) that gouerneth mee ſo farre from my proper Deuiſes, and Conceyptes, as I am conſtrayned to doe that which this ſecond Inſpiration leadeth mee vnto, and forceth my Mynde to receyue an Impreſſion: but what will be the ende thereof, as yet I knowe not. Notwythſtandinge, repoſinge mee in youre Vertue, and Honeſty, and acknowledgynge youre merite, I thincke my ſelfe happy to haue ſutch one for my Freende, that is ſo Fayre and comely a knight, and for ſutch I doe accept you vntill you haue obtayned of the Lady, my Mother, the ſecond poynċt, which may accompliſh that which is moſte deſyred of them, that for vertue's ſake do loue. And but for that you ſhall bee none otherwyſe fauoured of me, than hytherto you haue ben." "Tyll now haue I attended for thys ryght happye day of Ioy and Blyſſe (ſayd the Knyght) in token whereof, I doe kyſſe your whyte and delycate Hands, and for acknowledging the fauour that pre-ſently I do receiue, I make my vaunt to be the ſeruaunt of hir that is the fayreſt, and moſt curteous Gentlewoman, on thys ſide the Mountaynes." As hee had fyniſhed thoſe words they came to couer for Supper, where they were ſerued ſo honourably, as yf they had ben in the Court of the Monarch of Spayne. After Supper they went to walke abroade alongs the Riuer ſide, beſette wyth Wyllow Trees, where both the Beauty of the time, the runnyng Ryuer, the Charme of the Natural muſicke of birds, and the plea-ſaunt Murmure of the tremblyng Leaues, at the whiſtelyng of the ſwete Weſterne Wynd, moued them agayne to renew theyr Paſtyme after Dynner. For ſome dyd gyue themſelues to talke, and to deuyſe of deleċtable matter: ſome framed Noſegayes, Garlandes, and other prety poſyes for theyr Fryendes; other ſome did leape, runne, and throwe the Barre. In the end a great Lord, neighbor to Dom Diego, whoſe name was Dom Roderico, knowyng by his Fryend's Countenaunce to what ſaynt hee was vowed, and perceyu-

ing for whofe loue the feafte was celebrate, tooke by the hand a
Gentlewoman that fate nexte to fayre Gineura, and prayed hir to
daunce after a Song, whereunto fhee beeynge pleafaunt and wyfe,
made no great refufall. Dom Diego fayled not to ioyne wyth
hys myftreffe, after whome folowed the reft of that noble trayne,
euery of them as they thought beft. Now the Gentlewoman, that
was ledde into daunce, fong thys fong fo apt for the purpofe, as
if fhee had entred the heart of the Ennimy and Myftreffe of Dom
Diego, or of purpofe had made the fame in the Name of hir, whom
the matter touched aboue the reft.

Who may better fing and daunce amongs vs Ladies all,
Than fhe that doth hir louer's heart poffeffe in bondage thrall?
> The yong and tender feebleneffe
> Of myne vnfkilfull age,
> Whereof alfo the tenderneffe
> Doth feeble heart affuage:
> Whom Beautye's force hath made to frame
> Vnto a Louer's heft,
> So foone as firft the kindled flame
> Of louinge Toyes increft.

Who may better fing and daunce amongs vs Ladies all,
Than fhe that doth hir louer's heart poffeffe in bondage thrall?
> I haue affayed out to put
> The fier thus begoone,
> And haue attempted of to cut,
> The threede which loue hath fpoone:
> And new alliance fayne would flee
> Of him whom I loue beft,
> But that the Gods haue willed me
> To yeld to his requeft.

Who may better fing and daunce among vs Ladies all,
Than fhe that doth hir louer's heart poffeffe in bondage thrall?
> So amiable is his grace,
> Not like among vs all:
> So paffing fayre is his Face,
> Whofe hue doth ftayne us all:

And as the ſhining ſunny day
Doth eu'ry man delight,
So he alone doth beare the ſway,
Amongs eche louing wight.
Who may better ſing and daunce amongs vs Ladies all
Than ſhe that doth hir louer's heart poſſeſſe in bondage thrall?

Why ſhould not then, the fayreſt dame,
Apply her gentle minde,
And honor giue vnto his name,
Wyth humble heart and kinde?
Sith he is full of curteſie,
Indewd with noble grace,
And breſt replete with honeſty,
Well knowne in euery place.
Who may better ſing and daunce amongs vs Ladies all,
Than ſhe that doth hir louer's heart poſſeſſe in bondage thrall?

If I ſhould loue, and ſerue him than,
May it be counted vice?
If I retayne that worthy man,
Shall I be deemde vnwiſe?
I will be gentle to him ſure,
And render him myne ayde:
And loue that wight with heart full pure,
That neuer loue aſſayde.
Who may better ſing and daunce amongs vs Ladies all,
Than ſhe that doth hir louer's heart poſſeſſe in bondage thrall?

Thus the moſt ſacred vnity,
That doth our hearts combine:
Is voyde of wicked flattery,
The ſame for to vntwine.
No hardned rigor is our guide,
Nor folly doth vs lead:
No Fortune can vs twayne deuide,
Vntill we both be deade.
Who may better ſing and daunce amongs vs Ladies all,
Than ſhe that doth hir louer's heart poſſeſſe in bondage thrall?

And thus affured certaynely,
That this our loue fhall dure,
And with good lucke hope verely,
The fame to put in vre
The fowen feedes of amity,
Begon betwixt vs twayne,
Shall in moft perfect vnity,
For euermore remayne.

Who may better fing and daunce amongs vs Ladies all,
Than fhe that doth hir louer's heart poffeffe in bondage thrall?

Thys Song delighted the Myndes of many in that company, and
principally Dom Deigo, and Gineura, who felt themfelues tickled
without laughing: And the mayden reioyfed to heare hir felfe fo
greatly prayfed in fo noble a company, and fpecially in the prefence of hir friende who had no leffe pleafure by hearing the
praifes of his beloued, than if he had bin made Lord of all Aragon.
She for all hir diffembled Countenaunce could not hide the alteration of hir Mynde, without fending forth a fodayne chaunge of
colour, that forced a fayre and goodly taynt in hir Face.   Dom
Diego feeing that mutation, was fo ioyful as was poffible, for
thereby he knew and Iudged himfelfe affured of the good grace of
hys Miftreffe, and therefore wringing hir finely by the hands,
fayd vnto her very foberly Smiling: "What greater pleafure my
louinge Wench can there happen vnto your Seruaunt, than to fee
the accomplifhment of this Propheticall Song? I affure you that
in all my life I neuer heard muficke, that delighted me fo mutch
as this, and thereby doe vnderftand the good will of the Gentlewoman, which fo curteoufly hath difcouered yours towards me,
and the faythfull feruice whereof you fhall fee me from henceforth
fo liberall, as neyther goods nor life fhalbe fpared for your fake."
Ginuera who loued him with all hir heart, thanked him very
humbly, and prayed him to beleeue that the Song was truely
foonge, and that without any fayle, fhe that foonge, had thereby
manyfefted all the fecrets of hir mynde.   The daunce ended, they
fat theym downe rounde about a cleare Fountayne, which by
filent difcourfe, iffued from an high and moyfty rock, enuironned

with an infinite number of Maple trees, Poplars, and Afhes. To
which place a Page brought a Lute to Dom Diego, whereupon hee
could play very well, and made it more pleafauntly to found for
that hee accorded hys Fayninge Voyce to the Inftrument, Singing
this fong that followeth.

That I fhould loue and ferue alfo, good reafon doth require,
What though I fuffre loathfome grief, my life in woe to wrap?
The fame be th'only inftruments of my good lucke and hap,
The foode and pray for hungry corps, of reft th'affured hire.

By thought wherof (O heauy man) gufh forth of teares great
     ftore
And by and by reioyft agayne, my driery teares do ceafe:
Which guerdon fhall mine honor fure in that triumphant peace,
The fumme wherof I offer now, were it of price mutch more.

Which I do make withall my heart, vnto that bleffed wight,
My proper Goddeffe here on earth, and only miftreffe deere:
My goods and life, my brething ghoft within this carcafe here,
I vow vnto that maiefty, that heauenly ftarre moft bright.

Now fith my willing vow is made, I humbly pray hir grace,
To end th'accord betwene vs pight, no longer time to tracte:
Whych if it be by fured band, fo haply brought to paffe,
I muft my felf thrice happy count, for that moft heauenly fact.

Thys Song made the company to mufe, who commended the
trim inuention of the Knight, and aboue all Gineura prayfed him
more than before, and could not fo well refrayne hir lookes from
him, and he with counterchaunge rendring alike agayne, but that
the two wydowes their Mothers tooke great heede thereof, reioyfing greatly to fee the fame, defirous in time to couple them
togeather. For at that prefent they deferred the fame, in confideration they were both very young. Notwithftanding it had bene
better that the fame Coniunction had ben made, before Fortune

had turned the Wheele of hir vnſtablenes. And truely delay and
prolongation of time ſometimes bryngeth ſutch and ſo great
miſſchappe that one hundred times men curſſe their fortune, and
little aduyſe in foreſight of their infortunate chaunces that commonly do come to paſſe. As it chaunced to thoſe Wydowes, one
of them thinking to looſe hir ſon by the vaine behauior of the
other's daughter, who wythout the help of GOD, or care vnto his
wil, diſparaged hir honor, and prepared a poyſon ſo daungerous
for his Mother's age, as the foode thereof haſtened the way to the
good Ladye's Graue. Now whiles this loue in thys manner increaſed
and that the deſire of theſe two Louers, flamed forth ordinarily
in fire and flames more violent, Dom Diego all chaunged and
tranſformed into a new man, receiued no delyght, but in the ſight
of his Gineura. And ſhe thought that there could be no greater
Felicity or more to be wyſhed for, than to haue a Fryend ſo per-
feᵗ, and ſo well accomplyſhed wyth all thyngs requiſite for the
ornament and full furniture of a Gentleman. This was the occaſion that the young Knyght let no Weeke to paſſe without viſiting
his myſtreſſe twice or thryce at the leaſt, and ſhe did vnto hym
the greateſt curteſy and beſt Entertaynment, that vertue could
ſuffer a Mayden to doe, whych was the diligent Treaſurer and careful tutor of hir honor. And this ſhe dyd by conſent of hir
Mother. In lyk maner, honeſtie doth not permyt chaſte Maydens
to vſe long talk or immoderate ſpeach, with the fyrſt that be ſuters
vnto them, and mutch leſſe ſeemely it is for them to be ouer
ſqueimyſh Nice, wyth that man whych ſeeketh (by way of mar-
ryage) to wynne power and tytle of the Body, beyng in very
deede, or ought to be the moiety of theyr ſoule. Sutch was the
deſyres of theſe two Louers, which notwithſtanding was impeeched
by meanes, as hereafter you ſhal heare. For duryng the re-
bounding ioy of thoſe faire couple of Loyall Louers, it chaunced
that the Daughter of a Nobleman of the Countrey, named Ferrando
de la Serre, whych was fayre, very Comely, Wiſe, and of good
behauiour, by keepynge daily Company with Gineura, fell ex-
treamely in loue with Dom Diego, and aſſayed by all meanes to
do him to vnderſtand what the puiſſance was of hir Loue which
willingly ſhee meant to beſtowe vpon him, if it woold pleaſe hym

to honor hir fo mutch, as to loue hir with like fincerity. But the knight which was no more his own Man, beyng poffeffed of another, had with hys Lybertye loft his Wyts and Mynd to marke the affectyon of this Gentlewoman, of whom he made no accompt. The Maiden neuertheleffe ceafed not to loue him, and to proue all poffible wayes to make him hir owne. And knowing how mutch Dom Diego loued Hawking, fhe bought a hauke the beft in all the countrey, and fent the fame to Dom Diego, who wyth all his heart receiued the fame, and affectuoufly gaue hir thanks for that defired gyft, praying the meffanger to recommend him to the good grace of his miftreffe, and to affure hir felf of his faythfull feruice, and that for hir fake he would kepe the Hauke fo tenderly as the Balles of his eyes. Thys Hauke was the caufe of the ill fortune that after-wards chaunced to this poore Louer. For going many times to fee Gienura with the hauke on his fift and bearing with him the tokens of the goodneffe of his Hauke, it efcaped his mouth to fay, that the fame was one of the things that in all the World he loued beft. Truely this Word was taken at the firft bound contrary to his meaning, wherewith the matter fo fell out, as afterwards by des-payre he was like to lofe his Lyfe. Certaine dayes after, as in the abfence of the knight, talk rofe of his vertue and honeft condi-tions, one prayfing his proweffe and valyance, another his great Beauty and Curtefy, another paffing further, extolling the fincere affectyon and conftancy which appeared in him touching matters of Loue, one enuious perfon named Gracian fpake his mind of hym in this wyfe: "I will not deny but that Dom Diego is one of the moft excellent moft honeft and braueft knyghtes of Catheloigne, but in matters of Loue he feemeth to me fo walteryng and incon-ftant, as in euery place where he commeth, by and by he falleth in loue, and maketh as though he were ficke and would dy for the fame." Gineura maruelling at thofe words faid vnto him: "I pray you my frend to vfe better talk of the Lord Dom Diego. For I do thynk the Loue whych the Knight doth beare to a Gentlewoman of thys countrey, is fo firme and affured, as none other can remoue the fame out of the fiege of hys mind?" "Lo howe you be deceiued Gentlewoman" (quod Gracian) "for vnder coloure of diffymulate feruice, he and futch as he is doe abufe the fimplicity of young

Gentlewomen. And to proue my fayinge true, I am affured that
he is extremely enamored wyth the Daughter of Dom Ferrando de
la Serre, of whom he receyued an Hauke, that he loueth aboue all
other things." Gineura remembrying the words which certayn
dayes before Dom Diego fpake touching his hauke, began to fufpect and beleue that which Gracian alleaged, and not able to fupport the choler, whych cold Iealofy bred in hir ftomack, went
into hir Chaumber full of fo greate gryefe and heauyneffe as fhe
was many tymes lyke to kyll hir felfe. In the end, hopyng to
be reuenged of the wrong whych fhee beleued to receyue of Dom
Diego, determyned to endure hir fortune paciently. In the meane
tyme fhe conceyued in hir Mynd a defpyte and hatred fo great and
extreame agaynft the poore Gentleman that thought lyttle hereof,
as the former loue was nothing in refpecte of the reuenge by death
which fhe then defired vpon hym. Who the next day after his
wonted maner came to fee hir, hauing (to hys great damage) the
hauke on his fifte, which was the onely caufe of all her Iealofie.
Nowe as the knyght was in talke with the Mother, feeynge that
his beloued came not at al (accordyng to hir cuftome) to falute
him and bid him welcome, inquired how fhe dyd. One that loued
hym more than the reft, fayd vnto him: "Syr, fo foone as fhe
knewe of your comming, immedyately fhe wythdrew hir felf into
hir Chaumber." He that was wyfe and well trayned vp diffembled
what he thought, imagining that it was for fome lyttle fantafie,
whereunto Women wyllingly be fubiecte. And therfore when he
thought time to depart he toke leaue of the wydow, and as he was
goyng down the ftaires of the great Chamber, he met one of the
maides of Gineura, whom he prayed to commend him to hir miftreffe. Gineura duryng al this time tooke no refte, deuifing howe
fhee myghte cutte of cleane hir loue entertained in Dom Diego,
after fhe knewe that hee carryed the hawke on his fyft: beyng
the onely inftrument of her frenfie. And therefore thynkyng hir
felfe both defpyfed and mocked of hir Knyght, and that he had
done it in defpyte of hir, fhe entred into fo great rage and Choler
as fhe was like to fall mad. She being then in this trouble of
Mynde, behold hir Gentlewoman came vnto hir, and dyd the
knyght's meffage. Who hearing but the fymple name of hir fup-

poſed Ennimy, began to fighe ſo ſtraungely, as a Man would haue
thought hir ſoule preſently would haue departed hir Body. Afterwards when ſhe had vanquiſhed hir raging fit whych ſtayed hir
ſpeach, ſhe gan very tenderly to weepe, ſaying: "Ah traytor and
vnfaithful Louer, is thys the recompence of the honeſt, and firme
Amity whych I haue borne thee, ſo wyckedly to deceiue me vnder
the colour of ſo faint and deteſtable a Fryendſhip? Ah raſhe and
arrant Theefe, is it I vppon whom thou oughteſt to bend thy
wycked Trumperies? Doſte thou thinke that I am no better worth
but that thou prodigally ſhouldeſt waſte myne honor to bear the
ſpoyles thereof to hir, that is in nothing comparable vnto me?
Wherein haue I deſerued thys diſcurteſy, if not by louyng thee
more than thy beauty and fained loue deſerue? Diddeſt thou dare
to aduenture vppon me, hauyng thy conſcyence wounded wyth
ſutch an abhominable and deadly Treaſon? Durſte thou to offer
thy Mouth to kyſſe my Hand, by the mouth of another, to whome
thou haddeſt before dedicated thy lying Lyppes in thine owne
perſon? I moſt humbly thancke Almighty God that it pleaſed
him to let me ſee the Poiſon by thee prepared for the ruine of my
lyfe and honor. Ha foole, hope not to take me in thy Trap, nor
yet to deceyue me through thy ſugred and deceitfull Words. For
I ſweare by the Almyghty God, that ſo long as I ſhall liue, I will
accompte thee none other, but the moſt cruell and mortall Ennimy
that I haue in this world." Then to accompliſh the reſt of hir
carefull Minde ſhe wrote a Letter to giue hir farewell to hir olde
Friend Dom Diego. And for that purpoſe inſtruſted hir Page
with this Leſſon, that when the knyght ſhould come, he ſhould be
ready before hir lodging and ſay vnto him in the behalfe of hir,
that before he paſſed any further, hee ſhoulde read the Letter,
and not to fayle to doe the Contents: the Page which was malicious, and il affeſtioned to Dom Diego, knowyng the appointed
day of hys comming, wayted for hym a quarter of a mile from the
Caſtle, where he had not long taryed, but the innocent louer came,
agaynſt whome the page went, bearyng about him more hurtfull
and noyſome weapons than al the Theeues and robbers had in all
the Countrey of Catheloigne. In this manner preſenting his mys-
treſſe letters, he ſaid vnto him: "My Lord, madame Gineura my

miftreffe hath fent me vnto you: and bicaufe fhe knoweth how fearefull you be to dyfpleafe hir, prayeth you not to fayle to reade this Letter before you paffe anye further, and there wyth al to accomplyfh the effecte thereof." The knyght abafhed wyth that fodayne meffage, aunfwered the Page: "God forbid my fryend," (quod he) "that I fhould difobey hir by anye meanes, vnto whom I haue gyuen a full authority and puiffaunce over myne affectyons." So receyuing the letters, he kiffed them thre or four times, and openyng them, found that he loked not for, and red that whych he thought not off. The contents were thefe.

The letters of faire Ginuera, to the Knight Dom Diego.

There fhall paffe no day of my Lyfe, from makyng complaynts of the difloyall and periured Louer, who being more efteemed and better beloued than thou dydft deferue, haft made fo fmall accompte of mee, whereof I wyll be reuenged vpon my felfe, for that I fo lyghtly beleued thy wordes fo full of crafte and guyle. I am in mynd that thou henceforth fhalt flye to buzze and beat the Bufhes, where thou fufpecteft to catch the pray: for heere thou art lyke to be deceiued. Goe varlet, (goe I fay,) to deceyue hir whych holdeth thee in hir nets and fnares, and whofe Prefentes (althoughe of fmall Value) moued thee more than the Honefte, Vertuous and Chafte Loue, that Vertue hir felfe began to knytte betweene vs. And fith a Carrion Kyte hath made the fly further off, than the Wynde of the Ayre was able to bear thee, God defende that Gineura fhould goe aboute to hynder thy follyes, and mutch leffe to fuffer hir felfe to bee beguyled throughe thine Excufes. Nay rather God defend (except thou defireft to fe me dy) that thou fhouldeft euer bee in place where I am, affuryng thee of thys my mynde, neuer to be chaunged fo long as my foule fhall reft wythin my body: which giuing breath vnto my panting breaft, fhal neuer be other, but a mortall enimy to Dom Diego: and futch one as euen to the Death wyl not fayle to profecute the default of the moft traiterous and vnfaythfull Knyght that euer was gyrte in girdle, or armed with Sword. And behold the laft fauour that thou canft, or oughteft to hope of me, who lyueth not but onelye to martir and crucify thee, and neuer fhal beother but

> The greateſt Enimy, that euer thou haddeſt, or
>
> > ſhalt haue, Gineura the ſayre.

The myſerable louer had no ſooner red the Letter, but lifting vp his eyes to the heauens, he ſayd: "Alas, my God thou knoweſt well if euer I haue offended, that I ought to be banyſhed from the place, where my contentation is chyefly fixed, and from whence my heartſhall neuer departe, chaunce what myſſehappe and Fortune ſo euer ſhall." Then tournyng himſelf towards the Page, hee ſayd: "Sir Page my fryend, ſay vnto my Ladye, moſt humblye commending me vnto hir, that for this preſent time I wyll not ſee hir, but hereafter ſhe ſhall heare ſome newes from me." The page well leſſoned for the purpoſe, made hym aunſwere, ſaying: "Sir, ſhe hath wylled me to ſay thus mutch by mouth, that ye cannot do hir greater pleaſure, than neuer to come in place where ſhee is: for ſo mutch as the Daughter of Dom Ferrando de la Serre hath ſo catched you in hir nettes, that loth ſhe is your faithfull heart ſhoulde hange in ballance, and expeĉt the vncertaine Loue of two Ladyes at once." Dom Diego hearing the truth of hys miſſehap, and the occaſion of the ſame, made Lyghte of the matter for that tyme, till at length the Choler of his Miſtreſſe were abated, that thereby ſhee might know vpon how bryttle Ground ſhe hadde planted a ſuſpition of hir moſt faythfull and louing Seruaunt, and ſo retiring to his Houſe, altogither vexed and yll contented, he wente into hys Chaumber where with his Dagger he paunched the gorge of the poore birde, the cauſe of hys Ladies Anger, ſaying: "Ha vyle carraine kite, I ſweare by the bloud of him, that thou ſhalt neuer be the cauſe agayne, to make hir fret for ſutch a triflyng thing as thou art: I beleue that what ſo euer fury is hidden within the Body of this curſſed Kite, to engender a Plague, the ſame now is ſeaſed on me, but I hope to doe my Myſtreſſe vnderſtande what Sacrifice I haue made of the thyng that was ſent me, ready to do the lyke vppon mine owne fleſh, where it ſhall pleaſe her to commaund." So taking Inke and Paper, he made aunſwere to Gineura as foloweth.

The Letters of Dom Diego, to Gineura the faire.

But who would euer thynck (my Lady deare) that a Lyght Opinion could fo foone haue deuided your good iudgement, to condempu your Knight before you had heard what he was able to fay, for himfelf? truely I thought no more to offend you, than the man which you neuer knew, although you haue bene deceiued by colored words, vttered by thofe that be enuious of my happe, and Enimies of your ioy, who haue filled your minde full of falfe report. I fwere vnto you (by God, my good Lady) that neuer thinge entred into my fantafie more, than a defire to ferue you alone and to auoide the acquaintance of all other, to preferue for you a pure and entire heart. Whereof longe agone I made you an offer. In wytneffe whereof I humbly befeech you to beleue, that fo foone as you fee this Birde (the caufe of your anger and occafion of my mifhap) torne and pluckte in pieces, that my heart feeleth no leffe alteration or torment: for fo long as I fhall vnderftand your difpleafure to endure againft mee, affure your felfe my Life fhall abide in no leffe paine than my ioye was great when I franckly poffeffed your prefence. Be it fufficient (Madame) for you to know, that I neuer thought to offend you. Be contented I befeech you, with this facrifice which I fend you, if not that I doe the like vpon myne owne body, which without your good will and grace can no longer liue. For my lyfe depending vppon that only benefit, you ought not to be aftonned if the fame fayling his nourifhment doth pearifh, as fruftrate of that foode, propre, and apt for his Appetite : and by like meanes my fayd life fhall reuiue, if it may pleafe you to fpread your beames ouer mine obfcure and bafe perfonage, and to receiue thys fatiffaction for a fault not committed. And fo wayting a gentle aunfwere from your great curtefie, I humbly kiffe your white and delicate handes, with all humility, praying God fweete Lady, to let you fee how mutch I fuffer without defert, and what puiffaunce you haue ouer him that is all your

Faythfull and euer fervaunt

moft obedient, **Dom Diego.**

The letter clofed, and fealed, he deliuered to one of his fayth-full and fecret Seruaunts, to beare (with the deade Hauke) vnto Gineura, charging him diligently to take heede to hir counte-naunce, and aboue all, that faithfully he fhould beare away what fhe dyd fay vnto him for aunfwere. His man fayled not to fpeede himfelfe with diligence: and being come before Gineura, he pre-fented that which his maifter had fent hir. She full of wrath and indignation, would not once vouchfafe to reade the letter, and mutch leffe to accept the prefent which was a witneffe of the con-trary of that fhee did beleue, and turninge vnto the meffenger, fhe fayde: "My Frende, thou mayeft goe get thee backe agayne, wyth the felfe fame charge which thou haft brought, and fay vnto thy mayfter, that I haue nothing to doe with his Letters, his Excufes, or any other thing that commeth from his handes, as one hauing good experience of his fleyghts and deceipts. Tell him alfo, that I prayfe God, in good time I haue taken heede to the little fayth and truft that is in him for a countergarde, lightly neuer hereafter to bee deceiued." The feruyng man would fayne haue framed an Oration to purge his maifter, but the fierce Gentlewoman brake of his talke, faying vnto hym, that fhe was wel refolued vpon hir intent, whych was that Dom Diego fhould neuer recouer place in hir minde: and that fhee hated hym as mutch at that time as euer fhee loued him before. Vppon whych aunfwere the Mes-fanger returned, fo forrowfull for the Miffortune of his Mayfter (knowing hym to bee very innocent) as he knew full well into what defpayre his Mayfter would fall, when he vnderftode thofe pitifull and heavy newes: notwithftanding needes he muft knowe them, and therefore when he was come before Dom Diego, he recyted vnto hym from poynt to poynt his ambaffage, and deliuered hym agayne his Letters. Whereof the infortunate Gentleman was fo fore aftonned, as he was like to haue fallen downe dead at that inftant. "Alas," (fayd he) "what yll lucke is this, that when I thought to enioye the benefite of my attempte, Fortune hath reuolted to bryng me to the extremity of the mofte defparate man that ever lyued? Is it poffible that my good feruice fhould bee the caufe of my approached ouerthrow? Alas, what may true and faithfull louers henceforth hope for, if not the loffe of theyr tyme, when

after long deuoire and duetye, an Enuious fool fhall come to
depryue them of theyr ioy and gladneffe, and they feelyng the
bytterneffe of theyr abandoned farewell, one that loueth leffe
fhall beare away the fweete fruiéte of futch hope, and fhall pos-
feffe withoute deferte the glory due to a good and faythfull futer.
Ah fayre Gineura, that thou feeft not the griefe whych I do feele,
and the affeétion wherewith I ferue thee, and how mutch I would
fuffer to gayne and recouer thy good grace and fauor. Ha vayne
hope, which vntill now haft fylled me, with mirth and gladneffe,
altogether fpent and ouerwhelmed in the gaulle of thy bytter
fauour, and in the taft of thy corrupted lycour : better it had ben
for me at the begining to haue refufed thee, than afterwards
receiued, cherifhed, and fincerely beloued, to be banifhed for fo
light occafion, as I am ful fore afhamed to conceyue the fame
within remembrance : but fortune fhal not haue hir wil ouer me :
for fo long as I fhall liue I wyll contynue the feruaunt of Gineura,
and my lyfc I wyll preferue, to lette her vnderftand the force of
Loue : by continuaunce whereof, I wyll not fticke to fette my felfe
on fyre with the liuely flames of my paffions, and then withdrawe
the fyrebrandes of my ioy, by the rigour and frowardneffe that
fhall proceede from hir." When he had fynifhed his talke, he
began to figh and lament fo ftrangely, as his man was about to
go cal the lady his mother. In whom dyd appeare futch fignes, as
if death had ben at hand, or els that he had ben attached wyth
the Spirite of phrenfie. But when hee fawe hym aboute to come
agayne to himfelfe, he fayed thus vnto him : "How now, fyr, wyl
you caft your felfe away for the foolyfhe toy of an vndifcrete
girle, yll mannered and taught, and who perchaunce doth al this
to proue how conftant you would be ? No, no fir, you muft turne
ouer an other Leafe, and fith you bee determyned to loue hir, you
muft perfeuere in your purfute. For at length it is impoffible,
but that this Diamont hardneffe, muft needes bee mollified, if fhe
be not a Diuell incarnate, more furious than the wildeft beafts,
whych haunt the deferts of Lybia." Dom Diego was comforted
with that admonition, and purpofed to perfift in hys affeétion,
and therefore fent many meffages, giftes, letters, and excufes to
hys angry miftreffe Gineura. But fhe made yet leffe accompt

of them than of the firſt, charging the meſſangers not to trouble
themſelues about thoſe trifles, for ſhee had rather dye than ſee
hym, or to receyue any thyng from him, whom ſhe deadly hated.
When newes hereof came to the knyght, he was altogether impacient, and ſeeing the ſmall profite which he did gaine by purſuing
his folyſh opinion, and not able to beſtow his loue elſewhere, he
determined to die: and yet vnwilling to imbrue his hands with
his owne bloud, he purpoſed to wander as a vacabond into ſome
deſerte, to perfourme the courſe of his vnhappye and ſorrowfull
dayes, hoping by that meanes to quench the heat of that amorous
rage, either by length of tyme, or by death, the laſt refuge of the
myſerable. For which purpoſe then, he cauſed to be made two
pylgrims wedes, the one for himſelfe, and the other for his man,
and prepared al their neceſſaries for his voiage. Then writing a
Letter to his Gineura, he called one of his men, to whom he ſaid:
"I am going about certayne of myne affayres, whereof I will haue
no man to knowe, and therefore when I am gone, thou ſhalt tell
my Lady Mother what I ſay to thee, and that within twenty dayes
(God willing) I meane to retourne: moreouer I require thee, that
foure dayes after my departure, and not before, thou beare theeſe
letters to miſtreſſe Gineura, and if ſo be ſhe refuſe to receyue
them, fayle not to deliuer them vnto hir mother. Take heede
therefore if thou loue me, to do all that which I haue geuen thee
in charge." Afterwards he called his ſeruaunt vnto hym, which
had done the firſt meſſage vnto Gineura, which was a wiſe, and
gentle fellow, in whom the knight repoſed great affiaunce, to him
he declared all his enterpriſe, and th'ende whereunto his fierce
determination did extend. The good Seruaunt whych loued his
mayſter, hearing his intent ſo vnreaſonable, ſayde vnto him:
"Is it not enough for you ſir, to yelde your ſelfe a pray to the
moſt fierce, and cruell woman that lyueth, but thus to augment
hir glory, by ſeeing hir ſelfe ſo victorious over you? Are you
ignoraunt what the mallice of Women is, and how mutch they
triumph in tormenting the poore blynded ſoules that become their
Seruaunts, and what prayſe they attribute vnto themſelues, if by
ſome miſfortune they driue them to diſpaire? Was it without
cauſe that the Sage in times paſt did ſo greatly hate that Sexe,

and Kinde, as the common Ruine, and ouerthrow of men? What mooued the Greeke Poet to fing theefe verfes againft all forts of Women?

A common woe though filly woman be to man,
Yet double ioy againe fhe doth vnto him bring:
The wedding night is one, as wedded folk tell can,
The other when the knill for hir poore foule doth ring.

If not for that he knew the happineffe of man confifted more in auoyding the acquaintaunce of that fury, than by imbracinge, and chearifhing of the fame, fith hir nature is altogether like vnto Æfop's Serpent, which being deliuered from pearill and daunger of death by the fhepeheard, for recompence thereof, infected his whole houfe with his venomous hiffing, and rammifh Breath. O howe happy is hee that can mayfter his owne affections, and like a free man from that paffion, can reioyce in liberty, fleeing the fweete euill which (as I well perceyue) is the caufe of your defpayre. But fir, your wifedome ought to vanquifh thofe light conceipts, by fetting fo light of that your rebellious Gentlewoman, as fhee is vnworthy to be fauoured by fo great a Lord as you be, who defer-ueth a better perfonage than hir's is, and a frendlier entertainment than a farewell fo fondly giuen." Dom Diego, although that he tooke pleafure to heare thofe difcourfes of his faythfull feruaunt, yet he fhewed fo fower a Countenaunce vnto him, as the other with theefe fewe wordes helde his peace: "Sith then it is fo fyr, that you be refolued in your mifhap, it may pleafe you to accept mee to wayte vpon you, whither you are determined to goe: for I meane not to liue at mine eafe, and fuffer my mayfter, in payne, and griefe. I will be partaker of that which Fortune fhall prepare, vntill the heauens doe mitigate their rage vpon you, and your predeftinate mifhap." Dom Diego, who defired no better com-pany, imbraced him very louingly, thankinge him for the good will that hee bare him, and fayd: "This prefent Night about midnight, we wil take our Iourney, euen that way wheather our Lot and alfo Fortune fhall Guide vs, attendinge eyther the ende of my Paffion, or the whole ouerthrow of my felfe." Their intent they did put in proofe: for at Midnight the Moone being cleere when all thinges were at reſt, and the Crickets chirpinge through the Creauiſes of the Earth, they tooke their way vnſeene of any. And ſo ſoone as Aurora began to garniſh hir Mantle with colors of red and white, and the morning Starre of the Goddeſſe of ſtealing loue, appeared, Dom Diego began to ſigh, ſaying: "Ah yee freſhe and dewy Morninges, that my hap is farre from the quiet of others, who after they haue reſted vpon the Cogitation of their Eaſe, and ioye, doe awake by the pleaſaunte Tunes of the Byrdes, to perfourme by effect that which the Shadowe and Fantaſie of their Minde, did preſent by dreaming in the Night, where I am conſtrayned to ſeparate by great diſtaunce exceeding vehement continuation of my Torments, to followe wilde Beaſts, wandring from thence where the greateſt number of men doe quietly ſleepe and take their reſt. Ah Venus, whoſe Starre now conducteth me, and whoſe beames long agoe did glow and kindle my louing heart, how chaunceth it that I am not intreated according to the deſert of my conſtant minde and meaning moſt ſincere? Alas, I looke not to expect any thyng certayne from thee, ſith thou haſt thy courſe amongs the wandring ſtarres. Muſt the Influence of one Starre that ruleth ouer mee, deface that which the Heauens would to bee accompliſhed, and that my cruel miſtreſſe, deluding my languors and griefs, triumpheth ouer mine infirmity, and ouerwhelmeth me with care and ſorow, that I liue pyning away, amongs the ſauage beaſts in the Wilderneſſe? For ſomutch as without the grace of my Lady, all company ſhalbe ſo tedious and lothſom vnto me, that the only thought of a true reconciliation with hir, that hath my heart, ſhal ſerue for the comfort and true remedy of all my troubles." Whiles he had with theſe pangs forgotten himſelfe, hee ſawe that the day began to waxe cleere, the Sun already ſpreading his golden beames vpon the earth and therefore haſtely he ſet himſelf forthwards, vſing Bywayes, and far from common vſed trades, ſo neere as he could, that hee might not by any meanes be knowne. Thus they rode forth till Noone: but ſeeing their horſſe to be weary and faynt, they lighted at a village, farre from the high way: where they refreſhed themſelues, and bayted their horſſe vntill it was late. In this ſort by the ſpace of three daies they trauerſed the Countrey vntill they arriued to the foote

of a mountayne, not frequented almoſt but by Wilde and ſauage
Beaſts.   The countrey round about was very fayre, pleaſaunt,
and fit for the ſolitarines of the Knight: for if ſhadow pleaſed
him, hee might be delighted with the couert of an infinite number of fruiĉtfull trees, wherewith only nature had furniſhed
thoſe hideous and Sauage Deſertes.   Next to the high and wel
timbred Forreſts, there were groues and buſhes for exerciſe of
hunting.   A man could deſire no kinde of Veneſon, but it was to
be had in that Wilderneſſe: there might be ſeene alſo a certain
ſharpe and rude ſituation of craggy, and vnfruiĉtful rocks,
which notwithſtanding yelded ſome pleaſure to the Eyes, to ſee
theym tapiſſed with a pale moaſie greene, which diſpoſed into
a frizeled guiſe, made the place pleaſaunt and the rock ſoft,
according to the faſhion of a couerture.   There was alſo a
very fayre and wide Caue, which liked him well compaſſed round
about with Firre trees, Pine apples, Cipres, and Trees diſtilling
a certayne Roſen or Gumme, towards the bottom whereof, in the
way downe to the valley, a man might haue viewed a paſſing company of Ewe trees, Poplers of all ſortes, and Maple trees, the Leaues
whereof fell into a Lake or Pond, which came by certayne ſmal
gutters into a freſh and very cleare fountayne right agaynſt that
Caue.   The knight viewing the auncienty and excellency of the
place, deliberated by and by to plant there the ſiege of his abode,
for performing of his penaunce and life.   And therefore ſayd vnto
his ſeruaunt: "My friend, I am aduiſed that this place ſhall be
the Monaſtery, for the voluntary profeſſion of our religion, and
where we will accompliſh the Voyage of our Deuotion.   Thou
ſeeſt both the beauty and ſolitarineſſe, which do rather commaund
vs here to reſt, than any other place nere at hand."   The Seruaunt
yelded to the pleaſure of his mayſter, and ſo lightinge from their
horſſe, they diſfurniſhed them of their Saddles, and Bridles, gieuing
to them the liberty of the fields, of whom afterwards they neuer
heard more newes.   The ſaddles they placed within the Caue and
leauing their ordinary apparell, clothed themſelues in Pilgrimes
weedes, fortifying the mouth of the caue, that wilde beaſts ſhould
not hurt them when they were a ſleepe.   There the ſeruaunt
began to play the Vpholſter, and to make 2 little beds of moſſe,

whofe fpindle and wheele were of wood, fo well pollifhed and
trimmed, as if he had bin a carpenter wel expert in that Science.
They liued of nothing els, but of the fruicts of thofe wilde trees,
fometimes of herbs, vntill they had deuifed to make a crofbow
of wood, wherewith they killed now and then a Hare, a Cony, a
Kid, and many times fome ftronger beaft remayned with them for
gage: whofe bloude they preffed out betwene two pieces of wood
and rofted them againft the Sunne, feruing the fame in, as if it
had bene a right good Difhe for their firft courfe of their fober
and vndelicate Table, whereat the pure water of the fountayne,
next vnto their hollow and deepe houfe, ferued in fteade of the
good Wynes, and delicious Drinks that abounded in the houfe
of Dom Diego. Who liuing in this poore ftate, ceafed
night nor day to complayne of his hard fortune and curffed
plight, going many times through the Defertes all alone, the better
to mufe and ftudy thereupon, or (peraduenture) defirous that
fome hungry Beare fhould defcend from the mountayne, to finifhe
his life and paynefull griefes. But the good Seruaunt knowing
his Mayfter's forow and mifhap, would neuer go out of his fight
but rather exhorted him to retourne home againe to his goods
and poffeffions, and to forget that order of lyfe, vnworthy for futch
a perfonage as he was, and vncomely for him that ought to be
indued with reafon and iudgement. But the defperate Gentleman wilfull in his former deliberation, would not heare him fpeake
of futch retrayt. So that if it efcaped the feruaunt to be earneft
and fharpe agaynft the rudeneffe and fottifh cruelty of Gineura,
it was a paftime to fee Dom Diego mount in choller againft him,
faying: "Art thou fo hardy to fpeak il of the gentlewoman, which
is the moft vertuous perfonage vnder the coape of heauen? Thou
maift thancke the loue I beare thee, otherwife I would make thee
feele how mutch the flaunder of hir toucheth mee at the heart,
which hath right to punifhe me thus for mine indifcretion, and
that it is I that commit the wronge in complayning of hir feuerity."
"Now fir," fayd the feruaunt, "I do indeede perceyue what
maner of thing the contagion of loue is. For they which once
doe feele the corruption of that Ayre, think nothing good or
fauory, but the filthy fmel of that peftiferous meat. Wherefore

I humbly befeech you a little to fet apart, and remoue from
minde, that feare and prefumptuous dame Gineura, and by forgetting hir beauty, to meafure hir Defert and your griefe, you
fhall know then (being guided by reafon's lore) that you are the
fimpleft and weakeft man in the worlde, to torment your felfe in
this wife, and that fhee is the fondeft Girle, wholly ftraught of
wits, fo to abufe a Noble man that meriteth the good grace and
fweete embracement of one more fayre, wife and modeft, than fhe
fheweth hirfelfe to be." The knight hearing thefe words thought
to abandon pacience, but yet replied vnto him: "I fweare vnto
thee by God, that if euer thou haue any futch talke agayne,
eyther I will dye, or thou fhalt depart out of my company, for I
cannot abide by any meanes to fuffer one to defpife hir whom I
do loue and honor, and fhal fo do during life." The feruaunt
loth to offend his mayfter held his peace, heauy for all that in
heart, to remember how the poore gentleman was refolued to
finifh there, (in a defert vnknowen to his Freendes) all the remnaunt of his life. And who afwell for the euill order, and not
accuftome nourture, as for affiduall playnts and weepings, was
become fo pale and leane, as he better refembled a dry Chip, than
a man, hauing feeling or lyfe. His eyes were fonke into his Head,
his Beard vnkempt, his hayre ftaring, his fkin ful of filth, altogether more like a wilde and Sauage creature (futch one as is
depainted in brutal forme) than faire Dom Diego, fo mutch commended, and efteemed throughout the kingdome of Spayne. Now
leaue we this Amorous Hermit to paffionate and playne his miffortune, to fee to what ende the Letters came that he wrote to his
cruel Miftreffe. The day prefixed for deliuery of his Letters, his
feruaunt did his charge, and being come to the houfe of Gineura,
founde hir in the hall with hir mother, where kiffing his Mayfter's
Letters, hee prefented them with very great reuerence to the
Gentlewoman. Who fo foone as fhee knew that they came from
Dom Diego, all chaunged into raging colour, and foolifhe choller,
threwe theym incontinently vppon the grounde, fayinge: "Sufficeth it not thy Mayfter, that already twice I haue done him to
vnderftand, that I haue nothing to doe with his Letters nor
Ambaffades, and yet goeth he about by futch affaultes to encreafe

my difpleafure and agony, by the only remembraunce of his folly?"
The Mother feeing that vnciuile order, although fhee vnderftoode
the caufe, and knowinge that there was fome difcorde betweene
the two Louers, yet thought it to bee but light, fithe the Comike
Poet fayeth :

> The Louers often falling out,
> And prety warling rage :
> Of pleafaunt loue it is no doubt,
> The fure renewing gage.

She went vnto hir Daughter, and fayd vnto hir : "What great
rage is this : let me fee that Letter that I may reade it : for I haue
no feare that Dom Diego can deceyue me with the fweetenes of
his honny words. And truly Daughter you neede not fear to touch
theym, for if there were any Poyfon in theym, it proceeded from
your beauty that hath bitten and ftong the knight, whereof if he
affay to make you a partaker, I fee no caufe why he ought to be
thus rigoroufly reiected, deferuing by his honefty a better entertaynement at your hands." In the meane time one of the feruing
men toke vp the Letters, and gaue them to the Lady, who reading
them, found written as followeth.

The letters of Dom Diego, to miftreffe Gineura.

My deareft and moft wel beloued Lady, fith that mine innocency
can finde no refting place within your tender Corpfe, what honeft
excufe or true reafon fo euer I do alledge, and fith your heart
declareth itfelf to be Implacable, and not pleafed with hym that
neuer offended you, except it were for ouermutch loue, which
for guerdon of the rare and incomparable amity, I perceyue my
felfe to be hated deadly of you and in futch wife contemned, as
the only record of my name caufeth in you an infupportable
griefe and difpleafure vnfpeakeable. To auoide I fay your indignation, and by my mifhap to render vnto you fome eafe and contentment, I haue meant to diflodge my felf fo far from this
Countrey, as neyther you nor any other, fhal euer heare by fame

or true report, the place of my abode, nor the graue wherein my
bones fhall reft. And although it be an inexplicable heart's forrow
and torment, which by way of pen can not be declared, to be thus
mifprifed of you, whom alone I do loue and fhal, fo long as mine
afflicted foule fhall hang vpon the feeble and brittle threede of
life: yet for all that, this griefe falling vpon me, is not irkefome,
as the punifhment is grieuous, by imagining the paffion of your
minde when it is difquieted with difdayne and wrath agaynft me,
who liueth not, but to wander vpon the thoughts of your perfections. And forfomuch as I doe feele for the debility that is in
me, that I am not able any longer to beare the fowre fhockes of
my bitter torments and martyrdome that I prefently doe fuffer,
yet before my life doe fayle, and death doe feafe vpon my fenfes,
I haue written vnto you this prefent letter for a teftimoniall of
your rigour, which is the marke that iuftifieth my vnguiltyneffe.
And although I doe complayne of mine vnhappy fortune, yet I
meane not to accufe you, onely contented that eche man doe
know, that firme affection and eternall thraldome do deferue other
recompence than a farewell fo cruell. And I am wel affured,
that when I am deade, you will pitty my torment, knowing then,
although to late, that my loyalty was fo fincere, as the report of
thofe was falfe, that made you beleeue, that I was very far in loue
with the Daughter of Dom Ferrande de la Serre. Alas, fhall a
Noble gentleman that hath bene well trayned vp, be forbidden to
receiue the gifts that come from a vertuous Gentlewoman? Ought
you to be fo incapable and voyde of humanity, that the facrifice
which I haue made of the poore Birde, the caufe of your difdayne,
my repentaunce, my lawfull excufes, are not able to let you fee the
contrary of your perfuafion? Ah, ah, I fee that the dark and
obfcure vayle of uniuft difdayne and immoderate anger, hath fo
blindfold your eyes, and inuegled your mynde, as you can not
iudge the truth of my caufe and the vnrightoufnes of your quarell.
I will render vnto you none other certificate of myne innocency,
but my languifhinge heart, which you clepe betweene your hands,
feling futch rude intertaynment there, of whom he loaked for
reioyfe of his trauayles. But forfomuch then as you do hate me,
what refteth for me to do, but to procure deftruction to my felf?

And fith your pleafure confifteth in mine ouerthrow, reafon willeth that I obey you, and by deth to facrifice my life in like maner as by life you were the only miftreffe of my heart. One only thing cheereth vp my heart agayne, and maketh my death more myferable, which is, that in dying fo innocent as I am, you fhall remayne guilty, and the onely caufe of my ruine. My Lyfe will depart like a Puffe, and Soule fhall vanifh like a fweete Sommer's blaft: whereby you fhall be euer deemed for a cruell Woman and bloudy Murderer of your deuout and faythfull Seruaunt. I pray to God mine owne fweete Lady, to giue you futch Contentation, Ioye, Pleafure, and Gladneffe, as you do caufe through your Rigor, Difcontentment, Griefe, and Difpleafure to the poore languifhing Creature, and who for euermore fhall bee

Your moft obedient and affeéted

feruaunt Dom Diego.

The good Lady hauing red the Letter, was fo aftonned, as hir words for a long fpace ftaied within hir mouth; hir heart panted, and fpirite was full of confufion, hir minde was filled with forrow to confider the anguifhes of the poore vagabound, and fofter Hermit. In the ende before the houfhold diffembling hir paffion which mooued hir fenfe, fhe tooke her Daughter a fide, whom very fharply fhe rebuked, for that fhe was the caufe of the loffe of fo notable and perfeét a Knight as Dom Diego was. Then fhe red the Letter vnto hir, and as all hir eloquence was not able to moue that cruel damfell, more venemous than a Serpent agaynft the knight, who (as fhe thought) had not indured the one halfe of that which his inconftancy and lightneffe had wel deferued, whofe obftinate minde the mother perceyuinge, fayde vnto hir: "I pray to God (deare daughter) that for your frowardneffe, you bee not blinded in your beauty, and for refufall of fo great a benefit as is the alliaunce of Dom Diego, you be not abufed with futch a one as fhall dimme the light of your renoume and glory, which hitherto you haue gayned amongs the fobreft and modeft maydens." Hauing fayd fo, the wyfe and fage widow, went to the feruaunt of Dom Diego, of whom fhe demaunded what day his mayfter departed, which fhe knowing, and not igno-

raunt of the occafion, was more wroth than before: notwithftanding fhe diffembled what fhe thought, and fending backe his
feruant, fhe required him to do hir hearty commendations to the
Lady his miftreffe, which he did.   The good Lady was ioyfull of
them not knowing the contents of her fonne's letters, but looked
rather that he had fent word vnto his lady of the iuft hour of his
returne.   Howbeit when fhe faw that in the fpace of 20 dayes,
nor yet within a moneth he came not, fhee could not tell what to
thinke, fo dolorous was she for the abfence of hir fonne.   The
time paffinge without hearing any newes from him fhe began to
torment hirfelfe, and be fo penfiue, as if fhe had heard certayne
newes of his death.   "Alas," (quod fhe) "and wherefore haue the
heauens giuen me the poffeffion of futch an exquifite fruict, to
depriue mee thereof before I do partake the goodneffe, and
fwetenes therof, and before I do enioy the grifts proceding from
fo goodly a ftock.   Ah God, I fear that my immoderate loue is
the occafion of the loffe of my fonne, and the whole ruine of the
mother, with the demolition and waft of al our goods.   And I
would that it had pleafed God (my Son) the hunter's game had
neuer bene fo deere, for thinking to catch that pray thou thy
felfe waft taken and thou wandring for thy better difport, mif-
fing the right way, fo ftrangely didft ftraggle, that hard it is to
reduce thee into the right track agayne.   At leaft wife if I knew
the place, whereunto thou arte repaired to finde againe thy loffe,
I would trauell thither to beare the company, rather than to lyue
heere voyde of a Hufbande, betrayed by them whom I beft trufted
and bereft from the prefence of the my Sonne, the Staffe and
onely comfort of myne olde age, and the certayne hope of all our
Houfe and Family."   Now if the Mother vexed hir felfe, the Sonne
was eafed with no great reioyce, being now a free cittizen with
the Beafts, and Foules of the Forrefts, Dennes, and Caues, leauing
not the Profundity of the Woods, the Craggednes of the Rocks, or
beauty of the Valley, without fome figne or token of his griefe.
Sometime with a Puncheon wel fharpned, feruing him in fteede
of a Penknife, he graued the fucceffe of his loue vpon an hard
ftone.   Other times the fofte Bark of fome tender and new growen
fpray ferued him in fteede of Paper, or Parchment.   For there be

carued in Cyphres properly combined with a Knot (not eafily to
be knowne) the name of his Lady, interlaced fo properly with his
owne, that the fineft heads might bee deceyued, to Difciphre
the righte interpretation. Vpon a day then, as he paffed his
time (accordinge to his cuftome) to mufe vpon Myffehaps, and
to frame his fucceffe of loue in the Ayre, hee Ingraued thefe
Verfes vpon a Stone by a Fountayne fide, adioyning to his rude
and Sauage houfe.

If any Forreft Pan, doth haunt here in this place,
Or wandring Nymphe, hath hard my wofull playnt :
The one may well beholde, and view what drop of grace,
I haue deferu'de, and eke what griefes my heart do taynt,
The other lend to me fome broke, or fhowre of rayne
To moyft myne heart and eyes, the gutters of my brayne.

Somewhat further of many times at the rifing of the Sunne, he
mounted the Top of an high and greene Mountayne to folace himfelfe vpon the frefhe and greene graffe, where four Pillers were
erected, (eyther naturally done by dame Nature, or wrought by the
induftry of man,) which bore a ftone in forme four fquare, well
hewed, made and trimmed in maner of an Aulter, vpon which
Aulter he dedicated thefe verfes to the Pofterity.

Vpon this holy fquared ftone, which Aulter men doe call,
To fome one of the Gods aboue that confecrated is,
This dolefull verfe I do ingraue, in token of my thrall,
And deadly griefes that do my filly heart oppreffe,
And vex with endeleffe paynes, which neuer quiet is,
This wofull verfe (I fay) as fureft gage of my diftreffe,
I fixe on Aulter ftone for euer to remayne,
To fhew the heart of trueft wight, that euer liued in payne.

And vpon the brims of that Table, he carued thefe Wordes :

This Mafon worke erected here, fhall not fo long abide,
As fhall the common name of two, that now vncoupled bee,
Who after froward fortune paft, knit eche in one degree,
Shall render for right earneft loue, reward on either fide.

And before his Lodging in that wilde and ſtony Forreſt vpon the Barke of a lofty Beeche Tree, feeling in himſelfe an unaccuſtomed luſtineſſe, thus he wrote:

Th'encreaſing beauty of thy ſhape, extending far thy name,
By like increaſe I hope to ſee, ſo ſtretched forth my fame.

His man ſeeing him to begin to be merily diſpoſed, one day ſaid vnto him: "And wherefore ſir ſerueth the Lute, which I brought amongs our Males, if you do not aſſay thereby to recreate youre ſelfe, and ſing thereupon the prayſes of hir whom you loue ſo wel: yea and if I may ſo ſay, by worſhipping hir, you do commit idolatry in your minde. Is it not your pleaſure that I fetche the ſame vnto you, that by immitation of Orpheus, you may mooue the Trees, Rocks, and wylde Beaſtes to bewayle your misfortune, and witneſſe the penaunce that you doe for hir ſake, without cauſe of ſo haynous puniſhment:" "I ſee well," (quod the knight) "that thou wouldeſt I ſhould be mery, but mirth is ſo far from me, as I am eſtraunged from hir that holdeth me in this miſery. Notwithſtanding I will performe thy requeſt, and will awake that inſtrument in this deſert place, wherewith ſometime I witneſſed the greateſt part of my paſſions." Then the knight receyuing the Lute ſounded thereupon this ſong enſuing.

The waues and troubled ſcum, that mooues the Seas alofte,
Which runs and roares againſt the rocks, and threatneth daungers oft
            Reſembleth lo the fits of loue,
            That dayly do my fanſie moue.

My heart it is the ſhip, that driues on ſalt Sea fome,
And reaſon ſayles with ſenſeleſſe wit, and neuer loketh home,
            For loue is guide, and leades the daunce,
            That brings good hap, or breedes miſchaunce.

The furious flames of loue, that neuer ceaſeth ſure,
Are loe the buſie ſailes and oares, that would my reſt procure,
            And as in Skies, great windes do blo,
            My ſwift deſires runnes, fleeting ſo.

As fweete Zephyrus breath, in fpring time feedes the floures,
My miftreffe voice would ioye my wits, by hir moft heauenly powers,
    And would exchaunge my ftate I fay,
    As Sommer chaungeth Winter's day.

She is the Artique ftarre, the gratious Goddeffe to,
She hath the might to make and marre, to helpe or els vndo,
    Both death and life fhe hath at call,
    My warre, my peace, my ruine and all.

She makes me liue in woe, and guides my fighs and lookes,
She holds my fredome by a lace, as fifh is held with hookes,
    Thus by defpayre in this conceite,
    I fwallow vp both hooke and baite.

And in the deferts loe I liue, among the fauage kinde,
And fpend my time in wofull fighs, rayf'd vp by care of minde,
    All hopeleffe to in paynes I pyne,
    And ioyes for euer doe refigne.

I dread but Charon's boat if fhe no mercy giue,
In darkneffe then my foule fhall dwell, in Pluto's raygne to liue,
    But I beleue fhe hath no care,
    On him that caught is in hir fnare.

If fhe releafe my woe, a thoufand thankes therefore,
I fhall hir giue, and make the world to honor hir the more,
    The Gods in Skies will prayfe the fame,
    And recorde beare of hir good name.

O happy is that life, that after torment ftraunge,
And earthly forows on this mould, for better life fhal chaunge
    And liue amongs the Gods on high,
    Where loue and Louers neuer die.

O lyfe that here I leade, I freely giue thee now,
Vnto the fayre where ere fhe refts, and loke thou fhew hir how

I linger forth my yeares and dayes,
To win of hir a crowne of prayfe.

And thou my pleafaunt Lute, ceafe not my fongs to found,
And fhew the torments of my minde, that I through loue haue found,
    And alwayes tell my Miftreffe ftill,
    Hir worthy vertues rules my will.

The Fofter Louer.

The Fofter louer finging this fong, fighing fundry tymes betwene, the tricling teares ranne downe his Face: which thereby
was fo diffigured, as fcarfe could any man haue knowne him, that
al the dayes of their lyfe had frequented his company. Sutch
was the ftate of this myferable yong gentleman, who dronke with
hys owne Wyne, balanced himfelfe downe to defpayre rather than
to the hope of that which he durft not looke for. Howbeit like
as the mifchiefs of men be not alwayes durable, and that all thinges
haue their proper feafon, euen fo Fortune repentinge hir euill
intreaty which wrongfully fhee had caufed this poore penetenciary
of Gineura to endure, prepared a meanes to readauunce him aloft
vppon hir Wheele, euen when he thought leaft of it. And certes,
herein appeared the mercy of God, who caufeth things difficult
and almoft impoffible, to be fo eafy, as thofe that ordinarily be
brought to paffe. How may this example fhow how they which
be plunged in the bottome of defiaunce, deeming their life vtterly
forlorne, be foone exalted euen to the top of all glory, and felicity?
Hath not our age feene a man whych was by aucthority of his
Enimy iudged to dye, ready to bee caried forth to the Scaffolde
miraculoufly deliuered from that daunger, and (wherein the works
of God are to be marueyled) the fame man to be called to the
dignity of a Prynce, and preferred aboue all the reft of the people?
Now Dom Diego attending his fieldifh Philofophy in the folitary
valeys of the riche Mountayne Pyrene, was refcowed with an helpe
vnlooked for as you fhall heare. You haue hard how hee had a
Neyghbour and finguler Frend a Noble Gentleman named Dom
Roderico. Thys Gentleman amongs all his faithfull Companions
did moft lament the harde fortune of Dom Diego. It came to
paffe that 22 moneths after that the poore Wilde penitent perfon

was gonne on Pilgrimage, Dom Roderico tooke his Iourney into Gaſcoyne for diuers his vrgent Affayres, which after hee had diſpatched, were it that hee was gon out of his way, or that GOD (as it is moſt likely) did driue him thither, he approched towarde that Coaſte of the Pyrene Mountaynes, where that tyme his good Frende Dom Diego did Inhabite, who dayly grew ſo Weake and Feeble, as if God had not ſent him ſodayne ſuccour hee had gotten that hee moſt deſired, which was death that ſhould haue bene the ende of his trauayles and Afflictions. The trayne of Dom Roderico being then a bowe ſhot of from the ſauage Caben of Dom Diego, eſpyed the tractes of mens Feete newly troden, and beganne to maruayle what hee ſhould bee that dwelled there, conſidering the Solitude, and Infertility of the Place, and alſo that the ſame was farre of from Towne or Houſe. And as they deuiſed hereupon, they ſaw a man going into a Caue, which was Dom Diego, comming from making his complayntes vppon the Rock ſpoken of before. From which hauinge turned his face toward that parte of the worlde where he thought the lodging was of that Saynct, whereunto he addreſſed his deuotions, Dom Diego hearinge the Noyſe of the horſſe, was retired becauſe hee woulde not bee ſeene. The knight which rode that way, ſeeing that, and knowing how far he was oute of the way, commaunded one of his men to Gallop towardes the Rocke, to learne what people they were that dwelled within, and to demaund how they might coaſte to the high way that led to Barcelona. The Seruaunt approching neare the Caue, perceiued the ſame ſo well Empaled and Fortified with Beaſts ſkins before, fearing alſo that they were Theeues and Robbers that dwelled there, durſt not approche, and leſſe enquire the way, and therefore returned towards his mayſter, to whom hee tolde what hee ſaw. The knight of another maner of Metall and hardineſſe than that Raſcall and coward ſeruaunt, like a ſtout, Couragious, and valiaunt Man, poaſted to the Caue, and demaundinge who was within, he ſaw a man come forth ſo diſfigured, horrible to looke vppon, pale with ſtaring hayre vpright, as pitifull it was to behold him, which was the ſeruant of the foſter Hermit. Of him Roderico demaunded what he was, and which was the way to Barcelone. "Syr," aunſwered that diſguiſed perſon: "I know not

how to aunſwere your demaund, and mutch leſſe I know the
country where we now preſently be.   But ſir, (ſayde he ſighing)
true it is that we be two poore companions whom Fortune hath
ſent hither, by what il aduenture I know not, to do penaunce for
our Treſpaſſes, and Offences."   Roderico hearing him ſay ſo, began
to call to his remembraunce his Freende Dom Diego, although he
neuer before that tyme ſuſpeĉted the place of his abode.   He
lighted then from his horſſe, deſirous to ſee the ſingularities of the
Rocke, and the magnificence of the Cauiſh lodging, where hee
entred and ſawe him whom he ſought for, and yet for all that did
not know him : He commoned with him a long tyme of the pleaſure of the ſolitary life in reſpeĉt of theym that liued intangled
with the comberſome Follies of this World.   "For ſomutch" (quod
he) as the ſpirite diſtraĉted and withdrawen from Worldly troubles
is eleuate to the contemplation of heauenly thinges, and ſooner
attendeth to the knowledge and reuerence of his God, than thoſe
that bee conuerſaunt amongs men, and to conclude, the complaynts, the delights, ambitions, couetouſneſſe, vanities, and ſuper-
fluities that abounde in the confuſed Maze of Worldely troupe,
doe cauſe a miſknowledge of our ſelues, a forgetfulneſſe of our
Creator, and many times a negligence of piety and pureneſſe of
Religion.   Whiles the vnknowne Hermit, and the knight Roderico
talked of theſe thinges, the Seruauntes of Roderico viſiting all the
Corners of the deepe, and Stony Cell of thoſe Penitents, by Fortune
eſpied two Saddles, one of theym rychely wroughte and Armed
wyth Plates of Steele, that had bene made for ſome goodly Ienet.
And vppon the Plate well Wroughte, Grauen and Enameled, the
Golde for all the Ruſt cankering the Plate, did yet appear.   For
whych Purpoſe one of theym ſayde to the ſeruaunt of Dom
Diego : "Good Father hitherto I ſee neyther Mule, nor Horſſe, for
whom theſe Saddles can ſerue, I pray thee to ſell them vnto vs,
for they will doe vs more pleaſure, than preſently they do you."
"Maiſters (quod the Hermit,) if they like you, they be at your
commaundement."   In the meane time Roderico hauing ended his
talke with the other Hermit, without knowing of any thinge that
he deſired, ſayd vnto his men : "Now ſirs to horſe, and leaue wee
theeſe poore people to reſt in peace, and let vs goe ſeeke for the

right way which we fo well as they haue loft." "Syr," (quod
one of his men,) "there be two Saddles, and one of them is fo
exceeding fayre, fo well garnifhed and wrought as euer you faw."
The knight feeling in himfelfe an vnaccuftomed motion, caufed
them to be brought before him, and as he viewed and marked the
riche Harneffe, and Trappings of the fame, he ftayeth to looke
vppon the Hinder parte minionly wrought, and in the middeft of
the engrauing he red this deuife in the Spanifh Tongue.

Que brantare la fe, es caufa muy fea.

That is,

To violate or breake fayth, is a thing deteftable.

That only infcription made him to paufe a while. For it was
the Poefie that Dom Diego bore ordinarily in his armes, which
moued him to think that without doubt one of thofe Pilgrimes
was the very fame man to whom that Saddle did appertayne. And
therefore he bent himfelfe very attentiuely afterwardes to behold
firft the one, and then the other of thofe defert Citizens. But
they were fo altered, as hee was not able to know them agayne.
Dom Diego feeing his Freende fo neare him, and the defire that
he had to knowe hym, chafed very mutch in hys mynde, and the
more his Rage began to waxe, when hee faw Roderico approch
neare vnto hym more aduifedly to looke vpon hym, for hee had
not his own Affeations fo mutch at commaundement, but hys
Bloude mooued hys Entrailes, and mounting into the moft knowen
place, caufed outwardly the alteration which hee endured, to
appeare. Roderico feeing hym to chaunge colour, was affured
of that which before hee durft not fufpeat: and that which made
him the fooner beleeue that he was not deceiued, was a lyttle tuft
of haire, fo yelow as Gold, which Dom Diego had vpon his Necke,
whereof Dom Roderico takyng heede, gaue ouer all fufpition, and
was well affured of that he doubted. And therefore difplaying
himfelfe with hys armes opened vpon the necke of his friend, and
imbracing him very louingly, his face bedewed with tears, fayd
vnto him: "Alas, my Lord Dom Diego, what euill lucke from
Heauen hath departed you from the good company of them which
dye for forrow, to fee themfelues berieued of the Beauty, lyght
and ornament of their felowfhip? What are they that haue giuen

you occasion thus to Eclipse the bryghtnesse of your name, when
it oughte most clearely to shyne, both for theyr present pleasure,
and for the honour of your age? Is it from me sir, that you
oughte thus to hide yourselfe? Do you think me so to be blynd,
that I know not ryght well, that you are Dom Diego, that is so
renoumed for vertue and prowesse? I would not haue tarried here
so longe, but to carry away a power to reioyce two persons, you
being the one, by withdrawing your selfe from this heauy and
vnseemely Wyldernesse, and my selfe the other, to enioy your
Company, and by bearyng newes to your fryends, who sith your
departure, do bewaile and lament the same." Dom Diego seeing
that he was not able to conceyle the truth of that which was
euidently seene, and the louing imbracements of his best Friende,
began to feele a certayne tendernesse of heart lyke vnto that
whych the Mother conceyueth, when she recouereth hir Sonne
that is long absent, or the chaste wyfe, the presence of hir deare
Husband, when she clepeth him betwene hir armes, and frankely
culleth and cherisheth hym at hir pleasure. For whych cause not
able to refrain any longer for ioy and sorrow together, weping
and sighing began to imbrace him wyth so good and hearty
affection, as with good wyl the other had sought and longed to
knowe where he was. And being come againe to himself, he sayd
to his faithfull and most louinge friend: "Oh God, how vneasy
and difficult be thy iudgments to comprehend? I had thought to
liue here miferably, vnknowen to al the world, and behold, I am
here discouered, when I thought least of it. I am indeede" (quod
he to Roderico) "that wretched and vnfortunate Dom Diego, euen
that thy very great and louing fryend, who weary of his lyfe,
afflycted wyth his vnhap, and tormented by fortune, is retyred
into these desertes to accomplysh the ouerplus of the rest of his
il luck. Now sith that I haue satisfied you herein, I beseech you
that being content wyth my sighte, yee wyll get you hence and
leaue me heere to performe that lyttle remnant whych I haue to
lyue, without telling to any person that I am aliue, or yet to
manifeste the place of my abode." "What is that you say sir,"
(sayd Roderico) "are you so farre straught from your ryght wits,
to haue a minde to continue this brutal Lyfe, to depryue al your

friends from the ioy whych they receiue by inioying your company ? Think I pray you that God hath caused vs to be born noble men, and hauing power and authority not to lyue in Corners, or be buryed amid the flauery of the popular fort, or remain idle within great palaces or fecrete Corners, but rather to illuftrat and giue lyght with the example of our vertue to thofe that fhal apply themfelues to our dexterity of good behauior, and do lyue as depending vpon our edicts and commaundments : I appeale to your faith, what good fhall fuccede to your fubiects, who haue both heard and alfo knowne the benefit beftowed vppon them by God, for that hee gaue them a Lord fo modeft and vertuous, and before they haue experimented the effect of his goodneffe and Vertue, depriued of him, that is adorned and garnifhed with futch perfections ? What comfort, contentation and ioy fhall the Lady your mother receiue, by feelyng your loffe to be fo fodaine, after your good and delycate bryngyng up, inftructed with futch great diligence and vtterly berieued of the fruict of that education ? It is you fir, that may commaund obedience to Parents, fuccor to the afflicted, and do iuftice to them that craue it : Alas, they be your poore fubiectes that make complaints, euen of you, for denying them your due prefence. It is you of whom my good madame doth complayne, as of him that hath broken and violated his faith, for not comming home at the promifed day." Now as he was about to continue his oration, Dom Diego vnwilling to heare him, brake of his talk faying : " Ah fir, and my great Friend : It is an eafy matter for you to iudge of mine affayres, and to blame myne abfence, not knowing peraduenture the caufe thereof. But I efteeme you a man of fo good iudgement, and fo great a fryend of thinges that be honefte, and a Gentleman of great fidelity, as by vnderftanding my hard luck, when you be aduertifed of the caufe of my withdrawing into this folitarie place, you wyll rightly confeffe, and playnely fee that the wifeft and moft conftant haue committed more vaine follies than thofe don by mee, forced with like fpirite that now moueth and tormenteth me." Hauing fayd, he tooke afide Roderico, where he dyd tell vnto hym the whole difcourfe both of his Loue, and alfo of the rigor of hys Lady, not without weepyng, in futch abundaunce

and with ſutch frequent ſighes and ſobs interruptyng ſo hys ſpeach,
as Roderico was conſtrained to keepe him company, by remembryng the obſtinacie of hir that was the Miſtreſſe of his heart,
and thinkynge that already he had ſeene the effect of lyke miſſehap to fal vpon his owne head, or neare vnto the lyke, or greater
diſtreſſe than that which he ſawe his deare and perfect Fryend to
endure.   Notwythſtanding he aſſayed to remoue him from that
deſperate minde and opinion of continuance in the deſert.   But
the froward penitente ſwore vnto him, that ſo long as he liued
(without place recouered in the good graces of his Gineura,) he
would not returne home to his houſe, but rather change his being,
to ſeke more ſauage abode, and leſſe frequented than that was.
"For" (quod hee) "to what purpoſe ſhall my retourne ſerue where
continuinge mine affection, I ſhall fele lyke cruelty that I dyd in
time paſt, which wil bee more painful and heauy for me to beare
than voluntary exile and banyſhment, or bring me to that end
wherein preſently I am."   "Contente your ſelf I beſeech you, and
ſuffer me to be but once vnhappy, and do not perſwade mee to
proue a ſecond affliction, worſſe than the firſt."   Roderico hearing his reaſons ſo liuely and wel applied would not reply, onely
content that he would make him promyſe to tarry there two
monthes, and in that time attempt to reioyſe himſelfe ſo wel as
he could.   And for hys owne part, he ſwore vnto him, that he
would bee a meanes to reconcile Gineura, and brynge them to
talke together.   Moreouer, he gaue him aſſurance by othe, that
hee ſhoulde not bee diſcouered by hym, nor by any in his Company.   Wherewith the knyght ſomewhat recomforted, thanked
him very affectuouſly.   And ſo leauyng wyth him a fielde bed,
two ſeruaunts, and Money for his Neceſſities, Roderico tooke hys
leaue, tellyng hym that ſhortely he would viſite him againe, to his
great contentation, as euer he was left and forſaken with gryefe
and ſorrow, himſelfe makyng great mone for the vnſeemely ſtate
and myſerable plyght of Dom Diego.   And God knoweth whether by the way, he deteſted the cruelty of pitileſſe Gineura,
blaſphemyng a million of times the whole ſexe of Womankynd,
peraduenture not without iuſt cauſe.   For there lieth hydden (I
know not what) in the breſts of Women, which at times like the

Wane and increafe of the Moone, doth chaunge and alter, whereof a man can not tell on what foote to ftand to conceiue the reafons of the fame: whych fickle fragility of theirs (I dare not fay mobility) is futch, as the fubtilleft wench of them al beft fkilled in Turner's Art, can not (I fay deface) or fo mutch as hide or colour that naturall imperfection. Roderico arriued at his houfe, frequented many times the lodging of Gineura, to efpy hir fafhions, and to fee if any other had conquered that place, that was fo well affayled and befieged by Dom Diego. And this wyfe and fage knyght vfed the matter fo well, that he fell in acquaintance wyth one of the Gentlewoman's Pages, in whom fhe had fo great truft, as fhe conceyled from him very few of hir greateft fecretes, not well obferuing the preceipte of the wyfe man, who councelleth vs not to tell the fecretes of the mynde to thofe, whofe iudgement is but weake, and tongue very lauifh and frank of fpeach. The Knyght then familiar with this Page, dandled him fo with faire words, as by lyttle and lytle he wrong the Wormes out of his Nofe, and vnderftode that when Gineura began once to take Pepper in fnuffe againft Dom Diego, fhe fell in loue wyth a Gentleman of Bifkaye, very poore, but Beautyfull, young and luftye, whych was the Stewarde of the houfe: and the Page added further that hee was not then there, but woulde returne wythin three Dayes, as he had fent Woorde to hys myftreffe, and that two other Gentlemen woulde accompany him to cary away Gineura into Bifkaye, for that was their laft conclufion: "And I hope" (quod he) "that fhe will take me with hir, bicaufe I am made priuy to their whole intent." Roderico hearing the treafon of this flight and departure of the vnfaithful daughter, was at the firft brunt aftonned, but defirous that the Page fhould not marke his altered Countenaunce, faid vnto him: "In very deede meete it is, that the Gentlewoman fhould make hir owne choice of hufband, fith hir mother fo little careth to prouide for hir. And albeit that the Gentleman be not fo riche and Noble as hir eftate deferueth, hir affection in that behalfe ought to fuffife, and the honefty of his perfon: for the reft Gineura hath (thanks be to God) wherewith to intertaine the ftate of them both." Thefe wordes he fpake, farre from the thought of his hearte. For being alone by himfelf, thus he faid:

" O bleſſed God, how blinde is that loue, which is vnruled, and out
of order : and what difpayre to recline to them, which (voide of
reaſon) doe feede ſo fooliſhly of vayne thoughts and fond deſires,
in ſutch wiſe as two commodities, preſented vnto them, by what
ill lucke I know not, they forſake the beſte, and make choiſe of
the worſt. Ah Gineura, the faireſt Lady in all this Countrey, and
the moſte vnfaithfull Woman of oure time, where be thine eyes
and iudgement ? Whither is thy mynde ſtraied and wandred, to
acquite thyſelfe from a great Lord, faire, rich, noble, and vertuous,
to be giuen to one that is poore, whoſe parents be vnknowne, his
proweſſe obſcure, and birth of no aparant reputation. Behold,
what maketh me beleue, that loue (ſo wel as Fortune) is not onely
blynd, but alſo dazeleth the ſight of them that hee imbraceth and
captiuateth vnder his power and bondage. But I make a vowe
(falſe woman) that it ſhal neuer come to paſſe and that this Biſkaye gentleman ſhall neuer enioy the ſpoyles whych iuſtely bee
due vnto the Trauaile and faithfull ſeruice of the valyaunt and
vertuous knyght Dom Diego. It ſhal be hee, or elſe I wil dye
for it, whych ſhall haue the recompenſe of his troubles, aud ſhall
feele the caulme of that tempeſt, whych preſently holdeth hym
at Anker, amyd the moſt daungerous rockes that euer were." By
this meanes Roderico knew the way how to keepe promiſe wyth
his friende, which liued in expectation of the ſame. The two
dayes paſt, whereof the Page had ſpoken, the beloued of Gineura,
fayled not to come, and with him two Gallants of Biſkaye, valiaunt
Gentlemen, and well exercyſed in Armes. That Nighte Roderico
wente to ſee the olde Wydowe Lady, the Mother of the Mayden,
and fyndyng oportunity to ſpeak to the Page, hee ſaid vnto hym :
" I ſee my Friend, accordingly as thou diddeſt tell mee, that ye are
vppon departing, the ſteward of the houſe beeing now retourned.
I pray the tel mee, if thou haue neade of mee, or of any thyng
that I am able doe for thee, aſſuring thee that thou ſhalt obtaine
and haue what ſo euer thou requireſt. And therewithall I haue
thought good to tel thee, and giue the warning (for thine owne
ſake ſpecially) that thou keepe all thynges cloſe and ſecrete, that
no ſlaunder or diſhonour do followe, to blot and deface the Same
and prayſe of thy Miſtreſſe. And for my ſelfe I had rather dye,

than once to open my mouth, to difcouer the leaft intent of this enterpryfe. But tell mee, I praye thee, when do ye depart?" "Sir" (quod the Page) "as my Miftreffe faieth, to morow about ten or eleuen of the Clocke in the Euening, when the Lady hir Mother fhall bee in the found of hir firft fleepe." The knight hearyng that, and defirous of no better time, tooke hys leaue of the Page, and went home, where he caufed to bee fente for tenne or twelue Gentlemen, his Neighbours and Tenaunts, whom he made priuy of his fecretes, and partakers of that he went about, to deliuer out of Captiuity and miferie the chiefeft of all his Friends. The Nighte of thofe two Louers departure being come, Dom Roderico, which knewe the way where they fhould paffe, beftowed him felfe and his Company in Ambufh, in a little Groue, almoft three Miles of the Lodging of this fugitiue Gentlewoman: where they hadde not long tarried but they hearde the tramplinge of Horffe, and a certaine whifpring noife of People riding before them. Nowe the Nighte was fomwhat cleare, which was the caufe, that the Knighte amonges the thronge, knew the Gentlewoman, befides whome rode the Miferable Wretche that hadde ftolne hir awaye. Whome fo foone as Roderico perceyued full of defpyte, moued wyth extreme paffion, welding his launce into his reft, brake in the neareft way vpon the infortunate louer, with futch vehemency, as neither coate of Maile or Placard was able to faue his lyfe, or warraunt him to keepe company wyth that troupe which banded vnder Ioue's Enfeigne, was miferably flayne, by the guide of a blynd, naked, and thieuifh litle boy. And when he faw he had done that he came for, he fayd to the reft of the Company: "My Friends, thys man was careleffe to make inuafion vpon other mens ground." Thefe poore Bifkayes furpryfed vpon the fodayne, and feeyng the ambufhment to multiply, put fpurres to theyr horffe to the beft aduantage they could for expedition, leauing their Conduct or guid gaping for breath and geuing a figne that he was dead. Whiles the other were making themfelues ready to runne away, two of Roderico his men, couered with Skarfes, armed, and vnknowne, came to feafe vppon forrowfull Gineura, who beholdyng her fryende deade, began to weepe and crye fo ftraungely, as it was maruell that hir breath fayled

not. "Ah trayterous Theeues," (said fhe) "and bloudy Murderers,
why do ye not addreffe your felues to execute cruelty vppon the
reft, fith you haue done to death hym, that is of greater value
than you all? Ah my deare Fryend, what crooked and grieuous
Fortune haue I, to fee thee grouelyng dead on ground and I abyd-
ing in life, to be the pray of murderous Theeues and thou fo
cowardly beryued of lyfe." Roderico wyth his face couered, drew
neare vnto her, and fayde : "I befeech you Gentlewoman, to forget
thefe ftraunge fafhions of complaynt, fith by them ye bee not
able to reuiue the dead, ne yet make your ende of gryefes." The
maiden knowing the voyce of hym, that had flayne hir fryende,
began to cry out more fiercely than before. For whych caufe
one of the gentlemen in company with Roderico, hauing a blacke
counterfait beard with two lunets, in manner of fpeftacles, very
large and great, that couered the mofte part of his Face, approched
neare the bafhful maiden, and with bigge voice and terrible talk,
holding his dagger vpon hir white and delicate breaft, faid vnto
hir : "I fweare by the Almighty God, if I heare thee fpeake one
word more, I wil facrifice thee vnto the ghoft of that varlet, for
whome thou makeft thy mone, who deferued to end his daies vpon
a gallow tree rather than by the hands of a gentleman. Holde
thy peace therefore thou foolyfh girle, for greater honour and
more ample Benefite is meant to thee, than thou haft deferued.
Ingratitude onely hath fo ouerwhelmed thy good Nature, as thou
art not able to iudge who be thy friends." The gentlewoman
fearing death, whych as fhe thought was prefent, held hir peace,
downe alonges whofe Eyes a ryuer of Teares dyd run, and the
paffion of whofe heart appeared by affiduall fighes, and neuer
ceaffing fobbes, whych in end fo quallifyed hir cheare, that the
exteriour fadneffe was wholy inclofed wythin the mynd and
thought of the afflifted Gentlewoman. Then Roderico caufed the
body of the dead to be buryed in a lyttle Countrey Chappell, not
farre out of theyr way. Thus they trauayled two dayes before
Gineura knew any of them, that had taken hir away from hir
louer : who permytted none to fpeake vnto hir nor fhe to any of
hir company, beyng but a waiting maid, and the page that hadde
dyfcouered al the fecretes to Dom Roderico. A notable example

furely for ftolne and fecrete mariages, whereby the honour of the
contracted partes, is moft commonly blemyfhed, and the Commaundement of God violated, whofe word enioyneth obedience
to Parents in all ryghtfull caufes, who if for any lyght offence, they
haue power to take from vs the inheritance whych otherwyfe
naturall law would giue vs, what ought they of duety to doe,
where rebellyous Chyldren abufing theyr goodneffe, do confume
without feare of Liberty, the thynge that is in theyr free wyll and
gouernement. In like maner diuers vndifcrete and folyfh mothers
are to be accufed, which fuffer their daughters of tender and
chyldyfh age to be enamored of theyr feruants, not remembryng
how weake the flefh is, how prone and ready men be to do euyl,
and how the feducyng fpirite waytyng ftil vpon us, is procliue
and prone to furpryfe and catch vs wythin his Snares, to the intent
he may reioyce in the ruine of foules wafhed and redeemed wyth
the bloud of the Son of God. This troupe drawing neare to the
caue of Dom Diego, Roderico fent one of his men to aduertife
him of their comming, who in the abfence of his fryende, fylled and
fufteined with hope, fhortely to fee the onely Lady of hys hearte,
accompanyed wyth a merry and ioyfull Trayne, fo foone as hee
had fomewhat chaunged his wilde maner of Lyfe, he alfo by lyttle
and lyttle gayned a good part of hys lufty and frefh coloure, and
almoft had recouered that beauty, which he had when he firfte
became a Citizen of thofe defertes. Now hauing vnderftanded
the meffage fent vnto him by Roderico, God knoweth if with
that pleafaunt tydings he felt a motion of Bloud, futch as made
all his members to leape and daunce, whych rendred hys Mynde
aftonned, for the onely memorye of the thynge that poyfed hys
mynd vp and downe, not able to be wayed in equall Balaunce
whereof rather he ought to haue made reioyfe than complayne,
being affured to fee hir, of whome he demaunded onely grace and
pardon, but for recouery of hir, he durft not repofe any certayne
Iudgement. In the Ende hoyftyng vp hys head lyke one ryfen
from a long and found fleepe, hee fayd : " Praife be to God, who
yet before I dye, hath done me great pleafure, to fuffer me to haue
a fyght of hir, that by caufing my Matirdome, continueth hir
ftubburne manner of Lyfe, whych fhall procure in like fort myne

vtter ruine and decay. Vpon the approch of whom I ſhall goe
more ioyfull, charged with incomparable loue, to vyſit the ghoſts
beneath, in the preſence of that cruel ſwete, that now tormenteth
me with the ticklyſh tentation, and who ſometimes hath made me
taſt a kind of Hony ſugred with bytter Gal, more daungerous than
the ſuck of Poyſon and vnder the vermyllion rudde of a new
ſprouted Roſe diuiuely blowen forth, hath hydden ſecrete Thornes
the pryckes whereof hath me ſo lyuely touched, as my Wound
cannot wcll bee cured, by any Baulme that may be thereunto
applyed, without enioying of that myne owne miſſchappe, moſte
happy or wythout that remedy, whych almoſt I feele reſtyng in
death, that ſo long and oftentymes I haue deſired as the true
remedy of all my paynes and gryefe." In the meane whyle Dom
Roderico, whych tyll that tyme was not knowen vnto Gineura,
drew neare vnto hir by the way as he rode, and talked wyth
hir in this ſorte : " I doubt not (Gentlewoman) but that you think
your ſelf not wel contented to ſe me in this place, in ſutch company and for occaſion ſo vnſeemely for my degre, and ſtate, and
moreouer knowying what iniury I ſeeme to do vnto you, that
euer was, and am ſo affectionate and friendly to the whole ſtocke
of your race and Lynage, and am not ignoraunte that vppon the
firſte brunte you may iudge my cauſe vniuſt to carry you away
from the handes of your fryend, to bring you into theſe deſertes,
wylde, and ſolitary places. But if ye conſidred the force of that
true amity, which by vertue ſheweth the common Bondes of
hearts and myndes of Men, and ſhall meaſure to what end this
acte is done, without to mutch ſtaying vpon the lyght apprehen-
ſion of Choler, for a beginnynge ſomewhat troubleſom, I am
aſſured then (that if you be not wholly depryued of reaſon) you
ſhall perceiue that I am not altogether worthy blame nor your
ſelfe vtterly voyde of fault. And bycauſe we draw neare vnto
the place, whether (by the help of God) I meane to conduct you,
I beſeech you to conſider, that the true Seruaunt whych by all
ſeruice and duety ſtudieth to execute the commaundementes of
him that hath puiſſance ouer him, doth not deſerue to bee
beaten or driuen away from the houſe of his maiſter, but to be
fauored and cheriſhed, and ought to receyue equal recompenſe for

his feruice. I fpeake not this for my felfe, my deuotion beinge
vowed elfewhere, but for that honeft affection which I beare to all
vertuous and chafte perfons. The effect whereof I will not deny
to tell you in tyme and place, where I fhall ufe futch modefty
towards you, as is meete for a maiden of your age and ftate. For
the greatneffe of Noble Men and puifant, doth moft appeare and
fhew forth it felf, when they vfe Mildeneffe and Gentleneffe vnto
thofe, to whom by reafon of their Authority they mighte execute
cruelty and malice. Now to the end that I do not make you doubtfull long, al that which I haue done and yet meane to doe, is for
none other purpofe but to eafe the grieuous paines of that mofte
faithful louer that loueth at thys Daye vnder the Circle of the
Moone. It is for the good Knighte Dom Diego, that loueth you
fo dearely and ftill worfhippeth your Noble fame, who bicaufe he
wil not fhew himfelf difobedient, liueth miferably amonge bruite
beafts, amid the craggy rocks and mountaines, and in the deepe
folitudes of comfortleffe dales and valleis. It is to him I fay that
I do bryng you, protefting vnto you by othe (Gentlewoman) that
the misery wherein I faw him, little more than vi. Wekes paft,
toucheth me fo neare the heart, as if the Sacrifice of my lyfe
fufficed alone, (and without letting you to feele this painfull
voyage) for the folace of his martirdome I would fpare it no more,
than I do mine owne endeuor and honor, befides the hazarding
of the loffe of your good grace and fauour. And albeit I wel
perceiue, that I do grieue you, by caufing you to enter this painfull iourney, yet I befech you that the whole difpleafure of this
fact may bee imputed vnto my charge, and that it would pleafe
you louingly to deale with him, who for your fake vfeth fo great
violence againft himfelf." Gineura as a woman half in defpayre
for the death of hir friend, behaued hir felfe like a mad woman
void of wit and fenfe, and the fimple remembraunce of Dom Diego
his name fo aftonned her, (which name fhe hated far more than
the pangs of death) that fhe ftaied a long time, hir mouth not
able to fhape one word to fpeake. In the ende vanquifhed with
impacience, burning with choler, and trembling for forrow,
loked vpon Dom Roderico with an Eye no leffe furious, than a
Tigreffe caught within the Net, and feeth before hir face hir young

Fawnes murdered, wringing hir hands and beating hir delicate breſt, ſhe vſed theſe or ſutch like woordes: "Ah bloudy traitor and no more Knight, is it of thee that I oughte to looke for ſo deteſtable a villany and treaſon? How dareſt thou be ſo hardy to entreat me for an other, that haſt in myne owne preſence killed him, whoſe death I will purſue vpon thee, ſo longe as I haue life within this body? Is it to thee falſe theefe and murderer, that I ought to render accompte of that which I meant to doe? Who hath appointed thee to be arbitrator, or who gaue thee commiſ-ſion to capitulate the Articles of my mariage? Is it by force then, that thou wouldeſt I ſhould loue that vnfaithfull Knighte, for whom thou haſt committed and done this acte, that ſo longe as thou liueſt ſhal blot and blemiſh thy renoume, and ſhal be ſo wel fixed in my mind, and the wounds ſhal cleaue ſo neare my heart, vntill at my pleaſure I be reuenged of this wrong? No, no, I aſſure thee no force done vnto mee, ſhall neuer make mee other-wyſe dyſpoſed, than a mortall Enimy both to thee which art a Theefe and rauiſher of an other man's wife, and alſo to thy deſperate frend Dom Diego, which is the cauſe of this my loſſe: and now not ſatiſſied with the former wrong done vnto me, thou goeſt about to deceiue me vnder the Colour of good and pure Friendſhip. But ſith wicked Fortune hath made me thy Pryſoner, doe with me what thou wylt, and yet before I ſuffer and endure that that Traytor Dom Diego doe enioy my Virginity, I will offer vp my lyfe to the ſhadowes and Ghoſtes of my faythful fryend and hus-band, whome thou haſt ſo trayterouſly murdred. And therefore (if honeſtlye I may or ought entreate mine Enimy) I pray thee that by doynge thy duety, thou ſuffer vs in peace, and gyue lycence to mee, thys Page, and my two pore Maydens to depart whether we lyſt." "God forbid" (quod Roderico) "that I ſhould doe a Treſpaſſe ſo ſhamefull, as to depryue my deareſt fryend of his ioy and contentation, and by falſifiing my faith be an occaſion of hys death, and of your loſſe, by leauing you without company, wandring amids this wilderneſſe." And thus he continued his former diſcourſe and talk, to reclaime thys cruell Damoſell to haue pity vpon hir poore penytent, but he gained as mutch thereby, as if he had gone aboute to number the Sands alongs the Sea Coaſtes of

the maine Ocean. Thus deuifing from one talke to an other,
they arryued neare the Caue, which was the ftately houfe of Dom
Diego: where Gineura lyghted, and faw the pore amorous Knight,
humbly falling downe at hir feete, all forworne, pale, and dis-
figured, who weeping with warme teares, faid vnto hir: "Alas,
my deare Lady, the alone and onely miftreffe of my heart, do you
not thinke that my penaunce is long inoughe for the finne which
ignorauntly I haue committed, if euer I haue don any fault at
al? Behold [I befeech you (good ladie deare) what ioy] I haue
conceiued in your abfence, what pleafures haue nurfed mine hope,
and what confolation hath entertained my life: which truely
had it not bene for the continual remembraunce of your diuine
Beauty, I had of long time abreuiated the pains which do
renew in me fo many times the pangs of death: as oftentimes I think vpon the vnkindnes fhewed vnto me by making
fo litle accompt of my fidelity: whych can nor fhal receiue the
fame in good part, wer it fo perfeѐt as any affuraunce were able
to make it." Gineura fwelling with forrow and full of feminine
rage, blufhing with fury, hir eyes fparcklinge forth hir chollerick
conceypts, vouchfafed not fo mutch as to giue him one word for
aunfwere, and bicaufe fhe would not looke vppon him, fhe turned
hir face on the other fide. The poore and affliѐted Louer, feeing
the great cruelty of his felonous Myftreffe, ftill kneeling vpon
his knees, redoubling his armes, fetching Sighes with a voyce that
feemed to bee drawne by force from the bottome of his heart,
proceeded in thefe wordes: "Syth the fincerity of my fayth, and
my long feruice madame Gineura, cannot perfuade you that I
haue beene moft Obedient, Faythfull, and very Loyall feruaunt
towards you, as euer any that hath ferued Lady or Gentlewoman,
and that without your fauour and grace it is vnpoffible for mee
any longer to liue, yet I doe very humbly befeech you, for that all
other comfort is denied me, if there bee any gentleneffe and
curtefie in you, that I may receyue this onely grace at your hands
for the laft that euer I hope to craue: which is, that you being
thus greeuoufly offended with me, would do iuftice vpon that
vnfortunate man, that vpon his Knees doth inftantly craue the
fame. Graunt (cruell miftreffe) this my requeft, doe vengeaunce

at your pleafure vpon him, which willingly yeldeth himfelfe to death with the effufion of his poore innocent bloud to fatiffy you, and verily farre more expedient it is for him thus to die, by appeafing your wrath, than to reft or liue to your difcontentment or anoiaunce. Alas, fhal I be fo vnfortunate, that both life and death fhould bee denied me by one perfon of the world, whom I hoped to content and pleafe by any fort or meanes what fo euer reftinge in mine humble obedience? Alas gentlewoman rid mee from this Torment, and difpatch your felfe from the griefe you haue to fee this vnhappy Knight, who would fay and efteeme himfelfe moft happy (his life being lothfome vnto you) if he may content you, by death done by your owne handes, fith other fauour he cannot expect or hope for." The Mayden hardned in hir Opinion, ftoode ftill immoueable mutch like vnto a Rocke in the midft of the Sea, difquieted with a tempeft of billowes, and fomy Waues in futch wife as one word could not be procured from hir mouth. Which vnlucky Dom Diego perceyuing, attached with the feare of prefent death, and faylinge his Naturall force fell downe to the Grounde, and faintyng faied: "Ah, what a recompence doe I receiue for this fo faythfull Loue?" Roderico beholding that rufull fight, whileft the others went about to relieue Dom Diego, repaired to Gineura, and full of heauineffe mingled with fury, faid vnto hir: "By God (falfe fiendifh woman) if fo be that I doe chaunge my mind, I will make thee feele the fmarte, no leffe than thou fheweft thy felfe difhonourable to them that doe thee honour: Art thou fo careleffe of fo greate a Lord as this is, that humbleth himfelfe fo lowe to futch a ftrumpet as thou art: who without regarde either to hys renoume, or the honour of his Houfe, is content to bee abandoned from his noble ftate, to become a fugitiue and ftraunger? What cruelty is this for thee to mifpryfe the greateft humility that man can Imagin? What greater amends canft thou wyfh to haue, yea though the offence which thou prefuppofeft had ben true? Now (if thou be wyfe) chaunge thy Opinion, except thou wouldeft haue mee doe into fo many pieces, thy cruel corpfe and vnfaithful heart, as once this poore Knight did in parts the vnhappy hauke, which through thy folly did breede vnto him this diftreffe, and to thy felf the

name of the moſt cruell and diſloyall Woman that euer lyued. But
what greater benefite can happen vnto thee, than to ſee thys
Gentleman vtterly to forget the fault, to conceiue no ſiniſter ſuſpition of thy running away, crauing pardon at thy Hands, and is
contented to ſacrifice him ſelf vnto thine Anger, to appeaſe and
mytigate thy rage? Now to ſpeake no more hereof, but to proceede in that which I began to ſay, I offer vnto thee then both
death and Loue, chooſe whether thou lyſt. For I ſweare againe
by hym that ſeeth and heareth all thinges, that if thou play the
foole, that thou ſhalt feele and proue me to be the cruelleſt Ennimy
that euer thou hadſt: and ſutch a one as ſhall not feare to imbrue
his hands wyth the bloud of hir that is the death of the greateſt
friend I haue, and trueſt knight that euer bare armes." Gineura
hearing that reſolute aunſwere, ſhewed hir ſelſe to be nothing
afrayde nor declared any token of feare, but rather ſeemed to
haue encouraged Roderico, in braue and manniſh ſort, farre
diuers from the ſimplicity of a young and tender Mayden, as a
Man would ſay, ſutch a one as had neuer felt the aſſaultes and
troubles of adverſe fortune. Wherefore frouncyng her Browes,
and grating hir Teeth wyth cloſed fiſts, and Countenaunce very
bold, ſhe made him anſwere: "Ah thou Knight, whych once
gaueſt aſſault to commit a villany and Treaſon thinkeſt thou now
without remorſe of conſcyence to continue thy miſchyefe: I ſpeak
it to thee Villayne, whych hauing ſhed the Bloud of an honeſter
Man than thou art, feareſt not now to make me a Companion of
hys Death. Which thyng ſpare not hardily to accomplyſh, to
the intent that I liuinge, may not be ſutch a one as thou falſly
iudgeſt me to be: for neuer Man hitherto vaunted, and never
ſhall, that hath had the ſpoyle of my deareſt Iewell: from the
Fruiƈt whereof, like an arrant Thiefe, thou haſt depryued my loyall
Spouſe. Now doe what you lyſte: for I am farre better content
to ſuffer death, be it as cruel as thou art miſchieuous, and borne
for the diſquieting and vexation of honeſt Maidens then yelde vnto
thy furies: notwithſtanding I humbly beſeech Almyghty God, to
gyue thee ſo mutch pleaſure, contentation and ioy in thy loue, as
thou haſt done to me, by haſtening the death of my deare Huſband.
O GOD, if thou be a iuſt GOD, ſutch a one, as from whom we thy

poore Creatures do beleue al iuſtice to proceede, thou I ſay which
art the Rampire and refuge of al iuſtice, poure downe thy vengeance
and plague vpon theſe peſtiferous Thieues and murderers, which
prepared a worldely plague vpon me thine innocent damſel. Ah
wycked Roderico, think not that death can be ſo fearful vnto
me, but that with good hcart, I am able to accept the ſame,
truſting verily that one day it ſhal be the cauſe of thy ruine, and
the ouerthrowe of him for whom thou takeſt al theſe paines."
Dom Roderico marue+louſly rapte in ſenſe imagined the Woman
to be fully bente againſt hym, who then had puiſſance (as he
thought,) ouer hir own heart: and thinking, that he ſawe hir
moued with like rage againſt him, as ſhe was againſt Dom Diego,
ſtode ſtil ſo perplexed and voyde of ryghte minde, as he was
conſtrained to ſitte downe, ſo feeble he felt him ſelf for the onely
remembraunce of hir euyll demeanor. And whileſt this Pageant
was a doing, the handmayd of Gineura, and hir page, inforced to
perſuade their myſtreſſe to haue compaſſion vpon the Knight that
had ſuffred ſo mutch for hir ſake, and that ſhe would conſent to
the honeſt requeſts and good counſell of Roderico. But ſhe
which was ſtubbornely bent in hir fonde perſuaſions, made them
aunſere: "What fooles? are you ſo mutch bewitched, eyther with
the fayned teares of this diſloyall Knight, whych colorably thus
doth torment himſelfe, or els are yee inchaunted with the venomous honny and tirannicall brauery of the Theefe which murdered
my huſbande, and your mayſter? Ah vnhappy caytife mayden, is
it my chaunce to endure the aſſault of ſutch Fortune, when I
thought to liue at my beſt eaſe, and thus cruelly to tomble into
the handes of him, whom I hate ſo mutch as he fayneth loue vnto
me? And moreouer my vnlucky fate is not herewith content, but
redoubleth my ſorrowe, euen by thoſe that be of my trayne, who
ought rather to incourage mee to dy, than conſent to ſo vnreaſonable requeſts. Ah loue, loue, how euill be they recompenced
which faythfully doe Homage vnto thee? And why ſhould not I
forget all Affection, neuer hereafter to haue mynde on man to proue
beginning of a pleaſure, which taſted and felt bringeth more diſpleaſure than euer ioy engendreth delight. Alas, I neuer knewe
what was the fruiƈte of that which ſo ſtraungely did attach me,

and thou O trayterous and theeuifhe Loue, hafte ordayned a banket ferued with futch bitter difhes, as forced I am perforce to tafte of their egre fweetes : Auaunt fweete folly, auaunt, I doe henceforth for euer let thee flip, to imbrace the death, wherein I hope to find my greateft reft, for in thee I finde noughte elfe but heapes of ftrayninge Paffions. Auoyde from me all mifhap, flee from me ye furious ghoftes and Fayries moft vnkinde, whofe gaudes and toyes dame loue hath wrought to keepe occupied my louing minde, and fuffer me to take ende in thee, that I may liue in an other life without thee, being now charged with cup of griefe, which I fhall quaffe in venomous drincke foaked in the Sops of bitterneffe. Sharpen thou thy felfe, (O death vnkinde) prepare thy Darte, to ftrike the Corpfe of hir, that fhe may voyde the Quarelles fhotte agaynft hir by hir Aduerfary. Ah poore hearte, ftrip thy felfe from hope, and qualifie thy defires. Ceafe henceforth to wifhe thy Lyfe, feeing, and feelinge the appoynčted fight of loue and Life, combattyng within my minde, els where to feeke my peace in an other world, with him to ioy, whych for my fake was facrificed to the treafon of varlets handes, who for the perfite hoorde of his defires, noughte elfe dyd feeke but to foile his bloudy fifts with the pureft bloude of my loyall friend. And I this floud of Teares do fhead to faciate his felonous moode that is the iuft fhortening of my dolefull Dayes." When fhe had thus complayned, fhe began horribly to torment hir felfe that the cruelleft of the company were moued with compaffion, to fee hir thus ftrangely ftraught of hir wits : neuertheles they did not difcontinue by duety to folicite hir to haue regard to that which poore fayntyng Dom Diego dyd endure : who fo foone as wyth frefhe Fountayn water hee was reuiued, feeing ftill the heauineffe of his Lady, and hir increafed difdaine and choler againfte hym vanifhed in diuers foundings : which moued Roderico from ftudye deepe, wherein he was, to ryfe, whereunto the rage of Gineura had caft him downe, bicaufe forgetting all imaginarie affeċtion of his Lady, and propofing his duety before his eyes, whych ech Gentleman oweth to Gentle Damfels [and womenkind], ftyll beholding with honorable afpeċt the gryefe of the martyred wylderneffe Knyght, fighing yet in former gryefes, he fayd vnto Gineura, "Alas, is it poffyble,

that in the heart of ſo young and delicate a maiden, there may
bee harboured ſo ſtraunge fury and vnreaſonable rage? O God,
the effeĉt of the cruelty reſting in this Woman, painting it ſelfe in
the imaginatiue force of my mind, hath made me feare the like
myſſehappe to come to the cruell ſtate of this diſaduenturous
gentleman? Notwythſtanding (O thou cruell beaſt) thinke not that
thys thy fury ſhall ſtay me from doing thee to death, to rid thee
from follye and diſdayne, and this vnfortunate louer from deſpayre
and trouble, verily beleuing, that in tyme it ſhalbe knowne what
profit the World ſhall gayne by purgyng the ſame of ſutch an
infeĉted plague as is an vnkynd and arrogante hearte: and it ſhall
feele what vtility ryſeth by thyne ouerthrowe. And I doe hope
beſydes in tyme to come, that Men ſhall prayſe this deede of
myne, who for preſeruynge the Honoure of one Houſe, hath choſen
rather to doe to death two offenders, than to leaue one of them
aliue, to obſcure the glory and brightneſſe of the other. And
therefore" (ſayd he, tourning his face to thoſe of his traine,) " cut
the throte of this ſtubborne and froward beaſt, and doe the like to
them that be come with hir, ſhewe no more fauor vnto them all,
than that curſſed ſtrumpet doth mercy to the life of that miſerable Gentleman, who lieth a dying there for loue of hir." The
Mayden hearing the cruel ſentence of hir death, cryed out ſo loud
as ſhe coulde, thinking reſkue woulde haue come, but the poore
Wench was deceiued: for the deſert knew none other, but thoſe
that were abiding in that troupe. The Page and the woman ſeruaunt exclamed vpon Roderico for mercy, but he made as though
he heard them not, and rather made ſigne to his men to do what
he commaunded. When Gineura ſawe that their deathe was
purpoſed in deede, confirmed in opinion rather to dy, than to
obey, ſhe ſaid vnto the executioners: " My friends, I beſeech
you let not theſe innocentes abide the penaunce of that which
they neuer committed. And you, Dom Roderico, be reuenged
on me, by whome the fault, (if a woman's faith to hir huſband may
be termed a faulte) is don. And let theſe infortunate depart, that
bee God knoweth guiltles of any cryme. And thou my friend,
which lieueſt amonges the ſhadowes of faythfull louers, if thou haue
any feelinge, as in deede thou proueſt being in another world,

behold the pureneffe of mine heart and fidelity of my loue: who
to keep the fame inuiolable, do offer my felf voluntarily to the
death, which this cruell tyrant prepareth for me. And thou hangman the executioner of my ioyes, and murderer of the immortall
pleafures of my loue (fayd fhe to Roderico) glut thy vnfaciable
defire of bloud, make dronke thy mind with murder, and boaft of
thy litle triumph, which for all thy threates or perfuafible words,
thou canft not get from the heart of a fimple maiden, ne cary
away the victory for all the battred breach made into the ram-
pare of hir honour." When fhe had fo faid, a Man would haue
thought that the memory of death had cooled hir heate, but
the fame ferued hir as an affured folace of hir paynes. Dom
Diego being come to himfelf and feing the difcourfe of that tragedy,
being now addreffed to the laft act and end of that life and ftage
of faire and golden locked Gineura, making a vertue of neceffity,
recouered a lyttle corage to faue, (if it were poffible) the life of
hir, that had put hys owne in hazard miferably to end. Hauing
ftayed them that held the maiden, he repayred to Dom Roderico,
to whom he fpake in this wife: " I fee wel my good Lord and great
Friende, that the good will you beare me, caufeth you to vfe this
honeft order for my behalf, whereof I doubt if I fhould lyue a
whole hundred yeares, I fhall not be able to fatiffy the leaft of
the bondes wherein I am bound, the fame furpaffing all mine
ability and power. Yet for al that (deare friend) fith you fee the
fault of this miffehap to arife of my predeftinate ill lucke, and
that man cannot auoyde things once ordained, I befeech you do
me yet this good pleafure (for all the benefits that euer I haue receiued) to fend back again this gentlewoman with hir trayne, to
the place from whence you toke hir, wyth like affurance and conduct, as if fhee were your fifter. For I am pleafed with your
endeuor, and contented with my miffortune, affuring you fir
befides, that the trouble which fhe endureth, doth far more
gryeue my heart than al the paine which for hir fake I fuffer. That
hir forrow then may decreafe and mine may renue againe, that
fhe may lyue in peace, and I in Warre for hir cruel beauty fake,
I wyll wayt vppon Clotho, the Spynner of the threden life of man
vntil fhe breake the twyfted lace that holdeth the fatall courfe of

my dolefull yeares. And you Gentlewoman lyue in reſt, as
your poore ſuppliant, wretched Dom Diego, ſhalbe citizen of
wyld places, and vaunt you hardely that yee were the beſt beloued
maiden that euer liued." Maruellous truly be the forces of loue,
when they diſcouer their perfeꞔion, for by their meanes thinges
otherwiſe impoſſible be reduced to ſutch facility, as a man would
iudge that they had neuer bene ſo hard to obtaine, and ſo painefull to purſue: As appeared by this damſel, in whome the wrath
of fortune, the pynche of iealoſie, the intollerable rage of hir
fryendes loſſe, had ingendred a contempte of Dom Diego, an
extreame deſire to be reuenged on Dom Roderico, and a tedious-
neſſe of longer Lyfe. And now putting of the vaile of blynde
appetite, for the eſclariſhing of hir vnderſtandyng Eyes, and breakyng the Adamant Rocke planted in the middes of hir breaſt, ſhe
beheld in open ſight the ſtedfaſtneſſe, pacience and perſeueration
of hir great fryend. For that ſupplycation of the Knight had greater
force in Gineura, than all hys former ſeruyces. And full wel ſhe
ſhewed the ſame, when throwyng hir ſelfe vppon the Necke of
the deſperate Gentleman, and imbracyng hym very louyngly ſhe
ſayd vnto him: "Ah ſir, that your felicity is the begynnyng of
my great ioy of Mynd, whych ſauoreth now of ſweetnes in the
very ſame, in whom I imagyned to be the welſprynge of bytter-
neſſe. The diminutyon of one gryefe is, and ſhall bee the increaſe
of a bonde, ſutch as for euer I wyll call my ſelfe the moſte humble ſlaue of your honor, lowly beſeechyng you neuertheleſſe to
pardon my follyes, wherewyth full fondely I haue abuſed youre
pacience. Conſider a whyle ſir, I beſeech you, the Nature and
ſecrecye of loue. For thoſe that be blinded in that paſſion,
thynke them ſelues to be perfeꞔte Seers, and yet be the firſt that
commit moſt filthy faultes. I doe not denie any committed
wrong and treſpaſſe, and doe not refuſe therefore the honeſt and
gentle Correꞔtion that you ſhall appointe .mee, for expiation of
myne offence." "Ah my Noble Lady," (aunſwered the knight,
all rapt wyth pleaſure, and halfeway out of his wyts for ioy) "I
humbly beſeech you inflyꞔt vppon my poore wretched body no
further panges of Death, by remembryng the glory of my thought,
ſith the recitall bryngeth with it a taſt of the trauailes which you

haue fuffred for my ioy and contentation." "It is therefore,"
(quod fhe) "that I think my felf happy: for by that meanes I
haue knowne the perfect qualyties that be in you, and haue proued
two extremities of vertue. One confifting in your conftancy
and loyalty wherby you may vaunt yourfelf aboue hym that
facrificed his Lyfe vpon the bloudy body of his Ladye who for
dying fo, finifhed his Trauailes. Where you haue chofen a life
worfe than death, no leffe paynefull a hundred times a Day,
than very death it felf. The other in the clemency wherwyth
you calme and appeafe the rage of your greateft aduerfaries. As
my felf which before hated you to death, vanquifhed by your
courtefie do confeffe that I am double bound vnto you, both for
my lyfe and honor: and hearty thankes do I render to the Lord
Roderico for the violence he dyd vnto me, by which meanes I was
induced to acknowledge my wrong, and the right whych you had
to complayne of my beaftly refiftance." "Al is wel," fayd Roderico,
"fith without peril of honor we may returne home to our houfes:
I intend therefore (fayd he) to fend word before to the Ladies your
mothers of your returne, for I know how fo wel to couer and
excufe this our enterpryfe and fecrete iorneis, as by God's affiftance no blame or difpleafure fhall enfue thereof. And like as
(faid he fmiling) I haue builded the fortreffe whych fhot into
your campe, and made you flie, euen fo I hope (Gentlewoman)
that I fhalbe the occafion of your victorye, when you combat in
clofe campe, with your fweete cruel Ennimy." Thus they paffed
the iorney in pleafaunt talk, recompenfing the 2 Louers with al
honeft and vertuous intertainment for their griefs and troubles
paft. In the meane while they fent one of their Seruaunts to the
two widow Ladies, which were in greate care for their Children, to
aduertife them that Gineura was gone to vifit Dom Diego, then
being in one of the caftles of Roderico, where they were determined
if it were their good pleafure, to confumate their mariage, hauing
giuen faith and affiance one to the other. The mother of Gineura
could not heare tel of more pleafant newes: for fhe had vnderftanded of the foolyfh flyght and efcape of hir daughter, with the
fteward of hir houfe, wherof fhe was very forrowful, and for
grief was like to die, but affured and recomforted with thofe newes

ſhe failed not to mete the mother of Dom Diego, at the appointed
place whether the 2 louers were arriued two daies before. Ther
the mariage of that fair couple (ſo long deſired) was ſolempniſed
with ſutch magnificence as was requiſite for the ſtate of thoſe
two noble houſes. Thus the torment indured, made the ioye to
ſauour of ſome other taſte than they do feele, which without paine
in the exerciſe of loue's purſute, attaine the top of theyr deſires:
and truly their pleaſure was altogether like to him that nouriſhed
in ſuperfluous delicacy of meates cannot aptly ſo wel iudge of
pleaſure as he which ſometimes lacketh the abundance. And
verily loue wythout bitterneſſe, is almoſt a cauſe without effects,
for he that ſhall take away gryefs and troubled fanſies from
Louers, depryueth them of the prayſe of their ſtedfaſtneſſe, and
maketh vayne the glory of their perſeuerence: Forhee is vnworthy
to beare away the price and Garland of triumph in the Conflict,
that behaueth himſelfe like a coward, and doth not obſerue the
lawes of armes and manlike dueties incident to a combat. This
Hiſtory then is a Mirrour for Loyall Louers and Chaſte Suters, and
maketh them deteſt the vnſhamefaſtneſſe of thoſe, which vpon
the firſt view do followe with might and mayne, the Gentlewoman
or Lady that gieueth them good Face, or Countenaunce whereof
any gentle heart, or mynde, nourſed in the Schoolehouſe of vertuous education, will not bee ſqueymiſhe to thoſe that ſhall by chaſte
ſalutation or other incountry, doe their curteous reuerence. This
Hiſtory alſo yeldeth contempt of them, which in their affection
forget themſelues abaſing the Generoſity of their Courages to
be reputed of fooles the true champions of loue, whoſe like are
they that deſire ſuch regarde. For the perfection of a true Louer
conſiſteth in paſſions, in ſorrows, griefes, martirdomes, or cares,
and mutch leſſe arriueth he to his deſire, by ſighes, exclamations,
Weapings, and childiſhe playnts: For ſo mutch as vertue ought
to be the bande of that indiſſoluble amity, which maketh the
vnion of the two ſeuered bodies of that Woman man, which Plato
deſcribeth, and cauſeth man to trauell for hys whole accompliſh-
ment in the true purſute of chaſte loue. In which labour truly,
fondly walked Dom Diego, thinking to finde the ſame by his
diſpayre amiddeſt the ſharpe ſolitary Deſerts of thoſe Pyrene

Mountaynes. And truely the duety of his perfect friende, did more liuely difclofe the fame (what fault fo euer he did) than all his Countenaunces, eloquent letters or amorous Meffages. In like manner a man doth not know what a treafure a true Friende is, vntill hee hath proued his excellency, fpecially where neceffity maketh him to tafte the fwetenes of futch delicate meate. For a frend being a feconde himfelfe, agreeth by a certayne naturall Sympathie and attonement to th'affections of him whom he loueth both to particpate his ioyes and pleafures, and to forrowe his aduerfity, where Fortune fhall vfe by fome mifaduentures, to fhewe hir accuftomed mobility.

THE THIRTIETH NOUELL.

A Gentleman of Siena, called Anfelmo Salimbene, curteoufly and
gently deliuereth his enemy from death. The condemned party
feeing the kinde parte of Salimbene, rendreth into his hands his
fifter Angelica, with whom he was in loue, which gratitude and
curtefie, Salimbene well markinge, moued in Confcience, woulde
not abufe hir, but for recompence tooke hir to his wyfe.

WEE do not meane here to difcouer the Sumptuofity and Magnificence of Palaces, ftately, and wonderfully to the view of men,
ne yet to reduce to memory the maruellous effectes of man's Indus-
try to builde and lay Foundations in the deepeft Chanel of the
mayne fea, ne to defcribe their ingenious Induftry, in breaking
the Craggy Mountaynes, and hardeft Rocks, to eafe the crooked
Paffages of weary waies, for Armies to marche through in acces-
fible places. Onely now do we pretend to fhewe the effects of
loue, which furmount all Opinion of common thinges, and appeare
fo miraculous as the founding, and erecting of the Colliffæi,
Colloffæi, Theatres, Amphitheatres, Pyramides, and other workes
wonderfull to the world, for that the hard indured path of hatred
and difpleafure long time begoon, and obftinately purfued wyth
ftraunge cruelty, was conuerted into loue, by th'effect of concord,
futch as I know none, but is fo mutch aftonned, as hee maye
haue good caufe to wonder, confyderyng the ftately foundations
vppon which Kinges and great Monarches haue employed the
chyefeft reuenues of their prouinces. Now lyke as ingratitude
is a vice of greateft blame and difcommendation amongs men,
euen fo Gentleneffe and Kindneffe ought to beare the title of a
moft commendable vertue. And as the Thebans were accufed of
that crime, for their great Captaynes Epaminondas and Pelopidas.
So the Plateens (contrarywife) are praifed for their folempne obferuation of the Grekes benefits, which deliuered them oute of
the Perfians bondage. And the Sicyonians beare away the pryfe
of eternall prayfe, for acknowledgyng the good turnes receiued of
Aratus, that delyuered them from the cruelty of the tyrants. And

if Philippo Maria, duke of Milan, deſerued eternal reproch for his ingratitude to his wife Beatrix, for the ſecrete killing of hir, he being enryched with hir goodes and treaſures : a barbarous Turke borne in Arabia, ſhal carry the praiſe, who being vanquiſhed in Arabia, by Baldouine, kyng of Hieruſalem, and he and his Wife taken pryſoners, and his treaſures fallen into the hands of that good king, iſſued of the Loraine bloud, who neuertheleſſe ſeeing that the Chryſtian had deliuered him, and reſtored againe his wife would not be vanquiſhed in magnificence and liberalitye, and mutch leſſe beare the name of an vnkind prince, but rather when Baldouine was ouercome of the infidels, and being retyred within a certaine city, the Admiral of Arabie, came to him in the night, and tellyng him the deuice of his companions, conueyed hym out of the City, and was hys guide vntill he ſawe hym free from peril. I haue alleaged the premyſſes, bycauſe the Hiſtory whych I purpoſe to recyte, aduoucheth two examples not Vulgare or Common, the one of very great Loue, and the other of ſutch acceptation and knowledgyng thereof, as I thought it pity the ſame ſhould lurk from the Acquayntaunce of vs Englyſh Men. And that they alone ſhould haue the Benefite thereof whych vnderſtand the Italian tongue, ſuppoſing that it ſhall bryng ſome fruy&c and commodity to this our Engliſhe Soyle, that ech Wyghte may frame their lyfe on thoſe whych in ſtraung Countries far from vs, haue lyued ver-tuouſly wythout reproch that might ſoyle or ſpotte theyr name. In Siena then (an auncient, and very noble Citty of Toſcane, which no longe time paſt was gouerned by hir Magiſtrates, and liued in hir own lawes and liberties, as the Lucquois, Piſans, and Floren-tines do) were two families very rich, noble, and the chiefe of the Citty called the Salimbenes, and Montanines, of the Race and Stock whereof, excellent men in their Common wealth haue des-cended, very good and expert Souldiers for condu&e of Armies. Thoſe two houſes in the beginning were ſo great freendes, and frequented ſutch loue and familiarity, as it ſeemed they had bene but one houſe and bloude, dayly vſinge eche others company, and banketting one another. But Italy in all times being as it were a Store houſe of troubles, and a very marte of ſedition, bandes, and parcialities, ſpecially of ciuill warres in euery Citty, it coulde

not be that Siena fhoulde alone enioy hir liberty in peace, and
accorde of Cittizens, and vaunt hir felfe to bee free from knowledge of particular debate. For of warres fhee had good experience
againft the Florentines, who by long remembraunce haue don
what they coulde to make hir fubiect vnto them. Nowe the
caufe of that difcorde rofe euen by them which kept the Cittizens
in vnity and concord, and was occafioned by thofe 2 houfes the
nobleft, and moft puiffant of their common wealth. It is not
vnknowne to any man, that antiquity ordayned it to be peculiar
for nobility, to trayne vp there children in huntinge, afwell
to bolden and Nofell theym in daungers, as to make them ftronge,
and accuftomed in trauayle, and to force them fhun the delicate
lyfe and great Idlenes which accompany honorable houfes, and
thofe of gentle bloud, forfomutch as by the purfuite of Beaftes,
fleyghts of warre bee obferued : the Hounds be the fquare battell,
the Greyhoundes be the flanquarts and Wynges to follow the enimy,
the horfeman ferueth to gieue the Chace, when the Game fpeedeth
to couert, the Hornes be the Trumpets to founde the Chafe and
Retire, and for incouragement of the Dogges to run. To be fhort,
it feemeth a very Campe in battayle, ordayned for the pleafure
and paffetyme of noble youth. Neuertheleffe, by hunting diuers
miffefortunes doe arife, and fundry daungers haue happened by
the fame. Meleager loft his Lyfe for the victory of the wyld Bore
of Callydonia, Cephalus was flaine for kylling his deare beloued
Pocris, and Acaftus was accurfed for murdering the King's fonne
of whome he was the Tutour. William Rufus, one of our Englyfh
Kings, the fon of the Conquerour, was killed with an Arrow in the
New Forreft by a French Gentleman called Walter Tyrel, as he was
purfuing the Harte. Other hiftories reporte dyuers peryls chaunced
in hunting, but yet the fame worthy to be cheryfhed, frequented
and vfed by good aduife and moderate paftyme. So the huntinge
of the wylde Bore defyled the City of Siena, with the bloud of hir
owne Citizens, when the Salimbenes and Montanines vppon a daye
in an affembled company, incountring vpon a greate and fierce Bore,
toke hym by force of men and Beaftes. When they had don, as
they were banketting and communing of the nimbleneffe of their
dogs, ech man praifing his owne, as hauing done befte, there

rofe greate debate amongs them [vpon that matter], and proceeded
fo farre, as fondly they began to reuile one another with words, and
from taunting termes to earneft blowes, wherewith diuers in that
fkirmifh were hurt on both fides: In the end the Salimbenes had
the worffe, and one of the principall flayne in the place, which
appalled the reft, not that they were difcoraged, but attending
time and feafon of reuenge. This hatred fo ftrangely kindled
betwene both partes, that by lyttle and lyttle, after many combats
and ouerthrowes of eyther fide, the loffe lyghted vpon the Montanines, who with their wealth and rycheffe were almoft brought to
nothing, and thereby the rygour and Choler of the Salimbenes
appeafed, none being able to refift them, and in fpace of time
forgot all iniuries. The Montanines alfo that remayned at Siena,
liued in quyet, wythoute chalenge or quarell of their aduerfaries,
howbeit mutuall talke and haunt of others company vtterly
furceafed. And to fay the truth, there were almoft none to
quarell wythall, for the whole Bloude and Name of the Montanines
refted in one alone, called Charles the Sonne of Thomas Montanine, a young man fo honeft and well brought vp as any then
in Siena, who had a fyfter, that for beauty, grace, curtefy and
honefty, was comparable with the beft in all Thofcane. This
poore young Gentleman had no great reuenue, for that the patri-
monie of his predeceffors was wafted in charges for entertainement of Souldiers in the time of the hurly burly and debates aforefaid. A good parte alfo was confifcate to the Chamber of Siena
for trefpaffes and forfaitures committed: with the remayne he
fuftained his family, and indifferently maintained hys porte foberly
within his owne houfe, keping his fifter in decent and moderate
order. The Maiden was called Angelica, a Name of trouth, without offence to other, due to hir. For in very deede in hir were
harbored the vertue of Curtefy and Gentleneffe, and was fo wel
inftructed and nobly brought vp, as they which loued not the
Name or race of hir, could not forbeare to commend hir, and wyfhe
theyr owne daughters to be hir lyke. In futch wife as one of hir
chiefeft foes was fo fharpely befet with hir vertue and beauty, as
he loft his quiet fleepe, and luft to eate and drinke. His name
was Anfelmo Salimbene, who woulde wyllinglye haue made fute

to marry hir, but the difcord paft, quite mortified his defire, fo
foone as he had deuifed the plot wythin his brayne and fanfie.
Notwithftanding it was impoffible that the louer fo lyuely grauen
and roted in his mind, could eafily be defaced. For if once in a
day he had not feene hir, his heart did fele the torments of tofting
flames, and wifhed that the hunting of the Bore, had neuer decaied
a family fo excellent, to the intent he myght haue matched himfelf with hir, whome none other could difplace out of his remembraunce, that was one of the rycheft Gentlemen and of greateft
power in Siena. Now for that he durft not difcouer his amorous
griefe to any perfon, was the chiefeft caufe that martired moft
his hearte, and for the auncient feftred malice of thofe two families, he defpayred for euer, to gather either floure or fruict of that
affection, prefuppofing that Angelica would neuer fixe hir Loue
on him, for that his Parents were the caufe of the defaite and
ouerthrow of the Montanine houfe. But what? There is nothing
durable vnder the heauens. Both good and euyll haue theyr reuo-
lution in the gouernment of humane affayres. The amityes and
hatredes of Kynges and Prynces, be they fo hardened, as commonly
in a Moment hee is not feene to be a hearty Friende, that lately
was a cruell Foe, and fpyred naught elfe but the ruine of his
Aduerfary ? Wee fee the variety of Humayne chaunces, and then
doe iudge at eye what great fimplicity it is to ftay and fettle certayne, and infallible iudgement vppon man's vnftayed doings. He
that erft gouerned a king, and made all things to tremble at his
word, is fodaynely throwne downe, and dyeth a fhamefull death.
In like forte, another whych looketh for his owne vndoinge, feeth
himfelfe aduaunced to hys eftate agayne, by reuenge ouer his
Enimies. Calir Baffa gouerned whilom the great Mahomet, that
wan the Empire of Conftantinople, who attempted nothing without the aduice of that Baffa. But vpon the fodayne he faw him
felfe reiected, and the next day ftrangled by commaundement of
him, which fo greatly honoured him, and without iuft caufe did
him to a death fo cruell. Contrarywife Aragon the Tartarian
entring Armes againft his Vncle Tangodor Caui, when hee was
vpon the Poynct to lofe his Lyfe for his rebellion, and was conueyed
into Armenia to be executed there, was refcued by certayne Tar-

tarians the houfhold feruaunts of his dead vncle, and afterwards Proclaymed King of Tartary about the year 1285. The example of the Empreffe Adaleda is of no leffe credit than the former, who being fallen into the hands of Beranger the Vfurper of the Empyre efcaped his fury and cruelty by flight, and in the ende maried to Otho the firfte, fawe hir wrong reuenged vpon Beranger and all his Race by hir Sonne Otho the fecond. I aduouch thefe Hyftories to proue the mobility of fortune, and the chaunge of worldly chaunces, to th'ende you may fee that the very fame mifery which followed Charles Montanine hoyfted him aloft agayne, and when he looked for leaft fuccour, he faw deliueraunce at hand. Now to profecute our Hyftory: know yee that while Salimbene by little and little pined for loue of Angelica, whereof fhee was ignoraunt and careleffe, and albeit fhee curteoufly rendred health to him, when fometimes in his amorous fit he beheld hir at a Window, yet for al that fhee neuer fo mutch as gueffed the thoughts of hir louing enimy. During thefe haps it chaunced that a rich Cittizen of Siena, hauing a ferme adioyning to the Lands of Montanine, defirous to encreafe his Patrimony, and annexe the fame vnto his owne, and knowing that the yong Gentleman wanted many thinges, moued him to fel his inheritaunce, offring hym for it in ready money, a M. Ducates, Charles which of al the wealth and fubftaunce left him by his auncefter, had no more remaynyng but that countrey Ferme, and a Palace in the City (fo the rich Italians of ech City, terme their houfes,) and with that lytle lyued honeftly, and maintained his fifter fo wel as he could, refufed flatly to difpoffeffe himfelfe of the portion, that renewed vnto him the happy memory of thofe that had ben the chiefe of all the Common Wealth. The couetous wretch feeing himfelfe fruftrate of his pray, conceiued futch rancor againft Montanine, as he purpofed by right or wrong to make him not only to forfait the fame, but alfo to lofe his lyfe, following the wicked defire of tirannous Iefabell, that made Naboth to be ftonned to death to extort and wrongfully get his vineyard. About that time for the quarels and common dyfcordes raigning throughout Italy, the Nobility were not affured of fafety in their Countreis, but rather the common fort and rafcall number, were the chief rulers and gouerners of the common wealth, whereby the greateſt part of the Nobility or thoſe of beſte authority being baniſhed, the villanous band, and groſeſt kind of common people made a law (like to the Athenians in the time of Solon) that all perſons of what degree and condition ſo euer they were, which practized by himſelfe or other meanes the reſtablyſhing or reuocation of ſutch as were baniſhed out of their Citye, ſhould loſe and forfaite the ſumme of M. Florens, and hauing not wherewith to pay the ̃con-dempnation, their head ſhould remaine for gage. A law no doubt very iuſt and righteous, ſcenting rather of the barbarous cruelty of the Gothes and Vandales, than of true chriſtians, ſtopping the retire of innocents exiled for particular quarels of Citizens incited one againſt another, and rigorouſly rewarding mercy and curteſy, with execution of cruelty incomparable. This Citizen then pur-poſed to accuſe Montanine for offending againſt the law, bicauſe otherwiſe he could not purchaſe his entent, and the ſame was eaſy inough for him to compaſſe, by reaſon of his authority and eſtimation in the Citye: for the Endytemente and plea was no ſooner red and giuen, but a number of poſt knightes appeared to depoſe againſt the poore Gentleman, to beare witneſſe that he had treſpaſſed the Lawes of the Countrey, and had ſought meanes to introduce the baniſhed, with intent to kyll the gouerners, and to place in ſtate thoſe factious, that were the cauſe of the Italian troubles. The myſerable Gentleman knewe not what to do, ne how to defend himſelf. There were againſt him the Moone and the VII. ſtarres, the ſtate of the City, the Proctor and Iudge of the Courte, the wytneſſes that gaue euidence, and the law whych con-dempned him. He was ſent to Pryſon, ſentence was pronounced againſt him with ſutch expedition, as he had no leyſure to con-ſider his affayres. There was no man, for feare to incurre the diſpleaſures of the Magiſtrates, that durſt open hys mouth to ſpeake or make ſute for hys delyueraunce. Like as the moſt part of fryendes in theſe dayes reſembling the crow, that flyeth not but after carrian to gorge his rauenous Crop, and ſutch friends doe viſite the houſe of the fryend but for profit, reuerencyng him ſo long as he is in proſperitye, accordyng to the Poet's com-playnt.

Like as the pureſt gold in fieri flames is tried,
Euen ſo is fayth of fryends in hard eſtate deſcried.
If hard miſſehap doth thee affray,
Ech of thy friends do flie away,
And he which erſt full friendly ſemde to thee,
A friend no more to thy poor ſtate is hec.

And ſimple Wyghtes ought not to bee afrayde, and thynke amyſs if Fryendes doe flee away, ſith Prynces and great Lords incurre ſutch hap and Fortune. The great leader of the Romayne Armies, Pompeius, the honor of the people and Senate of Rome, what companion had he to flee with hym? Whych of his auncient friends toke paine to reſcue and delyuer him from his Enimyes hands which did purſue him? A king of Ægipt which had known and found this good Romane Prynce a kind and gentle fryend, was he that killed him, and ſent his head to his Victor and unſatible greedy gutte Iulius Cæſar, falſifying his promiſed fayth, and forgetting his receiued pleaſures. Amongs all the comforts which this pore Siena Gentleman found, although but a curſſed Traitor, was thys vnfaithfull and peſtiferous Camæleon, who came and offred him al the pleaſure and kindneſſe he was able to do. But the varlet attended conuenient tyme to make him taſte his poyſon, and to let him ſee by effect, how dangerous a thing it is to be il neighbored, hoping after the condempnation of Montanine he ſhould at pleaſure purchaſe the Lordſhippe, after whych with ſo open mouth he gaped. Ouer whom he had hys wyll: for two or three dayes after the recitall of the endytement, and giuing of the euydence, Charles was condempned, and his fine ſeſſed at M. Florins to be payed within xv. dayes, vntyl whych time to remaine in Pryſon. And for default of ſutch payment to looſe his heade, bicauſe he had infringed the Lawes, and broken the Statutes of the Senate. This ſentence was very difficult for poor Montanine to digeſt, who ſaw all his goodes like to be diſpoyled and confiſcate, complayning ſpecially the fortune of fayre Angelica his ſiſter, whych all the tyme of the impryſonment of hir deare brother, neuer went out of the houſe, ne ceaſed to weepe and lamente the hard fortune whereinto their family was lyke to fall by that new mifchaunce: "Alas," faid the fayre curteous damfel, "will the heauens never be appeafed but continually extend their wrathe vpon our deplored family, and fhal our miffehaps neuer ceafe? Had it not bene more tollerable for our confumed bloude, that the diffentions paft, had been tried by dent of fword, than to fee the prefent innocency of the young Gentleman my brother in daunger to be innocently accufed and put to death, through the vniuftice of thofe, which beare mortal malice to noble bloud, and glory in depryuation of the whole remembrance of the fame? O dampnable ftate that mufte hale the guiltleffe to the gibet and irreuocable fentence of thofe iudges remaining in a city, which men cal free, albeit a confufed multitude hath the vpper hande, and may fo bee, that Nature hath produced them to treade vnder foote noble Wightes for their Offences. Ah dear Brother, I fee well what is the caufe. If thou hadft not that lytle lordfhyp in the Countrey, and Pryncely Houfe in the City, no man would haue enuied thine eftate, or could haue charged thee with any Crime, which I would to God, thou badft not onely enterpryfed, but alfo broughte to paffe, to the intent thou mighteft haue ben re-uenged of the wrong which thefe cankred Carles ordinarily do vnto my Noble bloud. But what reafon is it that marchants and artificers, or the fonnes of villaines fhould rule a common Wealth? O happy Countreis where kings giue Lawes, and Princes fee by proued fight, thofe perfons which refemble them, and in their places beare the fway. And O unhappy wee, that be the flaues of a waiwarde ftate, peruerted by corruption. Why dyd our pre-deceffors minde to ftablyfh any lyberty at al, to thruft the fame into the confufed gouernment of the commons of our Countrey? We haue ftil the Frenchman at our tayle, or the people of our higheft Bifhop, or elfe thofe crafty Florentines, we be the common pray of al thofe that lift to follow the haunt, and that which is our extreameft mifery, we make oure felues the very flaues of them that of right ought to be reputed the vileft amongs us al. Ah deare Brother, that thy wretched tyme is come, the onely hope of our decayed family. Thou'hadeft neuer bene committed to Warde, had not thy falfe affured foes bene affure of witneffe to con-dempne thee. Ah that my life mighte raunfome thine, and re-

deme agayn thyne eſtate and ſuccor, thou ſhouldeſt be ſure that
forthwith Angelica would prepare hirſelf to bee the pray of thoſe
hungry rauenyng Wolues, which bleat and bellow after thy Lands
and Lyfe." Whyle this fayre Damſell of Siena in this ſort dyd torment hir ſelf, poore Montanine, ſeeinge that he was brought to
the laſt extremity of his deſired hope, as eche man naturally doth
ſeke meanes to prolong his lyfe, knowing that all other help fayled for hys delyueraunce except he ſold his land, aſwel to ſatiſfy
the fine, as to preuayle in the reſt of his Affaires, ſent one of the
gailers to that worſhipfull uſurer the cauſe of hys Calamity, to
offer him his Land for the pryce and ſum of a м. Ducates. The
pernicious and trayterous villain, ſeeing that Montanine was at
his mercy, and ſtode in the water up to the very throte, and knew
no more what to do, as if already he had tryumphed of hys life
and Land ſo greatly coueted, anſwered him in this manner : " My
friend thou ſhalt ſay to Charles Montanine, that not long ago I
would willingly haue giuen him a good Summe of Money for his
Ferme, but ſithens that tyme I haue imployed my Money to ſome
better profit : and albeit I was in minde to buy it, I would be loth to
give aboue 7. c. Florins, being aſſured that it cannot be ſo commodious, as my Money is able to bring yearely Gayne into my Purſe."
See how Auarice is the Pickpurſe of ſecret and hidden gayne, and
the very Whirlepoole of Honeſty, and Conſcience, couetinge nought
els but by vnrighteous Pray of other mens goods, to accumulate
and heape together. The aboundance whereof bringeth no greater
good hap vnto the gluttonous Owner, but rather the minde of
ſutch is more miſerable, and carryeth therewithall more decreaſe
of quiet, than increaſe of filthy muck. The couetous man beareth
no loue but to his Treaſure, nor exerciſeth charity but vpon his
Coaſers, who, than he would be diſpoſſeſſed thereof, had rather
ſell the life of his naturall Father. This deteſtable Villayne hauing ſometimes offered м. Ducates to Charles for his Enherytaunce,
will now doe ſo no more, aſpiring the totall Ruine of the Montanine Family. Charles aduertiſed of his minde, and amazed for
the Counſels decree, well ſaw that all thinges contraried hys hope
and expectation, and that he muſt needes dye to ſatiſfie the
exceſſiue and couetous Luſt of the Cormerant, whoſe malice hee

knew to bee fo vehement, as none durft offer him Money, by
reafon of the vnhappy defire of this neuer contented Varlet: For
which confideration throughly refolued to dye, rather than to
leaue hys poore Sifter helpleffe, and without reliefe, and rather
than he would agree to the bargayne tending to his fo great loffe
and difadvauntage, and to the Tirannous dealing of the wicked
Tormentor of hys Lyfe, feeing alfo that all meanes to purge and
auerre his innocency, was taken from him, the finall decree of the
Iudges being already paffed, he began to difpofe himfelfe to
repentaunce and faluation of his Soule, making complaynte of his
Mifhaps in thys manner.

To what hath not the heauens hatefull bin,
Since for the eafe of man they weaue futch woe?
By diuers toyles they lap our croffes in
With cares and griefes, whereon our mifchiefes groe:
The bloudy hands and Sword of mortall foe,
Doe fearch mine euill, and would deftroy me quite,
Through heynous hate and hatefull heaped spite.

Wherefore come not the fatall fifters three,
That draw the line of life and death by right?
Com furies all, and make an ende of mee,
For from the world, my fprite would take his flight.
Why comes not nowe fowle Gorgon full in fight,
And Typhon's head, that deepe in hell remaynes,
For to torment the filly foules in paynes?

It better were for mee to feele your force,
Than this miffehap of murdring enuy'es rage,
By curffed meanes and fall vpon my corfe,
And worke my ruine amid my flouring age:
For if I were difpatch'de in this defire,
The feare were gone, of blacke infernall fire.

O Gods of Seas, and caufe of bluftring winde,
Thou Æolus and Neptune to I fay,
Why did you let my Barke futch fortune finde,

That fafe to fhore I came by any way?
Why brake yee not, agaynft fome Rocke or Bay,
The keele, the fterne, or els blew downe the Maft,
By whofe large fayles through furging feas I paft?

Had thefe things hapt, I had not feene this houre,
The houfe of dole where wofull fprites complayne,
Nor vferers on me had vfde futch power,
Nor I had feene depaynted in difdayne,
The God of care, with whom dead Ghofts remayne.
Who howles and Skrekes in hollow trees and holes,
Where Charon raygnes among condemned foules.

Ah, ah, fince hap will worke my wretched end,
And that my ruine by iudgement is decreed:
Why doth not happe futch happy fortune fend,
That I may lead with me the man in deede,
That ftaynd his fayth, and faylde me at my neede,
For gayne of golde, as vferers do God knowes,
Who cannot fpare the dropping of their nofe?

I fhould haue flayne the flaue that feru'd me fo,
O God forbid my hands were brued in blood,
Should I defire the harme of friend or foe?
Nay better were to wifhe mine en'my good:
For if my death I throughly vnderftood,
I fhould make fhort the courfe I haue to run,
Since reft is got when worldly toyle is done.

Alas, alas, my chiefeft way is this,
A guiltleffe death to fuffer as I can,
So fhall my foule be fure of heauen's bliffe,
And good renoume fhall reft behinde me than,
And body fhall take end where it began,
And fame fhall fly before me, ere I flit
Vnto the Gods, where Ioue in throne doth fit.

O God conuert, from vyce to vertue now,
The heart of him that falſeth fayth wyth me,
And chaunge his minde and mend his maners throw,
That he his fault and fowle offence may ſee,
For death ſhall make my fame immortall bee:
And whiles the Sunne which in the heauens doth ſhine,
The ſhame is his, and honor ſhall be mine.

Alas, I mourne not for my ſelfe alone,
Nor for the fame of my Forefathers olde,
'Tys Angelike, that cauſeth me to mone,
'Tys ſhe that filles my breſt with fanſies colde,
'Tys ſhee more worth, than was the fliece of golde,
That mooues my minde and breedes ſutch paſſions ſtraunge,
As in my ſelfe I feele a wonderous chaunge.

Haue pitty Lord of hir and mee this day,
Since deſtny thus hath ſundred vs in ſpite,
O ſuffer not hir vertues to decay,
But let hir take in friendſhip ſutch delite,
That from hir breſt all vice be baniſht quite:
And let hir like as did hir noble race,
When I poore man am deade, and out of place.

Alas my hand would write theſe wofull lines,
That feeble ſprite denyes for want of might,
Wherefore my heart in breſt conſumes and pines,
With deepe deſires, that far is from man's ſight,
But God he ſees myne innocencie and right,
And knowes the cauſe of myne Accuſer ſtill,
Who ſeekes my bloud to haue on mee his will.

When Charles thus complayned himſelf, and throughly was
determined to dy, great pitty it was to ſee how fayre Angelica
did rent hir Face, and teare hir golden Locks, when ſhe ſaw how
impoſſible it was to ſaue hir obſtinate brother from the cruel

fentence pronounced vpon him, for whom fhe had imployed all hir wits and fayre fpeach, to perfwade the neereft of hir Kin to make fute. Thus refted fhe alone ful of futch heauineffe and vexation as they can think which fee themfelues depriued of things that they efteeme moft dere. But of one thing I can wel affure you, that if ill fortune had permitted that Charles fhould haue bin put to death, the gentle damfel alfo had breathed forth the final gafp of hir forowful life, yeldinge therewithall the laft end of the Montanine race and family. What booteth it to hold proceffe of long difcourfe? Beholde the laft day is come deferred by the Iudges, whereupon he muft eyther fatiffie the fine, or dye the next day after like a rebel and Traytor againft the ftate, without any of his kin making fute or meane for his deliueraunce: albeit they vifited the fayre mayden, and comforted hir in that hir wretched ftate, inftructing hir how fhee fhould gouerne hir felfe patiently to fuffer things remedileffe. Angelica accompanied with hir kin, and the maidens dwelling by, that were hir companions, made the ayre to found with outcries and waymentings, and fhe hir felfe exclaymed like a woman deftraught of Wits, whofe plaints the multitude affifted with like eiulations and outcries, wayling the fortune of the yong gentleman, and forowfull to fee the mayden in daunger to fal into fome mifhap. As thefe things were thus bewayled, it chaunced about nine of the clocke at night, that Anfelmo Salimbene, he whom we haue fayd to be furprifed with the loue of Angelica, returning out of the Countrey, where he had remayned for a certayne time, and paffing before the houfe of his Lady, according to his cuftome, heard the voyce of women and maydens which mourned for Montanine, and therewithall ftayd: the chiefeft caufe of his ftay was, for that he faw go forth out of the Pallace of hys Angelica, diuers Women making Moane, and Lamentation: wherefore he demaunded of the neyghbors what noyfe that was, and whether any in thofe Quarters were dead or no. To whom they declared at length, al that which yee haue heard before. Salimbene hearing this ftory, went home to his houfe, and being fecretly entred into his chamber, began difcourfe with himfelfe vpon that accident, and fantafying a thoufand things in his heade, in the ende thought that Charles

fhould not fo be caft away, were he iuftly or innocently condempned, and for the only refpect of his fifter, that fhe might
not bee left deftitute of the Goods, and Inheritaunce.   Thus difcourfing diuers things, at length he fayd: "I were a very fimple
perfon nowe to reft in doubt, fith Fortune is more curious of my
felicity than I could wifhe, and feeketh the effect of my defires,
when leaft of all I though vpon them.   For behold, Montanine
alone is left of all the mortall enimies of our houfe, whych to morrow openly fhall lofe his head like a rebell and feditious perfon,
vpon whofe Auncefters, in him fhall I be reuenged, and the quarell
betweene our two Families, fhall take ende, hauinge no more
caufe to feare renuing of difcorde, by any that can defcend from
him.   And who fhall let mee then from inioying hir, whom I doe
loue, hir brother being dead, and his goods confifcate to the
Seigniory, and fhe without all Maynetenaunce, and Reliefe, except
the ayde of hir onely beauty and curtefie?   What maynetenaunce
fhall fhe haue, if not by the loue of fome honeft Gentleman, that
for hys pleafure may fupport bir, and haue pitty vppon the loffe
of fo excellent beauty?   Ah Salimbene, what haft thou fayd?
Haft thou already forgotten that a Gentleman for that only caufe
is efteemed aboue al other, whofe glorious facts ought to fhine
before the brightneffe of thofe that force theymfelues to followe
vertue?   Art not thou a Gentleman borne, and Bred in noble houfe,
Iffued from the Loyns of gentle and noble Parentes?   Is it ignoraunt vnto thee, that it pertayneth vnto a noble and gentle heart,
to reuenge receyued Iniuries himfelfe, without feeking ayde of
other or elfe to pardon them by vfing clemency and princely
curtefie, burying all defire of vengeaunce vnder the Toumbe of
eternall obliuion?   And what greater glory can man acquire, than
by vanquifhing himfelfe, and chaftifing his affections and rage,
to bynde him which neuer thought to receyue pleafure or benefit
at his hand?   It is a thing which exceedeth the common order of
nature, and fo is it meete and requifite, that the moft excellent
doe make the effects of their excellency appeare, and feeke meanes
for the immortality of their remembraunce.   The great Dictator
Cæfar was more prayfed for pardoning hys enimies, and for fhewing himfelfe curteous and eafie to be fpoken to, than for fubdu-

inge the braue and valiaunt Galles and Britons, or vanquiſhing
the mighty Pompee. Dom Roderico Viuario, the Spaniard, although he might haue bene reuenged vpon Dom Pietro, king of
Aragon, for his infidelity, bicauſe he went about to hinder his
voyage agaynſt the Saracens at Grenado, yet woulde not Puniſhe
or Raunſome him, but taking him Pryſoner in the Warres, ſuffred
him to goe without any Tribute, or any exaction of him and his
Realme. The more I followe the example of mighty Perſonages
in thinges that be good, the more notorious and wonderful ſhall I
make my ſelfe in their rare and noble deedes. And not willing to
forget a wrong done vnto me, whereof may I complayne of Montanine? What thinge hath hee euer done agaynſt me or mine?
And albeit his Predeceſſors were enimies to our Family, they haue
therefore borne the penaunce, more harde than the ſinne deſerued.
And truly I ſhould be afrayde, that God would ſuffer me to tumble into ſome miſhap, if ſeeing one afflicted, I ſhould reioyce in
his affliction, and take by his decay an argument of ioy and pleaſure. No, no, Salimbene is not of minde that ſutch fond Imagination ſhould Bereue good will to make hymſelfe a Freende, and
to gayne by liberality and curteſie hir, which for hir only vertue
deſerueth a greater lord than I. Being aſſured, that there is no
man (except he were diſpoyled of all good nature and humanity)
ſpecially bearing the loue to Angelica, that I do, but he would
be ſory to ſee hir in ſutch heauineſſe and deſpayre, and would
attempt to deliuer hir from ſutch dolorous griefe. For if I loue
hir as I do in deede, muſt not I likewiſe loue all that which ſhe
earneſtly loueth, as him that is nowe in daunger of death for a
ſimple fine of a thouſand Florens? That my heart doe make ap-
peere what the loue is, which maketh me Tributary and Subiect to
fayre Angelica, and that eche man may knowe, that furious loue
hath vanquiſht kings and great monarches, it behoueth not me to
be abaſhed, if I which am a man and ſubiect to paſſions, ſo well
as other, doe ſubmit my ſelfe to the ſeruice of hir, who I am
aſſured is ſo vertuous as euen very neceſſity cannot force hir to
forget the houſe, whereof ſhe tooke hir originall. Vaunt thy
ſelfe then O Angelica, to haue forced a heart of it ſelfe impregnable, and giuen him a wound which the ſtouteſt Lads might

fooner haue depriued of lyfe, than put him out of the way of his
gentle kinde: and thou, Montanine, thinke, that if thou wilt thy
felfe, thou winneft to day fo hearty a frende, as only death fhall
feparate the vnion of vs twayne, and of all our pofterity. It is I,
nay it is I my felfe, that fhall excell thee in duety, poynting the
way for the wifeft, to get honor, and violently compel the mooued
myndes of thofe that be our aduerfaries, defiring rather vainely to
forgo myne own life, than to giue ouer the vertuous conceipts,
which be already grifted in my minde." After this long difcourfe
feeing the tyme required dilligence, hee tooke a thoufand Ducats,
and went to the Treafurer of the fines, deputed by the ftate, whom
he founde in his office, and fayde vnto him : "I haue brought you
fir, the Thoufande Ducates, which Charles Montanine is bounde
to pay for his deliueraunce. Tell them, and gieue him an acquit-
taunce, that prefently hee may come forth." The Treaforer woulde
haue giuen him the reft, that exceeded the Summe of a Thoufand
Florens: but Salimbene refufed the fame, and receyuing a letter
for his difcharge, he fent one of his Seruaunts therewithal to the
chiefe Gayler, who feeing that the Summe of his condemnation was
payd, immediately deliuered Montanine out of the Prifon where he
was faft fhut, and fettered with great, and weyghty Giues. Charles
thinckinge that fome Frier had bin come to confeffe him, and that
they had fhewed him fome mercy to doe hym to death in Prifon,
that abroade in open fhame of the world he might not deface the
Noble houfe whereof he came, was at the firft fight aftonned,
but hauing prepared himfelfe to die, prayfed God, and befought
him to vouchfafe not to forget him in the forrowful paffage,
wherein the ftouteft and coragious many times be faynt and in-
conftaunt. He recommended his Soule, he prayed forgieueneffe
of his finnes: and aboue all, he humbly befought the goodneffe
of God, that it would pleafe him to haue pitty vpon his Sifter, and
to deliuer hir from all Infamy and difhonor. When he was caried
out of Pryfon, and brought before the Chiefe Gayler, fodaynely
his Giues were difcharged from his Legges, and euery of the ftanders by looked merily vppon hym, without fpeakinge any Woorde
that might affray hym. That Curtefie vnlooked for, made hym
attende fome better thynge, and affured hym of that whych

before by any meanes hee durfte not thyncke. And hys expectation was not deceiued. For the Gayler fayde vnto hym: "Bee of
good Cheare Sir, for beholde the letters of your difcharge, wherefore you may goe at liberty whether you lift." In faying fo, he
opened the Pryfon, and licenced Montanine to departe, praying
him not to take in ill part his intreaty and hard impryfonment,
for that hee durft doe none other, the State of the City hauing fo
enioyned hym. May not ech Wyght now behold how that the
euents of loue be diuers from other paffions of the mind? How
could Salimbene haue fo charitably deliuered Montanine, the
hatred beyng fo long tyme rooted between the two houfes, if fome
greate occafion whych hath no name in Loue, had not altred his
Nature, and extinguifhed hys affection? It is meritoryous to fuccour them whome we neuer faw before, fith nature moueth vs to
doe well to them that be lyke our felues. But faith furmounteth
there, where the very naturall inclynation feeleth it felf conftrayned
and feeth that to be broken, whych obftynately was purpofed to
be kept in mynde. The graces, gentleneffe, Beauty, mild behauior and allurement of Angelica, had greater force ouer Salimbene, than the humility of hir Brother, although he had kneeled
a hundred tymes before him. But what heart is fo brute, but
may be made tractable and Mylde, by the Contemplation of a
thyng fo rare, as the excellent Beauty of that Siena Mayden, and
woulde not humble it felfe to acquyre the good graces of fo perfect a Damfel? I wyll neuer accufe man for beyng in Loue wyth
a fayre and vertuous Woman, nor efteeme hym a flaue, whych
painefully ferueth a fobre Mayden, whofe heart is fraught wyth
honefte affections, and Mynd wyth defyre tending to good ende.
Well worthy of blame is he to be deemed whych is in loue wyth
the outeward hew, and prayfeth the Tree onely layden with floures,
without regard to the fruict, whych maketh it worthye of commendation. The young maiden muft needes refemble the floure
of the Spryng time, vntill by hir conftancy, modefty, and chaftity
fhe hath vanquifhed the concupifcence of the flefh, and brought
forth the hoped fruicte of a Vertue and Chaftity not Common.
Otherwyfe, fhee fhall bee lyke the inrolled Souldyer, whofe valyance hys only mind doth wytnes, and the offer whych he maketh

to hym that doth regifter his name in the mufter bookes. But
when the effect of feruyce is ioyned wyth his attempt, and proofe
belyeth not hys promyfe, then the Captain imbraceth him, and
aduaunceth him, as a glaffe for his affaires from that time forth.
The lyke of Dames hauing paffed the affaults and refifted the
attempts of theyr affaylants which be honeft, not by force being
not requyred, but inclyned by ther owne nature, and the dyligence
of theyr chaft and inuincyble heart. But turne we againe vnto
our purpofe, Montanine, when he was delyuered, forthwyth wente
home to hys houfe, to comfort hir, whom he was more than fure
to be in great diftreffe and heauineffe for his fake, and whych
had fo mutch neede of comfort as he had, to take his reft. He
came to the gate of his Pallace (where beyng knowne that it was
Montanine) his fifter by any meanes coulde not bee made to
beleue the fame: fo impoffible feeme thynges vnto vs, which we
moft defyre. They were all in doubte, lyke as wee reade that
they were when S. Peter efcaped Herod's Pryfon by the Angel's
meanes. When Angelica was affured that it was hir Brother,
fobbes wer layde afide, fighes were caft away, and heauy weepings conuerted into teares of ioy, fhe went to imbrace and kiffe
hir Brother, praifing GOD for hys delyuerance, and making
accompt that he had ben raifed from death to lyfe, confidering
his ftoutnes of minde rather bent to dye than to forgo his Land,
for fo fmal a pryce. The Dames that wer kin vnto hym, and
tarried there in Company of the maiden half in difpayre, leaft by
difpayre and fury fhee might fall into outrage therby to put hir
lyfe in peril, with all expedition aduertifed their hufbands of
Montanine's Lyberty, not looked for, who repayred thither, as wel
to reioyce with him in his ioy and good fortune, as to make their
excufe, for that they had not trauayled to ryd him from that
mifery. Charles whych cared nothing at al for thofe mouth
bleffings, diffembled what he thought, thanking them neuertheleffe for their vifitation and good remembrance they had of hym,
for vifiting and comforting his fifter which honor, he eftemed no
leffe than if they had imployed the fame vpon his owne perfon.
Their friends and kinsfolk being departed, and affured that none
of them had payde his ranfome, hee was wonderfully aftonned

and the greater was his gryef for that he could not tell what hee was, whych withoute requefte, had made fo gentle a proofe of his lyberality: if he knew nothing, farre more ignoraunte was his fifter, forfomutch as fhe dyd thinke, that he had changed his mind, and that the horrour of death had made him fel his countrey inheritance, to hym whych made the firft offer to buy the fame: but either of them deceyued of their thought went to bed. Montanine refted not all the Nyght, hauyng ftill before his eyes, the vnknowne image of hym that had delyuered him. His bed ferued his turne to none other purpofe, but as a large field or fome long alley within a Wood, for walkes to make difcourfe of hys mynde's conceipts, fometimes remembryng one, fometimes another, without hitting the blanke and namyng of him that was his deliuerer, vnto whome he confeffed him felfe to owe hys feruice and duety fo long as hee lyued. And when hee faw the day begyn to appeare and that the Mornyng, the Vauntcurrour of the day, fummoned Apollo to harneffe hys Horffe to begynne his courfe in our Hemifphere, he rofe and went to the Chamberlaine or Treafurer, futch as was deputed for receypt of the Fines, feffed by the State, whom he faluted, and receyuing lyke falutation, he prayed hym to fhewe hym fo mutch pleafure as to tell hym the parties name, that was fo Lyberall to fatyffie his fine due in the Efchequer of the State. To whome the other aunfwered: "None other hath caufed thy delyueraunce (O Montanine) but a certain perfon of the World, whofe Name thou mayft eafily geffe, to whome I gaue an acquittance of thyne impryfonmente, but not of the iufte fumme, bycaufe hee gaue me a Thoufand Ducates for a Thoufand Florens, and woulde not receyue the ouerplus of the debte, whych I am readye to delyuer thee wyth thyne acquyttaunce." "I haue not to doe wyth the Money" (fayd Charles) "onely I pray you to tell me the name of him that hath don me thys great curtefy, that hereafter I may acknowledge him to be my Friend." "It is" (fayd the Chamberlayne) "Anfelmo Salimbene, who is to bee commended and prayfed aboue all thy parents and kinne, and came hither very late to bryng the Money, the furplufage whereof, beholde here it is." "God forbid" (fayd Montaine) "that I fhould take awaye that, whych fo happily was brought hither to rid me out of payne."

And fo went away wyth his acquittance, his mind charged with
a numbre of fanfies for the fact don by Salimbene. Being at
home at his houfe, he was long time ftayed in a deepe confideration, defirous to know the caufe of that gentle parte, proceeding from him whofe Parents and Auncefters were the capitall
Enimies of his race. In the end lyke one rifyng from a found
fleepe, he called to mynd, that very many times he had feene
Anfelmo with attentiue eye and fixed looke to behold Angelica,
and in eying hir uery louyngly, he paffed euery day (before theyr
gate) not fhewing other countenaunce, but of good wyll, and wyth
fryendly gefture, rather than any Ennimies Face, faluting Angelica at all tymes when he met hir. Wherefore Montanine was
affured, that the onely loue of Salimbene towards his fifter caufed
that delyueraunce, concluding that when the paffion doth proceede of good loue, feazed in gentle heart and of noble enterpryfe,
it is impoffible but it mufte bryng forth the maruellous effects of
vertue's gallantize, of honefty and curtefy, and that the fpyrite
wel borne, can not fo mutch hide hys gentle nourtoure, but the
fyre muft flame abroade, and that whych feemeth dyfficult to bee
brought to paffe, is facilitye, and made poffible by the conceiptes
and indeuors fo wel imployed: wherefore in the Ende not to bee
furmounted in Honefty, ne yet to beare the marke of one, that
vnthankefully accepteth good turnes, he determyned to vfe a great
prodigality vppon him, that vnder the name of foe, had fhewed
himfelfe a more faythful friend, then thofe that bare good face,
and at neede wer furtheft off from afflicted Montanine, who not
knowing what prefent to make to Salimbene, but of himfelfe and
hys fyfter, purpofed to impart his minde to Angelica, and then
vpon knowledge of hir wil to performe his intent. For which
caufe vnderftanding that his gracious enimy was gone into the
Countrey, he thoughte well to confyder of his determynatyon, and
to breake wyth hir in hys abfence, the better to Execute the fame,
vppon his nexte retourne to the Citye. He called Angelica afyde,
and beynge bothe alone together, hee vfed thefe or futch lyke
Woordes: "You knowe, deare Sifter, that the higher the fall is,
the more daungerous and greater gryefe he feeleth that doth fall
from highe than hee that tumbleth downe from place more low

and of leſſer ſteepenes. I ſpeak this, bicauſe I cal to mind the
condition, nobility, and excellency of our anceſters, the glorie of
our race, and riches of all our houſe, which conſtraineth me many
tymes to ſigh, and ſheade a ſtreame of teares, when I ſee the
ſumptuous palaces that were the homes and reſting places of our
Fathers, and grand fathers, when I ſee on al parts of this City, the
Armes, and Scutcheons painted and imboſſed, bearyng the mark
of the Antiquity of our houſe, and when I beholde the ſtately
marble tombes and braſen Monuments, in dyuers our Temples
erected for perpetuall Memorye of many knyghtes and generalles
of warres, that ſorted forth of the Montanine race : and chyefly I
neuer enter thys great Palace, the remnant of our inheritaunce and
patrimony, but the remembraunce of our auncefters, ſo glaunceth
ouer mine Hearte, as an hundred hundred tymes, I wyſh for death,
to thynke that I am the Poſt alone of the myſery and decay fallen
vppon the name and famous familye of the Montanines, whych
maketh me thinke our life to be vnhappy, being downe fallen from
ſutch felicity, to feele a myſery moſt extreame. But one thing alone
ought to content vs, that amid ſo great pouerty, yl luck, ruine
and abaſement, none is able to lay vnto our charge any thing
vnworthy of the nobility and the houſe, whereof we be deſcended,
our lyfe being conformable to the generoſitie of our predeceſſors :
whereby it chanceth, that although our poore eſtate be generally knowne, yet none can affirme, that we haue forligned the
vertue of them, which vertuouſly haue lyued before vs. If ſo
bee wee haue receiued pleaſure or benefit of any man, neuer
diſdained I with al duety to acknowledge a good turne, ſtil ſhun-
ning the vyce of ingratytude, to ſoyle the reputation wherein
hitherto I haue paſſed my lyfe. Is there anye blot which more
ſpotteth the renoume of man, than not confeſſing receiued benefites and pleaſures perfourmed in our neceſſity ? You know in
what peril of death I was, theſe few daies paſt, through their falſe
ſurmiſe which neuer loued me, and how almoſt miraculouſly I was
redemed out of the hangman's hands, and the cruel ſentence of
the vnryghteous Magiſtrate, not one of our kin offrynge themſelues in deede or word for my defenſe, which forceth mee to ſay,
that I haue felt of my Kin, which I neuer thought, and haue taſted

futch commodity at his hands, of whome I neuer durft expect or hope for pleafure, relief, aide or any comfort. I attended my delyueraunce by fute of thofe whome I counted for Kin and fryends, but the fame fo foon vanifhed, as the Neceffity and peryll were prefent. So preffed with woe, and forfaken of fryends, I was affrayde that our aduerfaries (to remoue all feare and fufpition in tyme to come) would haue purchafed my totall ruine, and procured the ouerthrowe of the Montanines name, by my Death, and approched end. But good God, from the place whereof I feared the danger, the calme arofe, which hath brought my Barke to the hauen of health, and at his hands where I attended ruine, I haue tafted affiance and fuftentation of myne honor and lyfe. And playnely to procede, it is Anfelmo Salimbene, the fon of our auncient and capital enimies, that hath fhewed himfelf the very loyall and faithful fryend of our family, and hath deliuered your brother by payment to the State, the fumme of a Thoufand Ducats to raunfome the life of him, who thought him to be his mofte cruel aduerfary. O Gentleman's heart in dede and gentle mind, whofe rare vertues do furpaffe all humaine vnderftanding. Friends vnited together in band of Amitye, amaze the World by the effects not vulgar in things whych they do one for an other. But thys furmounteth all, a mortall Ennimy, not reconcyled or requyred, without demaund of affuraunce for the pleafure which he doth, payeth the debts of his aduerfarie: which facte exceedeth all confideration in them, that difcouer the factes of men. I can not tel what name to attribute to the deede of Salimbene, and what I ought to call that his curtefy, but this muft I needes proteft, that the example of his honeftie and gentlenes is of futch force, and fo mutch hath vanquifhed me, as whether I fhal dye in payne or lyue at eafe, neuer am I able to exceede his lyberality. Now my life being ingaged for that which he hath don to mee, and hee hauynge delyuered the fame from infamous Death, it is in your handes (deare fifter) to practize the deuyfe imagined in my mind, to the intente that I may be onely bound to you for fatiffying the liberalitye of Salimbene, by meanes whereof, you which wepte the death and wayled the loft liberty of your Brother, doe fee me free and in fafety hauyng none other care but to be acquited of

hym, to whome both you and I be dearely bound." Angelica hearyng
hir brother fpeak thofe words, and knowing that Salimbene was
he, that had furpaffed all their kinne in amity and comforte of
theyr familye, anfwered her brother, fayinge : " I woulde neuer
haue thought (good Brother) that your deliuerance had come to
paffe by him whofe name euen now you tolde, and that our
Ennimyes breaking al remembraunce of auncient quarels, had care
of the health and conferuation of the Montanines. Wherefore if
it were in my power I would fatiffy the curtefy and gentleneffe
of Anfelmo, but I know not which way to begin the fame. I
being a maid that knoweth not how to recompenfe a good turne,
but by acknowledging the fame in heart : and to go to render
thanks, it is neither lawfull or comely for me, and mutch leffe
to offer him any thynge for the lyttle acceffe I haue to his
houfe, and the fmall familiarity I haue with the Gentlewomen of
his kinne. Notwythftanding, Brother, confider you wherein my
power refteth to ayde and helpe you, and be affured (myne honor
faued) I wyll fpare nothynge for your contentment." " Sifter "
(fayd Montanine) " I haue of long time debated with my felf
what is to be done, and deuifed what myghte be the occafion that
moued this young Gentleman to vfe fo greate kindneffe toward
mee, and hauing diligently pondred and waied what I haue feene
and knowne, at length I founde that it was the onely force of Loue,
which conftrained his affection, and altered the auncient hatred
that he bare vs, into new loue, that by no meanes can be quenched.
It is the couert fire which Loue hathe kindled in his intrailes, it is
loue whych hath rayfed the true effects of gentleneffe, and hath
confumed the conceipts of difpleafed mind. O the great force of
that amorous alteration, which vppon the fodain exchaung,
feemeth impoffible to receiue any more chaung or mutation. The
onely Beauty and good grace of you Syfter, hath induced our
gracious Enimy, the feruaunt of your perfections, to delyuer the
poore Gentleman forlorn of all good fortune. It is the honeft lyfe
and commendable behauiour of Angelica Montanine, that hath
incyted Anfelmo to doe an acte fo praife worthy, and a deede fo
kinde, to procure the deliuerance of one, which looked not for a
chaunce of fo great confequence. Ah gentle younge gentleman :

Ah pryncely minde, and heart noble and magnanimous. Alas how fhall it be poffyble that euer I can approche the honeft liberalitye wherwyth thou haft bound me for euer? My lyfe is thine, myne honour dependeth of thee, my goodes be tyed to thee. What refteth then, if not that you (fifter) voyde of cruelty do vfe no vnkyndneffe to hym that loueth you, and who for love of you hathe prodygally offred hys owne goodes to ryd me from payne and dyfhonor? If fo be, my lyfe and fauegarde haue ben acceptable vnto thee, and the fight of me dyfcharged from Pryfon was ioyful vnto thee, if thou gaueft thy willing confent that I fhould fel my patrimony, graunt prefently that I may wyth a great, rare, and precious prefent, requyte the Goodneffe, Pleafure and curtefye that Salimbene hath done for your fake: And fyth I am not able with goodes of Fortune to fatiffie his bountye, it is your perfon which may fupply that default, to the intent that you and I may be quytted of the oblygation, wherein we ftand bound vnto him. It behoueth that for the offer and reward of Money whych he hath imployed, we make prefent of your Beautye, not felling the pryce of your chaftity, but delyueryng the fame in exchaunge of curtefye, beyng affured for hys gentleneffe and good Nourtoure fake, hee wyll vfe you none otherwyfe, or vfurpe any greater authority ouer you, than Vertue permitteth in ech gentle and Noble hearte. I haue none other means of fatiffaction, ne larger raumfome to render free my head from the Tribute whych Salimbene hathe gyuen for my Lyfe and Liberty. Thynke (deare Sifter) what determinate aunfwere you wyll make me, and confider if my requeft be meete to be denyed. It is in your choife and pleafure to deny or confent to my demaund. If fo be that I be denyed and loofe the meanes by your refufe to be acquitted of my defender, I had rather forfake my Citye and Countrey, than to lyue heere wyth the title of ingratitude, for not acknowledging fo greate a pleafure. But alas, with what Eye, fhall I dare behold the Nobility of Siena, if by greate vnkyndneffe I paffe vnder filence the rareft friendfhip that euer was deuifed? What heartes forrow fhall I conceyue to bee pointed at wyth the finger, like one that hath forgotten in acknowledging by effecte, the receiued pleafure of my delyueraunce? No (fifter) eyther you muft bee the

quyet of my Minde, and the acquittance of vs bothe, or elſe muſt
I dye, or wander lyke a vagabond into ſtraunge Countries, and
neuer put foote agayne into Italy." At thoſe words Angelica
ſtode ſo aſtonned and confuſed, and ſo beſides bir ſelfe, like as
wee ſee one diſtraught of ſenſe that feeleth himſelf attached with
ſome amaze of the Palſey. In the end recouering hir ſprytes, and
bee blubbered al with teares, hir ſtomacke panting like the Bel-
lowes of a forge, ſhe anſweared hir brother in thys manner: "I
knowe not louyng Brother by reaſon of my troubled minde howe
to aunſwere your demaund, which ſeemeth to be both ryght, and
wronge, right for reſpeⅽt of the bond, not ſo, in conſideration of
the requeſt. But how I proue the ſame, and what reaſon I can
alleadge and diſcouer for that proofe, hearken me ſo paciently, as
I haue reaſon to complayne and diſpute vpon this chaunce more
hard and difficulte to auoyde, than by reply able to be defended,
ſith that Lyfe and the hazarding thereof is nothing, in regarde of
that which you wyll haue me to preſent with too exceeding prodigall Liberality, and I would to God that Life mighte ſatiſfie the
ſame, than be ſure it ſhould ſo ſoone be imployed, as the promiſe
made thereof. Alas, good God, I thought that when I ſawe my
brother out of Pryſon, the neare diſtreſſe of death, whereunto
vniuſtly he was thrown, I thought (I ſay) and firmely did beleue,
that fortune the Enimy of our ioy, had vomitted al hir poiſon, and
being deſpoyled of hir fury and crabbed Nature had broken the
bloudy and Venemous Arrowes, wherewyth ſo longe tyme ſhe hath
plagued our family, and that by reſting of hir ſelfe, ſhee had
gyuen ſome reſt to the Montanine houſe of al theyr troubles and
miſaduentures. But I (O miſerable wight) do ſee and feele how
far I am deuided from my hope, and deceiued of mine opinion,
ſith the furious ſtepdame, appeareth before me with a face more
fierce and threatning, then euer ſhe did, ſharpening hir ſelfe
againſt my youth in other ſort, then euer againſt any of our race.
If euer ſhe perſecuted our aunceſters, if ſhe brought them to ruine
and decay, ſhe now doth purpoſe wholly to ſubuerte the ſame, and
throw vs headelong into the bottomleſſe pit of all miſery, exter-
minating for all tegether, the remnaunte of our conſumed houſe.
Be it either by loſſe of thee (good brother) or the vyolent death

of me which cannot hazarde my Chaſtity for the pryce of myne
vnhappy life: Ah, good God, into what anguiſh is my mynde
exponed, and how doe I feele the force and Vyolence of froward
Fortune? But what ſpeak I of fortune? How doth hard lucke
infue, that is predeſtinated by the heauens vppon our familly?
Muſt I at ſo tender yeares, and of ſo feeble kinde make choyſe of
a thing, which would put the wyſeſt vpon Earth into their ſhifts?
My heart doth fayle me, reaſon wanteth and Iudgement hangeth
in ballaunce by continuall agitations, to ſee how I am dryuen to
the extremity of two daungerous ſtraits, and enuironned with
fearefull ieoperdies, forcibly compelled either to bee deuided and
ſeparated from thee (my Brother,) whome I loue aboue mine owne
life, and in whome next after God I haue fyxed and put my hope
and truſt, hauing none other ſolace, Comfort and helpe, but
thee, or elſe by keping thee, am forced to giue vnto an other, and
know not how, the precious treaſure which beyng once loſt, cannot be recouered by any meanes, and for the gard and conſerua-
tion whereof, euery woman of good iudgement that loueth vertue,
ought a thouſand times to offer hir ſelfe to death (if ſo many
wayes ſhe could) rather than to blot or ſoyle that ineſtimable
Iewell of chaſtity, wherewith our lyfe is a true lyfe: contrarywyſe
ſhee which fondly ſuffreth hir ſelf to be diſſeazed and ſpoyled of
the ſame, and looſeth it without honeſt title, albeit ſhe be a lyue,
yet is ſhe buryed in the moſt obſcure caue of death, hauing loſt
the honour which maketh Maydens march with head vpryght.
But what goodneſſe hath a Ladye, Gentlewoman, Maiden, or Wyfe,
wherein ſhe can glory, hir honour being in doubt, and reputatyon
darkened with infamie? Whereto ſerued the imperyall houſe of
Auguſtus, in thoſe Ladyes that were intituled the Emperour's
Daughters, when for their villany, theyr were vnworthy of the title
of chaſte and vertuous? What profited Fauſtina the Emperiall
Crowne vpon hir head, hir chaſtity through hir abhominable Life,
being rapt and deſpoyled? What wronge hath bene done to many
ſymple Women, for being buryed in the Tombe of dark obliuion,
which for their vertue and pudique Lyfe, meryted Eternall prayſe?
Ah Charles, my Brother deare, where haſt thou beſtowrd the Eye
of thy foreſeeing mynde, that without prouidence and care of the

fame due to honeſt Dames, and chaſt Damoſels of our Family, hauyng loſt the goodes and Fathers inheritance, wilt haue me in like ſort forgoe my Chaſtity, whych hytherto I haue kept with heedeful dilygence. Wilte thou deare Brother, by the pryce of my virginity, that Anſelmo ſhall haue greater victorye ouer vs, than he hath gotten by fight of Sword vpon the allied remnaunt of our houſe? Art thou ignorant that the woundes and diſeaſes of the Mynd, be more vehement than thoſe which afflict the Body? Ah I vnhappy mayden, and what ill lucke is reſerued for me, what deſtiny hath kept me till this day to be preſented for Venus' Sacri-fice, to ſatiſſy a young manne's luſt, which coueteth (peraduenture) but the ſpoile of mine honor? O happy the Romain maide, ſlayne by the proper hands of hir woeful Father Virginius, that ſhe myght notbe ſoyled with infamy, by the Lecherous embracements of rauenous Appius, which deſired hir acquaintaunce. Alas, that my brother doe not ſo, rather I woulde to God of his owne accord he be the infamous miniſter of my life ready to be violated, if God by his grace take not my cauſe in hand? Alas death, why doſt thou not throwe againſt my hearte thy moſt pearcing dart, that I may goe waite vpon the ſhadowes of my thryce happy Parents, who knowing this my gryefe, wyll not be voide of paſſion to helpe me wayle my woefull ſtate. O God, why was not I choaked and ſtrangled, ſo ſoone as I was taken forth the ſecret imbracements of my mother's Wombe, rather than to arriue into this miſhap, that either muſt I loſe the thing I deeme moſte deare, or die with the violence of my proper hands? Come death, come and cut the vnhappy threede of my woefull Lyfe: ſtope the pace of teares with thy trenchant Darte that ſtreame outragiouſly downe my face, and cloſe the breathing wind of ſighes, which hynder thee from doing thine office vpon my heart, by ſuffocation of my lyfe and it." When ſhe had ended thoſe Words, hir ſpeache dyd faile, and wax-ing pale and faint, (ſitting vppon hir ſtoole) ſhe fared as though that very death had ſitten in hir place. Charles thynking that his ſiſter had bene deade, mated with ſorrowe, and deſirous to lyue no longer after hir, ſeeing he was the cauſe of that ſownyng, fell downe dead vpon the Ground, mouing neither hand nor foote, as though the ſoule had ben departed from the bodye. At the noyſe

which Montanine made by reafon of hys fall, Angelica reuiued
out of hir fowne, and feeinge hir Brother in fo pytifull plyght,
and fuppofing he had bene dead for care of hys requeft, for beyng
berieued of hir Brother, was fo moued, as a lyttle thynge would
haue made hir do, as Thifbe dyd, when fhe viewed Pyramus to be
flayne. But conceyuing hope, fhe threw hir felfe vppon hir
Brother, curfing hir Fortune, bannyng the Starres of cruelty, and
hir lauifh fpeach, and hir felf for hir little loue to hir brother,
who made no refufall to dye to faue his Lande for reliefe of hir:
wher fhe denyed to yeld hir felfe to him that loued hir with fo good
affe&ion. In the end fhe applied fo many remedies vnto hir brother,
fometimes cafting cold water vpon his face, fometimes pinching
and rubbing the temples and pulfes of his armes and his mouth
with vineger, that fhe made hym to come agayne: and feeing
that his eyes were open, beholding hir intentiuely with the countenance of a man half in defpayre, fhe faied vnto him: "For fo
mutch brother as I fee fortune to be fo froward, that by no
meanes thou canft auoide the cruel lot, which launceth me into
the bottome of mortall mifery, and that I muft aduenture to
folowe the indeuors of thy minde, and obey thy will, which is more
gentle and Noble, than fraught with reafon, I am content to fatisfy
the fame and the loue which hitherto thou haft born me. Be of
good cheere, and doe wyth mee and my body what thou lift, giue
and prefente the fame to whom thou pleafeft. Wel be thou fure,
that fo fone as I fhal bee out of thy hands and power, I wyl be
called or efteemed thine no more, and thou fhalt haue leffe
authority to ftay me from doing the deuifes of my fantafie, fwear-
ing and protefting by the Almighty GOD, that neuer man fhall
touch Angelica, except it be in mariage, and that if he affay to
paffe any further, I haue a heart that fhall incourage my hands to
facrifice my Life to the Chaftitye of Noble Dames whych had rather
dye than liue in flaunder of dyfhonefty. I wyll die a body without defame, and the Mynde voyde of confent, fhall receiue no
fhame or filth that can foyle or fpot the fame." In faying fo, fhe
began againe to weepe in futch aboundance, as the humour of hir
brayne ranne downe by the iffue of bothe hir Eyes. Montanine
albeit forrowful beyond meafure to fee his gentle and chaft fifter

in futch vexation and heauineſſe, reioyſed yet in his mind, that ſhe had agreed to his requeſt, which preſaged the good lucke that afterwardes chaunced vnto him, for hys Lyberal offer. "Wherefore" (ſaid he to Angelica,) "I was neuer in my Lyfe ſo deſirous to liue, but that I rather chooſe to dye, than procure a thinge that ſhould turne thee to diſpleaſure and griefe, or to hazarde thine honor and reputation in daunger or peryll of damage, which thou haſt euer knowne, and ſhouldeſt haue ſtill perceyued by effect, or more properly to ſpeak, touched with thy finger if that incomparable and rare curteſy and Lyberality of Salimbene had not prouoked me to requyre that, which honeſtly thou canſt not gyue, nor I demaunde without wronge to thee, and preiudice to mine owne eſtimation and honoure. But what? the feare I haue to be deemed ingrate, hath made me forget thee, and the great honeſty of Anſelmo maketh me hope, yea and ſtedfaſtly beleue, that thou ſhalt receiue none other diſpleaſure, but to be preſented vnto him whome at other times we haue thought to be our mortal enimy. And I thinke it impoſſible that he wil vſe any villany to hir whome he ſo feruently loueth, for whoſe ſake he feareth not the hatred of his friends, and diſdained not to ſave him whome he hated, and on whome he myght haue bene reuenged. And forſomutch ſiſter, as the face commonly ſheweth the ſigne and token of the hearte's affection, I pray thee by any meanes declare no ſad countenaunce in the preſence of Salimbene, but rather cheere vp thy face, dry vp the aboundance of thy teares, that he by ſeeing thee Ioyfull and mery, may be moued to continue his curteſy and uſe thee honeſtly, being ſatiſſied with thy liberality, and the offer that I ſhall make of our ſeruice." Here may be ſeene the extremitie of two dyuers thinges, duety combatting with ſhame, reaſon being in contention with himſelf. Angelica knew and confeſſed that hir brother did but his duetye, and that ſhe was bound by the ſame very bond. On the other ſide, hir eſtate and virginall chaſtity, brake the endeuours of hir duety, and denyed to doe that which ſhe eſteemed ryght. Neuertheleſſe ſhee prepared hir ſelf to follow both the one and the other: and by acquitting the duety to hir brother, ſhe ordayned the meane, to diſcharge him of that which he was bound to his benefactor, determinynge neuer-

theleſſe rather to dye, than ſhamefully to ſuffer hir ſelfe to be
abuſed, or to make hir loſe the floure, which made hir glyſter
amongs the maidens of the city, and to deface hir good fame by
an acte ſo vyllanous.   But that ſpeciall rare vertue was more
ſingular in hir, than was that continency of Cyrus the Perſian
King, who fearing to be forced by the allurements of the excellent
beauty of chaſt Panthea, would not ſuffer hir to be brought into
his preſence, for feare that hee being ſurmounted with folyſh
luſtes, ſhould force hir, that by other meanes could not be perſuaded to breake the holy lawes of Mariage, and promiſed faith to
hir huſband.   For Salimbene hauing in his preſence, and at his
commaundement hir whome aboue al thyngs he loued would by
no meanes abuſe his power, but declared his gentle nature to bee
of other force and effect, than that of the aforeſaid king as by
reading the ſucceſſe of this hiſtorie you ſhal perceiue.   After that
Montanine and his ſiſter had vttered many other words vpon
their determination, and that the fayre maiden was appeaſed of
hir ſorrow, attending the iſſue of that which they went about to
begin : Anſelmo was come home out of the Countrey, whereof
Charles hauing intelligence, about the ſecond houre of the night,
he cauſed his ſiſter to make hir ready, and in company of one of
their ſeruants that caried light before them, they came to the
lodginge of Salimbene, whoſe ſeruaunt ſeeing Montanine ſo accompanied to knocke at the Gate, if hee did maruel I leaue for
you to think, by reaſon of the diſpleaſure and hatred which he
knew to bee betweene the two families, not knowing that which
had already paſſed for the beginning of a final peace of ſo many
controuerſies : for which cauſe ſo aſtonned as he was, he went to
tel his maiſter that Montanine was at the gate, deſirous ſecretly
to talk vnto him.   Salimbene knowing what company Charles
had with him, was not vnwilling to goe downe, and cauſing two
Torches to be lighted, came to his gate to entertaine them, and to
welcome the brother and the ſiſter, wyth ſo great curteſie and
friendſhip as he was ſurpryſed with loue, ſeeing before his eyes
the ſight of hir that burned hys heart inceſſantly, not diſcouer-
yng as yet the ſecrets of his thought by making hir to vnderſtand
the good wyl he bare hir, and how mutch he was hir ſeruant.

He could not tel wel whether he was incharmed or his eyes
dafelled, or not wel wakened from fleepe when he faw Angelica,
fo amazed was he with the ftraungeneffe of the fact, and arriuall
of the maiden to his houfe. Charles feeing hym fo confufed, and
knowing that the great affection he bare vnto his fifter, made him
fo perplexed and befides himfelf, faid vnto him : " Sir, we would
gladly fpeake with you in one of your Chambers, that there
myght be none other witneffe of our dyfcourfe, but we three
together." Salimbene which was wrapt wyth ioy, was able to make
none other aunfweare, but : " Goe we whether you pleafe." So
taking his Angelica by the hand, they went into the Hall, and from
thence into his chamber, whych was furnyfhed accordinge to the
ftate and riches of a Lord, he being one of the welthieft and chiefe
of the City of Siena. When they were fet downe, and al the feruants
gone forth, Charles began to fay to Salimbene, thefe words :
" You may not thinke it ftraunge (fir Salimbene) if againft the
Lawes and cuftomes of our Common Wealthe, I at thys tyme of the
Nyght doe call you vp, for knowyng the Bande wherewyth I am
bound vnto you, I muft for euer confeffe and count my felfe to be
your flaue and bondman, you hauing don a thing in my behalf
that deferueth the name of Lord and maifter. But what vngrateful
man is he that wil forget fo greate a benefit, as that which I haue
receyued of you, holding of you, life, goods, honor, and this mine
own fifter that enioyeth by your meanes the prefence of hir brother and hir reft of mind, not lofing our noble reputation by the
loffe prepared for me through vnrighteous iudgement, you hauing
ftaied the ruine both of hir and me, and the reft of our houfe
and kin. I am ryghte glad fir, that this my duety and feruice is
bounden to fo vertuous a Gentleman as you be, but exceeding
forry, that fortune is fo froward and contrary vnto me, that I am
not able to accomplifhe my good will, and if ingratitude may
lodge in mind of a neady Gentleman, who hath no helpe but of
himfelfe, and in the wyll of hys chaft fifter, and minde vnited in
two perfons onely faued by you, duety doeth requyre to prefent
the reft, and to fubmit al that is left to be difpofed at your good
pleafure. And bicaufe that I am well affured, that it is Angelica
alone which hath kindled the flame of defire, and hath caufed you

to loue that which your predeceffours haue deadly hated, that
fame fparke of knowledge, whycb our mifery could not quench
with all his force, hath made the way and fhewed the path whereby
we fhall auoide the name of ingrate and forgetfull perfons, and
that fame which hath made you lyberall towards me, fhalbe bountifully beftowed vpon you. It is Angelica fir, which you fee
prefent heere, who to difcharge my band, hath willingly rendred
to be your owne, fubmittinge hir felfe to your good wyll, for euer
to be youres. And I which am hir brother, and haue receiued that
great good wyll of hir, as in my power to haue hir wyl, do prefent
the fame, and leaue hir in your hands, to vfe as you would your
owne, praying you to accept the fame, and to confider whofe is
the gift, and from whence it commeth, and how it ought to be
regarded." When he had fayd fo, Montanine rofe vp, and without further talke, went home vnto his houfe. If Anfelmo were
abafhed at the Montanines arriuall, and aftonned at the Oration
of Charles, his fodain departure was more to be maruelled at, and
therwithal to fee the effect of a thing which he neuer hoped, nor
thought vpon. He was exceding glad and ioyfull to fee himfelf
in the company of hir, whome he defired aboue al things of the
world, but fory to fee hir heauy and forrowful for futch chaunce.
He fuppofed hir being ther, to procede rather of the yong man's
good and gentle Nature, than of the Maiden's will and lykynge.
For whych caufe taking hir by the hand, and holding hir betwene
hys armes, he vfed thefe or futch lyke words: "Gentlewoman,
if euer I had felt and knowne with what Wing the variety and
lyghtneffe of worldly thynges do flye, and the gaynes of incon-
ftant fortune, at this prefent I haue feen one of the moft manifeft
profes which feemeth to me fo ftraunge, as almoft I dare not
beeleue that I fee before myne Eyes. I know well that it is for
you, and for the feruice that I beare you, that I haue broken the
effect of that hatred, whych by inheritaunce I haue receiued
againft your Houfe, and for that deuotion haue deliuered your
Brother. But I fee that Fortune wyll not let mee to haue the
vpper hand, to bee the Conquerer of hir fodaine pangs. But you
your felf fhall fee, and euery man fhall know that my heart is
none other than noble, and my deuifes tend, but to the exploit of

all vertue and Gentleneffe: wherefore I pray you (fayd he, kiffing hir louingly) be not fad, and doubt not that your feruaunt is any other now, hauing you in his power, than he was when he durft not dyfcouer the ardent Loue that vexed him, and held him in feeble ftate, ful of defire and thought: you alfo may bee fure, that he hath not had the better hande ouer me, ne yet for his curtefy hath obteined victory, nor you for obeying him. For fith that you be myne, and for futch yelded and giuen to me, I wyl keepe you, as hir whome I loue and efteme aboue al things of the World, makyng you my Companion and the onely miftreffe of my goodes heart, and wyll. Thinke not that I am the Fryend of Fortune, and practife pleafure alone without vertue. It is modefty which commaundeth me, and honefty is the guide of my conceipts. Affure you then, and repofe your comfort on mee: for none other than Angelica Montanine fhall be the wyfe of Anfelmo Salimbene: and during my life, I wyll bee the Fryend, the defender and fupporter of your houfe." At thefe good Newes, the droufie and wandryng Spirite of the fayre Siena mayd awaked, who endyng hir teares and appeafing hir forrow, rofe vp, and made a very lowe reuerence vnto hir curteous fryend, thanking hym for hys greate and incomparable liberalitye, promifing all feruice, duetie, and Amitye, that a Gentlewoman ought to beare vnto him, whom God hath referued for hir Spoufe and hufband. After an infinite number of honeft imbracements and pleafaunte kiffes giuen and receiued on both partes, Anfelmo called vnto him one of his Auntes that dwelled within him, to whome he deliuered his new Conqueft to keepe, and fpedily without delay he fent for the next of his Kinne and deareft friends: and being come, he intreated them to kepe him company, in a very vrgent and weighty bufineffe he had to do, wherein if they fhewed themfelues dilygent in his requeft, doubtful it is not, but he addreffed fpeede for accomplifhment of his Enterpryfe. Then caufyng hys Aunte and welbeloued Angelica to come forth, he carryed them (not without their great admiration) to the pallace of Montanine, whither being arryued: he and hys Companie were well intertayned of the fayd Montanine, the Brother of fayre Angelica. When they were in the Hall, Salimbene fayd to hys Brother in law that fhould be: "Senio

Montanine, it is not long fithens, that you in company of my
faire Gentlewoman heere, came home to fpeake wyth mee, defirous to haue no man priuy to the effect of your conference. But
I am come to you with this troupe to difclofe my minde before
you al, and to manifefte what I purpofe to doe, to the intente the
whole World may know your good and honeft Nature, and vnderftand how I can be requited on them, which indeuor to gratifie
me in any thing." Hauing faid fo, and euery man being fet down
he turned his talk to the reft of the company in thys wife: "I
doubt not my friends and Noble Dames, but that ye mutch mufe and
maruell to fee me in this houfe fo late, and in your company, and
am fure, that a great defire moueth your minds to know for what
purpofe, the caufe, and why I haue gathered this affemblie in a
time vnlooked for, and in place where none of our race and kinne
of long time did enter, and leffe did meane to make hither their
repaire. But when you doe confider what vertue and goodneffe
refteth in the heartes of thofe men, that fhunne and auoide the
brutyfhneffe of Minde, to followe the reafonable part, and which
proprely is called Spirituall, you fhall thereby perceiue, that when
Gentle kynde and Noble Heart, by the great miftreffe dame Nature
be gryfted in the myndes of Men, they ceafe not to make appeare
the effect of their doings, fometyme producing one vertue, fometimes another, which ceafe not to caufe the fruicte of futch induftry both to blome and beare: In futch wyfe, as the more thofe
vertuous actes and commendable workes, do appeare abroad, the
greater dyligence is imployed to fearche the matter wherein fhe
can caufe to appeare the force of vertue and excellency, conceiu-
ing fingular delyghte in that hir good and holy delyuery, which
bryngeth forth a fruict worthy of futch a ftocke. And that force
of mind and Generofity of Noble Heart is fo firme and fure in
operation, as although humane thinges be vnftable and fubiect to
chaung, yet they cannot be feuered or difparcled. And although
it be the Butte and white, whereat fortune difchargeth al hir
dartes and fhaftes, threatning fhooting and affayling the fame
round, yet it continueth ftable and firme like a Rocke and Clyffe
beaten wyth the vyolent fury of waues rifing by wind or tempeft.
Whereby it chaunceth, that riches and dignity can no more ad-

uaunce the heart of a flaue and villaine, than pouerty make vile
and abafe the greatneffe of courage in them that be procreated of
other ftuffe than of common forte, whych daily keepe the maiefty
of their oryginall, and lyve after the inftincte of good and Noble
Bloude, wherewith their auncefters were made Noble, and fucked
the fame vertue oute of the Teates of Nourffes Breaffes, who in the
myddes of troublefome trauayles of Fortune that doe affayle them,
and depreffe theyr modefty, their face and Countenaunce, and
theyr factes full well declare theyr condition, and to doe to vnderftande, that vnder futch a Mifery, a Mynde is hydde which
deferueth greater Guerdon than the eigre tafte of Calamitye.   In
that dyd glowe and fhyne the Youthe of the Perfian and Median
Monarch, beynge nourffed amonges the ftalles and Stables of hys
Grandfather, and the gentle kind of the founder of ftately Rome
sockeled in the Shepecoates of Prynces fheepehierds.   Thus mutch
haue I fayd, my good lords and dames, in confideration of the
noble corage and gentle minde of Charles Montanine, and of his
fifter, who without preiudice to any other I dare to fay, is the
paragon and mirrour of all chaft and curteous maidens, well
trayned vp, amonges the whole Troupe of thofe that lyue thys day
in Siena, who beeyng brought to the ende and laft poynt of their
ruine, as euery of you doth knowe, and theyr race fo fore decayed
as there remayneth but the onely Name of Montanine: notwythftanding they neuer loft the heart, defire, ne yet the effect of the
curtefy, and naturall bounty, whych euer doth accompany the
mynd of thofe that be Noble in deede.   Whych is the caufe that
I am conftrayned to accufe our Auncefters, of to mutch cruelty,
and of the lyttle refpecte whych for a controuerfye occured by
chaunce, haue purfued them with futch mortall reuenge, as without ceafing, with all their force, they haue affayed to ruinate,
abolyfhe, and for euer adnichilate that a ryghte Noble and illuftre
race of the Montanines, amongs whome if neuer any goodneffe
appeared to the Worlde, but the Honefty, Gentleneffe, Curtefy and
vertuous maners of thefe twayne here prefente, the Brother and
fifter, yet they ought to be accompted amonges the ranke of the
Nobleft and chiefeft of our City, to the intent in time to come it
may not be reported, that wee haue efteemed and chearyfhed

Riches and droſſie mucke, more than vertue and modeſty. But
imitating thoſe excellent gouerners of Italy, whych held the
Romane Empire, let vs rather reuerence the Vertuous Poore, than
prayſe or pryſe the Rich, gyuen to vice and wickedneſſe. And
for ſo mutch as I do ſee you all to be deſirous to knowe the
cauſe and argument, whych maketh me to vſe this talke, and forceth mee to prayſe the curteſy and goodneſſe of the Montanines,
pleaſeth you to ſtay a lyttle with pacience, and not think the tyme
tedyous, I meane to declare the ſame. Playnely to confeſſe vnto
you (for that it is no cryme of Death, or heinous offence) the gyfts
of nature, the Beauty and comelyneſſe of fayre Angelica heere
preſent, haue ſo captiuate my Mind, and depriued my heart of
Lyberty, as Night and Day trauailing how I might diſcouer vnto
hir my martirdom, I did conſume in ſutch wyſe, as loſing luſt of
ſlepe and meate, I feared ere long to be either dead of ſorrow or
eſtranged of my right wits, ſeing no meanes how I might auoide
the ſame, bicauſe our two houſes and Families were at contynuall
debate : and albeit conflicts were ceaſed, and quarelles forgotten,
yet there reſted (as I thought) a certaine deſire both in the one
and the other of offence, when time and occaſion did ſerue. And
yet mine affection for all that was not decreaſed, but rather more
tormented, and my gryefe increaſed, hopeleſſe of help, which now
is chaunced to me as you ſhall heare. You do know, and ſo do
all men, howe wythin theſe fewe dayes paſt, the Lord Montanine
here preſent, was accuſed before the Seniorie, for treſpaſſes againſt
the ſtatutes and Edicts of the ſame, and being Pryſoner, hauing
not wherewith to ſatiſſie the condempnation, the Law affirmed that
his life ſhould recompence and ſupply default of Money. I not
able to ſuffer the want of hym, which is the brother of the deareſt
thing I eſteeme in the Worlde, and hauing not hir in poſſeſſion,
nor lyke without him to attayne hir, payed that Summe, and
delyuered hym. He, by what meanes I know not, or how he
coniectured the beneuolence of my deede, thynking that it proceeded of the honeſt Loue and affection which I bare to gracious
and amiable Angelica, wel conſideryng of my curteſy, hath ouercome me in prodigalitye, he this Nyght came vnto mee, with his
ſiſter my miſtreſſe, yelding hir my ſlaue and Bondwoman, leauyng

hir with me, to doe with hir as I would with any thing I had.
Behold my good Lordes, and yee Noble Ladies and cofins, and confider how I may recompence this Benefit, and be able to fatiffie a
prefent fo precious, and of futch Value and regard as both of them
be, futch as a right puiffant prince and Lord may be contented
wyth, a duety fo Liberall and Iewell ineftymable of two offered
thynges." The affiftants that were there, could not tell what to
fay, the difcourfe had fo mutch drawne their myndes into dyuers
fantafies and contrary opinions, feing that the fame requyred by
deliberation to be confidered, before lightly they vttred their
mindes. But they knew not the intent of him, which had called
them thither, more to teftify his fact, than to iudge of the thing
he went about, or able to hinder and let the fame. True it is, that
the ladies viewing and marking the amiable countenance of the
Montanine Damfell, woulde haue iudged for hir, if they feared
not to bee refufed of hym, whome the thing did touche moft neere.
Who without longer ftaye, opened to them al, what he was purpofed to do, faying: "Sith ye do fpende time fo long vpon a
matter already meant and determyned, I wyll ye to knowe, that
hauing regard of mine honour, and defirous to fatiffie the honefty
of the Brother and fifter, I mynde to take Angelica to my wyfe
and lawfull fpoufe, vniting that whych fo long tyme hath bene
deuyded, and making into two bodyes, whilom not well accorded
and agreed, one like and vniforme wyll, praying you ech one,
ioyfully to ioy with me, and your felues to reioyfe in that alliaunce,
whych feemeth rather a worke from Heauen, than a deede concluded by the Counfell and induftrie of Men. So lykewyfe all
wedded feeres in holy Wedlocke (by reafon of the effect and the
Author of the fame, euen God himfelfe, whych dyd ordayne it
firfte) bee wrytten in the infallible booke of hys owne prefcience,
to the intent that nothing may decay, whych is fuftayned wyth
the mighty hand of that Almyghty God, the God of wonders,
which verily hee hath difplayed ouer thee (deare Brother) by
makynge thee to fall into diftreffe and daunger of death, that
myne Angelica, beeing the meane of thy delyueraunce, myght
alfo bee caufe of the attonement which I doe hope henceforth
fhall bee, betwene fo Noble houfes as ours be." Thys finall de-

cree reueled in open audience, as it was, againſt their expeᴄtation, and the ende that the kindred of Anſelmo looked for, ſo was the ſame no leſſe ſtraunge and baſhfull, as ioyful and pleaſaunt, feeling a ſodain ioy, not accuſtomed in theyr mynde, for that vnion and allyaunce. And albeit that their ryches was vnequall, and the dowry of Angelica nothyng neare the great wealth of Salimbene, yet all Men dyd deeme him happy, that hee had chaunced vpon ſo vertuous a maiden, the onely Modeſtie and Integritie of whome, deſerued to bee coupled wyth the moſt honourable. For when a man hath reſpeᴄtc onely to the beauty or Riches of hir, whome he meaneth to take to Wyfe, hee moſte commonly doth incurre the Miſchiefe, that the Spyrite of dyſſention intermeddleth amyd theyr houſehold, whereby Pleaſuere vaniſhing wyth Age, maketh the riueled Face (beſet wyth a Thouſand wrynkeled furrowes) to growe pale and drye. The Wyfe lykewyſe when ſhe ſeeth her goodes to ſurmount the ſubſtance of hir wedded Huſband, ſhe aduaunceth hir hearte, ſhe ſwelleth wyth pryde, indeuoryng the vpper hand and ſouerainty in all thyngs, whereupon it riſeth, that of two frayle and tranſitorie things, the building which hath ſo fyckle foundation, can not indure, man being borne to commaund, and can not abyde a mayſter ouer hym, beyng the chyefe and Lord of hys Wyfe. Now Salimbene, to perfourme the effeᴄt of hys curteſie, gaue his fayre Wife the moytie of his Lands and goods, in fauoure of the Mariage, adopting by that meanes, Montanine to bee his Brother, appointing hym to be heyre of all hys goodes in caſe he deceaſed wythout heyres of his Body. And if Goᴅ did ſend hym Children, he inſtituted him to bee the heyre of the other halfe, which reſted by hys donation to Angelica his new espouſe : Whom he maried ſolempnely the Sunday folowing, to the great contentation and maruell of the whole City, which long time was affliᴄted by the ciuile diſſentions of thoſe two houſes. But what? Sutch be the varieties of worldly ſucceſſe, and ſutch is the miſchiefe amongs men, that the ſame which honeſty hath no power to winne, is ſurmounted by the diſgrace and miſfortune of wretched time. I neede not to alleage here thoſe amongs the Romanes, which from great hatred and malice were reconciled with the indiſſoluble knot of Amity ; forſomutch as the dignyties

and Honoures of theyr Citty prouoked one to flatter and fawne
vpon an other for particular profit, and not one of them attained
to futch excellencie and renoume, as the forefayd did, one of
whome was vanquyfhed with the fire of an amorous paſſion, whych
forcyng nature hir felfe, brought that to paſſe, which could neuer
haue bene thoughte or imagyned. And yet Men wyll accufe
loue, and painte hir in the Colours of foolyſh Furye and raging
Madneſſe. No, no, Loue in a gentle heart is the true fubiect and
fubſtance of Vertue, Curtefy, and Modeſt Manners, expellynge all
Cruelty and Vengeance, and nouriſhyng peace amongs men. But
if any do violate and prophane the holy Lawes of Loue, and per-
uert that which is Vertuous, the faulte is not in that holye Saincte
but in hym whych foloweth it wythout ſkyll, and knoweth not
the perfection. As hapneth in euery operation, that of it felfe is
honeſt, although defamed by thofe, who thinking to vfe it, doe
filthily abufe the fame, and caufe the groſſe and ignoraunte to
condempne that is good, for the folye of futch inconſtant fooles:
In the other is painted a heart fo voyde of the blody and abhominable finne of Ingratitude, as if death had ben the true remedy
and meane to fatiſſie his band and duety, he would haue made
no confcience to offer himfelfe frankly and freely to the dreadful
paſſage of the fame. You fee what is the force of a gentle heart
wel trained vp, that would not be vanquifhed in curtefye and
Lyberality. I make you to be iudges, (I meane you) that be con-
uerfant in loue's caufes, and that with a Iudgement paſſionleſſe,
voide of parciality doe dyfcourfe vppon the factes and occurrentes
that chaunce to men. I make you (I faye) iudges to gyue fentence, whether of three caried away the pryfe, and moſt bound his
companion by lyberall acte, and curtefie not forced. You fee a
mortall enimy forrow for the mifery of his aduerfary, but folycited
therunto by the ineuitable force of Loue. The other marcheth
with the glory of a prefent fo rare and exquifite, as a great
Monarch would haue accompted it for finguler fauor and prodigality. The maiden ſteppeth forth to make the third in ranke,
wyth a loue fo ſtayed and charity wonderfull towards hir brother,
as being nothynge aſſured whether he to whome ſhe offered hir
felfe were fo Moderate, as Curteous, ſhe yeldeth hir felfe to the

loffe of hir chaftity. The firft affayeth to make himfelfe a conquerour by mariage, but fhe diminifhyng no iote of hir Noble
mind, he muft feeke elfe where hys pryfe of victory. To hir a
defyre to kyll hir felfe (if thinges fucceeded contrary to hir minde)
myght haue ftopped the way to hir great glory, had fhe not
regarded hir virginity, more than hir own Lyfe. The fecond
feemeth to go half conftrained, and by maner of acquitall, and
had hys affectyon bene to render hymfelfe Slaue to hys Foe,
hys Patron and preferuer, it would haue diminifhed his prayfe.
But fithens inough wee haue hereof dyfcourfed, and bene large in
treatie of Tragicomicall matters, intermyxed and fuaged (in fome
parte) wyth the Enteruiewes of dolor, modefty, and indifferente
good hap, and in fome wholly imparted the dreadfull endes like
to terrible beginnings, I meane for a reliefe, and after futch fowre
fweete bankets, to interlarde a licorous refection for fweeting the
mouthes of the delicate: And do purpofe in this Nouell infuing,
to manifeft a pleafaunt difport betweene a Wydow and a Scholler,
a paffing Practife of a crafty Dame, not well fchooled in the difcipline of Academicall rules, a furmountinge fcience to trade the
nouices of that forme, by ware forefight, to incountre thofe that
by laborfome trauayle and nightly watch, haue ftudied the
rare knowledge of Mathematicalles, and other hidden
and fecrete Artes. Wifhing them fo well to beware,
as I am defirous to let them know by this rudi-
ment, the fucceffe of futch
attemptes.

THE THIRTY-FIRST NOUELL.

A Wydow called Miſtreſſe Helena, wyth whom a Scholler was in loue,
(ſhee louing an other) made the ſame Scholler to ſtande a whole
Wynter's night in the Snow to wayte for hir, who afterwardes by
a ſleyght and pollicie, cauſed hir in Iuly, to ſtand vppon a Tower
ſtarke naked amongs Flies and Gnats, and in the Sunne.

DIUERT we now a little from theſe ſundry haps, to ſolace our
ſelues wyth a merry deuice, and pleaſaunt circumſtaunce of a
Scholler's loue, and of the wily guily Subtilties of an amorous
Wydow of Florence. A Scholler returned from Paris to practiſe
hys knowledge at home in his owne Countrey, learneth a more
cunning Lecture of Miſtreſſe Helena, than he did of the ſubtilleſt
Sorbone Doctor, or other Mathematicall from whence he came.
The Scholler as playnely hee had applied his booke, and earneſtly
harkned his readings, ſo he ſimply meant to be a faythfull Louer
and deuout requirant to this Iolly dame, that had vowed his Deuotion and promiſed Pilgrimage to an other Saynct. The Scholler
vpon the firſt view of the Wydowe's wandring Lookes, forgetting
Ouide's Leſſons of Loue's guiles, purſued his conceipt to the vtter-
moſt. The Scholler neuer remembred how many valiaunt, wiſe
and learned men, wanton Women had ſeduced and deceyued. Hee
had forgot how Catullus was beguiled by Leſbia, Tibullus by
Delia, Propertius by Cynthia, Naſo by Corinna, Demetrius by
Lamia, Timotheus by Phryne, Philip by a Greeke mayden, Alexander by Thays, Hanniball by Campania, Cæſar by Cleopatra,
Pompeius by Flora, Pericles by Aſpaga, Pſammiticus the king of
Ægypt by Rhodope, and diuers other very famous by Women of
that ſtampe. Hee had not ben wel trayned in holy writ, or heard
of Samſon's Dalida, or of Salomon's Concubins, but like a playne
dealinge man, beleued what ſhe promiſed, followed what ſhe bad
him, waited whiles ſhe mocked him, attended till ſhee laughed him
to ſcorne. And yet for all theſe Iolly paſtimes inuented by this
Widdow, to deceyue the poore Scholler, ſhe ſcaped not free from
his Logike rules, not ſaife from his Philoſophy. He was forced

to turne ouer Ariftotle, to reuolue his Porphyrie, and to gather
his Wits about hym to requite this louing Peate, that had fo charitably delt with him. He willingly ferched ouer Ptolome, perufed
Albumazar, made hafte to Haly, yea and for a fhift befturred him
in Erra Pater, for matching two contrary Elements. For colde in
Chriftmaffe holy dayes, and Froft at Twelftide, fhewed no more
force on this poore learned Scholler, than the Sunne's heate in the
Feries of Iuly, Gnats, Flyes, and Wafpes, at Noone dayes in Sommer
vpon the naked tender Corpfe of this fayre Wyddow. The Scholler
ftoode belowe in a Court, benoommed for colde, the Wyddowe
preached a lofte in the top of a Tower, and fayne would haue had
water to coole hir extreme heate. The Scholler in his Shyrt bedecked wyth his demiffaries. The Wyddow fo Naked as hir Graund-
mother Eue, wythout vefture to fhroud hir. The Wyddow by
magike arte what fo euer it coft, would fayne haue recouered
hir loft Louer. The Scholler well efpying his aduantage when hee
was afked councell, fo Incharmed hir with his Sillogifmes, as he
made hir to mount a Tower, to curffe the time that euer fhe knew
him or hir Louer. So the Wydow not well beaten in caufes of
Schoole, was whipt with the Rod, wherewith fhee fcourged other.
Alas good Woman, had fhe known that olde malice had not bene
forgotten, fhe woulde not haue trufted, and leffe committed hir
felfe to the Circle of his Enchauntments. If women wift what
dealings are wyth men of great reading, they would amongs one
hundred other, not deale wyth one of thee meaneft of thofe that
be Bookifh. One Girolamo Rufcelli, a learned Italyan making
prety notes for the better elucidation of the Italyan Decamerone
of Boccaccio, iudgeth Boccaccio himfelfe to be this fcholler,
whom by an other name he termeth to be Rinieri. But whatfoeuer that Scholler was, he was truely to extreme in reueng, and
therein could vfe no meane. For hee neuer left the poore feeble
foule, for all hir curteous Words and gentle Supplication, vntill the
Skin of hir flefh was Parched with the fcalding Sunne beames.
And not contented with that, delt his Almofe alfo to hir Mayde,
by fending hir to help hir Miftreffe, where alfo fhe brake hir
Legge. Yet Phileno was more pityfull ouer the 3 nymphes and
fayre Goddeffes of Bologna, whofe Hyftory you may reade in the

49 Nouell of my former Tome. He fared not fo roughly with
thofe, as Rinieri did with thys, that fought but to gayne what
fhe had loft. Well, how fo euer it was, and what differency
betweene eyther of theym, this Hyftory enfuinge, more aptly fhall
gieue to vnderftande. Not long fithens, there was in Florence, a
young Gentlewoman of worfhipfull parentage, fayre and comely
of perfonage, of courage ftout, and abounding in goods of Fortune
(called Helena,) who being a widow, determined not to mary
agayne, bicaufe fhe was in loue with a yong man that was not
voyde of Nature's good gifts, whom for hir owne Tooth, aboue other
fhee had fpecially chofen. In whom (fetting afide all other care)
many tymes (by meanes of one of hir maydes which fhe trufted
beft) fhe had great pleafure and delight. It chaunced about the
fame time that a yong Gentleman of that Citty called Rinieri, hauinge a great time ftudied at Paris, returned to Florence, not to
fell his Science by retayle, as many doe, but to knowe the reafons of things, and the caufes thereof, which is a fpeciall good
exercife for a Gentleman. And being there honoured and greatly
efteemed of all men, afwell for his curteous behauiour, as alfo for
his knowledge, he liued like a good Cittizen. But it is commonly
feene, they which haue beft vnderftandinge and knowledge, are
fooneft tangled in Loue : euen fo it hapned with this Rinieri, who
repayringe one day for his paffetime to a Feafte, this Madame
Helena clothed al in blacke, (after the manner of Widowes) was
there alfo, and feemed in his eyes fo beautifull and well fauored,
as any woman euer he faw, and thought that hee might bee
accoumpted happy, to whom God did fhewe fo mutch fauoure,
as to fuffer him to be cleped betweene hir Armes : and beholdinge
her diuers tymes and knowing that the greateft and deareft things
cannot be gotten with out labour, he determined to ufe all his
endeuour and care in pleafing of hir, that thereby he might obtayne hir loue, and fo enioy hir. The yong Gentlewoman not very
bafhfull, conceyuing greater opinion of hir felfe, than was needefull, not caftinge hir Eyes towards the Ground, but rolling them
artificially on euery fide, and by and by perceyuing mutch gazing
to be vpon hir, efpied Rinieri earneftly beholding hir, and fayd,
fmiling to hir felfe : "I thinke that I haue not this day loft my

time in comming hither, for if I bee not deceyued, I fhall catch
a Pigeon by the Nofe." And beginning certayne times ftedfaftly
to looke vpon him, fhe forced hir felfe fo mutch as fhe could, to
feeme very erneftly to beholde him. And on the other part thinking, that the more pleafaunt and amorous fhe fhewed hirfelfe to
be, the more hir beauty fhould be efteemed, chiefly of him whom
fpecially fhee was difpofed to loue. The wife Scholler giuing
ouer his Philofophy, bent all his endeuour here vnto, and thinking
to be hir feruaunt, learned where fhe dwelt, and began to paffe
before hir houfe under pretence of fome other occafion : whereat
the Gentlewoman reioyfed for the caufes beforefayde, fayning an
earneft defire to looke vpon him. Wherefore the Scholler hauing found a certayne meane to be acquaynted wyth hir Mayde
difcouered his loue : Praying her to deale fo with hir miftreffe, as
he might haue hir fauor. The maide promifed him very louingly
incontinently reporting the fame to hir miftreffe, who with the
greateft Scoffes in the Worlde, gaue ear thereunto and fayd :
" Seeft thou not from whence this Goodfellowe is come to lofe al
his knowledge and doctrine that he hath brought vs from Paris.
Now let vs deuife therefore how he may bee handled for going
about to feeke that, which he is not like to obtaine. Thou fhalt
fay vnto him, when he fpeaketh to thee agayne, that I loue him
better than he loueth me, but it behooueth me to faue mine
honoure, and to keepe my good name and eftimation amongs other
Women." Whych thinge, if he be fo wife (as hee feemeth)
hee ought to Efteeme and Regarde. "Ah, poore Wench, fhe
knoweth not wel, what it is to mingle Hufwiuery with learning,
or to intermeddle diftaues with bookes. Now the mayde when
fhe had founde the Scholler, tolde him as hir miftreffe had commaunded : whereof the Scholler was fo glad, as he with greater
endeuor proceded in his enterprife, and began to write Letters to
the Gentlewoman, which were not refufed, although he could
receyue no aunfweres that pleafed him, but futch as were done
openly. And in this forte the Gentlewoman long time fed him
with delayes. In the ende fhe difcouered all this new loue vnto
hir frend, who was attached with futch an Aking Difeafe in his
heade, as the fame was Fraught with the Reume of Iealoufie :

wherefore fhe to fhewe hir felfe to be fufpected without caufe
(very carefull for the Scholler) fent hir mayde to tell him, that fhe
had no conuenient time to doe the thinge that fhould pleafe him,
fithens he was firft affured of hir loue, but hoped the next Chriftmaffe holly dayes to be at his commaundement: wherefore if he
would vouchfafe to come the night following the firft holly day,
into the Court of hir houfe, fhe would wayte there for his comminge.   The Scholler the beft contented man in the Worlde fayled
not at the time appoyncted, to go to the Gentlewoman's houfe:
where being placed by the Mayde in a bafe Court, and fhut faft
within the fame, he attended for hir, who Suppinge with hir friende
that night, very pleafauntly recited vnto him all that fhe had
determined then to doe, faying: "Thou mayft fee now what loue
I do beare vnto him, of whom thou haft foolifhly conceyued
thys Iealoufie.   To which woordes hir Freende gaue eare with
great delectation, defiringe to fee the effect of that, whereof fhe
gaue him to vnderftand by wordes."   Now as it chaunced the day
before the Snowe fell downe fo thicke from aboue, as it couered
the Earth, by which meanes the Scholler within a very little fpace
after his arriuall, began to be very colde: howbeit hopinge to receyue recompence, he fuffred it paciently.   The Gentlewoman a
little whyle after, fayd vnto hir Freende: "I pray thee let vs goe
into my chuamber, where at a little Window we may looke out,
and fee what he doth that maketh thee fo Iealous, and herken what
aunfwere he will make to my Mayde, whom of purpofe I wyll
fend forth to fpeake vnto him."   When fhe had fo fayde, they
went to the Window, where they feeing the Scholler (they not
feene of hym,) heard the Mayde fpeake thefe wordes: "Rinieri,
my Myftreffe is the angrieft Woman in the World, for that as yet
fhe cannot come vnto thee.   But the caufe is, that one of hir
Brethren is come to vifite hir this Euening, and hath made a long
difcourfe of talke vnto hir, and afterwardes bad himfelfe to Supper, and as yet is not departed, but I thinke hee will not tary
longe, and then immediately fhe will come.   In the meane tyme
fhe prayeth thee to take a little payne."   The Scholler beleeuing
this to be true, fayde vnto hir: "Require your Miftreffe to take no
care for mee till hir leafure may ferue: But yet entreat hir to make

fo mutch haft as fhe can." The Mayde returned and went to Bed,
and the Dame of the houfe fayd then vnto hir frend: "Now fir,
what fay you to this? Doe you thincke that if I loued him, as you
myftruft, that I would fuffer him to tarry beneath in this greate
colde to coole himfelfe?" And hauing fayd fo, fhe went to Bed
with hir frende, who then was partly fatiffied, and all the night
they continued in great pleafure and folace, laughing, and mocking the miferable Scholler that walked vp and downe the Court to
chafe himfelfe, not knowing where to fit, or which way to auoyde
the colde, and curffed the long taryinge, of his miftreffe Brother,
hoping at euery noyfe he heard, that fhe had come to open the
dore to let him in, but his hope was in vayne. Now fhe hauinge
fported hir felfe almoft till midnight, fayd vnto hir frend: "How
think you (fir) by our Scholler, whether iudge you is greater, his
Wyfedome, or the loue that I beare vnto him? The colde that I
make him to fuffer, will extinguifh the heate of fufpition whych
yee conceyued of my wordes the other day." "Yee fay true,"
(fayd hir frend,) "and I do affure you, that like as you are my delight, my reft, my comfort, and all my hope, euen fo I am yours,
and fhalbe during life." For the confirmation of which renewed
amity, they fpared no delights which the louing Goddeffe doeth vfe
to ferue and imploy vpon her feruaunts and futers. And after they
had talked a certayne time, fhe fayd vnto him: "For God's fake
(fir) let vs rife a little, to fee if the glowing fire which this my new
louer hath dayly written vnto me, to burn in him, bee quenched
or not." And ryfing out of their Beds, they went to a little Window
and looking downe into the Courte, they faw the Scholler dauncing
vpon the Snow, whereunto his fhiuering teeth were fo good Inftruments, as he feemed the trimmeft Dauncer that euer trode a Cin-
quepace after futch Muficke, being forced thereunto through the
great colde which he fuffered. And then fhe fayde vnto him:
"What fay you to this my frende, do you not fee how cunninge
I am to make men daunce without Taber, or Pipe?" "Yes in
deede," (fayd hir Louer) "yee be an excellent Mufitian." "Then"
(quod fhee) "let vs go downe to the dore, and I will fpeake vnto
him, but in any Wife fay you nothing, and we fhal heare what reafons and arguments he will frame to mooue me to compaffion, and

perchaunce fhall haue no little paftime to behold him." Whereupon they went downe foftly to the dore, and there without opening the fame, fhee with a fofte voyce out at a little whole, called
the Scholler vnto hir. Which hee hearinge, began to prayfe God
and thancke hym a thoufande times, beleeuing veryly that he
fhould then be let in, and approching the dore, faid: "I am heere
mine (owne fweete heart) open the dore for God's fake, for I am
like to die for Cold." Whom in mocking wife fhe anfwered : "Can
you make me beleue (M. Scholler) that you are fo tender, or that
the colde is fo great as you affirme, for a little Snow newly falne
downe? There be at Paris farre greater Snowes than thefe be, but
to tell you the troth, you cannot come in yet, for my Brother (the
deuell take him) came yefternight to fupper, and is not yet departed,
but by and by hee wyll be gon, and then you fhall obtayne the
effect of your defire, affuring you, that with mutch a doe I haue
ftolne away from hym, to come hither for your comfort, praying
you not to thincke it longe." "Madame" fayd the Scholler, "I
befeech you for God's fake to open the dore, that I may ftand in
couert from the Snow, which within this houre hath fallen in great
aboundaunce, and doth yet continue: and there I will attend your
pleafure." "Alas fweet Friend" (fayd fhe) "the dore maketh futch a
noyfe when it is opened, that it will eafily be heard of my brother,
but I will pray him to depart, that I may quickely returne agayne
to open the fame." "Goe your way then" (fayd the Scholler)
"and I pray you caufe a great fire to be made, that I may warme
mee when I come in, for I can fcarce feele my felfe for colde."
"Why, it is not poffible" (quod the Woman) "if it be true that you
wholly burne in loue for me, as by your fundry Letters written, it
appeareth, but now I perceyue that you mocke me, and therefore
tary there ftill on God's name." Hir frende which heard all this,
and tooke pleafure in thofe wordes, went agayne to Bed with hir,
into whofe eyes no flepe that night coulde enter for the pleafure
and fport they had with the poore Scholler. The vnhappy
wretched Scholler whofe teeth chattered for colde, faring like a
Storke in colde nights, perceyuing himfelfe to be mocked, affayed
to open the dore, or if he might goe out by fome other way: and
feeing it impoffible, ftalking vp and downe like a Lyon, curffed

the nature of the time, the wickedneſſe of the woman, the length
of the Night, and the Folly and ſimplicity of himſelfe: and conceyuing great rage, and deſpight agaynſt hir, turned ſodaynely
the long and feruent loue that he bare hir, into deſpight and
cruell hatred, deuiſing many and diuers meanes to bee reuenged,
whych he then farre more deſired, than hee did in the beginninge
to lye with his Widow. After that longe and tedious night, day
approched, and the dawning thereof began to appeare: wherefore
the mayde inſtruᶜted by hir miſtreſſe, went downe into the court,
and ſeemyng to haue pity uppon the Scholler, ſayd vnto hym:
"The Diuell take hym that euer he came hyther this nyghte, for
hee hath bothe let vs of ſleepe, and hath made you to be frozen
for colde, but take it paciently for this tyme, ſome other Nyght
muſt be appointed. For I know well that neuer thyng coulde
chaunce more diſpleaſantly to my Miſtreſſe than this." But the
Scholler full of dyſdayne, lyke a wyſe man which knew well that
threats and menacyng words, were weapons without hands to the
threatned, retayned in hys Stomacke that whych intemporate wyll
would haue broken forth, and wyth ſo quiet Woordes as hee coulde,
not ſhewynge hymſelfe to bee angry, ſayd: "In deede I haue ſuffred
the worſte Nyghte that euer I dyd, but I knowe the ſame was not
throughe your miſtreſſe fault, bicauſe ſhee hauing pitye vppon
me, and as you ſay, that which cannot be to Night, may be done
another time, commend me then vnto hir, and farewell." And thus
the poore Scholler ſtiffe for colde, ſo well as hee coulde, retourned
home to his houſe, where for the extremitye of the tyme and
lacke of ſleepe beyng almoſt deade, he threwe hymſelfe vppon his
bed, and when he awaked, his Armes and Legges had no feeling.
Wherefore he ſent for Phyſitions and tolde them of the colde he
had taken, who incontinently prouided for his health: and yet
for al their beſt and ſpedy remedies, they could ſcarce recouer
his Iointes and Sinewes, wherein they did what they could: and
had it not bene that he was yong, and the Sommer approching,
it had ben to mutch for him to haue endured. But after he was
come to Healthe, and grewe to be luſty, ſecrete Malyce ſtill reſting
in his breaſte, hee thought vpon reuenge. And it chaunced in a
lytle tyme after, that Fortune prepared a new accident to the

ſcholer to ſatiſfy his deſire, bycauſe the young man which was beloued of the Gentlewoman, not caring any longer for hir, fel in loue with an other, and gaue ouer the ſolace and pleaſure he was wont to doe to miſtreſſe Helena, for which deſpite ſhe conſumed herſelf in wepings and lamentations. But hir maid hauing pity vpon hir miſtreſſe ſorrowes, knowing no meanes to remoue the melancoly which ſhe conceiued for the loſſe of hir friend, and ſeing the ſcholler daily paſſe by accordinge to his common Cuſtome, conceiued a fooliſhe beliefe that hir miſtreſſe friend might be brought to loue hir agayne, and wholly recouered, by ſome charme or other ſleight of Necromancy, to bee wrought and brought to paſſe by the Scholler. Which deuiſe ſhe tolde vnto hir miſtreſſe, and ſhe vndiſcretely (and without due conſideration that if the ſcholler had any knowledge in that ſcience, he would helpe himſelfe) gaue credite to the words of hir mayde, and by and by ſayd vnto hir, that ſhee was able to bring it to paſſe, if he would take it in hande, and therewithall promiſed aſſuredly, that for recompenſe he ſhould vſe hir at his pleaſure. The mayde diligently tolde the Scholler hereof, who very ioyfull for thoſe newes, ſayd vnto himſelfe: "O God, prayſed be thy name, for now the time is come, that by thy helpe I ſhall requite the iniuries done vnto me by this wicked Woman, and be recompenſed of the great loue that I bare vnto hir:" And aunſwered the mayd: "Go tell thy miſtreſſe that for this matter ſhe neede to take no care, for if hir frend were in India, I can preſently force him to come hither, and aſke hir forgiueneſſe of the fault he hath committed agaynſt hir. And the maner, and way how to vſe hir ſelfe in this behalfe, I will gieue hir to vnderſtand when it ſhal pleaſe hir to appoinĉt me: and fayle not to tell hir what I ſay, comforting hir in my behalfe." The mayde caried the aunſwere, and it was concluded, that they ſhould talke more hereof at the Church of S. Lucie, whither being come, and reaſoning together alone, not remembring that ſhe had brought the Scholler almoſt to the poynĉt of death, ſhe reueyled vnto him all the whole matter, and the thing which he deſired, praying him inſtantly to helpe hir, to whome the ſcholler ſayd: "True it is lady, that amongs other things which I learned at Paris, the arte of Necromancie, (whereof

I haue very great fkill,) is one: But bycaufe it is mutch difpleafaunt to God, I haue made an othe neuer to vfe it, eyther for my
felfe, or for any other: howbeit the loue which I beare you, is
of futch force, as I cannot deny you any requeft, yea and if I
fhould be damned amongs all the deuils in hell, I am ready to
performe your pleafure. But I tell you before, that it is a harder
matter to be done, than paraduenture you belieue, and fpecially
where a Woman fhall prouoke a Man to loue, or a Man the Woman,
bycaufe it can not be done by the propre Perfon, whome it doth
touche, and therefore it is meete, whatfoeuer is done, in any wyfe
not to be affrayde, for that the cuniuration muft bee made in the
Nyght, and in a folytarie place wythout Companye : which thing
I know not how you fhal bee difpofed to doe." To whom the
Woman more amorous than wife, aunfwered: "Loue prycketh
mee in futch wife, as there is nothyng but I dare attempt, to haue
him againe, that caufeleffe hath forfaken me. But tel me I befeech you wherein it behoueth that I be fo bold and hardy." The
Scholer (fubtil inough) faid: "I mufte of neceffity make an image
of braffe, in the name of him that you defire to haue, which being
fent vnto you you muft, when the Mone is at hir ful, bath your felf
ftark naked in a running riuer at the firft houre of fleepe VII.
times with the fame image: and afterwards beyng ftil naked, you
muft go vp into fome tree or houfe vnhabited, and turning your
felfe towardes the North fide thereof wyth the image in your hand
you fhal fay VII. times certain words, that I wil giue you in writing, which when you haue done, two damfels fhal come vnto you,
the faireft that euer you faw, and they fhall falute you, humbly
demaundyng what your pleafure is to commaund them : to whome
you fhal willingly declare in good order what you defire : and take
hede aboue al things, that you name not one for an other : and
when they begonne, you may defcend downe to the place where
you left your Apparel, and array your felfe agayne, and afterwardes
retourne home vnto your houfe, and affure your felf, that before
the mid of the nexte Nyghte folowing, your Fryend fhall come vnto
you weepyng, and crying Mercye and forgyueneffe at youre
Handes. And know yee, that from that tyme forth, he wil neuer
forfake you for any other." The gentlewoman bearing thofe

words, gaue great credyte thervnto: and thought that already fhe
helde hir fryend betweene hir Armes, and very ioyfull fayd:
"Doubt not fir, but I wyll accomplyfh al that you haue inioyned
me: and I haue the meeteft place in the World to doe it: for vppon
the valley of Arno, very neare the Ryuer fyde I haue a Manor
houfe, fecretly to woorke any attempt that I lift: and now it is
the moneth of Iuly, in which tyme bathing is moft pleafaunt.
And alfo I remembre that not far from the Ryuer, there is a lyttle
Toure vnhabited, into which one can fcarce get vp, but by a certain Ladder made of chefnut tree, which is already there, whereuppon the fhephierds do fometime afcende to the turraffe of the
fame Toure, to looke for their cattell when they be gone aftray:
and the place is very folitarie out of the way. Into that Toure
wyll I goe vp, and truft to execute what you haue requyred me."
The Scholler which knew very well both the village whereof fhe
fpake, and alfo the Toure, right glad for that he was affured of his
purpofe, fayde: "Madame, I was neuer there, ne yet do knowe
the village, nor the Toure, but if it bee as you faye, it is not poffible to finde anye better place in the Worlde: wherefore when
the tyme is come, I wyll fend you the Image, and the prayer. But
I heartily befeech you, when you haue obtained your defire, and
do perceyue that I haue well ferued your turne, to haue me in
remembraunce, and to keepe your promyfe." Which the Gentlewoman affured hym to doe withoute fayle, and taking hir leaue of
him, fhe retired home to hir houfe. The Scholer ioyfull for that
his deuife fhould in deede come to paffe, caufed an image to be
made with certaine Characters, and wrote a tale of a Tubbe in ftede
of the prayer. And when hee fawe tyme he fent them to the
Gentlewoman, aduertifing hir that the Nyght folowyng, fhe muft
doe the thing he had appoynted hir. Then to procede in his
enterprife, he and his man went fecretly to one of his fryends
houfes that dwelte harde by the towne. The Woman on the other
fide, and hir Mayde repaired to hir place: where when it was
nyght, makyng as though fhe would go flepe, fhe fent hir Mayde
to Bed: afterwards about ten of the Clocke fhe conueyed hirfelf
very foftly out of hir lodgyng, and repayred neare to the Towne vpon
the riuer of Arno, and lookyng aboute hir, not feeing or perceiu-

ing any man, fhe vnclothed hir felfe, and hidde hir apparell vnder
a bufh of Thornes, and then bathed hir felfe VII. tymes with the
Image, and afterwardes ftarke naked, holding the fame in her
hand, fhe went towardes the Toure. The Scholler at the beginning
of the Nyghte beying hydden wyth hys feruaunt amongs the
willowes and other trees neere the Toure, faw all the aforefayde
thinges, and hir alfo paffing naked by him, (the whiteneffe of
whofe body furpaffed as he thought, the darkneffe of the night,
fo farre as blacke exceedeth white) who afterwardes behelde hir
Stomack, and the other partes of hir body, which feemed vnto him
to be very deleĉtable. And remembringe what would fhortly
come to paffe, he had fome pitty vppon hir, on the other fide, the
temptation of the Flefh fodaynely affayled, hym, prouoking him
to iffue forth of the fecret corner, to Surprife hir, and to take his
pleafure vpon hir. But calling to hys rememberaunce what fhee
was, and what great wrong hee had fuftayned, his mallice began
to kindle agayne, and did remoue his pitty, and luft, continuing
ftill ftedfaft in his determination, fuffring her to paffe hir Iorney.
The Wydow being vppon the Toure, and turning hir face towards
the North, began to fay the wordes which the Scholler had giuen
hir. Within a while after the Scholler entred in very foftly, and
tooke away the ladder whereupon fhe got vp, and ftoode ftill to
heare what fhe did fay and doe. Who hauing VII. times recited
hir prayer, attended the comming of the two damfels: for whom
fhe wayted fo long in vayne, and therewithall began to be ex-
treemely colde, and perceyued the dawning of the day appeare.
Wherefore taking great difpleafure that it came not to paffe as
the Scholler had tolde hir, fhe fpake theefe wordes to hir felfe:
"I doubt mutch leaft this Scholler will rewarde mee with futch
another night, as wherein once I made him to wayte: but if he
haue done it for that refpeĉt, he is not well reuenged, for the
nights now want the third part of the length of thofe, then, befides
the colde that he indured, which was of greater extremity." And
that the day might not difcouer hir, fhe woulde haue gone downe
from the Toure, but fhe found the Ladder to be taken away. Then
as thou the Worlde had molten vnder hir Feete, hir heart began to
fayle, and Fayntinge, fell downe vppon the tarraffe of the toure,

and when hir force reuiued agayne, fhe began pitifully to weepe
and complayne.   And knowing well that the Scholler had done
that deede for reuenge, fhe grew to be angry wyth hir felfe, for
that fhee hadde Offended another, and to mutch trufted hym whom
fhe ought (by good reafon) to haue accoumpted hir enimy.   And
after fhe had remayned a great while in this plight, then looking
if there were any way for hir to goe downe, and perceyuinge none,
fhe renued hir weeping, whofe minde great care and forrow did
pierce faying thus to hir felfe: "O vnhappy wretch, what will thy
brethren fay, thy Parents, thy Neyghbors, and generally all they
of Florence, when they fhall vnderftande that thou haft bene
found heere naked? Thy honefty which hitherto hath bene neuer
ftayned, fhall now bee blotted with the ftayne of fhame, yea, and
if thou were able to finde (for reamedy hereof) any matter of excufe (futch as might be founde) the wicked Scholler (who knoweth
all thy doings) will not fuffer thee to ly: ah miferable wretch,
that in one houre's fpace, thou haft loft both thy freende and
thyne honour. What fhall become of thee? Who is able to couer
thy fhame?"   When fhe had thus complayned hirfelfe, hir forrowe
was not fo great as fhee was like to caft hirfelfe headlong downe
from the Toure: but the Sunne being already rifen, fhe approched
neare one of the corners of the Walle, efpying if fhe coulde fee any
Boy keeping of cattell, that fhe might fend him for hir Mayde.
And it chaunced that the Scholler which lay and flept in couert,
awaked, one efpying the other, the Scholler faluted hir thus:
" Good morow, Lady, be the Damfels yet come?" The Woman feeing, and hearing him, began agayne bitterly to weepe, and prayed
him to come vp to the Toure, that fhe might fpeake with him. The
Scholler was thereunto very agreable, and fhe lying on hir belly
vpon the terraffe of the Touer, difcouering nothing but hir head
ouer the fide of the fame, fayd vnto him weeping: "Rinieri,
truly, if euer I caufed thee to endure an ill Night, thou art now well
reuenged on me; for although it be the moneth of Iuly, I thought
(becaufe I was naked) that I fhould haue frofen to death this
night for cold, befides my great, and continuall Teares for the
offence which I haue done thee, and of my Folly for beleeuing thee,

that maruell it is mine eyes do remayne within my head: And
therefore I pray thee, not for the loue of me, whom thou oughteſt
not to loue, but for thine owne ſake which art a gentleman, that
the ſhame and payne which I haue ſuſtayned, may ſatiſſy the
offence and wrong I haue committed agaynſt thee: and cauſe mine
apparell I beſeech thee to be brought vnto me, that I may goe
downe from hence, and doe not robbe mee of that, which afterwardes thou art not able to reſtore, which is, myne honor: for if
I haue deceyued thee of one night, I can at all times when it
ſhall pleaſe thee, render vnto thee for that one, many. Let
it ſuffice thee then with this, and like an honeſt man content thy
ſelfe by being a little reuenged on me, by making me to know
now what it is to hurt another. Do not, I pray thee, practiſe thy
power againſt a woman: for the Egle hath no fame for conquering
of the Doue. Then for the loue of God, and for thine honor ſake,
haue pitty and remorſe vpon me." The Scholler with a cruel heart
remembring the iniury that he hath receyued, and ſeeing hir ſo
to weepe and pray, conceyued at one inſtant both pleaſure and
griefe in his minde: pleaſure of the reuenge which he aboue all
things deſired, and griefe mooued his manhoode to haue compaſſion vpon the myſerable woman. Notwithſtanding, pitty not
able to ouercome the fury of his reuenge, he aunſwered: "Mis-
treſſe Helena, if my praiers (which in dede I could not moyſten
with teares, ne yet ſweeten them with ſugred woordes, as you doe
yours nowe) might haue obtained that night wherein I thought
I ſhould haue died for colde in the Court full of ſnowe, to haue
bene conueyed by you into ſome couert place, an eaſie matter it
had beene for mee at this inſtant to heare your ſuite. But if now
more than in times paſt your honor do waxe warme, and that it
greeueth you to ſtand ſtarke naked, make your prayers to him,
betweene whoſe Armes you ware not offended to be naked that
night, wherein you hearde me trot vp and downe your Courte,
my Teeth chattering for cold and marching vpon the Snow: And
at his handes ſeeke releefe, and pray him to bring your Clothes,
and fetch a Ladder that you may come downe: Force your ſelfe to
ſet your honor's care on him for whom both then, and now beſides
many other times, you haue not feared to put the ſame in perill,

Why doe you not cal for him to come and help you? And to
whom doth your help better appertayne than vnto him? You are
his owne, and what things will he not prouyde in this diftreffe of
yours? Or elfe what perfon will hee feeke to fuccour, if not to
helpe and fuccour you? Call him (O foolifh woman) and proue if
the loue which thou beareft him, and thy wit together with his,
be able to deliuer thee from my Folly, where (when both you were
togethers) you tooke your Pleafure. And now thou hafte Experience wheather my Folly or the Loue which thou diddeft beare vnto
him, is greateft. And be not now fo Lyberall, and Curteous of
that which I go not about to feeke: referue thy good Nights to thy
beloued freende, if thou chaunce to efcape from hence aliue: for
from my felfe I cleerely difcharge you both. And truly I haue
had to mutch of one: and fufficient it is for mee to bee mocked
once. Moreouer by thy crafty talke vttered by fubtill fpeache,
and by thyne vntimely prayfe, thou thinkeft to force the getting
of my good will, and thou calleft me Gentleman, valiaunt man,
thinkinge thereby to withdrawe my valyaunte minde from punifhing of thy wretched body: but thy flatteries fhall not yet bleare
mine vnderftanding eyes, as once wyth thy vnfathyfull promifes
thou diddeft beguile my ouerweeninge wit. I now to well do
know, and thereof thee well affure, that all the time I was a Scholler in Paris, I neuer learned fo mutch as thou in one night diddeft
teach mee. But put the Cafe that I were a valiaunt man, yet thou
art none of them vpon whom valiaunce ought to fhewe his effe&s:
and for the end of futch tormenting and paffing cruell beafts, as
thou art, only death is fitteft rewarde: for if a Woman made but
halfe thefe playnts, there is no man, but woulde affwage his reuenge. But yet as I am no Eagle, and thou no Doue, but a moft
venomous Serpent, I intend fo well as I can to perfecute thee mine
auncient enimy, wyth the greateft mallice I can deuife, which I
cannot fo properly cal reuenge, as I may terme it Corre&ion: for
that the reuenge of a matter ought to furmount the Offence, and
I will beftow no reuenge on thee: for if I were difpofed to apply
my mynde therevnto, for refpe& of thy difpleafure done to me,
thy Lyfe fhould not fuffife, nor one hundred more like vnto thine:
which if I tooke away, I fhould but rid the Worlde of a moft vile,

and wicked woman. And to fay the truth, what other art thou then a Deuill accept a little beauty in thy Face, which within few yeares will vanifhe and confume: for thou tookeft no care to kill, and deftroy an honeft man (as thou euen now diddeft terme me) whofe Life, may in tyme to come bee more profitable to the Worlde, than an hundred thoufand futch as thyne, fo long as the World indureth. I wil teach thee then by the paine thou fuffreft, what is it to mock futch Men as bee of fkyll, and what maner of thyng it is to delude and Scorne poore fchollers, gyuing thee warning hereby, that thou never fall into futch folly, if thou efcapeft this. But if thou haue fo great a will to come downe as thou fayeft thou haft, why doeft thou not throwe downe thy felfe headlonge, that by breaking of thy Necke (if it pleafe God) at one inftante thou rid thy felfe of the payne, wherein thou fayeft thou art, and make mee the beft contented man of the Worlde. For this tyme I wyll fay no more to thee, but that I haue done inough to make thee clime fo high. Learne then now fo wel how thou maift get down, as thou didft know how to mock and deceyue me." Whyle the Scholler had preached vnto hir thefe words, the wretched woman wepte continually, and the time ftil did paffe away, the Sunne increafing more and more: but when the Scholler held his peace, fhe replyed: "O cruell man, if that curffed nyght was grieuous vnto thee, and my fault appeared great, cannot my youth and Beauty, my Teares and humble Prayers bee able to mitigate thy wrath and to moue thee to pitty: do at leaft that thou mayft be moued and thy cruell minde appeafed for that onely act, let me once again be trufted of thee, and fith I haue manifefted al my defire, pardon me for this tyme, fith thou haft fufficiently made me feele the penance of my finne. For, if I had not repofed my truft in thee, thou hadft not now reuenged thy felf on me, which with defire moft fpytefull thou doeft full well declare. Gyue ouer then thine anger, and pardon me henceforth: for I am determined if thou wilt forgeue mee, and caufe me to come downe out of this place, to forfake for euer that vnfaithfull Louer, and to receiue thee for my only friend and Lord. Moreouer where thou greatly blameft my beauty, efteeming it to be fhort, and of fmal accompt, futch as it is, and the like of other women I know, not be regarded for other cauſe but for paſtime and pleſure of youthly Men, and therefore not to be contemned : and thou thy ſelf truly art not very old ; and albeit that cruelly I am intreated of thee, yet can I not beleue that thou wouldeſt haue me ſo miſerably to die, as to caſt my ſelfe down headlong, like one deſperate, before thine eyes, whome (except thou were a lier as thou ſeemeſt to be now) in time paſt I did wel pleaſe and like. Haue pitye then upon me, for God's ſake, for the Sunne begins to grow exceding hot, and as the extreame and bitter cold did hurt me the laſt Night euen ſo the heat beginneth to moleſt me." Whereunto the Scholler which kept hir there for the nonce, and for his pleaſure, anſwered : " Miſtreſſe you did not now commit your faith to me for any loue you bare, but to get that again which you had loſt, wherfore that deſerueth no good turne, but greater pain : and fondlye thou thinkeſt this to be the onely meanes, whereby I am able to take deſired reuenge. For I haue a thouſand other wayes and a thouſand Trappes haue I layed to tangle thy feete, in makynge thee beleue that I dyd loue thee : in ſutch wyſe as thou ſhouldeſt haue gone no where at any tyme, if thys had not chanced but thou ſhouldeſt haue fallen into one of them : and ſurely thou couldeſt haue falne into none of them, but would haue bred thee more anoyaunce and ſhame than this (which I choſe not for thyne eaſe, but for my greater pleaſure.) And beſides if all theſe meanes had fayled me, the pen ſhould not, wherewyth I would haue diſplayed thee in ſutch Colours, as when the ſimple brute thereof hadde come to thyne eares, thou wouldeſt haue deſired a thouſand times a Day, that thou hadſt neuer bene born. For the forces of the pen be farre more vehement, than they can eſteeme that haue not proued them by experience. I ſwear vnto thee by God, that I doe reioyſe, and ſo wil to the ende, for this reuenge I take of thee, and ſo haue I done from the beginning : but if I had with pen painted thy maners to the Worlde, thou ſhouldeſt not haue ben ſo mutch aſhamed of other, as of thy ſelfe, that rather than thou wouldeſt haue loked mee in the Face agayne, thou wouldeſt haue plucked thyne Eyes oute of thy head : and therefore reproue no more the Sea, for beeing increaſed wyth a lyttle Brooke. For thy loue, or for that thou wilt be mine own, I care not, as I haue already told thee, and loue him again if thou canft, fo mutch as thou wilt, to whome for the hatred that I haue borne, I prefently bear fo mutch good wyll agayne, and for the pleafure that he hath don thee now. You be amorous and couet the loue of young men, bicaufe you fee theyr Colour fomewhat frefh, their beard more black, their bodies well fhaped to daunce and runne at Tylt and Ryng, but al thefe qualities haue they bad, that be growne to elder yeares, and they by good experience know what other are yet to learn. Moreouer you deeme them the better horffemen, bicaufe they can iourney more myles a day than thofe that be of farther yeares. Truely I confeffe, that with great paynes they pleafe futch Venerial Gentlewomen as you be, who doe not perceyue (like fauage Beaftes) what heapes of euill doe lurke vnder the forme of fayre apparance. Younge men be not content with one Louer, but fo many as they behold, they do defire, and of fo many they think themfelues worthy: wherefore their loue cannot be ftable. And that this is true, thou mayeft now be thine owne wytneffe. And yong men thynkyng themfelues worthy, to be honoured and cherifhed of theyr Ladies, haue none other glory but to vaunt themfelues of thofe whome they have enioyed: whych fault maketh many to yeld themfelues to thofe that be difcrete and wife, and to futch as be no blabbes or Teltales. And where thou fayeft that thy loue is knowne to none, but to thy mayde and me, thou art deceiued, if thou beleue the fame, for al the inhabitants of the ftreete wherein thy Louer dwelleth, and the ftreete alfo wherein thy houfe doth ftand, talke of nothynge more than of your Loue. But many times in futch cafes, the party whome futch Brute doth touch, is the laft that knoweth it. Moreouer, young men do robbe thee, where they of elder yeares do gyue thee. Thou then (which haft made futch choyfe), remayne to him whome thou haft chofen, and me (whom thou flouteft) gyue leaue to apply to an other: for I haue found a Woman to bee my fryend, which is of an other difcretion than thou art, and knoweth me better than thou doft. And that thou mayft in an other world be more certaine of myne Eyes defire, than thou hitherto art, throwe thy felfe downe fo foone as thou canft, that thy foule already (as I fuppofe) receiued betwene the armes of the diuel hym felfe may

fe if mine eyes be troubled or not, to view thee breake thy Necke.
But bicaufe I think thou wilt not do me that good turne, I fay if
the Sunne begin to warme thee, remember the cold thou madeft
me fuffer, which if thou canft mingle with that heat, no doubt
thou fhalt feele the fame more temperate." The comfortleffe
Woman feeing that the Scholler's words tended but to cruell end,
began to wcepe and faid: "Now then fith nothing can moue
thee to take pity for my fake, at left wife for the loue of hir,
whom thou faieft to be of better difcretion than I, take fome
compaffion: for hir fake (I fay) whom thou calleft thy friend,
pardon mee and bryng hither my clothes that I may put them on,
and caufe me if it pleafe thee to come down from hence." Then the
Scholler began to laugh, and feing that it was a good while paft
III. of the clocke, he anfwered: "Well go to, for that woman's
fake I cannot wel fay nay, or refufe thy requeft, tel me where thy
garments be, and I wyll go feke them, and caufe thee to come
downe." She beleuing hym, was fome what comforted, and told
hym the place where fhe had beftowed them. And the Scholler
going out of the Toure, commaunded his feruaunt to tarry there,
and to take heede that none went in vntil he came againe. Then
he departed to one of hys friends houfes, where he wel refrefhed
himfelfe, and afterwards when he thought time, he layd him downe
to flepe. Al that fpace miftreffe Helena whych was ftyll vpon the
Toure, and recomforted with a lyttle foolifh hope, forrowful beyonde meafure, began to fit downe, feeking fome fhadowed place
to beftow hir felfe, and with bitter thoughts and heauy cheare in
good deuotion, wayted for his comming, now mufing, now wepyng,
then hopyng, and fodaynely difpayring the Scholler's retourne wyth
hir Clothes: and chaunging from one thought to another, like one
that was weary of trauel, and had taken no reft al the Nyght, fhe
fel into a litle flumbre. But the Sun whych was paffing hote,
being aboute noone, glaunced his burning beames vpon hir
tender body and bare head, with futch force, as not only it finged
the flefh in fight, but alfo did chip and parch the fame with futch
rofting heat, as fhe which foundly flepte, was conftrayned to
wake: and feling that raging warmth, defirous fomewhat to remoue hir felf, fhe thought in turning that all hir tofted flefh had

opened and broken, like vnto a fkyn of parchement holden againſt
the fire: befides with payne extreame, hir head began to ake,
with futch vehemence, as it feemed to be knocked in pieces: and
no maruel, for the pament of the Toure was fo paffing hotte, as
neither vpon hir feete, or by other remedy, fhee could find place
of reſt. Wherefore without power to abide in one place, fhe ſtil
remoued to and fro wepying bitterly. And moreouer, for that no
Wynd did blow, the Toure was haunted wyth futch a fwarme of
Flies, and Gnats, as they lighting vppon hir parched fleſh, did fo
cruelly byte and ſtinge hir, that euery of them feemed worſſe than
the prycke of a Nedle, which made hir to beſtirre hir hands, inces-
fantly to beate them off curſing ſtill hir felfe, hir Lyfe, hir friend
and Scholler. And being thus and with futch pain bitten and
afflicted with the vehement heat of the Sun, with the Flies and
gnats, hungry, and mutch more thyrſty, affailed with a thoufand
grieuous thoughts, fhe arofe vp, and began to loke about hir if
fhe could heare or fee any perfon, purpoſing whatfoeuer came of
it to call for helpe. But hir ill fortune had taken way al this hoped
meanes of hir reliefe: for the Hufbandmen and other Laborers
were al gone out of the fields to ſhrowd themfelues from the heate
of the day, fparing their trauail abrode, to threſh their corn and
doe other things at home, by reafon whereof fhe neither faw nor
hearde any thing, except Butterflies, humble bees, crickets, and the
riuer of Arno, which making hir luſt to drink of the water quenched
hir thirſt nothing at al, but rather did augment the fame. She fawe
befides in many places, woodes, fhadows and houfes, which lykewyfe did breede hir double grief, for defire fhe had vnto the fame.
But what fhal we fpeak any more of this vnhappy woman? The
Sunne aboue, and the hot Toure paiment below, wyth the bitings
of the flies and gnats, had on euery part fo dreſſed hir tender
corps, that where before the whiteneffe of hir body did paſſe the
darkeneffe of the Night, the fame was become red, al arayed and
fpotted wyth gore bloud, that to the beholder and viewer of hir
ſtate, fhe feemed the moſt yll fauored thyng of the Worlde: and
remayning in thys plyght without hope or councel, fhe loked
rather for death than other comfort. The Scholler after the
Clocke had founded three in the afternoon, awaked, and remem-

bring his lady, went to the Toure to fee what was become of hir, and fent his man to dinner, that had eaten nothing all that day. The Gentlewoman hearing the Scholler, repayred fo feeble and tormented as fhee was, vnto the trap doore, and fitting vppon the fame, pityfully weeping began to fay: "Rinieri, thou art be-yonde meafure reuenged on me, for if I made thee freefe all night in mine open Court, thou hafte tofted me to day vppon this Toure, nay rather burnt with heate, confumed me: and befides that, to dye and fterue for hunger, and thirft. Wherefore I pray thee for God's fake to come vp, and fith my heart is faynt to kill my felfe, I pray thee heartely fpeedily to do it. For aboue all things I defire to dy, fo great and bitter is the torment which I endure. And if thou wilt not fhewe me that fauor, yet caufe a glaffe of Water to be brought vnto me, that I may moyften my mouth, fith my teares bee not able to coole the fame, fo great is the drouth and heate I haue within." Wel knew the Scholler by hir voyce, hir weake eftate, and fawe befides the moft part of hir body all tofted with the Sunne: by the viewe whereof, and humble fute of hir, he conceiued a little pitty. Notwythftanding he aunfweared hir in this wife: "Wicked woman thou fhalt not dye with my hands, but of thine owne, if thou defire the fame, and fo mutch water fhalt thou haue of me for coolinge of thine heate, as dampned Diues had in hell at Lazarus handes, when he lifted up his cry to Abraham, holdinge that faued wighte within his bleffed bofome, or as I had fire of thee for eafing of my colde. The greater is my griefe that the vehemence of my colde muft be cured with the heate of futch a ftincking carion beaft, and thy heate healed with the coldneffe of moft Soote and fauerous Water diftilled from the orient Rofe. And where I was in daunger to loofe my Limmes, and life, thou wilt renew thy Beauty like the Serpent that cafteth his Skin once a yeare." "Oh myferable wretch" (fayd the woman) "God gieue him futch Beauty gotten in this forte, that wifheth me futch euill. But (thou more cruell than any other beaft) what heart hafte thou, thus like a Tyraunte to deale with me? What more grieuous payne coulde I endure of thee, or of any other, than I do, if I had killed, and done to death thy parents or whole race of thy ftocke and kin with moft cruel torments?

Truely I know not what greater tyranny coulde be vfed agaynſt a Trayter that had facced or put a whole Citty to the fword, than that thou haſte done to me, to make my fleſh to bee the foode and roſt meate of the Sunne, and the baite for licorous flies, not vouch-fafing to reach hither a fimple glaffe of Water whych would haue bene graunted to the condempned Theefe, and Manqueller, when they be haled forth to hanging, yea wine moſt commonly, if they aſke the fame. Now for that I fee thee ſtill remayne in obſtinate mind, and that my paſſion can nothinge mooue thee, I wyll prepare paciently to receiue my death, that God may haue mercy on my foule, whom I humbly befeech with his righteous eyes to beholde that cruell act of thyne." And with thofe woords, ſhe approched with payne to the middle of the terraffe, defpayring to efcape that burning heate, and not onely once, but a thoufande times, (befides hir other forowes) ſhe thought to fowne for thirſt, and bitterly wept without ceafing, complayning hir miſhap. But being almoſt night, the Scholler thought hee had done inough, wherefore he tooke hir clothes, and wrapping the fame within his feruaunt's cloke, he went home to the Gentlewoman's houfe where he founde before the gate, hir mayde fitting al fad and heauy, of whom he aſked where hir miſtreſſe was. "Syr," (fayd ſhe) "I cannot tell, I thought this morning to finde hir a Bed, where I left hir yeſter night, but I cannot finde hir there, nor in any other place, ne yet can tell wheather to goe feeke hir, which maketh my hearte to throb fome miſfortune chaunced vnto hir. But (fir quod ſhe) cannot you tell where ſhe is?" The Scholler aunfwered : "I would thou haddeſt bene with hir in the place where I left hir, that I might haue bene reuenged on thee fo well, as I am of hir. But beleue aſſuredly, that thou ſhalt not efcape my handes vntill I pay thee thy defert, to the intent hereafter in mocking other, thou mayſt haue caufe to remember me." When hee had fayde fo, hee willed his man to gieue the mayde hir Miſtreſſe Clothes, and then did bidde hir feeke hir out if ſhee would. The Seruaunte did his Mayſter's commaundment, and the Mayde hauing receyued them, knewe them by and by, and markinge well the fcholler's wordes, ſhe doubted leaſt hee had flayne hir Miſtreſſe, and mutch adoe ſhe had to refrayne from crying out. And the Scholler being gone,

fhe tooke hir Miftreffe Garments, and ran vnto the Toure.   That
day by hap, one of the Gentlewoman's labouring Men had two of
his hogges runne a ftray, and as he went to feeke them (a little
while after the Scholler's departure) he approched neare the Toure
looking round about if he might see them.   In the bufie fearche
of whom hee heard the miferable playnt that the vnhappy Woman
made, wherefore fo loude as he coulde, he cried out: "Who
weepeth there aboue?"   The Woman knew the voice of hir man,
and calling him by his name, fhee fayde vnto him: "Goe home I
pray thee to call my mayde and caufe her to come vp hither vnto
me."   The fellow knowing his miftreffe voice fayd vnto hir:
"What Dame, who hath borne you vp fo hygh? Your mayde
hath fought you al this day, and who would haue thought to finde
you there?"   He then taking the ftaues of the Ladder, did fet it vp
againft the Toure as it ought to be, and bounde the fteppes that
were wanting, with faftenings of Wyllowe twigges, and futch like
pliant ftuffe as he could finde.   And at that inftant the mayde
came thither, who fo foone as fhe was entred the Toure, not able
to forbeare hir voyce, beating hir hands, fhee began to crye:
"Alas fweete Miftreffe where be you?"   She hearing the voyce of
hir Mayde aunfwered fo well as fhee could: "Ah (fweete Wench)
I am heere aboue, cry no more, but bring me hither my clothes."
When the mayde heard hir fpeake, by and by for ioy, in hafte
fhe mounted vp the Ladder, which the Labourer had made ready,
and with his helpe gat vp to the Terraffe of the Toure, and feeing
hir Myftreffe refembling not a humayne body but rather a wodden
Faggot halfe confumed with fire, all weary and whithered, lying
a long ftarke naked vppon the Grounde, fhe began with hir Nayles
to wreke the griefe vpon hir Face, and wept ouer hir with futch
vehemency as if fhe had beene deade.   But hir Dame prayed hir
for God's fake to holde hir peace, and to help hir to make hir
ready: and vnderftanding by hir, that no man knewe where fhe
was become, except they which caried home hir clothes, and the
Labourer that was prefent there, fhee was fomewhat recomforted,
and prayed them for God's fake to fay nothing of that chaunce to
any perfon.   The Laborer after mutch talke, and requeft to his
Miftreffe, to be of good cheere, when fhee was ryfen vp, caried

hir downe vpon his Necke, for that fhe was not able to goe fo
farre, as out of the Toure. The poore Mayde which came behinde,
in goinge downe the Ladder without takinge heede, hir foote fayled,
and fallinge downe to the Grounde, fhee brake hir Thigh, for griefe
whereof fhe roared, and cryed out lyke a Lyon. Wherefore the
Labourer hauing placed his Dame vpon a greene banke, went to fee
what hurt the Mayde had taken, and perceyued that fhe had
broken hir Thigh, he caried hir likewife vnto that banke, and
placed hir befides hir miftreffe, who feeing one mifchiefe
vppon another to chaunce, and that fhe of whom fhe hoped for
greater help, than of any other, had broken hir Thigh, forrowfull
beyonde meafure, renewed hir cry fo miferably, as not onely the
Labourer was not able to comforte hir, but he himfelf began to
weepe for company. The Sunne hauinge trauayled into hys
Wefterne courfe, and taking his farewell by fettling himfelfe to
reft, was at the poynct of goinge downe. And the poore defolate
woman vnwilling to be benighted, went home to the Labourer's
houfe, where taking two of his Brothers, and his Wyfe, returned to
fetch the Mayde, and caried hir home in a Chayre. Then cheering
vp hys Dame with a little frefh water, and many fayre Wordes, he
caried bir vpon his Necke into a Chaumber, afterwardes his Wyfe
made hir warm Drinks and Meates, and putting of hir clothes,
layd hir in hir Bed, and tooke order that the miftreffe and maide
that night were caried to Florence, where the Miftreffe ful of lies,
deuifed a Tale all out of order of that which chaunced to hir, and
hir Mayde, making hir Brethren, hir Sifters, and other hir neighbours beleeue, that by flufh of lightning, and euill Sprites, hir face
and body were Bliftered, and the Mayde ftroken vnder the Arfe
bone with a Thunderbolt. Then Phyfitians were fent for, who
not without greate griefe, and payne to the Woman (which many
tymes left hir Skin fticking to the Sheets) cured hir cruell Feuer,
and other hir difeafes, and lykewife the mayde of hir Thigh :
which caufed the Gentlewoman to forget hir Louer, and from that
time forth wifely did beware and take heede whom fhe did mocke,
and where fhe did beftow hir loue. And the Scholler knowing
that the Mayde had broken hir Thigh, thought himfelfe fufficiently
reuenged, ioyfully paffing by them both many times in filence.

Beholde the reward of a foolifh wanton widow for hir Mockes and
Flouts, thinking that no greate care or more prouident heede
ougbt to be taken in iefting with a Scholler, than with any other
common perfon, nor well remembring how they doe know (not all,
I say, but the greateft parte) where the Diuell holdeth his Tayle:
and therefore take heede good Wyues, and Wydowes, how you giue
your felues to mockes and daliaunce, fpecially of Schollers. But
nowe turne we to another Wyddow that was no amorous Dame
but a fober Matrone, a motherly Gentlewoman, that by pitty,
and Money Redeemed, and Raunfomed a King's Sonne out
of myferable Captiuity, that was vtterly abandoned
of all his Friendes. The manner and meanes how
the Nouell enfuing fhall
fhewe.

THE THIRTY-SECOND NOUELL.

*A Gentlewoman and Wydow called Camiola of hir owne minde Raun-
ſomed Roland the Kyng's Sonne of Sicilia, of purpoſe to haue him
to hir Huſband, who when he was redeemed vnkindly denied hir,
agaynſt whom very Eloquently ſhe Inueyed, and although the Law
proued him to be hir Huſband, yet for his vnkindnes, ſhee vtterly
refuſed him.*

Bvsa a Gentlewoman of Apulia, maynetayned ten Thouſande
Romayne ſouldiers within the walles of Cannas, that were the remnaunte of the army after the ouerthrow there : and yet hir State
of Rycheſſe was faulſe and nothynge dimyniſhed, and left therby
a worthy Teſtimony of Lyberality as Valerius Maximus affirmeth.
If this worthy woman Buſa for Liberality is commended by auncient Authors : if ſhe deſerue a Monument amongs famous Wryters
for that ſplendent vertue which ſo brightly blaſoneth the Heroicall
natures of Noble dames, then may I bee ſo bolde amonges theſe
Nouels to bring in (as it were by the hand) a Wyddow of Meſſina,
that was a Gentlewoman borne, adorned with paſſing beauty and
vertues.   Amongs the rancke of which hir comely Qualities, the
vertue of Liberality gliſtered lyke the morninge Starre after the
Night hath caſt of his darke and Cloudy Mantell.   This Gentlewoman remayning in Wyddowes ſtate, and hearing tell that one of
the Sonnes of Federicke, and Brother to Peter that was then King
of the ſayd Ilande called Rolande, was caried Pryſoner to Naples,
and there kept in miſerable Captiuity, and not like to bee redeemed
by his Brother for a diſpleaſure conceyued, nor by any other,
pittying the ſtate of the young Gentleman, and mooued by hir
gentle, and couragious diſpoſition, and ſpecially with the vertue of liberality, raunſomed the ſayd Rolande, and craued no other
intereſt or vſury for the ſame, but him to huſband, that ought
upon his knees to haue made ſute to be hir ſlaue and ſeruaunte
for reſpect of his miſerable ſtate of Impriſonment.   An affiaunce
betweene them was concluded, and he redeemed, and when hee
was returned, hee falſed his former fayth, and cared not for hir :

for which vnkinde part, fhe before his Frends inueycth agaynſt
that ingratitude, and vtterly forſaketh him, when (fore aſhamed)
he would very fayne haue recouered hir good wil. But fhe like
a wife gentlewoman well waying his inconſtant mynde before
mariage, luſted not to taſte or put in proofe the fruicts and ſucceſſe thereof. The intire Diſcourſe of whom you fhall briefly and
preſently vnderſtand. ¶ Camiola a widow of the City of Siena, the
Daughter of a gentle Knight called Signor Lorenzo Toringo, was
a Woman of great renoume and fame for hir beauty liberality and
ſhamefaſtneſſe, and led a life in Maſſina, (an auncient Citty of
Sicile) no leſſe commendable than famous, in the company of hir
parentes, contenting hirſelf wyth one only Huſbande, while fhe
liued, which was in the tyme when Federick the thirde was Kyng
of that Iſle: And after their death fhe was an heyre of very great
wealth and ritcheſſe, which were alwayes by hir conſerued and
kept in maruellous honeſt ſort. Nowe it chaunced that after the
death of Federick, Peter ſucceedinge by his Commaundement, a
great Army by Sea was equipped from Meſſina, vnder the conduct
of Iohn Countee of Chiaramonte, (the moſt Renoumed in thoſe
dayes in Feats of Warre,) for to ayde the people of Lippary, which
were ſo ſtrongly and earneſtly beſieged, as they were almoſt all dead
and conſumed for hunger. In this Army, ouer and beſides thoſe
that were in pay, many Barons and Gentlemen willingly went vpon
their own proper coſtes, and charges, as well by Sea as Lande, onely
for fame, and to be renoumed in armes. This Caſtell of Lippari
was aſſaulted by Godefrey of Squilatio a valiaunt Man, and at that
time Admiral to Robert Kyng of Ieruſalem and Sicile: Which
Godefrey by long ſiege and aſſault, had ſo famiſhed the people
within, as dayly he hoped they would ſurrender. But hauing
aduertiſement (by certayne Brigandens which he had ſent abroade
to ſcour the Seas) that the Enimies Army (which was farre greater
than his) was at hand, after that he had aſſembled all his Nauy
togeather in one ſure place, he expected the euent of Fortune.
The Enimies ſo ſoone as they were ſeaſed and poſſeſſed of the
place, without any reſiſtaunce of the places abandoned by Godefrey, caried into the Citty at their pleaſure all their victualles.
which they brought wyth them, for which good happe and

chaunce the fayde Countee Iohn being very mutch encouraged
and puffed vp wyth pryde, offred Battell to Godefrey. Wherefore
he not refufing the fame, being a man of great corage, in the Night
time fortified his Army with Boordes, Timber, and other Ram-
piers, and hauing put his Nauy in good order, he encouraged his
Men to fight, and to doe valiauntly the next day, which done, hee
caufed the Ankers to bee wayed, and gieuing the figne, tourned the
prowees of hys Shyppes agaynft the Sicilians Army, but Countee
Iohn who thought that Godefrey would not fight, and durft not
once looke vpon the great army of the Sicilians, did not put his
Fleete in order to fight, but rather in readineffe to purfue the
enimies. But feeing the Courage, and the approch of theym that
came agaynfte him, began to feare, his heart almoft fayling him,
and repented him that he had required his Enimy to that which
he thought neuer to haue obtayned. In futch wife as miftrufting
the Battayle with troubled minde, changing the order giuen, and
notwithftanding not to feeme altogither fearefull, incontinently
caufed his Ships to be put into order after the beft maner he could
for fo little tyme, himfelfe gieuing the figne of battell. In the
meane while their enimies being approched neere vnto them,
and making a very great noyfe with Cryes and Shoutes, furioufly
entred the Sicilians, which came flowly forth, and hauing firft
throwne their Hookes and Grapples to ftay them, they began the
fight with Dartes, Croffe-bowes, and other Shot, in futch fort as
the Sicilians being amazed for the fodayne mutation of Councell,
and all enuironned with feare, and the Souldiers of Godefrey perceyuing the fame, entred their enimies Ships, and comming to
blowes, even in a moment all was filled with bloud, by reafon
whereof the Sicilians, then defpayring of themfelues, and they
that feared turning the prowes fled away : But neuertheleffe the
Victorye reclininge towardes Godefrey, many of their Ships were
drowned, many taken, and diuers Pinnaffes by force of their
Oares efcaped. In that fight died fewe people, but many were
hurt, and Ihon the Captayne Generall taken Pryfoner, and with
him almoft all the Barons, which of their own accordes repayred
to thofe Warres, and befides a great number of Souldiers, many
Enfignes as well of the field, as of the Galleyes, and fpecially the

mayne Standerd was taken. And in the ende, the Caftell being rendred after long Voyages, and great Fortunes by Sea, they were al chayned, caried to Naples and there imprifoned. Amongs thofe Prifoners, there was a certayne Gentleman named Rowlande, the Naturall Sonne of King Federick deceafed, a yong prince very comely and valyaunt. Who not being redeemed, taried alone in prifon very forrowfull to fee all others difcharged after they had payd their Raunfome and himfelfe not to have wherewith to fur- nifh the fame. For king Pietro (to whom the care of him apper- tayned by reafon he was his Brother), for that his warres had no better fucceffe, and done contrary to his commaundement, con- ceyued difpleafure fo wel agaynft him, as all others which were at that battell. Nowe hee then being prifoner without hope of any liberty, by meanes of the dampifhe pryfon, and his feete clogged with yrons, grewe to bee ficke and feeble. It chaunced by fortune, that Camiola remembred him, and feeing him forfa- ken of his brethren, had compaffyon vppon his miffehappe in futch wife, as fhe purpofed (if honeftly fhe might doe the fame) to fet hym at liberty. For the accomplifhment whereof without preiu- dice of hir honour, fhe fawe none other wayes but take him to hufband. Wherefore fhee fent diuers vnto him fecretely, to con- ferre if he would come forth vpon that condition, whereunto he wil- ingly agreed. And performing ech due ceremonie, vnder pro- mifed faith, vpon the gift of a ring willingly by a deputy efpoufed Camiola, who with fo mutch diligence as fhe could, payed two thoufand Crownes for his ranfome, and by that meanes he was deliuerd. When he was retourned to Meffina, he repayred not to his Wyfe, but fared as though there had neuer bene any futch talke beetwene theym: whereof at the begynninge Camiola very mutch maruelled, and afterwardes knowinge his vnkindeneffe was greatly offended in hir heart againft him. Notwithftanding to the intent fhe might not feeme to be grieued without reafon, before fhe proceded any further, caufed him louingly to be talked withal, and to be exhorted by folowing his promyfe to confum- mate the mariage: and feeing that he denied euer any futch Con- tract to be made, fhe caufed him to be fummoned before the Ecclefiafticall Iudge, by whome fentence was giuen that hee was

hir huſband euidence of his owne letters, and by witneſſe of certayne other perſonages of good reputation, which afterwards he
himſelf confeſſed, his face bluſhyng for ſhame, for that he had
forgotten ſutch a manifeſt benefit and good turne.   When the
kynde part of Camiola done vnto him was throughly known, he
was by hys Brethren reproued and checked for hys villany,
whereupon by their inſtigation, and the perſuaſion of his frends,
he was contented by humble requeſt to deſire Camiola to perform
the Nuptials.   But that gentlewoman which was of great corage
in the preſence of diuers that were wyth him, when he required
hir thereunto, anſwered him in this maner : "Rowland I haue
great cauſe to render thankes to almyghty God, for that it pleaſed
him to declare vnto me the proofe of thine vnfaythfulneſſe, before thou didſt by any meanes contaminate (vnder colour of
mariage) the purity of my body, and that through his fauour,
by whoſe moſt holy name thou wenteſt about to abuſe me by
falſe and periured Oth, I haue foreſeene thy Trumpery and
deceypt, wherein I beleeue that I have gayned more than I
ſhoulde haue done by thee in mariage.   I ſuppoſe that when thou
were in pryſon, thou didſt meane no leſſe, than now, by effect
thou ſheweſt, and diddeſt thinke that I, forgetting of what houſe
I was, preſumptuouſly deſired a Huſband of the Royal bloud, and
therefore wholly inflamed with thy love, did purpoſe to beguile
mee by denying the Trouth, when thou haddeſt recouered lyberty
thorough my Money, and thereby to reſerue thy ſelfe for ſome
other of more famous Aliaunce, being reſtored to thy former degree.   And thereby thou haſt gieuen proofe of thy will, and what
minde thou haddeſt ſo to do if thyne ability had bene correſpondent.   But God, who from the lofty Skyes doth beholde the
humble and low, and who forſaketh none that hopeth in him,
knowing the ſincerity of my Conſcience, hath gieuen mee the
grace by little trauayle, to breake the bands of thy deceipts, to
diſcouer thine ingratitude, and make manifeſt thine infidelity,
which I haue not done only to diſplay the wrong towardes me,
but that thy Brethren and other thy friends might from henceforth know what thou art, what affiaunce they ought to repoſe
in thy fayth, and thereby what thy frends ought to looke for, and

what thine enimies ought to feare. I have loft my Money, thou
thy good name: I haue loft the hope which I had of thee, thou
the fauour of the Kinge, and of thy brethren: I the expectation
of my mariage, thou a true and conftant Wife: I the fruits of
charity, thou the gayne of amity: I an vnfaythful hufband,
thou a moft pure and loyall Wyfe. Now the Gentlewomen of
Sicilia doe maruayle at my Magnificence, and Beauty, and by
prayfes aduaunce the fame vp into the heauens: and contrarywife euery of theym doe mock thee, and deeme thee to be Infamous. The Renoumed Wryters of ech Countrey will place me
amongs the ranke of the nobleft Dames, where thou fhalt be depres-
fed, and throwne downe amonges the Heapes of mofte vnkynde.
True it is, that I am fomewhat deceyued by deliuering out of
Pryfon, a yong man of Royal, and noble race, in fteede of whom
I have redeemed a Rafcall, a Lier, a Falfifier of his faith, and a
cruell Beaft: and take heede hardily how thou do greatly efteme
thyfelfe, and I wifh thee not to think that I was moued to draw
thee out of Pryfon, and take thee to Hufbande for the good qualities that were in thee, but for the memory of auncient benefits
which my father receyued of thine (if Federick, a king of moft
facred remembraunce were thy father, for I can fcarfly beleeue,
that a fonne fo difhoneft fhould proceede from fo noble a Gentleman as was that famous Prince.) I know well thou thinkeft
that it was an vnworthy thing, that a Widow not being of theRoyal
bloud fhould have to hufband, the fonne of a Kinge, fo ftrong
and of fo goodly perfonage, which I willingly confeffe: but I
would haue thee a little to make me aunfwere (at the leaft wife
if thou canft by reafon) when I payd fo great a fum of money to
deliuer thee from bondage and captiuity, where was then the nobility of thy Royall race? Where was thy force of Youth? And
where thy Beauty? If not that they were clofed up in a terrible
Pryfon, where thou waft detayned in bitter griefe, and forrowe,
and there with thofe naturall qualities, couered alfo in obfcure
darkneffe, that compaffed thee round about. The ill fauoured
noyfe and iangling of thy chaines, the deformity of thy Face
forced for lack of light, and the ftench of the infected Prifon that
prouoked fickneffe, and the forfaking of thy Frends, had quite de-

bafed al thefe perfections wherewith now thou feemeft to be fo
lufty. Thou thoughteft me then to be worthy, not onely of a
yong man of a royall bloud, but of a God, if it were poffible to
haue him, and fo foon as thou (contrary to all hope) didft once
vifite thy natural Countrey, like a moft peftilent perfon without
any difficulty, hafte chaunged thy mynde, and neuer fince thou
waft deliuered, once did call into thy remembraunce how I was
that Camiola, that I was fhee (alone) that did remembre thee:
that I was fhee (alone) that had compaffion on thy mifhap, and
that I was onely fhee, who for thy health did imploy all the goods
I had. I am, I am (I fay) that Camiola, who by hir Money raunfomed thee out of the hands of the Capitall enimies of thine Auncefters, from Fetters, from Pryfon: and finally deliuered thee from
Mifery extreme, before thou were altogether fettled in difpayre.
I reduced thee agayne to hope, I haue reuoked thee into thy
Countrey, I haue brought thee into the Royal Pallace, and reftored
thee into thy former Eftate, and of a Prifoner weake, and ill fauoured, haue made the a younge Prynce, ftrong, and of fayre
afpect. But wherefore haue I remembred thefe things, whereof
thou oughteft to bee very mindefull thy felfe, and which thou art
not able to deny? Sith that for fo great benefits thou haft rendred me futch thanks, as being my hufband in deede, thou haddeft the Face to deny me mariage, already contracted by the depo-
fition of honeft Witneffes, and approued by Lettres, Signed with
thine owne hand. Wherefore diddeft thou defpife me that hath
delyuered thee? Yea and if thou couldeft haue ftayned the Name
of hir with Infamy, that was thine onely Refuge, and Defender,
thou wouldeft gladly haue giuen caufe to the common people, to
thinke leffe than Honefty of hir. Art thou afhamed (thou Man
of little Iudgement) to haue to Wyfe a Wyddowe, the Daughter
of a Knight? O how farre better had it ben for thee to haue bene
afhamed to breake thy promifed fayth, to haue difpifed the holy
and dreadfull name of God, and to haue declared by thy curffed
vnkindnes, how full fraught thou art with Vice. I doe confeffe in
deede that I am not of the Royall bloud: notwithftanding from
the Cradle, being Trayned, and brought vp in the Company of
kinges Wyues, and Daughters, no great maruayle it is, if I haue

indued and put on a Royall heart and manners, that is able to get,
and purchafe royall Nobility: but wherefore doe I multiply fo
many wordes? No, no, I will be very facile, and eafie in that
wherein thou hafte ben to me fo difficult and hard by refifting
the fame with all thy power. Thou hafte refufed heretofore to be
mine, and hauing vanquifhed thee, to be futch, franckly of myne
owne accorde, I doe graunt that thou art not. Abide (on God's
name) with thy royall Nobility, neuertheleffe defiled with the fpot
of Infidelity. Make mutch of thy youthly luftineffe, and of thy
tranfitory beauty, and I fhal be contented with my Wyddow apparell, and fhall leaue the riches which God hath geuen me to Heyres
more honeft than thofe that might haue come of thee. Auaunt
thou wycked yong man, and fith thou art coumpted to be vnworthy of me, learne with thine own experience, by what fubtilty
and guiles thou maieft betray other dames, fuffifeth it for me to
be once deceyued. And I for my parte fully determine neuer to
tary longer with thee, but rather chaftly to lyue without hufband,
which lyfe I deeme farre more excellent than with thy match
continually to be coupled." After fhee had fpoken thefe words,
fhee departed from him, and from that time forth, it was impoffible eyther by prayers, or Admonitions to caufe hir chaunge hir
holy intent. But Rowland al confufed, repenting himfelf to late
of hys Ingratitude, blamed of ech man, his eyes fixed vpon the
grounde, auoyding not onely the prefence of his brethren, but of
all forts of people, dayly led from that time forth, a moft miferable
life, and neuer durft by reafon to demaunde hir againe to Wife,
whom he had by difloyalty refufed. The King and the other
Barons, marueyling of the noble heart of the Lady, fingularly
commended hir, and exalted hir prayfes vp into the Skyes,
vncertayne neuertheleffe wherein fhee was moft worthy of prayfe,
eyther for that (contrary to the couetous nature of Women) fhe
had raunfomed a yong man with fo great a Summe of Money,
or elfe after fhe had deliuered him, and fentence gieuen that he
was hir Hufbande, fhe fo couragioufly refufed him, as an vnkinde
man, vnworthy of hir company. But leaue we for a tyme, to
talke of Wydowes, and let vs fee what the Captayne, and Lieute-

naunt of Nocera can alledge vpon the difcourfe of his cruelties,
which although an ouer cruell Hyftory, yet depaynteth the fucceffe of thofe that apply their myndes to the Sportes of Loue, futch
Loue I meane, as is wantonly placed, and directed to no good
purpofe, but for glutting of the Bodye's delight, which
both corrupteth nature, maketh feeble the body,
lewdly fpendeth the time, and fpecially offendeth him who maketh proclamatiou, that
Whooremongers and adultrers fhal
neuer Inherite his
Kyngdome.

THE THIRTY-THIRD NOUELL.

Great cruelties chaunced to the Lords of Nocera, for adultry by one of them committed with the Captayne's wyfe of the forte of that Citty, with an enterprise moued by the Captaine to the Cittyzens of the same for Rebellion, and the good and dutyfull aunswere of them: with other pityfull euents ryfing of that notable and outragious vyce of whoredom.

THE furious rage of a Hufband offended for the chaftity violated in his Wyfe, furpaffeth all other, and ingendreth mallice agaynft the doer whatfoeuer he be. For if a Gentleman, or one of good nature, cannot abyde an other to doe him any kinde of difpleafure, and mutch leffe to hurt him in hys Body, how is he able to endure to haue his honour touched, fpecially in that part which is fo neere vnto him as his owne Soule? Man, and Wyfe being as it were one body and one will, wherein Men of good Judgement cannot well like the Opinion of thofe which fay that the honour of a lufty and couragious perfon dependeth not vpon the fault of a foolifh woman: for if that wer true which they fo lightly vaunt, I would demaund why they be fo animated and angry againft them which adorne their head with braunched Hornes, the Enfignes of a Cuckolde: and truely nature hath fo well prouided in that behalfe, as the very fauage Beaftes doe fight, and fuffer death for futch honeft Jealoufie. Yet will I not prayfe, but rather accufe aboue al faulty men, thofe that be fo fondly Jealous, as eche thinge troubling their mindes, be afrayde of the Flyes very fhadowe that buzze about their Faces. For by payning and moleftinge theymfelues with a thinge that fo little doth pleafe and content them, vntill manifeft, and euident proofe appeare, they difplay the folly of their minde's imperfection, and the weakeneffe of their Fantafy. But where the fault is knowne, and the Vyce difcouered, where the hufbande feeth himfelfe to receyue Damage in the foundeft part of his moueable goods, reafon it is that he therein be aduifed by timely deliberation and fage forefight, rather than with headlong fury, and raging rafhneffe

to hazard the loffe of his honour, and the ruine of his life and
goods. And lyke as the fayth and fidelity of the vndefiled Bed
hath in all times worthely ben commended and rewarded: euen fo
he that polluteth it by Infamy, beareth the penaunce of the fame.
Portia the Daughter of Cato, and wife of Brutus fhall be prayfed
for euer, for the honeft and inuiolable loue which fhe bare vnto
hir beloued hufband, almoft like to lofe hir life when fhe heard
tell of his certayne death. The pudicity of Paulina the wife of
Seneca appeared alfo, when fhe affayed to dy by the fame kinde
of death wherewith hir Hufband violently was tormented by the
vniuft commaundement of the moft cruel and horrible Emperoure
Nero. But Whores and Harlottes, having honeft Hufbands, and
well allied in Kin, and Ligneage by abandoning their bodyes, doe
prodigally confume their good Renoume: yea but if they efcape
the Magiftrates, or auoyde the wrath of offended hufbandes for
the wrong done vnto them, yet they leaue an immortall flaunder of their wicked life, and youth thereby may take example afwell to fhun futch fhameleffe Women, as to followe thofe
Dames that be Chafte, and Vertuous. Now of this contempt
whych the Wyfe beareth to hir Hufband, do rife very many times
notorious flaunders, and futch as are accompanied with paffinge
cruelties: wherein the Hufbande ought to moderate his heate,
and calme his choler, and foberly to chaftife the fault, for fo
mutch as exceffiue wrath, and anger, doe Eclipfe in man the light
of reafon, and futch rages doe make them to be femblable vnto
Brute, and reafonleffe Beaftes: meete it is to be angry for thinges
done contrary to Right, and Equity, but Temperaunce, and
Modefty is neceffary in al occurrentes, bee they wyth vs, or againft
vs. But if to refift anger in thofe matters, it be hard and difficulte,
yet the greater impoffibility there is in the operation, and effeƈt
of any good thinge, the greater is the glory that vanquifheth the
affeƈtion and maftereth the firft motion of the minde which is
not fo impoffible to gouerne, and fubdue to reafon, as many do
efteeme. A wife man then cannot fo farre forget his duety, as to
exceede the Boundes, and Limits of reafon, and to fuffer his
mynde to wander from the fiege of Temperaunce, which if he doe
after hee hath well mingled Water in his Wyne, hee may chaunce to

finde caufe of Repentaunce, and by defire to repayre his Offenfe augment his fault, finne being fo prompt and ready in man, as the crime which might bee couered with certayne Iuftice, and coloured by fome lawe or righteous caufe, maketh him many tymes to fall into deteftable Vice and Synne, fo contrary to mildneffe and modefty, as the very Tyraunts themfelues woulde abhorre futch wickedneffe. And to the ende that I do not trouble you with Allegation of infinite numbres of examples, feruing to this purpofe, ne render occafion of tedioufnes for you to reuolue fo many bookes, I am contented for this prefent, to bring in place an Hyftory fo ouer cruell, as the caufe was not mutch vnreafonable, if duty in the one had bene confidered, and rage in the other bridled and forefeene, who madly murthered and offended thofe that were nothing guilty of the Facte, that touched him fo neare. And although that thefe be matters of loue, yet the Reader ought not to bee grieued nor take in euill parte, that we bee ftill in that Argument. For we doe not hereby goe about to erect a Schoolehoufe of Loue, or to teache Youth the wanton Toyes of the fame. But rather bryng forth thefe Examples to withdraw the plyant, and tender Age of this our time, from the purfuite of like Follies, which may (were they not in this fort warned) ingender lyke effects that thefe our Hyftoryes do recoumpt, and whereof you fhall bee Partakers by reading the difcourfe that followeth. Yee muft than vnderftand, that in the time that Braccio Montone, and Sforza Attendulo florifhed in Italy, and were the chiefeft of the Italian men of warre, there were three Lords and brethren which held vnder their authority and Puiffaunce Foligno, Nocera, and Treuio, parcell of the Dukedome of Spoleto, who gouerned fo louingly their Landes together, as without diuifion, they maynetayned themfelues in great Eftate, and lyued in Brotherly concorde. The name of the Eldeft of thefe three Lordes was Nicholas, the fecond Cæfar, the yongeft Conrade, gentle Perfonages, wife and wel beloued fo well of the Noble men their Neyghbours, as alfo of the Cittyzens that were vnder their Obeyfaunce, who in the ende, fhewed greater loyalty towards them, than thofe that had fworne their fayth, and had giuen Pleadges for confirmation, as yee fhal perceyue by reading what infueth. It chaunced that the eldeft

oftentimes repayring from Foligno to Nocera, and lodging ftill in
the Caftell, behelde with a little to mutch wanton Eye, the Wyfe of
his Lieutenaunt whych was placed there with a good number of
dead payes, to Guard the Fort, and keepe vnder the Cittizens, if
by chaunce (as it happeneth vpon the new erection of Eftates)
they attemped fome new enterprife agaynft their Soueraygne
Lordes. Nowe this Gentlewoman was very fayre, fingularly delighting to be looked vpon : which occafioned the Lord Nicholas,
by perceyuing the wantoneffe and good wyll of the Myftreffe of
the Caftell, not to refufe fo good occafion, determining to profecute the inioying of hir, that was the Bird after which he hunted,
whofe Beauty and good grace had deepely wounded his Mind,
wherin if he forgot his duety, I leaue for al men of good iudgement to confider. For me thinke that this young Lorde ought rather fingularly to loue and cheryfh his liuetenaunt that faithfullye
and truftily had kept his Caftell and Forte, than to prepare agaynft
him fo Trayterous an Attempt, and Ambufhe. And if fo bee hys
fayd Lieutenaunt had bene accufed of felony, mifprifon, or Treafon
(yet to fpeake the trouth) hee might haue deliuered the charge of
his Caftell vnto an other, rather then to fuborne his Wyfe to folly.
And ought likewife to haue confidered that the Lieuetenaunt by
puttinge his truft in him, had iuft caufe to complayne for Rauifh-
ing hys Honoure from hym in the Perfon of hys Wyfe, whom hee
ought to haue loued wythout any affection to Infrindge the Holy
Lawe of Amitye, the breakinge whereof diffolueth the duety of
ech Seruaunt towardes his Soueraygne Lord and mayfter. To be
fhort, this blinded Louer yelding no' refiftaunce to loue, and the
foolifh conceipt which altereth the iudgements of the wifeft, fuffred his fanfie to roue fo farre vnto hys Appetites, as on a daye
when the Lieuetenaunte was walked abroade into the Caftel to
view the Souldiours and deade payes (to pleafure him that fought
the meanes of his difpleafure) hee fpake to the Gentlewoman his
Wyfe in this manner : "Gentlewoman, you being wife and curteous as ech man knoweth, needefull it is not to vfe long or Retho-
ricall Orations, for fo mutch as you without further fupply of talk
do clearely perceyue by my Looks, Sighes, and earneft Viewes, the
loue that I beare you, which without comparifon nippeth my

Hearte fo neare as none can feele the parching paynes, that the
fame poore portion of me doth fuffer. Wherefore hauing no
great leyfure to let you further vnderftand my mynde, it may
pleafe you to fhewe me fo mutch Fauour as I may be receyued
for him, who hauing the better right of your good grace, may
therewithall enioy that fecret Acquayntance, which futch a one
as I am deferueth : of whom yee fhall haue better experience if
you pleafe to accept him for your owne." This miftreffe Lieutenaunt which compted hir felfe happy to be beloued of hir Lorde,
and who tooke great pleafure in that aduenture, albeit that fhee
defyred to lette hym knowe the good will that fhe bare vnto
him, yet diffembled the matter a little, by aunfwering him
in this wife : "Your difeafe Sir is fodayne, if in fo little time
you haue felt futch exceffe of malady : but perchance it is your
heart that being ouer tender, hath lightly receyued the pricke,
which no doubt will fo foone vanifh, as it hath made fo ready
entry. I am very glade (Sir) that your heart is fo merily difpofed to daliaunce, and can finde fome matter to contriue the
fuperfluitie of tyme, the fame altering the diuerfity of man's com-
plexion, accordingly as the condition of the hourely Planet
guideth the nature of euery wight." "It is altogither otherwife
(aunfwered hee) for being come hither as a mafter and Lord, I am
become a feruaunt and flaue : and briefly to fpeake my minde, if
you haue not pitty vpon me, the difeafe which you call fodayne,
not only will take increafe, but procure the death and finall ruine
of my heart.", "Ah fir," (fayd the Gentlewoman) "your griefe is
not fo deepely rooted, and death fo prefent to fucceede as you
affirme, ne yet fo ready to gieue ouer the place, as you proteft,
but I fee what is the matter, you defire to laugh mee to fcorne,
and your heart craueth fomething to folace it felfe which cannot
be idle, but muft imploy the vacant tyme vpon fome pleafaunt
Toyes." "You haue touched the pricke (aunfwered the Louer) for it
is you in deede wherevpon my hearte doth ioy, and you are the
caufe of my Laughter and paffetime, for otherwife all my delights
were difpleafures, and you alfo by denying me to be your feruaunt, fhall abbreuiate, and fhorten my liuing dayes, who only
reioyfeth for choyfe of futch a myftreffe." "And bow (replied fhe)

can I be affured of that you fay? The difloyalty, and infidelity of man being in thefe dayes fo fafte vnited, fo haftely following one another, as the Shadow doth the Body, wherefoeuer it goeth." "Onely experience" (fayed he) "fhall make you know what I am, and fhall teach you wheather my heart is any thing different from my wordes, and I dare bee bolde to fay, that if you vouchfafe to do mee the pleafure to receyue mee for your owne, you may make your vaunt to haue a Gentleman fo faythfull for your frend, as I efteeme you to be difcrete, and as I defire to let you tafte the effect of mine affection, by futch fome honeft order as may be deuifed." "Sir" (fayd fhe) "it is well and aduifedly fpoken of you, but yet I thincke it ftraunge for futch a Gentleman as you be, to debafe your honor to fo poore a Gentlewoman, and to goe about both to difhonor me, and to put my life in pearill." "God forbid" (aunfwered the Lord Nicholas) "that I be caufe of any flaunder, and rather had I dye my felfe than minifter one fimple occafion whereby your fame fhould be brought in queftion. Only I doe pray you to have pitty vpon me, and by vfing your curtefie, to fatiffie that which my feruice and faythfull friendfhip doth conftrayne, and binde you for the comfort of him that loueth you better than himfelfe." "We will talke more thereof hereafter" (aunfwered the lieuetenaunt's Wyfe) "and than will I tell you mine aduife, and what refolution fhall follow the fumme of your demaunde." "How now Gentlewoman" (fayd he) "haue you the heart to leaue me voyde of hope, to make me languifh for the prorogation of a thing fo doubtful, as the delayes bee which loue deferreth? I humbly pray you to tell me whereunto I fhall truft: to the intent that by punifhing my heart for proofe of this enterprife, I may chaftife all mine Eyes by reuing from them the meanes for euer more to fee that which contenteth me beft, and wherein refteth my folace, leauing my minde full of defires, and my heart without final ftay, vppon the greateft Pleafure that euer man coulde choofe." The Gentlewoman would not loofe a Noble man fo good and perfect: whofe prefence already pleafed hir aboue all other thinges, and, who voluntarily had agreed to hys requeft, by the onely figne of hir Gefts, and Lookes, fayde vnto him fmilinge with a very good grace: "Doe not accufe my heart of lightneffe, nor

my minde of infidelity and treafon, if to pleafe and obey you, I
forget my duty, and abufe the promife made unto my Hufband,
for I fweare vnto you (fir) by God, that I haue more forced my
thought, and of long time haue conftrayned mine appetites in
diffembling the loue that I beare you, than I haue receiued pleafure, by knowing my felfe to be beloued by one agreeable to mine
affection.   For which caufe you fhall finde me (being but a poore
Gentlewoman) more ready to do your pleafure, and to be at your
commaundement, than any other that liueth be fhee of greater
Port, and regarde than I am.   And who to fatiffie your requeft,
fhal one day facrifice that fidelity to the iealous fury of hir hufband."   "God defend" (fayd the young Lord) "for we fhal be fo
difcrete in our doings, and fo feldome communicate, and talke
togeather, as impoffible for any man to difcry the fame.   But if
mifhap will haue it fo, and that fome ill lucke doe difcouer our
dealinges, I haue fhift of wayes to coloure it, and power to ftop
the mouthes of them that dare prefume to clatter and haue to do
with our priuate conference."   "All that I know wel inough fir"
(fayd fhe) "but it is great fimplicity in futch thinges for a man
to truft to his authority, the forced inhibition whereof fhall prouoke more babble, than rumor is able to fpreade for all his tattling
talk of our fecret follies.   Moreouer I would be very glad to do
what pleafeth you, fo the fame may be without flaunder.   For I
had rather dy, than any fhould take vs in our priuities and familier paftimes: let vs be contented with the pleafure that the eafe
of our ioy may graunt, and not with futch contentation as fhal
offend vs, by blotting the clereneffe of our good name."   Concluding then the time of their new acquayntaunce, which was the next
day at noone, when the Lieutenaunt did walke into the Citty, they
ceafed their talke for feare of his enteruiew.   Who (upon his retourne) doing reuerence vnto his Lord, tolde him that hee knewe
where a wilde Boare did haunte, if it pleafed him to fee the paftime.   Whereunto the Lord Nicholas fayned louingly to gieue eare
(although agaynft his will) for fo mutch as hee thought the fame
Huntinge fhould be a delay for certayne dayes to the enioying,
(pretended and affured) of his beloued.   But fhe that was fo mutch
or more efpryfed with the raging and intollerable fire of loue,

ſpeedily found meanes to ſatiffie hir louer's ſute, but not in ſutch
manner as was deſired of eyther partes, wherefore they were conſtrayned to defer the reſt vntill an other time.   This pleaſaunt
beginning ſo allured the Lord of Nocera, as vnder the pretence of
huntinge, there was no weeke that paſſed, but hee came to viſite
the Warrener of hys Lieutenaunt. And this order continuing without any one little ſuſpition of their loue, they gouerned theym-
ſelues wiſely in purſute thereof. And the Lord Nicholas vſed
the game and ſporte of Hunting, and an infinite number of other
exerciſes, as the running of the Ring, and Tennis, not ſo mutch
thereby to finde meanes to enioy his Lady, as to auoyde occaſion
of Iealoſie in hir Huſband, being a very familiar vice in all Italians,
the Cloake whereof is very heauy to beare, and the diſeaſe trouble-
ſome to ſuſtayne. But what? Like as it is hard to beguile an
Vſurer in the accoumpt of his money, for his continuall watch
ouer the ſame, and ſlumbring ſleepes vpon the Bookes of his
recknings and accoumpts, ſo difficult it is to deceyue the heart of
a iealous man, and ſpecially when he is aſſured of the griefe which
his head conceyueth. Argus was neuer ſo cleere eyed for all his
hundred Eyes ouer Iupiter's Lemman, as thoſe Louers be, whoſe
opinions be ill affected ouer the chaſtity of their Wyues. Moreouer
what Foole, or Aſſe is hee, who ſeeing ſutch vndiſcrete familiarity
of two Louers, the priuy geſtures and demeanors without witneſſe,
theyr ſtolne walkes at vntymely houres, and ſometimes theyr
embracements to, ſtrayght and common before ſeruants, that would
not doubt of that whych moſt ſecretly did paſſe? True it is that
in England (where liberty is ſo honeſtly obſerued as being alone
or ſecrete conuerſation gyueth no cauſe of ſuſpition) the ſame
mighte haue bene borne withall. But in Italy, where the Parents
themſelues be for the moſt part ſuſpected, (if there had bene no
facte in deede committed) that familiarity of the Lord Nicholas,
with hys Lieutenaunte's Wyfe was not ſuffrable, but exceded the
Bounds of reaſon, for ſo mutch as the Commoditie which they had
choſen for poſſeſſing of theyr loue, (albeit the ſame not ſuſpitions) animated them afterwards to frequent their familiarity and
dyſporte to frankly, and wythout diſcretion: which was the
cauſe that fortune (who neuer leaueth the ioyes of men wythout

giuing thereunto fome great alarme,) being enuious of the mutuall
delightes of thofe two louers, made the hufband to doubt of that
which hee would haue diffembled, if honor could fo eafily be lofte
wythoute reproch, as bloud is fhed without peryll of Lyfe, but the
matter being fo cleare, as the fault was euident, fpecyally in the
party which touched him fo neare as hymfelfe, the Lieuetenaunt
before he would enterpryfe any thing, and declare what he thought
defired throughly to bee refolued of that whych hee fawe as it
were but in a Cloude, and by reafon of hys conceyued Opynion
hee dealt fo warely and wifely in thofe affaires, and was fo fubtil
an efpiall, as one day when the louers were at theyr game, and in
their moft ftraite and fecrete embracements, he viewed them coupled with other leafh, than he would haue wifhed, and colled with
ftraighter bands then reafon or honefty did permit. He faw
with out beeing feene, wherein he felt a certaine eafe and contentment, for being affured of that he doubted, and purpofed to
órdeyne a fowre refection after their delightfome banket, the fimple louers ignoraunt by figne or coniecture, that their enterpryfes
were dyfcouered. And truely it had ben more tollerable and
leffe hurteful for the Lieuetenaunte, if euen then hee had perpe-
trated his vengeaunce, and punyfhed them for theyr wyckedneffe,
than to vfe the Cruelty wherewith afterwardes he blotted his
renoume, and foyled his hands by Bedlem rage in the innocent
bloud of thofe that were not priuye to the folly, and leffe guilty
of the wronge don vnto him. Now the Captain of the Caftel for
al his diffimulation in couering of bis griefe, and his fellony and
Treafon intended againft his foueraigne Lord, which he defired
not yet manifeftly to appeare, was not able any more from that
time forth to fpeake fo louingly vnto him, nor with futch refpect
and reuerence as he did before, which caufed his Wife thus to fay
vnto hir Louer : "My Lord I doubt very mutch leaft my hufband
doth perceiue thefe our common practizes, and fecrete familiar
dealings, and that he hath fome Hammer working in his heade, by
reafon of the Countenaunce, and vncheareful entertaynement which
he fheweth to your Lordfhip, wherefore myne aduyfe is, that you
retire for a certaine tyme to Foligno. In the meane fpace I wil
marke and efpye if that his alteration be conceiued for any matter

againft vs, and wherefore his wonted lookes haue put on this new
alteration and chaunge. All which when I haue (by my efpial
and fecret practize founded) I will fpedily aduertife you, to the
end that you may prouide for the fauegard of your faithfull and
louing feruaunt." The young Lord, who loued the Gentlewoman
wyth al his heart, was attached with fo great gryefe, and dryuen
into futch rage by hearyng thofe wycked Newes, as euen prefently
he woulde haue knowne of hys Lieuetenaunt, the caufe of his
dyfwonted cheare. But weyghing the good aduyfe whych his
woman had giuen him, paufed vppon the fame, and promyfed
hir to doe what fhe thought beft. By reafon whereof, gyuynge
warnyng to his Seruantes for hys departure, he caufed the Lyeuete-
naunte to be called before him, vnto whome hee fayd : "Captayne, I had thoughte for certayne Dayes to fporte and paffe my
tyme, but hearing tell that the Duke of Camarino commeth to
Foligno, to debate with vs of matters of importaunce, I am conftrained to departe, and do pray you in the meane time to haue
good regard vnto our affaires, and if any newes doe chaunce to
aduertife the fame wyth all Expedytion." "Sir" (fayd the Captayne) "I am forrye that now when our paffetime of hunting
myght yelde fome good recreation vnto your honour, that you
doe thus forfake vs, notwithftandyng fith it is your good pleafure, we will ceafe the chafe of the wylde Bore till your retourne.
In the meane time, I will make ready the Coardes and Tramelles,
that vppon your comming, nothing want for the Furniture of our
fport." The Lord Nicholas, feeing his Lieuetenaunt fo pleafauntly
difpofed, and fo litle bent to Choller, or iealous fantafie, was
perfuaded, that fome other toy had rather occupyed his Minde,
than any fufpition betweene his Wife and hym. But the fubtyll
Hufband fearched other meanes to be reuenged, than by kylling
him alone, of whom he receyued that difhonour, and was more
craftie to enterpryfe, and more hardie to execute, than the Louers
were wyfe or well aduifed to preuent and wythftande his fleightes
and pollicies. And albeit that the Wyfe (after the departure of hir
Fryend) affayed to drawe from him the caufe of his altered cheare
yet coulde fhee neuer learne, that bir hufband had any ill opinion
of theyr Loue. For fo many tymes as talke was moued of the

Lord Nicholas, hee exalted his prayfe vp into the Heauens, and commended hym aboue all his Brethren. All whych hee dyd to beguyle the pollycies of hir, whome he faw to blufh, and many times chaunge Colour, when fhe heard him fpoken of, to whom fhe bare better affe&tion than to hir Hufband, vnto whom (in very dede) fhe did owe the faith and integritie of hir body. This was the very toile which he had laid to intrap thofe amorous perfons and purpofed to rid the world of them by that meanes, to remoue from before his eyes, the fhame of a Cuckolde's title, and to reuenge the iniurie don to his reputation. The miftreffe of the Caftel feeynge that hir hufband (as fhee thought) by no meanes did vnderftande hir follies, defired to continue the pleafure, which either of them defired, and which made the third to die of phrenefie, wrote to the Lord Nicholas, the letter that followeth.

" My Lord, the feare I had, that my hufband fhould perceyue our loue, caufed me to intreat you certaine dayes paft, to difcontinue for a time, the frequentation of your owne houfe, whereby I am not little agrieued, that contrary to my wil, I am defrauded of your prefence, which is far more pleafaunt vnto me, than my hufband's flatteries, who ceafeth not contynually to talke of the honeft behauiour, and commendable qualyties that be in you, and is forry for your departure, bicaufe he feareth that you miflyke youre entertainement, whych fhould be (fayth he) fo gryeuous and noy-fome vnto him, as death it felfe. Wherefore, I pray you fir, if it be poffible, and that your affayres doe fuffer you, to come hither to the ende I may enioy your amayable prefence, and vfe the Liberty that our good hap hath prepared, through the litle iealoufie of my hufband your Lieuetenaunt : who I fuppofe before it be long wil intreat you, fo great is his defire to make you paffetime of hunting within your owne Land and territory. Fayle not then to come I befeech you, and we wyll fo well confider the gouernment of our affaires, as the beft fighted fhall not once difcry the leaft fufpicion thereof, recommending my felfe moft humbly (after the beft maner I can) to your good Lordfhip."

This Letter was deliuered to a Lackey to beare to the Lord Nicholas, and not fo priuily done, but the Lieutenaunt immediately efpied the deceipt which the fooner was difciphred, for fo mutch as he

dayely lay in wayte to find the meanes to reuenge the wrong done
vnto him, of purpofe to beate the iron fo long as it was hotte, and to
execute hys purpofe before his Wife tooke heede, and felte the endeuor of his Enterpryfe. And bicaufe that fhee had affayed by diuers
wayes to found his heart, and fele whether he had conceiued difpleafure againft the Lord hir louer, the Day after wherein fhe had
wrytten to hir friend, hee fent one of his Men in pofte to the three
Lordes, to requyre them to come the nexte Day to fee the paftime
of the fayreft and greateft wild Bore, that long tyme was bred in
the Forrefts adioyning vnto Nocera, Albeit that the Countrey was
fayre for courfinge, and that dyuers tymes many fayre Bores haue
ben encountred there. But it was not for this, that he had framed
his errand, but to trap in one toyle and fnare the thre brethren,
whom he determined to facrifice to the aulter of his vengeance,
for the expiation of theyr elder brother's trefpaffe, and for foyl-
ing the Nuptial bed of his feruaunt. He was the wylde Bore
whome he meant to ftrike, hee was the pray of his vnfaciable and
cruell Appetite. If the fault had ben generall of all three togethers,
he had had fome reafon to make them paffe the bracke of one
equall fortune, and to tangle them within one net, both to preuent
thereby (as he thought) his further hurt, and to chaftife their
leude behauiour. For many tymes (as lamentable experience
teacheth) Noble men for the onely refpecte of their Nobility, make
no Confcience to doe wrong to the honor of them, whofe reputation and honefty, they ought fo wel to regard as their owne.
Herein offended the good Prynce of the Iewes Dauid, when to
vfe his Berfabe without fufpition, he caufed innocent Vrias to
bee flayne, in lieu of recompence for his good feruice, and diligent
execution of his behefts. The children of the proud Romane
king Tarquinius, did herein greatly abufe them felues, when they
violated that noble Gentlewoman Lucrece, whom al hiftories do fo
mutch remembre, and whofe chaftity, al famous writers do commend. Vppon futch as they be, vengeance ought to be don, and
not to defile the hands in the bloud of innocents, as the Parents and
Kinfemen of deade Lucrece did at Rome, and this Lieutenaunt at
Nocera, vppon the brethren of him that had fent him into Corn-
wal, without paffing ouer the Seas. But what? Anger proceding

of futch wronge, furmounteth al phrenefie, and exceedeth al the
bounds of reafon, and man is fo deuoyd of Wyts, by feeing the
blot of defamation, to lyght vpon him, as he feeketh al meanes
to hurt and difpleafe him that polluteth his renoume. Al the
race of the Tarquines for like fact were banyfhed Rome, for the
onely brute whereof, the hufband of the faire rauifhed wife, was
conftrayned to auoid the Place of his natiuity. Paris alone
violated the body of Menelaus, the Lacedemonian kyng, but for
reuenge of the rauyfhed Greeke, not onely the glory and Rycheffe
of ftately Troy, but alfo the moft parte of Afia and Europa, was
ouertourned and defaced, if credyte may be gyuen to the recordes
of the Auncyent. So in this fact of the Lieutenaunt, the Lord
Nicholas alone, had polluted his bed, but the reuenge of the cruel
man extended further, and his fury raged fo farre, as the guiltleffe
were in greate Daunger to beare the penaunce, which fhall be
well perceiued by the difcourfe that foloweth. The Captaine then
hauing fent his meffage, and beyng fure of his intent (no leffe
than if he already had the brethren within his hold, vpon the
point to couple them together with his wife, to fend them all in
pilgrimage to vifite the faithfull forte, that blafon their loues in an
other worlde, with Dydo, Phyllis, and futch like, that more for
difpayre than loue, bee paffed the ftraictes of death) caufed to be
called before him in a fecrete place, al the fouldiers of the Fort,
and futch as with whome he was fure to preuayle, to whom not
without fheading forth fome teares, in heauie Countenaunce, he
fpake in this maner: " My Companions and Fryends, I doubt not
but yee bee abafhed to fee me wrapt in fo heauy plyght, and
appeare in this forme before you (that is to fay) bewept, heauy,
panting with fighes, and all contrary to my cuftome, in other
ftate and maner, than my courage and degree requyre. But when
ye fhall vnderftand the caufe I am affured that the cafe whych
feemeth ftraunge to you, fhall be thought iuft and ryght and fo
will perfourme the thing wherein I fhall employe you. Ye knowe
that the firft point that a Gentleman ought to regarde, confifteth
not onely in repelling the iniury done vnto the body, but rather it
behoueth that the fight begin for the defenfe of his honor, which
is a thinge that proceedeth from the Minde, and reforteth to the

Body, as the Inftrument to worke that which the fpyryte ap-
pointeth.   Now it is honour, for conferuation whereof, an honeft
man and one of good Courage feareth not to put hymfelfe in all
perill and daunger of death and loffe of goodes, referring himfelfe alfo to the guarde of that whych toucheth as it were oure
owne reputation.   In futch wyfe as if a good Captaine do fuffer
bys fouldier to be a wycked man, a Robber, a Murderer, and an
exacter, he beareth the note of dyfhonor albeit in all his doings
he gouerneth his eftate after the rule of honefty, and doth nothing
that is vnworthy his vocation.   But what? he being a head
vnited to futch members, if the partes of that vnited thing be
corrupt and naught, the head muft needes bear the blot of the
fault before referred to the whole Body.   Alas (fayd he fighing) what parte is more neare, and dearer to Man, than that
which is giuen vnto him for a Pledge and Comfort duryng his
Life, and which is conioyned to be bone of his bone, and flefh of
his flefh, to breath forth one Mynde, and to think with one heart
and equall wil.   It is of the Wyfe that I fpeake, who being the
moytie of hir hufband, ye ought not to mufe if I fay, that the
honoure of the one is the reft of the other, and the one infamous
and wycked, the other feeleth the troubles of futch mifchiefe, and
the Wife being careleffe of hir honour, the hufband's reputation is
defiled, and is not worthy of prayfe, if he fuffer futch fhame vn-
reuenged : I muft (Companions and good friends) here dyfcouer
that whych my heart would faine kepe fecrete, if it were poffible,
and muft rehearfe a thing vnto you, which fo fone as my Mouth
would faine kepe clofe, the Minde affayeth to force the ouerture.
And loth I am to do it, were it not that I make fo good accompt
of you, as ye being tied to me with an vnfeparable Amity, will
yeld me your comfort and Ayde againft him that hath done mee
this Villany, futch as if I be not reuenged vpon, needes muft I be
the Executioner of that vengeance vppon my felfe, that I am loth
to lyue in this difhonor, whych all the dayes of my life (without
due vltion) like a Worme wyll torment and gnaw my confcyence.
Wherefore before I goe any further, I woulde knowe whether I
myght fo well truft your aide and fuccour in this my bufineffe,
as in all others I am affured you would not leaue mee fo long as

any breath of life remained in you. For without futch affurance, I do not purpofe to let you know the pricking naile that pierceth my heart, nor the gryefe that grieueth me fo neare, as by vttering it without hope of help I fhall open the Gate to death, and dye without reliefe of my defire, by punifhing him, of whome I haue receyued an iniury more bloudy than any man can doe." The Souldiers whych loued the Captaine as theyr owne Lyfe, were forry to fee him in futch eftate, and greater was theyr dolour to heare wordes that tended to nothing elfe but to fury, vengeaunce, and murder of hymfelfe. Wherefore all wyth one accorde promyfed theyr helpe and mayne force towardes and againft all men for the bryngyng to paffe of that whych hee dyd meane to requyre. The Lieutenaunt affured of his Men conceyued heart and Courage, and continuing his Oration and purpofe, determyned the flaughter and ouerthrowe of thre Trinicien Brethren, (for that was the furname of the Lordes of Foligno,) who purfued his Oration in this maner: "Know ye then (my Companions and good Friends) that it is my Wife, by whome I haue indured the hurt and loffe of myne honour, and fhe is the party touched, and I am he that am moft offended. And to the ende that I do not hold you longer in fufpence, and the party be concealed from you, whych hath don me thys Outrage: ye fhall vnderftand that Nicholas Trinicio, the elder of the three Lordes of Folingno and Nocera, is he, that againft all ryght and equity hath fuborned the Wife of his Lieuetenaunt, and foyled the Bed of him, whereof he ought to haue ben the defender and the very bulwarke of his reputation. It is of hym my good Fryends, and of his that I meane to take futch Vengeaunce, as eternall memory fhall difplay the fame to all pofterity: and neuer Lord fhal dare to doe a like wrong to mine, without remembraunce what his duety is, which fhall teach hym how to abufe the honeft feruice of a Gentleman that is one of his owne trayne. It refteth in you both to holde vp your hand, and keepe your promife, to the end that the Lord Nicholas, deceiuyng and mocking me, may not truft and put affiance in your force, vnto whych I heartily do recommend my felfe." The Souldiers moued and incited with the wickedneffe of theyr Lord and with the wrong

done to him, of whom they receyued wages, fwore agayne to
ferue his turne in any exploit he went about, and requyred him to
be affured, that the, Trinicien Brethren fhould be ouerthrowne,
and fuffer deferued penaunce, if they might lay hands vpon them,
and therefore willed him to feke meanes to allure them thither,
that they might be difpatched. The Lieuetenaunt at these words
renuing a chearefull Countenaunce, and fhewing himfelf very
ioyfull for futch fucceffe after he had thanked his Souldyers, and
very louingly imbraced the chiefeft of them, reuealed hys deuifed
pollicy, and hoped fhortly to haue them at his commaundement
within the Fort, alleaging that he had difpatched two Meffengers
vnto them, and that his wife alfo priuily had fent hir page: vnto
whome he purpofed to gyue fo good a recompenfe, as neuer more
fhe fhould plant his hornes fo hygh, vnder a colour of gentle
entertaynement of hir ribauld and Friend. They were fcarce refolued vpon this intent, but newes were brought him, that the
next day morning, the three lords accompanied with other nobility
would come to Nocera, to hunt that huge wylde Bore, whereof the
Lieutenaunt had made fo greate auant. Thefe newes did not
greatly pleafe the Captaine, for fo mutch as he feared, that his
purpofe could not (conueniently) be brought to paffe, if the company were fo great. But when he confidered that the Lords alone,
fhould lodge within the Fort, he was of good cheare again, and
ftaied vpon his firft intent. The Triniciens the next day after
came very late, bicaufe the Lord Berardo of Verano duke of
Camerino, defired to be one, and alfo the two brethren taried for
Conrade, who was at a mariage, and could not affift the Tragedie
that was played at Nocera, to his great hap and profit. So this
troupe came to Nocera late, and hauing fupped in the City, the
Lord Nicholas, and the Duke of Camerino went to Bed in the Fort,
Cæfar the brother of Trinicio tarying behind with the Trayne, to
lodge in the city. Stay here a while (ye Gentlemen) ye I fay, that
purfue the fecrete ftelths of loue, neuer put any great truft in
fortune, which feldome kepeth hir promife with you. Ye had
neede therfore to take goode heede, leaft ye be furpryfed in
the place, wher priuily you giue the affault, and in the afte

wherein ye defire the affiftance of none. See the barbarous cruelty of a Lieutenant, which loued rather to kill his corriual in his cold bloud, than otherwife to be reuenged, when he faw him a bed with his Wife, purpofely that the example of his fury myght be the better knowne, and the fecret fclander more euident, from the roote whereof did fpryng an infinite number of Murders and mifchiefs. About midnight then, when all thinges were at reft vnder the darke filence of the nyght, the Lieutenant came to the Chamber of the Lord Nicholas, accompanied with the moft part of the Watch, and hauyng ftopt vp the yeoman of hys Chaumber, hee fo dreffed the Companion of hys Bedde, as for the firft proofe of his courtefie, he caufed hys Membres and priuy partes to be cut of, faying vnto him with cruell difdayne: "Thou fhalt not henceforth (wycked wretch) weld this launce into the reft, thereby to batter the honour of an honefter man than thy felf." Then lanching his ftomacke with a piercing blade, he tare the heart out of his belly, faying: "Is this the trayterous Heart that hath framed the plot and deuyfed the enterprife of my fhame, to make this infamous villaine without Life, and his renoume without prayfe?" And not content with this Cruelty, he wreakt the like vpon the remnaunt of his body, that fometimes the runnagate Medea did vpon hir innocent brother, to faue the Lyfe of hir felfe, and of hir friend Iafon. For fhe cut him into an hundred thoufand pieces, gyuing to euery Membre of the poore murdred foule hir word of mockery and contempt. Was it not fufficient for a tirannous hufband to be reuenged of hys fhame, and to kill the party which had defamed him, without vfing fo furious Anotamie vpon a dead body, and wherein there was no longer feeling? But what? Ire beyng wythout meafure, and anger wythout Brydle or reafon, it is not to be wondred, if in al his actes the Captayne ouerpaffed the iuft meafure of vengeance. Many would thinke the committed murder vppon Nicholas, to be good and iuft: but the Iuftice of an offenfe, ought not fo longe time to be conceyled, but rather to make him feele the fmart at the very tyme the deed is done, to the ende that the nypping gryefe of peftilent treafon wrought againft the betrayed party, be not obfcured and hydden by fodayne rage and lacke of

reafon rifing in the mindes firft motions, and thereby alfo the
faulte of the guilty, by hys indifcretion couered : otherwyfe there
is nothyng that can colour futch vice. For the law indifferently
doth punifh euery man, that without the Magiftrates order taketh
authority to venge his own wrong. But come we againe vnto
our purpofe. The Captayne all imbrued in bloude, entred the
Chaumber of the Duke of Camerino, whom with al the reft of
the ftrangers that were wythin the Caftle, hee lodged (without
fpeakynge any worde) in a deepe and obfcure pryfon. Beholde,
what refte they tooke that nyghte, whych were come to hunt the
Wylde Boare. For wythout trauaylyng farre, they were intrapped
in the fubtill engines and Nettes of the furious Lieuetenaunte, who
when the morning bedecked with hir vermilion cleare began to
fhewe hir felfe, when all the Hunters dyd put them felues in
readyneffe, and coupled vp theyr Dogges to marche into the
Fielde, beholde, one of the Captayne's cruell Minifters wente into
the City, to caufe the Lord Cæfar to come and fpeake with hys
brother Nicholas, and intreated him not to tarry, for that he and
the Duke were dyfpofed to fhewe hym fome difport. Cæfar
whych neuer fufpected the leaft of thefe chaunced murders,
defired not to be prayed agayne, but made hafte to the Butcherie
like a lamb, and in the company of the Wolues themfelues that
were in readyneffe to kyll hym. He was no fooner in the Court
of the Caftle, but feuen or eyght Varlets apprehended hym and
hys Men, and carryed hym into the Chaumber (bound lyke a
thefe) wherin the Membres of hys Myferable Brother were cut of
and difperfed, whofe corpfe was pitifully gored and arrayed in
Bloud. If Cæfar were abafhed to fee himfelfe bound and taken
pryfoner he was more aftonned when he perceyued a body fo
dyfmembred, and which as yet he knewe not. "Alas," (fayd he)
"what fighte is this? Is thys the bore whych thou haft caufed
vs to come hyther to hunt within our very Fort?" The Captayne
rifing vp, al imbrued wyth bloud, whofe face and voyce promifed
nothing but Murder to the miferable young Gentleman fayd : "See
Cæfar, the Body of thine adulterous brother Nicholas, that
infamous whoremonger, and marke if this be not his head : I
woulde to God that Conrade were here alfo that ye might all three

be placed at this fumptuous Banket, which I haue prepared for you. I fweare vnto thee then, that this fhould be the last day of all the Trinicien race, and the end of your Tirannies and wicked Life. But fith I cannot get the effect of that whych my heart defireth, my minde fhal take repaft in the triumph which Fortune hath ordeined. Curffed be the mariage and Wedding at Trevio, that hath hyndred me of an occafion fo apte, and of the meanes to difpatch a matter of futch importance as is the ouerthrow of fo many tirants." Cæfar at this fentence ftode fo ftil, as whilom dyd the wyfe of Loth, by feing the City on fire, and confume into afhcs: by the fight whereof fhe was conuerted into a ftone of Salt. For when he fawe that bloudy Pageant, and knew that it was his brother Nicholas, pity and feare fo ftopt the pipes of his fpeach, as without complayning himfelf or framing one word, he fuffred his throte to be cut by the barbarous captaine, who threw him halfe dead vpon the corps of his brother, that the bloud of either of them might cry vp to the heauens for fo loud vengeance as that of Abel dyd, being flain by the treafon of his neareft bro-ther. Beholde the dreadful begynnings of a heart rapt in fury, and of the mind of him that not refifting his fond affections, executed the terrible practizes of his owne braine, and preferring his fantafie aboue reafon, deuifed futch ruine and decay, as by thefe Examples the Pofteritye fhall haue good caufe to wonder. The lyke Cruelty vfed Tiphon towards his brother Ofyris by chopping his body in xxvi. gobbets, whereby enfued the decay of him and his, by Orus whome fome doe furname Appollo. And troweth the Captayne to loke for leffe mercy of the Brother of the other twayne that were murdered and of the Dukes kindred whome he kept Pryfoner? But he was fo blynded with Fury, and it may be, led by ambition'and defyre to be made Lord of Nocera, that he was not contented to venge his fhame on hym whych had offended, but affayed to murder and extinguyfh all the Trinicien bloud: the enheritaunce only remaining in them. And to come to the end of his Enterprife, this Italyan Nero, not content wyth thefe fo many flaughters, but thereunto adioyned a new Treafon affaying to win the Citizens of Nocera to moue rebellion agaynft their Lord, caufing them to affemble before the Forte, vnto whome

vppon the Walles, he vfed this or like Oration: "I haue hitherto
(my Maifters) diffembled the lyttle pleafure that my heart hath
felt to fee fo many true and faithful Citizens, fubiecte vnder the
wyll and unbrydeled luftes of two or three Tyraunts: who hauing
gotten Power and authority ouer vs, more through our owne folly
and cowardyfe, than by valiance, vertue and iuftice, either in them
or thofe which haue difpoyled this countrey of their auncient
liberty.   I will not deny but pryncipalities of longe entraunce and
Foundation deryued by fucceffion of inherytaunce, haue had fome
fpyce and kynde of Equity, and that Lordes of good lyfe and conuerfation ought to be obeyed, defended and honored.   But where
inuafion and feafure is againft ryght, where the people is fpoyled
and Lawes violated, it is no confcience to difobey and abolifh futch
monfters of nature.   The Romanes in the prime age of their Common Wealth ful wel declared the fame, when they banifhed out of
their City that proud race of the Tirant Tarquine, and when they
went about to exterminate al the rootes of cruelty and tyrannical
power.   Our Neighbors the Sicillians once dyd the like vnder the
conduct of Dion, againft the difruled fury and wilful cruelty of
Denis the tyrant of Syracufa, and the Atheniens againft the Chyldren of Pififtratus.   And ye that be forted from the ftocke of
thofe Samnites, which in times paft fo long heald vp their Heades
againft the Romane force, will ye be fo very cowardes and weake
hearted for refpect of the title of your feigniorie as ye dare not
with me to attempt a valiant enterprife for reducing your felues
into libertye, and to expell that vermyne broode of Tyraunts which
fwarme through out the whole regyon of Italy.   Wyll yee bee
fo mated and dumped, as the fhadow alone of a fond and incon-
ftant young man, fhall holde your Nofe to the Grindftone, and
drawe you at his luft lyke an Oxe into the ftall?   I feare that if ye
faw your Wiues and Daughters haled to the paffetyme and pleafure of thefe Tirauntes, to glutte the whoredome of thofe ftyncking
Goate Bucks, more Lecherous and filthy than the fenfeles fpar-
rowes: I feare (I fay) that ye durft not make one Sygne for
demonftratyon of your Wrath and dyfpleafure.   No, no (my
mayfters of Nocera,) it is hyghe tyme to cutte of the Hydra hys
heads, and to ftrangle hym wythin hys Caue.   The tyme is come

(I fay) wherein it behoueth you to fhewe your felues lyke Men, and no longer to diffemble the cafe that toucheth you fo neare. Confyder whether it bee good to follow myne aduyfe, to repoffede agayne the thyng whych is your owne, (that is) the Freedome wherein your Auncefters gloryfied fo mutch, and for which they feared not to hazarde theyr Goodes and Lyues. It wyll come good cheape, if you be ruled by me, it wyll redound to your treble Fame, if lyke Men ye follow my aduyfe, whych I hope to let you fhortely fee wythout any great peryll or loffe of your Citizens Bloud. I haue felt the effeƈt of the Trinicien Tirannye, and the rigor of their vnrighteous gouernment, which hauing begonne in me, they will not faile, if they be not chaftifed in time, to extend on you alfo, whome they deeme to be their flaues. In lyke manner I haue firft begon to repreffe their boldneffe, and to wythftande their leud behauior : yea and if you Mynde to vnderftande ryght from wrong, an eafy matter it will be to perfourme the reft, the time beinge fo commodious, and the difcouery of the thinge whereof I haue made you fo priuy, fo conuenient. And know ye, that for the exploit of mine intent, and to bryng you agayne altogether in Liberty, I haue taken the two Lords Nicholas and Cæfar pryfonners, attending till fortune do bryng to me the third, to pay him with like money and equall guerdon, that not onely you may bee free and fetled in your auncient priuiledge, but my heart alfo fatiffied of the wrong which I haue receiued by their iniuftice. Beleue (Maifters) that the thing whych I haue done : was not wythoute open iniury receiued, as by keepyng it clofe I burft, and by telling the fame I am afhamed. I wil kepe it fecrete, notwithftanding, and fhal pray you to take heede vnto your felues, that by vniuerfal confent, the mifchiefe may be preuented. Deuife what anfwer you wyll make me, to the intent that I by following your aduife, may alfo be refolued vpon that I haue to do, without Preiudice but to them to whome the cafe doth chyefly appertayne." Duryng al this difcourfe, the wycked Captayne kept clofe the Murder which hee had committed, to drawe the Worme out of the Nocerines Nofe, and to fee of what Mynde they were, that vppon the intellygence thereof, he myght woorke and follow the tyme accordyngly. Hee that had feene the Cytizens of Nocera after that fedytious Oration, would haue thought that he had heard a murmure of Bees, when iſſuing forth their Hyues, thcy light amidſt a pleaſauut Herber, adorned and beautyfied with diuers coloured floures. For the people flocked and aſſembled togythers, and began to grudge at the impryſonment of ther Lord, and the treaſon committed by the Lieuetenaunte, thynking it very ſtraunge that he which was a houſhold ſeruaunt durſt be ſo bold to ſeaſe on thoſe to whome he dyd owe all honour and Reuerence. And do aſſure you that if he had ben below, as he was vpon the rampire of the Walles, they had torne him into ſo many pieces, as he had made Gobbets of the Lord Nicholas body. But ſeing that they could not take him, they went about to ſeeke the deliueraunce of them, whome they thought to be yet aliue : and one of the chyef of the City in the Name of them all ſhortly and bryefly, aunſwered him thus: "If malice did not well diſcouer it ſelfe in the ſugred and Traiterous compoſition of thy woordes (O Captayne) it were eaſy inough for an inconſtant People (bent to chaunge, and deſirous of innoua- tions,) to heare and do that, which ſutch a traitor and flatterer as thou art doſt propoſe : but we hauing til now indured nothing of the Triniciens that ſauoreth of Tiranny, cruelty, or exceſſe, we were no leſſe to be accuſed of felony, than thou art guilty of Rebels cryme, by ſeaſyng vpon the Perſons of thy Lords, if we ſhoulde yelde credyt to thy Serpents hiſſing, or lend aide to thy traiterous practiſe, thou goeſt about againſt them who innoblyng thee are trayterouſly berieued of that which concerned their re- putation and greatneſſe. We be an honeſt People and faithfull Subiects. We wyll not be both Wicked and vnhappy at once, and without cauſe expell our heads out of our common Wealth. No though they ſhould perpetrate the miſchiefes whych thou haſt alleadged. Vppon ſutch Nouelties and ſtraunge facts we ſhall take newe aduiſe and Councell. To be ſhort, thou ſhalt pleaſure vs to ſet our Lordes at Lyberty, and thou like a wyſe man ſhalt doe thy duety, and ſatiſfy a People which eaſily can not endure that a ſubiecte do wrong to thoſe to whome he oweth obedience. And feare not to receiue anye euill of them, nor yet to feele anoyaunce, for wee wyll take vppon vs by honeſt meanes to craue pardon for thy fault how haynous ſo euer it be. But if thou continue thine

offence, be fure that the Lord Conrade fhall be aduertifed, and
with all our power we fhall fuccour him by force, to let thee feele
the Nature of Treafon, and what reward is incydent to the prac-
tizers of the fame." The Captaine albeit he was abafhed with that
aunfwere, and faw that it would not be wel wyth him if he did not
prouid fpedy remedy and order for his affayres, afwell for the
comming of the Lord Conrade, as of the brother of the Duke
Camerino, told the Citizens that within three or foure dayes he
would giue them a refolute aunfwer, and fo it might be, yelde
vnto theyr wylles, and delyuer them whom he had in holde. Thys
gentle aunfwere dyd nothyng ftay the Citizens for the accomplyfhment of that which they thought beft to do, knowing alfo that
the gallant had not commenced that Tragedy, but for other toyes
whych his vngracious head had framed for a further intended
Myfchiefe, for which caufe they affembled their Councell, and
concluded that one fhould ryde in pofte to the Lord Conrade, (the
third and remnaunt of the Brethren,) that hee myghte come to
take order for the delyueraunce of Nicholas and Cæfar whome
they thought he had referued ftill alyue in Captiuity. The
Nocerines fhewed this curtefie (not but that they woulde gladly
haue bene at lyberty, if the way had bene better troden,) afwell
for the lyttle truft they repofed in the Captayne, who they thoughte
would be no more gentle and faithfull, than he fhewed himfelfe to
be loyall to his Maifters, and for that Conrade was well beloued of
the Lordes his Neighbors, and fpecially of the impryfoned Duke
and his Brother Braccio Montone, who had the Italian men of
Warre at his pleafure, and that the Noble men woulde affifte him
wyth all their power. Wherefore they confidered that theyr
faireft and beft way, for auoiding of factions, was to kepe themfelues trufty and true, and by not hearkening to a Traitor, to bynd
their foueraigne Lord with futch duety and obedience, as the
vnkindeft man of the world would confeffe and acknowledg for
the confequence of a matter of futch importance. The feditious
captaine on the other fide, void of hope, and in greater rage than
hee was before, perfifted in hys folly, not without forefeeyng
howe hee myghte faue himfelfe, which hee had pollitikely brought
to paffe, if God had not fhortened his waye, by payment of Vfury

for hys Wyckedneffe, and by very dilygence of them in whome hee repofed his trufte, the manner and howe, immedyately doeth follow. So foone as he had gyuen ouer the Councell of the Citizens and a lyttle bethought him what he had to do, he called before him two yong Men, whom aboue al others he trufted beft. To thefe yong men he deliuered all his Gold, Syluer and Iewels, that they mighte conuey the fame out of the iurifdiction of his Lords, to the intente that when he faw hymfelf in daunger, he myght retire to the place where thofe gallants had before carryed his furniture, and mountinge them vpon two good fteedes, he let them forth at the Pofterne gate, praying them fo foone as they could to retourne aduertyfement of their abode, and that fpedily he would fend after them hys Chyldren and the reft of his moueables, tellyng them that he fpecially committed his Lyfe and goodes into their hands, and that in time and place he would acknowledg the Benefite don vnto him in that diftreffe. The two that were thus put in truft for fauegard of hys thyngs, promifed vnto him Golden Hilles and Miracles: but fo foone as they had loft the fight of theyr maifter, they deuifed another complotte and determined to breake faith to him, which was forfworne, and who made no confcience not onely to reuolt, but alfo cruelly to kill his foueraigne Lordes. They thought it better to ryde to Treuio, to tell the Lord Conrade the pitifull end of his brethren, and the impryfonment of the Duke of Camerino, than to feeke reft for him, whome God permitted not to be faued, for his heinous finne already committed, and for that which he mente to do vppon hys Wyfe. For all the dyligence that the Nocerines had made, yet were the Lieuetenaunte's Men at Treuio before them, and hauyng filled the Eares of Conrade with thofe heauy Newes, and hys Eyes with Teares, his Mynde with forrow, and Spyrite with defyre to be reuenged, and as Conrade was about to mount on horfe backe wyth the Trayne hee had, the Citizens were arryued to difclofe the Impryfonment of his brethren. To whome Conrade made aunfwere: "I would to God (my friends) that the tirant had ben contented with the litle cruelty wherof you fpeake, for then I would find the meanes to agree the parties vpon the knowledge of their variance. But (alas) his malice hath paffed further, and hath beaftly flain my brethren: but I fwear by the almighty God, that if he giue me life, I wil take futch, and fo cruell vengeaunce on him, as he fhall be a Glaffe to all his lyke, for punifhment of a fault fo horrible. Depart my frends, depart and get you home, difpofe your watch and gard about the Caftell, that the traiter do not efcape: and affure your felues that this your loue fhall neuer be forgotten, and you fhall haue of me not a Tirant as he malicioufly hath protefted, but rather futch a Lord, and better alfo, than hytherto ye haue me proued." If Conrade had not ben preffed with heauineffe, he had chaunted goodly Songes againft the Treafon of the Lieuetenaunt, and would haue accufed his Brother of indifcretion, for trufting him, whofe wyfe hee had abufed, and wel did know that he efpyed the fame. But what? The bufineffe requyred other things than Words: and extreame folly it is to nippe the Dead with taunts, or with vayne words to abufe the abfent, fpeciall where vltion and reuenge is eafy, and the meanes manifeft to chaftife the temerity of futch, and to be acquited of the wrong done vnto him that cannot do it hymfelfe. Conrade then toke his way to Tuderto, where then remained the Lord Braccio, and thereof was Lord and Gouernour, and had alfo vnder his gouernement Perugia, and many other Cityes of the Romane Church, and who wyth the dignity of the great Conftable of Naples, was alfo Prynce of Capua, to him the Trinicien Brother, all be fprent wyth Teares and tranfported wyth choller and griefe, came to demaunde fuccor for reuenge of the Lieuetenaunt's trefpaffe, faying: "For what affurance (my Lord) can Prynces and great Lordes hope henceforth, when their very feruaunts fhall ryfe, and by conftraining their Maifters, make affay to vfurp their feigniories wherein they haue no title or intereft? Is this a reuenge of wrong, in fteede of one to kill twaine, and yet to wifhe for the third to difpatch the World of our race? Is this to purfue his ennimy, to feeke to catch hym in trappe, whych knoweth nothing of the quarell, and to make hym to fuffer the payne? My two Brethren be dead, our Cofin Germaine the Duke is in pryfon, I am heere comfortleffe, all fad and penfife before you, whome lykewyfe this matter toucheth, although not fo near as it doeth me, but yet with lyke difhonor. Let vs go (my Lorde) let vs goe I befeech you to vifite our good hofte that fo rudely in-

treateth his Ghefts which come to vifite him, and let vs beare him
a reward, that he may tafte of our comming, let vs goe before hee
faue himfelfe, that with little trauayle and leffe harme to an other
the ribauld may be punifhed, who by his example if he longer
liue, may increafe courage both in Seruaunts to difobey, and in
Subiects to rebell, without confcience, agaynft their heads, and
gouerners? It is a cafe of very great importaunce, and which
ought to be followed with all rigor and cruelty. And he ought
neuer to bee fupported, comforted or fauored, which fhall by any
meanes attempt to reuolt or arme himfelfe agaynft his Prince, or
fhall conftrayne him or hir that is his Soueraygne Lord, or Mis-
treffe. Is not a Prynce conftituted of God to be obeyed, loued,
and cherifhed of his Subiects? Is it not in him to make and ordaine
lawes, futch as fhalbe thought needefull and neceffary for Common wealth? Ought not he then to be obeyed of his fubiectes and
vaffals? Ought they then to teach the head, and commaund the
chiefeft Member of their body? I do remember a tale (my Lord)
recited by Menenius Agrippa that wyfe, and Notable Romayne,
who going about to reconcile the commons with the Senate,
alleaged a fit and conuenable example. In time paft (quod he)
when the partes of Mankinde were at variaunce, and euery member would be a Lord generally confpiring, grudging and alleaging
how by their great trauayle, paynes, and carefull miniftery, they
prouided all furniture, and mayntenaunce for the belly, and that
he like a fluggifh Beaft ftoode ftill, and enioyed futch pleafures
as were geuen him, in this murmure and mutine, al they agreed
that the hands fhould not minifter, the Mouth fhould not feede,
the Teeth fhould not make it feruiceable, the Feete fhould not
trauayle, nor Heade deuife to get the fame: and whyleft euery of
them did forfake their feruice and obedience, the belly grew fo
thin, and the Members fo weake and feeble, as the whole body
was brought to extreme decay, and ruine, whereby (fayd Agrippa)
it appeareth that the feruice due vnto the Belly (as the chiefe
portion of man) by the other Members is moft neceffary, the
obeying and nurffing of whom doth inftil force and vigor
into the other parts through which we doe liue, and bee
refrefhed, and the fame difgefted and difpearfed into the vaynes,

and vitall powers ingendreth mature and fine bloud, and mayn-
taineth the whole ftate of the body, in comely forme and order.
By which trim comparifon, applyed to ciuile warre was deflected
and mollified the ftout corage and attempts of the multitude.
Euen fo agreing with Agrippa, if the Members grudge, and dis-
obey againft their chiefe, the ftate muft grow to ruine.   To be
fhort, in certaine haps a Trayter may be chearifhed, and that hath
falfified his firft fayth: but treafon and periury euermore be
detefted as vices execrable.   In this deede neyther the thing, nor
yet the doer hath any colour of excufe, the trefpaffe and caufe
for which it is don being confidered.   Suffifeth it Sir, for fo
mutch as there is neyther time nor caufe of further difcourfe, what
neede we to decide the matter, whych of it felfe is euident?   Beholde mee heere a poore Trinician Brother without brethren, ioy-
leffe without a Fort at Nocera.   On the other part confider the
Duke of Camerino in great diftreffe and daunger, to paffe that
ftrait of death my Brethren did.   Let vs goe (I pray you) to deliuer
the Captiue, and by reuenging thefe offenfes and murders, to
fettle my Citty in former State, and freedome, which the villayne
goeth about to take from me, by encouraginge my Subiects to
reuolt and enter armes, thereby to expel our houfe from the Title
of the fame."   As Conrade fpake thefe woords, and wyth great
grauity, and conftancy pronouncing fundry tokens of forrow, the
Coneftable of Naples, wroth beyond meafure for thefe vnpleafant
newes, and full of griefe and choller againft the trayterous Lieutenaunt, fwore in the hearing of them all, that he would neuer reft
one good fleepe vntill that quarell were auenged, and had quited
the outrage done to the Lord Conrade, and the wrong which he
felt in him for the imprifonment of the Duke of Camerino.   So
he concluded, and the Souldiours were affembled thorough out all
the parts of the Coneftable's Lands, vpon the ende of the weeke to
march againft the Fort of Nocera, the Cittizens whereof had layd
diligent Scout, and watch for the efcape of the Captayne, who
without bafhfulneffe determined with his men to defend the fame
and to proue fortune, making himfelfe beleeue that his quarell was
good, and caufe iuft to withftand them that fhoulde haue the
heart to come to affayle him.   The Conftable in the mean time

fent a Trumpet to Nocera to fummon the Captaine to furrender,
and to tell the caufe of his reuolt, and at whofe prouocation hee
had committed fo deteftable a Treafon. The Captaine well affured
and boldned in his Wyckedneffe, aunfwered that he was not fo
well fortified to make a furrender fo good cheape, and for fo
fmall a pryce to forgo his honor and reputation : and furthermore, that his wit was not fo flender, but hee durft deuife and
attempt futch a matter without the councel of any other, and that
all the deedes and deuifes paffed till that time, were of his owne
inuention. And to be enen with the wrong done to his honor by
the Lord Nicholas Trinicio, for the violation of his Wiue's Chaftity,
he had committed the Murders (tolde to Braccio) beyng angry,
that all the Tirannous race was not in his hand to fpyll, to the end
he mighte deliuer his Countrey, and put the Citizens in Liberty,
albeit that fondly they had refufed the fame as vnworthy of futch
a Benefite, and well deferued that the Tyrants fhould taxe them
at theyr pleafure, and make them alfo theyr common flaues and
Drudges. The Trumpet warned hym alfo to render to hym the
Duke, bicaufe he was guiltleffe of the facte, whych the Captayne
regarded fo little as he did the firft demaundes, whych was the
caufe (the Company being arriued at Nocera, and the Conftable
vnderftandyng the litle accompte the Caftell Gentleman made of
his fummons) that the battry the very day of theyr arriuall was
laid and fhotte againft the place with futch thunder and dreadfull
thumpes of Canon fhot, as the hardieft of the Mortpayes within,
began to faint. But the corage and litle feare of theyr chyefe,
retired theyr hearts into theyr bellyes. The breach being made
againe, the Conftable who feared to lofe the Duke in the Captaine's Fury, caufed the Trumpet to fummon them wythin to fall
to Compofition, that Bloudfhed might not ftirre theyr Souldioures
to further cruelty. But fo mutch gayned this fecond warnyng as
the firft, for which caufe the nexte day after the affault was
gyuen, where if the affaulte was valiant, the refiftaunce was no
leffe than bolde and venturous. But what can Thirtie or Fortie
Men doe agaynfte the Force of a whole Countrey, and where the
Generall was one of the moft valiaunte, and wifeft Captaynes of hys
tyme and who was accompanied with the floure of the Neapolitane

Fotemen. The affault continued four or fiue Houres, but in the
end the Dead payes not able to fuftayne the force of the affaylants, forfooke the Breache, and affaying to faue themfelues, the
Lieuetenaunt retired to the Kipe of the Fort, where his Wife continued prifoner, from the time that the two brethren were flaine.
Whiles they without, ruffled in together in heapes amonges the
defendauntes, the Duke of Camerino, with his Men, found
meanes to efcape out of Pryfon, and therewithal began furioufly
to chaftife the minifters of the difloyal Captaine, which in little
tyme were cut al to pieces. Conrade being within found the
Captayn's Father, vppon whom he was reuenged, and killed him
with his owne hands. And not content with that, caried into
further rage, and fury, he flafhed him into gobbets, and threwe
them to the dogs. Truly a ftraunge maner of reuenge, if the Captain's cruelty had not attempted like inhumanity. To bee fhorte,
horrible it is to repeate the murders done in that fturre, and
hurly burly. For they that were of the Captayne's part, and taken,
receyued all the ftraungeft and cruelleft punifhment that man
could deuife. And were it not that I haue a defire in nothing to
beely the Author, and leffe will to leaue that which he had wrytten
vpon the miferable end of thofe that were the minifters and
feruaunts to the barbarous tirrany of the Captayne, I would paffe
no further, but conceale that which doth not deferue remembraunce, except to auoide the example, which is not ftraunge, the
Cruelty of reuenging heart in the nature of Man, in al times grow-
inge to futch audacity, as the torments which feeme incredyble,
be lyable to credite as wel for thofe we reade in auncient Hiftoryes,
as thofe we heare tell of by heare fay, and chauncyng in our tyme.
Hee that had the vpper hand of his Enimy, not content to kyll,
but to eate with his rauenous teeth the heart difentraylde from
his aduerfary, was hee leffe furious than Conrade, by makinge
Anatomy of the Captayn's Father? And he that thruft Galleazze
Fogafe in to the mouth of a Canon, tying his Head vnto his Knees
and caufing him to be caried by the violent force of Gunpouder
into the City from whence he came, to bribe and corrupt certayne of hys enemies army, did he fhew himfelfe to be more
curteous than one of thefe? Leaue we a part thofe that be paft,

to touch the miferable ende wherewith Conrade caufed the laft
tribute of the Captain's fouldyers to bee payd. Now amongs
thefe fome were tied to the Tayles of wilde Horfes, and trayned
ouer Hedges, and Bufhes, and downe the ftiepnes of high Rocks,
fome were haled in pieces, and afterwards burnt with great Martyrdome, fome were deuyded and parted aliue in four quarters, other
fowed naked wythin an Oxe Hyde, and fo buried in Earth, vp to
the Chin, by whych torments they finifhed their Liues with fearful
gronings. Will ye fay that the Bull of Perillus, or Diomedes
Horffes, were afflictions more cruell than thefe? I know not what
ye cal cruelty, if thefe acts may beare the title of modefty. But
all thys, proceeded of wrath and difdayne of eyther partes. The
one dyfdayned that the feruaunt fhould be his head, and the other
was offended, that his foueraygne Lord fhould affay to take that
from him, which his duty commaunded him to keepe. Conrade
toke in ill part the treafon of the Captayn, who beyond meafure
was angry, that the Lord Nicholas had made him a brother of
Vulcan's order, and regeftred him in the booke of hufbands,
which know that they dare not fpeake. In fumme, the one had
right, and the other was not without fome reafon, and notwithftanding both furmounted the boundes of man's milde nature.
The one ought to content hymfelfe (as I haue fayd) for being
reuenged on him that had offended him, and the other of the
murder done, duringe the affault without fhewing fo bloudy
tokens of cruelty and fo apparent euidence of tiranny, vpon the
minifters of the brutall and bloudy Captayne, who feeing his
father put to death with futch Martirdome, and his men fo
ftraungely tormented, was vanquifhed with choller, difpayre and
impacyence. And albeit the Captayne had no greate defire to hurt
his Wyfe, yet was he furmounted with futch rage, as apprehending hir, and binding hir hands and feete, fhe ftyl crying him
mercy, and crauing pardon for hir faultes at the hands of God
and him, he threw hir downe from the higheft Toure of the Kipe
vpon the pauement of the Caftle courte, not without teares and
abafhment of al, which faw that monftrous and dreadful fight,
which the Souldiers viewing, they fired the Toure, and with fire
and fmoke forced the Captaine to come forth, and by lyke meanes

made him, his Brother and Chyldren to tread the daunce that his
Wyfe before had don.   Conrade by and by caufed thofe bodies to
be throwne forth for Foode to the Wolues, and other raueninge
Beafts, and Byrdes liuing vpon the pray of Carrion, caufing alfo
his Brethren honourably to bee buryed, and the Gentlewoman that
had borne the penaunce worthy for hir fault.   Sutch was the end
of the moft myferable, and worft gouerned loue, that I thinke
man hath euer red in wryting, and which doth clearely witneffe,
that there is no pleafure fo great but Fortune by chaunging and
turning hir Wheele maketh a hundred times more bitter than
defire of futch ioy doth yelde delyght.   And farre better it were
(befides the offence done to God) neuer to caft Eye on Woman,
than to bord or proue them, to rayfe futch Sclaunders and Facts
which cannot be recounted but with the horrour of the Hearers,
nor wrytten but to the great griefe of thofe that mufe and ftudy
vpon the fame: Notwithftanding for inftruction of our life, both
good and bad Examples bee introduced and offred to the view of
ech degree, and ftate.   To the end that Whoredome may bee
auoyded, aud bodily Pleafure efchued, as moft Mortal and pernicious Plagues that doe infect as well the Body and Reputation of
man, as the integrity of the Minde.   Befides that ech man ought
to poffeffe his own Veffel, and not to couet that is none of hys,
vnfeemely alfo it is to folicite the Neyghbor's Wyfe, to procure
thereby the difiunction and defaite of the whole bond of mariage,
which is a Treafure fo deare and precious, and carieth fo greate
griefe to him that feeth it defaced, as our Lord (to declare the
grauity of the Fact) maketh a comparifon of his Wrath agaynfte
them which run after ftraunge Gods, and applyeth the honour
due vnto him to others that doe not deferue the fame, with the
iuft difdayne, and ryghtfull Choller of a Iealous Hufbande, Fraught
wyth defpyght to fee himfelfe difpoyled of the Seafure, and Pos-
feffion onely giuen to him, and not fubiect to any other, whatfoeuer he be.   Learne here alfo (O yee hufbands) not to fly with fo
nimble Wing, as by your owne authority yee feeke reueng without
fearing the follies and fclaunders that may infue.   Your forrow is
iuft, but it behoueth that reafon doe guide your fantafies, and
bridle your ouer fodayne paffions, to the intent that yee come

not after to fing the doleful Song of repentaunce, like vnto this foolifh man, who hauing done more than he ought, and not able to retire without his ouerthrow, threw himfelfe into the bottom-leffe gulfe of perdition. And let vs all fixe faft in memory, that neuer vnruled rage, and wilful choller bringeth other benefit than the ruine of him that fuffereth himfelfe to runne headlonge into the fame, and who thinketh that all that is naturall in vs, is also rea-fonable, as though Nature were fo perfect a worckwoman, as in man's corruption fhe could make vs Aungels, or halfe Gods. Nature following the inftinct of that which is naturall in vs, doth not greatly ftray from perfection, but that is giuen to few, and thofe whom God doth loue and choofe. And Vertue is fo fel-dome founde, as it is almoft impoffible to imitate that perfection. And briefly to fay, I will con-clude with the Author of this prefent Hyftory.

Angre is a fury fhort,
To him that can the fame excell:
But it is no laughing fport
In whom that fenfeleffe rage doth dwell.
That pang confoundeth ech man's wits
And fhameth him with open fhame,
His honour fades in frantike fits,
And blemifheth his good name.

THE THIRTY-FOURTH NOUELL.

The horrible and cruell murder of Soltan Solyman, late the Emperor of the Turkes and father of Selym that now raigneth, done vpon his eldeſt Sonne Muſtapha, by the procurement, and meanes of Roſa his mother in lawe, and by the ſpeciall inſtigation of one of his noble men called Ruſtanus: where alſo is remembred the wilful death of one of his Sons named Giangir, for the griefe he conceiued to ſee Muſtapha ſo miſerably ſtrangled.

TWENTY two yeares paſt or thereabouts I tranſlated this preſent Hyſtory out of the Latine tongue. And for the rarenes of the Fact, and the diſnaturall part of that late Furioſe Enemy of God, and his Sonne Chriſt: I dedicated the ſame to the right honorable, my ſpeciall good Lord, with al vertues, and nobility, fully accomplyſhed, the Lord Cobbam Lorde Warden of the cinque Portes, by the name of Sir VVilliam Cobham Knyght. And bycauſe I would haue it continue in man's remembraunce thereby to renue the auncient deteſtation, which we haue, and our Progenitors had againſt that horrible Termagant, and Perſecutor of Chriſtyans, I haue inſinuated the ſame amongs the reſt of theſe Nouels. For of one thing I dare make warrantiſe, that auncient Writers haue not remembred, nor old Poets reported a more notorious or horyble Tragedy or fact executed againſt nature, then that vnnaturall murder done by the ſayd enemy of Chriſtianity, the late Soltan Solyman, otherwyſe called the great Turke. I remember the deſcription of Nero's Parricide vppon his louynge Mother, of purpoſe to behold the place of his byrth. I call to memory alſo the wycked Murther of Oreſtes, on hys Mother Clytemneſtra. I alſo conſider the vnfatherly part of Tantalus, who wyth the fleſh of his owne ſonne Pelops, feaſted the Gods. All which are not farre dyfferent from this peſtiferous Fury, and may wyth the ſame, and the lyke bee comparable by any Man heeretofore committed. This Hellyſh Champyon hys owne Sonne, of hys owne Seede, Naturally conceaued wythin hys mother's Wombe, vnnaturally in his owne preſence moſte Myſerably did kill. O pityfull caſe, But alas, voyde of pitty

to a pyttyleffe man. O cruell fact, but not ouer cruell to him that
liued a cruell Man. What Beaft be he neuer fo woode, or Sauage,
can fuffer his Yonglings to take harme, mutch leffe to doe them
hurte himfelfe? What fierce Lyoneffe can infefte hir owne Whelpe,
which with Naturall paines brought it into light? But what doe I
ftand vpon Lamentation of the cafe and leaue the bruteneffe of
this Madman far bruter then Lyons vnconfidered? The bruteneffe of
this fury fo farre ecceedeth Beafts, as Reafonable paffeth Vnreafonable. The fury of the Deuill, whom he ferueth, fo raged in his
tirannous life, as loe, he flue his owne Sonne. The care of God,
and Chrifte was fo farre out of his Sighte as hee fubuerted Nature.
The libidonous luftes of this Lecherous Infidell, fo furmounted the
bounds of reafon, as the fire thereof confumed his owne flefh.
This Enemy of Chrifte was fo bewytched as the dotage of his
infidelity confented to murder. And as tiranny like a Lord pos-
feffed his Brayne in huntinge after the bloud of Chriftians, so
Tiranny like an Enchaunter with the Sorcery of Feminine adula-
tion fhed the bloud of his owne begotten. Thus as tiranny was the
Regent of his life moft wicked, fo Tiranny was the Plague of his
owne generation. For as the Wryter of this Hyftory reporteth, it
was thoughte that the fame was done by Diuyne Prouydence.
And lyke as this vnhappy Father was a deadly Enemy vnto Chryft
and hys Church, fo this yonge Whelpe was no leffe a fheder of
Chriftian Bloud. No doubt a very froward Impe, and a towarde
Champion for the diuel's Theatre: and as it is fayd hereafter, fo
goodly a yong man in Stature and other externe qualities of the
body, as Nature could not frame a better. So excellent, and
couragious in Feates of armes as Bellona hirfelfe could not pro-
create a luftier. This Hiftory in the Latin tongue is written by
Nicholas Moffan a Burgonian borne, a man fo well in the warfare of good learning (as it appeareth) as in the feruice of the
warres well expert. Who being a Souldiour in Hercules warres
(the old Champyon of Chriftendome, and Pagan Enimy, Charles
the fifte) was fore wounded and taken Pryfoner in Bulgaria, in the
yeare of our Lord 1552, and continued Captiue till September,
1555, almoft three yeares. Whofe Mifery, Trouble, Famine,
Colde, and other Torments by him fuftayned, during the fayd time

if it fhould bee declared, perhaps woulde feeme incredible.   But
when the Turke had kept him in miferable bandes two yeares,
and faw he could not obtayne the Raunfome, whych he immefu-
rably requyred, at length fent him to the Caftell of Strigon, where
for a certayne time he remayned hampered with double chaynes
vpon his Necke, Handes, and Feete.   And within fometime after
hys comming thither he was made to toile in the day, like a common flaue, to hew and carry Woode, keepe Horfe, fweepe Houfes,
and futch other bufines.   Which Drudgery, he was glad to doe
afwell for exercyfe of his Members, which with colde yrons were
benommed, as alfo to get Breade to relieue his hunger.   For when
hee had done his ftinte, his Maifter gaue him Bread, Onions, Gar-
licke, Cheefe, and futch other fare: and at Night he was fent agayne
to Pryfon, where he was matched with a Mate, that for Debte
was condempned to perpetual Pryfon, of whom he learned many
things, afwel of their Lawes, Religion, warlike Affayres, and other
maners of the Turkes, as alfo of the order of this horrible Faƈt don
by Solyman.   And by the report of his fayd Companion in pryfon, he digefted the fame into the forme of this hiftory.   And
after this man had payed hys Raunfome, and was fet at lyberty, he
arriued into the partes of Chryftedome.   The Verity of whych is
futch, as it is not onely credyble bycaufe thys Man dyd wryte it,
who was three Yeares there refiaunt, and in manner aforefaid,
heard the truth thereof, but alfo is warranted, by fundry Marchant Men, Trauellers into farre Countreyes, faythfully verifiing
the fame to bee true.   And before I drawe to the dyfcourfe of the
Story, I will fet downe fome of the manners of Solyman's greateft
ftates and fauorites, and the pryncipal offices and honors of that
hellifh Monarchy.   As Muftapha, Machomet, Baiafith, Selim,
Gianger, Chruftam, and Hibrahim.   This Hibrahim was fo
dearely beloued with the Emperour Solyman as he exercyfed
the Office of Vefiri, whych is nexte to the Emperour, the chyefeft
in degree of honor.   Who by increafe of that Office, became more
wealthy in Treafure then Solyman himfelfe, whych when he perceyued, without any refpeƈt of the honorable office, or the honor
of the party, negleƈting in refpeƈt of richeffe (according to the
natural defire of Auarice, wherewith the greedy Appetites of the

ſtocke are endued) all religion, honour, Parents, countrey, friends or amity, he cauſed in his own preſence, his head to be ſtriken of, adding the treaſures of the ſaid Hibrahim to his owne Coaſers, and placed one Ruſtanus to ſucceede in his office. Beſides which honorable places ther be diuers degrees of honor, as Mutchtv, which is of that honor with them as the chief biſhop or Pope in other Countreies, and of ſutch authority with the Emperour, that aſwel in time of Peace, as alſo in Warres, he determineth vppon nothing without the counſel of Muchti. Baſcha (which we commonly call VVaſcha) is the Lieuetenaunt of a Prouince. But for-ſomutch as all other offices and dignities, depend only vpon the Emperor, and are beſtowed as he liſteth, none of them hauing any thing proper that he may call his owne: the ſayd Baſchas in all Prouinces, euery three yeare are chaunged after the diſpoſition of the Emperour, and continue no longer Gouernors, than the ſayd terme, without his ſpecial decree, and commaundement. And this chaunge and ſeueral mutation, is done for two cauſes. Firſt that notwithſtanding the ſayd Offices are beſtowed by turnes, yet they which are moſt excellente in prowes of Armes, and Valiaunce, are beſt in fauour, and are placed in the moſt fertile Countreyes. But the maner in the diſpoſition of the ſame Office is now degenerated, for where in tyme paſte the ſame were beſtowed vppon the beſt Captaynes and Souldyers, in theſe Days, are through Fauoure and Money, throughly corrupted. So that now amonges them all thynges for Money are venalia, ready to be ſolde, and yet the ſame vnknowen to the Emperour him ſelfe. The other cauſe, of the alteration and chaunge of the ſayd Baſchæ, and the Chyefeſt cauſe, as I haue learned is, leaſt through theyr longe abode in the ſayd Prouinces ſo to them aſſigned, by ſome incydent occaſion they myght entre familiarilie wyth the Chriſtians, and in ſucceſſe of tyme be conuerted. The Turkes haue alſo amonges them certayne Noble Men which in theyr Language they call Spahy, and it is the firſt degree of honour, but it hath no diſcent or ſucceſſion to the Poſterity, and they only deſerue the tytle thereof, whych in Warrelyke Affayres behaue them ſelues moſte Manfully, and who at length are preferred to another degree of honour, and are called Subaſche, which worde ſo farre as I can vnderſtande, may be referred to the Title of Baron. Next

to the fame Subafchæ here is another called Begg. But here is
meete to be knowne howe that woorde is taken amonges them two
wayes, for generally all they which excell other in any promotion
are called Beggi. That is to fay Lordes or Mayfters: but if it be
meaut fingularly or properly, then it fignifieth not fimply a Captaine (for they call a Captaine Aga) but alfo an Earle. And if the
fayd Begg chaunce to be endued by the Emperour with the order
of Knyghthoode, then hee is called Sanggakbegg. And they likewife are accuftomed to bee tranfpofed from County to county, as the
Bafchæ are, and the fame do not defcend to the heires, but when
the Earle is deade. And then both the promotion and county, are by
the Emperour giuen to another. And hereby it appeareth that no
man hath any thynge proper or his own, and therfore they cal
themfelues, Padifcahumcullari. That is to fay, the Emperour's
bondmen. Here alfo I ought to entreat of the manners of the
Turkes in theyr Warres, and the fundry offices therein. In what
forte they leuy, and mufter their Souldiers, the order of their
marching, the order in putting the fame in array, and by what
diligence they vfe their Skouts, and Wardes, all which had bene
neceffary to haue bene fpoken of, but that I might not be tedious.
And yet of one thing for a conclufion I entend to fpeake of, which is
of the Ianifchari. The fayd Ianifchari are the whole ftrength of
the Turkes battell, who neuer obtayne victory, but the fame is
aftributed to their valiaunce. They bee very expert, and fkilfull
in the vfe of fmall fhot, and great Ordinaunce, and in that kinde of
defence and munition, they chiefly excell. And as I haue red,
the Turke hath continually in wages thirty M. of the fayd Ianis-
chari. They haue aboue other many finguler Pryuiledges, in fo
mutch as the name of a Ianifcharus is in futch reuerence amongs
them, that notwithftanding any offence, or crime, done by them
worthy capitall death, they in no wife fhalbe punifhed, except
before the committing of the offence, they be depriued of their
eftate by their Captaynes. Thys Priuiledge alfo they haue aboue
others, that vnleffe they lye in Campe, they bee neuer compelled
to watch nor warde, without great neceffity do force them. And
for this they be hatefull and odious to other Souldiours. It is
fayd, that all they be Chriftian men's children. And in thofe
countreyes which he vanquifheth, he choofeth out the Boyes of

the fame, futch as he thinketh meete, and carrieth them away, and bringeth them vp in his owne trade, and lawes, with exercife of feates in armes, and being growen to ripe yeares, and man's ftate, they be alloted amongs the number of Ianifchari. And thus mutch touching the maners, dignities, and offices of that Turkifh broode : Now to the Hyftory. Bee it knowne therefore, that Solyman had of a certayne bonde Woman this Muftapha, to whom from his Youth hee gaue in charge the Countrey of Amafia. Who with his Mother continually refiaunt in the fayd countrey, became fo forwards in Feates of armes, as it was fuppofed of all men, that hee was gieuen vnto their countrey by fome heauenly prouidence. This Muftapha, with his Mother being placed in the fayd Countrey, it chaunced that the Kynge his Father was beyonde meafure wrapt with the beauty of another of his Concubins called Rofa, of whom hee begat foure fonnes, and one daughter. The eldeft of the Sonnes was called Machomet, to whom the Prouince of Caramania was affigned. The fecond, Baiafith, who enioyed the countrey of Magnefia. The third called Selymus, to whom after the death of Machomet the eldeft, the fayd Countrey of Caramania was appoincted. The fourth Iangir, whofe furname, by reafon hee was croke backed, notwithftanding his pregnant wit, was Gibbus. And the daughter he beftowed in mariage vppon Ruftanus Bafcha, who when Hibrahim was put to death, exercifed the office of Vefiri as is aforefayd (which office we vfe to call the Prefident of the Counfayle) and according to his natural difpofition to couetoufneffe, abufing the fayd office, altered and chaunged all maner of thinges belonging to the fame. He diminifhed the Souldiours wages, being by them called Ianifchari. He abated the ftipends of the Captayns, whom they nominate Saniachi. Hee alfo feaffed vpon the Prouinces yearely Taxes and Tributs. And herewith being not fatiffied, he ordayned a ftint vpon the charges of the king's houfhold, wherby he fought, but to accumulate vnto himfelfe, infinite treafures, gotten by deceiptfull extortion, through occafion whereof, he was fuppofed to be a faythfull, and diligent Seruaunte, and thereby greatly infinuated himfelfe into the king's fauour, little regardinge the hatred and difpleafure of others. In the meane time, this Rofa of whom mencion is made

before, perceyuing hir felfe before others to be beloued of the
Kinge, vnder the Cloake of devotion declared vnto Muchty (which
is the chiefe Bifhop of Machomet's religion) that fhe was affected
with a Godly zeale to builde a Temple, and Hofpitall for ftraungers,
to the chiefe God, and honor of Machomet: but fhe was not
minded to attempt the fame without his aduice. And therefore
fhee afked whether the fame would bee acceptable to God, and
profitable for the health of her foule. Whereunto Muchty
aunfwered: that the worke to God was acceptable, although to
hir foule it was nothing auaileable. Adding further, that not onely
all hir Subftance was at the Kinge's difpofition, but hir Life alfo,
being a Bondwoman. And therefore that worke woulde be more
profitable to the Kinge. With which aunfwere the woman in hir
mind dayly being troubled, became very penfiffe, like one that
was voyde of all comfort. The King being aduertifed of hir forrow
very gently began to comfort hir, affirming that fhortely he would
finde futch meanes, as fhe fhould enioy the effect of hir defire.
And forthwith manumifed hir and made hir free, a writing and inftrument made in that behalfe, according to their cuftome, to the
intent fhe might not be at commaundement any more to be yoked
in bondage. Hauinge in this forte obtayned this fauoure, the
fayd Rofa, with a great Maffe of Money determined to proceede
in hir entended purpofe. In the meane feafon, the Kyng wythout
meafure being incenfed with the defire of the fayd Rofa, as is
aforefayd, fent for hir by a meffenger, willing hir to repayre to
the Court. But the crafty Woman, vnfkilful of no pollicy, returned the Meffenger with fubtile aunfwere, which was, that he
fhould admonifh the King hir Lord and Soueraygne, to call to his
remembraunce afwell the lawe of honefty, as alfo the precepts of
his owne lawes, and to remembre fhe was no more a Bondwoman
and yet fhe could not deny but hir life remained at the difpofition of his maiefty, but touching Carnall copulation to be had
agayne with his perfon, that could in no wife be done, without
committing of finne moft heynous. And to the intent he fhould
not thinke the fame to be fayned or deuifed of hir felfe, fhe referred it to the iudgement of Muchty. Which aunfwere of repulfe, fo excited the inflamed affections of the Kyng, as fetting all

other bufineffe a part, he caufed the Muchty to be fent for.
And giuing him liberty to aunfwere, he demaunded whether his
Bondwomen being once manumifed, could not be knowen
carnally without violation of the lawes? Whereunto Muchty
aunfwered: that in no wife it was lawfull, vnleffe before he fhould
with hir contract matrimony. The difficulty of which Lawe in
futch forte augmented the Kyng's defires, as being beyond meafure blinded with Concupifcence, at length agreed to the marriage
of the fayd manumyfed woman, and after the Nuptial writinges
according to the cuftome were ratified, and that he had giuen
vnto hir for a Dowry 5000 Soltan Ducats, the marriage was concluded, not without great admiration of all men, efpecially for
that it was done contrary to the vfe of the Ottomane Ligneage.
For to efchew Society in gouernment, they marry no free or lawfull Wyues, but in their fteades to fatiffy theyr owne pleafures,
and libidinous Appetites (wherein moft vily, and filthely aboue any
other Nation they chiefly excell) they chofe out of diuers Regions
of the World the moft Beautifull, and fayreft Wenches, whom after
a Kyngly forte very honourably they bring vp in a place of their
Courte, which they call Sarai: and inftruct them in honeft, and
ciuile maners, with whom alfo they vfe to accompany by turnes,
as theyr pleafure moft lyketh. But if any of them do conceyue,
and bring forth childe, then fhe aboue all other is honoured, and
had in reuerence, and is called the Soltanes moft worthy. And
futch after they haue brought forth childe, are beftowed in marriage vppon the Pieres and Nobility, called Bafchæ, and Sangacæ.
But now to returne to our purpofe. This manumifed Woman being aduaunced through Fortune's benefit, was efteemed for the
chiefe Lady of Afia, not without great happineffe fucceeding in
al hir affayres. And for the fatiffiyng of hir ambicious entents,
there wanted but only a meane and occafion, that after the death
of Solyman, one of hir own children might obtayne the Empire.
Where vnto the generofity and good behauiour of Muftapha was
a great hinderaunce, who in deede was a yong man of great
magnanimity, and of Wit moft excellent, whofe Stomach was no
leffe couragious, than he was manly in perfon, and force. For
which qualities he was meruayloufly beloued of the Souldiours

and Men of warre, and for his wifedome and iuſtice very acceptable to the people. All which things this ſubtile woman confidering, ſhe priuely vſed the counſayle of Ruſtanus for the better
accompliſhing of hir purpoſe, knowing that he would rather ſeeke
th'aduauncement of his kinſman and the brother of his owne Wyfe
as reaſon was, then the preferment of Muſtapha, with whom ſhe
certaynely knew that Ruſtanus was in diſpleaſure. For in the
beginning, as he ſought meanes to extenuate the liuings of all
other (as is aforeſayd) ſo alſo he went about (but in vayne) to
plucke ſomewhat from Muſtapha. Whereby he thought that if
he ſhould once obtayne the gouernment, he would ſkarce forget
ſutch an iniury, and thereby not only in hazarde of his Office, and
dignity, but alſo in daunger of loſſe of his heade. All which
thinges, this wicked woman pondering in hir vngratious Stomacke
went about to inſert into the King's mynde, no ſmall ſuſpitions of
Muſtapha, ſaying that he was ambitiouſe and bolde vpon the
Fauour and good wil of all men (wherewith in deede he was greatly
endued) and reioyſing in his force, let no other thing to be expected, then oportunity of time to aſpire to the Kingdome, and to
attempt the ſlaughter of his Father. And for the better cloaking
of the matter, ſhe cauſed Ruſtanus at conuenient tyme, more at
large to amplifie and ſet forwards hir mallice, who alwayes had in
charge all principall and weyghty affayres. In whom alſo was
no lacke of matter to accelerate the accuſation and death of the
yong man. Moreouer to ſutch as were appoynćted to the ad-
miniſtration of the countrey of Syria, he priuely declared, that
Muſtapha was greatly ſuſpected of his Father, commaunding
euery of them dilligently to take heede to his eſtate, and of all
ſutch things as they eyther ſaw or perceyued in him, with all expedition to ſend aduertiſement, affirming that the more ſpight-
fully they wrote of him, the more acceptable it ſhould be to the
Kinge. Wherefore diuers times Ruſtanus being certified of the
kingly Eſtimation, Magnanimity, Wyſedome, and Fortitude of
Muſtapha, and of his beneuolence and liberality towards all men,
wherewith he greatly conciled their fauour, and how the ardent
deſires of the People, were inclined to hys election : he therefore
durſt not take vppon him to be the firſt that ſhould ſow the
ſeede of that wicked conſpiracy, but deliuering his Letters to the

vngratious Woman, left the reſt to the deuiſe of his vnhappy
brayne: But Roſa eſpying oportunity of time to ſucceede hir
vnhappy deſyre, ceaſed not to corrupt the Kyng's mynde, ſometimes with promiſe of the vſe of other Women, and ſometimes
with ſundry other adulations. So that if mention was made of
Muſtapha at any time, ſhe woulde take ſutch occaſion to open
the Letters, as might ſerue moſt apt for hir purpoſe. And ſhe was
not deceyued of hir expectation. For taking a conuenient time
not without teares (which Women neuer want in cloaked matter)
ſhe admoniſhed the Kinge of the pearill wherein he ſtoode, remembring amongs other thinges, how his Father Selymus, by ſutch
meanes depryued his owne Father both from his Kingdome, and
Life, inſtantly requiringe him by that example to beware. But
theſe Arguments of ſuſpition, at the firſt brunt ſeemed not proba-
ble to the Kyng, and therefore by this meanes the deuiliſhe Woman
could little preuayle, which when hir enuious Stomacke perceyued,
ſhe began to direct hir miſchieuous mynde to other deuiſes, ſeek-
ing meanes with poyſon to deſtroy the yonge man. And there
wanted not alſo, graceleſſe perſons, prompt and ready to accompliſh that miſchieuous fact, had not diuine prouidence reſiſted the
ſame. For Roſa ſent vnto Muſtapha a ſute of Apparell in the
name of his Father, which by marueylous craft was enuenimed with
Poyſon. But Muſtapha in no wyſe would weare the ſayd apparell
before one of his ſlaues had aſſayed the ſame, whereby he preuented the Miſchiefe of his vngratious Stepmother, opening to all
men the deceipt of the poyſon. And yet this peſtilent Woman
ceaſed not to attempt other Enterpriſes. She went about to purchaſe vnto hir the good will and familiarity of the Kyng in ſutch
ſort as the like neuer obtayned in the Courte of Ottoman, (for ſhe
vſed certayne Sorceries through the helpe of a Woman a Jewe
borne, which was a famous Enchauntreſſe, to wyn the loue of the
Kyng, and thereby perſwaded hir ſelfe to procure greater things
at his hands) in ſo mutch as ſhe obtayned that hir Children by
courſe ſhould be reſiant in their Father's Courte, that by theyr continuall preſence and aſſiduall flattering, they might get the loue
of their Father. So that if Muſtapha did at any time come to the
Court, by that meane ſhe might haue a better meanes to rid him
of his life, if not, to tary a time, wherein he ſhould be diſpatched

by the help of others. But Muftapha not repayring to the Courte
(for the Kyng's chyldren do not vfe to go out of their Countreys
affigned vnto them, without their Father's knowledge, nor to repayre to Conftantinople with any number of men of Warre, to
receyue their Inheritance till their Father be deade) fhe deuifed
another mifchiefe. For enioying hir former requeft, fhe recouered
another, alfo hauing brought to paffe that not onely in the Citty,
but alfo in the countrey, hir children fhould attend vppon theyr
Father. Yea, and Giangir the crokebacked fhould alwayes attend
on his father in his Warres. But the Stepmother's deuife for certayne yeares hanging as it were in ballance, at length Fortune
throughly fauoured hir wicked endeuours. For the Bafcha which
had the prote£tion of Muftapha, and the gouernment of the Prouince of Amafia, (For euery one of the Kyng's chyldren haue one
Bafcha, that is to fay a Liutenaunt, which doe aunfwere the people
according to the lawes and gieue orders for the adminiftration of
the Warres, and alfo euery one of them haue a learned Man to
Inftru£t them in good dyfcipline, and Pryncely qualities) the fayd
Bafcha I fay deuifed Letters wherein was contayned a certayne
treatife of Marriage, betwene Muftapha and the Kyng's Daughter
of Perfia, and how he had referred the matter to the Minifters of
the Temple, to the intent that if it had not good fucceffe, he fhould
be free from all fufpition, and fent the fame Letters to Ruftanus
who greatly reioyfed for that he hoped to bring his defyred purpofe to good effe£t. And fearing the matter no longer, incontinently he vttered the fame to Rofa, who both togethers, forthwith
went into the Pallace, and difcouered the whole matter to the
King. And to the intent they might throughly incenfe the Kyng's
mynde with fufpicions, that before was doubtefull, and deliberatiue
in the matter, to put him out of all doubt, they affyrmed that
Muftapha like an ambitioufe man, fought meanes to confpyre his
death being incenfed like a Madman to the gouernment of his
large Empyre, contrary to nature, and Law diuine. And to the
intent better creadit might be gieuen to their fubtile Suggeftions,
they alleaged the Treaty of Marriage betwene Muftapha and the
Kyng of Perfia, the deadly and auncient enimy of the Ottoman
Ligneage. For refpe£t whereof, he ought diligently to take heede

leaft by conioyning the power of the Perſians with the Sangachi, and Ianiſchari, which are the Captayns, and Souldiours, whoſe good willes he had with his lyberality already tyed to his fauour, in ſhort time, would go about to depriue him of his Kyngdome and Lyfe. With theſe accuſations and ſutch lyke they had ſo farre ſturred the king, as he himſelfe ſought the Death of his owne Sonne, in manner as foloweth.   Therefore in the yere of our Lord 1552, he cauſed to be publiſhed with al expedition throughout his prouinces, that the Perſians had made their vauntes how they woulde inuade the Countrey of Syria, win the Cityes there, and carry away the Captiues, and alſo would deſtroy euery place with fier and Sword, in ſutch ſort as no man ſhould withſtand them.   Wherefore to prouide againſt the ſayd proude and haultie Bragges, hee was forced to ſend Ruſtanus thyther with an Armie. The Souldiours being leuied, hee pryvily commaunded Ruſtanus in as ſecret manner as hee could and without any Tumulte to lay handes vpon Muſtapha, and to bryng hym bound to Canſtantinople.   But if he could not conueniently bryng that to paſſe, then to diſpatch hym of hys Lyfe by ſutch meanes as he could. Ruſtanus receyuyng thys wycked and cruell Commaundement, marched towardes Syria wyth a power. Wher when he arryued Muſtapha, hauing knowledge thereof ſetting all other buſineſſe a parte, beying accompanyed with the Luſtyeſt and beſt appoynted Men of Warre in al Turkey to the Numbre of ſeuen Thouſande, hee directed his Iorney alſo towardes Syria. Whereof when Ruſtanus had vnderſtandynge, and perceyued hee could not well accomplyſh the wycked deſire of the Kyng, immedyately retourned backe agayne to Conſtantinople in ſutch haſte that hee durſte not abyde the ſight of the Duſte rered into the Ayre by Muſtaphae's Horſe Men, and mutch leſſe hys commyng. When the Souldyers were retyred Ruſtanus declared to all Men that the Countrey was in good quyet, and pryuely repayred to the Kynge, and vttered to hym the cauſe of hys retourne, addynge further, that as farre as hee could ſee by manyfeſte Sygnes, and Coniectures, the good Wylles of all the Armye were inclyned to Muſtapha, and for that cauſe in ſo daungerous an Enterpryſe, hee durſte not aduenture with open Warres, but lefte all to the conſideration of hys Maieſty. This

reporte bred to the cruell Father (who nothynge degenerated
from the Naturall Tirannye of hys Aunceſtors) greater Suſpicions:
for reuengement whereof he moſt wickedly toke further aduiſe.
The yeare folowyng he commaunded an huge Army to be leuied
once againe makyng Proclamation that the Perſians with a greater
Power would inuade Syria, and therefore thought it mete that he
himſelf for the Common ſauegarde of them all, ought perſonally
to repayre thyther with a power to withſtande the indeuors of
his Ennimies. The Army being aſſembled, and al furnitures
prouyded in that behalfe, they marched forwardes, and within
fewe dayes after the cruell Father folowed. Who beynge come
into Syria, addreſſed a meſſenger to Muſtapha, to commaund
him forthwith to repayre vnto him, then being encamped at
Alepes. And yet Solymane could not keepe ſecret the mortall
hatred he bare to hys Sonne from others, although he imployed
dilygent care for that purpoſe, but that the knowledge thereof
came to the Eares of one of the Baſchæ, and others of Honour.
Emonges whome Achmet Baſcha pryuily ſent Woorde to Muſtapha, to the intent he myght take the better heede to hymſelf.
And it ſeemed not without Wonder to Muſtapha, that his Father,
wythout neceſſary cauſe, ſhoulde arryue in thoſe partes wyth ſo
great a Number. Who notwithſtanding, knowing hymſelfe
innocente, althoughe in extreame ſorrow and penſifenes of mynd
determyned to obey hys Father's Commaundement although he
ſhoulde ſtand in Daunger of hys Lyfe. For bee eſteemed it a
more honeſt and laudable part to incurre the Peryll of death in
Obedience to hys Father, than to lyue in contumelye by diſobedy-
ence. Therefore in that great anxietye and care of Mynde, deba-
tyng many thinges wyth hymſelfe: At length he demaunded of a
learned Man whych contynually was conuerſaunt wyth hym in his
Houſe (as is aforeſayde,) whether the Empyre of the whole World
or a vertuous Lyfe ought rather to be wyſhed for. To whom this
Learned Man moſt Godly aunſwered. That bee which dilygently
weyed the Gouernement of this Worlde, ſhall perceiue no other
Felycitye therein then a vayne and foolyſh apparence of goodneſſe.
"For there is nothyng" (quod he) "more frayle or vnſure then the
Worlde's proſperity. And it bryngeth none other Fruiċts but Feare,

forrow, troubles, fufpicions, murders, Wickedneffe, vnrighteouf‐
nes, fpoyle, Pouerty, Captiuity, and futch lyke whych to a man
that affecteth a bleffed Lyfe, are in no wyfe to be wyfhed for. For
whofe fake who fo lift to enioy them, leafeth the happines of that
Lyfe. But to whome it is gyuen from aboue to way and confider
the frayltye and fhortnes of thys ftate (which the Common People
deemeth to be a Lyfe) and to refift the vanityes of the World, at
length to embrace vertue, to them truely in heauen there is a
Place affigned and prepared of the higheft GOD, where hee fhall
inherite perpetuall Ioyes, and Felicity of the Lyfe to come." Wyth
whych aunfwer Muftapha beyng fomwhat prycked in confcience
wonderfully was fatisfied, as being tolde of him which feemed by
a certaine Prophecy to pronofticate his end. And tarrying vppon
no longer difputation, immedyately dyrected his Iourney towards
his cruell Father. And vfing that expedition he could, arriued at
the place where his Father encamped, and not farre from the fame
he pitched his pauilion. But this expedite arriuall of Muftapha
did inculcat a greater fufpicion in the wycked Father. And
Ruftanus was not behynde wyth lyes, and other fubtill informa‐
cions to fet forwardes the fame. And after he had called together
the common Souldiours and the chiefe men of Warre in the Army,
hee fente them to meete wyth Muftapha, who without any tarry‐
ing moft readily obeyed his commaundement, to put themfelues
in readines. In the mean time this crafty Verlet, fhewing by
outward countenance the hid enuy that lay fecrete in his heart,
forthwith repaired into the Kynge's Pauilion, and without fhame
or honefty told the King, howe almoft euery one of the principall
Souldiours of their owne accorde went to meete Muftapha. Then
the King being troubled in mind, went forth of his tent, and per‐
fuaded with himfelf that Ruftanus Wordes were true. Now
Muftapha lacked not fondry tokens of his vnhappy fate: For
not thre daies before he fhould take his iorney about the breake
of day in the morning being in flepe, he dreamed that he faw
Machomet clad in gorgious apparel, to take him by the hand, and
lead him into a moft pleafant place beutified with fundry turrets
and fumptuous buildinge hauing in it a moft delectable gardein,
who fhewing him al thofe things with his finger, fpake thefe

wordes: "Here" (quod he) "doe they reſt for euer, which in the
World haue lyued a Godly and iuſt Life, and haue bene Aduauncers
of Law and Iuſtice, and contempners of vice." And turning his
face to the other ſyde, he ſaw two ſwifte and broad Riuers, the one
of them boiled more blacke then Pitch. And in the ſayd Riuers
many were drowned, whereof ſome appeared aboue Water crying
with horrible voices, Mercy, Mercy. "And there" (quod he) "are
tormented all ſutch, which in the World moſt wyckedly haue committed Miſchiefe." And the chiefe of them he ſayed were Prynces,
Kinges, Emperours, and other great Men. With that Muſtapha
awaked and callyng the ſaied learned Man vnto him, vttered his
dreame. And pauſyng a lyttle whyle (for the ſuperſticious
Machometiſtes attribute mutch Credite to dotage of dreames)
being ful of ſorrow and penſifneſſe, at length anſwered That the
viſion was very dreadful, for that it pronoſticated extreame peril
of his life. Therefore he required him to haue diligent reſpect
thereunto. But Muſtapha beynge of great valiaunce and fortitude, hauing no regard to the aunſwer aforeſaid, couragiouſly
replied with theſe wordes: "Shall I ſuffer my ſelf to be vanquiſhed
with vaine and childiſh feare? Nay I wil rather take a good heart,
and make haſt to my Father. For I am aſſured that alwayes from
time to time I haue honored his maieſty accordyng to my duety,
in ſo mutch as neyther Fote trauelled, nor Eye looked, mutch leſſe
heart thought agaynſt his will to deſyre or couet to raigne,
except it had pleaſed the highe GOD to haue called hys Maieſty
from thys Lyfe to a better. And beſydes that my Mynde was neuer
bente after hys Death to beare rule, excepte Generall Election of all
the Army, to the intent I myghte entre the Imperiall Seate wythout
ſlaughter, Bloudſhed, or any other cruell fact, and thereby pre-
ſerue the friendſhip of my Brethren inuiolat, and free from any
ſpot of hatred. For I alwayes determyned, and choſe rather
(ſince my Father's pleaſure is ſo) to end my Life like an obedyent
Child, than continually to raigne, and be counted of al men,
obſtinate and diſobedient, eſpecially of mine enimies." When he
had ſpoken thoſe wordes, he made haſt to his father. And at his
arriual to the Campe, ſo ſone as he had pitched his Tent he apparelled himſelf al in white, and putting certain letters into his

bofome, which the Turkes vfe to do, when they go to any place (for in fuperfticions they vfe maruailous dotage) he proceded towards his father, entending wyth reuerence (as the manner is) to kiffe his hand. But when hee was come to the entry of the tent, he rememberd himfelf of his Dagger which he wore about him, and therefore vngirding himfelf he put it of for auoiding of al fufpicion. Which don, when he was entred the Tent, he was very curteoufly (with futch reuerence as behoued) welcomed of his father's Eunuches. And when he faw no man elfe, but the feat royal, where his father was wont to fitte readye furnifhed, with a forrowful heart ftode ftil, and at length demaunded where his Father was. Who anfwered that forthwith hee would come in prefence. In the meane feafon he faw feuen dombe men (which the Turke vfeth as Inftruments to kepe his fecrets, and priuily to do futch murthers as he commaundeth) and therewith immediately was wonderfully mafed faying: "Beholde my prefent Death." And therewith ftepped afide to auoide them, but it was in vaine, For being apprehended of the Eunuches and garde, was by force drawen to the place appointed for him to loofe hys Lyfe, and fodainly the domb Men faftened a Bowftryng about his Necke. But Muftapha, fome what ftriuing, requyred to fpeak but two Wordes with his Father. Which when the wicked parricide his Father hearde, beholding the Cruell Spectacle on the other fide of the Tente, rebuked the dombe Men, faying: "Wil you neuer execute my Commaundement, and doe as I bid you? Wyll you not kyll the Traitor, which thefe ten years fpace would not fuffer me to flepe one quyet Night?" Who when they harde him fpeake thofe cruell Woordes, the Eunuches and dombe Men threw him proftrate vpon the ground, and cording the ftring with a double knot moft pitifully ftrangled him. Which wycked and cruell facte being done, the Bafcha that was Lieuetenaunt of Amafia was alfo apprehended by the Kynge's Commaundement, and likewyfe beheaded in hys owne Prefence. This Facte also commytted, he caufed to be called before hym Gianger the Crokebacke, who was Ignoraunte of that was done, and Ieftynge wyth hym as though hee had done a thynge worthie commendation, bad him to go and meete his Brother Muftapha: who with a ioyful cheere made haft to meete him.

But when he came to the place and faw his infortunate Brother ly ftrangled and dead vpon the earth, it is impoffible to tell with what forrow he was affected. And he was fcafce come to the place, but his wicked Father fent Meffengers after him, to tell him that the Kyng had giuen him all Muftapha, his Treafures, Horfemen, Bondmen, Pauilions, Apparell: Yea, and moreouer the Prouince of Amafia. But Giangir conceyuing extreme forrow for the cruell murder of his deere brother, with lamentable teares fpake thefe words. "Oh cruell and wicked Dogge: yea, and if I may fo call my father, Oh Traytor moft peftilent, do thou enioy Muftapha, his Treafures, his Horfes, Furnitures, and the fayd Countrey to. Is thy heart fo vnnaturall, cruell, and wicked, to kill a yongue man fo notable as Muftapha was, fo good a Warriour, and fo worthy a Gentleman as the Ottoman houfe neuer had or fhall haue the like, without any refpect of Humanity or Zeale naturall ? By Saynct Mary I neede to take heede leaft hereafter in like maner thou as impudently do triumph of my death, being but a crokebacke and deformed man." When hee had fpoken theefe wordes, plucking out his Dagger, he flew himfelfe. Whereof when the Emperor had aduertifement, he conceyued infpeakable forrow. But for al that, his forrowfull heart vanquifhed not his couetoufe minde. For he commaunded all Muftaphe's Treafure, and other Furnitures to bee brought into his Tent. And the Souldiours thincking the fame fhould be gieuen amongs them made as mutch hafte to difpatche his commaundement. In the meane tyme Muftaphe's Souldiours (not knowing what was become of their Mayfter) feeing futch a number runne in heapes without order came forth of their Camp to withftande their foolifhe tumult, who very manfully, not without mutch flaughter withftoode the fame. And when the Fame of that Tragicall tumult was bruted amongs the King's souldiers, (who perceyuing the fame more and more to waxe hot,) they went forth to fuccour their fellowes, but the Onfet being gieuen on all fides, the fight on both parts was fo fierce, as in fhort fpace there were flayne very neere the number of two thoufande men befides the hurt and wounded, whereof the number was greater. Howbeit this Broyle had not bene thus ended, had not Achmat Bafcha, a graue and wife man, and for his experimentes in the Warres of great aucthority amongs the

ſouldiers driuen them back, and repreſſed their fury.   Who turning himſelf towards Muſtaphe's ſouldiers with ſmiling countenaunce and milde words appeaſing their furious ſtomacks ſpake
theſe wordes : " Why my deere brethren and freends wil yee now
degenerate from your olde accuſtomed wiſedome, ſufficiently tried
in you theſe many yeares paſt, and will now reſiſt the commaundment of the great Soltan the lord and ſoueraigne of vs all ? I cannot
chuſe (as God ſhal help me) but meruayle what ſhould mooue you
whom hitherto I haue proued to be ſo notable and valiant men,
and in this ciuile conflict, you ſhould bende your force vpon your
own frends, and raiſe vp ſutch a ſpectacle to the Ottoman enemy,
againſt whom heretofore you haue very proſperouſly and manfully
fought, and therewith by mutuall ſlaughter to make them reioyſe
whom heretofore with the like, you haue made heauy and penſiue.   Therefore my fellowes as you tender your own valiaunce
and Magnanimity, take heede, that by your own folly you do not
leſe the eſtimation of your wonted fortitude and wiſedome,
wherein hitherto you haue excelled all men.   And reſerue your
force, which you now more than inough haue vſed amongs your
owne Fellowes till you come againſt your Enemies, where you ſhall
haue a more laudable, and better occaſion to vſe it."   With
theſe woordes and the like ſpoken by Achamat Baſca, the Souldiours were ſomewhat appeaſed, and all thinges were franckely
ſuffered to bee carried out of Muſtapha hys Pavylion to the Kynge's.
But when the death of Muſtapha came to the knowledge of
the Ianiſchari, and the reſt of the Army, forthwith began another
ſedition.   And after the Trumpets had blowen the onſet, there
was ſutch a Tumult and ſtyrre amongs the Souldiours, mixte wyth
ſundry Lamentations, and Teares, that like Madmen with great
violence, they ran into the Courte, with theyr Swords naked in
theyr hands ready bent to ſtrike.   And this renued and ſudden
ſtyrre ſo terrified the Knyg, that hee wiſte not what to do who for
all the dampes would needes haue fled.   But being perſuaded of
his Counſelloures to tarry, hauing throughe Neceſſity, gotten
occaſion to attempt that whych in the tyme of hys moſt ſecurity
he durſt ſcarce haue enterpryſed, went forth, and with ſterne
Countenaunce, ſpake to hys Souldyers in this manner.   " What
rumors, what tumultes, and what mad partes are theſe, wherewith

ſo proudely in this ſort ye diſquiet me? What meane theſe
enflamed countenances? What ſignify theſe haulty geſtures,
theſe proude and angry lokes? Doe you not remembre that I am
your King that hath Power and Authority to gouerne and rule
you? Are you determyned in this ſort to ſpot your Auncyent and
inuincible valiaunce, and the notable Warrefare of your predeces-
ſours, with the bloud of your Emperour?" And while the King
was ſpeaking theſe Words, the ſouldiers boldly anſwered, how
they confeſſed him to be the ſame, whome many yeares ago they
choſe to be their Kinge, and for that hee alleaged how they
had with their good ſeruice in the Warres acquired vnto him many
great conqueſts and had diligently kepte the ſame: all that they
did of purpoſe that he ſhould vſe towards them againe a godly
Authority and iuſt Gouernment, and not vnaduiſedly ſhould lay
his bloudy handes vppon euery iuſte Man, and ſo to ſtaine and
defile himſelfe with the Bloud of Innocents. And againe, where
he laide to their charge, that they were iſſued from their Cabanes
armed with Weapon, they affirmed the ſame to be done in a iuſt
quarell, euen to reuenge the ſlaughter of innocent Muſtapha, and
for that they ought not to haue ſutch a Kynge as ſhould worke
his anger vppon them that had not deſerued it. Further they
required that they might cleare themſelues openly of the offence
of Treaſon, whereof falſly they were accuſed by Muſtapha, his
Enimies, and to haue their accuſer to be brought forth in open preſence. And ſayde more that before he perſonally did appeare
before the Iudgement Seat Face to Face to giue euidence, *ſub
talionis pœna*, accordinge to the Law, they would not vnarme nor
yet diſaſemble themſelues. [And whiles theſe things were debated
betwene the emperor and the ſouldiers, the cruelty of the fact, ſo
moued] all men to teares, that the Kyng him ſelfe ſeemed to take
great repentaunce for his horrible deede, and promyſed the Souldiours that they ſhould haue their requeſts, and went about with
fayre perſwaſions to mittigate (as mutch as lay in him) their furious ſtomakes. Howbeit the Souldiours gaue diligent heede to
their watch and warde euery man in his place appoynted, that the
king might not ſecretly conuey himſelfe away, and ſo deceyue
theym of his promiſſes, and the expectation of their requeſts. In

the meane time the Kyng depriued Ruftanus of all his offices, and
promotions, and tooke away from him the priuy Signet whereof
he had the keeping, and deliuered it to Achmat Bafcha. Ruftanus
amafed with the terror and feare of the Souldiours, thinking himfelfe fcarce in good fecurity amongs his owne men, fecretly conueyed himfelfe to Achmat Bafcha his Pauilyon, and afked counfell of him what was beft to be done in fo doubtfull, and daungerous a cafe. Who aduifed him therein to haue the kyng's aduice,
and as he commaunded him fo in any wyfe to doe. Which counfayle marueyloufly fatiffied the mynde of Ruftanus. And without any longer delay by certaine Meffengers which were his faythfull, and familier Freends required the King's aduife. Whereunto
the King aunfwered that forthwith without longer tariaunce he
fhould auoyde his fyght, and abfent himfelfe from his Campe.
Who replied that without Money and other furnitures, he could
not conueniently execute hys commaundement. But the King
had hym to do what hee lift, for he woulde in no wife gieue hym
leaue to haue any longer time or fpace to deliberate the matter.
At length Ruftanus without further ftay, as guilty of his curfed
deuifes, accompanied with eyght of his truftieft Frends directed
his Iorney to Conftantinople, and vfing mutch expedition (as
feare in fearefull matters putteth fpurres to the horfe) came to
Conftantinople: and there with Rofa and other the Confpiratours
expected the euents of Fortune not without daunger of their
liues. Moreouer it was fayd that Solyman, whofe Confcience
bewrayed the beaftlynes of his abhominable facte, being pricked
with a fuperfticious repentance, determined to trauel on pilgrimage to Mecha, and proceding in his voiage, he was driuen by
meanes of the Perfians force to go to Hierufalem there to offer
facrifice for the death of his Sonne, which they call Corba. But
now to conclude, and fomewhat to fpeake of Muftapha or rather
by way of admonition this one thing to fay of him, that the fayde
Muftapha was fo acceptable and well beloued of all men for his
warlike experience, and for his redineffe to fheade Chriftian bloud,
that they fuppofed the like would neuer be in the Ottoman houfe
more towards to enlarge, and amplyfie their Empyre, or promyfed
greatter thinges for the perfourmance thereof. In fo mutch as

then they difpayred fo of their Enterprifes, as this Prouerbe rofe
vp amongs them, Gietti Soltan Muftapha, which fignifieth an
vtter difpayre in thinges which they thought before to goe about.
Therefore we haue good caufe to reioyce for the death of thys
cruell enimy that fhould haue raygned, and to thinck the flaughter
of him not to be done without God's fpeciall prouidence, who in
this forte hath prouided for vs. And at length to be wife, and
abftayne from ciuile Warre and diffencions. And with common
Force to fet vppon this wicked Tarmegant, confidering that he is
not only a generall Ennimy to our Countrey and Lyfe, but alfo to
our Soules. Which thing if we do, it will not be fo hard a matter
to withftand the force of this enemy of Chriftendome, as if we doe
not, it wyll be daungerous through our continuall difcorde to gieue
him occafion to inuade the reft of Europe, and fo with his
tiranny bring the fame to vtter deftruction, which God
that is omnipotent forbid, who bring vs to vnity
through his Sonne Iefus Chrifte,
Amen.

THE THIRTY-FIFTH NOUELL.

*The great curtefie of the Kyng of Marocco, (a Citty in Barbarie)
toward a poore Fiſherman, one of his Subieƈts, that had lodged
the Kyng, being ſtrayed from his Company in hunting.*

For ſomutch as the more than beaſtly cruelty recounted in the
former Hyſtory, doth yelde ſome ſowre taſte to the minds of thoſe
that be curteous, gentle and well conditioned by nature, and as
the Stomacke of him that dayly vſeth one kinde of meate, be it
neuer ſo delycate and daynty, doth at length lothe, and diſdayne
the ſame, and vtterly refuſeth it: I now chaunge the Diet, leauing murders, ſlaughters, deſpayres, and tragicall accidents, and
turne my ſtile to a more pleaſaunt thing, that may ſo well ſerue
for inſtruƈtion of the noble to follow vertue, as that which I haue
already written, may riſe to their profit, warely to take heede they
fal not into ſutch deformed and filthy faults, as the name and
prayſe of man be defaced, and his reputation decayed: if then the
contraries be knowne by that which is of diuers natures, the
villany of great cruelty ſhalbe conuerted into the gentleneſſe of
milde curteſie, and rigor ſhalbe condempned, when with ſweete-
neſſe and generoſity, the noble ſhall aſſaye to wyn the heart,
ſeruice, and affeƈted deuotion of the baſeſt ſorte: So the greatneſſe and nobility of man placed in dignity, and who hath puiſ-
ſaunce ouer other, confiſteth not to ſhew himſelfe hard, and
terrible, for that is the manner of Tyraunts, bicauſe he that is
feared, is conſequently hated, euyll beloued, and in the ende forſaken, of the whole World, which hath bene the cauſe that in
times paſt Prynces aſpiring to great Conqueſts, haue made their
way more eaſie by gentleneſſe and Curteſie, than by fury of armes,
ſtabliſhing the foundations of their dominions more firme and
durable by thoſe meanes, than they which by rigor and cruelty
haue ſacked townes, ouerthrowne Cities, depopulated Prouinces,
and fatted Landes with the bodies of thoſe, whoſe liues they haue
depriued by dent of ſword, ſith the gouernement and authority
ouer other, caryeth greater ſubieƈtion, than puiſſance.   Where-

fore Antigonus, one of the fucceffors of great Alexander (that
made all the Earth to trembe vppon the recitall of hys name) fee-
ng that hys Sonne behaued himfelfe arrogantly, and wythout
modefty to one of hys Subiects, reproued and checked hym, and
amongs many wordes of chaftifement and admonition, fayd vnto
him : "Knoweft thou not my Sonne, that the eftate of a Kyng is
a noble and honourable feruitude?" Royall wordes (in deede)
and meete for a Kyng : For albeit that eche man doth reuerence to
a Kyng, and that he be honoured, and obeyed of all, yet is hee for
all that, the Seruaunt, and publike Mynifter, who ought no leffe
to defend hys Subiect, than the Subiect to do him honour and
Homage. And the more the Prynce doth humble himfelfe, the
greater increafe hath his glory, and the more wonderfull he is
to euery Wyght. What aduaunced the Glory of Iulius Cæfar, who
firft depreffed the Senatorie State of gouernment at Rome? Where
his Victoryes atchieued ouer the Galles and Britons, and afterwardes ouer Rome it felfe, when he had vanquifhed Pompee? All
thofe ferued his tourne, but his greateft fame rofe of his Clemency
and Curtefie : By the whych Vertues hee fhewed himfelfe to be
gentle, and fauorable euen to thofe, whom hee knewe not to
loue him, otherwife than if hee had beene their mortall Enimy.
His Succeffors as Auguftus, Vefpafianus, Titus, Marcus Aurelius,
and Flauius were worthily noted for clemency : Notwithftanding I fee not one drawe neere to the great Courage, and Gentleneffe, ioyned wyth the finguler Curtefie of Dom Roderigo
Viuario the Spanyarde Surnamed Cid, towarde Kyng Pietro of
Aragon that hindred his expedityon agaynft the Mores at Gren-
adoe. For hauing vanquyfhed the fayde King, and taken hym
in Battell, not onely remitted the reuenge of his wrong, but alfo
fuffered hym to go wythout raunfome, and tooke not from him
fo mutch as one Forte, efteemyng it to bee a better exploite to
winne futch a King with curtefie, than beare the name of cruell in
putting him to Death, or feafing vpon his land. But bicaufe acknowledging of the poore, and enriching the fmal, is commendable in a Prynce, than when he fheweth himfelfe gentle to his lyke,
I haue collected this difcourfe and facte of Kynge Manfor of
Marocco, whofe Chyldren (by fubtile and fained religion) Cherif

fucceded, the Sonne of whom at this day inioyeth the kingdomes
of Su, Marocco, and the moſt part of the iſles confinynge vpon
Æthiopia. This hiſtory was told by an Italian called Nicholoſo
Baciadonne, who vppon this accydent was in Affrica, and in
trafike of Marchandyſe in the Land of Oran, ſituated vppon the
coaſt of the South ſeas, and where the Geneuois and Spanyards
vſe great entercourſe, bicauſe the countrey is faire, wel peopled,
and wher the inhabitants (although the ſoyle be barbarous) lyue
indifferent ciuilly, vſing great curteſie to Straungers, and largely
departing their goodes to the poore, towards whom they be ſo
earneſtly bente, and louing, as for theyr Lyberality and pytiful
almeſſe, they ſhame vs Chriſtians. They meinteine a greſt numbre
of Hoſpitalles, to receiue and intertaine the poore and neady,
wherein they ſhew themſelues more deuout than they that be
bounde by the law of Ieſus Chriſte, to vſe Charity towardes theyr
brethren, with more curteſie and greater myldneſſe. Theſe Ora-
niens delight alſo to record in wryting the ſucceſſe of thinges that
chaunce in their time and carefully referue the ſame in Memorie,
whych was the cauſe that bauyng regiſtred in theyr Chronicles,
(wrytten in Arabie letters, as the moſt part of thoſe Countreyes do
vſe) this preſent hiſtory, they imparted the ſame to the Geneuois
marchants of whom the Italian author confeſſeth to haue receyued
the copie. The cauſe why the Geneuois marchant was ſo diligent
to make the enquirie, was by reaſon of a City of that prouince,
builte through the chaunce of thys Hiſtorye, and which was called
in theyr Tongue, Cæſar Elcabir, ſo mutch to ſay as, A great Pallace. And bycauſe I am aſſured, that curteous Myndes will
delyght in deedes of Curteſie, I haue amonges other the Nouelles
of Bandello, choſen by Francois de Belleforeſt and my ſelf, dis-
courſed thys, albeit the matter be not of great importance. For
greater thynges and more notorious curteſies haue bene done by
our own Kinges and Prynces. As that of Henry the eight a Prynce
of notable memorye in hys Progreſſe into the North the xxxiii.
yeare of his raigne, when he dyſdayned not a pore Miller's houſe
being ſtragled from his trayne, buſily purſuing the Hart, and ther
vnknowne of the Miller, was welcomed with homely cheare, as
hys mealy houſe was able for the time to miniſter, and afterwardes

for acknowledging his willing Mynde, recompenced him wyth
daynties of the Courte, and a Pryncely rewarde. Of Edwarde the
thyrde, whofe Royall Nature was not difpleafed pleafauntly to vfe
a Waifaring Tanner, when deuyded from his Company, he mette
hym by the way not far from Tomworth in Staffordfhire, and by
cheapening of his welfare fteede (for ftedineffe fure and able to
carry him fo farre as the ftable dore) grewe to a price, and for
exchaunge the Tanner craued fiue fhillings to boote betwene the
Kings and his. And when the King fatiffied with difport, defired
to fhew himfelf by founding his warning blafte, affembled all hys
Traine, and to the great amaze of the poore Tanner, (when he was
guarded with that Troupe) he well guerdoned his good Paftime
and familiar dealing, with the order of Knighthoode and reafonable reuenue for the maintenaunce of the fame. The lyke
Examples our Chronicles, memory, and reporte plentifully doe
auouche and witneffe. But what? this Hyftory is the more rare
and worthy of notyng, for refpect of the People and Countrey,
where feldome or neuer Curtefie haunteth or findeth harborough,
and where Nature doth bryng forth greater ftore of monfters, than
thinges worthy of praife. This great King Manfor then was not
onely the Temporall Lord of the Countrey of Oran and Marocco,
but alfo (as is faide of Prete Iean,) Byfhop of his Law and the
Mahomet Prieft, as he is at thys Day that raighneth in Feze, Sus,
and Marocco. Now thys Prynce aboue all other pleafure, loued
the game of Hunting. And he fo mutch delighted in that paffetime, as fometime he would caufe his Tentes in the myd of the
defertes to be erected, to lye there all Nyght, to the end, that the
next day he might renew his game, and defraud his men of idle-
neffe, and the Wild beafts of reft. And this manner of Life he
vfed ftill, after he had done Iuftice and hearkened the complaintes
for which his Subiectes came to difclofe thereby theyr griefes.
Wherein alfo he toke fo great pleafure, as fome of our magiftrates
do feeke their profite, whereof they be fo fqueymifhe, as they
be defirous to fatiffy the place whereunto they be called, and
render all men their righte due vnto them. For wyth theyr
Bribery and Sacred Golden Hunger, Kings and Prynces in thefe
dayes be ill ferued, the people wronged, and the wycked out of

feare. There is none offence almoſt how villanous ſo euer it be, but is waſhed in the Water of Bribery, and clenſed in the holly drop, wherewith the Poets faine Iupiter to corrupt the daughter of Acrifius faſt cloſed within the braſen Toure. And who is able to refiſt that, which hath ſubdued the higheſt powers? Now re-turne we from our wanderings: This greate Kynge Manſor on a day aſſembled his People to hunt in the mariſh and fenny Countrey, that in elder age was not farre of from the City of Alela, which the Portugalles bolde at this preſent, to make the way more free into the Iſles of Molucca, of the moſt part wherof their King is Lord. As he was attentife in folowing a Beare, and his paſtime at the beſt, the Elements began to darke and a great tempeſt roſe, ſuch as with the ſtorme and violent Winde, ſcattered the trayne far of from the King, who not knowing what way to take, nor into what place he might retire, to auoid the tempeſt, the greateſt that he felt in al his life, would with a good wil haue ben accom-panied as the Troiane Æneas was, when being in like paſtime and fear he was conſtrayned to enter into a Caue wyth his Queene Dido, where he perfourmed the Ioyes of hys vnhappy Maryage. But Manſor beeynge without Companye, and wythout any Caue at Hande, wandered alonges the Champayne ſo carefull of hys Lyfe for feare of Wylde Beaſtes, whych flocke together in thoſe deſertes as the Courtiers were penſiue, for that they knew not whether theyr Prynce was gone. And that which chiefly grieued Manſor was hys being alone without guide: And for all he was well mounted, he durſt paſſe no further for fear of drownyng, and to be deſtroyed amiddes thoſe Marſhes, whereof all the Countrey was very ful. On the one ſide he was fryghted with Thunderclaps, which rumbled in the ayre very thicke and terryble: On the other ſide the lightning continually flaſhed on his face, the roring of the Beaſtes apalled him, the ignoraunce of the way ſo aſtonned him, as he was affraide to fall into the running Brokes, which the outragious raignes had cauſed to ſwell and ryſe. It is not to be doubted, that oriſons and prayers vnto hys greate prophet Mahomet were forgotten, and doubtfull it is whether he were more deuout when he went on Pilgrimage to the Idolatrous Temple of Moſqua. Hee complayned of ill lucke, accuſing Fortune, but chiefly hys owne folly, for giuing himfelfe fo mutch to hunting, for the defire whereof, hee was thus ftraggled into vnknowen Countreyes. Sometimes he raued and vomytted his Gall agaynft his Gentlemen and houfhold feruaunts, and threatned death vnto his guarde. But afterwards, when reafon ouerfhadowed his fenfe, he faw that the tyme, and not their neglygence or little care caufed that difgrace. He thoughte that his Prophet had poured downe that tempeft for fome Notable finne, and had brought him into fuch and fo dangerous extremity for his faults. For which caufe he lifted vp his Eyes, and made a thoufand Mahomet mowes, and Apifh mocks (according to theyr manner.) And as he fixed his eyes aloft vp to the heauens, a flafh of lightning glaunced on his Face fo violently, as it made him to holde downe his head, lyke a lyttle Chyld reproued of his maifter. But he was further daunted and amazed, when he faw the night approche, which with the darkenes of his cloudy Mantell, ftayed hys pace from going any further, and brought him into fuch perplexitye, as willingly he would haue forfaken both his hunting and company of his Seruants to be quit of that Daunger. But God carefull of good Myndes (with what law fo euer they be trayned vp,) and who maketh the Sunne to fhine vpon the iuft and and vniufte, prepared a meanes for his fauegarde, as you fhal heare. The Affricane King beyng in his traunce, and naked of all hope, necefſity (which is the cleareft loking glaffe that may be found,) made him diligently to loke about, whether he could fee any perfone by whome he might attayne fome fecuritie. And as he thus bent himfelfe to difcry all the partes of the Countrey, he faw not far of from him, the glimpfe of a light which glimmered out at a little Window, whereunto he addreffed himfelfe, and perceiued that it was a fimple Cabane fituate in the middeft of the Fennes, to which he approached for his fuccor and defenfe in the time of that tempeft. He reioyfed as you may think, and whither his heart lept for ioy, I leaue for them to iudge which haue affayed like daungers, how be it I dare beleue, that the faylers on the feas feele no greater ioy when they arriue to harborough, than the king of Marocco dyd: or when after a Tempeft, or other peril, they difcrye vppon the prowe of their fhyppe, the bryghtneffe of

fome clyffe, or other land. And thys king hauing felt the tempeſt
of Wind, raine, haile, lyghtenyng, and Thunder claps, compaſſed
round aboute with Marſhes and violent ſtreames of little Riuers
that ran along his way, thought he had found Paradiſe by chaunc-
ing vpon that ruſticall lodge. Now that Cotage was the refuge
place of a pore Fiſher man, who lived and ſuſteined his Wife and
children with Eeles which he toke alongs the ditches of thoſe deepe
and huge Marſhes. Manſor when he was arrived at the dore of
that great pallace couered and thacked with Reede, called to them
wythin, who at the firſt would make no anſwer to the Prynce that
taried there comming at the Gate. Then he knocked againe, and
with louder voyce than before, which cauſed this fiſher man,
thinkynge that he had bene ſome rippier (to whom he was wont
to ſell hys ware, or elſe ſome ſtraunger ſtrayed out of his way,)
ſpedily went out, and ſeeinge the Kinge well mounted and richlye
clothed, and albeit he tooke him not to be his foueraigne LORD, yet
he thought he was ſome one of his Courtly Gentlemen. Wherefore hee ſayde: "What Fortune hath dryuen you (ſir) into theſe ſo
deſerte and ſolytarye Places, and ſutch as I maruell that you
were not drowned a hundred tymes, in theſe ſtreames, and bogges
whereof this Marriſh and fenny Countrey are full?" "It is the great
God" (aunſwered Manſor) "which hath had ſome care of me, and
will not ſuffer me to peryſh without doynge greater good turnes
and better deedes than hitherto I haue don." The King's comming thither, ſeemed to Prognoſticate that whych after chaunced,
and that God poured downe the Tempeſt for the Wealth of the
Fiſher man, and commodity of the Country. And the ſtraying of
the Kyng was a thyng appoynted to make voyde thoſe Marſhes,
and to purge and clenſe the Countrey: Semblable chaunces haue
happened to other Prynces, as to Conſtantine the great, beſides
his City called New Rome, when he cauſed certayne Marſhes and
Ditches to be filled vp and dryed, to build a fayre and ſumptuous
Temple, in the Honor and Memory of the bleſſed Virgin that
brought forth the Sauior of the World. "But tel me good man"
(replyed Manſor) canſt thou not ſhew me the way to the Court,
and whether the King is gone, for gladly (if it were poſſible) would
I ride thither." "Verily" (ſayd the Fiſher Man) "it will be almoſt

day before ye can come there, the fame beinge ten leagues from hence. "Forfomutch as thou knoweft the way" (aunfwered Manfor) "doe me fo great pleafure to brynge me thither, and be affured that befides the good turne, for which I fhall be bound vnto thee, I will curteoufly content thee for thy paynes." "Sir" (fayd the poore man) "you feeme to be an honeft Gentleman, wherfore I pray you to lyght, and to tarry heere this Night, for that it is fo late, and the way to the City very euyll and comberfome for you to paffe." "No, no," (fayd the King) "if it be poffible, I muft repayre to the place whither the King is gone, wherefore doe fo mutch for me as to bee my guide, and thou fhalt fee whether I be vnthankfull to them that imploy their paynes for mee." "If Kyng Manfor" (fayd the Fifher man) "were heere hymfelfe in Perfon and made the lyke requeft, I would not be fo very a foole, nor fo prefumptuous, (at this time of the Nyght) to take vppon me without Daunger to bryng hym to his Palace." "Wherefore?" (fayed the Kyng) "Wherefore? (quod you), bicaufe the Marfhes bee fo daungerous, as in the Day tyme, if one know not wel the way, the Horfe, (be hee neuer fo ftronge and Lufty,) may chaunce to fticke faft, and tarry behynd for gage. And I would be forry if the King were heere, that he fhould fall into Peryl, or fuffer any anoyance and therewythall would deeme my felfe vnhappy if I did let hym to incur futch euyll or incombrance." Manfor that delighted in the communication of this good man, and defirous to know the caufe that moued him to fpeak with futch affection, faid vnto him: "And why careft thou for the Life, health, or preferuation of the Kynge? What haft thou to doe wyth him that wouldeft be fo forry for hys ftate, and carefull of his fafety." "Ho, ho," faid the good man, "doe you fay that I am carefull for my Prince? Verily I loue him a hundred tymes better than I do my felfe, my Wife or children whych God hath fent me: and what sir, do not you loue our Prince?" "Yes that I doe" (replyed the Kyng,) "for I haue better caufe than thou, for that I am many times in his company, and liue vpon his charge and am entertayned with his wages. But what nedeft thou to care for hym? Thou knoweft him not, hee neuer did thee anye good turne or pleafure: nor yet thou nedeft not hope henceforth to haue any pleafure at his hands."

"What?" (faid the Fifher man) "muft a Prince be loued for gaine
and good turnes, rather than for hys Iuftice and curtefie? I fee
wel that amongs you maifter Courtiers, the benefits of kings be
more regarded, and their gifts better liked than their vertue and
nobility, which maketh them wonderful vnto vs: and ye do more
efteme the gold, honor and eftates that they beftow vpon you,
than their health and fauegard, which are the more to be confidered, for that the King is our head, and GOD hath made him
futch one to kepe vs in Peace, and to be carefull of our ftates.
Pardon me if I fpeake fo boldly in your prefence." The kyng
(which toke fingular delight in this Countrey Philofopher,)
anfwered him: "I am not offended bicaufe thy words approche fo
neare the troth: but tel me what benefit haft thou receiued of
that king Manfor, of whome thou makeft futch accompt and
loueft fo wel? For I cannot thinke that euer he dyd thee good,
or fhewed thee pleafure, by reafon of thy pouerty, and the little
Furnyture within thy houfe in refpect of that which they poffeffe
whome hee loueth and fauoreth, and vnto whome he fheweth fo
great familyaritye and Benefite." "Doe tell me fir" (replyed the
good man) "for fo mutch as you fo greatly regard the fauoures
which Subiects receiue at theyr Prynces handes, as in deede they
ought to doe, What greater goodneffe, richeffe, or Benefite ought I
to hope for, or can receyue of my King (being futch one as I am,)
but the profite and vtility that all we whych be his vaffalles do
apprehend from day to day in the Iuftyce that he rendereth to
euery Wyghte, by not fuffering the puiffant and Rich to fuppreffe
and ouertread the feeble and weake, and him that is deuoid of
Fortune's goods, that indifferency be maintayned by the Officers, to
whom he committeth the gouernement of his Prouinces, and the
care which he hath that his people be not deuoured by exactions,
and intollerable tributes. I do efteeme more his goodneffe, clemency
and Loue, that he beareth to his fubiects, than I doe all your
delycates and eafe in following the Court. I moft humbly honor
and reuerence my king in that he being farre from vs, doeth
neuertheleffe fo vfe his gouernment as we feele his prefence like
the Image of God, for the peace and vnion wherein we through
him do lyue and enioy, without difturbaunce, that lytle whych

God and Fortune haue gyuen vs. Who (if not the king) is he that doeth preferue vs, and defend vs from the incurfions and pillages of thofe Theues and Pirates of Arabie, which inuade and make warre with their neighbours? and there is no friend they haue but they would difpleafe if the King wyfely did not forbyd and preuent their villanies. That great Lord which kepeth his Court at Conftantinople and maketh himfelf to be adored of his people like a God, brideleth not fo mutch the Arabians, as our king doth, vnder the Protection and fauegard of whome, I that am a poore Fifher man, do ioy my pouerty in peace, and without fear of theeues do norifh my litle family, applying my felfe to the fifhing of Eeles that be in thefe ditches and fenny places, which I carry to the market townes, and fell for the fuftenance and feeding of my wife and children, and efteeme my felf right happy, that returning to my cabane, and homely lodge at my pleafure, in whatfoeuer place I do abide, bicaufe (albeit far of from Neigh-boures,) by the benefite and dilygence of my Prince, none ftaye my iourney, or offendeth me by any meanes, whych is the caufe (fayd he lifting vp his hands and eyes aloft,) that I pray vnto God and his great Prophet Mahomet, that it may pleafe them to preferue our King in health, and to gyue him fo great happe and contentation, as he is vertuous and debonaire, and that ouer hys Ennimies (flying before him,) he may euermore be victorious, for noryfhing his people in peace, and his children in ioy and Nobility." The King feeing that deuout affectyon of the paifaunte, and knowyng it to be without guile or Hypocrifie, would gladly haue difcouered himfelf, but yet willyng to referue the fame for better opportunity, he fayd vnto him : "Forfomutch as thou loueft the king fo well, it is not impoffible but thofe of his houfe be wel-come vnto thee, and that for thy Manfor's fake, thou wilt helpe and do feruice to his Gentlemen." "Let it fuffife you" (replyed he) "that my heart is more inclined to the King, than to the willes of thofe that ferue him for hope of preferment. Now being fo affectionate to the king as I am, thynke whyther hys houfe-holde Seruauntes haue power to commaund me, and whither my willing mynde be preft to doe them good or not. But mee thynke ye neede not to ftay heere at the gate in talke, being fo wet as you be: Wherefore vouchfafe to come into my houfe, which is youre owne, to take futch fimple lodging as I haue, where I wyl entreat you, (not according to your merite) but with the little that God and his Prophet haue departed to my pouerty: And to morrow morning I will conduct you to the City, euen to the royall Palace of my Prynce." "Truly" (anfwered the King) "albeit neceffity did not prouoke me, yet thine honefty deferueth well other reputation than a fimple Countrey man, and I do thinke that I haue profited more in hearing thee fpeake than by hearken-yng to the flattering and babbling tales of Courting triflers, which dayly employ themfelues to corrupte the eares of Prynces." "What fir?" (fayd the Payfant) "thynke you that thys poore Coate and fimple lodging be not able to apprehend the Preceptes of Vertue? I haue fometimes heard tell, that the wife auoyding Cityes and Troupes of Men, haue wythdrawne themfelues into the defertes, for leyfure to contemplate heauenly thynges." "Your fkyll is greate," replyed Manfor: "Goe we then, fith you pleafe to doe me that Curtefie as this night to be myne hofte." So the king went into the Ruftical Lodge, where infteede of Tapiftery and Tur-key hangings, he fawe the houfe ftately hanged with fifher Nets and Cordes, and in place of rich feeling of Noble mens houfes, he be-held Canes and Reedes whych ferued both for the feeling and couering. The Fifher man's Wife continued in the kitchen, whileft Manfor hymfelf both walked and dreffed his owne horfe, to which horfe the Fifher man durfte not once come neare for his Corage and ftately trappour, wyth one thing he was abundantly refrefhed, and that the mofte needefull thing which was fire, whereof there was no fpare, no more then there was of Fifhe. But the king which had been dayntely fed, and did not well tafte and lyke that kynde of meat, demaunded if hys hunger could not be fupplyed with a lytle Flefh, for that his ftomacke was anoyed with the onely fauoure of the Eeles. The poore man, (as ye haue fomewhat per-ceiued by the former difcourfe) was a pleafaunt fellow, and delighted rather to prouoke laughter than to prepare more dainty meat, faid vnto the king: "It is no maruell, though our kinges do furnifhe themfelues with Countrey men, to ferue them in their Warres, for the delicate bringing vp and litle force in fine Courtiers. Wee, albeit the Raine doth fal vppon our heads, and the Winde affaile euery part of our bodies all durtie and Wet, doe not care either for fire or Bed, wee feede vpon any kinde of meate that is fet before vs, withoute feeking Sauce for increafing of our appetite: and we (beholde) are nimble, healthy, lufty, and neuer ficke, nor our mouth out of taft, where ye do feele futch diftemperaunce of ftomacke, as pity it is to fee, and more ado there is to bring the fame into his right order and tafte, than to ordeine and dreffe a fupper for a whole armie." The king who laughed (with difplayed throte,) hearing his hofte fo merily difpofed, could haue been contented to haue heard him ftill had not his appetite prouoked him, and the time of the Night very late. Wherefore he faid vnto him: "I do agree to what you alleage, but performe I pray thee my requeft, and then wee will fatiffie our felues with further talke." "Well fir" (replyed the king's Hofte,) "I fee well that a hungry Belly hath no lufte to heare a merry fong, whereof were you not fo egre and fharpe fet, I could fing a hundred. But I haue a lytle Kidde which as yet is not weaned, the fame wil I caufe to bee made ready, for I think it cannot be better beftowed." The fupper by reafon of the hofte's curtefie, was paffed forth in a thoufand pleafant paffetimes, whych the Fifherman of purpofe vttered to recreate hys Gueft, bicaufe he fawe hym to delight in thofe deuyfes. And vppon the end of Supper, he fayd vnto the King: "Now fir, how like you this banket? It is not fo fumptuous as thofe that be ordinarily made at our Prynce's Court, yet I thynke that you fhal flepe wyth no leffe appetyte than you haue eaten with a god ftomack, as appeareth by the few Woords you have vttered in the tyme of your repaft. But whereunto booteh it to employ tyme, ordeyned for eating, in expenfe of talke, whych ferueth not but to paffe the tyme, and to fhorten, the day? And meats ought rather to be taken for fuftentation of Nature then for prouocation or motion of thys feeble and Tranfitorye Flefhe?" "Verily" (fayd the King) "your reafon is good, and I doe meane to ryfe from the Table, to paffe the remnant of the Nyght in reft, therewyth to fatiffie my felfe fo well as I haue wyth eatyng, and do thanke you heartily for your good aduertyfement." So the King went to Bed, and it was not long ere hee fell a

sleepe, and contynued tyll the Mornynge. And when the Sunne
dyd ryfe, the Fifherman came to wake hym, tellyng hym that it
was tyme to rife, and that hee was ready to bryng him to the
Court. All this whyle the Gentlemen of the kinge's Traine were
fearching round aboute the Countrey to fynde his Maiefty, makyng
Cryes and Hues, that he myghte heare them. The kyng knowyng
their voices, and the noyes they made, went forth to meete them,
and if his People were gladde when they founde him, the Fifherman was no leffe amazed to fee the honor the Courtyers did vnto
his Gueft. Which the curteous king perceiuing, fayd vnto
him : "My Friend, thou feeft here, that Manfor, of whome yefternight thou madeft fo great accompt, and whome thou faidft, that
thou didft loue fo well. Bee affured, that for the Curtifie thou
haft done him, before it bee longe, the fame fhall be fo well
acquyted, as for euer thou fhalte haue good caufe to remembre it."
The good man was already vpon his marybones befeeching the
King that it would pleafe bim pardon hys rude entertainement
and his ouermutch familiarity whych hee had vfed vnto him. But
Manfor caufing bim to rife vp, willed hym to depart, and fayed
that within few dayes after he fhoulde beare further Newes. Now
in thefe Fennifh and marryfh groundes, the Kyng had already
builded diuers Caftles and lodges for the pleafure and folace of
hunting. Wherefore he purpofed there to erect a goodly City,
caufing the waters to be voyded with greate expedition, whych
City he builded immediately, and compaffyng the circuite of the
appoynted place, with ftrong Walles and depe Ditches, he gaue
many immunities and Pryuiledges to thofe, that would repayre to
people the fame, by meanes whereof, in litle tyme, was reduced to
the ftate of a beautifull and wealthy City, whych is the very fame
that before we fayd to be Cæfar Elcabir, as mutch to fay : "The
great Palace." This goodly worke beinge thus performed Manfor
fent for his hoft, to whome hee fayde: "To the end from henceforth
thou mayeft more honourably entertaine Kyngs into thy Houfe,
and mayeft intreate them wyth greater fumptuofitie, for the better
folacyng of them wyth thy curtefy and pleafaunt talke, beholde
the City that I haue buylded, which I doe gyue vnto thee and thyne
for euer, referuing nothyng but an acknowledgement of good wil,

to the end thou mayſt know that a Gentleman's mind nouſled in
villany, is diſcouered, when forgetting a good turne, he incurreth
the vice of Ingratitude." The good man ſeeing ſo liberall an offer
and preſent worthy of ſutch a king fell downe vppon his knees,
and kyſſing his foote with al humility, ſayd vnto him : " Sir if
your Liberality did not ſupply the imperfection of my Meryte, and
perfourmed not what wanted in me, to attayne ſo great eſtate, I
would excuſe my ſelfe of the charge whych it pleaſeth you to
gyue mee, and whereunto for lacke of trayning vp, and vſe of
ſutch a Dignity, I am altogether vnfit. But ſith that the graces
of GOD, and the gyftes of Kynges ought neuer to bee reiected, by
acceptynge thys Benefite wyth humble thankes for the clemencye
of your royall Maieſtye, I reſt the Seruaunt and ſlaue of you and
yours." The king hearing hym ſpeake ſo wiſely, took hym vp,
and imbraced him, ſaying : " Would to God and his great Pro-
phete, that all they which rule Cityes, and gouerne Prouinces, had
ſo good a Nature as thine then I durſt be bolde to ſay, that the
People ſhoulde lyue better at theyr eaſe, and Monarches without
charge of conſcience, for the ill behauyors of theyr Officers. Lyue
good man, lyue at thine eaſe, maynteine thy people, obſerue our
lawes, and increaſe the Beauty of the City, whereof from this time
forth wee doe make the poſſeſſer. And truly the preſent was not
to bee contempned, for that the ſame at this day is one of the
faireſt that is in Affrica, and is the Land of the blacke People, ſutch
as the Spaniards call Negroes. It is very full of Gardeins, furniſhed with aboundance of Spyces brought from the Moluccas,
bicauſe of the martes and faires ordeined there. To be ſhort,
Manſor ſhewed by this gift what is the force of a gentle heart,
which can not abyde to bee vanquiſhed in curteſie, and leſſe
ſuffer that vnder forgetfulneſſe the memorye of a receyued good
turne be loſt. King Darius whilome, for a little garment, receiued
in gift by Silofon the Samien, recompenced him wyth the gaine
and royall dignity of that City, and made him ſoueraine Lord
thereof, and of the Iſle of Samos. And what greater vertue can
illuſtrate the name of a noble man, than to acknowledge and pre-
ferre them, which for Natural ſhame and baſhfulneſſe, dare not
beholde the Maieſty of their greatneſſe ? God ſometymes with

a more curteous Eye doth loke vpon the prefents of a poore man,
than the fat and rych offerings of him that is great and wealthy?
Euen fo a benefite, from what hand foeuer it procedeth, cannot
chofe but bryng forth the fruicts of his Liberality that giueth the
fame, who by vfing largeffe, feleth alfo the like in him to whom
it is employed.   That magnificence no long time paft vfed the
Seigniorie of Venice, to Francefco Dandulo, who after he had
dured the great difpleafures of the Pope, in the name of the whole
City, vpon his returne to Venice, for acknowledgment of his pacyence, and for abolifhmente of that Shame, was wyth happye and
vniforme Acclamatyon of the whole ftate electcd, and made Prince,
and Duke of that Common wealth.   Worthy of prayfe truly is he,
that by fome pleafure bindeth another to his curtefie: but when
a Noble man acknowledgeth for a benefit, that which a Subiect is
bounde to gieue him by duty and feruice, there the proofe of
prayfe carryeth no Fame at all.   For which caufe I determined to
difplay the Hyftory of the barbarous King Manfor, to the intent
that our Gentlemen, noryfhed and trained vp in great ciui-
lytie, may affay by their mildeneffe and good education,
to furmount the curtefie of that Prynce, of whom
for this time wee purpofe to take our
Farewell.

CONCLUSION,

AN ADUERTISEMENT TO THE READER.

------◆------

WHAT thou haſt gained for thy better inſtruction, or what conceiued for recreation by reading theſe thirty fiue Nouells, I am no
Iudge, although (by deeming) in reading and peruſing, thou
mayſt (at thy pleaſure) gather both. But howſoeuer profite, or
delight, can ſatiſſy mine apoyntment, wherefore they were preferred into thy hands, contented am I that thou doe vouchſafe
them Good leſſons how to ſhun the Darts, and Prickes of inſolency
thou findeſt in the ſame. The vertuous noble may ſauor the
fruits and taſte the licour that ſtilleth from the gums or buds of
Vertue. The contrary may ſee the bloſſoms fall, that blome from
the ſhrubs of diſloialty and degenerat kinde. Yong Gentlemen, and Ladies do view a plot founded on ſured grounde, and
what the foundation is, planted in ſhattring Soyle, with a faſhion
of attire to garniſh their inward parts, ſo well as (ſpareleſſe) they
imploy vpon the vaniſhing pompe. Euery ſort and ſexe that
warfare in the fielde of humayne life, may ſet here the ſauourous
fruict (to outwarde lyking) that fanſied the ſenſuall taſte of
Adam's Wyfe. They ſee alſo what griefts ſutch fading fruicts
produce vnto poſterity: what likewiſe the luſty growth and
ſpring of vertue's plant, and what delicates it brauncheth to thoſe
that carefully keepe the ſlips thereof, within the Orchard of their
mindes. Diuers Tragical ſhewes by the pennes deſcription haue

bene difclofed in greateft number of thefe Hyftories, the fame
alfo I haue mollified and fweetened with the courfe of pleafaunt
matters, of purpofe not to dampe the deynty mindes of thofe that
fhrinke and feare at fuch rehearfall. And bicaufe fodaynly
(contrary to expectation) this Volume is rifen to greater heape
of leaues, I doe omit for this prefent time fundry Nouels of mery
deuife, referuing the fame to be ioyned with the reft of an other
part, wherein fhall fucceede the remnaunt of Bandello, fpecially
futch (fuffrable) as the learned French man François de Belle-
forreft hath felected, and the choyfeft done in the Italian. Some
alfo out of Erizzo, Ser Giouani Florentino, Parabofco, Cynthio,
Straparole, Sanfouino, and the beft liked out of the Queene of
Nauarre, and other Authors. Take thefe in fo good part with
thofe that haue and fhall come forth, as I do offre them with good
will curteoufly correcting futch Faults, and Errors, as fhall
prefent themfelues, eyther burying them in the Bofome
of Fauor, or pretermitting them with the beck
of Curtefie.

FINIS.

BALLANTYNE PRESS: EDINBURGH AND LONDON.